The Scorpion's DAUGTHER

The
Scorpion's
DAUGTHER

Stephen Francis Montagna

ARPress
45 Dan Road Suite 5
Canton MA 02021

Hotline: (888) 821-0229
Fax: 1(508) 545-7580

Ordering Information:
Quantity sales. Special discounts are available on quantity purchases by corporations, associations, and others. For details, contact the publisher at the address above.

Printed in the United States of America.
ISBN-13:   Paperback   979-8-89389-244-4
                eBook   979-8-89389-245-1

Library of Congress Control Number: 2024906450

Table of Contents

The greatest monument to fallen soldiers are not constructed of polished marble and crowned by ornate, bright shining placards. The true monuments to fallen soldiers are resting deep in the steamy jungles or silently washing on the sandy beaches far from our shores, and they are crowned by a lone rifle sticking in the ground with a tattered and rusting helmet on top as its brass placard honoring his or her unselfish sacrifice. Wherever a fallen soldier is buried marks the greatest monument to his or her dedication to duty and the protection of the fallen soldier's loved ones and country. A soldier does not fight because he hates who is standing before him. He fights because he loves the ones and his country standing behind him.

God bless all our fallen soldiers and the loved ones they have left behind to remember and give that soldier immortality by remembering their ultimate sacrifice for God, country and family. God rests his hand on the shoulder of any man or woman who picks up a weapon and dresses in our country's uniform and defends our great country and freedom from all threats!

SUPPORT OUR WOUNDED WARRIOR PROJECT

The Scorpion's Daughter was born from the pages and is the continuation of my novel "The Sting of the Scorpion", but as is the Sting of the Scorpion, The Scorpion's Daughter is a complete and finished novel in its own right. Both these novels follow and are lead into by my novel "Eagle's Nest".

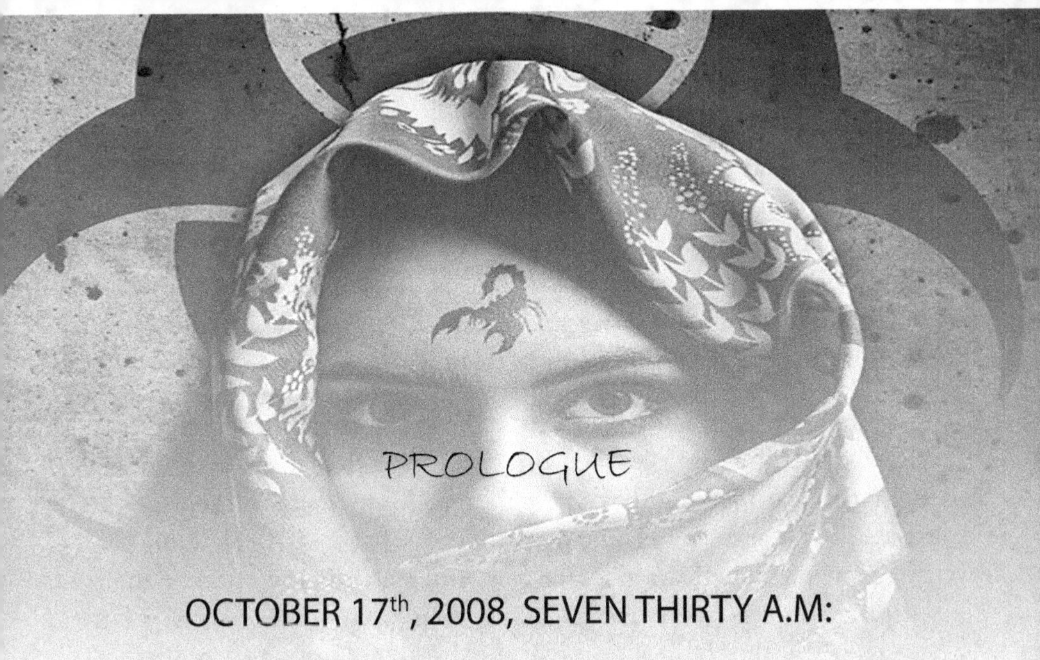

OCTOBER 17th, 2008, SEVEN THIRTY A.M:

A desert camouflaged armored United States Army Humvee slowly and cautiously entered the small town of ar-Ramadi in Iraq. There were four heavily armed American soldiers riding in the lead humvee vehicle, and the soldiers seemed to be hunting for bear. One soldier had his body hanging half out of the upper turret type structure on top of the heavy jeep, and he was manning the heavy fifty caliber machine gun. The trooper was on alert against a possible insurgent attack on them or his fellow soldiers. Four more armored Humvees were stationed near the mouth of the main street of the Iraqi village just outside the town. They were being supported by a pair of Bradley Fighting Machines, and twenty other heavily armed support soldiers.

Even though much of this area of Iraq was considered secured and safe to move freely around in without much fear of an insurgent attack against the American soldiers, and Iraqi soldiers recently took over the security operations of the area in question. The concerned American soldiers were taking nothing for granted for this operation the troopers were out on. Especially because of the mission the soldiers were dispatched on by Army Command earlier this morning.

The slow-moving Humvee traveled at ten miles an hour as the heavy war machine entered the village, and the driver was looking for the building they were instructed to visit. The Americans identified the building as being constructed about center of the tiny town near a large water fountain, where the local villagers drew drinking water from. The small town was clean and many local stores were open for business this early in the day. The street was about overflowing with Iraqi civilians going about their daily work and business. Arguments raged between Iraqi buyers and sellers of wares in the middle of the streets.

Iraqi children ran wildly across the street causing the Humvee to slow further. Iraqi music filled the street and mingled with arguments raging in the town, and crying children. Many males old enough to serve in the army or insurgency stopped what they were doing and stared at the American machine as it entered their town. Some males displayed sneers with hatred lacing their eyes, while others waved pleasantly at the soldiers riding in the threatening machine of war.

The driver kept his eyes glued out the windshield; he did not want to run over a child running in the street before his machine. The other soldier in the front seat watched for the building they were searching for. After another hundred yards, the passenger called out to the driver.

"Sergeant, on the right side, that's the house we're looking for. The one with the blue door and all the people standing in front of it is the target building we're looking for."

"Great, that's fucking great Corporal; this is all we fucking needed on this suck ass mission. A bunch of half crazed fucking Iraqi assholes blocking us from speaking to this female we were dispatched to speak with, dammit. I don't know why the hell we got stuck notifying this Arab bitch about her stinking Father's death. He was nothing more than a damn terrorist killing our soldiers back in the States. I though and still believe we should take her in to custody and pump the shit outta her ass until we find out all the damn information about her Father we need to know, Corporal. This is one shit filled miserable mission we're on man."

"I know Sergeant, but we have orders and when they call, we haul."

"What the hell are you, a commercial for the Army? Notify our backup, inform them we found the dump and we're stopping. Tell them they betta be ready to lend a hand double quick, if we come under attack in this shit filled village. Look at those bastards. They're acting like they want to kill, cook and eat our asses for breakfast." The Sergeant barked at his Corporal.

The Corporal informed his backup as ordered by his Sergeant, and before the Sergeant pulled his Humvee to a stop, two Apache fast attack helicopters showed up and hovering over the parked Humvee. The machine took up a protective standoff position over the humvee and the four American soldiers getting out of the ground machine.

The Sergeant in command looked up and breathed a sigh of relief as he grumbled at his fellow soldier. "Well, at least I see Command's taking this mission seriously."

The two soldiers from the rear of the humvee took up flanking and guard positions, remaining with their machine parked in the middle of the street, and the soldiers kept the sergeant and corporal under cover. Ready to react in case their brother soldiers came under attack from any of the gathered and angry mob of Iraqis in front of the home the soldiers were ordered to visit.

Ever though the Iraqis were acting hostile towards the American soldiers, they were wise enough to open a path through their ranks, so the soldiers could approach the home.

Sergeant Thomas Doocy cautiously walked through the ranks of the gathered Iraqi mostly male civilians as if he didn't notice them standing on either side of him. The soldier walked up to the front door of the home and raised his hand, but the door opened before he could knock on it. The Sergeant took a step back and stared at the door until it was completely opened, and an elderly woman was standing and blocking the doorway.

The Sergeant shook his head, angered over the way the elderly woman was blocking his way, and then the soldier got control of his emotions and nearly barked at the old woman. "Ma'am, I'm looking for a woman named Ayesha al-Qaysi. I've been informed this woman lives here, Ma'am. I've been assigned a number of items I must hand to her personally."

As the Sergeant spoke calmly to the old woman, an Iraqi man standing behind her translated the American's words to Iraqi for the mother of the woman the soldier wished to speak with. Without responding to the American's words, the mother stepped aside and a stunningly beautiful woman came out from the interior of the house, and stopped before the soldier.

"Yes, I am Ayesha al-Qaysi, ugly foreign soldier. Why have you come to upset me at such a terrible time in my life, lowly infidel? Have you cursed soldiers not done enough harm and damage to my country since you invaded my country of Iraq? You have to bother me at the trying time of knowing my beloved Father was killed in the land of Satan not long ago, Mista?"

Ayesha's words angered the Sergeant. He was furious by her thinking he was causing harm to her country. The Sergeant wondered why this woman did not understand he was placing his life on the line to free her and her people of the terrible leadership of Saddam Hussein. Fighting to keep control over his rage, the soldier removed the anger from his eyes, as he put his hand out and offered the Iraqi beauty a package and remarked in a polite voice. "Ma'am, these are the personal effects of your Father, Colonel Hamoodi al-Qaysi, Ma'am. They were shipped to my Command by the authorities in the United States, and I was ordered to deliver them to you. I'm sorry for your Father's death, but he was doing the Devil's work in my country, Ma'am."

Sergeant Doocy could not stop his words until he delivered the insult his heart demanded.

More anger seeped in the cold black eyes of the woman as she hated this American more now he branded her father doing the devil's work in the United States. A number of gathered male civilians in the street and on Ayesha's property, grumbled over the American's insulting remark, but the Iraqi's were smart enough to hold their ranks due to the other soldiers in their town, and the pair of helicopters hovering so near where they were bunched up on Ayesha's property.

It was Ayesha's turn to control her emotions as she reached out and took the package from the soldier. She looked at the package for several seconds without uttering a word to anyone in ear shot of her, and then she turned her back on the Sergeant and other soldiers, and walked back inside the home, rudely dismissing the soldier and what he had done for her. Instantly, a number of male Iraqi's moved in front of the Sergeant and blocked him from seeing in the home until the door closed behind them. Not knowing what to do next to display his respect for the woman, the Sergeant turned to his Corporal and barked at him.

"We did our duty, what say we get out of here before one of these sand swimmers decided to play a fucking hero, and he starts World War Three on our asses, because of this Iraqi chick."

The two soldiers headed back for their humvee and climbed in it and left the Iraqi village as quickly as they could leave. This time the soldier driving the machine at a speed the soldiers preferred, so they became a harder target to hit if any insurgents were operating in the area, and they wanted to attack an American convoy. In no time the lead humvee linked up with the rest of their company, and vehicles and helicopters headed back for their headquarters, and the safety the Fort offered the soldiers.

CAMP LEJEUNE, JACKSONVILLE NORTH CAROLINA. MONDAY, OCTOBER 21ST, 2008

Marine Colonel Bruce Leadbetter, the commander of the elite and highly trained Special Forces soldiers, chose this day to go over the latest AAR, or After Action Report filed by Captain Robert Walker, over the attempted terrorist attack on the Miami Sea Port Terminal in Florida. This was the first time in months the Colonel had his entire MNRRF Multi-National Rapid Response Force assembled before him, and he intended to make the best of their time together, before he was forced to release the troops on liberty for who knew how long. The last action Road Kill, Captain Walker's nickname for the unit, along with Mutt, Lieutenant Frank Hall, Buckethead, Sergeant Vincent Lombardo, No Neck, Sergeant Robert Abbott, and Sergeant Dorothy Ramirez, who was held hostage by the Iranian terrorist attack of almost two years ago. But it was still on the Colonel's mind, because he never had a chance to evaluate the hard hitting action in Florida with his elite strike force.

Even Toby, the civilian country and western singer was invited to attend this military briefing, along with the other elite troops from the colonel's strike forces, who didn't take part in that terrorist attack. The singer was requested there by Walker, who felt he owed the civilian a debt of gratitude, because the singer joined forces with him and his soldiers in their attempt to free his girlfriend from the Persian attackers. The singer helped stop the attack on the United States with Walker's troops, and the civilian did it without regard to his safety on the dangerous mission.

Colonel Leadbetter stood on the top step of the porch to his office in front of the grinder area of the massive military base. The grinder was where the Colonel worked his soldiers to death, in his efforts to form them into the greatest fighting and strike unit in the armed services. He looked over his gathered soldiers and was proud of them. Finally, the officer stepped down from the porch and walked out to his troops. Walker was standing before the formation of soldiers.

He headed right for his Captain, and when he was standing before the man. He stopped moving and ripped off a sharp salute which the captain returned equally as sharp as the commander grumbled at his Captain. "Well Mr. fucking big shot celebrity soldier, I'm pleased to see you still know how the hell to properly respect your Commanding Officer, Mister."

Leadbetter looked off to Walker's right and picked up Mutt, and barked at him. "And you Mr. Bullshit, there's still no fucking hope of my getting respect from your ass I see, buster!"

Mutt grinned back at his commander, but he still refused to salute the Colonel first.

"Arrr… Getting back to you Captain Walker, I'm pleased over the way you and your lowlife pukes handled those Persian terrorists in Miami, Mister. You and the fools you surrounded yourself with, did an outstanding job for your country and for the Marine Corps. But you and I are going to have a private little chitchat on the do's and don'ts of taking a fucking civilian on a military operation with your ass, Mister." Colonel Leadbetter shot a harsh but brief glare at the singer standing with General John White, the Chairman of the Joint Chiefs of Staff.

The country singer, who liked to go by Tee K (Toby Keith), looked at his feet to get out of the angry stare from the Colonel. This action caused General White to lean closer and mumble to the singer. "Take it easy son, the Colonel's only busting yours and Walker's horns a little. Once he's finished dressing down his troops, we're heading to the White House. It seems the President wants to pin a few medals on you people who did that act in Miami. I'll tell you this much Toby, if you ever want to hang up your guitar and serve your country. I'd be proud to offer you a position in this bunch of special ops troops I assembled before you. Due to your actions with Walker, you cemented a position with the group. I can assure you each and every one of these troopers would be more than proud to have you as part of their force. What say to my offer sir?"

"General White, I'm flattered over the offer to join your fine troops, sir. But I'm comfortable with my chosen field, sir. To tell you the truth General, one mission with these soldiers, is more than enough to last me two lifetimes." He flashed a quick smile at the military officer.

"I hear you son, I understand where you're coming from. These soldiers are the best of the best, and it takes a special breed of person to want to linkup and stand a post with these troops, sir. These soldiers take command of any mission that other branch of the service can't handle, and accomplish that mission no matter what operation it happens to be sir." General White replied as he placed a proud smile on his lips as he glanced at the troops of mixed male and female members from all over the world.

Colonel Leadbetter noticed the General speaking with the civilian singer, and he ignored the two as he continued speaking to his troops. "Okay Walker, I don't know how the hell you discovered these fucking terrorists and what they were up to in the States, Mister. But I'm pleased you were where you were when you were there. I still can't get over the fact of you using a damn civilian puke in this operation, Mister. You're damn lucky the dopey civilian didn't get busted up any, or it'd be your ass on the fucking swing I'd be firing at, buster. Be that as it may, you still did an outstanding job, and that's what happen when you people walk around my beloved United States with your fucking eyes opened, and your heads on a swivel. I'll tell each one of you swinging dicks and bouncing tits, if Walker and the people he had with him didn't find those assholes down there. We'd be burying American civilians by the fricking truckload.

"Okay people, its Zero, Six, Fifteen Hundred Hours, so this is what I'm going to allow you pack of assholes to do on my beloved base. You people are free to go to mess and after you chow down, we're going to discuss the operation Captain Walker and his people engaged in detail in Florida. We're going to examine each action and come up with where his people could have acted and reacted a little more efficiently on this fucking mission. We're also going to discuss the dangers of allowing a stinking civilian to join in on a military operation. If that shit happens again, I'm warning each one of you fucking misfits, you'll rule the day your mamma's ever fucked your papa's and produced the likes of you Squids. Head out and eat, we'll reassemble on the grinder at Zero Eight Hundred Hours. Any Squids not assembled in front of me at that time, will be shot on general principles. Is that clear?"

"Yes sir." Was the reply from the gathered but rather bored looking elite group of soldiers.

"I can't hear you fucking people! Sound off like you assholes have a pair!" Colonel Leadbetter suddenly roared at his troops as he started stomping up and down in front of the formation, glaring at his troops.

"Yes sir." Was screamed back by the troops the second time.

"That's better, at least I know now you people are the soldiers I fucking trained, dammit. Before I dismiss you screaming squirrels, I have to introduce you people to a number of new recruits who don't possess enough brains in their damn noggin's to stop them from volunteering to join up with our unit. I believe Walker and a few others of you pukes know these new soldiers. But for the benefit of those who never met this new batch of pukes, here they are. The first soldier who thinks he's a good enough to join our troops is Sergeant William Glenallen." The Colonel stopped speaking and waited for the soldier to step out of the ranks. When he did, he went on with his words.

"That's enough bullshit, who the hell do you think you are, someone special, get back in the ranks before I hop you in the ass! Ahhh… the second recruit is Sergeant Carl Youngblood, just nod your head and stay in the ranks, Mister." The Colonel growled at the second soldier because he did not want to waste time waiting for the soldier to step out to be recognized.

"That's good enough for the likes of you. The third soldier's named Sergeant Stephen Stringold, the fourth replacement soldier to the unit is Sergeant Edward London, and the last fool who wants to linkup with our unit is Sergeant Michael Nettestad. I'm warning you people, if any of you assholes harm these new soldiers before they're accepted in our ranks, you'll be answering to me, personally. You'll have plenty of time once they're part of our unit to corrupt them. Okay, go and choke down food and get back here at your assigned time. You're dismissed!" Colonel Leadbetter placed his hands on his hips as he stared at the soldiers until they disappeared from his sight, and then he turned his attention to General White and the civilian.

General White walked towards and then right past the Colonel as he and the civilian entered the Colonel's office and living quarters, and then they waited for the Colonel to come in and speak with them.

"Great, now I have to deal with the fucking General and his civilian puke." Leadbetter complained to himself as he followed the two men into his office.

General White looked over his shoulder and snapped at the officer lagging behind him. "Stop your fucking grumbling and get your ass in here double quick, Colonel. We have a number of matters to discuss then I want to get back to Washington ten minutes ago. Colonel, once you're finished ripping your troop's new asshole, I want Walker, Hall, Abbott, Lambardo, and Ramirez and this gentleman here sent to Washington. They have a meeting set with the President scheduled for tomorrow. Right now the President and I are at peace with one another, and I want to keep it that way, Colonel. So no one I ordered to Washington better be late, or it'll be your ass I'll mow down if you catch my drift." General White offered as he seated himself in the Colonel's chair, leaving the colonel and civilian standing for the moment.

"General White, I have to inform you I'm still uncomfortable having this civilian puke hanging around my beloved base, and him still being part of my soldiers, sir. This is a military installation General

White, and a civilian puke no matter what he did for or with my soldiers, has any business observing what's going on with our troops, sir. I protest the fact he's dressed in civilian clothes and acting like he's part of my troops, General White." Leadbetter placed a look on his face that left no doubt in the General or civilian's mind he hated the civilian.

Drawing in a breath, General White allowed a quick smile as he offered to his excited Colonel in a calmer voice. "Colonel Leadbetter, I understand what you're saying sir. I happen to agree with the fact we have a civilian watching what's going on with your, err… pardon me Colonel, our Special Operations Soldiers, Sir. But taking in account this gentleman here was a major part of stopping a terrorist action that would've equaled, if not surpassed the sneak attack on the Twin Towers in New York. I'm of the mind to offer you that this gentleman has earned the right to be standing with our elite troops, sir. Furthermore Colonel Leadbetter, Bruce, I want to explain to you why I have come to the base…"

"By your leave General White." Leadbetter offered as he dared to interrupt his commander.

"You do have a set of brass balls to interrupt me, Mister. Go ahead with your bitch Colonel, you paid for your attitude you're displaying before me, sir."

The still angry Colonel did not miss a beat as he went on with his steamy words. "General White, if you must insist having this damn civilian, err… gentleman standing with my troops, sir. At least order the puke to dress in a military uniform and swear him in as a soldier, sir. In that way I have some control over his damn ass sir, and I can treat him as I do the rest of the soldiers under my command, General White Sir. It's my right to request this man get dressed in a military uniform and service, or he has to get the hell off my base. General White, I demand you order this gentleman to dress in a…"

This time the Chairman of the Joint Chiefs of Staff interrupted his lesser officer as he roared. "Colonel Leadbetter, you demand from me sir! Allow me to inform you of something here and now, Mister.

You demand nothing from me Colonel Leadbetter! Let me further inform you of something else you might not understand properly, Mister. You're in no position to demand anything from me, sir. Colonel Leadbetter, this man has earned the fucking right to be honored by me and you and the President of the United States, as well as from the rest of the soldiers in our command, sir.

"Colonel Leadbetter, I believe you're pushing our friendship a bit too far sir. I warn you, remember your position in this conversation! Besides Colonel, I don't really give a flying fuck what you might and might not like or even think around here, sir. You're here for one reason and one reason only, Colonel. That's to carry out my orders as they're issued and received by you, and like it, Mister. If you have anything else to add to this conversation, now is the time to air your complaints, and I'll have you replaced as the Commandant of this installation, and you'll spend the rest of your days in the service counting polar bears at the North Pole, Colonel. Do I make myself perfectly clear on this fucking subject, Colonel Leadbetter?"

Colonel Leadbetter went to full attention and ripped off a salute to his commanding officer as he replied. "You made your feelings perfectly clear over this err… gentleman, General White."

"Great, now that we got that straightened out Bruce, why don't you and Alan take a seat so we can speak of what's expected of your troopers and this gentleman, sir." General White smiled at both of the men standing before him, and then he waited for them to take their seats.

AT THE SMALL IRAQI TOWN OF AR-RAMADI, OCTOBER 22ND, 2008

Tuesday morning, Ayesha al-Qaysi woke as usual at five thirty a.m. and walked around the home like a Zombie in a coma. She was in a state of shock at how her father was slaughtered by the Americans on the civilian road in the United States. In all her life, she always believed her father invincible, bulletproof. She could not bring her mind to accept the fact that her father was dead. She walked in the kitchen and looked for her mother, she was still asleep. Ayesha remembered how her mother reacted when the Americans brought her husband's personal effects home. How proud she was of watching her daughter take the remains of her father, and then turn away from the Americans like they were not standing outside the door.

Suddenly, Ayesha started frantically looking around the kitchen for the personal effects of her father. For a moment she grew upset, the package was not where she laid it five days ago. Searching for the package, she discovered it on the table by the couch in what was the living room of their home. Ayesha smiled as she wondered if her mother moved the package to the table, as she looked at it she glanced at the wall above the package and noticed the picture of her father. He was smiling and dressed in his uniform of the Republican Guard of Iraq.

Ayesha smiled at the picture because her father looked more handsome dressed in his Iraqi military uniform. She remembered how her father fought the Americans as they invaded Iraq both times. He was wounded when the Americans invaded Iraq the second time and he linked up with General Hassan al-Zahar, and the Iraqi General sent the hit team to the United States to kill the President in an effort to stop the stifling sanctions strangling the life out of the devastated Iraqi people and country. Although she never met Colonel Abdulaziz Majd al-Adwani, he was what her father referred to as the terrorist in command of the special hit team sent to America.

Ayesha al-Qaysi remembered how her father hated this Colonel with a passion, because her father refused to have anything to do with anyone involved in terrorism, and their ugly actions. Her father complained he was a soldier, and a soldier's fate was tied to the battlefield. It was not connected to sneaking around assassinating a leader of another country from the shadows.

Ayesha lowered her eyes until they rested on the package wrapped in the green paper, as she remembered her father and how savagely he died. The assassination attempt the Iraqi terrorists carried out against the President of the United States failed, and Colonel al-Adwani escaped the United States after the other terrorists he was in command of, were killed by police officials and soldiers. Once the members of his cell were killed, al-Adwani made his way to General al-Zahar's headquarters in Iraq, and the Iraqi Colonel used the General to offer him safety from the searching Americans. But the Americans dared to invade Iraq again, and they arrested the terrorist Colonel, and the soldiers fled Iraq with the Colonel as their prisoner. During the attack, General al-Zahar was killed and the retreating Americans left her father standing in the middle of the streets of Dawral, swearing the death of al-Adwani and the soldiers who invaded Iraq again.

Ayesha al-Qaysi remembered how her father announced he was going to organize another hit team, and they were going to enter the United States and kill Colonel al-Adwani. So he could not inform the American public that President Saddam Hussein was the one behind the order to kill the American Leader. She remembered her father swearing on his Qur'an he would kill every American soldier involved with the killing of General al-Zahar, and the taking of al-Adwani as their prisoner back to the United States. How confident her father was over being able to seek his revenge on the hated Americans when her father left to enter the United States and carry out his oath.

A tear ran down her cheek as she remembered how she waited for word on how her father was doing killing the terrorist Colonel, along with the cursed American soldiers. Ayesha al-Qaysi reflected how she watched the news everyday in hopes of hearing of her father's success in the United States. She also remembered how fear took over her when it was announced two American soldiers were killed in North Carolina, and a third soldier wounded. Then the terrible news of the Iraqi terrorist hit team responsible for the death of Colonel al-Adwani, was stopped before they could kill the Iraqi Colonel, and most of the hit team was killed in their failed attempt. Then she feared for her father's life. She refused to leave the TV for a moment, until it was announced Colonel Hamoodi al-Qaysi and his female companion were killed on the side of a road in the United States called I-95, as the sun was setting in the country.

Then, over the years that past, Ayesha recalled how she heard of the trial of the Iraqi Colonel and his hanging, and the second invasion of Iraq that nearly destroyed Iraq's feared Army, and the hanging of her President, Saddam Hussein. She remembered how long they waited before the body of her father was returned to them, so they could offer him a proper burial. She hated the fact she could not open the coffin to see her father's face before they laid him asleep forever. It took the United States over a year and a half to return her father's body, and by that time all that was left were bones. How she cursed America and their leader for keeping her father's body from them for so long.

Every time Ayesha al-Qaysi spotted an American military patrol entering her village, or saw these invading foreigners walking proudly around her country on TV, she had all she could do not lifting a weapon against them, and seek revenge against them for her father's death, and the destruction of her country. She cursed the despised Americans whenever they were displayed on her TV, and she knew how much she hated every one of the invaders of her country. How arrogant the Americans seemed to be behaving in her country, entering any building they wanted to search while ignoring the respects and customs the male Iraqi's showed wives and women.

The insults suffered by the Iraqi civilians at the hands of the occupying American soldiers. Killing Iraqi man and male children under the guise they were thought to be insurgents, and shooting up their religious sights. Everything the infidel soldiers of the United States and her allies were doing in her country, made her hate them more with every passing day and moment of time. How she hated the United States and her brave soldiers, and how it was eating at her soul every second of the day, consuming her being.

Ayesha al-Qaysi was standing in the dim lighted living room, and was accompanied by her two trusted and loyal female friends, who entered her home the moment she flipped on the light. Sadiya Sadjadpour and Shafiqu al-Quraishy, the same age as their suffering friend over her father's death. All three women were twenty five years old, and they were thought to be the most beautiful women in the village. The three were chased by all eligible male Iraqis of the town.

Ayesha's two girlfriends stood behind her as Ayesha stared at the package containing her father's personal effects. As strange as it felt, Ayesha was almost afraid to open the package. She couldn't help but fear what she might find in the package. She entertained the thought the Americans might have placed a bomb in the package to complete their revenge against her father, by killing the rest of her father's family.

As Ayesha stared at the package, Sadiya moved forward and rested her hand on her friend's shoulder and offered. "Go ahead Ayesha and open the package. I'm certain it's what your Father had on his person when he was murdered by the hated American police. Please Ayesha open the package, maybe there's a message to you from your Father."

Ayesha looked into the eyes of her girlfriend, and was greeted with a warm smile.

"Yes Ayesha, open the package and see if your Father sent you something special to remember him with for all times, sister." Shafiqu added to her friend's voice and offer as she too smiled at her upset girlfriend, and then she waited for her to open the item.

Drawing in a breath to calm her nerves, Ayesha took a step forward and reached out and rested her hands respectfully on the package. In her mind's eye, she could see her father's face in the dim glow of the room, and it gave her the inner strength to pick up the package in both hands.

Sadiya and Shafiqu also moved forward so they could see the contents of the package as their sister opened it. They thought of Ayesha's father and what he attempted to do in the United States.

Ayesha began to open the package, but could not stop her hands from trembling. The green wrapping ripped easily, and as soon as she ripped the front the package opened, all three women drew in their breath. Lying on the top of the items in the package, sat Colonel Hamoodi al-Qaysi's Qur'an. The cover and pages were worn, a testament to how many times the Colonel searched for solace between the pages of the sacred book. A tear slid down Ayesha's cheek, she noticed the blood stain on the cover and understood her father had the holy Book on his person when the police took his life from her in their country. She picked up the Book as if it was made of porcelain, and she was afraid her hands might cause the Book to crumble between her fingers.

"You see Ayesha your Father sent to you the most important thing in his life. To have your Father's Qur'an should make his passing easier for you to endure, my poor sister. Each time you pick up the Book to pray, you'll be remembering your Father's great sacrifice for Iraq and her children. Please sister; take care of the Book, it's the sacred words of the Prophet Muhammad Himself. Between the grand pages, it tells us how to deal with the hated infidels out to destroy the Islamic fate and her faithful children, sister." Shafiqu offered to Ayesha as she looked at the sacred Book, and she noticed the blood stain on the upper corner of the prayer book.

"What else is in the package?" Sadiya asked, she was the impatient and bold one, and she was the one who usually led the others to the trouble they got in.

Ayesha gave a harsh look, nearly a sneer at her girlfriend and then began to rummage through the rest of the package after she laid the Holy Qur'an on the table. Ayesha also found her father's wallet with a number of pictures of his friends in the military service of Iraq. More tears escaped her eyes when she found a picture of her father standing with a pretty female military officer, and both seemed like they were smiling at her. Other items of her father's were in the package, a pen, American cash, and the medal her father won during his fight against the Coalition Forces when they invaded Iraq in the Desert Storm War.

There were a number of other items resting inside the package, but nothing special, so Ayesha allowed the covering to slide off the couch. She could not take her eyes off her father's copy of his Holy Qur'an, she felt it was a personal link to his spirit she was certain was sharing Paradise with Muhammad and Allah.

"Well sister, there wasn't much your Father sent home to remember him with. I'm willing to bet the cursed infidels kept much of what your Father had at the terrible time of his death. How I hate the Americans and their occupation of our country!" Sadiya offered to her best friend.

"You don't know what you're talking about, my evil sister! Her Father sent Ayesha his prized possession, his Qur'an. Only you wouldn't see the gift Ayesha's Father bestowed on her." Shafiqu snapped at Sadiya as she gave her a nasty look to stop her from saying more to Ayesha.

"Please Shafiqu, after all the time you known Sadiya, I'd think you'd know by now how she allows her mouth to rule her unwise words and actions. I'm certain Sadiya didn't mean to insult me by her choice of words, she's wild. I always said you can't tame what's meant to be wild, and Shafiqu, Sadiya was born to be the most wild of us, my sister of life." Ayesha offered as she smiled first at Shafiqu, and then at Sadiya as warm and lovingly.

Shafiqu returned Ayesha's smile, and then looked at her other girlfriend and noticed the smile on her lips. Shafiqu knew the three of them loved each other dearly.

Sadiya moved near to Ayesha and picked up the wrapping from the package and snarled. "I'll burn this piece of filth the infidels wrapped around your Father's items, anything from the hated Americans don't deserve to be allowed to remain in a faithful follower of the Qur'an's home."

"What are you going to do with your Father's Qur'an?" Shafiqu asked as she picked up the Book, and opened it to her favorite passage and began to read it to herself.

"Shafiqu, my Father's copy of his Holy Qur'an will be a special part of my life until I no longer exist on this earth, and I returned to the sands that gave birth to me. I'll be buried with the sacred Book resting on my unworthy chest. Everywhere I go, I'll carry my Father's Book of the Qur'an. It'll bring me the peace of mind and strength to believe my Father's presence once offered me, my sister." Ayesha replied as she took the sacred Book from Shafiqu, and closed it and placed it in her pocket. It was good the Holy Book was a small copy of the Qur'an, it fitted perfectly in her pocket by her heart.

"What are we going to do? Are we going to make the hated Americans pay for killing your Father, Ayesha? I know your Father would want us to do something against the lowly infidels for this insult against his country." Sadiya remarked while allowing anger to cloud her eyes.

"My Father's spirit is demanding we seek revenge against the hated Americans, and all who follow the misbegotten United States evil ways. What course my revenge is going to take, I don't know. But some way somehow, I'll have my revenge against the infidels for killing my Father like they have and what their cursed occupying forces are doing to my country. I hated having to sit and watch the fools hang our President as if he was nothing more than a common criminal. My revenge will befall the cursed heads of the new leaders of Iraq, who are nothing more than puppets for the United States, my sisters." Ayesha al-Qaysi growled as she looked from one woman's eyes to the other, and lightly patted the Qur'an hidden in her pocket.

"Ayesha, you speak words resting in the hearts of the people of Iraq, my sister of the desert sands. It pleases me that you feel the same as we, and from the look in your eyes. It seems we're going to do something against the cursed soldiers occupying the lands of our beloved country and ancestors. I have other friends who feel and believe as we do; it'd only take my letting them know of our intent, to lock their loyalty to our cause. All you have to do is give me the word Ayesha, and I'll let them know they're needed for our fight against the Crusader soldiers." Sadiya offered as she pumped up her chest and smiled at Ayesha.

Ayesha turned and looked in the eyes of Sadiya, and offered. "Of course you'd know many of our sisters waiting their time to act against the Coalition forces occupying our country. If I'm looking for someone to start trouble for us, all I have to do is look to you and your friends. Yes, I'll finish what my Father had started against the filthy infidels who invaded our country, and I fear we'll need all the help we can muster. But Sadiya, I believe we'll have the needed number of faithful male followers of our country. As much as I'd like to use women for our cause to attack the hated Americans, we have no knowledge of where we might get our hands on weapons and explosives we need for our attacks against the foul infidels."

"Ayesha, we could align ourselves with al-Qaeda of Iraq. I'm certain they'll be happy to give us weapons and explosives for our war against the Americans. Who walk around our country as if it was theirs to trespass upon." Sadiya offered, hoping she was being helpful to Ayesha and her plans to attack the American soldiers occupying Iraq.

Stunned to her soul, Ayesha stared at Sadiya before she was able to reply to the troubling words as she replied. "My wayward sister of the desert, what makes you believe I'd go to the hated al-Qaeda of Iraq for help fighting the Americans occupying Iraq? What makes you think I'd go to a larger evil against the Arab lands of the Middle East, to rid Iraq of this lesser evil of the American infidels? At least we know the extent of the American evil facing the Islamic world. But al-Qaeda in Iraq, Heaven only knows where their evil efforts will end before they become at peace with the world for the sake of the Middle East and her children.

"No my Sunni sister, you must learn to curb your enthusiasm a little better. We must never allow ourselves to think al-Qaeda in Iraq is the salvation of the Arab world or the Middle East. If we allow ourselves to follow those evil brokers of death, it'd surely lead to the complete destruction of all Arab races. My sister, I fear if al-Qaeda of Iraq continues to attack every nation of the world, it'd only be a matter of time before all other nations of the world, including many Arab nations, would turn on the al-Qaeda forces and destroy the evil followers of Usama bin Laden, and his unholy ways on the earth.

"As it's believed in our world, if you follow the Vulture it would surely lead you to death, and Usama bin Laden is the true Vulture of the Arab world. We have to maintain our distance from al-Qaeda and what the fools stand for. We have enough problems facing us with the Americans, without drawing in them fools. Besides, we have no need of the al-Qaeda fighters or their evil weapons. We have enough of our own fighters in Iraq to carry our fight with the hated occupying forces. Between our sisters and brothers, we'll win our fight. Besides, our brothers will afford us the weapons we need to defeat the Americans who invaded our lands, sisters." Ayesha offered Sadiya, and Sadiya offered Ayesha one of her warming smiles that lit up her whole face.

THE SPECIAL OPERATIONS CAMP STATIONED AT CAMP LEJEUNE, NORTH CAROLINA. TUESDAY, OCTOBER 22ND, 2008, SEVENTEEN TENHUNDRED HOURS EST

Captain Robert Walker, along with the other soldiers who comprised the elements of the elite, specially organized Multi National Rapid Response Force. The soldiers entered their barracks for the first time since reporting to the base under Colonel Leadbetter's orders. The group of one hundred and fifty highly trained selected soldiers entered the barracks with half heading for the upstairs area of the barracks. The soldiers ordered to the ranks of Walker's troops, followed the Marine Captain in the building. They had no idea where they were to bunk down, and until he ordered them where to go and who to be with, they decided to follow him.

Walker entered the separate room he used for his private quarters in the enlisted man's barracks. Even though he was an officer, he refused to be separated from the foot soldiers he came up with in the ranks of the service since enlisting. He was followed in the room with his usually close group of soldiers, Mutt, Lieutenant Frank Hall, Walker's girlfriend, Sergeant Dorothy Ramirez, Buckethead, Sergeant Vincent Lambardo, and No Neck, Sergeant Robert Abbott. But this time the other soldier's girlfriends followed them in the room. Blind Date, Sergeant Regina Raphael, on loan to the elite soldiers from the French REP, or Regiment Etranger de Parachutistes of the French Foreign Legion Paratroopers, followed the others.

The beautiful female French soldier was seriously dating Mutt, ever since he lost his girlfriend in the hard hitting action branded 'Operation Sandstorm' that took place in Iran a number of years back. Ice was another young and beautiful female soldier, Sergeant Diane Morrison, who was wounded in another action the group was involved in recently, and was almost forced out of the unit because of the severity of her wounds. She was dating the massive No Neck off and on, and Baby Tee, Sergeant Teri Dorland, who received her unit nickname because of how small her breasts were, was also sort of dating the equally as massive soldier branded Buckethead. These soldiers were tight and when you saw one of the soldiers, you usually saw the rest of them.

When the other soldiers were comfortable in Walker's quarters, Ghost, (Sergeant Walter Casper) strolled in and sat down on top of the small refrigerator and grinned at the rest of the troopers. The Ghost was one of the most dangerous soldiers in the group, and he was always picked as lead scout or pointman for any action the soldiers engaged in.

"Man, that fucking Colonel's really getting on our asses lately." Mutt complained.

"That's because you and some of the uther usual fuckups from the unit keep on screwing up our exercises, stupid. You above all of us should know what the hell's expected of us out there, when we're going through this so called special urban training crap we're stuck dealing with lately, you asshole." Walker fired at his friend as he glared at the dangerous soldier.

"Don't pick on Mutt like that Walker. You know damn well he wouldn't be able to pull his foot outta the mud if someone didn't help him, baby." Ice offered in a sweet but vicious tone as she got on Mutt's case for screwing up their exercise earlier in the day.

"Hey bitch, you wanna keep running your fucking mouth you might as well put it to betta use." Mutt growled at the female soldier.

"Hey man, don't get on Ice's case, she gives good headache." Buckethead remarked.

"C'mon and knock it off will you." Walker grumbled at the other soldiers, and then added to his words. "Look people, the sooner we get this new training crap down pat, the sooner we can get the hell offa this base and back home until we're needed again by our commander."

Sergeant Dorothy Ramirez was clinging to Walker ever since he and the other soldiers rescued her from the latest batch of terrorists who invaded the United States. Ghost noticed how Ramirez wasn't letting go of her lover's body and remarked. "Well it's great to have Bonnie and Clod back together. I don't mind telling ya, you two shitbirds scared the crap outta us, Raz. I still don't know how the hell you allowed yourself to get captured by a bunch of A-rab assholes in the first place, girl. We were stuck listening to the whole fricking mess go down on radio as it took place, and we couldn't do crap about it to help you birds out. Nevertheless, it was a great action and you people did well doing your act."

Walker stared at the Ghost, and then nodded over his complement.

Mutt was grinning from ear to ear, he was happy they were able to get Ramirez away from the terrorists there to carry out a terrorist action in Miami a few months back, and he added to the conversation. "Hey Ghost, Adam and Evil over there did well. You shoulda seen Walker go after the stinking terrorist like the lousy dudes owed him money. And, when we armed Evil, she wanted to go afta the remaining terrorist assholes with hatred and, a severe want for fucking blood in her heart. All the while we were tracking the scumbags Walker was nuts, he was driving so fast I was afraid we were gonna go back in time."

"I didn't know you were so worried about me during that mess in Miami, Robert. Oh you're wonderful." Ramirez chanted as she looked in his eyes with love and tears clouding her eyes.

"What the hell did you think I was doing while you were running all over the place with them A-rab, pardon me, Persian terrorists? I love you and besides girl, if anything happened to you, think of all the trouble I woulda had breaking in a new chick to hang with…" Walker cut his words short as Ramirez punched him in the short ribs over his stupid remark, but she still smiled at her soldier as she waited for him to catch his breath.

One of the new soldiers shifted his weight, and this action drew Walker's attention to the five soldiers standing together, and he barked at them. "You FNG's (Fucking New Guys) betta get the fuck outside and pick out a place and bunk to deck down on until we're the hell offa this base. Any of our people out there will help and even move around if you guys decide to stick together until you get to know us betta, man."

CHAPTER TWO

Sergeant William Glenallen was leading the other soldiers to Walker's unit, and he nodded at Walker, and then he and the other soldiers made a move to leave Walker's quarters. They were stopped dead in their tracks when Ghost growled at the other soldiers in the room. "Hey Walker, not for fucking nuthin man, but aren't we gonna at least name the new pukes, before the dudes join the rest of the soldiers out there? It's gonna cause a helluva riot if the uther guys ask them their nicknames and they ain't got one branded to their sagging asses yet." For some reason, the Ghost was angry as hell over something, and he was not trying to hide the fact in the least.

"Shit, there's no problem Ghost, I merely forgot to tell ya buddy. We met these pukes while we were on leave in the Keys. They stayed with us for a weekend before reporting to base. When they linked up with us, they informed me they came with tag names, so there's no reason for us to bother taking the time to name them before they join our people.

"That's great, what the hell are you hanging onto their stinking names for?" The Ghost snapped at Walker as he lit up a smoke.

"Hey man you betta get the vinegar outta your fucking tone when addressing my ass. What the fuck's got your ass heated up, Ghost?" Walker snarled after he had enough of the Ghost's tone.

The new guys did not know what to make of the confrontation between Walker and the other soldier. They decided to take a backseat and keep their mouths shut until they calmed down.

"I'm fucking hot because you and the uther pricks got involved in a defending action with a mess of fucking terrorists who invaded our country with evil intent in their minds, and we weren't able to lend a hand to you guys. I'm further pissed because now we had to report to base for this added bullshit training. How the fuck many times do we hafta go over the same kinda crap before they understand we know what the fuck we're doing in the field of battle? Let some assholes try and hit us again in the States, and they'll end up the same way the uther assholes that you went up against. Fucking dead Walker."

"Ghost, we didn't have any uther choice. The pukes hit us first. So we couldn't take time to draw in the rest of you guys, and we'll continue our fucking training until we can carry any operation off successfully even in our fucking sleep, so you betta get used to it. But you're right about wanting to know the new guy's unit names, man." Walker turned his attention to the five new guys and aimed his words at the one he took as the chosen leader of the group.

"Sergeant Glenallen, I order you to inform the Ghost and the uthers your nicknames, before the stinking Ghost has a fucking baby on us. I'm telling you new guys, that's one soldier you don't want or need pissed off at ya ass. He'll never back offa ya for a second until he's satisfied he got back at ya properly." Walker turned to the Ghost and gave him a smirk which forced Ghost to fire back at Walker.

"You're getting to be quite the fucking comedian around here lately, buddy. With twenty thousand stinking comedians outta work and here you are trying to be one of the assholes, wiseass. You new pukes, get on with giving out your fucking names before you gotta deal with my ass!" The Ghost growled at them.

"Don't get on our fucking asses soldier. Just because you're having a little lip shit trouble with the Captain, that's your problem not mine man. I did my stinking time in the service to be respected by every soldier I come across, even you so back the fuck offa my ass for something bad happens to your ass, buddy." Glenallen growled at the Ghost, not liking the way the dangerous soldier was speaking to him. Only because the Sergeant did not know anything about the Ghost and fighting skills he commanded, gave Glenallen the strength to reply to the Ghost the way he was speaking to him.

Walker smiled over the balls the new soldier was displaying to the Ghost, and the rest of the soldiers in the room, because he knew the Ghost would never attack another American soldier unless it was in self defense. He decided to allow the new guy to handle the situation with the Ghost, and if it started to get out of hand then he would step in and calm down both soldiers before it came to blows between them.

Every soldier in the room with Walker were staring at the Ghost, waiting to see how he was going to respond to the new soldier's warning.

The Ghost stared at the new guy until he allowed a smile, and then he remarked at the new guy in a much calmer voice this time. "Look buddy, you got fucking guts and guts are enuf to allow you to survive, especially in our unit. I'll let you get away with this shit this time, but in the future if you talk down on me, especially in front of any soldier in my unit, you betta have your hospitalization in order, cause you're gonna need it by the time I'm through with ya ass. What's your tag name so we can get rid of you new pukes so we and the regulars can get down to business round here."

Sergeant Glenallen stared at Ghost for a few tense moments, and decided to let it go as he replied. "My fucking nickname's High Spade, I got tagged with it because I'm black…"

"It fits ya good man." The Ghost snapped, and grinned at the soldier speaking to him.

"Funny man and you said Walker was trying to be a fucking comedian, huh soldier? Anyway, I'll introduce the other soldiers by their tag names as I point to the soldiers. Sergeant Carl Youngblood was tagged with the moniker of Sleeper, that's because he's the only soldier I know who can sleep in a moving Humvee heading in for an action. Sergeant Steve Steingold standing next to Youngblood was hit with Mule because he was always saddled down with the heavy weapons for the unit when we were on a mission. Sergeant Edward London was tagged with Small Change, that's because every time we went to a gin mill, he'd only carry change, and we got stuck paying for his drinks for the night.

"The last soldier behind me is Sergeant Michael Nettestad, and he received the tag name of Sweat Stain. He was given the name because anytime we went on an operation he was the first one to soak his uniform with sweat and started to stink up a storm." Glenallen spread his hands apart and smirked at the angry looking soldier he now knew as the Ghost.

"Well it seems the names fit you people and I see no reason to suggest changes unless you people screw up while we're on a mission." The Ghost grumbled as he went back to his cigarette, and rudely dismissing the new soldiers as he ignored their presence in the room.

Sergeant Glenallen turned back to Captain Walker as he looked at the Captain, to make certain his last orders did not change because of the slight confrontation with the other soldier.

Walker smiled at the new soldier, and offered him in a calm voice. "Sergeant you have your orders so I suggest you get busy carrying them out. The rest of us have a number of uther items we hafta to go over, and you new guys didn't earn the right to sit in on any skull sessions yet. Once you people are accepted in the unit, and you guys prove to us you're worth your dog tags. Then and only then will you people be included in any future training exercises or missions we get sent on. You guys have to prove your worth to us before you're accepted into the unit. You're dismissed, get out there and meet up with the rest of the soldiers."

The Captain stared at the new soldiers until they filed out if his office, once they were out, Walker turned on the Ghost and got on his ass. "Hey man, what the hell was that shit about, you asshole? You know betta than to display a case of the ass in front of any new pukes to the unit, buster. You embarrassed the shit outta my ass, I can't afford to have the new shits thinking my unit's out of fucking control, and I take lip shit from anyone in the damn unit. You made me feel like I wasn't the man every one of you puds had to worry about, and you weakened my standing with the new fucking soldier as well, buster."

"Arrr… I'm pissed in general, Walker. You know something, I'm getting sick and tired of being forced to report to this base anytime some brass hat wants to have us play soldier, and impressing their asses. I ain't got a life of my fucking own anymore, dammit! Every time I get interested in something or one, it seems like I get ordered back to base for more of this so-called special training bullshit they keep trying to shove down our throats, Walker. By the time I get back home again, whatever the hell I was getting involved in is either outdated, or some uther puke finished my idea off, and he got paid for what I was attempting to do with my life, man.

"I'm tired of this bullshit of playing soldier and running all over the damn world putting down another bunch of nuts who think they can take over the world, or they wanna hurt Americans. I think it's about time for some uther units of the service to step up to the plate and take some of the heat offa our shoulders for a change, Captain. That's why I'm so pissed off, Walker. This shit sucks the big one I'm telling ya, man."

"What the hell can I tell ya? This shit comes with our choice of trade, so you betta get used to it if you wanna hang with the rest of us grunts, and stop complaining while you're at it." Walker grumbled at the dangerous soldier known as the Ghost.

THE OVAL OFFICE, THE WHITE HOUSE, WASHINGTON D.C. THURSDAY, OCTOBER 24th, 2008. 7:30 A.M.

This meeting was classified as the President's DBR or Daily Briefing Report on current terrorist threats thought to be leveled against the United States, or any of her interests or allies throughout the world. The special meetings were ordered by the President, and it was scheduled for every Thursday morning without fail. It was a meeting of the President's National Security Council, and the permanent members consisted of the President, Vice President, the Secretary of the State, Secretary of Defense, the Chairman of the Joint Chiefs of Staff, and the Director of the Central Intelligence Agency.

The meeting also included the Director of the National Security Agency, the NSA, and the Security Advisor along with a host of other important Presidential and Cabinet members and aides, secretaries and a number of certain military advisors. Usually the meeting was held in the Situation Room constructed some seventy nine feet under the East Wing of the White House. But the President hated that room, and he only used it during national emergencies, or other threatening situations of late.

The President was seated behind the antique oak desk and his eyes were leveled on the face of the CIA Director, John Raincloud. The Director was fishing around in his briefcase, he was looking for the report he prepared for the President for this meeting. Everyone else attending the meeting busied themselves with other matters until the CIA Director's presentation started.

The President sat back in his chair and looked at General John White, the current Chairman of the Joint Chiefs of Staff, and the President smiled. He marveled at John's last name of White, because the Chairman was a huge black man. The President was pleased to have this powerful General working so closely with him. John was instrumental in solving a number of vital military operations successful for his Administration since he was first elected as Command in Chief of the United States. President Albert Cole diverted his eyes away from his General and looked at other people he surrounded himself with. He was pleased with everyone, and their loyalty to him and to the United States.

The lone civilian attending this meeting was Doctor Joel Russbinder, the President remembered drafting the doctor and sent him on the mission to Iran where the General's soldiers went after Iran and their secret nuclear development complex. He ordered the doctor to join his counterterrorist program, and he made the doctor the leader of NEST or Energy Department's Nuclear Emergency Search Team. The President's thoughts were interrupted by the CIA Director as he cleared his throat. Signaling he was ready to begin his report to the other members.

"Errr… yes Director Raincloud, you may begin your report if you don't mind. Excuse me I was taking a few moments while I waited for your report to begin." The President offered politely to the full blooded large Sioux Native American in a polite tone of voice as he smiled at the huge man as he waited for him to begin his briefing.

"No problem Mr. President, with all due respect sir, I fear my report for this week might be lengthily in duration, but we have a lot to go over, Mr. President." Director Raincloud picked up his file folder with the blue border and opened the cover.

The President looked at the BBTS or Blue Border Top Secret file and noticed a number of pages and realized the Director was not kidding over the length of his report.

"Mr. President and other members of the National Security Council, the security code document number for this briefing is One, Seven, Two, Two. But before I start my presentation, please allow me to say I'm honored to be allowed to address the members of this meeting on this fine day. Mr. President, as you and everyone living in the United States and the world, realizes how well the war in Iraq is shaping up and progressing, sir. Violence against our ground troops and Iraqi civilians has dropped to under twenty percent, sir.

"Mr. President we have al-Qaeda in Iraq on the run, and many Sheik leaders are bringing the young males of that country under their control, and stopping most violence in the country, sir. We have electric flowing to seven provinces unabated, and there are no serious threats on the board at this time. Of course sir, there's still radical fractions hitting us with car bombs and ambushes, but they're getting few and far in between of late, Mr. President."

"Yes Mr. Raincloud, I'm pleased at the way the Iraqi war is progressing. But it took a long time to get in the positions with that war we find ourselves in, sir. I don't mind telling you John, it almost destroyed my Administration until our General got control over there, sir." The exhausted looking American Leader offered as he let out his breath in a rush.

"Quite right Mr. President, the war in Iraq weighed heavily on all our minds, as well with the American public, sir." Director Raincloud replied as he gave General White a quick nod before continuing with his presentation. "On the other hand Mr. President, Iran's still giving us problems, and Iran's a major contributor in keeping Iraq in a constant state of unrest and turmoil, sir. We're tracking Iran's smuggling routes on which she's supplying the Shiite troublemakers with a flow of weapons and explosives to attack our military, and the leaders of Iraq with, sir."

"Yes John, I'm aware of the problems Iran's causing in this region of the Middle East. I don't mind informing you it's a matter of time before we have to come to grips with Iran and her nuclear ambitions, sir. If we and the Security Council members of the United Nations don't do something about their program and soon, Israel will jump the gun and start a major war in the Middle East. I wish to hell we could talk sense with the Religious leaders. The nut running that country is pushing his nation further down the path of war with us and the world, Director Raincloud. If the Iranian President gets his hands on refined plutonium, he's going to construct nuclear weapons, and that's sure as hell going to force Israel's hands to react against this nuclear threat to their nation's security.

"I fear if the Iranian President gets his hands on enough of the crap, every terrorist fraction in the world will end up with some of it, and we'll be facing a flood of dirty bombs exploding in many of our major cities, Director Raincloud." The President complained as he absentmindedly picked up a pencil and began twirling it between his fingers. It was a habit he picked up, and anyone who noticed the President doing this knew he was upset.

General White was allowing Director Raincloud to offer this report to the Security Council members, even though it crossed into his field of responsibility also. But the two men had discussed the report before Director Raincloud began offering it to the President and the other members of the council. Both of them agreed it was a better offering if one of them made the presentation to the members, and if any members had questions, they could ask either of them for a more detailed explanation later on.

Director Raincloud allowed the President a few moments to calm down before going on with his report. With a deep breath Director Raincloud went on. "Yes Mr. President, we agree with the concerns you raised, and in my report I do address some of them. Mr. President, my office has coordinated closely with General White, and we ran a number of detailed scenarios covering an all-out major war with Iran, along with a number of surgical strikes carried out against their nuclear facilities throughout Iran, sir. One of our biggest nightmares would be an all out land invasions of that Persian country, sir."

"Director Raincloud, shouldn't General White be giving this part of the report, sir? I believe you might be stepping on his toes a might by venturing down this area of the report without his input, Director Raincloud." The President offered with concern as he looked at the comfortable looking General seated at the meeting.

"With all due respect Mr. President," General White replied as he went to his feet, and continued speaking to the concerned President. "John and I discussed this report beforehand sir, and we came to the conclusion it'd be an easier report for everyone to follow if one of us gave this presentation to the members of this council, sir. I'd be more than pleased to respond to any questions or concerns from other members, sir. If they have troubling concerns after John has finished with this briefing, Mr. President Sir."

"Very well then General White, since you and John have discussed this situation and both of you agreed. Then I'll listen to John and if I have any questions, I'll aim them at you at the conclusion of this meeting, sir." The President almost growled at his General as he turned his attention back to the other man, and then he waited for Director Raincloud to continue with his report to the council.

General White returned to his seat the moment the President turned to Director Raincloud.

The instant the President looked at him, Raincloud continued where he left off with his briefing for the commander. "Mr. President, if we're forced to engage Iran on the ground, it's believe it'd take us over three years with a reinstated draft system set in place, to muster the over one million ground soldiers we'd need to enjoy a successful engagement with Iran, sir. It's estimated our ground forces would suffer a severe causality rate of over five thousand occupying forces a year. For the duration of a possible ten year stay in Iran until a stabile government could be installed that might be powerful enough to take command of the fractured country, and release our ground troops from further stay in that country, sir. That's what's believed we'll be looking at if we're forced to put boots on the ground in the country of Iran, Mr. President Sir…"

"In your personal opinion Mr. Raincloud, is this the only door we have opened to us, if we're forced to engage Iran in a battle on the ground over their damn nuclear ambitions, and their constant interference with the inner workings of Iraq, sir? Placing troops on the ground and then going inside that country for the kill factor, Director Raincloud." The President asked as he sat forward and looked in the eyes of the large CIA Director.

"That's not the way I see it Mr. President. I believe General White is in a better position than I to answer that last question more intelligently than I can answer it for you, sir." The CIA Director Raincloud offered confidently, but hating to have to turn his briefing over to the General, he believed it was necessary to answer the President's question completely.

"I see why you two believed it was better to allow one of you to do this briefing for the members, Director Raincloud. I hate being shifted over to the General to hear the answer to my question. It disrupts the flow of this conversation, sir. Okay General White, it looks like the balls now in your court sir. I believe it's necessary to hear from our General on this subject of ground forces being deployed inside Iran. Do you want me to repeat my question of Director Raincloud, General White Sir?" The President asked as he turned his attention to the General and stared at him.

When the President looked at him, General White rose and took a military attention stand before the President as he began to speak. No sooner did he begun speaking when the President cut him off and offered to the members attending the meeting. "Gentlemen, from this time further in this meeting, there's no need to stand when addressing any member of this council. Please General, retake your seat and be comfortable. I'm certain you're more comfortable and at ease speaking from a chair than to be forced to stand at attention addressing us, sir. This is an important meeting General, but there's no reason to stand on formalities. They're so boring."

"Thank you Mr. President, but it'll not be necessary for you to repeat your question, sir." The General replied as he sat and placed his folder before him on the desk and began reading from a page. "Mr. President, my people have been busy running a number of in-depth detailed scenarios involving a number of surgical strikes utilizing a flood of over fifteen thousand cruise missiles launched from our naval warships stationed in the Persian Gulf, Red Sea and Mediterranean, sir. We came to the conclusion any attack on Iran thought possible, will cause serious problems for my overstretched and depleted Military Forces, sir. We're in the mist of two wars as it stands, and I don't need a third war taking place unless it's absolutely necessary, Mr. President.

"Any attack against Iran whether it involves air or and ground forces and other assets on Iran, will cause more instability in the vastly troubled region of the Middle East, and it could have the opposite effect we're after, Mr. President. Such as forcing normally stable and peaceful Arab countries to maybe joining forces with Iran against us, or at least stop us from using their soil and military bases to launch our attack against Iran from, Mr. President. But if we're forced into a direct confrontation against Iran, it's been decided we'll employ the use of over ten thousand fighter planes and heavy bombers from aircraft carriers and military bases stationed well in the strike zone of the Middle East, and as far away as the United Kingdom and Italy, sir.

"These military assets will key in on selected and identified military targets spread throughout Iran, such as the Iranian Revolutionary Guard Headquarters which controls much of the military operations of Iran, and Iran's known and located nuclear sites, Mr. President. Once the major attacks on these installations were carried out successfully, we'll be forced to place special operation soldiers on the ground in Iran. In an attempt to better assess the extent of damage we inflicted on their military and nuclear operations, Mr. President. And, to secure any installations we deem necessary to secure, until we can evaluate what they were up to in Iran, sir.

"Furthermore Mr. President, many problems facing us, have been successfully cleared up and addressed by Director Raincloud's detailed report for the members of the Security Council, and the outstanding work of his office and well-trained people, sir. We have over eighty percent of Iran's nuclear facilities and military operations targeted in for first attention in the event of hostilities against the Iranian nation, sir. Some of Iran's nuclear operation is unknown to us as viable targets, Mr. President. But I assure you we're working diligently trying to locate all missing pieces of this puzzle before we're forced to act militarily against Iran, sir. If and when you decide to open our attack against the Persian nation, by that time we'll have located one hundred percent of their nuclear facilities and military installations in the country, sir.

"What we know for certain is, the Iranian government has buried their most vital nuclear facilities and operations deep underground in a number of secluded civilian sections of their vast desert, and other nuclear installations are dispersed throughout Iran, and that's one of the many reasons why we developed the twenty five thousand pound ground penetrating weapon we threatened to use in Iraq, Mr. President.

"We have certain reliably information mapped out the Iranian government constructed a number of important nuclear facilities and operations near schools, hospitals, and Mosques in hopes of deferring our attack against these structures because of the likely collateral damages that'll be suffered by Iran's civilian population, in the event of hostilities against our countries, sir. If and when we're forced to take matters into our hands and you give us, the military the green light to hit these selected military and strategic targets in Iran for destruction, Mr. President."

"This is all good to understand, General White. But what happens if Israel decides we're not moving fast enough against Iran to satisfy their needs to protect themselves and their nation's security against a possible nuclear attack, or future threat from Iran. By the way General White, you were supposed to report to me on the expected time before Iran's able to produce enough weapons grade plutonium to enable their technicians to start constructing their nuclear weapons and capabilities for their long range missiles, sir. Which I remind you General White are more than capable of hitting not only our military assets throughout the

Middle East region. But the missiles will be able to strike in the heart of Israel, General White?" The upset American Leader complained as he held his general in his angry stare for the moment.

"Mr. President, as far as we can ascertain, Iran's at least two years from having the capabilities of producing enough weapons grade plutonium to develop and arm ten long range missile delivery systems, sir. Israel and her want to stop Iran from developing nuclear capabilities of their own, have created a smorgasbord of serious situations to deal with, Mr. President. Problems we don't quite know how to begin to deal with." The General stared at the President.

"How's that, General White? Remember General, Israel's our only true ally in this region, and we desperately need Israel to remain an active state and ally, in case we have to go in the Middle East in force, and we can no longer depend on Saudi Arabia to offer us platforms to work from in the region, sir." The President remarked as he again sat forward and this time held his General in his harsh glare as he waited for his reply.

"With all due respect Mr. President, if Israel decides to attack Iran to end Iran's nuclear ambitions, it's all going to come down on our shoulders anyhow sir. Any attack on the Iranian nuclear installations by Israel, would serve to set their nuclear operations and ambitions back a few years at best, and Iran will be more belligerent and harder to handle than ever to deal with, if Israel does attack first, Mr. President. That's because Israel doesn't possess the military assets necessary to destroy all nuclear threats from Iran like we do, sir. Also Mr. President, any military operation against Iran carried out by Israel will cause a devastating retaliation by the Iranian military dealing with and closing down the Strait of Hormoz as they did during the war with Iraq.

"Iran would cut their nose off to get back at Israel and us, by blocking their own oil exports in a foolish attempt to close down the Persian Gulf to all commercial oil transportation against the world, Mr. President. The Strait of Hormoz is the Middle East chokepoint and main lifeline to the world and it'll bring back the horrors of small Iranian speed boats attacking civilian oil tankers at sail on the waters of the Persian Gulf, sir. If Iran does close down the Persian Gulf to commercial oil tanker traffic, it'll cause the price of crude oil to soar to as we estimated at nine hundred dollars a barrel, depending on how long any war with Iran lasts in the Middle East, sir. Couple their attack speed boats with the Chinese made Silk worm missiles they have stationed in and around the Strait, adding their large military base completed in the same area of the Gulf, Mr. President. Iran will drive the commercial oil tanker traffic on the Persian Gulf nuts on the world.

"Yes Mr. President our reaction would be to escort civilian commercial shipping through the Straits with our Naval Warships as we done the last time Iran closed the Straits against the world. But Mr. President there will be so many attacks on the commercial shipping, and some attacks will surely get through our defenses no matter how well we try and protect the civilian shipping from Iranian attacks, sir.

"Mr. President, I haven't brought up the problem of floating and moored mines released in the Persian Gulf waters, sir. The last time Iran chose to close the Persian Gulf against the flow of world oil, we had two Naval Warships heavily damaged by these damn mines, sir. They were all over the Gulf almost in uncountable numbers. We placed heavy machine gun mounts stationed on both sides of a number of our naval ships of war on picket duty in the Persian Gulf. These weapons will help to set off discovered floating mines in the Persian Gulf waters, sir. Although we're certain Iran won't be able to cause the havoc she once did the last time she chose to close the Persian Gulf waters. This is based on the assumption Iran will be forced to use the old and outdated technology to attack commercial shipping using the Gulf waters, and we're further advanced than when they did this act the last time against us, Mr. President.

"But the problem we'll face with Israel attacking Iran is as follows, Mr. President. If Israel attacks Iran on her own accord, she'll be employing American made F-15s and F-16s, and would be dropping American made bombs on the military and nuclear targets in Iran during the length of her operation against that Persian country, sir. So even if we stand on the sidelines and watch Israel attack Iran, we'll still get the blame one way or the other as happens when we have a problem in the Middle East, Mr. President." General White took a second to catch his breath, and allow the President or anyone else attending the meeting a break to ask him or Raincloud questions they might have troubling them over their presentation to the members of the council.

"Excuse me a moment please General White, I seem to remember a report I read a few months back about some new type missile system Israel had developed, sir. I believe they were classified as long-range missiles if my memory serves me correctly, sir." The President offered with a little concern lacing his voice as he stared in the eyes of his powerful military officer, and waited for the General's reply.

"Quite right Mr. President and that suggestion opened another scenario for us to contend with. I have to offer Israel does indeed have in their arsenal a new missile system they have branded the Jericho Three missile system. And yes, the system is a long range missile unit, and what we know of the system and Israel's intent to employ it against Iran's nuclear development and installations. Mr. President, I ran a detail report I'll offer you after this meeting has concluded sir, but I'll fill you in on what we understand at this time, sir.

"Mr. President, we come to the conclusion if Israel employs this new weapon system against Iranian sites, she'd be capable of destroying Iran's nuclear development, and Israel wouldn't have to resort to the use of warplanes to get the job done. Israel could mount either high explosives or her nuclear weapons on the tips of the missiles, and she could devastate Iran's nuclear ambitions in a full day's operations, sir. To tell you the truth Mr. President, we'd rather Israel employs this system when she decides to take the Iranian nuclear situation into her own hands, sir."

"Why is that General White?" The President asked with concern.

"Mr. President, if Israel employs this missile system she developed basically on her own, with minor assistance from us mind you, Mr. President. The Arab world would have to place the blame for the attack solely on the shoulders of the Israel leaders, sir. That'd enable us to step in and help broker a cease fire and settlement against retaliation strikes between the surviving Arab nations against the Israel government, sir…"

"General White, why wasn't I informed of this missile system the Israeli's developed, sir? I'm warning you General White, heads will roll if I discover vital information such as this is withheld from me as you military types seem to like doing, when you people believe this crap will upset me if I found out about it." The angry America Leader said dryly at his military officer as he held him in his gaze.

"Mr. President, you received an initial report on this weapon system the moment the Israeli military came seeking our help in the development of this system with them, sir. I believe it was sent to you as a low level report, and I don't see any reason to lift that report up to a priority alert, sir. The missile systems takes some heat from the Middle East off our shoulders, if the Israeli's use it against Iran, Mr. President." The General replied to the seated President.

The Director of the NSA sat forward and the President acknowledged his want to ask a question. "Yes Director, do you have something you want to ask the General, sir?"

"Yes I certainly do Mr. President." Bill Blaylocke replied he was the National Security Director who took over this position when Norman Griffin was killed in the failed attempted assassination of the President as he boarded Air Force One a few years back.

"Please, the General's here to answer any questions as well as give his briefing to us, sir."

"Thank you Mr. President." The smallish Director offered politely to the American Leader, and shifted his eyes and looked at the military officer, and remarked to him with a snap in his voice. "General White, before you ask sir, allow me to respond that we at the NSA are aware of this Israeli missile system, sir. But that's not the reason I requested to speak with you, sir. General White, I agree with the concerns you brought forth at this meeting sir, all but one."

"And which one is that, Mr. Director?" The General snapped back at the man.

"General White, you voiced a fear Israel will attack Iran with or without our consent or help, before they act against the Persian nation, sir. Why is that General White? You know Israel's under strict orders not to involve military assets we sold them in any attacks against any Arab neighbors for this reason you breached with us, sir. Israel knows full well if she does use some of our military equipment in any out of country attacks. Israel will forfeit a large part of our military and monetary support of their actions displayed in the Middle East, sir."

"Evidently Mr. Director, you're not privy to the latest statements from the outgoing Prime Minister of Israel, sir. The Israeli Prime Minister didn't mince words with his press statement made to the general population of his country, sir. He stated emphatically Israel doesn't need the help or consent of the United States to attack Iran, the moment he felt Israel's security was being threatened by Iran, or her attempts to secure nuclear weapons for their long range missile systems, sir." The General remarked smugly, feeling he was one upping the NSA Director.

The Security Director accepted the slight rebuff with a scowl, but he didn't respond to the General's stinging words aimed at him at the meeting.

When the military officer did not get the reaction he was looking for from the Director, he went on with his presentation once he got the look from the President to get on with it. "Yes Mr. President, the outgoing Prime Minister of Israel wants to do something before he leaves office, in an attempt to clean up his name, and what better way to make this name than by attacking Iran before he leaves office, sir. Israel set the table to use the military equipment she brought from us when she invaded Lebanon a number of years back, Mr. President.

"Israel's no longer concerned with using equipment we sold them to attack her Arab neighbors. You must keep in mind no matter what Israel does over the Iranian nuclear issue, we have to maintain support of the Israeli nation, and we have to allow Iran and the Arab world to understand this. We know direct talks with the Iranians on any political level will net us nothing with the present leadership in place against us and our interests in the Middle East, Mr. President. With each failed attempt to talk sense with the Iranians, serves to strengthen

Israel's want and need to take matters into her own hands and act in Israel's best security interests in the Middle East, sir."

"General White, let's place Israel on the side burner for the time being at this meeting. We know full well what's coming down the chute sooner or later, and what we'll do about it when it happens, sir. I want to know what's happening in Afghanistan and our never-ending search for Usama bin Laden." The President snapped at his military officer.

"With all due respect Mr. President, I believe Director Raincloud should takeover this part of the presentation, sir. He has his operatives working on the ongoing bin Laden situation, sir." The General replied as he turned and looked at the well-respected CIA Director.

Director Raincloud began to speak the moment the President set his eyes on him. "Mr. President, the war in Afghanistan's working out quite well for us, sir. Though it's true the Taliban's making a number of serious problems for our troops on the ground. I'm as certain as you and everyone seated at this meeting, when we do the troops surge in Afghanistan, most of these problems will come to a quick end for us and our allies involved in that country, Mr. President. At least that's what we're banking on sir."

"Excuse me Mr. Raincloud, but I'm more interested in the bin Laden problem than I am in the Afghanistan situation, sir. I can't impress upon you how important it is to my Administration to bring this man to justice. Don't forget I'm up for reelection this year, and bin Laden would be a feather in my cap if we were to capture or kill him, sir." The President moaned as he held Director Raincloud in his harsh gaze as he waited for his reply.

"Mr. President, there are many in this country and spread throughout the world who no longer believe the leader of al-Qa'eda doesn't matter, and he's no longer a serious threat to the United States or our Allies, sir. But I can assure you Mr. President they're laboring under a false delusion sir. True bin Laden no longer holds the esteem and power he once mastered in the world of terrorism, sir. Even in the Muslim world his popularity dropped off drastically, and his followers and a large number of younger jihad factions have slowly drifted from his sphere of influence, and these new jihadists ventured off to do their own acts of terrorism, and they taken to denouncing bin Laden as their leader lately, sir. Many extremely radical and young elements of the Islamic followings moved away from bin Laden and al-Qaeda's control over them, sir.

"Usama bin Laden's once threat he held over the free world has deteriorated from a well structured and maintained group of terrorist leaders controlling everything their fighters done and do, and he enjoyed the ability of moving huge sums of untraceable cash to a mess of unofficial terrorist cells of misguided young radicals, sir. Who try to emulate their predecessors control by dreaming up and carrying off devastation attacks on civilian targets aboard that could bear the al-Qaeda's trademarks imprinted on them sir.

"But these new batch of wannabe terrorists assembled a scattered and loosely knitted global arrangement between themselves, a sort of who's who in the jihad leadership which is almost impossible for us to trace to their grassroots origins and brain thrust, and destroy them, sir. In reality Mr. President, al-Qaeda and their leader bin Laden, still remains a believable source of inspiration and copycat image to follow to the young Muslims who dreamed of hurting anyone who doesn't believe in their religion and their wants and beliefs. With this gradual moving from the bin Laden leadership and control by these new young groups of Muslims who want to takeover for their once leader, has forced our intelligence and United Kingdom's MI-5 to begin looking to their and our homegrown terrorists followers, sir.

"The so called homegrown terrorist is the largest and latest real time threat against our nation's security and the hardest for us to detect, mainly because their plot to hurt the United States and her people can't be stopped in time, sir. This is because the plots are hatched in the fanatic's head, and it leaves no trail for us to follow until it's left in blood, sir. But again I remind you Mr. President, the death of bin Laden's influence over these younger jihadist nuts and the other copycat militants, has been exaggerated and underestimated by many top brain thrust of the intelligence arena, sir. Bin Laden is enjoying a powerful controlling influence over many of these young and leaderless jihad groups that may be a bit stronger than when bin Laden originally fled from Afghanistan, and bin Laden moved his terrorist operations into the lawless and remote area of Pakistan, sir.

"Yes Mr. President, the Taliban's enjoying resurgence in Afghanistan, and they and bin Laden are enjoying the safety the rugged lawless areas of Pakistan offers them. And they're also enjoying the lack of military attention the Pakistan government's deploying against them. But we'll get the sonofabitch sooner or later and have no doubt about that, Mr. President. It's only a matter of time before we get our hands on him, and we'll bring bin Laden and his followers to justice, sir. The scales of justice will be balanced against him and his cronies, and that you can bank on, sir." It was at this point in his presentation Director Raincloud decided to take a break, and see if anyone attending his offerings had questions of him before he went on with his report. When no one asked him questions, the CIA Director continued his presentation.

"**M**r. President, many so called independent terrorist operators, insurgents and militants took to setup their brand of terrorist networks without bin Laden's blessings or guidance. Nevertheless Mr. President, these independent jihad operators and other nuts still look to al-Qaeda and bin Laden for inspiration and further terrorist training and organizational skills, and the money they need to fund operations and attacks against the free world, sir. These homegrown terrorists are hitting us with a number of problems trying to track and hunt the bastards down before they're successful in attacks against us or our allies, sir. They're a bunch of loosely fitted fanatical actors, and their youth make them more brazing and dangerous than bin Laden and his wingnuts.

"Many homegrown terrorists are nothing more than a bunch of lonely wayward kids, and they're attacking their own country in an attempt to push their radical beliefs and wants. Their close affiliation with al-Qaeda and its leadership is giving these homegrown terrorists the efforts and will to attack surrounding nations from their homelands, sir. I need not remind you what happened in the United Kingdom when their homegrown nuts started to attack the trains and stations, and the car bombs they never got to set off, sir.

"Mr. President, we have evidence that a number of these young terrorists from the United Kingdom traveled to Pakistan for special terrorists training, and targets the al-Qaeda leadership wanted hit before they returned and attacked their homeland, sir. These are the problems we're facing, sir. These young radical attackers aren't relying so much on computers and cell phones for communications and their organization, and this is making it much harder for us to track and hunt them down, sir. We're currently tracking a number of this new generation of wannabe Jihadists making trips to Pakistan to be trained by the al-Qaeda terrorist organization, and then head back to their homelands to carry out their attacks against free countries, sir...."

"Now we're getting to where I wanted this briefing to head, Director Raincloud. I want to know what the hell we're doing about Pakistan, and the protection their country's offering to these terrorists basically operating free of military reprisals in that country, sir." The upset President snapped as he interrupted the Director's presentation.

"With all due respect Mr. President, Pakistan's the real problem we're forced to deal with in our ongoing war against terrorism and the al-Qaeda terrorist organization, sir. The FATA or Federally Administered Tribal Areas operating inside the Pakistan border, offer safe havens for al-Qaeda and Taliban followers to operate safely from. For them to forward their training of this new breed and future young group of Jihad terrorists we're forced to deal with. Mr. President, we're becoming alarmed over the large number of Western recruits showing up in some tribal regions in Pakistan for special terrorist training to make them more active terrorists against freedom, and working with the al-Qaeda forces, sir.

"Once these leaderless Jihadists reach the safety of the lawless and ungoverned FATA regions in Pakistan, they receive instructions from bin Laden's group, and he can guide them to almost anywhere in the world as long as these new batch of nuts have access to the internet, sir. Since the Nine, One, One attack, the leading prick of the al-Qaeda organization released a number of videos urging this new breed of terrorists to attack us, and some ranting and raving has been acted on by the new breed of Jihadist he's in control of, sir.

"Mr. President, lately bin Laden and his group of thugs, turned their attention towards the government of Pakistan and we're applauding this action, sir. If bin Laden's successful in turning Pakistan's protection against him and his followers, the Pakistani military will take a much more serious and active role in hunting him and his followers down and killing them off, sir. We know bin Laden was the force behind the assassination of the future female Prime Minister of Pakistan, sir. We further understand bin Laden's active in his want to destroy the government of Pakistan, Mr. President. Once he weakens the Pakistan government enough, he believes he'll be able to do in Pakistan, like what he did in Afghanistan, until we moved in and destroyed their operations in Afghanistan.

"Thank God Mr. President because of the outstanding programs you have installed throughout the United States, it's been pretty much impossible for al-Qa'eda forces to successfully hit us inside our borders, sir. What with the intense intelligence gathering capabilities we're currently employing against al-Qaeda, and adding the crossover to other security offices such as sharing information with the NSA, FBI, and the Homeland Security Agency and the other Intelligence Agencies. We know exactly what each office is doing to combat terrorism in our borders, sir. We tightened up our border's security and we're keeping an eye on immigrants who try to sneak into the United States across the border with Mexico and Canada, and with the civilians reporting suspicious acting people they detect to these Intel Agencies, sir. We basically got a good handle on the situation in the States, Mr. President.

"Even though we're successful with efforts against the al-Qaeda terrorist forces Mr. President, bin Laden's still hell bent with slaughtering any people from free countries, and they're resorting to attack global economies lately, sir. Bin Laden's turning to any means in an effort to harm the West or our allies or interests. Al-Qaeda and their cohorts started to resort to an assortment of new and more deadly weapons and tactics to create fear and alarm to any country who don't agree with their radical beliefs, sir."

"Director Raincloud, I believe you have drifted a might from the point I was interested in hearing about, sir. I was wondering what efforts we're employing in our ongoing search for bin Laden and his pack of murderers, sir. But since you brought up the Pakistan situation, I believe I want to know more about what's happening inside that nation, and what if anything they're doing trying to get control of their nation, and booting Usama and the rest of his thugs out of that nation, sir." President Cole offered as he again sat forward and he looked at Raincloud.

"Yes Mr. President, as we've been witnessing taking place over the past few months. Pakistan's suffering from her own form of homegrown and unwelcome terrorism being turned against her government and people, sir. A series of devastating car bombings occurred this year, along with machine gun attacks on her politicians and civilians, and countless suicide attacks on crowded public areas gave the new President of Pakistan fits and concerns to deal with, sir. Pakistan's becoming the frontline in the ongoing war on terrorism for the rest of the world, Mr. President.

"I further fear until the Pakistani government realizes this fact she'll never join us in this war for the survival of the free world. I feel bad for the new President of Pakistan, Mr. President. He's caught between a rock and a hard place, trying to maintain his strong ties with the United States, and yet the Pakistan President's trying to appease the more radical Muslim factions inside his borders, sir. He's further caught in the middle of crosshairs, because he has to deal with our growing impatience with Pakistan's failed campaign against the Taliban and al-Qaeda forces and bin Laden, and their attacks and excursions in Afghanistan from the Pakistan side of the border.

"The Pakistani President understands it's only a matter of time before we lose patience with him and his backassward country and Administration, and we take matters into our hands if he doesn't get his nation under control in the near future, and their country might and could end up like Afghanistan, sir. With our and NATO Forces bringing civilization and security back to his fragmented country if he can't get the job done for himself, Mr. President.

"This failure of the Pakistan leadership to get control over Taliban and al-Qaeda forces has caused some Special Forces soldiers to mount a series of military excursions on the Pakistan side of the border with our blessings I might add, Mr. President. We understand the hard hitting lightening fast raids inside Pakistan is going to strengthen the lawless Islamic border tribes with their festering hatred of us, and adding their die hard allegiance to al-Qaeda and Taliban forces operating inside their country. Mr. President, you have to take into consideration Pakistan with our help, assisted the Taliban and Mujahedeen fighters against the Russian forces when they attacked Afghanistan. Our support of the Taliban ended when they started to try to takeover control over Afghanistan, but Pakistan's support never ended for the Taliban fighters, and that's why many people in Pakistan are supporting the Taliban and al-Qaeda forces against us, sir.

"With the current form of incursions we're forced to carry out against the terrorists operating inside Pakistan, is starting to cause some serious problems with the Pakistan military, who took to firing weapons at our military forces when we actually invade Pakistan in pursuit of Taliban or al-Qaeda forces operating inside that country, sir. If only to try and hit the Taliban and al-Qaeda forces where they're hiding in that country, Mr. President. Our Special Forces troops are working under strict orders not to return fire on any Pakistani military troops unless absolutely necessary for self defense and safety, Mr. President.

"Their civilian and more radical elements are taking a strong stance against these military raids into their country from the Afghanistan side of the border, sir. We weighed both side of the equation, and came to the conclusion it's well worth the hard feelings if we can hit the terrorist's where they're sleeping, Mr. President."

"Err… excuse me for interrupting you Director Raincloud. Do you know how many excursions our Special Forces soldiers committed in Pakistan, in their search for bin Laden and of his criminals, sir?" "Mary Hirshfield asked from her seat as she flashed a smile at the CIA Director.

The CIA Director turned to see the Vice President as he replied. "Although General White's in a much better position to reply to that question Ms. Hirshfield, I know the numbers of excursions our special operation forces committed into Pakistan, Ma'am. As of this day there had been twenty seven air incursions inside Pakistan airspace Ma'am, mostly carried out by our unmanned drone aircraft, which caused the death of fifteen important leaders of the al-Qaeda terrorist organization, Ma'am. Our Special Forces troops entered Pakistan soil twelve times when they detected al-Qaeda forces on the move inside

Pakistan, and these soldiers knew they could hit them hard and get out of Pakistan intact, Ma'am.

"We also gathered word the surviving al-Qaeda leadership is hoping these raids carried out by our troops in Pakistan, will alienate the Arab tribal leaders more, along with the more radical and younger terrorist elements of that country against the Pakistan government, Mr. President. These attacks into Pakistan by our soldiers and drones, helped to disrupt our troubled relations with the troublesome Pakistan military and her civilians and leaders. There was a recent poll taken in Pakistan, and it came out three out of ten Pakistani civilians reject any form of cooperation, and a better working relationship between their military forces and ours working in Afghanistan, sir.

"Also taking place Mr. President is a crisis developing in Pakistan, because of the rash of terrorist attacks carried out on her civilian population mostly by Taliban militants operating inside that country, and with their civilians asking why they should become an active part of our ongoing fight against world terrorism. Mr. President, their questions are being answered by the devastating attacks from the Taliban and al-Qaeda forces aimed against Pakistani people in their country, sir." Director Raincloud turned to the President and gave him a quick look, and then he went on with his report for the council.

"At this moment Mr. President, Pakistan's economy is in shambles, and the new President spent more time locked behind bars than he did with any political life he enjoyed thus far, sir. He once claimed to be outright insane in an attempt to try and avoid further criminal prosecution and imprisonment because of his criminal past, Mr. President. Couple this with the assassination of Prime Minister Bhutto finishing off a year of turmoil and murder and all sorts of hell occurring inside Pakistan, helped to strengthen and clean up our image inside that country, and it served to tarnish the terrorist's role in Pakistan for the time being, sir.

"Mr. President, I must take this time to inform you and the rest of the members of this esteem council that we've been busy intercepting a series of cries and concerns originating from many cities for the government to start making Pakistan a safe country for their civilized people to move about and make a living in, sir. It's beginning to turn for us, but the process is going at a slow and very laborious pace, sir. Mr. President, trying to speak any sense into the members of the Pakistan government is like spitting in the wind and ducking, sir. Even though Pakistan had its fair share of terrorist attacks carried out against their civilian population and government, sir. Pakistan's still trying to take on a dual role of enabling the wanted terrorists to openly and freely operate inside their country, sir.

"It's been a helluva mess in Pakistan, and there are no signs of it getting any better in the near future for them or us, Mr. President. The ever expanding war carried out against global terrorism has shifted its attention back towards the borders of Afghanistan and Pakistan, where it started. Ever since we were able to bring some form of security to Iraq, and with the Taliban resurging power in certain areas in Afghanistan, has forced us to turn our eyes and attention to Pakistan. It's Pakistan that gives us more problems to mount than Afghanistan ever has, and this is because of the mountainous and lawless region of Pakistan under influence of a band of Arab tribal leaders who not many of Pakistan's military troops want to go up against and engage in combat, Mr. President." Director Raincloud again took a quick breath, and he paused to see if anyone had any questions of him. When none came, he continued with his report again.

"Mr. President, one must realize the forces involved with protecting al-Qaeda and the Taliban fighters operating freely in the Pakistan border, sir. It's been a long belief in the Arab world, and especially in Afghanistan and Pakistan, whenever a visitor visits a home in either Arab countries sir. The visitor's welcomed to the home and he's offered protection of the owner of that home and villagers of the town to all ends of hospitality, sir. The owner of the home is willing to give up his life to protect the visitor to his home and country from harm. In this case the hospitality's being offered to al-Qaeda and Taliban militants hiding inside Pakistan, sir.

"This fact is giving protection to al-Qaeda forces and bin Laden and his leadership operating in Pakistan. With this protection afforded to the terrorists, gives the attackers power to be able to assault cities and towns, and against our military forces in Afghanistan, and these attacks are keeping us from bringing security to Afghanistan as we brought to Iraq and her people.

"On the other hand, Pakistan's starting to come apart at the seams in that nation, sir. The economy's in terrible condition, and there's unrest rapidly growing among the youth of that nation, couple this with the rash of devastating terrorist attacks recently occurring against that nation. Along with their own breed of young homegrown terrorist actions that government must deal with, and adding Pakistan's nuclear weapons and fears that threat posses to the free world if any of these damn weapons of mass destruction happen to fall in the hands of either or both al-Qaeda and Taliban. Forces me to believe Pakistan's standing on the doorstep of an all-out civil war occurring inside that country that'll virtually tear the troubled nation apart from one end to the other, sir. This is a serious threat we have to keep in the back of our minds at all times, sir.

"If a civil war breaks out inside the border of Pakistan Mr. President, it'll offer al-Qaeda and Taliban forces a new political platform to operate safely from. Much like they did when they once controlled everything occurring inside Afghanistan a few years ago. Before we stepped in and placed an end to that control when we invaded Afghanistan for revenge for the Nine, One, One attack bin Laden masterminded and his assholes carried out in New York, Mr. President.

"Another problem we've been forced to deal with Mr. President is the fact with our military incursions carried out in Pakistan by airforce and assets on the ground. It served to raise the hatred and anger of the Pakistani peoples against us, and it's so bad that a vital military supply line from Pakistan to Afghanistan supplying ammunition and fuel and other military necessities and supplies for our troops and NATO forces in Afghanistan. Was blocked temporally by hordes of young Pakistani civilians for a few days, until their military units got a handle on the kids and they opened the supply route again, sir. Since the first blocking of vital supply lines in Pakistan Mr. President, it has almost become a common place thing nearly every week with these kids attempting to block our supply vehicles from getting supplies to our troops in Afghanistan, sir.

"I guess the Pakistani civilians and her youth feel since they got away with it once, it opened the flood gates to carry out this harassment against our troops when they want to make a name for themselves, or cause us fits with supplies getting to our troops, Mr. President. Since these attacks on our supply line began, we've been laying pressure down on the Pakistani government to curtail the Taliban and al-Qaeda forces, and their operations inside their country, to get some pressure off our military forces in Afghanistan, sir. The Pakistani President made a number of lame and lackluster attempts to stop the insurgent's operation in safety of Pakistan from crossing over the border and hitting Afghan and our military targets in Afghanistan, Mr. President.

"Mr. President, the Pakistani President and government displayed some minor success against the Taliban and al-Qaeda forces operating inside that country, sir. Most Western leaders believe the Pakistani government hasn't done nearly enough to enable us to get the upper hand on these terrorist groups operating in the borders of Pakistan, in our attempt to end their savage reign they're enjoying over their civilian population, sir. True Mr. President, we, along with the Afghanistan government, are trying to open some form of close and vital communications with the lesser fanatical elements of the Taliban followers. The main thrust and hardliners of the Taliban militants and al-Qaeda forces are still resisting our efforts in this area to bring about some sort of a peaceful settlement between their forces and Afghan government, Mr. President.

"Presently Mr. President, our main focus is leveled on the Pakistani government. That's because of their lack of control over the ungoverned tribal regions of their country that provides sanctuary for the Afghan, al-Qaeda and Taliban insurgents to operate from, sir. The breakthrough we're searching for, hinges on the new but weak Pakistani government to adopt a military strategy where they eliminate those sanctuaries that serve as an extension to the Afghan field of battle, sir. We're trying to convince the Pakistanis of something they already understand, Mr. President.

"The al-Qaeda, Taliban and Afghan insurgents and terrorist fractions are the single serious threat to the security and peace of both troubled nations, Pakistan and Afghanistan, and against the world, Mr.

President. Nothing for both nations will get better until we eliminate the growing threat from these terrorist groups, sir. This is what caused us to step up military efforts bringing the war to the terrorists using Pakistan as their staging grounds, to continue their terrorist attacks against our military forces and Afghan government. Mr. President, we have to be prepared to increase our incursions into Pakistan by employing Predator drones, as well as employing other military aircraft assets and ground forces, until we can destroy all the al-Qaeda and Taliban forces and what they represent in Pakistan, sir. Even if we have to do this without the Pakistani government's blessing and consent, Mr. President.

"Mr. President, we have to step up pressure on the new Pakistani government, sir. Because if we continue to allow al-Qaeda and the Taliban forces to continue carrying out their disruptive incursions in Afghanistan against our and NATO troops, and continue creating havoc and mayhem in the areas we established a form of security in. It'll be a matter of time before the Afghans not causing us trouble, join forces with the troublesome insurgents because they're sick and tired of an endless war in their country. We're going to lose gains we have established in Afghanistan after these years of fighting in that country. It's getting tense and we're continuing to do all we can in our ongoing efforts to destroy the Taliban and al-Qaeda forces, but we can only do so much, because we're basically operating with one hand tied behind our backs. We have to stop the incursions from Pakistan into Afghanistan by the damn insurgents, sir.

"It's almost like Vietnam where we couldn't bomb certain areas of that country, even though we knew the VC were concentrating military supplies and efforts as a staging ground in the areas we weren't allowed to bomb. Here, we can chase the damn Taliban and al-Qaeda fighters until they make it to Pakistan, and then we have to break off our engagement because they have freedom to operate inside that country, and we can't get our hands on them, sir. If we could carry out a bombing campaign in Pakistan where the terrorists are hiding, within three week's time, the Taliban and al-Qaeda forces will be just a bad memory, Mr. President.

"We have to force the Pakistani military to start dealing properly with al-Qaeda and Taliban insurgency situation in their borders, rather than their sitting on the sidelines watching as our ground troop's chase and enter Pakistan, to get at the terrorist attackers from the Afghan side of the border. Mr. President, we have to be prepared to carry out other measures in our efforts..."

"Excuse me for interrupting your presentation, Director Raincloud. Why haven't the Pakistani military taken control of the al-Qaeda and Taliban situation you're speaking of in their country, sir? The Pakistani government has to realize it's in their best interests to eliminate the problem the terrorist forces are causing their country." The Vice President asked with concern.

"That's a good question Madam Vice President, and I'll try to answer it to the best of my ability, Ma'am. I'll address my answer to the President, Ma'am." Raincloud replied as he turned to the President before speaking. "Mr. President, the Pakistani government's loaded down with her own batch of problems, but the real problem lies with their military getting the upper hand on the insurgents in their country. The Pakistani military isn't geared to handle the al-Qaeda and Taliban forces, because their brain thrust and set is built in and around the fear and concern over India invading Kashmir, and the Pakistani military having to enter an all-out war with India.

"The Pakistani military doesn't understand the first thing about how to control a successful domestic counterterrorist operation against these insurgents in their country, sir. Before you ask the question I know is on your mind Mr. President, on numerous occasions my office made it clear to the Pakistani leadership and military, we stand ready to give them our best military advisors to train their military on how to deal with the terrorists in their country and killing their innocent civilians, sir. So far, they haven't agreed to our offer of help.

"Mr. President, the crackdown on the terrorist forces by the resurgent Pakistani government, and serious efforts now being put forth and employed by the Pakistani military. These actions forced a large numbers of the Pakistani civilian population living in this troubled region to cross the border with Afghanistan to get distance from the fighting, sir. The Pakistan military have been engaging the terrorist fighters in their country quite regularly and seriously of late, sir. However Mr. President, the Pakistani military command is trying to dump this crap on our shoulders, by reporting to their people we're not doing enough to stop the Taliban and al-Qaeda forces from crossing the Afghanistan border and creating problems for their government, sir.

"Also Mr. President, the Taliban turned their attention to the internet to report to their followers of their success they're enjoying in Afghanistan. I find this move interesting on their part, sir. Because when the Taliban were in control of Afghanistan, they'd put to death anyone caught working on computers, or and especially the internet, sir. How things change when one is on the run from justice, Mr. President. But their sudden use of the internet created a new problem for our side, Mr. President. When Taliban insurgents are successful in carrying out an attack against our military operations in Afghanistan, they put it out on the internet.

"Many times the Taliban reports are out before we had the chance to investigate and find out if the attack they're talking about took place, sir. The Taliban are resorting to the use of improved IED's (Improvised Explosive Devices) employed against our troops in the field, adding to the rising death toll of our soldiers. The bastards are planting the devices inside buried culverts constructed to drain the flooded areas that run under the roads, so we can't detect them before they explode, sir. They're also employing two hundred to five hundred pounds of explosives in attacks against our troops, and they enjoyed some success defeating the new mine resistant, ambush protected vehicles we branded MRAP's.

"They're the heavy machines designed with the special super harden V-shaped hull to deflect roadside explosives that detonate under or near the machine. Although the machines were developed to stand up to roadside bombs, they weren't designed to stand up to such powerful explosives being employed against them, and in some attacks against these vehicles, they've either been flipped in the air or blown in half, either crushing or seriously injuring the soldiers trapped inside the machine, sir. Before you ask Mr. President, it's believed these roadside weapons are being imported to Pakistan from Iran, sir. It seems the Iranian government turned their eyes and military efforts towards the insurgents working in the Pakistan border against us, sir.

"Mr. President, there's one more part of this report I want to deliver, but as it stands sir. Not all the evidence is in yet to formulate a more accurate plan of a future terrorist attack, sir. But I'll offer what I have assembled so far for your approval, and you can direct me in what you want me to do about this information, Mr. President. Over the past two months sir, a number of special operatives been busy intercepting a number of mixed and sometimes confusing communications going on between a few well known al-Qaeda leaders, and a terrorist group operating inside the Pakistan border, sir. From what we pieced together so far about these communications, we believe an attack against India is in the works from this Pakistani terrorist group."

The President showed he was paying attention to his CIA Director's words as he offered. "Director Raincloud, don't tell me another Nine, One, One attack is in the works from these assholes, this time planned against India, sir."

"It's believed so Mr. President, allow me to explain this clearly for you, sir. Lately, we've been intercepting a number of back and forth communications originating from within an old terrorist organization still operating in the Pakistani borders, sir. The terrorist group goes by the name of Lashtar-E-Taiba, and we have reason to believe this terrorist organization's operating under the wing and protection of al-Qaeda leaders in Pakistan. Most communications we intercepted and deciphered thus far Mr. President, point to the leaders of this organization issuing orders to their field operatives to begin preparing to attack India's interest in of Mumbai, sir.

"Mr. President, we've been in constant contact with the Indian Counterterrorism Agency and their forward Commanders in the field, sharing this information with the Pakistani government. As it stands at this point Mr. President, it's believed these terrorists are preparing to hit the capital city of India with small weapons and hand grenades aimed against civilian targets, sir."

"Jesus Christ Director Raincloud, I can't believe we're discussing a possible terrorist attack on an Indian city so calmly, sir. What the hell are we doing to try and protect our civilians visiting India's capital, sir?" The President growled at the CIA Director, not trying to show his disgust over a terrorist attack in the offerings.

"Mr. President, we've been communicating with our Embassy in India, and issued a warning for all American civilians visiting the capital to take care in their actions, and further ordered them to remain in their rooms in hotels, and not to be seen walking on the streets of Mumbai, sir. At this moment sir, we're operating under a medium alert warning, and will until we assemble a more immediate threat aimed against our civilians there, sir. If and when this intercept comes, we'll order our civilians in India to hide, or get out of the country all together, Mr. President." Director Raincloud offered as he maintained direct eye contact with the American Leader.

"Dammit to hell, this war in that region is going to be the death of me yet, Director Raincloud. What is the Afghan government doing providing security for their country so we can start pulling our boys out of the danger zone?" The President moaned as he waited for his reply.

"Mr. President, I'd like to answer that question, sir. I fear John will go a bit light on his response, sir." General White offered from his seat.

"Please do General White." President Cole replied to his military leader.

"Mr. President, the Afghan government's crippled in their organization and governmental skills, and it doesn't show any signs of improving in the near future, sir. With the rampart and out of control corruption and poverty consuming most of the country, this situation in turn has help to fuel the expansion of the opium poppy crops, Afghanistan's main cash crop of the country. Because of its ease at growing and handling of the huge cash crop once it produces its form of death, sir. We're also being hampered by the lackluster and poor protection attitudes of the other allied nations who placed their soldiers in Afghanistan to assist us in our war against terrorism in this region, sir.

"Most troops from NATO nations aren't interested in engaging the Taliban or al-Qaeda insurgents in pitch battle, for fear of losing soldiers to the fighting occurring in that country, sir. Mr. President, if we're able to get some NATO Forces to shoulder more of the responsibility and burden of fighting in the borders of Afghanistan and Pakistan. That action would free up more of our soldiers, so they could train the Afghan police and military in earnest to defend themselves against the Taliban and al-Qaeda forces, Mr. President. And, that'll enable them to shoulder more of their country's security situations for a change. Mr. President, the only thing missing from Afghanistan is their nation's security efforts, sir. Once the civilians of that country start to feel they're secured in their country's borders. Then and only then will the civilians begin to rebuild their country to an operating nation, Mr. President..."

"Excuse me for interrupting again General White. But I believe I have absorbed about everything that's been offered to the council at this meeting by you and Director Raincloud, sir. You both gave me quite a bit to mill over, General White. But it's getting late and I have a number of scheduled meetings setup for later on today I must prepare myself for, sir. What say we place an end to this meeting? But I want you and Director Raincloud to place everything spoke about today on hard paper, so I can review it at my leisure and then consider what I want to do about this troubling situation you have pointed out to me, sir?

"Then I'll be able to give you a much better response to these problems raised before me, sir. I don't mind telling you my brains are scrambled for the rest of the day sir, and I have a mess of meetings I must attend to, General White. Everyone, I want to thank you for attending this special meeting and your input was extremely valuable. You'll excuse me if I leave and attend to projects set up for the day. Mary, you're with me, I need you for the first two meetings for today, young lady." The President replied as he rose to his feet, and waited for his Vice President to join him and they quickly left the room.

THE SPECIAL OPERATIONS CAMP STATIONED AT CAMP LEJEUNE, NORTH CAROLINA. THURSDAY, OCTOBER 24, 2008

It was five p.m. by the time the special operations troops were released from their day of added training. The exhausted elite soldiers filed in their barracks with many of them not even thinking about eating their evening meal, because they were so spent. The soldiers staying on the second floor of the barracks separated from the other troopers, and headed upstairs to wash their aching bodies in the hot water of the showers. The barracks was flooded with curses and complaints over the way the soldiers were being trained and driven for future missions they might be sent out on by their commander, Colonel Bruce Leadbetter and his staff.

Captain Robert Walker headed for his quarters in the front section of the barracks on the first floor, and as usual he was followed in by his chosen few troopers he was always with. Sergeant Dorothy Ramirez was moving behind Walker, and Mutt, Lieutenant Frank Hall, Blind Date, Sergeant Regina Raphael, and the Ghost, Sergeant Walter Casper, followed them in the room. The moment Walker sat down by the small desk in the room, the complaints started.

"Hey Walker, when the hell are we gonna get the fuck offa this stinking base and head home for some fun and games, man? I'm getting tired of playing soldier I feel they're keeping us on base for spite." No Neck, Sergeant Robert Abbott grumbled as he made himself comfortable, and then he glared at the Captain. The female soldier Ice, Sergeant Diane Morrison was by Neck who she was interested in romantically.

The way Neck barked at him got Walker's blood going, and he snarled at the large soldier. "Hey pal, you wanna talk to me you betta get the heat outta your fucking tone, or you're gonna find yourself raking the grass with your damn comb. I told you crybabies once we get this training crap down pat, and we act like we know what the fuck we're doing, we'll be released on leave. If you wanna head home then you do betta on the training course. We're only getting stuck here because you shitbirds keep screwing up out there stupid, so you only have yourself to blame, man."

Casper did not like the anger in the other soldiers so he offered while trying to calm the other two down. "Say Road Kill, not for nuthin but I'd like to know when we might be finishing up with this training crap myself. It feels like we were stuck on this damn base for a year already, and I wanna get back to the real world and start living a civilian life again, man."

Walker turned to the Ghost and saw his smile and relaxed and offered him. "I feel ya pain, and feel the same way you do, man. I wanna get home and start living my life again. I'll clue you in on something you might not know man, from what Colonel Leadbetter told me the uther day, it looks like we'll be pulling leave in early December. Although he's not happy with the way this urban training shit's going down so far. The stinking Colonel told me he wasn't gonna keep us stuck on the base for the Christmas holidays, buddy. I know once Command release us from active duty, we're gonna be on leave until the middle of next year, barring uther crap coming down the chute and screwing up our leave."

There was a collective release of breath as the soldiers kicked back. Then they started to go over the latest training session, trying to figure out where they might make improvements, so Colonel Leadbetter would get off their back and release them on leave.

THE SMALL IRAQI TOWN OF AR-RAMADI, FRIDAY, OCTOBER 25th, 2008

Ayesha al-Qaysi woke at the crack of dawn as usual. For some reason she was excited about this day, but did not understand why. Ever since she woke, she had a haunting feeling something good was going to happen, and she was looking to push the day along to see what that good might be. She was all smiles as she rushed around the home and decided to make breakfast for her mother. She had no idea of events taking place in the Iraqi desert on this morning.

An Iraqi boy of thirteen from her village named Saad Ihsaan, headed to the desert looking for anything he could find to sell on the black market, to make his poor family money. Saad was known in the village as a desert scavenger, always going to where a noted tank battle between the invading Coalition Forces came across a column of stalled Iraqi tanks and armored vehicles. So far, the young man found many minor military items, and once when he was scrounging in one of the burned out hulks of an Iraqi war machine, and he found a slightly burned wallet from an obviously dead Arab soldier with over a hundred dollars worth of Iraqi money stuffed in it.

Saad knew Ayesha since he was born, and many times when he was growing up, Ayesha baby sat him for his mother. Saad knew of Ayesha's anger at the American soldiers who seemed to be everywhere in Iraq. On this day, Saad vowed he was going to find weapons for Ayesha to hide, in case she wanted to take revenge on the Americans for the death of her father. He wanted to impress Ayesha by finding weapons, and headed to the desert in search of them.

As always it took Saad Ihsaan four and a half hours to make it to where the small war was fought. There were fifteen Iraqi tanks left destroyed and rusting on the sands of the desert, along with nineteen smaller armored support vehicles. Although the American soldiers removed all the weapons they found inside the destroyed war machines, there was hope a few weapons were missed, and this was the young male's driving force on this day.

Just as Saad climbed over the steep sand dune to where the destroyed armor was left to rust in the desert, he took a pull from the bottle of water he carried. He was sweating heavily, and because of the blowing winds last night, the desert landscape seemed all wrong to him. This time instead of running down the other side of the dune, he had to go to his right and run along the spine of the dune until it sank closer to the desert floor. But the winds uncovered dead Iraqi soldiers covered over by the blowing sand during the long ago battle. The soldier's bodies were skeletons, but he was hoping to find missed weapons buried by the sands.

There was something strange about the area where the three dead soldiers rested on the ground. The sand was flat, but the area was not a hidden road or possible abandoned landing strip. The way the sand was shaped and hard packed, Saad was certain it was a manmade feature. The child slowed his pace and started to cautiously walk to the first dead Iraqi's body. His want to impress Ayesha gave him the strength to approach the bodies in fear of them. The air was wrong in the area, like there was stale air coming from the ground beneath his feet, and there was a foul smell he put off to the decayed bodies of the Iraqi soldiers. The young child walked up to the first body as if he was afraid the soldier was going to come back to life, and then beat him for bothering his long sleep.

Saad looked in the eyeless sockets of the skinless skull, and let out his breath in a rush, knowing this dead soldier would never again beat another Iraqi child. The soldier's bent helmet laid three feet from the body, and the uniform was rotted and obviously ripped apart by a horde of desert scavengers who ate the flesh of the soldiers slaughtered by the invading Americans.

He reached out with his foot and lightly touched the first body with his sandal. What decayed skin was left on the arm fell free of the bones, and almost caused the child to lose his stomach. Never before did he ever see a body in such a state of decay. The Iraqi child saw many bodies of soldiers and the tortured civilians of Iraq in his short lifetime, but never in the condition like these poor forgotten bodies were in. It was almost like the dead soldiers were left lying on the sand to serve as a warning to anyone who might come across them.

Fear drove the child away from the first body, because there was almost nothing left of his uniform that once covered the bleached white bones. There was no need for him to search this body. Saad stepped over the body and headed for the next one. This soldier's uniform was nowhere near as rotted as the first one, and he had dreams of finding cash on this body. Without thinking, he knelt down by the body and he carefully opened the breast pocket, he could see something was resting in that pocket of his uniform.

Saad's lips parted in a smile as he removed the soldier's wallet. He placed his weight on his heels as he rested kneeling on the sand, and opened the tattered wallet. He never read the name on his military ID, he was more interested in any riches the soldier might have had on his person at the time of his death. The child pulled out papers, a faded military pass and a picture of the soldier's obvious wife. In a side pocket, he found what he was looking for. The soldier had some American cash, a total of one hundred dollars. Again a smile as he realized this soldier had to be an officer to have such a bounty on his person.

Once he removed the cash, he tossed the wallet on the sand as he rose and stepped over this body and walked towards the last soldier lying in a heap. This soldier was almost as rotted as the first body he looked at, but there was some uniform spread out by the body. Saad check the cloth from the body and found the wallet of this soldier. Desert scavengers gnawed on the leather for whatever food value it might receive from the leather. There was no money in this wallet, but it was full of military papers. He pulled the papers out of the wallet in search of more cash, and he released the papers to the winds of the desert. The child had no interest in the papers he released as they blew over the sand and disappeared from view.

Disappointed in his poor find on this last body, the child stood and before he left the area, he studied the landscape. It still stuck him as more than strange the shape of the area, and he decided to check it out a little further. Saad understood Saddam Hussein constructed many secret weapon bunkers buried in the sands of the desert, and he was wondering if he might have just stumbled over one of these caches. This thought and his want to impress Ayesha, gave him the strength to remain in the area of death, and search it. Ayesha needed weapons in her desire to hurt the American soldiers occupying his country.

Cautiously, Saad walked around the flat area where the bodies of the soldiers lay. He was dragging his foot over the sand in search of any openings to an underground bunker. Twice in his search of the area did he have to step over a body of a soldier lying on the sand. He started to stomp his feet on the hard packed sand, and where he stomped his feet, it sounded like the desert. He was about to give up his dreams of finding a hidden catch of weapons, when his next foot stomp sounded like he was standing over a hollow. He immediately dropped to his knees and he drove his hands into the soft sand.

Not six inches under the sand, his hands ran over a smooth surface and he started clearing the sand from the area. The sand felt good to his hands as he uncovered what looked to be a concrete slab. With sweat running down his face and burning his eyes from the heat and adrenaline filling his body, he tried to find the opening he was in search of. Not being able to find it, Saad Ihsaan rose and continued stomping his feet on the sand. Wherever he stomped, the same hollow sound replied. His stomping was leading him towards a mound of sand, the only rise in the flat area he was searching. As he headed for the mound, the hollow sound was getting louder. He was three feet away from the mound when he stomped his foot once more, and a shift in the mound of sand drew his attention. Saad went to drive his hands in the mound, and his fingers bent inwards when they hit the concrete covering hidden by the loose sand.

It took Saad an hour digging before he found the opening to the underground bunker. But the Iraqi child had no idea how far the papers he removed from the soldier's wallet traveled in that amount of time, driven by the blowing wind of the desert. Three pages were blown over a mile away from where they were released in the wind.

Saad uncovered the opening to the bunker, and struggled with the concrete cover, his mind raced with wonders of delight over what he might find hidden under the sand. His mind went from a catch of gold, to a horde of weapons then to food supplies to feed his family. With almost superhuman strength, the ninety five pound boy shoved the one hundred pound slab of cement out of his way, uncovering the entryway to the chamber. He had to blink to get his eyes accustomed to the darkness as he entered the opening. To his amazement, he discovered a candle standing near the opening, and there was matches as well.

With trembling hands, Saad took the candle and matches and lit it. He placed one foot before the other and climbed down the steps as he entered the darken tomb. The candlelight made the child see where he was going in the bunker, and soon he found three other candles and lit them. There was enough light for him to see everything in the bunker and to his disappointment, all he discovered were countless stacks of bottles and stainless steel metal containers, and each had the skull and cross bones printed on the warning label. There were three AK-47 assault rifles in the bunker, and the child carried them over to the opening and stacked them. Saad Ihsaan was disappointed over the catch of useful weapons he discovered, and found himself trying to read the warning labels. What was stated as stored in the containers did not impress him, and he was about to leave the underground enclosure when a small vial drew his attention.

The reason this vial drew his attention was because it was separated from the others, and housed in a glass enclosure. It looked special so he moved to the vial. He noticed the markings on the glass, and saw a larger container with the same warning printed on it. Even though Saad did not understand what the warning was, he understood he had discovered something important, something that might assist Ayesha and her hatred for the American soldiers occupying Iraq.

He removed the glass protection from the vial and took the tube from the stand. He tried to open the container, but it was sealed by a tamper proof cap, so he shrugged and stuffed it in his pocket. His trying to remove the cover broke the seal of the vial, and once it was in his pocket, a trace of yellow liquid housed inside the tube, seeped out and stained his pocket. Saad decided to leave the bunker and gathered the assault weapons and carried them up the steps. The fresh but hot air revived him, and he laid the weapons on the ground and struggled to slide the slab over the opening to the bunker, he took sand and hid the opening under the desert as best he could. He did this in case Ayesha wanted to see where he found what was hidden in the glass vial.

When he hid the opening to the underground to his approval, he stood and started to walk in the direction that led him to the area. Saad looked to the sun and was amazed over the time he used exploring the bunker. He felt it was nearing two in the afternoon, and he was a few hours from his town. He quickens his pace because he wanted to be out of the desert before the sun went down, and the scavengers, animal and human came out of their hiding places, and preyed on any poor soul they found wandering in the desert in the darkness of night.

THE IRAQI TOWN OF AR-RAMADI IN THE ANBAR PROVINCE, THURSDAY, OCTOBER 24th, 2008 AT 1:30 P.M.

Ayesha al-Qaysi was surrounded as she was all day by Sadiya Sadjadpour and Shafiqu al-Quraishy. The two Iraqi women were concerned about their sister, so they decided to protect her more from herself than any other threat to her person. They knew she was suffering from her father's death at the hands of the American police. The three women were cleaning Ayesha's mother's home. Her friends were making pests of themselves all day by not allowing their upset friend to do anything with cleaning of the home.

The two women prepared the afternoon meal for Ayesha, her mother and two of her brothers who both women hated with a passion. They were angry with the brothers because they were not interested in seeking revenge against the hated American soldiers in Iraq for the death of their father. The two women barely spoke to the brothers as they prepared the meal. Even Ayesha was having a hard time trying to speak to her brothers, because of their lack of interest to revenge themselves against the Americans who killed their father in the United States.

Ayesha was bored with her friends and all the attention they were showering her with. She wanted time to be alone with her grief over her father's death. But her friends would not give her a moment to herself. She even tried to hide in her bedroom, but the two concerned women invaded her room and tried to speak to her until she gave up and came out of her room. Slowly, Ayesha gave in to the attention her friends were lavishing on her, knowing they were concerned about her well being, and that was why they would not leave her alone.

It was starting to get late, and the home was stuffy and hot, so Ayesha announced she was going to go outside for fresh air. The moment she walked to the door, her friends were behind her and when she spotted them, she snapped in a huff. "I was wondering if my watchdogs were going to escort me outside. Come, you bothered me all day, so you might as well finish my day off being with me until I turn in for the night, unless my nosy sisters plan to sleep with me too."

Her words caused her friends to laugh as they followed her with Sadiya, the forward one retorting. "If I thought I could get away with it, I'd sleep with you one night, Ayesha. I'm certain I could teach you things on the art of making love to a woman if you know what I mean."

"I told you that you better watch out for this one, my desert sister. I knew she was the wild one out of the three of us, but I never dreamed she was that wild, Ayesha. Sadiya, you better choose your words a little more wisely, if any males hear you offering to sleep with a woman, you'll be stoned to death for that sin, even if it was spoken in jest." Shafiqu warned her friend as she held her in her angry gaze.

The women walked out of the home just as Saad walked into the Iraqi town from the desert. The three women noticed the young lad's excitement as he rushed up to the three lovely women. Saad took the time to hide the Russian made assault rifles outside the town before he entered it, he still carried the vial in his pocket, but the tiny glass tube was empty of it once deadly contents. Saad smiled at Ayesha as he announced proudly to her. "Ayesha, I have found something in the desert that will make you very happy."

Immediately, the child started to wheel and deal with the Iraqi female as he replied. "My eyes saw much on this foul day, but alas my stomach is empty I fear, sister."

"Can you believe the Gaul of this little young desert scavenger, sister? He dares to offer you something that'll please you, and then he tries to pick your pocket of money at the same time, in order to hear what he offers for your pleasure. I think we should beat the fool for daring to insult you in this manner, Ayesha." Sadiya snarled at the young male as she glared at the Iraqi lad.

"Hold your tongue Sadiya, I want to hear what Saad found in the desert. Saad, here is a coin to help fill your aching stomach."

"Ayesha, my stomach thanks you for the meal it'll enjoy because of this one coin." Saad replied as he took the coin and it instantly disappeared into his robe.

"Then your tongue better tell me what I want to know if you value your throat, to use it to pass the food to your empty stomach." Ayesha grumbled, knowing Saad makes a good living with what he discovers on the desert. She noticed the child was shaking slightly and she stared at his face and decided she did not like the color of his skin and added. "Saad, what makes you tremble like the wash on the line, young fool?"

"I don't know what's making me tremble. I think I'm suffering from exhaustion, I remained in the desert longer than I planned, Ayesha." Saad replied as he tried to control his trembling.

"Never mind this small talk, what is it you offer our sister that'll bring her pleasure, desert jackal?" Sadiya snapped as she again glared at the young man.

Saad looked at Sadiya and told his inquisitor. "I was not speaking to you, I know about you and how wild you are and live your life, woman. Your threats are wasted on my faithful ears, I fear you not, witch of the sands. If you continue to speak disrespectful against me, I'll have your back opened by the sting of the lash. I'll tell you what I found in the desert, but I'll tell Ayesha and you can listen if you want, I'll not answer you witch."

"Enough of this bickering Sadiya and allow Saad to inform us of what he discovered in the desert, my troublesome sister born with a tongue that stings like the tail of the scorpion. Saad, tell me what you found on your visit to the desert, I'm interested and if I gain pleasure from your find, you'll find me generous, my desert brother who wants to help her sister in my times of need." Ayesha said as she smiled at the young man. She was happy with the distraction Saad was causing her, because it stopped her two friends from bothering her like they did all day.

"Sister Ayesha, I can tell you what I discovered, but I think it'd be wise to show you than tell you. First I believe I need water, for some reason I'm thirsty on this unending day of sun and sands blowing in my face." Saad replied as he returned Ayesha's smile with his own.

"Arrrr… Ayesha, I believe this young fool of a bragger with the wagging tongue, is doing nothing more but wasting our time offering us something of no worth. I don't believe the desert jackal has discovered anything of value, sister. I know about you, nasty little desert sand flea. I know you look in women's homes in the middle of the night in hopes of seeing that woman undressing, you little pervert. I'll stop you from wasting our time like you're doing, evil monster. If you want to see a woman's breasts, look and be gone before I beat you and open your back with the stinging lash, desert dog." Sadiya snapped as she pulled down the front of her blouse and exposed her breasts to his gaze.

Saad found it impossible not to grin as Sadiya's breasts danced inches from his eyes.

"Please Sadiya pickup your blouse before you get all of us in trouble with the village elders and males. If they to see what you're doing before Saad, it'll be your back opened by the sting of the lash. Sadiya, will you please go in my home and retrieve Saad a glass of water to end his thirst?" Ayesha stared at Sadiya until she lifted her blouse, and then she disappeared in her home. When Sadiya was gone, Ayesha asked him in a pleasant voice.

"Saad Ihsaan, before Sadiya returns and argues with you further, what have you found in the desert on this troubling day, my desert brother?"

"Sister Ayesha, I found three automatic weapons. I hid them outside the village. They are safe until you take possession of them, my sister."

Ayesha smiled as she bent and hugged Saad's head to her chest, and kissed him on the forehead. She was suddenly alarmed when she kissed Saad, she was able to tell he was running a fever. Nevertheless, she thanked him by offering how important he was to her future plans.

"This is wonderful news my little brother. These weapons are the first we have and they'll help us bring the war to the cursed American Armies who have invaded our country. With your help Saad, we're becoming a real threat against the god cursed infidels, and you become an important cog in our future plans against them. You must tell me where you have these weapons hidden, and do you have ammunition for these weapons, my Iraqi brother?"

"Alas my sister, I have the weapons and they're safe, in my haste to leave the area I found them, I failed finding any ammunition for the weapons. I'm sorry Ayesha, I feel I let you down by not looking around the bunker for bullets." Saad cried as he wiped at his forehead, stopping the sweat from running in his eyes with the back of his hand.

"Saad, don't feel bad for not looking for ammunition, you're a young man and how would you know what was needed for these weapon's worth? You said something interesting to my ears. Saad, you mentioned you found an underground bunker in the desert. Saad, you must drink your water, and then take me to where you discovered this bunker. There might be other things of worth to my cause in there you're not aware of, brother. Here, drink water and then take me to this bunker you discovered, young warrior of Iraq." Ayesha presented to the Iraqi lad as she took the water from Sadiya, and offered it to the sweating and shaking child.

Saad drank the water without coming up for air then replied. "Sister, the weapons are hidden outside the village and we can reach them in a few minutes. I fear we'll have to put off our trip to the desert until tomorrow. The bunker's an hour and a half's walk from our village, and it'll be dark and dangerous to go there tonight. Besides, I'm exhausted and not feeling well, and I'll use this night to rest by bones so I can take you to the bunker tomorrow. Come, I'll take you to the weapons and you can take them to your possession and do what you like with them, sister."

Sadiya and Shafiqu looked at Ayesha with confusion in their eyes, and with a quick nod, the two women fell in line with Ayesha and they followed her and Saad out of the village. The other women did not trust Saad, and Sadiya resented Ayesha for allowing the young desert scavenger to help them with their plans to attack the Americans in Iraq. She hated the little man because she felt he was robbing the dead of the desert.

The three women allowed Saad to lead the way, and they talked amongst themselves as they followed the lad. Ayesha was concerned over the child's health and his complaint of feeling ill when she spoke to him a few moments ago. But her thoughts were interrupted by Sadiya as she snarled at Ayesha following her to where the child hid the weapons.

"Look at the little dog of a male walking before us like he's doing. He's acting like all the stupid males of our village, so cocky with his cursed swagger and confidence, like he owned the women of Iraq. Ayesha, I don't understand why you're allowing this jackal pup to help us like this. He's going to cause trouble for us in the future. He's too young and I fear he might open his worthless mouth, and the hated ears that report to the American soldiers will hear him speaking, and they'll betray our plans to the lowly infidels if we're not more careful dealings with this one." Sadiya complained bitterly.

"I understand your fears, but Saad has proven how useful he'll be for our cause..." Ayesha's words were cut off when Saad nearly stumbled before them.

"Sadiya, I hope our Iraqi brother's alright, I fear for his health." Ayesha added as she reached out and prepared to catch Saad if he did fall off his shaky feet.

"I fear your concerns are wasted on that desert scavenger, nothing will happen to the likes of him. As it is written in the great Book of the

Holy Qur'an, only the worthy will suffer from an early death." Sadiya offered as she made no attempt to help Ayesha, if she had to help the lad as he slowly led them out of the village. It was after five p.m. by the time they headed out to the desert where Saad hid the weapons, and the women knew Saad was right not wanting to head to the desert at this time of the day.

They walked about a mile from the village before the shaking Saad held up his hand, and then he slowed his pace and began to search for his hidden catch of weapons. The women stopped walking and watched the young lad as he searched the sand until he turned and looked at Ayesha and announced. "Ayesha, here is where I have the weapons hidden." He dropped to his knees and began digging in the sand.

Ayesha kept her eyes glued to the child because she still did not like the way he was acting, and she noticed the color of his skin and knew something was wrong with Saad.

The child's smile grew as he pulled the first weapon from under the sand.

Sadiya noticed the child buried the weapons without protecting them from the sand and complained. "There, what did I tell you about this one? The fool has no idea what he's doing with these weapons? Anyone with half a brain would've known not to bury them without protecting them from the sand. Now we have to take apart the weapons and clean them before we dare use them against the enemies of Iraq. I think we should reconsider allowing this desert scavenger to be part of our plans against the hated infidels who occupy our beloved Iraq, sister."

"Please Sadiya, you must learn how to control your unconquered temper. True, Saad should've protected the weapons from the sand before he buried them, but at least he found weapons we'll use in our fight against the hated American soldiers who have invaded our country. You better get used to working with Saad, I've decided he'll be an active part of our fight against the infidels, and that's all I'm going to say about it, Sadiya!" Ayesha glared at Sadiya because she was growing cross with her and her complaining about Saad and the help he was offering them.

Shafiqu smiled because of the anger Ayesha aimed at Sadiya, she was also getting angry over the way Sadiya was acting. She was feeling Sadiya was getting cold feet with their plans, and that was why she was doing so much complaining.

Saad watched as Ayesha yelled at Sadiya with a smile, as he held the first weapon in his hands and offered it to Ayesha.

Ayesha turned to Saad and returned his weak smile as she took the weapon and shook the sand from the automatic weapon. She looked at the lad and noticed how badly he was sweating and again grew concerned over his health. Thinking of taking some work from the child's shoulders, she snapped at Sadiya. "Sadiya, retrieve the other two weapons where Saad placed them, and it'll be your responsibility to clean them of sand for our use against our enemies. I don't like the way Saad looks, and I want to return him to the village so his mother can look after him." Ayesha turned to Saad and offered.

"Saad, I fear you'll have to be ready to return to the area where you found these weapons tomorrow morning. I want to get an early start and I want you rested and prepared for our trek to the bunker you told me about. I plan to leave the village at eight a.m., and I expect you to be ready at that time, my little Iraqi brother of the hot burning desert sands."

Whether or not she realized it or not, but she was taking command of the other women, and the young lad. She knew what she was going to do, and nothing was going to stop her. Ayesha had the first weapons she needed, and she was putting her plan forward.

OUT IN THE DESERT FIFTEEN MILES
NORTH OF AR-RAMADI

It was nine twenty-five p.m. when a caravan of American military vehicles pulled up and made a protective circle of their war machines. The exhausted Unit of Marines decided to take a short break from their never ending search for insurgents using the desert to regroup and organize for another attack against their fellow soldiers, or Iraqi soldiers, civilians or police officers trying to bring peace to Iraq.

The Marines dismounted their armored vehicles and used this time to light up smokes and stretch their legs to get the blood flowing in them. Security guards took up positions to protect the soldiers as they enjoyed their little break, before heading off to search the desert for other troublemakers. One soldier walked away from the others because there were women in their unit, and he had to relieve himself. As he was taking a leak he noticed a few slips of papers blowing across the sand and thought that strange. According to his maps there was no civilian population near his position for fifteen miles in all directions of the compass. When the soldier finished he chased down the pages, hoping they might be pictures of naked women.

The Marine almost had to jump on the page to catch it as it continued to be blown across the sand by the wind. When he unfolded the paper he shook his head because it was covered with words written in Arabic, and he could not read a lick of the scribble. But something struck him about the paper and he felt this page might be importance to their Intel people. Because there was an official looking Iraqi military stamp printed on top of the crumbled up page.

The Marine brought the paper to their temporary camp and allow Sergeant Coleman to read it. He knew she understood and was able to read and write Arabic words. With the paper in his hand, the Lance Corporal rushed back to camp and called out to the female Sergeant. "Hey Jess, I found this paper and I think it might be important, Sarge. It has an official looking Iraqi military stamp on the damn thing. It's written in their fucking scribble Sarge."

"Hand it over and I'll tell you if you found something, Corporal. You probably found a map describing where there's a mountain of hidden gold, Corporal." Sergeant Coleman offered with a smile because she did not think the Corporal found anything of importance.

The Sergeant pressed the crumbled paper out on her leg as she read the page smiling the smile disappeared as she got deeper into the military document. Slowly standing as she grasped the importance of the document, the Sergeant barked at the Lance Corporal without taking her eyes from the document. "Bobby, where the hell did you say you found this damn thing? We have to get in touch with Command and tell them what we have."

"It was where I was taking a leak, what's up Sarge?" The Corporal replied as he looked over his shoulder and pointed to where he found the paper.

"Were there any more papers in the area with this one?"

"Yeah Sarge, there was a couple of papers flying around. Why Sarge?" The Corporal asked.

"Corporal, take Billy and Ray and collect any papers you see out there. I want all the papers you find brought to me immediately, soldier. Carl, raise Command HQ and tell them they have to patch me through to Intel, STAT. This shit's hot, very hot. We might have found the missing WMD's (Weapons of Mass Destruction) the old President said was hidden in the desert, Mister. Get going you three and take anyone else you need, but find me all the papers you see out there. Carl, get on the radio PDQ, we found something that's gonna make many people happy."

Carl followed the Sergeant's orders and raised command over the radio, and when he started to speak to the Lieutenant on duty, and informed the officer what they discovered, he transferred the call to S-1 or Intelligence Division.

A very bored sounding Major answered. "Yeah this is Major Raffidy, identify yourself and inform me the reason for this call. We're very busy here."

"Yes Sir Major Raffidy, this is Sergeant Jessica Coleman, sir. We're on patrol in sector M-3 at coordinates One, Three, Seven at Niner, Four, One, sir. We found a paper and from what I can tell of the document, sir. It's a list of a number of chemical and biological weapons the Iraqi military was secretly working on."

When the Sergeant reported her position, the still bored sounding Major checked the map and mumbled as he listened to the Sergeant's report. "Man Sarge that's way the fuck out there… Huh, repeat last part of your report from slip of paper on, Sergeant." The Major growled as he stood and made a number of hand signals to his aide. He had to get the General to listen to the report from the Marine, so he could tell the Major his next orders.

"Major Raffidy Sir, we found a paper and it's written in Arabic and has the official Iraqi military stamp on top of the page, sir. It's a detailed list of chemical and biological weapons the Iraqi military was working on somewhere near our position, sir."

"Sonofa fucking bitch, okay Sergeant Coleman, you're in command of that unit…"

"I am in command of the unit, and have been since we were ordered to search this section of the desert, Major…" Sergeant Coleman offered as she interrupted him.

"Shut the fuck up and listen Sergeant, you and your unit are now working for S-1, soldier. You're to secure the entire area where you're hunkered down and find any other papers at your location, Sergeant. I'll have a flood of Intel Operatives out there by the time your radio shuts down. If you found what I think you found, your unit's going to be as popular as the unit that found Saddam fucking Hussein hiding in his little rathole. I'm dispatching helos as we speak mark your location with red smoke so they can find you easier. I'll have the wheels moving from my end and by this time tomorrow that paper will be sitting on the President's desk. Good work soldier, secure your position, assistance is on the way and I'll clear your actions with your Commander, Sergeant."

"Yes Sir Major Raffidy, I'm ordering our location marked with red smoke, send your people, sir. Out." Sergeant Coleman replied in the dead receiver.

The moment she was off the radio with the Intel Officer, the Sergeant barked a batch of orders to the soldiers with her unit. "Okay, we have to secure our position. No one comes in or out of the area without our knowing and controlling it. We have to prepare for company ICO's sending people to take over the area and operation on our asses we're now working for Intel. Let's look alive and carry out your orders as received, troopers."

It took less than an hour for the first operatives to show up at the Sergeant's position, and the new soldiers took command of the five pages the soldiers discovered. The Americans had no way of knowing they were setting up shop twenty miles away from the underground bunker.

The commander of the specialized soldiers took possession of the Iraqi military pages and placed them in a secured lock box, and then sent it on its way by helicopter back to his command center. When the General of Intelligence Unit read the papers, he immediately realized what the soldiers discovered in the desert, and he placed the documents in a security bag and marked it with a Blue Border Top Secret label, and then he sent it on its way to CIA Headquarters stationed at Langley Virginia.

CIA HEADQUARTERS, LANGLEY VIRGINA, SATURDAY OCTOBER 27th, 2008

CIA Director John Raincloud looked at his watch and was surprised to see it was five thirty p.m., and he decided to call it a day. He wrapped up what work he had on his desk and placed a call to his secretary and announced. "Mary, what are you still doing hanging around, girl? You should've left the office an hour ago. How many times do I have to tell you because I'm burning the midnight oil, you don't have to stay? You have a family to attend to."

"John, how long have you known me sir? Quite a long time and by now you must know I'd never leave the office while you're still working, unless you order me personally. Or you send me on a mission, sir. What's up sir, I'm certain you didn't bother me for remaining at my post while you're still working, John?" Mary fired back at her boss, she was with him long enough not to allow him to get on her, because he did not realize the time.

"Whew, you're getting worse than my wife. Mary, I'm wrapping things up for the day and going home and catch up on some sleep after I share a drink and supper with my wife. Your day is done as of now. I'll see you back here at nine a.m. sharp tomorrow morning. I don't want to see you here before that time or else, Mary."

"I take it you're coming in late for work tomorrow, John? That's the only way I'll not show up at my appointed time, sir. If you're going to be here at your normal time then so am I, Director Raincloud." Mary asked and warned the Director.

"Since when do you know of me turning up late for work, young lady? I'll be here at my usual time." Director Raincloud replied in his intercom with a smirk, he knew what was coming next from his hot blooded Italian secretary.

"Well Mister, if you're reporting to work at seven thirty Director, I'll be arriving at the same time, sir." Mary retorted over the intercom, informing the man she wasn't afraid of his growling.

"You have me young lady, I was just offering you a later start for the day, that's all…"

"Excuse me Director, a currier just stepped in the office sir. I have to see what he has this late in the day, sir. Hold on while I attend to the messenger, sir." Mary offered as she interrupted the director, and let go of the intercom and asked the currier. "May I be of assistance, sir?"

"Yes Ma'am, I have a BBTS for the Director, Ma'am. You have to sign for the delivery after I checked your ID before I release it, Ma'am." The bonded currier replied.

Mary pulled her CIA identification card she just put away in preparation of leaving her office and flashed it to the man, and then she signed the document and took possession of the special carrier pouch, and dropped it on her desk and she escorted the currier out of her officer.

The CIA Director heard the outer office door close, he got up and he headed for Mary's office to see what was delivered, and who sent it to him and what the delivery was about.

Mary noticed the Director standing behind her and moaned. "Well John, so much for going home for the night. You have a BBTS delivery and it came from ICQ in Iraq."

"Uh oh, I wonder what this dispatch is about." John grumbled as he went to Mary's desk and took the leather pouch. He tucked it under his arm and walked back in his office to open it.

"I'll bring you in a cup of coffee, John." Mary said to the Director's back.

Before he closed the door the Director ordered. "Mary, since this dispatch came from Iraq, it's obviously military in nature. Maybe it might be a good idea to get General White's backside here, young lady. If I have to do overtime tonight, I might as well drag his ass along. Can you get him on the horn before you start that coffee, sweetheart?"

"I'll place a call to his office and see if the General's in or if he's available, Director. If not I'll locate him in the field or at home, and request he comes over to the office, Director." Mary replied as she returned to her desk, and dialed the General's contact number. The phone rang six times before she hung up, and hit the General's cell number. She knew the General always had his cell phone on his person.

The phone rang three times before it was answered by the powerful military officer and Mary immediately recognized the General's voice and offered. "General White, Director Raincloud wants you to report over to his office immediately if possible, sir. He just received a security dispatch from Iraq, and he wants you to go over it with him, General White. It seems important and he wants your opinion of the dispatch.

CHAPTER FIVE

Gennal John White, the current Chairman of the Joint Chiefs of Staff was surprised to receive a call from the CIA Director's secretary, especially at this time of the day. He listened to her words and then replied as he checked his watch to see what time it was. "Jesus H. Christ, doesn't the Director ever go home to sleep? Mary, I got caught out of position, and it's going to take me the better part of an hour to get over to his office. Will John wait, or does he want to put this meeting off until tomorrow morning like normal people work?"

"General White, the Director ordered me to request you to come to his office, sir. If you want to put this meeting off until tomorrow morning, may I suggest you speak to the Director, sir. And, see if he's willing to put off this meeting until morning, General White?" Mary offered with a snap in her voice, she was not accustomed to anyone wanting to put off a called meeting with her boss when he called them in for one.

"Yeah, I'll do that. Sorry if I bothered you with this problem, Mary." General White noticed her tone, and gave her a case of attitude back. The General did not like anyone taking liberties with him. He abruptly broke off the communications with the secretary and dialed the Director's number so he could pitch his bitch with the CIA Director.

John answered the call. "Yeah John, I need you at the office, sir. I just received an emergency communication from one of my operatives in Iraq. He stamped it hot and used the security tape on

75

the communication, sir. So I think it is imperative you get over here as soon as possible, so we can go over this report together, sir."

"Dammit John, don't you go home for the night and sleep?" General White complained as he let out his breath in a rush over the phone.

"To be truthful General White, I was on my way out of the office when this dispatch arrived, and the way I look at it. If I have to do night work then I want company, sir. How long before you can get here, General?" Director Raincloud offered with a hint of a rush for the General.

"Shit, okay John I should be able to get there within the hour, sir. It's that important sir?" The General replied as he let out his breath in a sort of a hiss.

"I won't know for certain until I open the communication, General." The Director replied smartly as he allowed a smile, knowing his friend was on his way to his office no matter how much he bitched about it.

"You win this round, but let me tell you something mister. The first chance I get my friend, I'm going to have your ass working some serious overtime the next time I need you to keep me company for the damn night, John." General White offered with a hint of a laugh in his voice as he broke off the conversation with the Director. Then he ordered his Marine drive with a growl to get him over to the CIA headquarters as quickly as possible.

The driver let out his breath, angered over that he was going to pull overtime. He was scheduled to take his wife out to get a jump on their Christmas shopping for the children. Without being ordered, the driver put the siren on and jumped in and out of traffic.

Director Raincloud did not wait for General White to arrive before he opened the communication. It was cleared for his review so it was not written in code, and he started to go over the top secret document. He was so into what he was reading he did not pick up Mary come in with coffee. Seeing the Director so involved in what he was reading, she placed the cup on his desk, and backed out of his office to allow the Director privacy to read the report.

The CIA Director rose to his feet as he continued to read the document and took a break and hit the intercom button and snapped at his secretary. "Mary, get Doctor Russbinder on the horn. You can reach the Doctor at the NEST (Nuclear Emergency Search Team) Headquarters."

"Will do sir, and I'll inform you when I have the doctor on the line, Director."

"Do that Mary, and if you can't locate him at his Headquarters, try his cell. I have it on the phone under the seven key. I'd like to speak to the Doctor before the General arrives if possible. This communication concerns him as well." The Director broke off his communication and went back to reading the document. The Director could not believe what he was reading.

Mary placed a call to NEST Headquarters and was informed the doctor was on his way home for the day. She hit the seven key and it automatically dialed the doctor's private cell number. The phone rang three times before it was answered by an exhausted sounding voice. "Yes, this is Doctor Joel Russbinder, who am I speaking with please?" The CIA Director's number did not come up on his caller ID screen.

"Doctor Russbinder, this is Mary, Director Raincloud's secretary, sir. The Director asked if you'll hold the line while I patch you through to the Director, sir. He's waiting to speak to you."

Just as Mary spoke to the doctor, General White strolled in the office and she smiled as she hit the intercom and announced. "Director, I have Doctor Russbinder on line Seven, and General White has arrived, sir."

"Crap, okay I'll speak to the Doctor and allow the General to come in." The Director moaned as he picked up the receiver of the phone.

General White did not wait to be allowed in the office as he opened the door. He walked across the office and plopped down in the chair across from the Director and lit up a smoke, and watched as the Director answered the phone after nodding to him.

As the full blooded Native American CIA Director answered the phone, he turned the report around on his desk, and then slid it so the Chairman could read the dispatch while he spoke to the doctor. "Ahhh… Doctor Russbinder Sir, I'm pleased I was able to get in touch with you this late in the day, sir."

"Good afternoon or should I say good evening, Director Raincloud. It's a pleasure to speak with you again, sir. You're lucky to get me at this time of the day I was on my way home for the night. We had one devil of a day and I'm exhausted and want to get home and put my feet up and relax, before turning in for the night." The doctor complained as he checked the time.

"Doctor Russbinder, I'm sorry to burst your bubble sir. I'm ordering you to report to my office, and I'll not take no for an answer. Before you ask the reason why, allow me to explain sir. I just received a communication from one of my operatives working in Iraq, and I need your opinion on what the soldiers had discovered, sir. I believe we might have found the smoking gun to the weapons of mass destruction that nut was hiding all over his damn country, Doctor Russbinder." Director Raincloud replied in the phone, and turned to the General and watched his expression change as he heard the reason why he called for the doctor to report to his office.

"Is this an emergency situation Director Raincloud? I wanted to get home for the night sir."

"From now on Doctor, any call I place to you is to be classified as an emergency, sir? What do you think I was calling you for, if I didn't think this was an emergency Doctor? How soon can you arrive at my office, Doctor?" The CIA Director snapped in the phone, he was that angry because the doctor was daring to question him.

"I'm sorry Director Raincloud and I should be able to get to your office in the next half an hour, sir." Doctor Russbinder ignored the ugly way the Director was speaking to him. Over the past few years he butted heads with the Chairman of the Joint Chiefs of Staff on a number of occasions, and he was getting used to the way these powerful people spoke to him when they were excited about something they deemed an emergency for the country.

"Get here that quick, Doctor!" Director Raincloud snarled as he broke off the connection with the doctor, and began speaking to the military officer. "You heard my conversation with the Doctor. He's nothing but a royal pain in the damn can, General White."

"Don't I know that, John. Gees, why so formal and I believe you were hard on that puke on the horn? Remember what the President warned us about him John, he wants us to treat the asshole with the utmost of respect. What's this shit about I'm reading here, John? From what I was able to gather from this report so far, it seems we might be speaking about some kind of designer biological weapon that nut was working on in his country. From what I read, it seemed like he was designing this damn thing to attack just the Iranians. Man, that sonofabitch really hated the Iranians, even though I can't blame him, sir. They're so damn hard to work and talk sense with, sir." The General replied as he shrugged and stared at the Director.

"That's what I was able to gleam from the document. That's why I sent for the Doctor, he has to clear this up for us so we can brief the President on what we might have found in Iraq, sir. By the way John, would you like a cup of coffee sir? I believe we're going to get stuck here for most of the night. General." Raincloud offered as he picked up his cup to discover the coffee was cold.

"Hell John if we're going to get stuck here all night, I believe I'll need something stronger than a cup of coffee, sir." The General snapped back at the Director.

"Will a shot of Rye do the trick, General? That's all I have in my office, sir. If you remember right, we polished off the Scotch last time we pulled an all nighter, and I'm afraid I never got a chance to replace the bottle." The Director replied as he gave him one of his famous smiles.

"A shot of Rye will do the trick nicely John. Do you want to go over this report, or do you want to put it off until the Doctor arrives, so we don't get stuck going over this thing twice in one night, Director?" General White retorted as he watched his friend pour them a shot of whiskey.

"Man that's hot Chief." The General was the only man in Washington who could get away with calling Raincloud "Chief" as he complained and downed his drink in one quick gulp, and then he repeated his question to the Director. "You didn't answer do you want to review this report before the Doctor arrives?"

"I think we should go over it so we sound like we know what we're questioning the Doctor about over this report, when we jump his ass when he gets here." The Director replied as he sipped his drink and asked the General if he wanted another.

"Naw, one belt's good enough. I don't want to be three sheets to the wind before the Doctor gets here, and we can get his opinion of this document." The military officer replied with a snap in his tone as he opened the document again, and finished reading the short report.

"Jesus H. Christ John, if Saddam Hussein was able to perfect this damn designer biological weapon, he would've been able to wipe Iran off the face of the earth in a month's time. Did the soldiers find any of this crap with these papers? I trust you have a flood of your own people out there looking for this crap if it exists?" General White grumbled, showing no concern the CIA Director was notified about the biological find in Iraq, before the soldiers under his command reported the discovery to his office in the Pentagon first.

"General White, from what I read of the report, it seems the Iraqi technicians were able to prefect this weapon. They never got the chance to release it against the Iranians, because your soldiers hit Iraq before he could do his act with the stuff. As of yet I have no reports any searchers were able to locate where the madman had hidden the crap in the desert. One thing I can assure you General, none of my people will come out of this area until they have located the crap if it exists. We can't allow anyone to find this crap and release it in the air, especially if they don't know what the hell the crap can do to a country. That sonofabitch was hell bent on destroying Iran. I can't believe they were able to prefect such a dangerous weapon as this."

"Wait a minute we're acting as if this crap exists, and we don't know if the Iraqi technicians were able to perfect this stuff. Even if the assholes were successful in developing this crap, how do they know if it's going to work the way they think it will. Chief, I don't want to go off half cocked on this one, it's too damn important for us to overreact to this report. I think we have to sit tight and wait for the Doctor to get here, and once he reviews this shit. He can tell us how serious a situation we might have on our hands and be facing in the future." General White offered to the Director, not believing there was a possibility of the Iraqi technicians developing a so called designer biological weapon that would concentrate and kill one particular race of people, and not affect anyone else who comes in contact with the weapon.

"Hmmm, perhaps you might be right at that General. There's no sense pushing the panic button until we can determine how deadly this possibility is, sir. I wonder what's keeping that Doctor. He should be here by now, dammit."

No sooner did the Director utter the words than the doctor entered his outer office. Mary smiled at the exhausted doctor as she rose and offered. "Good evening Doctor Russbinder, General White and Director Raincloud are waiting in his office. How are you tonight, sir?"

"Don't tell me General White's in the office, Ma'am. I don't know about that Officer. No matter how hard I try to please him, I just can't seem to make him like me, Ma'am. What should I do, go in or do you have to announce me first?"

"I'll show you to the Director's office Doctor Russbinder. No one can enter the Director's office on their own, sir. Don't take it to heart what the General might say to you, sir. You have to understand he has many soldiers in harm's way, and he's never pleasant to be around when he has soldiers on a battlefield, sir. He's really a nice and concerned man." Again, Mary flashed one of her soul warming smiles as she led him into the Director's office.

"I was made to understand there were different ways to think and speak about the General. I never heard him referred to as a nice man to be around, Ma'am." Doctor Russbinder offered Mary while trying to make light of his situation, as he followed her into the Director's office.

Mary smiled at the doctor as she led him into the office. The moment Director Raincloud and General White saw the doctor coming into the room. They both stood with Director Raincloud taking the lead offering his hand to the doctor.

Director Raincloud allowed the doctor a few moments to settle in and get comfortable, and then he handed him the report while offering. "Doctor Russbinder, I trust you know General White, sir? Anyway Doctor, this report's the reason why I sent for you, sir. A Marine patrol happened across these Iraqi papers blowing around the desert of Iraq while on normal patrol, Doctor. What I need to know from you is, if the crap printed on those pages could be a reality, sir. Once you determined if this biological weapon might have been perfected by the Iraqi technicians, I'd like your best guestimate on the amount of devastation this damn weapon could do to a specified race of people, sir."

"Please don't tell me another nation's leader has placed an order for his scientists to work on a new form of weapon of mass destruction, Director Raincloud." Doctor Russbinder moaned as he took the papers from the CIA Agent, and stared him in the eyes.

"Spare me the astonished looks, Doctor Russbinder. By now it has to come to you as no big surprise that Saddam Hussein ordered his scientists to continue their work of developing weapons of mass destruction for that madman to employ against us, or any other nation, sir. I thank God he's where he should be, rotting in his damn grave, Doctor. Just read the report and inform me of your opinion if it was possible for the Iraqis to develop what we're referring to as a designer biological weapon of mass destruction, sir."

"Give me a few moments to review these items sir, maybe I'll be able to give you my best thoughts on what I read, Director Raincloud. Of course you understand without any product to run a number of tests on, I'll be guessing if the Iraqis were able to develop this weapon of mass destruction, sir. As you know we have many projects in progress ourselves, but because they're on the drawing board that doesn't mean we have perfected the projects, Director Raincloud." Doctor Joel Russbinder grumbled and did not wait for a reply from the Director as he started to read the small stack of papers he was handed by the Director.

Director Raincloud got the General's attention and with a quick hand movement. Then the Director asked the General if he wanted another shot of Rye, or anything else to drink or something to eat to hold him over until they left his office.

General White shook his head no as he watched the doctor plop heavily in an empty chair in the office and started to go over the papers the soldiers discovered in Iraq. It did not bother the General the doctor barely acknowledged him in the Director's office. It was no secret the General hated working with the doctor, or any other civilian on military situations.

Both men watched as the doctor's facial expressions changed with each paragraph he read. When the doctor started to sweat and his facial expressions turned to one of serious concern, both men paid closer attention to the doctor until he was finished reading the papers.

Letting out his breath in puffs, the shaken doctor tried to get control over his labored breathing as he set the papers on the director's desk. Then he looked Director Raincloud dead in the eyes.

"For the love of the Christ Child Doctor Russbinder, tell us what you think the damn Iraqis were working on, sir! I don't have all fucking night to wait for you to blurt out what you might have discovered in that mess of papers, Mister."

"Please General White allow the Doctor a few moments so he could collect his thoughts. I'm certain the Doctor will tell us soon enough, General." Director Raincloud complained at the military officer while not taking his eyes off the doctor's face. He knew the answer, but he had to hear it come from the doctor before he acted on it.

Drawing in a breath and holding it for a moment, not bothering to look at the General who snarled at him. Doctor Russbinder replied to the CIA Director's request. "Of course you understand my profession lies in the nuclear field, Director Raincloud, General White, and the only reason I was linked up to the chemical and biological field is due to the President's order…"

"I understand that crap Doctor Russbinder. Get on with your damn report to my ass, sir. If it's what I believe it is, I have to immediately inform the President what we might have discovered in Iraq, sir. After all, the reason for our troops to enter the nation of Iraq was to find his stash of weapons of mass destruction, which we might be holding the proof in our hands at this moment, Doctor." Director Raincloud snarled at the concerned looking civilian doctor.

The way director Raincloud spoke to the doctor brought a smile to the General as he allowed the Director to deal with the civilian operative. That was how much he hated working with civilians on a project.

"Yes Director Raincloud, you have to understand my response will be based on speculation. That's because I don't have any of the product so I can run vital tests on the product then offer you a more positive and detailed response to the seriousness of the problem you introduced…" Doctor Russbinder offered in a concerned tone, but was cut off by the Director as he grumbled.

"C'mon Doctor Russbinder, I'm not getting any younger waiting for you to inform me what you think the damn Iraqis were working on." Director Raincloud snapped at the doctor.

"Yes by all means Director Raincloud, I'm sorry for delaying my response, sir. I had to make up my mind before I replied to this startling information I just read, sir. From the papers I reviewed and test results contained in them, sir. I'm afraid I'm forced to believe the Iraqis were able to perfect a so called designer biological weapon of mass destruction, sir.

"To classify this discovery as a possible designer biological weapon is the perfect way to describe this terrible discovery, sir. I don't know if you fully understand the significance and upsetting ramifications attached to this startling discovery, Director Raincloud. If the Iraqis were successful in developing a weapon that attacked and destroyed one specific race of people, think of the severe implications of the new and extremely deadly weapon of mass destruction, sir. If the Iraqi technicians were able to design a weapon that just attacked and killed Persian born peoples, what's stopping them from alternating this weapon to attack let's say, Italians, Japanese, or any other race of people of the world who Saddam Hussein might have held a feeling of resentment or hated against, Director Raincloud? The troubling ramifications of this are endless I'm afraid, sir."

"Allow me to inform you Doctor, I understand the ramifications of this weapon, but what I wanted to know is; is it possible they perfected this weapon, sir?" Raincloud snorted nastily.

"Director Raincloud, I have to reply it's more than possible the Iraqis developed this designer weapon of mass destruction, sir. Director, I believe they perfected this weapon and I further offer we have to do everything in our power to discover where Saddam Hussein has hidden this weapon. And, we have to destroy the entire batch of the biological strain along with the paperwork explaining how they come about to perfect this weapon, sir."

"That's all I wanted to hear, Doctor Russbinder. You're free to go at this point, Doctor. I'm going to keep the General with me, and I'm going to send a flash message out to the President, and in this message I'm going to demand an emergency meeting with his National Security Council and us three, for the first moment available tomorrow morning, sir. Doctor, I'm ordering you to keep your day opened, I'll notify you when the President will be able to make time for us to meet at the White House, sir. You'll have to give your report to the Man in person, and then we'll see how he wants to respond and handle this situation." Director Raincloud offered and held the doctor in his gaze until he rose.

Without waiting to be sent for, Mary appeared at the door and led the doctor out of the Director's office as fast as the doctor could leave.

The moment the doctor was out of his office, Director Raincloud dropped in his chair and grumbled at the military officer. "Well John, what do you think about this latest problem, sir?"

"I can tell you one thing Chief I'm not going to wait for the President to decide what he wants to do about this shit. I'm activating soldiers in Iraq, and I'm going to assign them to discover where that nut hid this shit in his country. I don't give a fuck if they tear up the entire desert in this region with machines, they'll find this crap or they'll spend the rest of their lives looking for this shit. I can't allow this crap to fall in the wrong hands, or have it somehow opened because the fool who might find it, did not know what he discovered. Like the Doctor said, the ramifications of this weapon could be earth shattering, John."

"I agree General excuse me while I send a flash to the White House." The Director reached for his phone and dialed, in seconds a voice on the other end offered in the receiver.

"This is the White House Chief of Staff's desk, how may I direct this call please."

"Yes, good evening Walter, is the President available, this is Director Raincloud, son?"

"Good evening Director Raincloud. I'm afraid the President turned in for the night, and he left strict orders not to be disturbed unless it was a matter of the utmost importance, sir. Director Raincloud, it's past eleven p.m. and you know the President turns in at ten unless he's entertaining, or there's an emergency he's working on, sir."

"Walter you're going to have to wake him, it is imperative I speak with him immediately. You can classify it as an emergency, and that should keep your ass out of the fire when you wake him." Director Raincloud replied in the phone.

After a few moments of hesitation, Walter offered. "Director Raincloud, no one informed me this was going to be a workstation that can claim my life, sir. You know how the President gets when I wake him once I was ordered not to interrupt him under any circumstances, sir."

"Hey look friend, you wanted to work in the damn White House, son."

"Yes I did Director, but I never knew how dangerous it could be for my health working here."

"Look Walter, just go and wake the man and tell him I have to speak to him immediately."

"Okay Director Raincloud, I hope you have a place for me when the President fires me for waking him tonight, sir. He's not going to be in a good mood once I wake him from his sleep, sir." Walter complained as he left his phone and hit the button for the private elevator that took him up to the third floor of the White House and President's sleeping quarters. It took him three minutes before he was standing at the door to the President's bedroom. He tapped lightly on the door, and then he waited to be yelled at from within.

"What! Who the hell's waking me now dammit! I left strict orders I wasn't to be disturbed tonight, dammit." The President grumbled as he got out of bed and headed for the door in a huff.

"Errr Al, don't you think you should put your robe on, dear?" President Cole's wife asked as she fired one of her best smiles at her lover from the bed as she got up on one elbow.

"The hell with that, when someone wakes me in the middle of the night, they get me the way I come." Albert returned his wife's smile as he opened the door to find Walter waiting on the other side. Again the President had to smile because of the way Walter was standing in the hallway. He looked like he was looking for some place to hide.

"Mr. President, please excuse me for waking you sir, Director Raincloud is on the phone and he wants to speak to you. I told him you retired for the night, but he insisted I wake you."

The anger left the President. "You did right to wake me Walter, if the Director's on the phone, I have to respond. I'll take the call in the Johnson Room. Err… Walter, since I'm up, I'd like a warm glass of rum and one of my cigars please."

The American Leader followed Walter to the second floor and entered the President Johnson Room and there was a warm fire glowing in the white marble fireplace to take the chill out of the room. A glass of heated rum and a cigar was set out for the President to enjoy which caused him to smile. He sat and when the light went on, he answered the phone. "Yes Director Raincloud, what's the reason for this late night call I'm certain couldn't wait until tomorrow when it would have been a more proper time for you to communicate with me, sir? I know how you are sir, so speak to me Director Raincloud."

"I'm sorry for waking you Mr. President. We discovered certain and crucial information that had to be brought up to your attention immediately, sir. The documents I'm referring to could be a world changing situation, sir." Raincloud informed the President what they discovered in Iraq, and by the time he finished his report, the President was wide awake and upset as he growled.

"Director Raincloud, you did right waking me tonight. I'll set up a meeting with my National Security Council for eight a.m. sharp tomorrow morning. I want everyone you need from your side to attend the meeting. I want Doctor Russbinder to attend this meeting also, Director. You get hoping on your side, and I'll get the wheels in motion from my side, Director Raincloud. Err… what about General White, Director?"

"He's with me Mr. President." Director Raincloud replied with a smirk in his tone.

"I should've known you two are as thick as thieves. I'm pleased we don't have to inform the General of this meeting for tomorrow morning, Director Raincloud."

"Yes Sir Mr. President, we're continuing to go over this report so we can make a more intelligent report to the Council and yourself, Mr. President." Director Raincloud offered to the President as he looked at the General and nodded, informing the officer there was a meeting scheduled for tomorrow with the Security Council.

"Very good Director Raincloud, I guess we covered everything we had to go over for now. Until morning sir, good night Director, give my regards to the General please."

"I certainly will Mr. President, and have a good night's sleep sir. I'm sorry for waking you, but you can understand the reason, sir." Director Raincloud replied to the President, but found he was speaking to a dial tone.

"That's that General, we have a meeting for eight a.m. tomorrow with the President and his war council." Director Raincloud offered as he turned his attention to the officer.

MONDAY, OCTOBER 28th, 2008 THE WHITE HOUSE, EIGHT A.M.

General John White with CIA Director John Raincloud and Doctor Joel Russbinder walked into the Oval Office together, with the director acting like he was in command of the meeting. The President decided to hold this meeting in the office instead of the Situation Room seventy-five feet below the East Wing of the White House. He hated the room with a passion, it was stuffy and the air always gave him a headache when he was forced to use the room for another meeting.

The President nodded to Director Raincloud as they entered the oval room. The President was not surprised to see the doctor accompanying them and he remained silent until the three were seated and settled in for the meeting. The Vice President, Mary Hirshfield was seated to the President's left as usual for any meeting, and she was the only one who sat behind the President's desk with him. She wanted a better view of everyone attending the meeting because of the importance the President placed on the hastily called meeting.

When everyone was comfortable, the President began by addressing the meeting. "Good morning ladies and gentlemen, I guess you're all wondering why I called you here for this emergency meeting of our Security Council. I called everyone here because our ever alert and on guard CIA Director Raincloud, has discovered something in Iraq's desert that's of serious concern and consequence to the world. If what the Director has discovered is true, we have a grave situation on our hands. A situation that needs, correct that, demands our immediate attention and action. I'll no longer keep you in suspense, please Director Raincloud you have the floor, sir. Please begin your report to the council, sir." The President turned to the CIA Director and smiled as he waited for his report to begin.

Director Raincloud went to stand but he was waved back to his seat by the President as he offered to him and the others. "Please everyone let's place formalities on the floor for this meeting. It's not necessary for anyone to stand when they're addressing the rest of us today. Please Director Raincloud, you have the floor and I promise not to interrupt you again, unless it absolutely necessary sir."

"Thank you and good morning to you and everyone attending this meeting, Mr. President. Please allow me to introduce Doctor Joel Russbinder to all here. Although he has attended a number of these special meetings in the past, I wanted to refresh your memories on who this man is. Mr. President, last night I came to have a report forwarded to me by one of my operatives in Iraq, sir. The report held information so devastating to the world that I called Doctor Russbinder to my office, and allowed him to review this information to make certain it was viable intelligence, before I disturbed the President's sleep…"

"Director Raincloud, you dared to wake Albert up last night? When I last spoke to him, he threatened he was going to have anyone who interrupted his sleep sent to the North Pole to count Polar Bears. This report must be important, please continue Director Raincloud." Vice President Hirshfield said with a grin. The Vice President's words served to do what she intended, it caused everyone to chuckle, and it relieved the tension everyone was feeling at the meeting.

"Yes Ms. Hirshfield Ma'am, I was the one who woke the President last night, because I classified this information as a national emergency and serious threat, Ma'am. I'm going to turn the meeting over to the Doctor. I believe he's the one who could best display the gravity of this discovery my operatives found in the Iraqi desert, Ma'am. Please Doctor Russbinder, if you'd be so kind, you may begin to inform us of your findings of what we have discovered hidden in Iraq yesterday, sir."

Doctor Russbinder nodded at the Director then cleared his throat before speaking to the others. When he was ready he offered. "Mr. President, as the Director informed you, I was called to his office last evening, sir. He was concerned over the information he had in his possession, sir. I met the Director with General White, and the Director allowed me to read the report causing him alarm, sir. He asked me for my professional opinion of what he discovered, sir. Mind you Mr. President, I have none of this product available to run a number extremely vital tests on, so I'm afraid at this time my report is based solely on pure speculation..."

"I understand that Doctor Russbinder. Give us as much information as you can, based on the report handed to you by Director Raincloud, sir." The President offered in a polite voice.

"Yes Sir Mr. President, based solely on the once secret Iraqi military report I reviewed for Director Raincloud last night, sir. It's my professional opinion the discovery of this designer biological weapon is a very serious..."

"A designer biological weapon my God in Heaven Doctor Russbinder. Don't tell me some nut developed a designer biological weapon? What the hells a designer biological weapon anyhow, sir? What was the damn thing designed for, other than killing masses of innocent civilians as all biological and chemical weapons are designed for, Doctor Russbinder? God dammit sir, it seems all we're doing lately is jumping from one frying pan to another, sir." The National Security Director, William Blaylocke complained as he stared at the doctor.

Doctor Russbinder returned the National Security Advisor Director's stare before replying. "Yes Director Blaylocke, you're right feeling all biological and chemical weapons are designed for one thing and one thing only sir, to kill masses of soldiers on the field of battle, or civilians in targeted cities. So I guess you can offer all biological and chemical weapons are a form of a designer weapon of mass destruction, sir. In this case Director Blaylocke, it seems some technicians working in Iraq have successfully constructed a complete designer biological weapon in the true sense of the word, sir…"

"What the hell are you talking about, Doctor Russbinder! What the crap do you mean by a designed biological weapon, sir? Are you telling me someone designed a weapon of mass destruction aimed at a certain nation, sir?" Director Blaylocke offered as he continued to glare angrily at the doctor, not trying to hide the anger trapped in his chest.

"In a way Director Blaylocke that's exactly what I'm informing you of, with one difference in my presentation, sir. This designer biological weapon we're discussing isn't designed to attack a certain nation. It's designed to attack a certain race of people, and anyone with the ancestry linked to that certain race of people under attack by this weapon, no matter where they might live throughout the world. Will be in danger of death if this weapon was developed, and it's somehow released in the air by accident or design, Director Blaylocke." Doctor Russbinder snapped at the upset National Security Director as he returned his concerned glare.

"Jesus Christ Doctor Russbinder, doesn't the world have enough problems to worry about from the miserable weapons of mass destruction we developed over the past years? Now we have to shake in our beds at night with worry about some nut attacking a full race of people, because that nut has a hardon for someone, and he wants revenge against that someone and his people. God dammit Doctor Russbinder, we have to do something about this weapon before we find it offered to the likes of a bin Laden, or the other asshole controlling the civilian population of Iran, Doctor. Dammit to hell!" Director Blaylocke growled as he flung his hands in the air in disgust over the alarming information he was hearing from the doctor.

"Director Blaylocke, I understand where you're coming from, and the concerns you're voicing at this meeting, sir. Displaying anger and outrage over this situation won't help, and will serve to stop me from completing my report to the President, and the rest of you sir. What I have to inform the President of over this discovery by Director Raincloud's operative in Iraq has earth shaking ramifications, and if this biological weapon is released, Heaven only know what form of changes this weapon might take once it's released against its intended target, sir…"

This time it was the President who interrupted the doctor's presentation. "Doctor Russbinder you seem to be extremely worried about this weapon changing its characteristics if it's released in the air, sir? Is this a fact and am I correct in my assumption of the fears you're suffering, sir?"

"Mr. President, that's exactly what I'm afraid of happening with this item, and until I had a chance to examine some product of this extremely dangerous weapon, I'll continue worrying about this fact, sir. These designer chemical and biological weapons are nothing new to us working in the field, nothing new at all Mr. President. I can't tell you how many times in the past years we ourselves tried to design one of these specialized weapons that'd attack only a certain race of people, sir. We've been successful with most of our efforts to develop a number of these types of weapons we're speaking about at this council meeting, Mr. President. The weapons have always displayed they'd work well once released against our enemy in the field of battle, Mr. President.

"This is where our concerns were raised, and the results forced us to abandon further development of these specialized designer type weapons, Mr. President. Once we perfected a weapon that'd affect anyone of say Russian nationality, we ran countless and verities of tests on this discovery, with each test we conducted with the product we developed. It displayed a sincere want and effort to change its original design, and soon we discovered if we tried to use such a weapon on the battlefield, the longer it survived in a growing environment sir. The more it wanted to and did force a change from its originally designed purpose…"

"Excuse me for interrupting your presentation, Doctor Russbinder. You're making it hard for me and the others to follow what you're offering us, sir." The President remarked then went on with his words aimed at him. "Please Doctor Russbinder, you have to understand there are some of us who don't understand what you're speaking about, Doctor. If it's possible, can you use layman terms when explaining what you call the ramifications of this newly discovered weapon of mass destruction, sir. I and everyone else here would like to know as much as possible about this weapon. It'd make it easier for us to follow your words and understand them, Doctor."

"Excuse me Mr. President, I'll try and make my presentation clearer and more understandable and much easier for those unfamiliar with the field I'm speaking about, sir. As I stated Mr. President, the development of a designer chemical or biological weapon to attack say a certain race of people is nothing new to us, nothing new at all Mr. President. But we've been forced to abandon further such research on these types of weapons, because we discovered once the perfected weapon was released into what we call a controlled and favorable growth atmosphere condition, before the chemical or biological weapon ran its short life expediency, sir.

"The deadly strain of the weapon would always try, or would successfully mutate into a more complex and far more dangerous weapon than originally designed for, that wanted to change its original target and designed intention, sir. The longer the product existed in this controlled growth environment, the more the developed product wanted to turn into a weapon that'd eventually attack any and all living things on the face of the earth sir, whether that living thing was of human or animal in nature, Mr. President.

"No matter how we tried to coax the designer weapon into remaining in the state it was originally designed for, Mr. President. The longer the weapon existed in a growing and free environment, the more the weapon wanted to change into a more serious threat that'd eventually attack any living thing on the face of the earth, sir. Mr. President, the sole reason we originally wanted to prefect one of these designer weapons, was the aim if we were forced to employ one such weapon on the battlefield or against a nation in whole, we could design the product to attack just the enemy we're facing on the field of battle and no one else, sir.

"We tried to develop these specialized types of weapons so if they were released on the earth. They'd only destroy the enemy we were facing, before the weapon ran its course and died off, and any innocent civilian hopefully wouldn't be affected by the release of the weapon against the enemy, sir. I assure you Mr. President we weren't the only nation attempting to develop this type of weapon, sir. We never dreamed to develop a chemical or biological weapon of this type, until evidence that the Russians were attempting to develop their own product of a new form of a designer weapon of mass destruction. Once we realized what the Russians were attempting to develop, of course we have to put our hat in the race, and we try to develop one first Mr. President.

"As is always the case and what happens when any nation tries to develop a form of a new weapon of mass destruction, Mr. President. We're forced to join in on the project, and we desperately try to develop the same type of weapon, before any other nation was capable of developing the weapon first, and employing the damn thing against our troops in the field, sir. It's the threat if you use this type of weapon of mass destruction against us, we'll use it against you. Thus the deterrent factor takes over as it did with the development of the nuclear weapon age, sir. We still suffer from this aged old and very foolish belief if you were to ask me, Mr. President. If the Russians were capable of developing a new form of weapon of mass destruction, the Russian leadership and military would immediately use it against us, before we're capable of developing the same type weapon as a determent to further development or deployment of their weapon.

"Mr. President, you have to understand the way we might be able to develop a successful antidote to any newly developed chemical or biological weapon is, sir. We have to develop the base product or weapon first, sir. After all Mr. President, any possible antidote to a biological or chemical weapon is a concoction of a weaker version of the same type weapon introduced into a cow or horse, and when the weapon didn't destroy the host body, Mr. President. It meant the infected host developed a successful resistance to the weapon, and we then use the host's blood to develop the true antidote for military and civilian use, sir."

"Please Doctor Russbinder, we don't need you to explain what's necessary in the development of an antidote to a chemical or biological weapon, sir. I want to know what the hell could and would happen if this so called designer biological weapon was released in the atmosphere, Doctor. When I was first informed of this new weapon, I wanted to believe what was the true threat the supposed weapon posed to the world. I don't mind telling you Doctor Russbinder, when Director Raincloud informed me of this new weapon and its intended target I felt what the hell's the harm, Doctor? I felt if the weapon would only attack the Iranians, what's the worry? The Iranians are so much trouble to the world anyhow, Doctor Russbinder.

"But now Doctor Russbinder, after hearing the possible threats posed by an intentional release of this biological weapon might mutate into a weapon that could attack anything living on the face of the earth. I understand the severe ramifications you're bringing forth to our attention at this council meeting, Doctor Russbinder. And, those ramifications are going to cause me to react against this threat with everything I have available, sir." The President stopped speaking after interrupting the doctor for the third time during his presentation. The President turned from the doctor and the moment his eyes locked on the face of his Chairman of the Joint Chiefs of Staff, he started to speak in a commanding tone to the military officer.

"General White, you heard enough of this presentation from the Doctor as obviously I have, sir. We have to react against this discovery, and we have to act against it with everything we have stored in the arsenal, sir. General White, I believe you'll have to activate your entire Multi National Rapid Response Forces for this emergency, sir. I'm ordering you to have these soldiers shipped to Iraq. I want your best people on this one General, if this damn thing's released from its confinement before we find the surviving crap. We'll be burying innocent civilians of the world with tractors in pits by the thousands, by the fucking thousands I tell you, General White! You better get on this one immediately, sir." The President stopped speaking to his military officer, and held him in his glare until the General reacted to his orders.

General White rose and saluted his Commander in Chief. Then General White turned on his heels and stormed out of the Oval Office as if the devil were chasing after him. The General did not realize it. CIA Director Raincloud was right on his heels as he left the room. When the General walked out of the White House, it was at this point he realized the Director was with him, and snapped at his friend as he stopped by his staff car and held the door for the Director. Signaling he wanted to speak to him further over this situation they raised with the President.

"God dammit John, it looks like I have to place my soldiers in harm's way again, because of that flaming asshole once running Iraq. I thought we were finished with threats from that fucking madman when we stretched his damn neck a few years ago. That sonofabitch is going to haunt me right to my grave. I don't think the world will be over the endless problems that man caused the world." The General shook his head over his complaint and the thought of deploying his soldiers against this new world threat.

Director Raincloud got comfortable in the rear seat of the staff car and waited for the General to join him. Once the Chairman was seated, the Director offered. "General White, we know we're going to suffer problems created by Saddam Hussein for years to come. The nut set up his country in that matter, to create problems for any nation even if he was no longer in command of that country. As for your Special Forces soldiers sir, that's why we have that system set in place and operational. To send these specially trained effective soldiers out, so they can nip any world threatening situation off in the bud, before it gets out of hand and the world has to sweat. These soldiers understand why and what they were trained for, and they expect to walk in the shadow of death every time we send them on a mission, General White…"

"You sound like a commercial for my soldiers. John, I know why and how we trained these young kids we're making into soldiers. I just hate to be forced to send these soldiers out to wipe the ass of some nut that had dreams of taking over the world. I deployed these kids more times than I care to admit, and I think each one of them has done their job to the best of their abilities. It might be time for some other nation's kids to take some weight of fighting off my troop's shoulders for a change." General White glared at his friend, and started to go over his future orders to his soldiers and mission.

Director Raincloud knew what the General was doing, and gave him peace by his silence, to formulate his thoughts before they got back to his office in the Pentagon. The driver did not have to be told where to head, he headed for the General's office. It took them seventy five minutes to reach the Pentagon due to heavy traffic and the driver had to fight all the way to the General's office.

The driver pulled the staff car under the protective overhang at the North door of the Pentagon, and then the driver shot out of the car and he rushed around and opened the door for the General and Director. The soldier saluted the General and got growled at for his efforts. "Keep yourself available for the rest of the day and even the night, mister! I have no idea if I might need you again to get me back over to the Big House, (White House) soldier."

"Yes Sir General White." Was all the driver replied as he held the door open for the officer and maintained his at attention stance. Director Raincloud nodded at the young man and received a smile.

General White charged for his office, the Director was actually having a problem trying to keep up with the fuming officer. The General charged into his office and barked at his secretary. "Mary, get that pain in the damn ass Colonel Leadbetter on the horn." After growling at his secretary, the General went in his office and threw his briefcase on the floor and plopped in his chair and let out his breath in an exhausted sigh. Once he was seated, the General looked at the worn out Director and gave him the look that stated, 'well what the hell are you looking at'?

Director Raincloud took a seat in the General's office and stared at the General waiting for him to speak.

CAMP LEJEUNE, NORTH CAROLINA. MONDAY, OCTOBER 28th, ELEVEN FORTY FIVE A.M.

Colonel Bruce Leadbetter was going over the report filed by Captain Robert Walker about their last training exercise when his phone rang. Pissed off over the interruption, the Colonel swung his feet off his desk and leaned forward and picked up the receiver and spat. "Yeah, this is Colonel Leadbetter, who the hell is this and why are you bugging my ass? I have enough crap on my shoulders without having to answer this damn phone." The Colonel was angry Sergeant John Kirkpatrick did not answer the phone before he had to.

"Colonel Leadbetter, this is Mary, General White's secretary, sir. I don't mind saying, you sound in an awful foul mood on this fine day, sir. I hope everything is going well for you at the base, Colonel Leadbetter. It seems everyone in Washington are on edge lately with all that's taking place in the world." Mary offered while giving the Marine colonel a sort of slap in the face for the way he answered the phone.

"Yes I am in a foul mood at that Ma'am, and I have a feeling my mood isn't going to get any better over this call from your boss, Ma'am. Sorry for the way I snapped at you earlier, Ma'am. It's been one helluva day and my troops down here are pushing me over the falls with every training exercise I put them through, Ma'am."

"I'm sorry you're being so upset by your soldiers, Colonel. Anyway Colonel Leadbetter, the reason for this call is General White wants to speak with you, sir. Please hold the line while I transfer this call to his office, Colonel…"

"Do you have any idea what the General wants, Mary?" The Colonel interrupted.

"Again I'm sorry to inform you Colonel Leadbetter, I'm not privy to that information, sir. The General only ordered me to get you on the line and that's all, Colonel. Please hold the line while I transfer your call to the General's office, sir. If we're disconnected for any reason sir, you'll call back immediately Colonel Leadbetter, and I'll send your call to the General's office, sir."

"Yeah sure Ma'am." The Colonel snarled in the phone, angry he was unable to get information from the secretary before he was forced to speak to his commanding officer.

General White drew in his breath and was about to speak to the Director when the red light blinked on his phone. "Excuse me this has to be the Colonel." The General picked up the phone and barked. "Good morning Colonel Leadbetter, how is your day working out, sir?"

"As always General White, the kids don't want to understand one thing of what the hell I'm trying to teach them with this new urban warfare tactics, sir. Have no fear though General White, they'll learn everything I want them to know, or I'll have their damn hides for my trophy closet, General. Err… General White, I'm certain you didn't call to find out how the hell the specialized training was progressing, sir. To what do I own to this call, and where and when do we have to ship out to pull someone's buns out of the fire, sir?" The Colonel did not try to hide the fact he understood this call from his commander was a call to send his troops on another mission.

THE SMALL IRAQI TOWN OF AR-RAMADI, TEN MINUTES TO EIGHT, MONDAY, OCTOBER 28th, 2008

Although Ayesha al-Qaysi wanted to head to the area where Saad Ihsaan found the weapons, so she could see what other items of use to her cause might also be hidden there. She had a minor family emergency that delayed her leaving for the bunker until this day. She wanted to give Saad more time to regain his strength before they headed to the desert. She was as usual surrounded by her two adopted Iraqi sisters, Sadiya Sadjadpour and Shafiqu al-Quraishy, and they seemed like they were waiting for her to tell them what to do. All three women were waiting for Saad Ihsaan to arrive, so he could take them to where he found the weapons.

It was Sadiya who spotted Saad slowly walking towards them as if he did not have a care in the world, and she snapped nastily at her beautiful girlfriends. "Look sisters, here comes the lowly one who wants to be thought of as a man."

Ayesha turned to Sadiya and groaned at her. "For the love of Allah Sadiya, I wish you wouldn't be so nasty to Saad, he's helping us and deserves our respect for his aide."

"I can't help it sister, I despise the foul fool because he thinks he's a man, and he's helping us as if we couldn't carry out our plans without his worthless help."

"Ayesha, I fear you're wasting your words on Sadiya's ears. She'll only do what she wants, no matter the outcome to her and her sisters." Shafiqu remarked.

"I fear only Allah's mighty wrath if I fail in the quest He has laid out for us to follow in life, Shafiqu who has such a big mouth and attacks me with your words!" Sadiya snapped at her friend, giving her the nastiest look as she glared at her.

"Don't start trouble with me now Sadiya, you'll not find me as understanding as Ayesha is. I'll not tolerate your insolence directed at my person. I'll respond with…"

"Enough bickering between my two foolish sisters, if we're to be successful in our dream to seek revenge on the lowly heads of loathsome American soldiers, who occupy our country as if they have a right to be controlling us. We three are going to have to learn to work together without bickering between us. Be still sisters, the young one is about on us, and we need his help to begin our attacks on the hated Americans." Ayesha hissed at her friends as her eyes studied the frail body of the young Saad Ihsaan as he approached her. She was concerned for the child's health and she did not want anything to happen to him until he brought her to the location where he found the weapons in the bunker.

Saad Ihsaan walked up to Ayesha because he liked her best out of the three women he was working with, and he smiled at her.

Ayesha returned Saad's smile as she asked the lad. "My little brother of the desert, I ask you how you're feeling on this day. The last time we spoke, you seemed like you were coming down with something, and I was worried if you were going to be in good health to take me out to the desert where you located the items we need."

"I thank you for your concern for my health, Sister Ayesha. It's good to understand someone truly cares about you. Fear not, I'll go to the land of Paradise at my appointed time, and not before, sister." Saad was actually in love with Ayesha, he had a crush on her and he was trying to speak like an adult to her whenever they met.

"I thank you for your brave words my little brother of the sands, I must ask you how your health is. We have a long trek to where you have found the weapons, Saad." Ayesha offered as she smiled at the young Iraqi lad.

"I must offer my health has cost me a little concern for two days. But today I feel well and I'll have no problem taking you out to the place where I found the underground bunker, Ayesha." Saad offered as he straightened his back and pumped up his chest as he tried to show her he was in fine health today.

The young man's actions could not hide that he was suffering from ill health before Ayesha's eyes. She had no way of knowing Saad Ihsaan was fatally infected by the altered biological weapon, and inside his body the weapon was changing its original designs, and was beginning to change, so the biological bug could destroy his body even though he was not of the Iranian nationality.

"Err… Ayesha, I must ask a question if you don't mind, sister." Shafiqu asked as she stepped forward so she could better see Ayesha's face as she addressed her.

Ayesha turned to the other woman and replied. "What is the question you must ask of me that's weighing so heavily on your mind, sister?"

"You said to Saad he was going to take you out to the location where he found the weapons in the bunker. Am I to take it Sadiya and myself will be ordered to remain in the village until you return with new discoveries? You know we want to go in the desert with you."

"Yes I did say that and that's what you and my other sister will do, that's because you and Sadiya shall remain in the village until our return. Before you get upset with my decision, allow me to explain my reason. I want you and Sadiya to remain behind is twofold. The first and most important reason is; if all four of us leave for the desert we might arouse suspicion from the village elders. They might send male fools to find out why three women set off for the vastness of the desert. The second reason is basically the same, if all of us head out and happen across an American patrol, they might become concerned we were up to no good and detain us. Sisters, if Saad and myself head in the desert and we come across Americans, they'll think a sister and her brother left the village to have peace and quiet. That's why you two must remain behind please."

Sadiya went to speak against Ayesha's decision, but she was immediately cut off when Ayesha turned and offered. "Sadiya, I won't get involved in an argument with you over my decision. It's my decision and it has been cast on the sands of the desert. I'm sorry, but Allah is the only one who might be able to change my mind. Please remain in the village until we return."

Sadiya looked into Ayesha's eyes then giving in with her orders, she drew in a breath and held it as she shook her head yes at Ayesha, as she complied with her last order.

"Thank you for supporting me, sister. I need the backing of my two faithful friends." Ayesha offered as she placed her attention on Saad Ihsaan and said. "My little brother, are you certain you're in good enough health to take this trek to the unending desert with me?"

"Of course I am Ayesha, why do you ask me such a foolish question? I'm in good health."

"By the great gray beard of the Prophet, the master of a thousand flees speaks with the tongue of a liar and a braggart. Betray not the sacred sands of Mecca, because even I can see the foul beggar of no importance looks like he's having trouble keeping his worthless eyes opened, let alone listening to what we're discussing, Ayesha." Sadiya snapped as she flung her arms in the air and shook her head in disgust over Ayesha displaying concern over the child who she loathed almost as much as she hated the American soldiers occupying Iraq.

Ayesha turned and she glared angrily at Sadiya, but she did not say anything because she was that upset with her. But her look was more than enough to silence Sadiya and she lowered her head and fell silent.

Ayesha turned her attention back to Saad again, and offered in a calm voice. "Come my little brother of the desert sands. I want to leave the village before the Almighty and always angry Eye of Allah (the sun) raises high in the cloudless sky, and it bakes the sands until we can no longer walk on the burning grains. My foolish sisters will remain in the village while you bring me out to where you found the weapons we'll use against the lowly Kafir, the non-believers and enemy of our sacred country of Iraq." Ayesha stepped aside to allow Saad Ihsaan to lead the way for her out of the village and into the vastness of the desert.

Both Sadiya and Shafiqu watched as the two left the edge and safety of the village, and walked into the unending sands of the desert. Neither woman wanted Ayesha to leave them behind. But they were ordered by their sister to remain behind, and that was what they were planning to do, even though their hearts was with their sister in the desert.

Ayesha allowed Saad to set the pace. She was still concerned for the health of the young lad and she had no idea what was troubling him. Saad did not know what was ailing him either, all he knew was his stomach was upset and burning, and every joint in his body seemed to be hurting as if they were being pulled apart. He was forcing himself to place one foot in front of the other. What he wanted to do was remain in bed and not move a muscle until his body stopped hurting. Nevertheless, he forced himself to lead the way for Ayesha in the desert.

The two walked slowly over the soft sand for over three hours, and Ayesha was able to tell Saad was suffering pain and she was feeling sad for the struggling young child, she called out. "Saad, I'm exhausted, I suggest we take a little break and have some water to share. Once we rest for a few minutes, we can start again for this place you discovered. How much further is it from where we're stopped, Saad? I fear the Eye of Allah will be very angry on this day, and the desert won't be a pleasant place to be."

Saad stopped walking and glanced towards the sky then moaned as he let out an exhausted sigh. "Yes, it seems the Eye of Allah will be very angry on this day. From where we're standing, I'd say we're another two and a half hours to where I found the hidden bunker. I believe I'll take the break as you suggested and enjoy a sip of water before we go on."

"I'm sorry Saad, I didn't understand this place was so far out in the desert. I thought you told me the bunker was only a few hours from our village."

"I'm sorry the bunker is further than I let on. That was to keep the location hidden from that witch who hates me so in our village. Whoever built this bunker was as wise as the Prophet, and he chose a very secluded and safe place for it. I believe we rested long enough to regain strength. The Eye of Allah is getting high in the sky and soon it will be too hard to keep walking in the coming heat of the day." Saad offered as he forced his body to start walking. With each step he took,

Saad moaned. Each second that passed, it seemed the pain in his body grew in intensity.

After another hour of walking in the desert, Ayesha noticed something flying in the far off in the distance, but it was so far from where they stood it looked like a tiny speck floating in the sky. She called out an alarm to Saad three steps in front of her. "Saad stop walking, there's something floating in the sky and I want to know what it is, before we go any further in the desert. I don't want to stumble into a trap, little one."

FIFTEEN MILES NORTH OF THE IRAQI TOWN OF AR-RAMADI

Sergeant Jessica Coleman had every soldier from her search unit in the desert looking for more pages from the report on the biological weapon. They found seven pages from the report, and each page was more important and chilling than the last. The female Sergeant just ended yelling at the Corporal who found the original page of the report, because he was complaining about the stifling unbearable heat of the desert. The Sergeant was glaring at the Corporal when she noticed the first of three helicopters rapidly closing in on her position. The moment she noticed them, she bellowed at the other soldiers. "Look alive, we have more Spooks (CIA Agents) coming in. This mess is going to be their problem once they secured the area, thank God. We're trained to kill, not to waste our time walking around the desert looking for loose papers."

The Sergeant had to shield her eyes with her hand so she could watch as the helicopters closed in on where she was standing. The blowing sand forced in the air from the beating rotors made her to turn her head to the side, so it did not sting the exposed sections of her face.

The instant the wheels from the unmarked black painted special Blackhawk helicopter touched down on the sand, a man dressed in a military uniform with no rank or unit markings visible on it, jumped out and he stomped his way towards her. The man did not walk like a soldier, and the rotating blades of the helicopter and blowing sand kicked up by the rotor, did not seem to bother the man either. He walked up to the female Sergeant and growled nastily while ignoring the first agent sent to oversee the Marines looking for more Iraqi papers. "Who the fuck are you Sergeant, and are you in command of these god damn mud skippers here?"

"Yes sir, I'm Sergeant Jessica Coleman, and I'm in command, sir. Who are you sir?" The Marine Sergeant replied as she went to attention and saluted the man.

"Don't ever fucking salute me in the damn field, stupid. God dammit soldier, if there's any snipers out there, you just fucking identified me as someone in command of your damn troops. Never mind who the fuck I am, you're here to answer my questions, not ask them Sergeant. Sergeant Coleman, call your lazy ass people in. I want to talk to the asshole who found the original paper you sent to Intel. Get it done soldier!"

"Yes sir, all soldiers assemble. Look alive and assemble double quick." The Sergeant bellowed while seething over the way the spook spoke and disrespected her before her troops.

While he waited, the agent spoke with the other operative sent out hours after the soldiers found the first paper from the Iraqi report. It took a few moments for the Marines to assemble before their Sergeant and stranger, in that time two more unmarked special Blackhawks landed near the first spooling obvious CIA chopper, and a flood of new soldiers also with no identifying unit insignias or ranks on their uniforms, poured out of the machine and took up a protective position surrounding their leader, and the Marines. The new soldiers took up a threatening stance like they were going to attack the Marine unit they were surrounding.

When the Marine unit was assembled, the stranger barked at the female commander. "Okay Sergeant Coleman, call the damn soldier who found the first paper to the front. I want to get this damn show of the fucking road, so I can get the hell out of this lousy desert, Sergeant."

"Yes sir, Lance Corporal Hicks, front and center." The Sergeant barked without turning to face her troops, and then she waited for Hicks to join her before the stranger.

Corporal Hicks snapped to attention, he heard the agent giving it to his Sergeant moments ago, so he did not salute either person before him. He flashed a smile at the stranger glaring savagely at him like he was going to rip his head off his shoulders if he said the wrong words to the man.

The stranger dressed in the unmarked military uniform yelled at the soldier. "What the fuck are you smiling at, asshole? What the hell kind of fucking Marine unit are you people for the love of God? A smiling Marine, you're a god damn killer mister, not a grinning fucking asshole. You like your two stripes pinned on your damn sleeve?"

"Yes sir." Lance Corporal Hicks replied as he wiped the smile from his lips, and then he glared at the tall stranger.

"If you want to keep the fucking strips, I suggest you identify yourself immediately. Before I bust you all the way back to PFC, and if you don't understand what the fuck the letters means buster, it fucking means Praying For Civilian, asshole. Who the hell are you?"

"Yes I'm Lance Corporal Robert Hicks, Sir." Hicks sharpened his attention stance.

"Well Lance Corporal Robert Hicks, where did you discover the first paper?"

Hicks looked around, and then offered to the stranger. "Sir, I found the paper about twenty five yards in that direction from where we're standing, sir. The Sergeant had me mark the place where I found the paper with that pipe stuck in the sand, sir." Hicks pointed to the spot and waited for the next question.

The agent looked at where Hicks was pointing and noticed the two foot tall pipe sticking out of the sand and remarked. "It's good to see your fucking Sergeant's keeping her head on a swivel. Get out of my face. Sergeant Coleman, how many papers have your assholes found?" The stranger snapped as he looked at the female Sergeant now.

"We found a total of eleven pages, sir. I checked them and they all pertain to what the Iraqi military was secretly working on out here, sir." Sergeant Coleman replied proudly.

"God dammit, you can read this fucking Arab scribble crap, Sergeant Coleman?"

"Yes sir, well sir." Sergeant Coleman replied with a sort of grin.

"That's great Sergeant, I didn't know any walking sandbags could read English, let alone this crap the Arabs write. Sergeant Coleman, since you can read this shit and know what these reports contain, I'm classifying you and your Marines as a security risk as of this moment. You people will no longer take orders from your Marine Command. Any and all orders you people will obey, will come from my lips alone. Do you fucking read that order, Sergeant Coleman?"

"Yes sir." Was all Sergeant Coleman replied to the fuming CIA Operative.

"Very good Sergeant, err… what's the closest god damn Iraqi town to this position, or didn't you think to consider that situation, Sergeant Coleman?" The lead CIA Agent growled while using the Sergeant's last name more as an insult leveled against her, than as a sign of respect as he looked around. All the agent could see for miles in all directions were massive sand dunes and blowing scrub grass and lizards and a sea of sand.

"Yes sir, the closest Iraqi town to this position is the village of ar-Ramadi, sir."

"Sergeant Coleman, have you requested a patrol to rip that damn Iraqi town apart, in case these papers came for that rat's nest. If these papers came from that town, you might have discovered where that madman once running this country hid this crap we're looking for, Sergeant!"

"No sir, I didn't take the time to secure the nearest town to this position, sir. I was ordered to locate any papers we could discover, and that was what we were doing, sir."

"Jesus H. Christ, I see you don't have the brains you were born with Sergeant! Get on your radio and get in contact with Command and have them order a unit of Marines to enter that fucking village, and rip the damn thing apart stick by stick if need be, Sergeant. I want that village disassembled if necessary by these soldiers we're sending there to search the place. The Marines aren't to leave a stone unturned in their search of that dump, if this crap's hidden in that town, I want it found. Do you understand your god damn orders as received!" The agent snarled at the female Sergeant.

"Yes sir I understand my orders." The fuming Sergeant grumbled at the CIA Agent.

"Get it done while I get the rest of my people out in the damn area and find what you dumb ass Marines were unable to find, Sergeant Coleman. My troops only, five will keep an eye on these mud Marines. The rest of you will get out in the area and see if any of these assholes missed some papers. The way I see it, we have eleven pages from this report, and we have the last page of the damn thing that's marked sixty. That means there are forty nine pages of this damn report missing, and I want every fucking page found by you people ten minutes ago. You'll stay out here until every page of this report is accounted for, or you people are too old to fart dust. Get going and follow your orders!" The CIA Agent glared at his specialized soldiers as they quickly fanned out into the surrounding area, and started searching for the rest of the Iraqi military report.

THE IRAQI DESERT

Ayesha al-Qaysi stared at the tiny speck in the air until she realized it had to be a helicopter. Because of the way it was flying and obviously went into a hover mode, and then the machine lowered and disappeared from view behind a sand dune. Every nerve in her body was on alert because she feared maybe the American soldiers were looking for her and Saad. Her concentration was interrupted by Saad as he cried and pointed towards the sky. "Sister of the sands, I see two more specks in the sky, and they seem to be heading to where the first speck disappeared behind the mountain of sand."

Ayesha looked at Saad and noticed him pointing in the direction he was looking in, and she looked in the same place. She had to shield her eyes with her hand from the glare from the blazing sun again. There were no clouds in the sky and it was easy for her to see the two other specks moving towards the first one. The two new specks were heading for the same place when the first helicopter disappeared moments before behind the sand dune.

"What could they be my sister of the hot burning sands?"

"The foul things are American helicopters. I fear the lowly infidels are looking for us. We better get a move on it little one. I don't want one of the loathsome American machines to fly over and discover us standing in the middle of the desert staring at their flying machines, as if it was an angel coming from Paradise to rescue us. How much further are we from this bunker you discovered, Saad? I warn you my little brother, if a helicopter comes our way, we're going to have to bury ourselves under the sand and hide until the cursed thing leave us in peace." Ayesha grumbled as she watched the first of the two new specks start to lower from the sky and then disappeared where the first one went.

"What good will our burying ourselves under the sand do, sister who obviously does not understand the ways of the sand?" Saad said as he tried to fix the desert robe a traveler of the sands wore to protect them from the sun, or biting of the hard blowing sands of the desert.

"Defiled one what a foolish question to ask me? It'll hide us from the searching eyes of the god cursed non-believers who think they own the sacred lands of Iraq." Ayesha snapped at Saad.

"It's as I offered sister. Even if we pulled every grain of sand from the desert on our shoulders and we're buried under tons of it. The hated American soldiers will be led to us by following the footprints we left in the sand as we walk for the bunker I discovered, Ayesha." Saad flashed a smile as he looked behind her at the two sets of footprints marring the flat sands leading to where they were standing at the base of a long sand dune.

Ayesha looked behind her and stared at the long line of footprints they were leaving in the sand, and then she offered. "It seems this foolish woman can learn wise things from her little Iraqi brother. How long will these prints scaring the sand last, before they disappear from the wind and the desert is back to normal, Saad?"

"I fear there's much you must learn about the desert and ways of the sand, sister. Most of our footprints are already erased by the winds of the desert. These prints we see only go back about a quarter of a mile. It'll not take long before the wind changes these prints until they look nothing like human footprints, and the hated American searchers will overlook the prints as plain marks in the sands below them, sister."

"You are wise beyond your young years my little brother. But perhaps we should quicken our pace so we can be out of this area, in case one of these helicopters heads our way. I want to be inside the bunker before any god cursed infidels come at us. I'll tell you my brother I'm going to help the desert winds hide our footprints a lot quicker." With that said Ayesha removed her protective howli and dropped it to the surface of the sand and then dragged the fabric behind her. The cloth distorted the footprints so much they looked like slight depressions in the sand as the two Iraqis quicken their pace for the bunker.

Saad smiled over what Ayesha was doing, he was proud of her because she was starting to show smarts needed by everyone to survive in the vastness of the desert. But he was worried about her because she was exposing so much of her exquisite silk like skin to the burning Eye of Allah, and he was concerned she would dehydrate before they reached the safety and coolness of the buried bunker they were searching for. Again, Saad Ihsaan looked to the sky then to the marking sand dune that brought him to the bunker the first time, and he felt they were less than fifteen minutes from the hidden place. He forced himself to place a foot before the other and walk, knowing they would reach the bunker before the sun could harm Ayesha's exposed skin.

The pain and shortness of breath was robbing him of his strength, and by the time they slid down the dune, and ended up walking on the hard flat area before the bunker, Saad was barely able to go on. Ayesha drew in her breath as she looked at the remains of the bodies of the

Iraqi soldiers killed trying to protect the bunker from the Coalition Forces who attacked her country.

Since the last time Saad visited the secluded area, the desert scavengers were again at work eating what was left of the bodies. The only meat left on the bones was the skin that turned hard as leather under the blistering sun. Even the once foul smell from the bodies was no longer as offensive as it was the first time Saad was at and found the bunker.

Ayesha turned her eyes away from the bodies of the soldiers who died protecting her country from the American invaders, as she called to Saad checking the remains for riches he might have overlooked the last time he searched the bodies. "Come with me little brother, who is defiling the honored bodies of our soldiers. Leave them and come here and show me where the entry of the bunker is resting. We're on a mission that would freeze the blood of a coward, and we must carry on until our dreams are realized, and we have successfully driven the cursed infidels who dared to invade Iraq in the want for our riches.

"Hurry Saad, my skin is burning off my foul bones through the shirt on my worthless back. We have to get out from under the Eye of Allah before we die from its revenge, or the cursed American helicopters fly over us and send one of their foot patrols to investigate what we're doing this far out in the vast desert, foolish one. Come here and show me where the entry to this bunker rests beneath the boiling sand under my feet I said."

Saad left the bodies and rushed to Ayesha's side. From this position, he started to search the area for where he found the entry to the bunker. He spotted an area that looked familiar and rushed to the spot and got on his hands and knees and began to move sand out of his way. Since the last time he was by the bunker, the harsh winds of the desert changed the landscape to where he was having a little trouble finding the opening to the underground lair beneath his feet.

Ayesha allowed the young child a few moments of searching the sand before she approached him and got down on her knees and started to move sand with him. After ten minutes of searching the sand, Ayesha snapped at the young Iraqi. "What is this you young fool of the desert that you don't know where the god cursed opening to the bunker truly lies, Saad? I'm beginning to believe Sadiya was right when she said you speak with the tongue of a worthless liar. Are we in the right place or not, Mista?"

"Ayesha don't lose faith in me, I'm nothing but dirt under your feet my sister. I'm certain this is the area where I found the entry to below the sand. Have no fear, I'll find the opening I know exists in this area, sister." Saad pleaded even though ever muscle in his body was killing him, and it was hard for him to breathe.

"I fear nothing but Allah's great wrath, little fool." Ayesha growled as she stared at the young man digging in the sand, and added. "You better find this opening before the cursed American soldiers see us digging in the sand like rutting pigs."

Ayesha's words of anger gave him the strength to push his painful body further, and he moved to his right and started to search in this area. After a few more moments of searching, a swirl of sand started to disappear in the sand and Saad moved over to this spot and drove his hands in the sand. His fingertips touched the concrete plate he placed over the opening to the bunker, and he dug in the sand with a new fever. In seconds, he cleared and then removed the plate and pulled the door to the bunker up, and the stale air instantly assaulted his nose. It smelled of oil, urine and from the many different chemicals and weapons locked under the earth for so long.

Ayesha saw the young child remove wood slats from under the sand and she moved a little closer to where he was working. When Saad opened the concrete door to the bunker, Ayesha smiled as he placed his foot on the concrete step leading into the bunker. She followed the lad deeper into the bunker and watched as the child started feeling around the darkness for the candle he left behind. When he found it, he lit it with the matches he brought with him. It took a few moments for their eyes to adjust to the dark room, and the coolness of it was refreshing their overheated bodies and returning their strength.

Ayesha found another half-burned candle on a table and lit it off Saad's candle, and she started to look around the filthy room of stale air and foul odors. She found a kerosene lantern, but the fuel had long ago evaporated and it was no use to them. She discarded it and searched the room and in no time she found five more candles and had them lit, this was enough light to allow them to move around the cluttered room safely, and see everything stored in the large concrete tomb.

Everywhere Ayesha looked in the large cement room, she noticed countless numbers of vials and racks of test tubes, rubber tubes, jars and stacks of papers thrown helter skelter over the floor, and a bank of useless computers and rows of file cabinets. Most of the computers were destroyed by the Iraqi soldiers before they fled the secret bunker. She noticed a number of electrical plugs on the walls, but obviously the generator that produced the electric for the bunker was removed by the soldiers who abandoned the bunker years ago, or by desert scavengers who would steal anything they could cart off with them of any worth. Nevertheless, Ayesha moved to a wall switch and flipped it on and looked at the lights hanging from the ceiling. She was praying to Allah they would work, they did not.

As her eyes grew more accustomed to the dim light, she noticed more items stored inside the bunker. She walked over to a pistol resting on a desk and checked to see if there was any ammunition in it, and then she tucked the weapon in her robe. She moved along the desk until she came across a run of stainless steel tables and two microscopes and a slop sink. She checked but no water came out of the taps. She never thought of checking on Saad as her eyes continued to scan the interior of the dank concrete room. Her mind was working overtime, thinking she was going to find that one weapon she could use against the American soldiers that would make the difference, and drive them out of her homeland.

Saad was so exhausted and in so much pain he sat down on an overturned box and tried to get his breathing under control, and try and absorb some of the pain he was suffering. He rested his pounding head against the concrete wall and allowed the coolness help his throbbing headache. The young child closed his eyes as his life drained from his body.

Ayesha was desperately searching the interior of the structure for more of the AK 47 Kalashnikov assault rifles that might have been left behind when the workers and Iraqi soldiers left the bunker when the American Forces first attacked her country that seemed like a lifetime ago now. In the back of her mind, she was angry that some of the Iraqi soldiers ordered to defend the bunker, obviously fled or had given up to the lowly American Forces when they attacked the area, because of the few weapons they found hidden in the place. She had no interest or idea what might be in the countless glass vials she was passing. She was only interested in finding weapons to use to fight the infidel invaders of her country. All the while she searched the bunker she paid no attention to the slowly dying boy.

She smiled when she found boxes of ammunition for the weapons Saad found. This discovery brought Saad back to her mind and for the first time since they entered the bunker, she cast a glance at the boy. She was shocked by what her eyes beheld. He was sitting on a box leaning his head against the concrete wall with his eyes closed. He was covered with sweat, and his body was trembling and jerking. She immediately stopped her search of the bunker and she went over to the lad and had to shake him with her hand to get the child's attention. His eyes slowly opened and Ayesha said. "What's wrong with you? You should've been refreshed by the cool but stale air of this foul dungeon we're in. Answer me fool, what's wrong with you?" Ayesha did not know why, but she was concerned and scared at the same time. She wondered if something inside the bunker was making the child sick.

"Sister, I don't know what is wrong with me, all I know is I can't breathe properly, and my body hurts all over. I fear I'm dying in this foul place of Satan." He replied in a voice barely over a whisper, as he struggled to speak and breathe.

Ayesha looked over her shoulder at the chemicals stored inside the bunker, and a thought entered her mind and she asked him. "Saad, you didn't touch any of this foul stuff in this filthy bunker did you? Paradise only knows what some of this stuff might be, and what it could do to your body if you touched it, my little desert brother."

CHAPTER SEVEN

"Ayesha, I only removed the weapons I found in the room, because I felt you'd have need of them. That's all I touched here, sister." Saad whispered with great effort.

"Saad, are you certain you touched nothing else in this foul place? I have to be honest, I don't like the way you look and the way you're acting. I don't want to be forced to carry you back to the village so the doctor can have a look at you, and discover what's ailing your body, child."

"I told you I touched nothing but the god cursed weapons I found hidden inside the bunker for your cause, sister. I was afraid to touch anything inside this foul place." He mumbled as he searched his mind to see if he did touch something hidden in the bunker. He looked in Ayesha's blue eyes as he continued to search his mind, and then remembered the small glass vial he stuffed in his pocket and offered to her weakly.

"My concerned sister of the sands, I took something with me, I took it because it was in an interesting glass case. I have it with me. Do you want to see what it is my sister?"

"Saad, I want to see it at once, it might be what has made you sick, child." Ayesha snapped at the lad because she understood he was dying right before her eyes.

Saad Ihsaan painfully sat forward and then he dipped his sweat soaked hand beneath the many folds of his desert Trobe, and went fishing in his pocket until he found what he was looking for. With a weak smile of victory crossing his parched lips, he removed the small vial from under his robe and then he offered it to the pretty woman. The child did not understand the danger he carried in his pocket.

The instant Ayesha saw the vial she pulled away from it as if she was looking into the eyes of the devil. She instantly recognized it as a medical item from the bunker. She looked around the room and noticed a pair of plastic gloves lying on a table and rushed for them. Putting the gloves on, she returned to Saad's side, and took the vial from him and carefully studied it as she turned the small vial around in her hand. Ayesha let out her breath in a rush of disgust as she announced. "This thing can't be the evil thing making you ill. The foul thing is empty Saad."

Saad sat forward on the box as he tried to focus his eyes on the vial as he cried. "Sister, it was full of a liquid when I took it a few days ago. Ayesha, the liquid in the glass tube made it shine in different colors, and that's why I took it. Believe me my sister it was once full of something."

"What happened to the foul liquid that was inside the tube? Do you think it might have evaporated, or could it have leaked out in your pocket, foolish one?"

"Hummm, I believe it leaked out in my pocket, come to think of it, I remember my pocket being wet, and I thought it was from sweat. Since the bottle's empty, now I know why my pocket was wet." He offered, summoning his last bit of strength in his body.

"My Iraqi brother, there's no way for me to know what this stuff was since the vial is empty. You said you removed it from this cursed place when you first discovered the bunker. Where was it you found this filth stuff? If you don't have the strength in your body, point out the area you found this in." Ayesha snapped at the lad.

Again, summoning up the last bit of his strength that was left in his hurting body, he cautiously scanned the chamber until he noticed the wide sphere of stainless steel resting on the table where he found the glass vial. He raised his hand as if it weighted a ton, and then he slowly extended his finger and pointed to where he found the item Ayesha was asking him about and she was so concerned about the vial.

She turned her eyes to where Saad was pointing, and noticed the highly polished stainless steel tables with a lone shiny metal cylinder sitting on it and she asked. "Saad, over there by that metal cylinder is where you say you found this evil looking glass thing I hold in my hands?"

She helped him to lean back until most weight of his body was again leaning against the cool concrete wall, and once he was comfortable she left his side and rushed over to the table. Gone from her mind was the want to locate weapons she could use to fight the American soldiers. Now, the only thought in her mind was to find out what was in the vial, and if it was the cause of Saad's illness. She did not want Saad to die, especially if the sickness killing him was because he found the weapons she needed to fight the occupying forces taking over Iraq.

Ayesha rushed over to the table as she wiped the sweat from Saad's body from her hands on her robe. She could not believe how much the child was sweating, and looked around in her effort to locate another glass vial so she could discover what was stored in it. There were no others to be found on the table. Then her eyes focused on the only thing there, the stainless steel cylinder and she cautiously examined it, looking for the way to open the item. She noticed the twist locking arm and placed her hands on it and gave it a twist. The locking device moved and once it moved, it was easy to twist until the cylinder opened in two pieces. Locked inside the cylinder was a larger vial that she believed was what Saad discovered inside the small glass vial, was filling the larger bottle she was staring at.

She would not touch the bottle with her bare hands for fear of what it was killing Saad, might affect her if she touched the bottle. She allowed the suspended bottle in one half of the cylinder to remain unmolested as she studied it. Saad was correct the liquid inside the bottle had different dancing colors raised by the flickering light from the candles in the bunker. She knew she discovered something evil and extremely dangerous, she realized whatever the item was she might be able to employ it against the invading American soldiers. Over the years, she heard countless stories of Saddam Hussein and his unending efforts to create chemical, biological and nuclear weapons of mass destruction.

Her mind was screaming she might have found one of those weapons, and she had to discover what it was so she knew how to use it against the enemy. She rested the bottom half of the cylinder with the bottle in it on the table, and placed the top part of the cylinder down. Once both halves were safe, she started to look for paperwork identifying what it was she was looking at.

She ripped apart stacks of paper as she read the start of each page, until she realized it did not pertain to the item she was concerned with. The other part of her driving force was discovering what the item was, so she would be able to save Saad's life.

After briefly reading about a hundred reports, she was about to give up when she picked up a file folder she dropped to the floor, in her haste to find what she was looking for. She opened the folder and there was one sheet of paper in it, it was the one she was looking for. Most of what she read she did not understand, when she came to the part describing what the deadly compound would do to anyone born Persian, she knew she found an extremely dangerous weapon to unleash against the hated American soldiers. Her mind did not realize the lethal weapon would only kill Persian born people, because she wanted it to destroy the hated foreign soldiers moving freely all over her country.

She made up her mind, she was going to take the item to her village, and was going to push, drag, or carry if she had to, Saad to their village so he could receive the medical help needed to save his life. She dropped the report to the floor because it meant no more to her. She understood she had to secure the cylinder and item contained inside it by putting the two halves of the cylinder together, and then she was going to help Saad on his feet, and they would leave the evil bunker. Before an American patrol happened along and discovered the chamber and them in the desert.

Ayesha went back to the table, and put the two ends of the cylinder together then she tightened the lock down device as tight as she could get it. Once this was completed, she turned to the child in the bunker with her. She rushed to his side and had to shake him until he opened his eyes. She did not realize her activity was making her sweat as well.

The concerned young female Iraqi looked at Saad's distorted and pained face as she dabbed at the sweat covering his ashen white face with the sleeve of her robe. She did not like the color of his skin, or the way the child was breathing and his breath smelled wrong, bad to her. He was breathing lightly and labored and it was almost impossible for her to even detect him breathing. She cooed softly to Saad in a sweet voice. "My poor little Iraqi brother, how are you feeling? Do you think you'll have the strength to walk back to our village, Saad? I need to know this so I know how to handle you when we leave this evil place of the devil. I have to get you home so you can get medical help as quickly as possible."

There was almost no strength left in Saad's crippled and frail body, and he struggled to speak as he mumbled to Ayesha barely over a whisper. "Sister, I can walk under my power back to our village, so don't trouble yourself over my health. I'll not allow a cold stop me from helping my sister with her cause to free our country of the invading infidels, Ayesha. Besides, there's nothing wrong with me only I'm tired, that's all Ayesha."

She smiled at the courage Saad was displaying as she wiped his forehead with the arm of her robe and replied. "I don't believe how strong you are. I believe you're putting to shame the worthless male adults from our village, by the strength you're displaying for your sister over your health. Come Saad you must get to your feet, we have to leave this cursed place of evil and misery. I fear the American helicopters we saw so many miles away, are closing in on us, and we have to be gone from this evil place before they locate this bunker and come to investigate it.

"Saad, I'll help you on your feet so we can leave this terrible place constructed to destroy human lives. Once you're standing on your own, I need to take that cylinder with us. So I need you to walk as best you can so we can leave this place of hate. I'll not be able to carry the cylinder and help you walk, so you have to be strong for me, Saad. Come get to your feet Saad."

THE IRAQI TOWN OF AR-RAMADI

Twelve Blackhawk troop transport helicopters hovered at the far end of the Iraqi village of ar-Ramadi, as the helicopters lightly touched down, twelve soldiers poured out of each machine. At almost the same moment the helicopters landed, a convoy of mixed Humvees and military trucks and two Bradley Fighting Machines pulled up by the spooling helicopters. The soldiers formed in a protective stance, and entered the village supported by heavily armed Humvees and Bradley machines. The troops banged on the door to the first home of the village, and when the door was answered, the soldiers forced their way in the home and began to search it. Two fast attack Apache helicopters showed up and hovered over the soldiers entering the village.

The Marines entered the village like an invading Army as they searched the town from top to bottom, to make certain the biological weapon they were searching for, was not developed or stored in the village. The commander remained by the lead Humvee, and watched his soldiers entered home after home and searched every inch of them. Some Marines entered the Mosque and other gathering place in the town, though they were carefully entering an Iraqi place of worship. After three hours of searching, the Marines started gathering around their commander.

The civilians were ordered to assemble by the water fountain in the center of the town. It was the only source of water for the entire village, and the civilians remained there for the full time the search took to be carried out by the soldiers. The Marines found the three AK 47's Saad found for Ayesha, and removed them from where Shafiqu hid them. The two women stared at the soldiers with hatred locked in their eyes all the time the foreign troopers were in their village.

When the Marine Sergeant reported to his commander the search of the village had not found any sign of the weapon of mass destruction being in the village. The commander ordered his Marines to saddle up and then the soldiers and machines left the village as quickly as they entered it a few hours before. The Marines left the Iraqi civilians gathered by the water fountain, and none of them dared move away from it until the American soldiers were out of their village. The angry civilians dispersed to check their homes and see what damage the soldiers caused them. The village was filled with curses and closed fists shaken in the air, aimed at the Marines as their machines disappeared.

The moment the Marine Commander was back inside his Humvee, he immediately reported to his command of their failure to locate the item of concern. Command reported this fact to the lead CIA Agent working in the field along with Sergeant Coleman's Unit of Marines still searching in the desert for any more of the military papers.

THE UNIT OF MARINES IN THE DEEP DESERT

Sergeant Jessica Coleman's Radio Operator called out, and then informed her there was an incoming call for the agent. She looked at the agent, and then led him over to their Radio Operator. The CIA Agent took the mike and glared at the operator, informing him to leave and then he answered the incoming call with a growl. "Yeah, this is Special Agent Peter Stockten, go ahead with your damn traffic, Mister!"

"Yes Agent Stockten, we searched the village of ar-Ramadi from head to toe, and we found no sign of the item being in the village, sir. We found nothing. This was a waste of time and effort. I believe the answer to your interest lies closer to where you found the evidence, sir. Over."

"Yeah, I'm beginning to believe that myself. You have done well and your people are dismissed from any further duty to this incident, sir. I'll handle it from my side from now on." The agent broke off the communication without the proper disconnect codes, he was that angry. He turned back to Sergeant Coleman and barked at her in a savage voice.

"Okay Sergeant, I'm releasing your pack of assholes from detention, and you're to order your idiots to linkup with my people, and they're to assist them and follow every damn order from my people as if they were issued from God Almighty, Sergeant. Give your orders we're heading into the miserable desert. I'll have provisions airlifted to us when we need the damn things, Sergeant." The agent glared at the Sergeant until she jumped to follow his orders.

Agent Stockten watched in anger as the Marines formed up with his people, and he whirled his arm in the air, and three helicopters built up takeoff power until they were able to life off the ground. Stockten took over the Sergeant's lead machine as the soldiers and his people got on board the Humvees. When they were ready to go, the agent got on the radio and informed the pilots the direction he wanted to head off in. He remembered the direction Lance Corporal Hicks pointed when he first asked him where he found the paper. Stockten also got in touch with his command and demanded to speak to a weather expert, and ordered the man to make up a chart of winds in this region for the past seven days. He was basing his request on the condition of the pages. The condition informed him the pages were not blowing around on the desert sands for a long period of time.

Agent Stockten felt that if he had the track of the winds for the last seven day, he would be able to better pinpoint where the papers came from at least that was what he was banking on as he ordered the driver to head out with the helicopters leading the way for his convoy. When the report came in, he checked the wind charts and found they were mainly blowing in his direction from the west, so he ordered the driver to head in that direction until ordered to do otherwise.

The Marines in the Humvee with the agent stared at the man with hatred in their eyes. None of them like the way the spook was speaking or treating them, but they were powerless to do anything about it. At least two Marines swore the first sign of trouble they got into, this agent was going to be the first one going to get hit by a drive by bullet and left where he fell.

THE HIDDEN IRAQI MILITARY BUNKER

Ayesha al-Qaysi was having trouble getting Saad Ihsaan to stand under his own power. Once he was on his feet, she shoved him towards the opening of the bunker. When Saad was outside the complex, she when back inside the dark chamber and lifted the polished metal cylinder, and also tried to take one ammunition box for the AK-47s. It was impossible for her to take both items, so she left the rounds behind. Once she was out of the bunker, she scanned the sky in all directions in search of any sign of the American helicopters they spotted a few hours before. She smiled because she saw nothing in the air. She then grabbed Saad's hand and pulled him out of the area. The child was dragging his feet in the sand, barely moving on shaky legs with her help to keep him moving away from the area.

She resorted to cursing at the lad to make him move faster. Nothing she did or cursed worked on Saad, because he was moments from death. Ayesha was struggling with the added weight of Saad leaning heavily on her body, and trying to carry the nearly twenty pounds of metal cylinder in her other hand. She was happy because the wind of the desert was beginning to kick up, and she looked behind and saw the wind was blowing the sand hard enough to cover her tracks almost as quickly as she and Saad made them in the sand. She struggled with Saad until they were about ten miles away from the bunker, and then she dropped him against a sand dune.

The steep sand dune was blocking most of the howling wind assaulting their bodies. She carefully placed the heavy cylinder down on the sand, and then she checked on Saad's fading health. The child was not moving at all now, and he was barely breathing. She removed the hood of the desert robe from his head, so she could better see his face, and what she saw upset her to all ends. Saad's eyes were mere slits and blackened and his face was sunken in, and he did not even look like Saad any longer.

The skin on his face was as white as the sand, and blood was seeping out of the corners of his eyes, the side of his mouth and his nose. She turned his head and noticed blood seeping out of his ear. She was fighting the want to heave her guts over what was happening to Saad's body. She did not know why this reaction was happening to the young lad. She picked up his eyelids and his eyes seemed lifeless and stationary, and the child had the look of death in them. A deep and sudden breath drawn in by the child, and then his body rattled and settled down on the sand for the last time in his young life, as his hands fell off his chest and hung lifelessly by his sides. One look at the child and she knew Saad Ihsaan had died.

Her first instincts were to bury the child from her village in the sand so the desert scavengers did not defile his body. A movement off to her right and high in the air drew her attention. She concentrated on the small speck and realized there were three specks. One word escaped her lips and it was drowned out by the whirling wind. "Americans!" She watched the three helicopters for a few moments and they seemed to be heading directly at her. The track of the helicopters was going to carry them a few miles above the bunker she and Saad left a few hours ago. She knew the American soldiers were looking for her and Saad, and her breathing became labored as she thought of her next moves to avoid being picked up by her enemy.

She looked at Saad's frail body and felt sad because he was the first Iraqi freedom fighter to give up his life for her dream to attack the hated American soldiers who had invaded her country. She said a silent pray from the Holy Qur'an for Saad's soul, and then she bent and laid his body out in a comfortable position, and carefully straightened the desert robe so it protected his body the best it could. She picked up the hood and pulled it up until it covered his head. Even though they were on the protected side of the massive sand dune, she knew it would not take long what wind got between the dunes to cover over the body with the blowing sands of the desert.

She then picked up the heavy metal cylinder and started off in the desert again. As little as she knew of the harsh ways of struggling to survive in the vast desert, she understood enough to stay on the leeward sides of the tallest sand dunes, so she could hide her presence from the searching helicopters, and protect herself from the hard winds of the sandstorm rapidly developing until she reached the safety of her village. Fighting the harsh blowing and ever shifting sand under her feet, was making it extremely hard for her to continue to get back to her village with her weapon locked in her arms.

In the back of her mind, she could not help feeling bad for leaving Saad's body on the sand. But she also could not take time to bury him, or the American soldiers would have discovered her, and she was still too near the underground bunker for her to deny she knew anything about the secret complex under the sand. She was pushing herself forward, constantly looking over her shoulder to see where the American helicopters were at. She felt she was opening the distance between her and the flying machines, because the specks looked smaller now. Nevertheless, she kept pushing forward to the safety of her village.

THE CONVOY OF AMERICAN HUMVEES AND HELICOPTER FLYING COVER FOR THE MILITARY VEHICLES AND SEARCHING THE DESERT

The pilot reported to the agent in command of their mission. "Agent Stockten, the wind's really picking up sir. It looks like we're in for a bit of blow. My visibility's going to hell in a handbag, sir. I'm suggesting we set down and wait out this upcoming blow, sir. I'm getting concerned the sand might get in the intakes of my engines and knock out our motors. Advise if you want to continue with this mission or if we can set down and wait this thing out, sir. Over."

"Yeah, I see the wind picking up. Tell you what Commander, look around and find a safe place to huddle and wait this bullshit wind storm out, sir. You damn pilots are my eyes in the sky, and I need you people up there while I'm on this shit filled operation. You have my permission to seek shelter Commander I'll pass on your request to the other Humvees. You lead the way and when we see you set down, we'll circle your machines with ours and try to protect your helicopters with our machines from the sands. Out."

"Roger your last Agent Stockten, will comply with orders as received, sir. I noticed while we were heading this way a large sand dune to our portside about seven miles off, sir. I feel if we put down there, the sand dune will protect us from the sandstorm developing, sir." The pilot replied over the radio to the lead agent.

"Lead the way and cut down the chatter on the damn horn. And, don't refer to me as an Agent, I'm Number One for the rest of this mission to all concerned."

"Roger that last Number One, commencing my turn as of this point, sir."

Stockten had to turn his head to see the direction where the helicopters were turning, and then he barked at the driver of his humvee. "Follow the helicopters, they're heading for cover."

The fuming soldier did not bother to respond to the orders from the nasty agent, all he did was turn and look straight ahead and cursed the spook under his breath.

Little did the CIA Agent know, the helicopters and his vehicles were heading for the same sand dune protecting the bunker.

It took the soldiers and war machines an hour and fifteen minutes to reach the sand dune. The helicopters were on the ground by the time the Humvees pulled up behind the protection offered by the huge mound of sand. By the time the soldiers and humvees reached the protection, the wind and sand was whipping up, and it was almost impossible to see where they were going. The helicopters landed as close to the mound of sand as they could get, and the Humvees pulled up and surrounded the unprotected sides of the helicopters. No soldiers wanted to get out of the protection offered by the machines, but Sergeant Coleman took command of her troops, and she ordered them out to form a protective ring around the vehicles. Stockten approved of the Sergeant's orders, but he did not want the Marines out there by themselves. He took command of the radio and ordered five of his people out of the machines to help the Marines.

Sergeant Coleman's Marines fanned out to their usual defensive positions they took when the machines were parked. They hunkered down and tried to protect themselves against the hard blowing sands. The Marines had protective glasses on and their noses and lips were protected by a special hard plastic mask, made to keep the sand out of their mouths and noses. The soldiers also wore ear protection against the roar from the wind and blowing sand.

Private Edward Wilson was the furthest soldier out from the group, and he was classified as the pointman for the detail. He had his head bent and aimed the top of his helmet into the teeth of the wind.

All the while he was bent down on a knee he cursed the Sergeant, agent and anything else he could think of to curse. He hated the desert when the winds blew. It made everything they did so much harder to accomplish. The Private looked at the hard packed sand under his feet and thought it was hard enough to land a plane on it. He took control of his rifle with one hand and with the other he tested the sand's hardness. Then he looked to his right and noticed the flat area extended far enough to land a plane safely on it. Then he looked in the other direction and the flat area continued for over a mile easy.

The Private found himself wondering if this area was a sort of landing strip made for Iraqi warplanes years ago before the Desert Storm War Games. He started to pay closer attention to the area and all he could see of it. The width of the flat area was wide enough to land a set of planes side by side. But the soldier thought it strange there were three small sand piles in the middle of the flat area, and he also noticed a small depression in the sand the wind was blowing over but not filling in. The Private had to squint in his protective goggles while he tried to see through the whipping sand. The bumps of sand lying nearly in the middle of the flat area kept drawing his attention, and he struggled off his knee and then he moved towards the first small pile of sand. The strong wind almost blew him over, but he fought to maintain his balance until he was bent over by the sand pile.

Once he was there, the Private reached out to see if the sand was as hard as the flat area. It was soft, and the blowing sand was adding to the back of the bump in the sand. Now, the Private thought something might be buried under the sand. Remembering the many stories he heard about the Iraqis raping the museums when they attack the country the second time. The Private's thoughts went to wondering if he might have found some items of worth.

With a smile the excited Private forced his hand under the sand, and when his gloved fingers felt something under it, he felt he found something worth a fortune. The soldier grabbed hold of what his fingers touched, and when he pulled his hand from under the sand, he had a denuded leg bone minus the foot. Shocked over his discovery, the Private pulled away from the pile as he dropped the bone. Then he pulled out his handheld radio and reported to his Sergeant. "Holy shit

Sergeant Coleman this is Private Wilson, Ma'am. Come in Sarge, this is important."

Sergeant Coleman was in the command Humvee with the agent and two of his people when her handheld came to life and she replied. "Go Private, what do you have? Over." The Sergeant knew it had to be something for the Private to contact her.

"Hey Sarge, I just found a part of god damn body under a sand pile out here, Ma'am. Over."

"Who is it, is it a dead soldier, or some civilian who might have lost his way and died out here in this god forsaken place, Private? Over." The concerned Sergeant asked the Private.

"I don't know Sarge I didn't ask the bag of bones who the hell he was yet, Ma'am. Over."

"Funny Private it's a good thing you're low man on the totem pole, or I'd bust you for your last remark, Mister. Can you see the whole body? Is it dressed in a uniform or civvies, wiseass?"

"I don't know, all I found was a leg bone I think, and it has nothing on it Ma'am. Over."

"Well dig the damn thing out until you can tell either way and get back to me double quick, wiseguy. Is the one you found the only body out there, or are there more with it, Private? Over." The female Sergeant growled her questions to the Private over the radio.

"It's the only one I see, there's at least two more piles of sand out here like the one I found this dead dude under, Ma'am. Do you want me to check the others out as well Ma'am? Over."

"Find out if the first one's a military or not, and then check out the other two piles. I'm coming out to help you, Private." The Sergeant replied in her radio.

"Yes Ma'am." The Private offered as he held his weapon with one hand, and with the other he started to move the sand from the buried body until he uncovered most of the remains. He stopped digging when he found pieces of an Iraqi uniform by the bones. Once he discovered this he got up and moved over to the next pile and started to dig in that one. Lance Corporal Hicks, the nearest soldier to Private Wilson, moved over and helped him dig in the sand. By the time Sergeant Coleman reached the two soldiers, they uncovered enough of the three soldiers to identify them as Iraqi troopers, and they were obviously killed many years ago judging by the condition of the bodies.

The Sergeant walked up to the two soldiers trying to protect herself from the blowing wind, and snapped in almost a scream to be heard over the roar from the raging wind. "What the hell do you have?" The Sergeant was followed by the spook in command of their mission.

"Ma'am, the three stinking bodies are definitely Iraqi soldiers and from the looks of the bodies, they've been dead a helluva long time, Sarge. What should I do with the damn things, Ma'am?" The Private reported and asked at the same time, because he was the one who found the bodies. Corporal Hicks stood with his mouth shut and grinning because the lead spook was in the wind along with the soldiers, and the agent was eating a ton of sand by the spoon full because he did not have protection the Marines had.

"You can eat the fucking things for all I care. I don't give a fuck what you do with their bodies. You can leave them where they lay for any good they are to us, buster. What I do care about, is what the hell these three soldiers were doing all the way the hell out here in the middle of fucking nowhere, soldier. From what I can see of what's left of their bodies, these pukes weren't soldiers trained for offensive actions. They look more like they were out here to guard something or someone, dammit. Because there's nothing out here within miles of this place, we have to be standing close to whatever the hell these assholes were out here to protect. Sergeant!" The angry lead agent growled as he turned to face the female soldier.

When he had the Sergeant's attention, Stockten added to his words, screaming to be heard over the roar of the wind drowning out his words. "Get everyone out of those fucking machines. I want this entire area searched, and if we don't find anything the first time, we're going to search the area again and again until we find what the hell these asses were out here protecting."

"Sarge, there's something else I noticed and want to show you, Ma'am…"

"Look asshole, you'll address your god damn report to my ass from this point on, buster. Fuck your bitch Sergeant. What the hell did you want to tell her, stupid?" The lead agent hissed nastily as he cut off Private Wilson's words to his Sergeant and glared at him.

Private Wilson looked at his Sergeant and she nodded and he reported with a snap to the agent. "Okay pal you got it. Look fella I spotted a slight depression by the third downed body. It looks like it might be a hole in the damn ground, and it's being filled by this blowing sand."

"Lead me over to this god damn depression." The agent shot back at the Private.

"It's over there man." Private Wilson pointed and he got growled at again.

"Don't point at the damn thing, bring me over to the fucking place, you fucking asshole you! You Marines are dumber than a box of fricking monkey nuts, I swear."

His last words angered the Marines who gathered around their discovery, and if it was not for the Sergeant giving them the cool off look. The agent and the rest of his people could have ended up joining the bodies of the dead Iraqi soldiers lying on the sand.

IN THE MIDDLE OF THE DEEP DESERT

Ayesha was struggling desperately while carrying the over twenty pound metal cylinder, and trying to walk in the ever shifting sand with the hollowing wind pushing her forward, because it was blowing in the same direction she was heading. It had been quite a while since the last time she looked over her shoulder to see where the helicopters were, or if they saw her and were coming after her. There was so much sand blowing she was not able to see her hand in front of her face. She was please Saad insisted she wear the Howli, because that was the only thing protecting her from being sand blasted by the harsh blowing sands.

She decided if the American soldiers picked her up in the desert, the helicopters would be forced out of the air until calm returned to the sand. So she knew she had the time of the sand storm to get to the safety of her village, before the helicopters were able to be airborne again. Even though the wind was blowing harder than moments before, she did not seek to hunker down until the blow was over. She wanted out of the desert as soon as possible.

Walking around the side of another sand dune, she found herself out of the harsh wind, she took this time to remove the hood of her Howli and look about. She wanted to make certain she was heading away from the bunker towards her village, and not walking in circles. She took this time to swallow the last bit of water she carried to the desert, now time was working against her. With the wind blowing this hard and her walking in it, it would not take long for her to dehydrate and lose her strength and die a terrible death. Once she finished her water reserve, she discarded the skin container and tried to get her bearings. Not being able to see any identifying landmarks, she had to resort to her compass. When she discovered she was walking due north at one hundred and eighty degrees, she understood she was heading directly for the safety of her village.

Even though she had no idea how close she was to her town, the knowledge of her heading for it filled her with new strength, and she shoved off on her trek again. With a deep sigh, she placed one foot in front of the other and started to walk again.

IN THE VILAGE OF AR-RAMADI

Once the American soldiers left the village, both Sadiya Sadjadpour and Shafiqu al-Quraishy became alarmed over their friend and the young lad out in the desert. The wind around the village was blowing as hard as it was in the middle of the desert. The women understood some ways of the land of sand, and they knew their friends were walking through the midst of a harsh sand storm. Once the anger they suffered because of the search of this village by the American soldiers left their bodies, they started to search their minds on how they could help their friends find the village through the blowing sand.

The two women spoke of their fear to an elder and told him of their dilemma. The elder suggested they get a few smudge pots and burn diesel fuel, so the burning fuel would send up columns of black smoke in the air, and hope it would show the missing children the way home.

Sadiya and Shafiqu loaded their arms with pots and rushed to the end of the village where their friends entered the desert. They placed the pots on the sand and one of the males of the village came out carrying five gallons of diesel fuel. He opened it and poured liquid in each pot. The sand was blowing harder at the edge of the village. Then the male struggled to light rags on fire, and once they were burning he dropped one after the other in the pots.

Seven columns of black smoke rose into the air, even though the wind was blowing the smoke, anyone near would see it and come to where the smoke was coming from. The male had enough of the sand biting in his face and he left the women looking towards the desert. Both women stood by the burning smudge pots, and covered their eyes and stared out in the desert, searching for the first signs of either of their friends.

Ayesha was beginning to doubt she would ever find her village as she struggled in the blowing sand, and she began to curse everything she held dear. She believed Allah would never allow her to die alone in the vastness of the desert, not with her God knowing what her plans were. She tried to talk herself into believing Allah would protect her, even though she was beginning to fight off desperation in the search for her village.

The male who filled the pots with fuel, returned to the women for a few moments and handed Sadiya a large cow bell and ordered her to ring it. He told Sadiya the noise would travel further in the desert than the smoke with the wind interfering with it. Both women thanked the man as he rushed for the safety of his home to protect him from the blowing sand.

Sadiya began to ring the bell and when her arm got tired, she passed the bell to Shafiqu, Sadiya continued to scream Ayesha's name out over the roar of the wind. Both women refused to leave, they decided this was the least they could do for Ayesha, to assist her in finding the village. Sadiya wanted to go in the desert to search for Ayesha and Saad, but Shafiqu refused to let her enter the desert. She warned her friend they were waiting for Ayesha, and she did not want to be forced to start looking for her as well, if she lost her way in the desert searching for their missing friends.

Reluctantly, Sadiya gave up her bid to enter the desert to search for Ayesha.

As she struggled to trudge along in the harsh blowing wind and sands, she stopped dead in her tracks. She thought she heard something and uncovered her ear and turned her head away from the roar of the wind, using the side of her hood as a scoop so she could hear better. All she heard was the roar of the wind. She was about to fix the hood of her robe when she heard the noise again. Uncovering her eyes, she started to search the area where she thought she heard the noise from. She had to squint and her mind informed her there was black smoke in the air a distance from where she was standing. Now, her mind was warning her that the smoke might be coming from the American war machines searching for her and the child.

She wanted to head in another direction to avoid the smoke and possible enemy soldiers waiting to capture her. Again she was stopped leaving the area by the noise. Now, she swore the noise she heard was the sound of a bell, and no Americans would ring a bell and give away their position, if they were searching for her. As she listened to make certain it was a bell, she was able to hear someone calling, even though she could not make out what the caller was saying.

After listening to the sound of the bell she was hearing for some time, along with someone calling out to her, she realized someone was calling her name. She smiled as she closed the hood of her robe around her head and rushed to who she believed were her friends looking for her in the desert. She fell to the sand three times in her haste to find her friends, all three times she fell she protected the metal cylinder locked in her aching arms. She was fearful if the cylinder fell and broke open, the biological weapon inside would escape and not only kill her, it would kill everyone living in her village, and maybe even in her entire country.

The smoke was getting thicker, and she was able to see two shapes in the blowing sand. She smiled and increased her movement. The knowledge she was this close to the safety of her village and friends, removed the fatigue she was suffering from her body. She forced herself forward even though every muscle in her body caused her pain. The overwhelming weight of the container in her arms felt as if it weighed a ton. As exhausted as she was, she refused to put the cylinder down, it was hers and she was going to use it against the American invaders.

She was ten feet from the two shapes she still could not make out clearly she knew they were Sadiya and Shafiqu. Her friends did not realize she was only a few feet from them, because the sand was blowing that hard. Finally, it was Shafiqu who saw something moving before her, and stopped ringing the bell and called out to the aberration she saw moving before her. "Ayesha, is that you my sister?"

Giving into her exhaustion, Ayesha allowed her body to collapse to the sand as she called back to her friend. "Yes Shafiqu, it is I, and I have survived the endless walk in the desert. I'm afraid I cannot walk another step though my sister."

Sadiya and Shafiqu dropped what they had in their hands and moved forward to assist their friend with Shafiqu calling out. "You stay where you are and we'll come to you. We have water and it'll give you strength, my wayward sister of the vast desert."

Ayesha allowed her body to stretch out on the sand as she tried to gather her strength. Her hands never released the strangle hold on the cylinder in her arms. Breathing heavily wrapped up in the desert robe, she struggled to get her breathing under control. Suddenly there were hands on her body pulling her over on her back. There were more hands working on the hood of her robe as they uncovered her face. The next thing she realized was someone pouring warm water in her mouth, and trying to stop the sand from landing on her face. Shafiqu was cooling her off.

Sadiya was looking around her thoroughly fatigued sister on the sand for the young Iraqi male. She was unable to locate the child which caused her to ask. "Ayesha, where is the little foul one who cost you so much pain on this cursed day?"

Ayesha was struggling to get her breathing under control, and the strength in her body. She summoned up the strength to reply to Sayida's question. "Sadiya, I fear Saad is the first Martyr to lay down his life for our just cause, sister."

"I don't understand how did the beggar of no importance die while you were in the desert, Ayesha? Did you run into trouble with the cursed American soldiers, did they kill the lowly dog of an unbeliever?

Are you hurt my sister who does not know better than to come out of the desert when the winds are angry?" Sadiya asked the exhausted Ayesha.

"You never know when to close your foul mouth sister! Now is not the time to flood our sister with questions of no worth. Come Ayesha, we have to get you out of this endless blowing wind. You need to rest and regain your strength and refresh and renew yourself. Give me this, what is this foul can you carry like it's a new born child you cradle in your arms, Ayesha?" Shafiqu asked as she tried to take the metal cylinder from Ayesha.

Ayesha refused to relinquish her death like hold on the cylinder as she pulled it even closer to her body and she replied. "Shafiqu, it's the answer to ridding Iraq of the cursed Crusaders who dared to invade our country. With this great weapon, we'll be able to kill all the hated American soldiers in masses. So many their civilians back home will demand their government remove their cowardly soldiers from our sacred lands."

Shafiqu leaned a little on her knees and then she stared at the cylinder for a few moments, and then offered with concern lacing her voice. "My foolish young sister, what power is possessed in such a small tin can like that'll have power over the might of the American soldiers? From what I saw of the lowly infidels, they fear nothing not even their own God. I fear you're weaving a tall tale, one I'm unable to believe."

"My unbelieving Shafiqu, I'm too exhausted to explain the awesome power contained in the walls of this container I hold in my arms. Once I had a chance to rest and regain my strength, I'll inform you of the power contained within this cylinder. For the moment Shafiqu, you'll have to trust in my faithful words until I can have a chance to prove all I say to you is true, sister."

"You're correct Ayesha who has come back to us from the deep desert, we have to get you out of this god forbidden desert, before its sand and heat takes you away from the ones who love you. Come sister and allow me to help you to your feet. Ayesha, give the cursed metal can to Sadiya and she'll carry it for you, you must be exhausted from your long trek." Shafiqu said as she offered Ayesha her hand and the women struggled to their feet with Ayesha crying.

"No one will take possession of this cylinder but me while I breathe a breath in my worthless body. What happened in the village while I was gone from home for so long, sister? I thank my two faithful sisters for their concern over my wellbeing, and lighting the signal fires that helped guide this wayward one home safely. If I didn't see the smoke from the smug pots and hear you calling out to me, I fear I would've wandered the desert until I was called home to Paradise by Allah's breath and will."

"Much has taken place in our village while you were walking the desert. Far too much happened to explain it to you here. There'll be plenty of time to tell you of what happened in the village. Then you can explain the power you have in that metal can you carry." Shafiqu replied as she allowed Ayesha to lean heavily on her body, and began guiding her to their village.

Sadiya was looking behind her in hopes Ayesha was wrong, and the village troublemaker would come walking out of the desert to join them. For the first time in her life, Sadiya realized how much she liked the young lad, even though she spends much of her life cursing Saad while he was growing up in their town.

Shafiqu was having trouble struggling with Ayesha's body leaning heavily against her that Sadiya stepped forward and helped her walk from the other side of Shafiqu. This made the three women better able to walk together and in no time, they walked down the main street of the village with the wind pushing them forward. The two helped Ayesha to her front door and when they knocked, her mother answered and one look at her daughter she took over care of Ayesha. Shafiqu and Sadiya allowed the mother to take her from them and when she slammed the door in their faces, they turned and headed for the safety of their homes in the village.

THE SAND FLAT DEEP IN THE IRAQI DESERT

Corporal Wilson led Agent Stockten and Sergeant Coleman through the blowing sands to the slight depression, and one look in it from the agent, and he immediately took command of the situation and barked orders to both Marines and the rest of his people.

"Coleman, have your damn people form a protective ring around this depression, no one gets near it without my permission, dammit. None of your walking sandbags are allowed within fifty feet of the damn thing. My people get your asses over here and start digging in this fucking sand. I want to know what the hell's under our damn feet. I believe we stumbled over what we're looking for in this miserable desert. Get a move on it, you Marines are under command of your Sergeant. If I see any of you coming near where we're working, I'll have the lot of you shot on the spot. This is a top secret classified area, and you fucking Marines are here to protect my people while we work on this damn place, period!"

Agent Stockten was forced to step aside as a number of his special unit moved in and started to dig in the sand with shovels they stole from the Marines. It was a losing cause though, as fast as the agents dug the sand out of the opening, the wind blew it right back in it on them. Seeing this, Stockten roared. "I need a few of your fucking Marines over here, Sergeant Coleman."

Again, the lead agent said the Sergeant's name as if it was a four letter word as he waited for her to assign a few Marines to his unit. When four angry Marines stood at attention before the agent, he roared at them. "You people get over there and start up three of your vehicles and move the damn things here and form a windbreak around where my people are working in the fricking ground. Get the damn thing done before I have the lot of you shot on general fucking principles. Move it or lose it."

The Marines moved to follow their orders though they hated taking orders from the spook.

Stockten moved to where his people were digging in the sand and losing more ground than they were gaining, because of the blowing sand. One of his people offered with a smirk. "Agent Stockten, we found a set of concrete steps leading underground. I hope we didn't find a tomb."

"Well let me tell you something, if this is a tomb it had modern day Iraqi soldiers guarding it for some damn reason. Keep your fucking wise cracks to yourself and get in there and dig. I want to know what we found." The agent was being kinder to his people, but not much though.

One of the pilots walked over to the agent and leaned his head closer to the man as he offered. "Number One, I have a secured call coming in for you on my radio, sir."

"Thanks, at least I know you have the brains you were born with, or you wouldn't be able to fly that damn thing with the skill you have. Which helicopter should I use, mister?" The lead agent barked at the pilot.

"The lead one is my machine sir." The pilot growled back at the agent as he glared at him.

"Spare me the fucking look Commander and let's go. You people have no god damn idea what the hell we're looking for. If you people did, you'll probably crap your damn pants." The agent did not back down from the larger helicopter pilot.

The pilot did not reply to the insult as he followed the agent to his helicopter. The door guard opened the side door when the agent was near the helicopter. Stockten climbed in and the moment the soldier inside pointed to the radio, he barked at the pilot. "Commander, get your people out of this damn machine, I need privacy when I'm speaking to fucking Command."

Without missing a beat the pilot ordered his people out of the helicopter. The moment he was alone, Stockten snarled in the radio. "Yeah, this is One, Three, go with your traffic, sir. Over."

"It's good to see you're in one of your usual good moods, Stockten. You missed your ordered check in, and I was calling to see what was going on out there, sir. Over."

"Yeah Command, it looks like we might have found what we were sent out to find, sir. I can't confirm it at this time though, I should know for certain within the next three to four hours, sir. Over." The agent said in a calmer tone, taking the rebuff from his commanding officer to heart.

"Outstanding, the moment you know for certain if you found the package. Let me know and I'll flood your location with more security and protection and technicians than you can count. Have you run into any insurgents or other troublemakers?" The commander asked.

"None whatsoever Command. With the wind blowing like it is, we didn't even come across a fucking camel walking around out here, sir. I'm going to need more supplies and provisions. It looks like we might be out here for quite some time, sir." Stockten offered.

"You tell me what you need and I'll have it shipped out to you before you can pull the pants out of the crack of your ass, sir. I'm going to need your exact GPS position, sir. Agent Stockten, I can't tell you how important your mission is to the security of the world, sir. I had a conversation with General White, he informed me of the ramifications this thing could cause if it's released by accident or on purpose, sir. This thing could wipe out all life on the earth if we can't confine the crap. I have to warn you of Directive Three, One, One, Seven sir…"

"What the hell is Directive Three, One, One, Seven sir? I never heard of that one sir."

"I wouldn't think you did Agent, it was ordered by the Chairman of the Joint Chiefs of Staff, General John White, sir. Directive Three, One, One, Seven calls for the complete destruction of the nation of Iraq with a combined nuclear attack by forces of the United States and Russia, to sterilize the region and kill this package before it could spread to any other nation of the Middle East if released, sir. Yes Agent Stockten, you heard me correctly sir.

"I included Russia because they have a stake in this damn nightmare. General White has been in contact with his military counterpart in Russia once he had information this package was discovered, and he informed the Russian General of this threat from Iraq. It took the Russians fifteen minutes to agree with the General's proposal to destroy Iraq and any other nation of the Middle East, if it becomes infected by the package, and if needed to control a release of the package before it escapes to the rest of the globe, sir."

"Well the damn General's doing his job right if he was able to get the damn Russians to agree to anything we need to do that quickly. Command, I have to get back to my people and see what the hell we might have discovered here sir. Like I said, the moment we know for certain what the hell we're dealing with sir I'll get back to you." Stockten complained because he wanted to break off his communications with his command and get back to work.

"Before I allow you to break off this communication Agent Stockten, I need to inform you of another turn of events. General White informed us he intends to deploy his specialized Rapid Response Forces if you discover this package. Those soldiers will be assigned to hunt down any items not contained if you catch my drift, sir." The agent's commanding officer added to his report to the CIA Operative over the radio.

"Who the hell is this fucking General that he commands the power to remove an assignment that should be handled by the CIA from us, sir?" Stockten hissed hotly into the radio.

"Listen up Stockten, the General I'm speaking of is the Chairman of the Joint Chiefs of Staff, sir. He commands the power to takeover this operation at a drop of the hat. Besides Agent, he owns the President's ear and this order originates from the White House. It looks like we'll be forced to take a back seat on this one once you discovered where this package is stored in Iraq."

"That's great then I suggest you pull me and my people the hell out of this damn desert and off the front of the dime, and allow this General's fucking pack of pet's takeover the operation, Commander.

I'm not going to place my people in danger continuing to look for this crap, so some glorified Army unit can step in and take the credit for finding and containing this cr…"

"The specialized unit we're speaking about is comprised of mainly Marines, but it does cross the other branches of the service, Agent Stockten. It includes specially trained soldiers from twenty different nations who have volunteered their soldiers to make up this special unit of fast attack soldiers, sir. That's why the unit was branded the Multi Nation Rapid Response Force, Stockten." The commander interrupted his agent as he informed him of the command power this General had under his command.

"Jesus H. Christ, you mean to tell me that I'm going to be forced to turn over this crucial operation to a bunch of thick headed glory hunting Marine bastards, and that bastard unit includes soldiers from certain countries I consider enemies against the United States, sir? What the hell next am I going to be stuck dealing with on this operation, sir." Stockten growled, not believing the last orders his commander issued him.

"That's what you'll do and you'll like it, Agent Stockten. I know how you feel about this order and it rubs me the wrong way as well, I assure you. General White doesn't want the CIA's fingerprints on this train wreck. Agent Stockten, that's why he wants to deploy these specialized soldiers. He's of the mind if anything goes wrong with this operation, he could say the Marines were operating under their own direction, in that way he'll keep the President out of the cross hairs, and protects us at the same time. As much as I don't like these orders, I'm able to see where the General's coming from, and Heaven knows with Congress riding our asses, we need to remain out of the lime light on any mission we're sent on, sir.

"Especially with the flap we're receiving from Congress over the harsh treatment we dished out on the terrorists we're holding at Gitmo and other special prisons throughout the world. I say the hell with it and allow the Marines get the black eye if anything goes wrong with this mess."

"Commander, it seems I have no other choice in the matter. I'm forced to step aside when these soldiers get out here, sir. Do you have any idea when these Rapid Response Forces are scheduled to arrive, and they take command of this operation, Commander?" The agent snapped.

"From what I was led to believe about these soldiers, the specialized units are being detained at Camp Lejeune, once you discover where this crap originated from, Agent Stockten. These troops will be shipped over to Pope Airforce Base at Fort Bragg, and then they're to be shipped out to your position once the location of this crap is discovered and confirmed, Agent Stockten." The commander replied.

"Allow me to get back to my people so I can see what the hell we discovered. That way I and my people can get the hell out of this desert and allow this pack of thick headed Marines takeover my operation, sir." Agent Stockten growled in the radio, not hiding he was angry as hell over the fact he was giving up command of the operation to locate and security the biological danger.

"Will do Agent Stockten and there's another thing I want to discuss with you, and I warn you while I'm at it, sir. You need to change your lousy disposition and attitude against these soldiers heading your location, sir. You have to understand, they're carrying the approval seal not only from the Chairman of the Joint Chiefs of Staff.

"They're coming with the approval from the President. Also, from what I understand about these soldiers, they'll respond to any threat against them with lethal force. Whether that threat comes from the enemy of our country or from anywhere else, and that includes your attitude and that of the paramilitary units under your direct command. I'm warning you Stockten, I don't need any extra paperwork you'll cause if you push these soldiers too far, and they attack you and your people. Go easier on these damn soldiers or you'll be dealing with me at the end of this operation, sir. Do you get my warning loud and clear, Agent?" The commander growled at his lead agent.

"Yeah, I hear your orders Commander. I'll treat these soldiers like I do my people. Relax and allow me to do my fucking job and stop detaining me further from accomplishing my mission." The agent snapped at his control and let out his breath in a rush of anger.

"Look Pete, I read the complaints filed against you over the way you treat your people when I deploy you as a Field Commander. I want you to treat these soldiers once they're deployed to your position, like you treat your kids and wife. This is a direct order Agent. If I get negative feedback over the treatment of these soldiers by you or your people, the lot of you will answer to me, and then to General White. Do you read me and hear my warning Agent Stockten?"

"Yes I read you loud and clear Commander. I'll treat these fucking crybabies like I do my own children, sir. Jesus H. Christ Commander, if these soldiers can't take a little heat from me. Why the hell are you sending them fucking people out here for, sir? They're going to eat a ton of shit once they're deployed in this hell hole of a fucking nation, sir." The agent in charge snarled while shaking his head in disgust.

"I'm warning you once more Stockten, you'll treat these soldiers with kid gloves, or you'll answer to me." The commander warned in a heated tone.

"I hear you, and if these damn Marines are heading out here, dammit. Allow me to get back to my god damn people so I can conclude my end of this fucking operation, sir."

"You do that Stockten, and remember while you're working with these specialized soldiers to treat them like they were your own kids. I don't need the President or Chairman coming down on my ass because you couldn't control yourself, and live with turning your operation over to these soldiers being sent out there to relieve you. These soldiers are highly qualified to takeover this mission and carry it out to its completion, Agent Stocken. Be sure to watch your mouth also, I don't need to read anymore complaints about that mouth of yours, sir."

CAMP LEJEUNE, NORTH CAROLINA. ZERO ELEVEN FORTY EIGHT HUNDRED HOURS, MONDAY OCTOBER 28th, 2008

Because of the time difference between the United States and Iraq, it was October 28th as Colonel Bruce Leadbetter continued his conversation with the Chairman of the Joint Chiefs of Staff, General John White. The worried Colonel listened as the General informed him of their upcoming "Rapid Fire" mission to Iraq. "Colonel Leadbetter, we discovered a threat to the United States, and to the world, sir. It seems a unit of Marines discovered a partial Iraqi military report floating around the desert, confirming the fact some Iraqi technicians had successfully developed a biological weapon solely designed to attack people of the Persian nationality.

"Before you ask Colonel, we had Doctor Russbinder check out what we have of this report so far sir. The Doctor's of the mind this biological designer weapon will mutate into a weapon of mass destruction, if it's ever released that would eventually attack and destroy every living soul and animal in the world, Colonel. There are no known antidotes for this item because we don't know what makes up the composition of the damn thing, until we can get our hands on some product of the weapon, and find out what the hell makes the damn thing tick, sir.

"It's the same old thing and you know what I'm going to need from you and the rest of your troops to find what the damn Iraqis have developed, Colonel. So I'm not going to go over all the particulars with you at this time, sir. I have a list of orders for you so listen up. I need you to get your troops packed up and shipped out to Pope Airforce Base ten minutes ago. Once we locate where this crap's stored in Iraq, your troops will take the crap and control it until we have it transferred back here for examination. Russia's aware what we're going after, and in the need to maintain the balance of power between our two nations, we're going to share this item with them, so they don't feel like we're one up on them.

"Our people are going to be the ones who'll be in control of this crap until we can have it transferred over to the Center for the Biological Security stationed at the University Of Pittsburg Medical Center better known as CBSUPMC, for special handling and dissecting. We're hoping those people can come up with a working antidote for this crap, just in case we don't get the complete product, and someone gets their grubby little hands on some of this shit. And, by either accident or on purpose, they try to destroy one certain race of people, or the world entirely if they release the shit to the air, sir.

"Arrr… this problem's for the others to solve, our job's to find the lot of this crap and get it here to the States, and your people are the ones who'll do the job, Colonel Leadbetter. Once your people arrive at Pope, they'll hunker down until I can set up transportation out to the Middle East. Your troops will be shipped to Kuwait and wait there until they receive orders to enter Iraq and take command of the operation currently in the hands of a Special Agent Peter Stockten, Colonel.

"From what I hear of this Agent working with the Marine's who originally found the damn report, he's a real bastard to work with and he might give our people more than a little bit of grief over taking his command from his ass, sir. Colonel Leadbetter, you're going to have to control not only this pain in the ass Agent we're forced to work with, but you're also going to be forced to control your pack of live wires at the same time, sir. I don't need a fire fight taking place between a bunch of CIA Paramilitary Operatives and your people out in the field, Colonel. I want you to especially keep Captain Walker away from this special agent, sir.

"I don't have more information than this Colonel Leadbetter, all I can tell you for certain are to get your troops over to Pope, and then have the troops hunker down until I have further orders for them, sir. I'll get your troops out to Kuwait the first opportunity I get, so your soldiers will be closer to the theater of consideration, and I can get them in motion quicker than if I have to wait until the last moment to deploy your troops from the States to Kuwait, sir. Colonel Leadbetter, we're going to brand this mission I'm sending your troops on as 'Operation Rapid Fire', and you'll be in command of the mission, and you'll have the power to pull in any military assets working in Iraq you deem necessary, to complete your mission successfully, sir.

"I have to warn you of this threat, Colonel Leadbetter. You'll probably engage insurgents or the new phase of enemy combatants for these packs of assholes operating in the borders of Iraq, sir. If you engage any of these nuts, you'll call in fixed wing or rotor aircraft, or other strike packages you need, and end any engagement, Colonel. You can draft any other needed units from the Marines or Army operating in any sector of Iraq you have to investigate, sir.

"Your mission Colonel Leadbetter is far more important than any operation taking place in Iraq, and you have the power to draft any military assets or strike packages other missions are employing for the success of your operation, sir. Errr... wait a moment Colonel, I have a report coming in from Pope Airforce Base, probably concerning your troops and transports. Don't hang up on me I'll be back to you momentarily Colonel." General White ordered and placed the Colonel on hold and answered the other call then he was back to his Colonel.

"Colonel Leadbetter, the people over at Pope did a super human job and they have the aircraft needed to transport your troops out to Kuwait standing by on the base, sir. Get your people on the move, sir. I'll keep you informed of any new developments in Iraq over this crap from my side, while your troops are in transit for Kuwait. Colonel Leadbetter, I have people jumping down my damn throat and have to get back to the President, and inform him of what I set in motion for this operation. I have other people I have to light a fire under over this damn mess. Colonel Leadbetter, I'll get back to you, sir." General White ordered as he broke off the communication with no further words to the lesser officer.

Colonel Leadbetter hung up and sat back as he thought of his next move. Sergeant John Kirkpatrick, the Colonel's aide was sitting in his office, and he asked his commander with a slight hesitation. "Errr Colonel..., do you want me to head over to the barracks and get our people ready to ship out for Pope, sir?"

The Colonel put his hands behind his head and stared at his Sergeant for a few moments, and then he replied to the NCO. (Non Commissioned Officer) "Naw Sergeant Kirkpatrick, that's orders I have to give to these assholes. I better shake it up we have people waiting for our pack of misfits at Pope, Sergeant. I want you with me in case some of these damn hotheads don't like the orders." He sat forward and rose and headed out of his office with the Sergeant following.

Sergeant Walter Casper, was standing outside the barracks enjoying a smoke and a little private time from the mayhem taking place in the barracks. He spotted the Colonel and Sergeant heading for their barracks and dipped inside and reported to Walker.

Sergeant Casper searched the barracks until he noticed Walker standing with Sergeant Dorothy Ramirez, his main squeeze, along with Lieutenant Frank Hall. Seeing his Captain in the barracks, the Ghost rushed down the hallway and stopped by his side. The moment Walker noticed the Ghost standing by him, he snapped at the soldier. "I see by the stupid ass look on your puss you got some shit news for my stinking ass, pal. What got you fired up? You see something you didn't like or what, Ghost?"

"Walker, the fucking Colonel and his little henchman are heading for our barracks. I think someone's in heat for something around here, man." The Ghost stopped speaking to see how Walker was going to react to what he told him. The Captain did not have a chance to reply to the Sergeant before the angry Colonel came charging into the barracks, and he immediately started to bark orders to anyone he laid his eyes on.

Colonel Leadbetter kicked a shit can out of his way as he charged into the living area of the barracks, and screamed at his troops. "Okay you pack of Squids your holidays in my beloved Corps are over as of this moment. Paint it up, we have a new mission dropped in our laps, and we're heading for Pope ten minutes ago." The Colonel glanced at one of the female soldiers and spotted she was sitting on her bunk without a top on, and he snarled nastily at her in particular.

"Sergeant fucking Dorland, it's a damn good thing you have small tits, it hard for me to tell you're a damn woman with tits like that, soldier. You better get some damn rags on them damn things before I have what is on your chest chopped off, and have that fat molded into a makeshift dick and slammed between your legs, and make a real soldier out of your ass. Get dressed before I lose my temper and order you out on the damn grinder like that for all our other soldiers to get a gander of them tits of your, soldier!"

"Eat me Colonel, I'm in my barracks and I can relax anyway I choose." Sergeant Dorland, Baby Tee, snapped at the fuming colonel with as much venom in her tone as he used on her.

"You fucking people will never learn how to properly respect your Commanding Officer I see, dammit. It's 'Sir, eat me Colonel Leadbetter, Sir' to you and you better remember that before I do eat you for fucking breakfast, sister. Then I'll shit your junk out when I want to get rid of your damn aftertaste, Dorland." The Colonel glared at the female soldier until she uncrossed her legs, and got off her bunk and slipped in the shirt of her uniform. The Colonel went back on the attack on the rest of his troops.

"Walker! Where the fuck are you at? I need to speak to you double quick buster!"

Walker stepped out from between Mutt and Ramirez's racks and growled at the officer. "I'm down here, what's up Colonel? You mentioned we have a new mission, sir?"

"Get your slimy ass down here on the double quick and speak to me face to face, mister! I'm not going to scream my orders out to you, buster. Why weren't you in your private quarters when I first entered this damn barracks? Why the hell do you think you were given private quarters in the first place in these barracks? You're an Officer and as such you have to start separating yourself from the rest of this ripraft in here, shitbird." Colonel Leadbetter waited until Walker walked down the length of the barracks. The Captain took his time walking over to the Colonel, it was an act of defiance and it made the Colonel angrier at him.

"If you don't get a fucking move on it buster, I'm going to have your ass strapped to a god damn hell fire missile, and then order to fire the fricking thing off to get your ass moving a helluva lot faster than you're moving, Captain."

Walker's obvious busting of the Colonel's horns made his fellow soldiers laugh until the commander turned and glared at them. They made themselves look busy to get out from under the angry stare from their commanding officer.

Walker continued his walk over to the angry looking Colonel and he actually had the balls to take the time to light up a cigarette in front of the irate Colonel. The officer did not hesitate, he had to get control over his livewire or lose the respect of the other soldiers in the barracks. He slapped the cigarette out of Walker's mouth. The Captain smirked at the officer, and asked the Colonel again. "What's up Colonel Leadbetter?"

"I'll tell your slimy ass what the fuck's up, in your quarters so these shitbirds don't hear us speaking. Being this close to these Screaming Eagle's makes my damn skin crawl and turns my stomach sick." Colonel Leadbetter and Sergeant Kirkpatrick stepped aside and allowed Walker to pass them, and they followed him in his quarters. The moment Walker closed the door after the Colonel and Sergeant entered his room, the Colonel hissed at Walker in a savage voice.

"I'll take one of them fucking cigarettes, mister. Walker, I'm warning you in no uncertain terms, mister. I don't give a rat's ass how we speak to one another when we're alone and no one can hear us going at it. But you have to learn to respect me in front of the rest of your war wacky bastards and bitches out there, sir. Arrr… fuck it that's not what I'm here for. Walker, we have a situation rapidly developing around our asses, and your soldiers are going to have to get this situation under control in a fast hurry, sir."

"Where are we heading this time around, Colonel Leadbetter Sir?" Captain Walker asked with little concern in his tone. He and his troops were so used to going on missions at the drop of a hat that nothing surprised him or them any longer.

"Now where the fuck do you think your people are heading, buster? Iraq!"

"I guess it's time for us to get another sand enema I see, sir. What's going down in sand land again, sir?" Walker asked his commanding officer.

"Walker, I surrounded your ass with the cream of the crap out there that I successfully stole from all other Branches of the Armed Forces, and it looks like this time you're going to need the entire unit for this one. I don't have very much in the way of positive information about this upcoming mission at it stands, sir. All I have orders for, is to get your criminals over to Pope for immediate deployment to Kuwait. What I do know about this operation is we're going to be on a fucking nother bug hunt, and this time it could have worldwide ramifications.

"As of this time, we have a group of Spooks operating in the desert, and they might've located where this crap was hatched. Our orders will be to take command of the operation from the damn Spooks, and if they discover any of this crap was removed from the hatchery. We'll have to find the missing shit no matter where it might be hidden in that country. It looks like we'll have card blanch on this one, and we can pull in any assets we need to complete our mission, Captain.

"Well that's all I have on the upcoming mission at this point, Captain. I suggest you get out there and get some heat under the asses of your pack of damn criminals." The Colonel offered as he stood and dropped the cigarette on the floor and stepped on it. Then he and Sergeant Kirkpatrick left Walker's office.

Walker watched as the two soldiers left his office then he waited a moment for the enviable to happen. His wait was not long before some of his people entered the room to see what the Colonel wanted with him. As usual, Sergeant Ramirez was the first soldier in his office, she was followed by Mutt, No Neck, (Sergeant Robert Abbott), he was followed by Buckethead, (Sergeant Vincent Lambardo). That soldier was followed by the Ghost and Blood Clot, (Sergeant Richard Burnbach) the unit's medic.

The room quickly got overcrowded and forced Walker to order the medic. "Blood Clot, stand by the damn door and stop any uther assholes from trying to squeeze in here, before we can't breathe in here for crap sake. Leave the damn door opened so the rest of the troops can hear my fucking orders, so I don't get stuck repeating them for those guys out there. The rest of you listen up. We received orders to report to Pope, and it looks like we're heading for fucking Iraq on another damn bug hunt, people…"

Walker's report was interrupted by the moans from the soldiers in his office, and standing in the barracks living area.

"Okay, I'll give you people that one but not another so keep quiet until I finished briefing you people. Everyone's going on this mission, so you have to get packed and be ready to ship out to Pope that fucking quick. Move it because I have a helluva lot of uther crap I hafta look after, before I'm ready to shove off. You people know what they say, when they call, we fucking haul. Move it people, because I don't know when the hot shot Colonel and his private ass will return, and we betta be ready to ship out when he does, full equipment and weapons." Walker warned his elite troopers then he stared at them until they got a move on it.

THE SECRET IRAKI BUNKER CONSTRUCTED IN THE MIDDLE OF THE IRAQI DESERT

The moving of the heavy military vehicles did the trick, and the machines blocked most of the wind driving the agent's crazy while digging in the sand. Once the wind was pretty much blocked by the machines, they were able to move the sand from the opening of the bunker. When the opening was cleared of sand, they got out of Stockten's way and allowed him to sidestep into the dank opening. Agent Stockten had his MP-5 weapon in his hands, and cautiously moved into the bunker. He had no way of knowing if there were Iraqi soldiers or insurgents hiding in the bunker, and he was taking nothing for granted.

Agent Peter Stockten was followed down the concrete steps by the rest of his agents equally on guard for a possible ambush or other trouble inside the bunker. Once it was determined no enemy soldiers or insurgents were hiding inside the structure set to attack them as they entered the place. Stockten roared at the soldiers bunching up behind him on the steps.

"Williams, get outside and order one of the fucking Marines to drag a portable power plant by the opening to this place. I want some fucking lights strung out in here so we can see what the fuck we're doing here, dammit. From the looks of this fucking thing, it looks like the place where the damn Iraqi technicians were working on their fucking chemical and biological weapon projects. I can see a mess of test tubs and other medical and technical equipment stored down here. Get a move on it Lieutenant, I need lights down here. Damn, I see a string of overhead lights so that'll make it easier for us to illuminate this damn rathole down here."

It took Williams and three Marines ten minutes to get the portable generator setup and running by the mouth of the bunker. One Marine knew something about electrical work, and was allowed in the bunker to tap the power into the original lighting system. Once Stockten was able to see what he was doing, he ordered the Marine out and he and his agents began taking the place apart with their bare hands, with the AIC Agent In Charge dishing out the orders to his people.

"Okay gentlemen, you people know what we're here looking for, so rip this fucking place apart and find me the damn evidence we need, and hopefully some of the remaining product of this damn crap. I don't care if we're stuck in this fucking place until we're old enough to fart dust and retire. No one's going to leave this fucking place until we find what we're sent out here to look for. Get busy and find this missing crap before those other assholes get here and those troops relieve us from duties on this mission. I'll be dipped in shit before I give up my god damn Command to a bunch of fucking thick headed Marine soldiers too damn stupid to pull their own feet out of the fucking mud. Get busy and find this shit, we're time poor here and I want this shit found now, god dammit!"

As Special Agent Peter Stockten gave orders to his agents, he leaned his MP-5 machine gun against a table and started to search the interior of the bunker for signs of the weapon of mass destruction. The agent wanted to find product, or papers showing the item was stored in or born in the bunker, before Walker and his crew arrived, and they relieved him of his mission.

Colonel Masterson, second in command of the special agents, was arms deep in a mess of papers in his search of the bunker. Finding reports scattered all over the floor, and the file cabinets in total disarray, he complained to his superior. "Agent Stockten, it seems like we're a few days late and a dollar short getting here, sir. From the looks of this dump, it seems like it's been picked clean, sir. Not many papers have been on the floor for a long period of time because of their condition. I don't believe we're going to find a damn thing that might set us on the right track to find this missing shit, sir."

"Don't hand me that Masterson, with all the papers scattered around this place. There has to be something about the crap here. Keep looking we have to find it. As poor as the technicians were at protecting paperwork and product, there has to be something left in this dump. Keep looking, and remember we're piss poor on fucking time, those damn Marines have to be heading here as we speak, Colonel Masterson. I want evidence of this crap before they get here!"

"Yes sir." Masterson replied as he continued reading reports lying on the ground.

"God dammit keep looking, we have to get something before those damn Marines relieve us. I want evidence and I want it right now for fuck's sake!" Stockten roared at his agents. He was becoming frustrated with this search because of the pressure he had on his shoulders over being relieved from his duty by Marines. He hated the feeling and was taking it out on his people.

A Second Lieutenant, standing by the table where Ayesha removed the metal cylinder from earlier in the day, noticed the clean spot on the table. The rest of the surface was covered with a thick layer of dust, and he absentmindedly started examining the area a little closer. The officer did not realize he was stepping on sheets of paper scattered over the floor around the table. He did notice the burned-out candle on the table, and the run off wax had no dust covering it, which made him feel it was just burned off, some dust was burned by the once flame. This discovery made the Lieutenant look even closer at the round impression in the dust.

Agent Stockten was on the floor on his hands and knees, reading report after report he picked up. When he finished reading the report and if it did not pertain to his needs, he tore the papers in half once he discovered they were not what he was looking for in the bunker. Or the report he read contained nothing in the way of needed intelligence for his people. He ripped them in half so no other agents would waste their time reading a report already gone over by someone else in the bunker. Taking a break, Agent Stockten looked around the interior of the bunker to make certain his people were actively involved in the search of the bunker. Noticing his Lieutenant looking at the table and obviously wasting his time there, he barked angrily at the officer.

"Lieutenant, we're searching for fucking papers in this damn dump, not a damn table, mister. If you don't want to do your fucking job, get the hell out there with those stupid Marines and bake in the fricking sun and suck down sand, mister. I told you we're working against time."

With the severity of the way Stockten was snarling at him brought the Lieutenant out of his daydream. "Err… I believe I might have found something not quite right over here, sir."

The echo of the Lieutenant's words did not stop ringing inside the bunker before Stockten was standing by the officer's side, and he snapped at the kid. "What the fuck do you think you found, Lieutenant? Show me what you got, and explain it to me at the same time."

"Look Agent Stockten, something was obviously recently removed from the surface of this table, and it couldn't have been removed long ago, sir. See the surface it's still covered with about a half an inch of dust and sand. All except for this circle impression on the table see here sir. Where the dust is mounted up Agent Stockten, it's loose and slightly burned. Look at the handprints and finger marks left where I believe whatever was removed from the table, was taken as early as possibly today, sir. Also Agent Stockten, look at the melted wax from the candle, there's no dust covering the burned out wax, and that makes me believe whoever was in here, used this candle as late as today to see where he or she was, and what he or she was doing before we entered the bunker and also how…"

"Lieutenant, I don't give a rat's ass what you might or might not believe. I agree with your assumption of an object being removed from this table and not long ago at that. This find makes me believe someone was in this bunker, and we missed his ass by mere hours, dammit. Okay Lieutenant, I'll take over this discovery and here's what I want you to do. Take two Agents and get out to those damn helicopters. The first moment they can get in the air once this damn wind stops blowing, get them up and hunting Lieutenant. Head out in the three different directions of the compass, you don't have to cover the point we used getting here. I want the entire desert searched for the prick or pricks that were in this damn bunker earlier today. If we were forced to hunker down because of the sandstorm, he or they must have hunkered down too."

CIA Agent Stockten noticed the sour look clouding over his officer's face, and it forced him to offer to the young man to calm him down a little. "Lieutenant Bryant, this isn't a punishment order I'm issuing you, sir. I'm placing you in Command of an extremely important part of this search and discovery mission. If we don't find any product that we're aware is in this damn country from this miserable weapon of mass destruction, and might still be remaining in this fucking bunker. Then there's a damn good possibility and I bet the fucks that were in here earlier today, must have removed the remaining product from this fucking dump. Pick out the other Agents you want to assist you in the search for these missing pricks, and get the hell out there and follow your orders as received, mister."

A smile replaced the sour look then the Lieutenant called out the names of the agents he wanted with him. Then the three agents nearly ran up the cement steps leading out of the bunker.

Stockten watched the agents leave the bunker, and called out to the remaining agents still searching the bunker. "Listen up people, we have a lead and there are plenty of papers that needs going over for evaluation and saving or discarding, if the damn documents mean nothing to our mission. I want every fucking document read and read again and then discarded if that report isn't connected to the item we want, or if you deem it's a useless report not worth hanging on to for further Intel purposes or consideration, gentlemen. I want this entire area of the damn bunker searched thoroughly before any of you guys spread out and start searching the rest of this fucking place for the evidence we need. Move it out like you people have a purpose for being in this damn place for the love of God."

Agent Stockten stared at his agents in the bunker as they gathered around where he was standing, and they started picking up page after page of Iraqi reports from the floor, and reading them carefully. Each agent in the bunker was capable of reading, speaking and writing Arabic. When the agents were working again, Agent Stockten joined in with reading the masses of papers from the floor of the filthy bunker as he picked up the first page to read.

Even though it was cooler inside the bunker, the agents were sweating and suffering from heat exhaustion. None of the agents dared to take time to take water, or a breather for fear of receiving the wrath of Stockten, who was just as tired and in need of water as the others were.

Agent Lieutenant Carl Bryant and the two agents with him, crawled out of the narrow opening of the bunker, and each agent headed for one of the helicopters. Lieutenant Bryant entered the command helicopter and ordered the pilot to liftoff as soon as possible. The wind died down dramatically, and the pilot didn't ask questions as he increased power to his spooling machine. In seconds, the black painted CIA helicopter was at full military takeoff power, and it slowly lifted off the ground. The lead helicopter was followed by the other two machines of war, and the pilot asked the Lieutenant. "Where we heading? What are my orders?"

"I want you to head due south of our position, we're looking for anyone walking around in the desert, sir. We came to the conclusion someone was inside the bunker as early as today, and we missed them by mere hours. We have orders to take them in if we discover anyone out there. The other helicopters and agents are to head east and west our location with the same orders, Commander." Lieutenant Bryant replied to the pilot as he shot a quick smile at him then waited for the commander to relay his orders to the commanders of the other machines.

"Will do sir, I'll relay orders to the other pilots so there's no doubt of their orders, sir."

"Do that Commander." Lieutenant Bryant remarked as he made himself comfortable by the side open door of the machine, and started looking for signs of someone who walked, or was trying to hide from the biting winds of the sand storm that died down.

As the three helicopters left the area of concern where the Marines and agents were working in the hidden bunker, Agent Stockten and the rest of his people read any Iraqi reports they picked up from the floor. Agent Stockten was fighting the uneasy feeling that maybe he opened his mouth a bit too soon to command. He was beginning to believe what they found was a secret military and medical bunker, originally designed to take care of wounded or exhausted Iraqi soldiers brought to this facility for medical treatment and care. The more Stockten read of the countless discarded military reports, the more he was beginning to believe it was a medical and rehab and supply bunker.

As desperation was setting in, and Stockten was about ready to call for his first break in their search of the bunker. One agent suddenly called out in an excited voice. "Fucking bingo, bingo, bingo. I found a report concerning the product we're looking for, Agent Stockten."

Stockten was standing by the other agent's side in a flash as he actually ripped the report from his hand and quickly read it. The fatigue he was suffering from instantly left his exhausted body as the excited agent read a report dated January 1st, 2001. It stated the Iraqi technicians tried the first batch of the Biological Agent they had branded P, One, Three, Five on a captured Iranian prisoner they shipped to the bunker just for the experiment. The lead agent read the ugly effect the deadly biological agent had on the Persian prisoner, and he was appalled over the report.

He read where the weapon was released on the helpless Persian prisoner, and was simultaneously exposed to an Iraqi prisoner, and only the Iranian was attacked and suffered terribly for a few moments, and then he died by the biological weapon. The report went on to state the Iraqi prisoner was killed once it was determined the agent did not affect him, and the technicians had no further need of the prisoner classified as a deserter.

Stockten drew in his breath as he read the effects of the biological agent attacking the body of the Iranian subject. It stated raw blood poured out of the mouth, nose, ears and rectum of the naked subject three minutes after initial exposure to the weapon and the subject's breathing became labored in the process. Wracking pain and uncontrollable convolutions assaulted the subject's body until death occurred within five minutes from the exposure time to the weapon.

An autopsy was performed on both subjects exposed to the weapon, and the Iranian's body displayed all major organs in the body was disrupted and or ruptured, and the Persian was believed to have died from drowning in his own blood and other bodily fluids. The report on the slaughtered Iraqi prisoner stated the Iraqi displayed no ill effects from the exposure to the biological weapon. All three reports were stapled together, and it confirmed this was the place where this biological weapon was developed and tested on helpless human subjects.

With a sigh of relief, Agent Stockten roared at the CIA Agents working in the bunker. "Now this was what we were sent here to fucking find! And, if there's one report on this shit, there has to be others stored inside this damn dump. We have to keep looking for anything pertaining to the item we have a fixed name for, gentlemen. It was branded by the Iraqi developers as P, which I believe stands for Persian, One, Three, Five. Keep your eyes opened for anything that has this letter and group of numbers attached to it."

"Agent Stockten, I just read a report with those numbers printed on the top of the page. It's around here somewhere sir." Another agent called out as he dropped to his knees, and fished through the mess of papers he discarded. In a minute he found the paper he was looking for, and handed it to his commanding officer.

Stockten took the report and read it. There were three pages to the detailed report, and two pages were missing according to the numbers printed at the top of the pages Stockten had. With anger flooding his words, Stockten growled savagely at the agent who found the report. "There are two pages missing from this fucking report. Find them or you're going to find yourself walking out of this fricking desert by yourself when we're done here, mister."

The other agent went back to searching the masses of pages he went through scattered about on the floor of the bunker by his feet, as Agent Stockten reread the stunning report he had locked in his hands. It was a report covering the biological discovery, and the amount of biological weapon the Iraqi technicians were able to produce of the weapon to date. Of course, the page covering the amount of the weapon produced at this once secret facility was missing, and this added to Stockten's anger.

He brought the report over to the table that had the round impression in the dust, and laid out the three pages, with the other report he had in his possession after he wiped off the layer of dust covering the table with his other hand. The lead agent reread the reports line by line in hopes he might have overlooked something important the first time he read them. Now Stockten knew for certain this bunker was the place where the Iraqi technicians and military personal developed this deadly product. He was determined he was going to locate the biological agent once produced at this site, and he was going to come out of this mess he was trapped in, smelling like a rose to his commanders. Agent Stockten believed he would have all the I's dotted and Tees crossed before the Marine troops came out to the bunker to relieve him of his duties and mission.

The three helicopters with no identifying markings imprinted on them, took off in a tight formation and once airborne, the machines split up and each headed for their assigned directions to carry out their search for the subjects and what they might have in their possession. Agent Bryant was looking out the window searching the flat featureless surface of the desert for signs someone recently moved on it. The agent cursed because the sand storm erased all signs of anything once moving on the endless sea of sand stretching to the horizon below his helicopter.

The special agent suggested to the pilot he make a sweeping turned to the east, and instructed the pilot to swoop out to the west as they maintained their heading due south at the same time. The Lieutenant wanted to make certain he did not miss tracks in the sand, or anyone moving on the desert. He was thrilled to death his commander placed him in command of the helicopters, and he was sure as hell going to find what his commander sent him to locate.

The Marine door guard suggested the Lieutenant close his side door and look out the window, so they could keep the heat from the desert out of the interior of the helicopter. The Lieutenant did not want to close the door for fear he might miss someone moving or footprints in the sand below them. Even the door guard was helping the Lieutenant search for his target from the compartment area of the war machine. Even though the wind was just about kicking up from the sand storm, there was nothing moving on the sand. Even the usual lizards were still hiding under the sand while waiting it out for the end of the blowing sands to come.

The door guard moved over to the Lieutenant and mumbled to the officer. "Talk about nothing but fucking sand out there, sir. I don't see how anything can live out here, or want to."

"I hear you, but they do and we have to find the ones who beat us to the bunker and removed the shit, before Agent Stockten has our asses for supper, Sergeant. By the way Sergeant, I'm sorry for the way my commander's treating you Marines. He has a lot of shit weighing heavy on his mind, and until he finds what he's looking for. He's going to be a fucking bear to deal with. I appreciate the help you're giving me, Sarge. I need all the eyes I can get to help me locate our missing packages out there. Boy, I can't wait until this damn mission is behind us.

"This is the first time in my life I been this deep out in the desert, Sarge. Dammit, I can't get my bearings Sarge everything is so flat and colorless out there. There are no noticeable landmarks that can help me determine where the hell we're heading, Sarge." The Lieutenant mumbled as he continued to stare out the opened side door of the Blackhawk helicopter for any signs of civilization, or someone hunkering down to wait out the hard blow of the desert.

"I know what you mean Lieutenant, if we didn't have our damn GPS and compasses working at all times, we'd be hard pressed to know where the hell we're heading ourselves, sir. I'll tell you this much though Lieutenant Bryant. I wouldn't want to get lost out there by myself, sir. I don't see anyone surviving in the desert for long, unless you know what the hell you're doing down there, sir. Well will you look at what we have here for Pete's sake Lieutenant, our first sign of something alive and kicking out there on the damn desert, sir." The Marine Sergeant pointed to a lone camel that just stirred out from under the mound of sand that covered her over when the wind was blowing so hard from the sand storm hours ago.

"Yes, and I wish to hell and back it had a rider on its back, Sergeant. I wonder if the camel threw the rider off when the sand started to blow. Do you think we should land and check it out, Sergeant?" The concerned Lieutenant asked the well seasoned Sergeant with concern.

"No way in hell Lieutenant. After all the time I spent in the damn desert, it's quite easy to tell this camel is a wild one, sir. You see the way it's plugging along, it shows she hasn't had a rider on her back for quite some time, sir. I'm willing to bet the damn thing escaped her master a long time ago, and it's been wandering around the desert looking for food and water, and probably a mate while she's at it, sir. Sooner or later some Arab will come along and find the damn thing and capture it, and then force the camel to do his bidding for the rest of its life, sir."

"Damn Sarge, I don't think I'll get the eye for things you Marines have." Bryant complained as he watched the camel struggle walking in the sand deposited on the desert by the sandstorm.

"You'll get used to the ways of the desert soon enough if you're out here long enough, Lieutenant. I feel you people are going to be out here for some time looking for this shit, sir. A lot longer than you guys think you're going to be stuck working out here that is, sir. I believe our mission just started, and it has a long way to go Lieutenant Bryant."

BACK INSIDE THE UNDERGROUND IRAQI BUNKER

CIA Special Agent In Charge Peter Stockten was fuming because the two pages from the report were still missing. He was using his time reading the accumulated report for a third time, when an agent called in an excited voice. "Agent Stockten, I have another page to your report."

"Outstanding, bring the damn thing over here. So I can see if it's the fucking page I need, dammit." The lead agent snapped at his fellow special agent.

"Agent Stockten, I found a second page marked number four, sir. I believe it's the last page to the report you have, sir." A second agent offered as he stood up, and hustled over to the commanding officer and handed him the page he found.

Stockten grabbed the two pages and then he carefully laid them out on the table next to the other three he had and they were the pages from the report he wanted.

With a grin of triumph, Stockten read the pages. He was surprised this report was written in English for some reason. The only thing he could come up with was this technician must have not been able to read Arabic, so the report was printed out in English. He was looking for the one item he was searching for throughout the lengthily report. The first page had what he needed, and his grin grew into a smile as he announced to the other CIA Agents.

"Gentlemen, according to this fucking report we pieced together, it seems the damn Iraqi technicians were successful and able to produce a certain amount of the weapon known as P, One, Three, Five, and it was a total of thirty-six ounces of the damn agent. It further states one ounce of this crap was stored in a test tube, so the asshole technicians had a percentage of the product at easy access in hand's reach. So the damn technicians were able to continue their experiments buts on Persian souls they dragged here to kill with this shit. The report states the remaining thirty five ounces of this crap was contained in a sealable heavy stainless steel metal cylinder that measured some twelve inches across and nineteen inches high.

"The fucking report goes on and states that this stainless steel cylinder is registered as being left inside this bunker when the assholes first abandoned this miserable place when our people were closing in on the dump. I have to finish the report and maybe it'll clue me in on where the hell this shit was being stored inside this place, by these asshole technicians in the first place, dammit. Maybe it's being hidden in a secret place or a hidden safe.

"For the love of the Christ Child, at least we know what the fuck we're looking for here, dammit. The report explains the delivery system as being simple exposure to the air and is wind dispersed. We're going to be forced to be extremely careful dealing with and handling this shit once we locate it, and we get our hands on it. I want all eyes looking sharp for this stainless steel cylinder until we discover where these assholes had the crap hid in here. Check this place out thoroughly, go over the place with a fine tooth comb for hidden safes or specially constructed containment structures. I'm certain these pricks didn't leave this shit in the fucking open, being it is so damn lethal. The Iraqi technicians had to fear an accidental spill of the shit, so I'm certain it has to be stored in a safe place. At least I pray to the Christ Child the damn fools had the smarts to protect this crap while they worked on the production of the god damn product..."

"Agent Stockten, didn't the Lieutenant say he was looking at a circle shape in the dust on the table you're using as your workstation, sir?" One of the agents asked his commander.

"Dammit you're right, and it was here someplace. I hope some of the impression is still there so we can judge if this was the place where they had the crap resting." Stockten growled as he removed the papers from the surface of the table, and examined the surface carefully. Sure enough, the clean faint round impression was still able to be seen on the table, and Stockten snarled. "God dammit, does anyone have a fucking tape measure on them? I want to measure this impression and see if it's the size as what's written on this fucking report."

Another special agent in the bunker moved to Stockten's side and offered him a measuring tape. Stockten grabbed the ruler and measured the impression on the table. A cold sweat broke out on his brow as he read the distance was twelve inches.

The same agent who handed Stockten the measuring tape, looked at his feet and noticed a slim metal object lying on the floor near him. He had no idea what he was looking at, but bent down and picked up the metal shape and fingered it in his hand while studying it with his eyes.

Stockten understood he had discovered where the weapon was stored, and he was looking to jump on someone to funnel his anger, and when he noticed the agent fumbling around with an object, he snarled. "What the fuck are you playing with, god dammit? We have one helluva important mission we're on, and you're wasting your time playing with a metal object. Throw the damn thing away and look for any information we might discover in here about this damn weapon…"

A third agent was an expert on medical procedures and handling of dangerously contaminated materials, called to his commander. "Agent Stockten, I wouldn't be so fast to tell Agent Michaels to discard that item, sir. I saw those types of items, it's a special stand designed to hold a test tube in the upright position for safe storage, until the technician decides to place the test tube in a safer holding place, sir. Or Agent Stockten, the technician working with the product for further experimentation stored inside the test tube in question, sir. After hearing an ounce of the product was stored in a test tube for further development by the technicians, sir. I'm willing to bet that stand was the one holding the test tube with the available product stored in it, sir."

When Michaels heard what the agent said to his commander, he dropped the object and frantically wiped his hands on the sides of his filthy uniform. He was in fear he might have contaminated himself by handling the item used to hold the test tube with the weapon stored in it.

The other agent noticed Michaels fearful reaction and smiled, because he wanted to reassure the young man by offering. "Agent Michaels, there's no need to be worried about contamination from the biological weapon on that test tube stand, sir. I believe the weapon was left unattended for so long, it probably lost its deadly characteristics by this time. Even if the product was an active strain of the weapon, it had to be handled cautiously by the technicians who developed the product, sir. Or the technicians and security people who worked in this bunker would have surely been killed by the weapon, and we wouldn't be wasting our time looking for the crap, sir.

"Relax Michaels, if you're still concerned about picking up any contamination from the subject, sir? All you have to do is go and wash your hands with the chemical I have. It's Decontaminating Solution Two, and it'll wash away any active residue from your hands, sir." The concerned special agent offered Michaels a plastic container. Then he watched as Michaels thoroughly washed his hands with the fluid.

"That's good advice Agent Levy offered. From this point forward, gentlemen. I want everyone to get dressed in your biological and chemical protection contamination gear while working in this damn bunker. No one is to touch any item or surface in this dump with their unprotected hands, or I'll lop the damn things off on you. I want everyone working in here dressed in their self contained breathing and protective environment suits. I should've ordered everyone to get dressed in this equipment before I allowed you to enter this damn bunker in the first place for Christ's sake. Get outside and get dressed in your NBC (Nuclear, Biological, and Chemical) gear, and then get back in here search this dump with a fine tooth comb, people.

"Maybe whoever the hell was in here before us, moved the crap to another location in the miserable place, and the item is still here. Has anyone thought to check the air for chemical or biological contamination, or do I have to do all the thinking for you people, god dammit?"

Agent Levy responded to his commander's concerns by calling back to him with a snap. "Agent Stockten, I was the second man to enter the bunker behind you as was my duty, sir. Even though you broke rules and regulations governing entering a possible contaminated environment by not allowing me to enter first, I allowed it to happen sir. It's my responsibility to scan the interior of the bunker or any site we're investigating for contamination remaining here or elsewhere, sir. As I followed you in the bunker, I used my handheld Bendix BxINBCAD detector and ran a detailed spectrum of the air confined in the interior of this bunker, sir.

"There was a slight radiation level picked up of three mili-renkins per hour, which I classified as coming from the stainless steel stored inside the bunker. It's far below danger levels to our people's health, sir. I checked the air for any released chemical or biological weapons residue harmful or fatal to our health. I picked up a number of readings on chemicals in the air. They're classified as coming from normal items stored or used in the bunker such as plastics, cleaning solutions and other normal items used in everyday life, Agent Stockten. Most elements I'm picking up have a number of dual purposes, and give off the same readings if they're used for normal living or use in chemical weapons combinations, Agent Stockten.

"These commonly used and usually non-lethal chemical element traces I'm picking up, can be used in the construction of a number of BCW or Binary Chemical Weapons. I'll explain this statement further for you and the other agents, so they know what I'm talking about, Agent Stockten. A binary chemical weapon is one that's formed from the mixing of two usual non-lethal elements commonly referred to as precursor, sir. Marrying the combination of the two non-lethal elements through a chemical reaction, the mixture becomes lethal after the munitions are mixed together, and fired or launched at their intended target, sir.

"These binary chemical weapons are stored and then transported with only one of the needed chemical elements stored inside the weapon's housing, sir. The second element is carried in special containers and then added to the weapon at the firing or launch sight and time, sir. This safety precaution is carried out to eliminate any possible accident and or contamination to the soldiers employing the weapon against their target. As I stated Agent Stockten, I believe the trace elements

I'm picking up were used by the Iraqi technicians inside the bunker for normal cleaning procedures only, sir.

"I noted and investigated a number of interesting items discovered inside the bunker that proves beyond a shadow of a doubt, the Iraqi technicians was or were preparing to work on a number of selected chemical and biological weapons. The items I'm referring to is a noted Neutron Spectroscope and rather expensive Raman Spectrophotometer which is a portable machine commonly used for the identification of chemical agents stored in glass containers and ampoules found in usual CAIS or Chemical Agent Identification Sets, sir.

"I further noticed a stockpile of the chemical known as Pyridostigmine Bromide, which is the drug commonly issued and taken by some United States and Allied troops during the Persian Gulf War, sir. To help protect the soldiers against a possible release of chemical nerve agent recognized as Soman, known to be in the hands of the Iraqis, and threats were made to employ this weapon of mass destruction when we began our Operation Desert Storm against Iraq, sir.

"Placing these discoveries aside for the moment Agent Stockten, I took it on myself and I ran a complete and very detailed spectrum analyst of the air contained inside the bunker while continuing to search for a biological strain residue that could still be active and harmful to our people's health in the air trapped in the bunker, sir. During the detailed analyst I picked up three parts per billion of air density of the biological element identified as Anthrax. This is far below possible dangerous levels against our people's health working in here, sir. Our people were inoculated against the Anthrax threat long before we came to Iraq, which is standard orders for our military units in the field of activity, sir.

"Agent Stocken, I classified this threat as non-existent and no active threat against our people searching the interior of this bunker. I also picked up a minute level of the biological agent commonly referred to as Aflatoxin, sir. Before you ask about this item, this biological agent is a combination of several different and extremely dangerous carcinogenic toxic substances produced, and usually stored in agricultural crops by active mold spores and are…"

"What the fuck would the god damn Iraqi assholes be doing with that crap in this damn bunker? They can't grow crops in the middle of the fucking desert." Agent Stockten growled at the reporting agent as he held him in his angry glare.

Agent Levy chuckled over his commander's remark as he explained further. "Agent Stockten, there could be a number of reasons for a reading of this element being discovered in here, sir. Of course the first thought that comes to mind, is the Iraqi technicians were working on this item for future use of this agent against agricultural crops grown in another country they wished to attack, and destroy that nation's crops in the field. Or they could've been planning to cause sickness to humans who eat produce contaminated with this substance. As you're obviously aware, there's been plenty of concern about al-Qa'eda getting their hands on a biological strain that'd contaminate our crops in the fields in the United States…"

"Yeah Agent Levy, I'm aware of the concerns of that fact in the States. We always feared someone especially the assholes from al-Qa'eda would try an attack on our crops. Could that be what these assholes were working on here, before their end came and we got them before they released this shit against the earth, Agent Levy?"

"That's always a possibility Agent Stockten. But in this case I'm willing to believe because of the lack of continual maintenance and upkeep of this structure. The molds I'm picking up started to grow because of the lack of fresh air and sunlight getting inside the bunker, and their spores are releasing and causing this reading I'm currently picking, sir. From all the reports we have read over the years, there's no mention of the Iraqi technicians working on Afltoxins, sir. I can actually smell the molds growing inside the bunker, Agent Stockten." Agent Levy reported confidently to his commanding officer.

"Then Agent Levy, it seems you know your way around the inside of the test tube, sir. Am I to believe there's nothing in the air in this dump dangerous or fatal to my people's health, sir?" Agent Stockten growled at the other agent.

"Not at the minor levels I'm picking up with my monitor. I'm keeping my detector on and constantly scanning the air, sir. I'll continually be monitoring the air because with the disruptions and activities our people are creating inside the bunker, there's a possibility one of our people might disturb something that could harm us that might have been sealed by the dust trapped inside this structure. After all Agent Stockten, we're working in a possible biological, chemical or nuclear contaminated environment that could become extremely dangerous to our health at the drop of the hat, sir.

"Agent Stockten, we don't know for certain there might be a biological or chemical booby trap left behind by the Iraqi soldiers and technicians when they abandoned this structure when the war started against them, sir. There's a possible chance they left a little gift behind to kill anyone who stumbled over this once secret installation as we've done, Agent Stockten. By the way sir, my findings have to be reported to the CBDC or Chemical and Biological Defense Command at the Aberdeen Testing Grounds stationed at Maryland as soon as possible, sir. That way Command will know what to inoculate other CIA Agents or soldiers against that certain item Command's planning to send here to help us search for this biological weapon."

"That's a good point Agent Levy, and that's why I'm going to keep our people stuffed in their fucking self-contained environmental survival suits until we have removed all information from this damn bunker, and we're in control of this product of the biological weapon we know the Iraqi technicians branded P, One, Three, Five, sir. You better get outside yourself and get dressed in your contamination gear." Stockten snapped and glared at Levy as he waited for the officer to leave the bunker with the other special agents. Levy did not leave, instead he offered.

"What about you Agent Stockten? Are you going to leave the bunker and get dressed in your protective gear, sir? I don't see you preparing to get out of the bunker." Levy stared at his commander while waiting for his reply.

"Look here you worry about your fucking self and our people and I'll worry about myself, Agent Levy. I told you I see you know your way around the inside of a fucking test tube. I also see you don't know your way out of a damn test tube. I can't work in that crap and I'm not going to get dressed in it until we locate the product, and we have it in our control, Agent Levy." Stockten snapped at the other agent staring at him in hopes he would leave the bunker as ordered.

Not seeing Stockten making preparations to leave the bunker as ordered. Levy growled at his commander. "Agent Stockten, you're my Commanding Officer for this mission, sir. But I happen to be the Medical Officer for this operation. Being as such Commander, I can override your orders if I deem them as endangering our Agent's lives, or yourself. Yes I understand the protective gear's heavy and cumbersome and hard to work in. But I'm ordering you to get in the gear for your safety. I warn you in no uncertain terms Agent, if you refuse to follow my orders.

"I'll have no choice but to relive you of command of this operation, Agent Stockten. Then I'll ban you from the interior of this bunker for the duration of the search, if you continue to refuse to protect yourself against contamination that might be lurking in this structure! Agent Stockten, it's for your health and well being that I'm ordering you to follow my orders immediately, sir."

Agent Peter Stockten continued to glare at the other agent, and then released his breath in a hiss. "Agent Levy, I'm not going to get in a fucking pissing contest with you over this order you just blurted at my ass, mister. I'm warning you, if you pull your medical rights and Command over my ass or this operation, I'll have your ass shot on the spot. Then I'll continue working my way and my people until my mission has been completed as ordered. Am I making myself perfectly clear to you on my point I'm making here?"

"Colonel Stockten Sir, I'm of the same rank as you, and I've been a Colonel a year longer. That makes me Senior Officer on site. Am I to take it you're threatening a Superior Officer with physical and deadly harm, sir?" Agent Levy asked warningly as he glared at Stockten as he waited for his reply, not believing the threat warning from his commander.

"Abso fucking lutely I am, and make no mistakes about my threat, Colonel Levy! If you're so damn worried about contamination released inside this damn bunker, I suggest you get your ass the hell out of this bunker on the double quick. Then get dressed in your protective gear before you reenter this dump. Or you allow other of our Special Agents to enter this fucking installation without wearing their protective equipment, sir."

After a few moments of intense silent stare down by both officers, Levy broke off the heated confrontation and groaned. "Very well Agent Stockten, I'll do as you ordered, sir. I'm warning you, I'll be making a report of this incident and your threat to have me shot to Command. I'm certain they'll take proper steps leading to your dismissal, and possible prison time, Colonel!"

"Oh God, sniff, sniff a single tear running down the side of my god damn cheek. You do whatever the hell you deem necessary to make you feel any better over my orders, Colonel Levy. Just get your ass the hell out of this fucking bunker. You're ordered not to return to the interior until you're properly dressed and protected against any situation trapped inside here. I'll take my chances the way I see fit, Colonel. Now get a move on it before I lose my temper and do something you regret later on, sir."

Agent Levy shook his head as he let out his breath in a rush and he turned on his heels and stormed out of the bunker to get dressed in his protective clothing. Colonel Levy knew he was not going to make any reports to command over Stockten's actions or threats, because he was as guilty by not ordering his agents to get dressed in their protective clothing, before allowing them to enter the bunker when it was first discovered. His job for this mission was to protect the agents and check for chemical, biological or nuclear contaminated environments the agents might stumble over, before allowing them to check their discovery.

The other operatives that left the bunker when ordered to get protected started coming back in the bunker. To the last man, they looked at their commander and were upset he was not taking steps to protect himself against possible contamination.

Stockten noticed the looks but ignored them as he barked orders. "Spare me the fucking looks, get busy, you people know what we're searching for, so find the shit we're looking for."

BLACKHAWK HELICOPTER ONE, ONE, SEVEN

CIA Agent Carl Bryant was staring out the window of the helicopter searching the flat barren surface of the vast desert for any possible footstep impressions or locating someone walking in this region. Since they lifted off, the only thing they came across was the lone camel wandering the desert after the sandstorm blew itself out. The Sergeant who relieved the agent that commanded the door guard position of the helicopter so he could help search the bunker, was looking over the Lieutenant's shoulder, looking for signs of life on the wasteland of the desert.

The CIA helicopter made a wide swinging turn so it could head due east and continue to head south at the same time. The machine started to fly over a huge sand dune that was a straight drop off on the leeward side of it. The sheer height of the sand dune protected the leeward side from being assaulted by the recent hard blow, and when the helicopter cleared the edge of the dune. The alert Sergeant was the first one to call out in an excited voice to the almost daydreaming special agent.

"Look at the side of the sand dune, Lieutenant. If I didn't know any better, I'd swear two people walked down the side of that sand dune, and it wasn't long ago at that. We can still see their footprints in the sand, so they have to be around here someplace, sir."

Agent Bryant looked in the direction the Sergeant was pointing in, and he concentrated his vision on the side of the sand dune. Sure enough, here and there was definitely a set of recent footprints still visible in the soft sand. Bryant picked up the mike and snapped in it and then ordered the pilot of the helicopter. "Commander, I want you to make another pass over the sand dune we just flew over, sir. We spotted something and we want a better look at it. Be prepared to land on a moment's notice if ordered, sir. If I order you to land, I want you to make contact with the other helicopters and order them to our position. If it's what I believe we spotted, we're going to need all the help we can get searching the area, sir."

"Roger that Agent Bryant. Will do as ordered sir, beginning my turn now sir." The commander of the helicopter replied and carried out his last order.

The pilot placed his machine in a hard turn which forced Bryant to grab the overhead handhold so he did not go tumbling out of the machine. All the while Bryant was inside the helicopter, he never placed the seatbelt on. He was more concerned with the freedom to search the sand for human life than his safety. When the helicopter leveled off and the pilot aligned the machine with the sand dune, the agent let go of the handhold and stared at the huge dune.

The Sergeant was standing over the Lieutenant's shoulder again, and when they were near enough to the dune. He again pointed out the footprints in the sand and announced. "You see the marks, they have to be footprints even though they're messed up from the winds, Lieutenant. I suggest we land and check out the area. If I was someone caught by a hard blow, I sure as hell would've found a safe place to hunker down until the storm blew itself out, sir. What better place to wait it out other than a leeward side of a sand dune like this one, Lieutenant Bryant."

"I agree with you Sergeant Jarrett." Bryant replied with a snap as he read the Sergeant's name off his uniform ID, and picked up the mike to the intercom. "Commander, land this thing by the sand dune, sir. I want to check out the area closer, sir. We found something that needs further looking at. Contact the other helicopters and have them linkup and land with us. I have a feeling we're going to need all the eyes we can get for this search, sir. Over."

"Roger last Agent Bryant. I have my co-pilot calling in the other helicopters to our position, sir. Landing as ordered, sir." The pilot offered to the CIA Agent in command.

The pilot placed his machine in hover mode then backed away a little from the sand dune and then landed in a flat area some fifty yards away from the base of the massive sand dune. The special agent waited until the machine was on the sand before jumping out of the helicopter, he was followed by the Sergeant. By the time they made it to the side of the dune, the other two helicopters were preparing to land by their helicopter. The sand the machines kicked up landing was almost as bad as the sand storm they just experienced.

The Sergeant moved before the Lieutenant and led the way and scrutinized what was left of the footprints. Even though they were badly distorted, it was easy for the seasoned Marine Sergeant to recognize them as footprints. He turned and smiled at Bryant as he announced. "Judging by what's left of the damn footprints, I'd say they were made by our friend who visited the bunker and left before we arrived on scene, sir."

"I agree again with you Sergeant. I have to make contact with my Commander and make a report on what we just found here. I'm certain he's going to growl like hell for bugging him. But what the hell Sarge, we found something that needs reporting." With that said the CIA Agent removed his handheld radio and keyed the mike and nearly yelled in the mike so he could be heard over the roar from what was left of the winds of the sand storm.

"One, Niner, One reporting in, come in Commander One. Over sir."

Agent Peter Stockten was reading every word printed on the reports he found in the bunker, while keeping an eye on the other agents when his radio sparked to life. The commander recognized his Lieutenant's call in numbers and he grabbed his radio and barked. "Yeah, this is One, what the hell do you have, mister? Over Lieutenant."

"One, we discovered a preserved set of footprints on the leeward side of a large sand dune, sir. We make it two people were moving in the area about the time the sand storm hit, sir. I have the other two Charlie's converging my Papa Papa, (location) to aide in search of the area for possible subjects and item we want, sir." The Lieutenant reported to his commanding officer.

"What the hell are you bothering me for with this fucking crap? Lieutenant Bryant, can you bring in the footprints?" Stocken growled at Lieutenant.

"Err… no sir." Bryant replied with a slight stutter in his tone over the radio.

"Of course you can't. Report back when you have something more solid to report. OUT!" Stockten angrily demanded as he broke off the communication.

"Man that one has to get himself a new fucking personality real quick like, Lieutenant." The grinning Sergeant offered the young agent with a smirk.

"I know what you mean Sergeant. Look sir the rest of our people are here so why don't you take some of them and work over that area of the dune, while I take the rest and work the area in that direction, Sergeant." Bryant replied as he ignored his comment and pointed in the opposite direction he was sending the Sergeant and his crew in.

"Errr… you want me to command your people, Lieutenant Bryant? Are you certain they're going to go along with my orders, sir?" The sergeant asked with surprise in his tone.

"Look Sergeant, I don't care who the hell's giving orders around here. Let me explain it to you so you understand where I'm coming from. I have to locate these subjects so no one is in command of this operation. I want everyone looking for these subjects, being with you Sarge, you've proved you understand the ways of the desert better than I and my people. That's why I want you to lead half the group, while I lead the other half. I need results, not who's leading who around here, sir. You got it Sergeant?" Agent Bryant asked.

"I understand your logic Agent Bryant, and agree with it sir. C'mon, the first seven of you guys are with me. Let's move people, we have subjects to locate on the ground and take in custody, so we can get the hell out of the damn desert." The Sergeant offered as he took the lead and moved his group in the direction of his area of responsibility.

Agent Bryant watched the older Marine Sergeant and others leave and then ordered. "Come on, we'll start our search in this direction, keep your eyes opened. We have two possible subjects in the area. If we don't find the subjects, at least we'll have a lead on where they were and maybe the direction they went in. Let's get going."

The second group headed out with each man looking for any signs of the missing people. There was little in the way of tracks left in Bryant's area. But his group continued searching by every scrub brush or mound in the sand they came across, hoping to flush out the missing subjects who might be hunkered down and hiding from the sand storm or searchers, and they were using the sand and desert robes to hide under until the wind died down.

Sergeant John Jarrett and his group went to the other end of the massive dune to begin their search of the area, and none of them found any further signs of anyone moving on the sand. The wise Sergeant felt he was heading in the right direction the missing people headed off in, because he was still sort of protected from the less blowing wind by the dune. Not finding anymore footprints, the Sergeant held up his hand and stopped forward progress of his group. He turned to the rest of his group and said. "It looks like we're going to have to spread out and search more of this area, if we plan to find anything of help to us. I got a gut feeling we're on the right path to find these two pricks. The first two of you guys go out about fifty yards and search out there, and the next two go out twenty five yards from this position and search from there, the rest of you follow me and we'll check out this area."

The Sergeant waited until the four CIA Agents peeled off from the group and headed further away from the sand dune. Then the Sergeant started his search with the remaining agents in his smaller group. There were so many slight piles or bumps in the sand in this area the Sergeant and his group could not check everyone of them, they did not have time for this search.

The two agents who went the furthest away from the base of the dune were studying the sand for any disturbances or footprints. One agent drifted about ten yards further out than the ordered fifty yards, and he was heading to a large scrub brush. Something drew his attention to it and when he got up to the bush, he discovered a clear footprint protected by the bush. He looked around the area before calling he discovered two footprints, but they were coming from only one person now. When he was certain he found something, he called out to the Sergeant.

"Sergeant Jarrett, I found other footprints over here sir."

The call did not only get the Sergeant's attention, but it also got the attention of Agent Bryant and the rest of his group. Lieutenant Bryant turned while ordering the other agents searching with him. "Let's get over to the Sergeant's group, they must have found something there." The Lieutenant's group rushed over to the Sergeant as he and his people made their way to the agent who just found the new set of footprints in the sand. The agents linked up at about the same time by the excited agent.

The Sergeant and Lieutenant looked at the footprints the other agent was pointing out. They listened as he explained what he discovered by the bush. "Sarge, Lieutenant, I believe the two subjects must have separated closer to the base of the sand dune, sir. I'm certain these footprints are from only one person now, sir. I have two right foot impressions and one left, and none of the prints are overlapping, which makes me believe they were made by one person."

The Sergeant who had more experience searching the desert for enemy combatants replied. "I agree with your assumption, these footprints were made by the same person. Let's look around the area and see if we can find out where they separated behind us. Maybe one of them was hurt and he's still in the area. Check out any mounds in the sand. The sonofabitch could be lying under the sand at our feet using his damn robe to allow him to breathe under the ground. These bastards can survive in the desert like we survive in the cities back home, people."

The other agents looked at Bryant to see if he was going to change the Sergeant's orders, and when he didn't say anything, the others headed off as ordered. The Sergeant remained standing by the Lieutenant and when the agents were searching, the Sergeant remarked to Bryant. "Something's wrong here sir."

"What do you mean Sarge?"

"I see no reason for these two creeps to separate like they had obviously done, sir. When you're in a shit storm like the one we just had. You want all the company you can have in case something goes wrong, and one of them has to help the other out, Lieutenant Bryant. I think one of the missing bastards must have somehow been injured, and the sonofabitch is still hanging around in the area someplace, sir."

"Where can anyone hide in the middle of nowhere, Sarge?" Lieutenant Bryant asked as he started to look around the area surrounding him.

"You know how the A-rabs are and how they're trained to survive in the desert, sir. They use their desert robe for everything from a stinking tent, to a cover lying on the sand, and they let the sand cover them so they're protected from the winds of a sand storm, or discovery Lieutenant."

Lieutenant Bryant scanned the area and noticed many small mounds of sand that could be hiding an insurgent from view. He turned back to the Marine NCO and offered with concern. "Sarge, we're going to be forced to check out each and every mound of sand in the area. If it's like you just said and one of these two we're searching for, might have been injured and left behind. We have to locate him so we can find out if they were the ones in the bunker and they removed that damn cylinder my Commander wants, sir."

"We better start poking a stick in all these stinking mounds to see if anyone's hiding under them, Lieutenant Bryant."

POPE AIRFORCE BASE STATIONED AT FORT BRAGG, NORTH CAROLINA

The caravan of Marine Humvees pulled up to the Green Monster loading ramp of Pope Airforce Base and as usual, Captain Robert Walker was the first one out of the military machines and he looked around. He noticed the medical tent set up off to the side of the landing strip on base, and spotted the five massive C-5 Galaxy transport aircraft resting on the landing strip.

Colonel Bruce Leadbetter walked up behind Captain Walker and lightly rested his hand on his shoulder as he announced. "Walker, everyone from the outfit has to report to the medical tent before boarding the transports. We have orders from General White to have booster shots for many biological and chemical agents we might be forced to deal with on this latest bug hunt. You're in charge of seeing every one of these nuts gets these booster shots, mister."

Just as the Marine Colonel said the words, Sergeant Dorothy Ramirez walked up to the two officers and complained to her commander. "Gees Colonel Leadbetter, how the hell many times are we going to be forced to put this crap in our bodies, sir? As I remember sir, many of these inoculations are still being used under the IND Investigational New Drug status, and since we were forced to sign that damn agreement where we allow these shitting things to be introduced to our bodies. We have to follow your orders as received. Even though we have no idea what the hell the medics are pumping into our bodies, or what harm these drugs are doing to us now, or in the future, Colonel Leadbetter."

"Jesus H. Christ, am I going to have trouble with you again over this shit, Sergeant? Every damn time we have to receive these fucking booster shots, you immediately bust my horns again, and you know damn well you're going to get the same answer you got the last time you busted my horns over this same problem, Sergeant. Look sister, you knew damn well what you were signing when you first agreed to allow the Doctors to introduce this protection against most biological or chemical weapons under the Investigation New Drug Division. So again, it's too late to bitch about it now. There are two things you can do about it Sergeant, follow orders and like it. Or you'll be wearing my boot as a seat cushion in that lovely little ass of yours, Sergeant! Do you have anything else to offer me over this subject, Ramirez?"

Sergeant Ramirez went to say something more to her commanding officer. But she was cut off by Walker before she said something she might regret later on to their angry commander, who took the stance he was just waiting to jump all over her.

"Colonel Leadbetter, my people will visit the medical tent as instructed for their booster shots, sir." Walker glanced at Ramirez and smiled to calm her down before she set off the other troopers in their group. He knew they would back Ramirez over her gripe to show her they were backing her against the Colonel in any bitch she threw at him.

Ramirez noticed the look on Walker's face and she allowed her shoulders to sag, and when Colonel Leadbetter saw she backed down, he growled. "That's better Sergeant, now follow your fucking orders, and get the rest of your screaming squirrels on board those damn trash haulers (transport planes) for debarkation to Kuwait, Sergeant!"

The female Sergeant went to an attention stance, and ripped off a salute at Colonel Leadbetter. She then turned on her heels and snapped at the soldiers gathered behind her. "You heard the Colonel, everyone over to the tent for bug protection then board the aircraft. We're heading for Kuwait for assignment in Iraq. Snap to it, we have a job."

There were many bitches from the elite group of soldiers as they assembled in front of the medical tent, and one by one they entered it. Walker, standing by the commanding officer's side offered. "You know Colonel some of them shots are gonna make my people sick as dogs, sir. I hate starting any mission with my troops not at one hundred percent power."

"What can I tell you Captain, them are the fucking breaks. Your troops have been trained to operate wounded, so what's the point you're trying to make, mister?"

Walker was about to reply to the Colonel's bitch when Doctor Joel Russbinder, the head of NEST or Nuclear Emergency Search Team walked up to their side. Since the doctor was drafted into this elite Special Operations soldiers, he was placed in command of any bug or chemical weapons searches by General John White, Chairman of the Joint Chiefs of Staff.

Upon seeing the doctor prepared to leave with his troops. It was Colonel Leadbetter's turn to complain as he growled. "Oh great, now we're going to be stuck with this pain in the ass civilian on another military operation, god dammit!"

Doctor Russbinder smiled at the officer as he replied. "It's good to see you again, Colonel."

"Yeah what fucking ever, mister. What the hell did I tell you, Doc? I told you I didn't give a good god damn if you're a civilian or not. When you speak to me you'll salute my ass, unless we're in the field. Would you like to try it again?" Colonel Leadbetter groaned at the doctor.

"Excuse me Colonel Leadbetter it's been a while since the last time I was on a mission with your troops, sir. I guess I forgot your protocol, Colonel." With that said, Doctor Russbinder ripped off a professional looking salute to the waiting commanding officer.

"That's better Doctor Russbinder, you'll get the hang of it the longer you're with my troops, sir. I was warned in advance by General White that you were going to be joining us on this latest bug hunt, and the same orders goes for your ass as well, Doctor. Get your backside over to that medical tent and get your boosters. Then get on board the lead aircraft and wait for me, and then I'll brief you on our orders for this operation, Doctor."

"Colonel Leadbetter, I was likewise briefed by General White for this operation. I have the necessary emergency equipment we'll need being delivered to Kuwait as we speak, sir. So I believe I know what's going on." Doctor Russbinder replied confidently to the Colonel.

"I don't give a flying fuck what the hell you and General White spoke about before you linked up with me and the rest of my troops, mister. This military operation Doctor is mine, and mine alone to carry out, and I'll brief you on what I want you to do for this mission, sir. Forget every damn thing General White told you about before you arrived here Doctor, unless he's here going with us on this one, sir. I'm the head cheese you have to listen to around here, sir.

"Let me tell you something Doctor, if you don't follow my orders and you get in trouble on this mission. I'll leave your ass where you stepped in the shit. As I told you Doctor Russbinder, I hate having a damn civilian puke on any military operation I'm in command of. You civilian types are nothing more than fucking armatures and a military mission's no place for untrained people like yourself, Doc. Do I make my feelings clear on where you stand on this operation, Doctor Russbinder?" Colonel Leadbetter snorted at the doctor.

"I guess we're going to do nothing more but clash heads like the last time I was on a mission with your troopers until this operation's completed, Colonel Leadbetter." Doctor Russbinder shot back nastily at the commanding officer of the operation, as he hardened his glare at the officer, and he let out his breath at the same time.

"That makes my fucking boat float, you puke. At least we're going to be at each other's throats until we're out in the field, and you prove your worth to me and my soldiers, Doctor Russbinder. Do you have a problem with that and any other orders? If you do, we could always settle our differences here. That way I won't have to be responsible for your sagging ass in the field. You'll be dead here, Doctor. What's your pleasure civilian, that is if you got the balls you were born with, you'll take me up on my offer to relieve you of this duty?"

"I see we're going to have the same argument we did the last time I was on a military mission with your troops, Colonel. I'll give you the same answer I gave you then. Since I've been appointed by the President of the United States to head my office and since General White is the one who ordered me to go on this mission with you and your soldiers, Colonel. I suggest those people are the only ones who can relieve me of this duty, Colonel." Doctor Russbinder placed his hands on his hips as he glared at the officer. He was driving home to the colonel he was aware he was on a military operation by using the colonel's phase when he referred to their operation.

"What's this shit you're shoving in my face? Are you growing a set of balls, Herr Doctor? You dare insult me by glaring at me with your fucking hands on your hips? Gees Doc, you're beginning to display guts, and guts are enough in my book to respect you. I hope you have the balls to backup your stance you're adopting against me. Your actions earned you a seat in that aircraft, Doc. Be on it before I board the trash hauler, or you'll find your ass standing on this tarmac when the aircraft leave for our operation, Doctor!" The Colonel shot back at the doctor as he smiled over the victory he won over the civilian by making him lose his temper.

While the Colonel and civilian were going at it, Walker left them and went to the medical tent to receive his boosters and protection for the mission. When he was done he headed for the lead aircraft, boarded it and waited for the other soldiers ordered on the first plane. He knew the aircraft would not takeoff until the Colonel was on board, and gave the order to takeoff. He had to admit he was pleased the Colonel was going on this mission as an active member.

Colonel Leadbetter waited for his soldiers to receive their boosters for bug problems, and he entered the tent and received his. Once the Colonel was done with his shots, he stomped to the lead aircraft and boarded like he was angry at the world. The moment the officer was in the troop area, he looked for Walker. Spotting him with Ramirez he headed for him. The canvass metal seats were set up four people across and Colonel Leadbetter remained standing and glaring at the Mutt, (Lieutenant Frank Hall) and No Neck, (Sergeant Robert Abbott) until they got the message and stood and moved out of their seats. Ramirez was sitting by Walker's right side by a window, so she was out of the Colonel's way and he did not bother her to leave.

When the other soldiers left, Colonel Leadbetter took the seat closest to Walker and plopped down and let his breath out. Then he barked at the Captain. "Walker, did that pain in the ass civilian puke get on board this damn thing?"

"Yes Sir Colonel, he's seated seven aisles back with Blood Clot (Sergeant Richard Burmbach, the unit's medic) and a few of the uther soldiers, sir. I believe he's going over some dangers we might face on this mission with our medic, Colonel. Why sir?"

"I wanted to make certain the sonofabitching civilian was on board the aircraft that's all. Captain, it seems we have another mission involving a bug hunt. One of these days these damn assholes who want to conquer the world will learn, the good will stop their evil aims, mister. I hope another nation will step up to the plate and shoulders some responsibilities of keeping a lid on the world." Colonel Leadbetter growled as he tried to make himself comfortable on the narrow canvass and pipe makeshift seats in the cargo bay of the transport aircraft.

Walker stared at the Colonel then replied to his bitch. "Colonel not for nuthin, but you're starting to sound like a damn commercial, sir. You know as well as I and the rest of the troops in this trash hauler, the only people who'll stop the next nut from trying to take over the world, is us. We're the ones who have been trained for this type of work and as long as our units are kept in place and good to go. There's no reason in hell for any uther nation to step up to the plate and take some of the heat offa our asses, Colonel Leadbetter."

Colonel Leadbetter did not respond to his remarks, instead he leaned forward and he looked around Walker at Ramirez and grumbled at her. "What about you Sergeant, you over your little snit, or are your tits still tied up in a fucking knot?"

"Look Colonel Leadbetter, it'd be just like you to rub the way I feel about the Doctor's sticking this crap in our bodies, sir. I took the damn shots even though it was against my better judgment, so let it go at that, sir." Sergeant Ramirez warned her commander hotly.

"I wanted to see if you were still hot as hell about it, that's all, sister." The Colonel snapped as he aimed a sarcastic smirk at the female Sergeant.

"Let me tell you something about us women, that you obviously still don't understand sir. What you give a woman she'll make it greater in return for her male counterpart, sir. If you give her sperm, she'll give you a baby. If you give her a house, she'll give you a home, Colonel. If you give her a bag of groceries, she'll give you a great meal. If you give her a smile, she'll give you her heart, sir. She'll multiply and enlarge whatever she's given two fold. So Colonel Leadbetter, if you give her crap, you better be ready to receive a ton of shit in return, Sir." She smiled the vicious sweet smile a woman gives any man when she's trying to make her point with him, as she stared at her commanding officer like she was daring him to reply.

"Yeah, right, okay, whatever Ramirez, and let me tell you something about me you evidently don't understand, sister. The day I become afraid of a fucking man, woman or beast is when I'll hang up my fucking nuts forever, sister. Walker!" Colonel Leadbetter snapped as he turned to him. "You and the rest of these screaming squirrels of yours are the best of the best, sort of the cream of the crap so to say, and that's why we have been chos…"

"Colonel, you're making me blush here, sir." Walker offered with a smirk as he interrupted the Colonel, and noticed the look he gave him and added. "What Colonel, I have the fucking humility gene inside me sir."

The Colonel shook his head slowly and snarled at his smart ass Captain. "Walker, you and the rest of God's lunatics are going to send me over the fucking falls yet, buster. Now you made me forget the point I was trying to make with your ass. Arrr… fuck it, I have a number of other points to go over with you for this mission, and I want you and your girlfriend to pay attention to everything I have to offer you shitbirds. Besides me, you shitbags are going to be the main cogs for this entire operation, and it'll be up to you birds to keep this pack of criminals in line and focused on our mission when they're out of my sight."

The Colonel stopped speaking and drew in a huge gulp of air, and then he went on with his conversation. "Walker, as you're aware, the Boss at Fort Fumble, (military slang for the Pentagon) General White branded this mission Operation Rapid Fire, and you know what this mission's about, another damn bug hunt. This bug hunt's extremely important to everyone involved. It's discovered Saddam Hussein's pack of assholes developed a designer biological weapon designed to attack one specific race of people. In this case, this weapon was and is aimed at the Persian or Iranian peoples. Mind you Captain it wouldn't hurt my feelings in the least if it only took out the assholes running that country. But since it's aimed at the entire race of Iranians, we have to stop it from being deployed against them, sir.

"Walker, we can't allow this biological weapon to be used accidentally or on purpose against any race of people. Especially because we've removed the madman once in command of Iraq, and it'd be a helluva injustice to Iran for this weapon to destroy his enemy, if he's able to do it from his damn grave. This goes to show you how much Saddam hated the Iranians, the nut he was. Anyhow Walker, we have to locate all remaining product of this weapon of mass destruction, and after we do our experiments to understand what this weapon is capable of doing, we'll destroy the damn lot of it in the fires of hell it was created to cause.

"We have a number of Spooks in the field looking for this crap, and they believe they discovered where this item was developed in Iraq. They're involved in maintaining control of the site until we get there and relieve them and see what they uncovered. I hate like hell when the CIA assholes get there before we do Captain, they always seem to fuck things up. Now don't get me wrong about the CIA Operatives, Walker. They're one helluva paramilitary outfit and they know what they're doing. But sometimes their operations cross over and end up interfering with our actions. That's when they cross swords with my ass, Walker...."

"Yeah, and don't bring it up to me. I know the operatives got the short end of the shit stick when Congress investigated them for their harsh treatment of the damn terrorists being held at Gitmo. Let me tell you Walker, if Congress thinks the CIA were harsh in their interrogations of them lousy pricks. They should've allowed me to interrogate the flaming assholes. I wouldn't leave enough of them behind to bring to trial. Instead of shaking the hands of the CIA Operatives for keeping our asses safe and not hit again in the States, Congress decided to bring some operatives to court and place them as ineffective units, and exposing their names and identities to our enemy.

I feel Congress is guilty of aiding and abetting our enemy by going after the CIA, dammit. The bleeding hearts they think they are. Our enemy must be laughing themselves sick over the treatment of the CIA.

"While we're on this subject let me finish my bitch, Walker. We're a country of conscious and we're committed to protecting our civilians under any circumstances, and it's a must for us to keep the threat of terrorism on the front burner. If we relax our guard for one moment, we'll be forced to witness the destruction and deaths of innocent men, women and children, murdered in the most barbaric of ways.

"The word for these evil doers is branded as terrorist, but they're saboteurs and in any war, saboteurs are not offered protection of the laws governing soldiers or civilians of any nation. To be politically correct, these terrorists are in reality, mass murderers of the innocent. There can't be any laws protecting terrorists, saboteurs or mass murderers. These animals gave up that right of legal protection when they murder their first innocent man, woman or child, dammit.

"The laws of war and military conduct were made to govern soldiers carrying out their country's bidding, not to offer protection to mass murderers and terrorists. When bin Laden remarked he makes no distinction between soldiers dressed in their country's military uniforms and innocent civilians, he displayed his contempt for any freedom loving civilized person in the world. Such deplorable and utter contempt for the lives of the innocent civilians, show how low this evil man and his followers live their lives. Bin Laden drafted young Arab men and has turned them into Jihads and incorporated them into a system constructed around a misled romantic and religious cause. But in actuality these Jihads are nothing more than frontline soldiers for these beasts who want to destroy the freedoms enjoyed by any peace loving nation of the world.

"People like bin Laden and his followers can only sleep at night if they believe they're causing other nations to force their civilians to live their lives in bondage in fear of him. Savages like bin Laden and his followers want people to believe in his God, in his beliefs, and to move the free peoples of the world back to the Stone Ages. Bin Laden sends his misled soldiers to murder in the names of Allah and his messenger

Muhammad. Bin Laden fails to inform his Jihads when they reach the gates of Paradise, Allah and Muhammad will be waiting with fistfuls of lightning bolts and thunder, their revenge against these Jihads for employing their names as the means for them to murder without thought or conscious. The terrorist are the infidels and violators to the printed words in the Holy Qur'an. In Allah's mercy, Allah values all life He created and He'll resent anyone using His name for the sake of murder, especially murder of the innocent.

"Any country's leaders living under the illusion if they do nothing against the damn terrorists, if they don't condemn the terrorist's evil ways and put up with the terrorist existence in their borders, or they bend a knee to these murderers and their future threats. Their nation will never come under attack by these creatures of the black world. The more nations these animals attack and remove freedoms from, the more nations these mass murderers will attack, until no nation is free from their evil actions.

"The only way to defeat these hate mongers and brokers of death and destruction, is for all nations to come together as one and form a wider Multi Nation Rapid Response Force. Much like the one we organized and you people are part of, comprised of elite specialized soldiers from the United States, Russia, Japan, China, France, the United Kingdom, Italy, Spain, and Saudi Arabia to mention a few. Along with any other nation who wants their country's children to enjoy the God given right and enjoyment of living in a world where they can chose their God to respect, and chose the way they want to live their lives in peace. A good example to follow is how the Sri Lankan military ended the twenty year threat of terrorism from the Tigers terrorist.

"They ended the threat and listened to no one while doing it. I feel we have to remove the useless Security Council of the United Nations who never agree to a situation. Because of political or monetary agreements and considerations, and we have to turn over the power of the Security Council to nations of clear conscious, and this power should be centered in The Hague, the Neverlands for a more direct action.

"This suggested expanded Multi Nation Rapid Response Force has to be allowed to work under the no borders call, where a free loving nation has to do is call for intervention from the Rapid Response Force soldiers, and after a hearing in the neutral nation at The Hague, and once the hearing's completed. The MNRRF soldiers are sent to the country having problems with terrorist organizations, and the specialized soldiers neutralize the terrorist activities by any means to eliminate the threat to that infected nation, whether it's in the borders of the United States or Russia. This is the only way to break the backs of terrorism, and it might teach the terrorists to change the beliefs and laws of one nation by entering the political arena, rather than paralyzing a free nation by employing terrorism and the death of the innocent. We have to force the terrorist to duck their heads or they'll be blown off on them.

"Terrorism Walker is like a mean junkyard dog, it can't be fought with ASPCA rules. Any nation's who wants to eliminate terrorism from their land, has to remove the chain from their bigger and meaner dog, meaning the Rapid Response Force, and allow them to fight it out in the pit of hell without tying your meaner dog's hands behind their backs. Bleeding hearts who want to offer legal protection to these mass murderers have to hold their damn tongues and stop trying to offer these fucking animals legal protection under civilized laws, when the terrorists operate outside the actions of the civilized world. When these murderers only reason for living is to remove these same civilized rights and laws from the nations they hate so much. This proposed expanded MNRRF has to enjoy the backing by the agreeing nations, and supported one thousand percent with all military assets needed to be employed to defeat the terrorist organizations.

"The murderers operate with no civilized laws governing their cowardly sneak attacks and actions against civilians, and the terrorists should in return have no civilized laws protecting their worthless lives. The host country allowing these animals to live and organize in that nation and attack other countries from their soil, has to suffer stifling sanctions and if need be. The military weight of every free nation to fall on their damn shoulders until that nation reacts, and they destroy the sanctuaries these mass murderers enjoy in the host nation.

"God dammit Captain Walker, I believe what it'll take other fucking nations of the world to witness before they finally realize the only way to truly destroy the damn terrorist organizations and their constant threats of death and destruction, is by banding together for the common cause of eliminating all terrorism. I hate to think how many other god damn nations will only react once they have suffered their own Nine, One, One cowardly sneak attack by these damn animals. Before those other nations finally take the threat posed by terrorism seriously, and they react to these mass murderers properly and with evil intent.

"Walker, any god damn terrorist taken in custody alive before or after a terrorist attack, has to be treated in the same savage manner he chose to live his damn life, and any means necessary has to be employed against the surviving terrorist, to gather vital information on future terrorist attacks planned by these animals. The people who complain the loudest obviously never lost a loved one to the terrorist attacks. These flaming assholes who complain about the harsh treatment of the poor and misunderstood fucking terrorists still being held at Gitmo, receive at the hands of their jailers.

"Are only spreading the damn cheeks of their asses wide while waiting for another spineless Nine, One, One sneak attack in our country, and yet they still offer these fucking animal's protection and the rights of law they want to remove from the rest of us. I'm telling you in no uncertain terms Walker, even a home grown terrorist a civilian from our country, has to be treated as a saboteur and terrorist. He has to be tried in a military court and the military has to melt out his justice for actions in the savage way he lived his life.

"Dammit, I say we should give the arrested terrorist to the survivors or widowers of their attack, and how they want to treat these pricks has to be accepted by all. I assure you Captain there'd be no need for any exhausting trials for these animals, and the survivors and widowers will get the information of future terrorist attacks against any nation before they happen from these cowards, before they're sent on their way for their maker's judgment of their actions. Again I say, treat the terrorists like they treat the innocent, with contempt and utter distain for their existence, period. Let the fucks see their leaders lied to them about virgins waiting to boff."

The Colonel stopped speaking to Walker because the transport plane went to takeoff power.

THE SITE WHERE THE THREE CIA HELICOPTERS LANDED

This section of the Iraqi desert was as barren as most areas in the vast deserts of the world, and the CIA crews were searching the sand for the remaining insurgent they were classifying the missing person. The CIA Agents had no idea they were searching for a dead Iraqi child.

The ones working with the Marine Sergeant John Jarrett, was poking into any slight mound of sand with their hands, or sticks they found in the area. Looking for the one who they believed was left behind by the other mover. Lieutenant Bryant and the rest of his special agents were working nearest to the foot of the massive sand dune. The Lieutenant split his people up in groups of twos, and a pair of agents searching ten feet away from the base of the dune, when one of them noticed a piece of cloth sticking out from under the sand.

Sliding his weapon off his shoulder, the agent brought the MP-5 assault weapon around to a firing position, as he cautiously headed for the slip of cloth he spotted buried under the sand. The cloth was sticking out from under the sand, and the agent working with this one noticed the actions of his fellow agent. He followed suit by preparing his weapon for firing, as he followed the other agent's lead as he cautiously approached the mound of sand.

When the two agents were standing shoulder to shoulder looking at the fabric, the one asked the other. "Ray, what do you think you got under there? It's definitely cloth sticking out."

"I think we found the missing subject and the sonofabitch is hiding under the sand like a rat. Okay pal, we see you under the sand, I'm ordering you to crawl out from under there with your hands on your head, and don't give me problems. We have you covered and if you make any stupid moves, we'll kill you. Get out from under there." The agent repeated his orders in Arabic in case this one did not understand English.

The moment the agent called out to who he believed was hiding under the sand, every agent from the group stopped what they were doing, and they turned to this agent ordering someone. Once they saw him aiming a weapon at the sand, the other agents and Sergeant surrounded the two agents and small mound of sand. They were aiming their weapons at the pile waiting for the subject to follow their orders and come out from under the sand.

The Sergeant was by the Lieutenant's side and reached out and forced the other agent's weapon up as he took command of the situation. He knelt on the sand and carefully studied the cloth. The Lieutenant got down on a knee and he cautiously asked the Sergeant in a low voice with concern. "What do you think, Sergeant? Do you think there's someone under that cloth, or is it something someone discarded?"

"As sure as I know there's sand in the fucking desert, there's someone under there, Lieutenant. I'm not seeing any movement, so either this guy's deaf or he's dead, sir." The Sergeant grumbled as he would not remove his eyes from the strip of cloth for a second.

"What are you going to do Sergeant?" The Lieutenant asked the well seasoned soldier as he stared at him and the Sergeant continued to study the mound of sand.

"I'm gonna pull the lousy sonofabitch out from under the sand, and see if we can find out who he is, and what the hell he was doing this far out in this damn desert. Here's what I want your people to do. I want them to keep this guy covered, tell them kids not to shoot my ass if they have to go postal on this sonofabitch under there, Lieutenant. I'm gonna grab hold of the cloth and pull the prick out from his hiding place like the rat he is. Lieutenant, I don't want your trigger happy bastards shooting this guy or me, unless he reacts and tries to shoot first, sir. We hafta take this guy alive if he's breathing, so we can question the prick and see who he is, and what he's doing in the desert." Sergeant Jarrett offered while not removing his eyes from the cloth sticking out from under the sand.

The Lieutenant straightened up and relayed the orders the Sergeant just issued him to the agents surrounding the mound of sand. Once he was certain the others knew what was expected of them, he again knelt by the Sergeant and offered. "Do it Sarge, we're ready for anything sir."

"Okay people standby, I'm gonna pull this guy's ass out from under the sand. If he tries to run, jump on his ass and beat it to the sand where he came out from. Here we go, get ready for anything happening from this little prick under there." Slowly reaching out his hands after shaking them to get his circulation going, the NCO grabbed the piece of cloth and pulled gently on it until he got enough of the cloth out so he could wrap it around his mitt size hand. When he had a good hold on the cloth, he was ready he gave a hard tug on the fabric.

Because the Howli was wrapped so protectively around the small frame of the young child, the boy's body came flying out from under the sand as the Sergeant pulled on it. The sheer force the Sergeant used and the light weight of the child's body, caused the Sergeant to fall backwards, and he ended up sitting on his ass on the sand with the Howli wrapped body of the child lying at his feet. Instantly, two agents fell on top of the robe and tried to pin the body of the thought to be insurgent on the sand, while the Sergeant struggled back to his feet, and roared at the agents. "You two people feeling any movement under that damn robe?"

"No sir, the body isn't moving a muscle under us sir. I definitely feel a body in the fabric though, it's still as death." The agent lying right on top of the body offered as he continued to hold the small body down on the sand.

"Then get the hell offa him so we can unwrap the prick and see who we have, fella." The angry Sergeant ordered as he took a defensive stance over the body and prepared to attack it, if the Iraqi tried to give them any trouble.

Reluctantly and cautiously, the two agents took their weight off the body, and then they stood and aimed their weapons at the pile of cloth.

"Gees, will you people relax a little, dammit. Evidently this guy isn't moving so he's either too weak to respond, or he's dead. Either way we have control of the sonofabitch." The Sergeant growled as he went down on a knee again, and he started to run his hand over the cloth. When he realized the body under the cloth was lying on his belly, he reached out and rolled the body over until it was on its back. Once he had him in this position, the Sergeant began to cautiously unwrap the body of what he believed was an Iraqi soldier, as he kept his eyes open for a weapon or reaction from the person.

As he removed the heavy Howli from the limp body, the Marine Sergeant bitched at the CIA Lieutenant. "Man, this little prick's wrapped up in there tighter than a god damn Alabama tick digging in on the backside of a stinking deer, sir. No wonder these fucking guys can bury themselves so deep under the sand and live through it until they want to crawl out from under it, sir. Uh oh!" The concerned Sergeant suddenly mumbled as he uncovered the face of the child, and he noticed the condition of the body.

"What's wrong Sergeant, is he dead, sir?" The Lieutenant asked with concern.

"This one's deader than a doorknob, sir. The prick has dried blood coming from his eyes, nose, mouth and both his ears, sir. This dead one's nothing more than a child, Lieutenant. I wonder if he somehow escaped from the Iraqi technicians after being exposed to this biological weapon we are in search of, and the poor kid made it all the way out here with the help of someone else. When the kid croaked, the other one left his dead ass behind and took off like his asshole was shooting sparks. Lieutenant, I believe we have an infected and contaminated body here. We have to act accordingly before we become contaminated by this shit ourselves, if we ain't crapped up by the shit already, sir." The now worried Sergeant replied as he stood and moved away from the dead body of the kid.

"Shit, God dammit, okay let's get away from the body and get dressed in our protective gear. Then we have to place this body in a sealed airtight bag and prepare it for E-vac back to the bunker. Then we'll see what Stockten wants to do with it. Let's get a move on it and I want everyone checked for contamination when we get back to the bunker with this body."

The CIA Agents scattered and rushed back to the spooling helicopters and they quickly got dressed in their environmental suits and separate breathing apparatus. The engines of the helicopters were never shut down on a mission. This was a precaution in case they were forced to liftoff and defend the agents on the ground if they came under attack from insurgents in the area. Once the agents were protected against possible contamination, only the medical agents were allowed near the body of the child, so they could examine it to see if they could decide how the child had died.

The Sergeant standing by the Lieutenant again, offered in case he did not understand his duty on this mission. "Lieutenant Bryant, you know we hafta get this body back to our people in one fucking piece, sir. If he's contaminated by this biological weapon, our people are gonna need his blood so they could work on some kinda antidote against this shit. I hope they can work with his blood after this prick's death. So we hafta be more than cautious with his body, sir. I wonder what a damn kid like this was doing way the fuck out here, and how he might have become contaminated by this shit, Lieutenant Bryant?"

"I'm aware of that Sergeant Jarrett I was briefed before I started on this operation. That's why I had at least one medical agent on board each helicopter. It's their responsibility to prepare the body for transport back to the bunker, so we can begin examining the body of the child. As for the body being that of a child, I can't answer that question. Knowing how little regard the Iraqi military offered their people, if this kid's an Iranian, I could only imagine what they done to his body, Sarge. What do you think Sergeant, how old do you think this kid was?"

"I don't know I'm not good at setting an age for a person, yet alone some damn kid, sir. If I was to venture a guess about his age, I'd say he's no older than fifteen, probably younger, maybe something like fourteen or thirteen or even younger, I really don't know, sir. I'll tell you this much though Lieutenant, I don't care how old the damn kid was. All I see is another dead Iraqi who won't live long enough to come at us as an insurgent with a weapon, and he can't kill any of my people in his condition, sir." The Sergeant growled as he flipped the protective mask over his head, and then he hooked up the air line from the tank on his back to the mask, so he could breathe properly in the protective equipment.

"Man Sergeant, that was colder than the other side of the pillow. He's only a kid, and he's dead from what I believe was through no fault of his own. Have you gotten so hard and non-caring over all this death that a dead child no longer affects you, Sarge?" The Lieutenant asked as he stared at the Sergeant while waiting his response.

"Yeah Lieutenant Bryant, a death of a kid bugs the shit out of my ass, sir. But I saw many times what a child carrying a fucking weapon is capable of doing to a soldier, if that soldier allows his feeling for that kid to affect his betta judgment, and take the kid out first, sir. The kids of this lousy ass backward country have been trained since leaving their mother's breast to kill, especially Americans, sir. So as I said, this kid's no longer a threat to me or any of my fellow soldiers, Lieutenant Bryant. It's that easy to say sir." The Sergeant yelled so he could be heard through his protective hood and mask system.

"I hope I never become as cold hearted as you, Sergeant." The Lieutenant replied hotly.

"Take my word for it Lieutenant Bryant, if you stay in this country long enough, you'll become that hard yourself, sir. C'mon Lieutenant, we hafta see if we can be of assistance to the medics working with the body, sir." The Sergeant offered as he rested his hand on the officer's back, and turned him so they could see what the medics were doing with the child.

The Lieutenant allowed himself to be led over to the body by the Sergeant.

By the time the Lieutenant and Sergeant returned to the body of the child resting on the sand, the medics were working on the body. The boy was stripped and other agents burning the clothes and desert robe. The Lieutenant almost wrenched in his survival suit when he saw the condition of the frail body. His chest was an angry and dark black and blue color, even his arms and hands showed the same coloring. He looked at the child's legs and the muscles showed signs of being held in a taught condition, looking like stalks of black and blue. Even the child's toe and fingernails were black, and the Lieutenant could swear he noticed blood under the blacken nails of the body. It seemed the child's whole body was assaulted by the biological agent.

The most telling and chilling thing about the child's battered and bloody body was his face. It was frozen in a mask of sheer terror and unmanageable pain, as if the child screamed his life out of his body. When one of the medics forced the distorted mouth of the child opened, more raw blood freely poured out and the medic captured most of it and he placed it into a sealable secure plastic bag. The medic then laid the bag down on the chest of the child. The medics then turned the body on the side and one ran a clean white cloth between the cheeks of his backside, it instantly turned red from raw blood. The medics were placing every item they used on the child's body in sealable secured bags for later examination.

When the medics finished their examinations of the small body, they then quickly prepared it and the items they used on it into heavier sealable bags they removed from the helicopters. The body was the hardest to slip into the huge bag, and once the head disappeared inside the clear body bag, it was sealed air tight with the use of a special heating iron. The body looked smaller as it was stuffed in the bag. When everything was sealed and ready for transport, the medic walked up to the Lieutenant and offered.

"Lieutenant Bryant, the body and items contaminated by our examination, are stored and ready for transport back to our temporary base, sir. I have to tell you Lieutenant Bryant. The way I see it sir, the body was definitely exposed to the biological weapon, sir. Also Lieutenant, the way we packed the body and items up, sir. I'd say there's no way for us to pick up contamination from the body or items we accumulated thus far, Lieutenant. As an added precaution to our actions sir, I'd keep everyone, even the pilots dressed in their protective environment suits, and far from the body and items we have until we delivered the body and items back to the bunker and our Commanding Officer, Lieutenant Bryant." The medic warned as he looked at the small body being loaded inside the helicopter.

"That's a wise suggestion and I'll follow it to the letter, sir. By the way sir, was it possible for you to tell if this child was Iranian?" The Lieutenant asked the medical agent as he stared at him through the goggle ports in the protective mask.

"That's the strange thing about the child and this nightmare, sir. If I was a betting man Lieutenant Bryant, I'd bet the ranch he was Iraqi ancestry, sir. If this weapon was originally designed to attack Iranian or Persian born peoples, how did it kill this kid, Sir?"

"Doctor, we were briefed this biological weapon can change its properties at a drop of a hat, and go after anyone it wants to destroy. That's why this operation's carrying such a priority on it sir, and we're expendable on this mission as long as we find all this shit that exists, and get it in something that won't threaten life. Doc, I suggest you get the body and items of contamination on board the third helicopter, and I'll have the other two machines take the agents who don't have to be near this body, sir. That way Doc, if anything goes wrong and this biological weapon attack us, only the agents with the body and pilot and co-pilot of that helicopter are at risk, sir."

"Thanks a lot Lieutenant Bryant, when you said we were expendable. I didn't know you meant the medics, sir." The other agent complained at the officer.

Bryant smiled through his protective mask as he replied. "I'm sorry to say it this way, sir. But that's the way I'm going to order it be carried out until our commander relieves me of this duty, Doctor. Please sir, you have to get the body and items you used, loaded on board the classified medical helicopter, so we can get back to the bunker and our people, sir. I'm certain by this time Stockten's probably eating his way through his protective equipment. If you'll excuse me, I have to make my report to the Commander before he skins me a live, sir. Be ready to shove off, we'll be lifting off the moment you have the body and items stored in the medical helicopter. Everything's waiting on you and your medics to finish with the kid, sir."

"I'll have the body and items stored on the chopper before you give the order to liftoff, sir." Looking over his shoulder, the doctor noticed his medics loaded the body, and they were moving the rest of the contaminated items to the helicopter, and added. "Lieutenant Bryant, the body has been placed on board the machine, and my people are finishing up now sir."

"Outstanding, we'll lift off in five minutes. As I stated, excuse me while I make contact with Agent Stockten and inform him what we discovered here, sir. Doc, I think I'm going to order the other helicopter to continue searching for the package we obviously missed, while our helicopters return to the bunker, sir. Excuse me Doctor."

Agent Bryant moved over to his command helicopter and pulled the mike outside the machine, so he could make contact with Stockten. The harsh wind from the once fierce sandstorm had completely died off, and it was dead calm as the Lieutenant made his call. "Errr... this is Spotter One to Lead Control. Come in. Over."

CIA Colonel Peter Stockten was staying on the backs of his people, tearing the interior of the bunker apart in their continuing search for information on the weapon branded P, One, Three, Five, when his secured radio went off. Stockten charged for the table and grabbed the radio and barked in a savage tone. "This is Lead, report Spotter One. It's about fucking time you got back to me. What the hell do you have, and it better be what I sent you out there for. Or don't bother coming back to this place until you carried out your orders properly, Lieutenant."

"Lead, we found a body of a believed to be small Iraqi child sir. Discovered evidence proves he was not alone out here, sir. The one with the child obviously left when he died, sir. We believe he was infected by the item we are in search of sir. We have the body and items used to examine the body, stored on board the medical helicopter, and we are preparing to lift off and head back to the bunker with the body and items of examination, sir. I'm going to keep one helicopter searching for the missing subject who was with the dead one, while my machine and medical helicopter head back to the bunker, sir…"

"You'll do no such thing. I'm ordering only the medical helicopter to come back to the bunker, and your machine and the other one will continue searching until you located, and taken as your prisoner the missing subject in question, Lieutenant. I want that package brought back here, and I want it brought here in one piece, Lieutenant. We have to question the package to find out what these two were doing here. And, if the package is the one who removed the object from this bunker. Lieutenant, you have your orders, follow them as received. That's all I have for you Lieutenant, and if you don't find our package, don't return mister."

"I'll follow orders as received. I have the medical helicopter lifting off." The Lieutenant offered as he whirled his fingers in the air, giving the signal to liftoff to the pilot then he went back to his conversation with the Agent in Charge. "Lead, I and the other machine will be lifting off and we'll not return your position until we located our missing package, sir. Out."

Agent Peter Stockten did not wait for the Lieutenant to finish his statement, he broke off the report by disconnecting the radio, and then he went back to searching the bunker.

The young CIA Lieutenant watched as the medical helicopter slowly lifted off, and he set the mike back in place in the helicopter. It was at this point he noticed the pilot was staring at him as if waiting for further orders, as he struggled out of his protective clothing and he offered to the pilot of the helicopter. "Commander Peterson, you and the co-pilot can get out of your protective gear. We're going to continue the search for the missing package who was with this speed bump (military slang for a dead body) we just shipped out to the bunker, sir. We have orders not to report back to the bunker until we have located the other person that was with the kid when he died and we taken him prisoner, sir."

"I can't say I'm unhappy getting out of this crap, Lieutenant. Do you have any idea where you might want to search for the other package, sir?"

"I guess we'll start due West of this location, Commander. I know ar-Ramadi was searched by Marines yesterday. So there's no sense going over the same grounds twice, sir. We have to check the map and see if there are any Iraqi towns or villages west of our location, Commander." The Lieutenant offered with a smile.

"Will do Lieutenant, you better order your people on board the helicopters if we have orders to continue our search by Agent Stockten, sir."

POPE AIRFORCE BASE STATIONED AT FORT BRAGG, NORTH CAROLINA

Captain Robert Walker was on board the transport aircraft along with Colonel Bruce Leadbetter, they were forced to stop speaking because of the roar coming from the massive engines, as the aircraft headed for its proper altitude. When the aircraft leveled in flight, it was quiet enough for the officers to speak, and the Colonel started off. "Walker, I have a little slide show for you and your pack of criminals. It'll display a detailed map of the area of Iraq in question for this operation. I'll go over the map with you, and you can go over them with these nuts of yours, sir. It'll highlight towns or Iraqi villages we have to check out if we're forced in the field to find this crap. We'll also view a video of the search area of our responsibility for this mission."

"Captain, I want you to pay attention to the video, because it's an up to date of the area of investigation, and we're going to pick out possible ambush sites Iraqi insurgents might use against us while we're in the field. This is going to be a free fire mission throughout, which means if you or these other shit sacks come under enemy fire, you won't need permission to return fire on the attackers. Make no mistake about it Walker, this is an important operation, and we're going to find ourselves in Iraq in the shit, until all traces of this weapon are accounted for. Even if we have to retire from the service in Iraq, Captain.

"I have permission from General White to pull in any air or ground assets and strike packages operating in Iraq from any mission they're assigned to, to support this operation. We have command for this entire mission and we will succeed, or your ass will be the first one I'll take my anger out on if you catch my drift. Are you paying attention?" Colonel Leadbetter suddenly roared at Walker because he did not ask one question, and the Colonel wanted to make certain he was working off the same sheet of music he was for this operation.

"Heaven help me, I am Colonel Leadbetter. Back off on my ass will ya, Colonel. I'm paying attention to every damn word you're saying, sir. That's only because I'm desperate sir." Walker replied with a smirk.

"Look wiseass, there's no room for any clowning a fucking round on this operation. We have a shit filled detail that could cost us our lives if we screw up on this one. At least assure me you're starting out on this damn operation in a serious mood, buster." The military officer stopped speaking at this point, and held Walker in his angry gaze.

"Yeah Colonel Leadbetter, whatever you say goes, sir. If you don't know it by now sir, it's time you understand when I or these uther soldiers step foot out on a mission we're assigned to. We turn into professional soldiers with no horse shit between us, and we get the job done, sir."

The Colonel continued to glare at Walker until he felt his message was sent then he went on with his orders. "One of these days Walker, I might get the respect due me from you and the rest of these shit sacks you command. Arrr… what the hell, this mission sucks as it is, so there's no sense making it harder for you and these pukes. Walker, we have to go over a lot of crap and we have little time to accomplish it.

Be prepared to hit the ground in Iraq running, because I want to take command of this operation from the Spooks working it until we reach them, Captain."

"I agree Colonel, I hate like hell when we have to work side by side with the Spooks, sir. They give me the fucking heebe jeebies, sir." Walker remarked.

"Let me tell you Walker, the CIA Spooks give everyone the heebee jeebies. That's why I want to take command of this operation the moment we touchdown in Iraq, Captain. Let's take a break and get something to eat, once we've eaten it's going to be all business until we touchdown in Iraq." The Colonel growled at Walker then made a hand signal and airmen began running sandwiches and sodas out for the Marines trapped in the cargo area of the transport plane.

The Colonel left Walker's side and started to work with one of the Airmen. The young Airman was setting up the projector so he could go over the mission with Walker. By the time the elite soldiers finished choking down food, the Colonel was ready to begin his presentation to the soldiers on board the trash hauler aircraft.

"Okay you pack of screaming eagles, pay attention. When I call eyes, every eye on board this trash hauler better be watching my ass, if you people know what's good for the lot of you. Because if you shit sacks don't hear my first order, you birds better be able to read minds, I won't repeat an order for a second time. Once we're in the field and active, I'll be keeping my eye on you shitbirds, and if I see one of you out of place, I'll put a cap in your ass myself. Eyes!" The Colonel looked at the faces of his elite soldiers on board the aircraft, and when he was certain he had their attention, he began his presentation about their operation.

"That's good I'll brief you on our mission. Some of you shit squares might not know where we're heading, it's Iraq. It seems that madman once running the place and we settled his hash, had his people working on a special type of biological weapon. This weapon was classified as a new breed of designer weapon of mass destruction. It was designed to kill only Iranian or Persian born peoples. Well, the brain thrust at

Fort Fumble received reports discovered by one of our patrols in the desert on this item. They're of the belief once this weapon's introduced to the air, it'll morph into a more destructive weapon that'll change it properties, and the item will start to kill every soul on the face of the earth…"

Some soldiers groaned because they were going out on another bug hunt, but the Colonel overlooked the grumbling as he went on with his briefing. "That's right people we're going on another bug hunt. This one comes with the blessing of the President, which means we're free to use any means necessary to locate this item. We'll be in command of any American armed forces operating in Iraq. Our orders come from top of the ladder, from General White. He ordered us to locate every microbe of this shit, even if we have to level a city, village or Iraqi town we have to invade to accomplish our mission, troopers.

"Once we're deployed in Iraq, we'll split our forces into three companies. One company of troops will be back up for the other two companies who might get in trouble with any of these jackasses who call themselves fucking insurgents. Shit, I forgot, it's no longer insurgents, its enemy combatants, dammit. We have to make nice nice to these damn popping jays who want to kill, cook and then eat our asses. The assholes who don't want to call a spade a spade, we have to come up with pleasant names to call our damn enemy now. Anyway, if any forces engage or get engaged by insurgents err… enemy combatants in the field of operation. I don't want you people to be involved in a long drawn out engagement with these flaming assholes. You're to call in fixed wing or rotary aircraft, and allow the fly jockies to destroy any resistance you might come across in the field.

"Nothing you people might come across in Iraq is to be allowed to interfere with our mission. You're to eliminate any problems with extreme prejudice, and you'll move on to your next objective for this operation. You will be moving in Humvees or by ankle express (Foot) and if you discover information about this item, call in trash haulers and they'll move you to your next objective. We have to find this shit, and we have to find it double quick before it's released to the air by accident or on purpose. Okay people look at the map displayed on the screen. The first mark is the position where the Iraqi papers were discovered in the desert." He focused in on the location until it showed where the Marine patrol was stationed, and then he went on with his report. "When our patrol discovered the papers blowing around out there, they reported their find to Command, and Command turned the find over to the fucking CIA Spooks…"

Another groan from the soldiers. This time the Colonel reacted. He wanted to make certain he had the soldier's attention, and when the second gripe was voiced, he reacted angrily. "What the fuck was that shit? Are you asses griping about our fucking mission? Listen up you criminals, any of you ball sacks and bouncing tits have a problem with our mission, are free to get off this aircraft right the fuck now, dammit. I gave you crybabies the first groan, if I hear another gripe from you people, you'll regret the fucking day your daddy's porked your mamas. I know how you hate working with CIA Spooks. I do also but it's our job to relieve the Spooks from the main part of this mission, and take command of the operation from that point on.

"Once we're in command of this shit filled mission, if any Spooks get caught up in your cross hairs, kick them in the ass and move on. The next location I'm focusing in on the map is where the Spooks discovered a supposed underground bunker in Iraq. It's in this location where they were able to discover where this biological weapon was cultivated into a working weapon of mass destruction by the Iraqis. The Spooks found reports of experiments the technicians carried out on a number of defenseless Persian and Iraqi prisoners they're still working on this bunker looking for evidence on this item we'll be looking for… Huh, what the hell was that you said?"

An Airman interrupted the Colonel's report and whispered in his ear then the Airman handed him a video tape and turned on his heels and left the angry Colonel.

Colonel Leadbetter handed the airman working the projector the tape and announced to his troops. "We received an up to date report, it seems a detachment of other Spooks discovered a body of an Iraqi kid in the desert. The body showed signs of being exposed to some form of biological or chemical weapons that caused his death."

Lieutenant Frank Hall, was sort of paying attention to the Colonel's presentation. He was also bothering his main squeeze on the aircraft, Sergeant Regina Raphael. Raphael was on loan to the Rapid Response Forces from France, nicknamed Blind Date. The two soldiers were sitting with Buckethead (Sergeant Vincent Lambardo), and he was with a female soldier he was interested in dating. Sergeant Teri Dorland, nicknamed Baby Tee because of the size of her breasts. Mutt turned to Blind Date and grumbled. "When I get to I stinking raq, I'm gonna find me an A-rab chick and see how these sand swimmers fuck." He was trying to get a raise out of his girlfriend.

"That's disgusting I don't know why I allow myself to be interested in you, Mista."

"Hey man, in case you didn't understand what she said, it means she didn't like what you just said, asshole. Now you're gonna have to make it up to her, or spend this whole mission rubbing your own dick, stupid." Buckethead mumbled at his fellow soldier.

Their conversation caught the attention of Colonel Leadbetter and he attacked the soldiers he felt were not paying attention to his warning. "If you assholes don't shut the fuck up over there and put your eyes back on this screen. I'll have the damn things plucked out of your noggins and glued to the screen so I know at least your eyeballs are paying attention. You soldiers just pulled the unloading supervision of the trash haulers. The rest of God's lunatics better be looking at me if you know what's good for you guys. I warned the lot of you I'll not repeat an order.

"Okay people, As I said I was informed the Spooks located a body of a young child, and the body displayed signs of being infected with this biological weapon we'll be searching for in that lousy country. This latest discovery makes it more important we locate any remains of this weapon. If it was used once then whoever used the damn thing will surely use it again.

"Okay, on the screen is displayed the location where the Spooks found the kid's body, so when we reach this bunker. Walker will command a company of soldiers and head out for this second location to see if you people can discover any evidence the Spooks might have missed. If not, Walker and his troops will spread out from this location and search for whoever the hell infected this kid with this crap, or was with him when he died. Walker's group will be the command unit for the operation, and he'll control the follow-on units. The follow-on units will coordinate their operations with Walker's group. Walker, your One Charlie (Satellite Controller and Communications) soldier for this operation will be Sergeant Burgwald.

"All units will funnel their communications with Burgwald, he was handpicked for this operation because he knows his way around the damn system expertly. Command will work through Burgwald while you people are in the field doing your act. Also, each unit will have an ATO or Air Tasking Officer from the Airforce attached to your unit. The fly jockey will be the one who'll communicate with aircraft platforms called in to assist you people if you Boots come under attack from enemy combatants stalking the area. The reason we're taking an airforce person with us, is because he's in tune with the procedures to bring the required strike platform weapons to bear on enemy attackers. The airforce personnel are to be treated with the utmost of respect by you fucking people, period!

"Walker, you'll pick out your point personal and assign any soldier to duties that'll bring the best possible success rate for this operation. Also, you'll…" The Colonel's report was interrupted a second time when the lights in the cargo area blinked, and the pilot's voice came in over the aircraft's intercom and warned.

"To all personnel on board this aircraft, you're instructed to remain in your seats and all unnecessary electrical usage will be interrupted for the duration of the in flight refueling procedures for this flight. We're beginning our first in flight refueling. Also, our orders were changed since takeoff. We're no longer scheduled to land at our original site at Garcia, we're instructed to accept three in flight refuelings and are ordered to land at the Kuwait military airfield, and from there you'll debark this aircraft and begin your penetration of Iraq at that time. All lights in the cargo bay will be turned off until all aspects of the in flight refueling had been completed. All personnel are instructed to return and remain in your seats until ordered to do otherwise by the Cargo Master. Refueling will commence in ten minutes of flight. Cargo Master is now in command of all personnel in the cargo bay area until further notice. That is all."

All the while the pilot was making his announcement to the Special Forces soldiers, Colonel Leadbetter glared at the intercom. He was fuming the pilot interrupted the orders to his people. When the pilot finished his instructions, he growled at his troopers. "Well, that settles that crap for the time being, you people heard the head cheese for this damn flight, and you'll follow his orders as if they came directly from me. Make yourselves comfortable, because the first moment I'm able to speak to your clods again, I'm going to drill into those noggins what we're doing on this mission."

THE UNDERGROUND IRAQI BUNKER IN THE MIDDLE OF THE DESERT

CIA Special Agent In Command Colonel Peter Stockten, decided to leave the stuffy air of the bunker for a while, and was now standing outside waiting for the medical helicopter to bring the body of the Arab child to him. Stockten had his medical staff standing by; he wanted a detailed autopsy carried out on the dead child, so the medic's understood what they might be facing if this biological weapon was ever released against them, or the world.

Agent Stockten was lighting his second cigarette when he heard the beat from the helicopter before he located it in the blazing sun. When he spotted the machine coming in for a landing, he barked at his medics. "Okay, you people better look alive, the body of that kid's about here. When you guys get the body, you'll bring it into the tent and rip it apart. I want to know how the kid died, and what this damn biological weapon did to his body. I'll have my ID personal check out the kid's clothes and personnel property to see if we can discover who the hell this kid is, and where he came from. I need answers and I need them ten minutes ago."

As the helicopter touched down, the medical staff moved in dressed in their protective gear, and removed the body from the machine. Agent Stockten, still refused to dress in his protective gear, watched from a safe distance as the medics hustled the kid's body into the tent and closed the flap. As foolish as the command agent was acting over wearing the protective NBC gear. He was no fool and he was giving the tent a wide berth. He knew he would not go anywhere near the medical tent or the kid's personal effects while they were exposed to the air.

Agent Stockten remained outside the bunker because he believed they discovered everything there was to be found about the biological weapon. He moved to where his cook prepared meals for the CIA Agents, and had something to eat and drink. It was noon and he looked up at the blazing sun and cursed the country. Then he found himself wondering when the Marines scheduled to relieve him and his people of their mission, was going to arrive on the site. He started to think what he was going to have his agents do when the Marines arrived, and how much help he was going to offer them, and if there would be trouble between his agents and the bull-headed Marines.

The lead agent lost all thoughts of time and when a medic came out of the tent and jumped into the decontamination shower. Stockten found himself walking as close as he would get to the medical tent. He watched the medic wash his protective clothing, and struggle out of the protection and breathing device. He waited where he was until the medic walked to him, and then he growled at the man. "Well, you finished with the damn autopsy on that Arab kid?"

"Yes Agent Stockten, as much as I needed to know for now that is, sir. What we discovered and been able to put together, more than half the kid's body was disrupted, swollen and or ruptured by the invading biological weapon, sir. We found traces of the weapon still active in the liver, heart and lungs of the body, sir. It seems more than half the child's major organs were ruptured, and the child actually died by drowning on his own blood. From what I can see of the invasion of the weapon in the child's body, he must have suffered for a long time, and endured a terrible death before succumbing to the affects of the weapon assaulting his body."

Agent Peter Stockten cocked his head to the side and stared at the medic before asking. "Sir, something you said has me a bit confused about the death of the kid."

"If you tell me what's troubling you, perhaps I can clear it up for you sir." The medic replied.

"Yeah, you said only half his damn body was being disrupted and affected by the damn biological weapon. How come every organ in the kid's body wasn't affected by the invading weapon, sir? Perhaps there's something there that might offer us a possible use, or maybe even a clue on how to better protect ourselves against this fucking thing if it ever gets out, sir, sir." The lead agent questioned the medic.

"You're correct with that statement Agent Stockten, and that puzzled me as well, sir. At least it confused me until I was informed by the ID personal the kid wasn't a full blooded Iraqi born, sir. It seems the kid's Father was European and only his Mother was of Iranian ancestry. This information forced me to believe only the Iranian dominated organs were affected by the weapon, sir. I must warn you Agent Stockten, the remaining traces of this weapon active in the kid's body, seems to be working on changing its properties. It was slowly starting to affect the European dominated parts of the body. This reinforces the belief the biological weapon would mutate in the body, and quickly become a weapon that'd be a threat to the population of the world, sir." The medic replied as he stared deeply in the commanding officer's eyes until he felt Stockten realized the ramifications he was informing him about.

"God dammit! I was hoping we'd have time before this damn thing started to change its properties. From what I get you telling me, this weapon's foaming at the mouth to kill any host it's introduced to. It'd react quickly in efforts to do what the weapon was designed. To fucking kill every living soul and thing on the face of the earth." Stockten complained as he pitched his cigarette angrily at the ground and ground it into the sand in a fit of rage with the heel of his boot.

"You obviously don't understand what we discovered during our autopsy of the child's body, Agent Stockten. I have my people working on the body to see if they could discover anything else that might help us protect ourselves from the affects of this biological weapon, sir. They'll continue working on the body until they dissected every organ of the body, so my medics could understand how the weapon caused the death of the kid, sir. Agent Stockten, we have parts of the active weapon quarantined, and with the blood from the body. We can start to work on an antidote against the weapon. I'm afraid I don't have the proper personal available to enable me to carry out the procedures that has to be accomplished to create an antidote against the weapon."

This information hit Stockten hard and he growled at the medic. "Look Mister, all you have to do is inform me of the personnel you need to work on a damn antidote against this fucking crap. I'll have their asses shipped out here double quick, sir. Come with me and tell me who you want shipped out here to assist you with this crap. I have to get to a fucking radio and get in contact with Command, and have these people transferred here as quickly as possible, sir."

"Yes Agent Stockten, I'm going to need blood work and toxicology personal along with diagnoses and experimental equipment and experts that'll make my work easier to accomplish, while we continue looking for a possible antidote for this…"

"Yeah yeah Doc, allow me to make contact with my command and I assure you. You'll have everything and one you need and more without asking for it a second time. I'm certain the bigwigs will want us to work on this crap in Iraq, rather than bringing this shit to the United States, sir." Stockten grumbled as he made way for his communication center. Since the sand storm stopped blowing, his agents set up a working center outside the helicopters and humvees.

Stockten picked up the mike and growled in it. "This is Lead to Command. Over."

"This is Command, sent your traffic Lead. Over."

"Yeah Command, we discovered a downed person and we're able to retrieve a proportion of the item in question active for closer examination, sir. My medics are complaining they don't have the proper personal and equipment needed to carry out their needed experiments on the item, sir. I have requests from my medics to be filled by Command, if you want us to continue with our work on this item in Iraq, Command."

"I read you, Lead. Lead I have orders for you to carry out, sir. You're instructed to see if your medics are able to release two samples of this active product, yet maintaining possession of a third sample for them to work on in Iraq, sir. We're trying to set up three different examination points to see if all three examination centers will agree with their finding, sir. We need a response to this request of you and your medics, Lead. Report back Lead. Over."

Stockten did not respond as he turned to the medic and snapped at the man. "You heard what they want from you, can you fill their request so I can respond in the positive to Command, sir?"

After thinking about his reply, the medic offered confidently. "Yes sir, I can cut off two samples of the active biologic from the blood, Agent Stockten."

Stockten returned to his radio. "That's a Roger on request of my medics. He offers he can send two samples of active product anywhere in the States you want it delivered, Command."

"Good Lead, here is what you're to do. Prepare two samples of product for delivery to the States. One sample is to be sent to main headquarters at Quantico. Your second sample is to be hand delivered to the Center for the Biological Security at the University Of Pittsburg Medical Center. I'll inform the Doctors of the item being shipped out to them, and warn them of the dangerous item. Lead as for your medics and request for equipment and expert personnel, sir. The moment I break off this communication, I'll have everything and one and more your medical teams need and want in the form of personal and equipment, shipped to your position immediately, sir. You have your orders, carry them out as received, Lead. Over and out Lead."

"Well fuck you in the ass too buster! Cut me off like that dammit, I should cut your fucking balls off for that insult." Stockten growled at the dead mike, then he turned back to the looking medic and ordered him. "You heard the fucking orders from Command, I suggest you get your ass back in that damn tent and make those two samples available for shipment to the United States, sir. How the hell soon can you have the samples ready to go, sir?"

"Agent Stockten, I can have the samples ready for shipment in fifteen minutes, sir."

"Good, that's outstanding. I'll have transportation for the samples setup by the time you're done preparing the samples for transit. You better get on with your work, sir." Stockten ordered.

SIX C-5 TRANSPORT AIRCRAFT LANDING AT A SECLUDED MILITARY BASE ON THE BORDER BETWEEN IRAQ AND KUWAIT

Four a.m. October 29th, 2008. The flight of military transport aircraft carrying the Rapid Response Force troopers, landed almost unnoticed but by a few military personnel stationed on the Kuwaiti military base. The moment the engines shut down, a line of humvees pulled up and personnel from the Kuwaiti Airbase pitched in and helped the Special Forces soldiers unload their gear, then the troopers loaded them in the humvees. Colonel Bruce Leadbetter and Captain Robert Walker were the first officers off the aircraft, and watched as the humvees pulled up to where they could be loaded with the specialized equipment. What neither officers noticed were the five black painted and no identifying marks humvees at the end of the convoy. These five machines were the CIA Medics ordered to follow the Marines to the Iraqi bunker.

It took more than an hour to have the humvees loaded with the soldiers and equipment then the convoy crossed the Kuwaiti border to the all but destroyed country of Iraq. Colonel Leadbetter was in the lead humvee busting the horns of the driver, trying to get him to move the machine faster for the soldiers. He wanted nothing more in life than to get out to the bunker and relieve the Spooks from duty, and his troops take command of the operation.

Many soldiers tried to sleep in the backs of the humvee troop transport vehicles. No soldiers displayed very much concern over their extremely dangerous mission. All the soldiers knew was they were being sent on another operation for their country's security, and the only thing that mattered to them was the successful conclusion of that mission. Some of the soldiers were enjoying what there was to see of the scenery from Kuwait. Once the group of elite soldiers and machines entered the deep desert, everything was going to look the same. Nothing but a sea of endless sand waiting them there, along with mountainous sand dunes and blowing tumbleweed, lizards and temperatures so hot. The soldiers would be able to cook bacon and eggs on the fenders of their war machines.

After an hour of traveling through the endless desert, the complaints started from the upset soldiers being bounced around the hard riding machines. The longer the soldiers and machines traveled through the desert, the more complaints came from the soldiers. Even Colonel Leadbetter was starting to get pissed off over the time they were to travel before arriving at their assigned location, and CIA Spooks waiting their arrival.

THE CENTER FOR BOLOGICAL SECURITY AT THE UNIVERSITY OF PITTSBURG MEDICAL CENTER. WEDNESDAY, OCTOBER 30th, 2008, EIGHT A.M.

General John White, Chairman of the Joint Chiefs of Staff arrived at the Medical University at the same time the package from Iraq arrived at the College campus. The powerful General wanted to make certain the doctors at the University knew what they were working on, and how dangerous the item was. The Chairman did not want anyone taking anything for granted when it came to working on the deadly biological weapon, P, One, Three, Five.

The General was greeted at the parking lot by Doctor Johan Rosenblum, who introduced himself to General White. After the pleasantries were exchanged by both men, General White got right down to business as he offered to the elderly doctor in a warning voice. "Err… Doctor Rosenblum, I suppose you're kind of troubled as to why a military man requested and came to pay you a visit at the University today, sir. Please allow me to explain why I decided to visit you, sir.

The reason is of a major national security situation sir, and I'm going to need your assistance and knowledge on this matter, Doctor."

"To be quite truthful General White, I was concerned as to why I was informed to be expecting a visit from the Chairman of the Joint Chiefs of Staff. Don't tell me you're here to draft me in the armed service. I believe I'm too old for active duty, General." The elderly doctor offered.

General White gave out with a laugh as he replied. "No sir, not at all sir I'm not here to draft you in the service, sir. The reason I'm here sir is as follows. I have to be honest and blunt with you over this situation, Doctor Rosenblum. Doctor, a Marine patrol operating in Iraq stumbled over an extremely important Iraqi military document displaying a certain number of technicians were working on and perfected what we branded as a designer biological weapon, geared to attack a certain race of people, sir. Since the accidental discovery of this document Doctor Rosenblum, we discovered an underground bunker where the Iraqi technicians perfected the designer weapon, sir. Doctor, we also discovered a dead child in the desert, and his body was showing definite signs of being infected by this weapon I'm speaking about, sir."

"I don't mean to interrupt you General White, since we're speaking about a sensitive subject, sir. Perhaps it'd be a wiser idea if we went to my office where we can speak more openly, and without fear of being overheard by either the facility or the student body of the College, General White. The last thing I feel we need at the University is a panic over what we're speaking about, General White." The cautious doctor offered the General as he turned and headed for his office.

General White did not reply to the doctor's remark. Instead he nodded and followed the elderly doctor down the hallway of the college, until the doctor turned and entered a private office. Once the men were seated and comfortable, Doctor Rosenblum asked the military officer in a pleasant voice. "Can I offer you any refreshments General White? A cup of coffee or tea perhaps, I'm afraid I don't have anything stronger I can offer in my office, General White."

"A cup of coffee will do just fine Doctor Rosenblum, thank you sir." General White replied as politely allowing a slight smile.

After pouring the General a cup, Doctor Rosenblum returned to his seat and made a temple out of his fingers, and stared at the huge black military officer over his hands, as he waited for the General to inform him of why he was receiving a visit from the Chairman.

Sipping his coffee, the General rested the cup on the desk, and announced in a confident tone. "Doctor Rosenblum, I can see by your expression you're wondering why I'm here. Please allow me to explain sir. You should be receiving a sample of a biological weapon discovered in Iraq later on today, sir. Doctor Rosenblum, I can't begin to inform you how dangerous this weapon is, and what the ramifications to the world might be, if this weapon is released in the atmosphere. I have a sample of this weapon being delivered to your University today Doctor, and it'll be your job to assess the characteristics of this weapon, and what it can and can't do, and how much of a threat this item is to the security of the world, sir. I know how you people hate to work with chemical or biological weapons Doctor Rosenblum, and believe me sir. If I had any other office I could send this crap to, I would've never ordered a sample to be delivered to you, sir.

"Anyway, Doctor Rosenblum, as I stated, I need your facility to examine this weapon of mass destruction, I need to know how to defeat it if at all possible. I also need your people to come up with some form of a working antidote against this damn thing at the same time. Believe me Doctor, if I didn't think this was of a national or global situation, I would've never bothered you with this so dangerous an item, sir. I received an assessment on this weapon from Doctor Joel Russbinder, the head of our NEST or Nuclear Emergency Search Team, placed in command of searches for either nuclear, chemical or biological agents throughout the world, sir. Doctor Russbinder's accompanying my soldiers in the field to discover all product of this weapon, sir. His report was based on the reports the Marines discovered by accident in Iraq. Doctor Russbinder didn't have any active product to analyze properly as you'll soon have, sir.

"This is why I'm at your College and took it on myself to order a sample of this product delivered to your University, Doctor Rosenblum. I need you to work on this item, and I need your threat assessment and contagion rate as soon as possible. Allow me to further explain how crucial your report will be, sir. Doctor, I considered naturalizing a certain section of Iraq with a nuclear blast if we're unable to discover the remaining product of this deadly weapon, sir. This decision was based on Doctor Russbinder's report delivered to the President, sir. The President was in complete compliance with this decision to use nuclear weapons to sterilize and burn off any remaining product of this weapon wherever it might be hidden in Iraq, Doctor. Believe me Doctor this situation is that serious for us to be considering the use of nuclear weapons to erase every trace of this damn thing, sir."

General White took a quick breath. He understood the doctor was rocked to his soul over the information he was delivering. The officer had no choice in the matter he needed this doctor's help and needed it immediately. He was about to begin his words again when a young man entered the doctor's office, and he informed him they'd received a special delivery from the military, and a pair of angry looking soldiers were waiting outside the building, demanding to speak to him personally.

The doctor dismissed the young man with a flick of his hand, and then he turned to the General and mumbled at the officer. "General White, I take it the two soldiers outside belongs to you? Two soldiers are waiting to speak with me, General."

General White shook his head in the affirmative because he did not inform the doctor the two soldiers outside were CIA Operatives.

"I guess we better get out there and see what they have, General White. I'm going to have the package delivered to the isolation ward where we experiment on infectious items brought to the University. I couldn't allow something of such concern to be brought through the main doors of the school, sir. Shall we go?" He offered as he waited for the General to join him.

"By all means Doctor Rosenblum, all you have to do is inform me where you want the package delivered to on the property, and the soldiers will get it there safely, sir. By the way Doctor, you have to understand this item's being classified as a national security event under the Homeland Defense Act sir, and only yourself and few handpicked by you team of doctors are to work on this item, sir. The fewer Doctors you need assisting you, the better it'll be to enable us to maintain a security lid on this item, Doctor. All experiments on this item identified as P, One, Three, Five, has to be carried out on a top secret level. No one and I mean no one is to know of the existence of this item under the threat of death, Doctor Rosenblum." General White warned the doctor as the General got up and followed the doctor out of his office.

The doctor and military officer met the soldiers by the main entry doors to the college, and the doctor informed the soldiers where they were to deliver the package on the site. When he was finished dealing with the soldiers, Doctor Rosenblum turned to the General and offered in a shaking voice. "General White, will you accompany me to the isolation ward of the campus?"

"No Doctor Rosenblum, I believe you have the ball in your park, and you have to hit the ground running, sir. It's up to you and your colleagues on how you want to handle your experiments with this item. I need your test results as soon as possible, Doctor. Your finding will inform me on whether or not I'll have to get my troops out of the threatened area, and release a nuclear cleansing of the region in question, Doctor. I'm sorry to be forced to inform you of this, sir. But these soldiers will remain with you at all times until they're relieved and a second set of soldiers takeover duties of security over this item and school, sir. All the while you're working on this item sir the soldiers will be supplying security for your experiments on this item, Doctor Rosenblum." General White placed a sort of smile on, trying to soften his order to the doctor.

"Gees General White, I don't know how some of our more radical students on campus will react to seeing soldiers on the Campus, sir. Some of these kids have a problem with any form of military presence, especially on campus property, General." The doctor's look intensified as he stared in the General's eyes.

"I'm as sorry about how some students will react over the fact there'll be soldiers on campus property all the while this biological weapon is in your possession, Doctor Rosenblum. Not only will these soldiers remain on campus as ordered while this item is here, sir. They'll be armed and operating under strict orders to employ deadly force against anyone who might challenge their authority, or try to invade their area of responsibility Doctor Rosenblum.

"Again, I'm sorry for this severe an order issued on your campus, Doctor Rosenblum. As I stated Doctor, this item is being classified as a national security situation, and an extremely serious threat and I'll protect the secrecy and security of this item no matter what I have to order, to accomplish this fact sir. I cleared it with the leaders of the campus about having armed soldiers on campus while this item is being worked on by your staff, sir. Your leaders intend to address the student body later on today, and make a good reason to have the soldiers present at the college, sir. I'm sorry Doctor Rosenblum, but I have to get going sir.

"I'm scheduled to meet with the President later today, and I have to get my ass back down to Washington PDQ sir. Good luck with your experiments on this item Doctor, and remember this sir. I need the results of your experiments with this product ten minutes ago, sir. Also Doctor Rosenblum, you better be prepared to deliver a report to the President in person, once you have completed your experiments on the item, Doctor." General White announced in a sharp voice as he put his hand out and he shook hands with the shaken civilian doctor.

When they were finished speaking and shaking hands, General White turned and he quickly disappeared from the doctor's sight. His staff car was parked on the other side of the building, and he had to rush a little to get to it, so the driver could return him to Washington before his scheduled meeting with the President. The trip down to Washington went without a hitch, the traffic was light and the driver only employed his siren once, to get a slow moving car out of the speed lane. General White smiled remembering the look on the civilian doctor's face when he left him.

THE UNDERGROUND BUNKER IN THE IRAQI DESERT

CIA Agent In Command, Colonel Peter Stockten was still outside the once secret Iraqi bunker. He was keeping an eye on his medical team as they continued to work in the tent on the child's remains, and examining his personal items. Although Stockten refused to step a foot closer to the medical tent than he was standing, he was getting constant updates on the medic's work on the body by the agents in the medical tent. Stockten was using the excuse that he was waiting to hear what the medics turned up on the child's death, to stay outside the concrete bunker.

The air in the dim lit cement structure made breathing hard to endure, and Stockten refused to go on an independent air supply system which would force him to dress in the rest of the protective environmental equipment. The fresh air he was breathing did not do very much for his bad mood, and the commander ended up barking at any other of his special agent or soldiers assisting his people he came across.

As Stockten took the time to light his umpteenth cigarette when he noticed a dust cloud raised about a mile away from his location. Angrily, he pitched the half smoked cigarette at the ground, knowing someone was heading for his location.

A second agent ran up to his commanding officer and he announced in an excited voice while slightly out of breath. "Agent Stockten, we just picked up a convoy of military vehicles heading for our position, sir. I believe it has to be the detachment of Marines scheduled to relieve us of our duties at this bunker, sir."

"No shit Shirlock, it has to be the pain in the ass Marines coming to relieve us of our duties on this messed up operation. Dammit, I was hoping to have some answers for this shit before these assholes showed up and stopped me from completing my orders. You better warn the others that company's coming, and order them to treat these assholes properly. Anyone guilty of giving these fucking soldiers a hard time will answer to me. Get on with your orders and warn the others about these troops coming at us." Agent Stockten glared at his fellow agent until the young man and took off to carry out his orders.

Stockten walked out before the helicopters and cleared his setup and was standing in a position where he would be the first to greet the Marines. All the while he waited for the soldiers to reach his position, Stockten cursed his command, commander and soldiers coming to relieve him of command for this so important an operation. One thing Stockten hated with a passion was to be pulled off any mission without completing it. This was the second time in his life this was happening, and this one was the most insulting to his massive ego. Because Stockten was not turning this operation over to another group of operatives from his company, he was turning it over to a bunch of thick headed killer Marines.

When Stockten felt he was out far enough and stopped walking and lit up another cigarette, he settled down to wait for the rapidly approaching military vehicles.

Colonel Leadbetter, along with Captain Walker, Sergeant Ramirez, Lieutenant Hall and Sergeant Abbott were riding in the lead vehicle, and the angry Colonel growled at the driver, Sergeant Nirajima. "Hey stupid, stop this damn thing by that lone prick who looks like he's out there waiting for our asses to arrive."

"Owe Colonel Leadbetter, that jab hurt my fucking feelings, sir." McNip moaned over the slug the Colonel aimed at him by calling him stupid.

Colonel Leadbetter ignored McNip's complaint as he focused his eyes on his main target of the CIA Spook obviously waiting for his troops to arrive on the site.

McNip slowed his vehicle down, and the other vehicles connected with the Marines slowed. The black painted humvees did not slow, they shot past the Marine vehicles and continued heading for the encampment at full speed.

Agent Stockten watched the vehicles pass him at high speed, and nodded to a driver delivering more of his specialized people out to the Iraqi site. His attention was forced back to the lead vehicle of the convoy as it came sliding to a stop four feet from the lead operative. Leadbetter was pissed McNip allowed his vehicle to come so close to the man before he stopped it, and he smacked McNip on his head and barked. "You're fucking lucky you didn't run over that puke out there. As soon as I settle up with this shit sack, me and you are going to have a little chat."

McNip ignored the Colonel's warning as he watched Walker and the Colonel jump out of the machine. The two officers walked up to Stockten and the Colonel allowed Walker to break the ice with the man. His words immediately embarrassed the Colonel as he grumbled. "Hey buddy, you the fucking resident penis around this here dump, buster?"

Walker's words infuriated the special agent, and before he was able to get control over his rage. Stockten fired right back at the grubby-looking Marine. "Now you look here fucker, I happen to be the Special Agent in Command Colonel Peter Stockten, of this damn operation, and I demand the respect due me. You fucking thick headed Marine bastard you." Stockten took on the stance of an attacking linebacker, and glared at the young and proud looking soldier.

Walker accepted the threat from the agent and he took on the defensive posture as he replied. "Look buster, make your fucking move on my ass but take your time, man. I never rush a man who has a death wish to carry out. If you want your wife to cash in on your death bennies, I suggest you don't take too much time making your move on my ass. I never offer respect until the puke I'm looking at earns it. If you wanna earn my respect make your move on my ass. Or are you all fucking talk and no frigging action? You people cost the Marine Corps many a good soldier drafted by your gutless fucking outfit, and I wouldn't mind avenging my brothers by talking it out on your fricking ass, pal."

Colonel Leadbetter had to laugh as he watched the two jackasses squaring off against each other like a pair of school kids fighting over a woman. When he felt it was starting to get out of hand, he remarked. "Captain Walker, stand down if you know what's good for you, soldier.

You, Special Agent in Command whoever the fuck you are, you should know better than to take a stance of attack against one of my soldiers. Why the hell don't the two of you assholes learn to play together? We have enough bad guys out there who want us dead without us killing off each other. Agent man, you better look over my shoulder before you decide to make a move on my Captain's ass." Leadbetter stepped aside so the special agent could see what he was referring to.

Stockten looked behind the Colonel and what he saw chilled him to his soul. Every trooper in the convoy was out of their machines, and they took a defensive stance against him and the rest of his agents on the site. They were protecting the officers he was in a confrontation with. The Marines had their weapons cocked, locked and ready for action. Swallowing his pride and spit, the agent took a calmer stance as he replied to the Colonel's warning.

The moment he noticed the agent allowed his shoulders to sag, he spoke up. "Special Agent in Command, I'm Colonel Bruce Leadbetter, and I'm in command of this Marines detachment. This Captain you want a piece of is Captain Robert Walker, and he'll be in command of the soldiers who'll go in the desert in search of the biological product. Now Special Agent, I want this transition of power from your command to mine to go without a fucking hitch. Make no mistake about it though I'll take command of this fucking operation, with or without your cooperation. I know it must be going against your grain for us dumb Marines to takeover this operation from your ass, but them are the fricking breaks. How do you want this damn thing to go down, with a hand shake or us breaking some fucking heads around here, sir?"

Agent Stockten had no other choice. He was facing down over what looked like more than one hundred and fifty heavily armed soldiers prepared to attack. Not only was he outnumbered, he could not allow his people to attack Marines. He would never be able to explain it to his commander. Letting his breath out in a rush, the lead agent offered the Marine. "Colonel Leadbetter, allow me to introduce myself, sir. My name is Colonel Peter Stockten, sir. I'm operating under orders to turn over my command of this operation to you and your soldiers, Colonel. However, my Agents will be at your service prepared to lend assistance to you and your troops, sir. Since we found the biological weapon and are most familiar with this weapon. I believe it'd be in your best interest in keeping us on the mission to assist you, Colonel."

Colonel Leadbetter was unable to hide the slight smile he was enjoying, because he realized this CIA Agent was actually begging him to remain attached to this operation. Over his many years of dealing with operatives from the CIA, this was the closest one of their Spooks ever came to begging him for anything. Fighting off the want to get on the once proud agent's ass again, he got control of his feelings and then offered with a touch of sarcasm he offered. "Yeah Special Agent Stockten Sir, it's a pleasure to meet you sir. After listening to you, I happen to agree your Agents might be of assistance to my people at that, sir. Besides Agent, you people have the only access to a helicopter in the area, and until I'm supplied with my helicopters, I'll commandeer your machine. So that order is going to force your Agents to remain at this location until I have no further need of your people, sir.

"Would you excuse me for a moment Agent Stockten?" Colonel Leadbetter asked and responded before the agent replied. He turned to Walker and snapped at his officer. "Okay Walker, the show's over. Get your people deployed and setup and secure this position. Errr... remember Captain, these people here are classified as civilian contractors, and they're to be treated with the utmost of respect. I'll be holding you responsible if any of your Screaming Eagles get out of hand, Walker. You have permission to utilize any civilian contractors in any duties you might want to assign them to. If some contractors give you problems Captain, you'll report their infraction to Agent Stockten here, and he'll handle his people from that point. You have your orders, so carry them out Captain." He gave Walker the harsh look that informed him he better get a move on it.

Walker went to a full attention stance and ripped off a sharp salute to his commander then he headed for the bulk of his troops. He smiled when he noticed none of his troops relaxed their attack stance, and were still cautiously eyeing the CIA Agent with a want for action. He moved up to the Mutt and vented at him. Everything he was doing was to impress the CIA Agents who stopped what they were doing and were staring at the soldiers who invaded their position.

"Mutt, you hafta get our people out and have them relieve the damn Spooks. You know our orders so get on carrying them out before the Colonel gets on my ass, because of you dragging your frigging feet. Assign the most likely soldiers to the more important positions. The rest of them can do the backup crap for the other troops. Have the troopers who won't be entering the damn bunker dig in. Who knows, we might get hit by a pack of stinking enemy combatants, and I want to be well prepared for any contingencies, man. C'mon man, we gotta get a move on it, because the stinking Colonel's gonna get tired of speaking to the head cheese, and he's gonna come after us for dragging our damn feet."

"You got it." The Mutt replied and then he went after some troops and bitched. "Hey Buckethead, you got the stinking duty to relieve the Spooks by the damn helicopter. You're to secure the machine for our use. Neck, get inside the damn bunker and see what the hell the Spooks down there are up to. No one enters the damn bunker without NBC (Nuclear, Biological or Chemical) protective gear. The rest of you people pick out one of the uther Agents and follow them around like they're your bitches. They're to do nothing around here without the Colonel or Walker's permission. If I see one of these Spooks walking around and he isn't being trailed by one of our people, someone's ass is gonna be caught in a fucking sling for it. Move it out people.

"Any soldier who doesn't have a damn Spook to follow, are ordered to dig in and form a defensive security ring around this position. Remember, we're in fucking sand land and there are plenty of enemy combatants hanging around who want to cook and eat our damn asses. The heavies, you people know who you are, you're to set up your heavy M-50's, so you birds can lay down a cross and suppression fire to any points of our position, in case we come under attack by any assholes from this messed up country. Let's get a move on it you guys know what we need to setup for protection, so get it done." The Mutt snapped at the soldiers and removed his spade from his backpack and picked out a safe place, and started to dig a foxhole.

Captain Walker watched his second in command dish out the orders and he remained silent. He felt it was about time the Mutt who was a Lieutenant, started to take some crap from his shoulders. The

Mutt was the only other officer besides himself and Colonel Leadbetter on this mission. Something the Mutt was doing suddenly caught Walker's attention, and he walked over to his friend, and when he was standing on the rim of the hole the Mutt was digging, he growled at Lieutenant Hall.

"Hey stupid, not for nuthin, but what the hell do you think you're fucking up to man?"

"Hey man, I got cold chills running up and down my spine, because I'm stuck here in this god forsaken country again. I'm digging a fucking foxhole, what the hell do you think I'm doing. I'm gonna dig this fucking thing so damn deep that I might be classified as AWOL by the time I'm frigging done with the damn thing. It's gonna be that damn deep man." Again, the Mutt flashed one of his famous smiles at Walker as he stopped digging so he could speak to him.

Walker smiled because of the way the Mutt framed his bitch, and then he grumbled at him. "Look stupid, you ain't gonna hide your can in some damn hole in the ground, asshole. I'm gonna need you inside the damn bunker with me, and also out here keeping an eye on the rest of these pain in the asses, if I happen to be busy and can't do it for myself. C'mon Mutt, you're the only uther Officer I got on this fucking operation besides the stinking Colonel, and you're gonna hafta take some of this crap offa my back. You can use Ramirez if you need help dealing with our people. She knows how to handle anyone who might give you any stinking trouble. Put her in command of the female soldiers if you couldn't figure that one out for yourself.

"Besides Mutt, we're not gonna be at this position for a long time I believe. Remember, we hafta get out to where the uther Spooks found the body of that kid, and we hafta check that area out and then we'll begin our search for this missing shit from there. That's another reason why you're wasting your time digging that hole in the damn ground. Mutt, I didn't know you were part mole anyway. Get your ass outta there and keep by my side, and when the Colonel orders us outta here, I won't hafta go looking for your stinking butt."

All the while Walker was griping at the troublesome Mutt, he remained standing in the middle of the shallow hole he was digging, and when he heard what Walker ordered him. He threw the shovel at the mound of sand he created. The spade dug into the soft sand and remained sticking in the pile as he bitched at Walker. "Oh man Walker, I'm beginning to really hate this stinking shit. How the hell come I'm always one of the assholes who hasta go running all over the fucking place looking for the damn bad guys? I'd like one of these missions I can dig in and wait for the mess to be over with, without my having to be exhausted and beat up from the feet up to boot. This shit's starting to suck the big high one man."

McNip joined Walker as he got on the Mutt's case and yapped at him to add his two cents. "You know something man, you're starting to become a constant complainer."

The Mutt glared at the half Japanese soldier, and then vented. "Hey Homes, don't you gotta go home and stir fry a fucking cat or something, buddy."

His remark angered McNip and he started to bitch. "You know man, I got a good mind to come in that damn hole and…" McNip's words were cut off by Walker as he grumbled at him.

"Hey man you're starting to circle the stinking drain for your last ride. If you have a good mind you'd know betta than to get involved in an argument with the stinking Mutt. He'd stay in your face longer than a stinking blackhead. Enuf screwing around already, Mutt, get your ass outta that hasty and follow me. McNip, if you don't have something to do, I'll find ya something and you won't like it I can assure ya, buddy. Get on with your other duties."

The Mutt struggled out of the shallow foxhole, and then he walked past McNip, he stopped long enough to give him a dirty look. Then he caught up to Walker heading for the rest of his troops to get them moving.

THE SMALL IRAQI TOWN OF AR-RAMADI

t took the beautiful, and still thoroughly exhausted and beaten up Ayesha al-Qaysi two full days of complete bed rest and drinking vast amounts of water, to help her fight off the terribly disabling effects of her very trying day of walking in the deep desert with the child Saad Ihsaan. Even though she had her body covered up with the desert robe, she still suffered severe sunburn to her face and her hands and lower arms. All through her time of suffering and rehabilitation, she was constantly surrounded by the ever present Sadiya Sadjadpour and Shafiqu al-Quraishy, and neither woman would leave her side for a moment while she was recuperating. Even her mother was extremely concerned over her lovely daughter's weaken health and state, and she too was making a real pest with her beautiful daughter trying to get her to drink more water, eat food and rest.

On Wednesday October 30th at seven a.m., Ayesha woke and decided she had enough of lying around the home doing nothing but resting. She sat up and cast her eyes at the stainless-steel cylinder resting by the foot of her bed. She did not realize what she have found in the desert, and the ramifications this discovery held for the world. When she rested her feet on the floor, she almost stepped on Sadiya, and this woke the other woman. When Sadiya sat up, she woke Shafiqu also sleeping on floor of Ayesha's room. All three pretty women looked at each other, and started giggling as Shafiqu offered Ayesha her hand to help her get out of bed. Shafiqu could not help it and she found herself staring at Ayesha's peeling but lovely face, and she felt terrible for her sister so badly sunburned on her face and neck by the Eye of Allah (the sun) in the desert.

Ayesha al-Qaysi did not pay much attention to the metal cylinder as she allowed the other two women to lead her to the kitchen. Shafiqu al-Quraishy wanted her sister to have something to eat. With the energy Ayesha was displaying thrilled Shafiqu to no ends, and she wanted her to start recovering her strength by having more to eat.

Shafiqu led her to the kitchen table and sat her down, and started preparing eggs for her breakfast meal. Neither of the two young women were able to speak to Ayesha about her ordeal in the deep desert, or the upsetting loss of Saad Ihsaan. They did not know how he lost his life, and they were interested in learning about this, and what was inside the cylinder. Shafiqu placed the eggs in front of Ayesha, and settled down and watched her eat. Ayesha did not realize how hungry she was until she started to eat. When she finished, she stretched her arms over her head and groaned. Shafiqu took this as a good sign and asked her Iraqi sister the question troubling her. "Ayesha, how did the young one die in the desert with you?"

Tears started to build in her eyes as she allowed her mind to wander, and remembered the terrible bleeding Saad was doing. She had no idea why he was bleeding and dying before her eyes. Drawing in a sad breath, she replied. "Shafiqu, I don't know why Saad died. I see no reason for his death, something must have attacked his body and he died terribly. I was completely helpless to offer him any comfort, and I was forced to stand by and watch him die while I was holding him in my arms and crying over him."

Shaifqu shared her sister's grief. "Ayesha, do you think something inside the place where the child found the weapons, might have caused his death?"

"That is a wise question and it's one I'm unable to answer. Your words make sense, whatever killed the child had to be inside the bunker." She offered while choking back tears.

Ayesha's reply did not warn her of what she said but they registered in Shafiqu's mind, and a fearful chill filled her body as she said. "Ayesha, if what killed the child was in what you called a bunker, does that mean what killed him might be affecting you?"

Her half smile instantly left her lips as her mind mulled over what Shafiqu just said to her. She was unable to stop the shaking of her body as she suddenly feared for her life, and the death the child suffered before her eyes. Now she feared the same thing that killed the child, was slowly killing her, and she faced the same terrible death in her future. Her thoughts turned to the steel cylinder of death she had in her bedroom. A fear filled her as she wanted to get rid of the cylinder and what it contained. She wondered and made up her mind, she was going to go to the village elder and tell him of what she found, and ask him what she should do with the cylinder.

Shafiqu saw the look change on her face and grew more concerned for her health as she asked. "You seem upset perhaps if you tell me what's troubling your mind. I might be able to set your mind at ease for you my desert sister."

"I fear there's nothing you could offer that would bring peace of mind to me, Shafiqu. Only my faith and belief in Allah will bring me peace of mind. This is something I must work out for myself. If I'm infected with the same fate that killed Saad then that's something I must suffer alone. It makes me understand I might have precious little time allotted to me by Allah's merciful will. One thing I must do is bring the gift I received from the desert to the Town Elder, and see what he instructs me to do with it. He's a very wise and well-educated man, and he'll know what I must do with my gift, and how to properly use it against our enemy." She offered as she shifted her eyes to her bedroom and the cylinder of death.

"I know nothing of this gift you speak of my sister. I'll tell you this though Ayesha, when you go to meet the Village Elder, I and our other sister will accompany you to keep you safe. I heard stories about the foul Elder and how he treats pretty women, and what he demands of them for his help. I'll not allow that lowly dog to disrespect your body, sister." Shafiqu snapped as she allowed her face to display the anger she felt in her heart for the Elder.

Shafiqu's remark brought a smile to her lips as she replied. "Fear not for how the foolish infidel will treat my body. I assure you, with the gift I'll place at his feet, enjoying a woman's treasures will be the last thought in the old man's mind." Another laugh and she continued speaking. "I tell you to fear not for me, I heard the many foul stories about the old Village Elder. He'll have no success with me I assure you my sister."

"Be that as it may Ayesha, Sadiya and myself will accompany you to the old Elder's home. Errr..., would you be so kind as to inform me of what this gift you found in the desert might be, you said it came from Allah's Hand." Shafiqu asked while fishing around for information.

"I have no problem telling you what this gift is, if I knew what it is. The only thing I can tell you for certain is, it's a weapon that might erase the cursed invaders of our country in one wave of Allah's powerful Hand. That's all I can tell you about this gift. I believe it was offered to me through Allah's great wisdom, and it might be the only weapon we have powerful enough to attack the lowly infidels who rule our country under the guise of offering the peoples of Iraq freedom. All we have done is trade one mass evil for another, we lost President Saddam Hussein, and he was replaced by the massive numbers of hated American soldiers, and they're more of a threat to Iraq's future than President Hussein ever was. Come with me my sister, I'll get out of these filthy rags and dress in proper clothes to visit the foolish Elder.

"Once I'm dressed, we'll request a visit with the old fool of the village. I heard he likes women properly dressed in his presence, if a respectful Arab woman will ever be honored by the old man and his evil ways. I know he'll make us jump through hoops before we're allowed a visit. He believes he's that important to the pulse of Iraq's future. We'll humor the old man to draw his vast knowledge and help on how and where we'll employ this great weapon against all enemies of Iraq. Come my sisters, we'll shower and change into the correct clothes for our visit to the great fool. I hate to tell my sisters, but you two are as filthy as I feel. I don't believe you changed your clothes for as long as I. Come, we have to prepare for our visit with the old fool." Ayesha got up from the table invigorated by the strength of freeing Iraq from the occupational American soldiers, and the woman rushed for her bedroom.

When she entered her bedroom, she pulled her clothes from her body and once naked, she rushed to the bathroom and took a quick shower. She scrubbed her body, feeling the sand from the desert had permeated ever pour of her silk like skin. She washed her long hair and got out of the shower and dried herself. As she headed for her bedroom with just a towel around her exquisite body, she passed Shafiqu who was naked and heading for her shower.

"My foolish sister of the desert, you better be a little more careful when walking around my home like that, Shafiqu. You must remember that I have five nosy and very foolish brothers, and any one of them would do anything to see you naked like this, my sister." Ayesha warned her favorite sister as she slapped her on her naked rump, which caused her to shake her rearend back at her, and giggle as she rushed by her to shower.

The slap made Shafiqu remarked. "I have news for you my foolish sister who now thinks she's all powerful. I'm certain your worthless brothers saw me naked more than once in their foul and wasted lives. This is not the first time I showered in your home."

"Ohhhh, you're more evil than I believed, my devilish sister." Ayesha added as she left Shafiqu and entered her bedroom to get dressed. The women knew her brothers left for work hours before. When she entered her bedroom, she smiled at Sadiya who was topless, and laid out the clothes she felt she should dress in for her visit with the Elder.

Ayesha could not take her eyes off Sadiya's outstanding body, her lovely skin was absolutely flawless, and had the lovely olive hue Arab women of the Middle East enjoyed. Her breasts were perfect with no hint of sag, her waist small. Sadiya was a perfect woman to be enjoyed by some lucky Iraqi male. She had to shake her head to break the trance Sadiya's exquisite body enveloped her in. When her head was cleared, she announced. "Sadiya, let me see what you prepared for me for my visit with the foul Elder. He's such an evil old man."

"I chose the clothes I believe should impress the old fool, and make his mouth water at the same time, seeing what he's unable to enjoy." Sadiya offered proudly.

Ayesha walked to the bed as she allowed the towel to fall free of her body, and she bent over the bed and picked up the blouse Sadiya picked out for her. Looking at it she became embarrassed by the blouse, it was one of few she owned that displayed her charms, while allowing her a semblance of decency. She looked to Sadiya and announced. "Wow Sadiya, I would've never picked out this blouse to wear before the old fool. I'll have to be extra cautious if I have to bow to the old fool, if I'm not careful his eyes will see what I keep sacred for my future husband. If I'm going to wear that blouse, I'll have to wear my Kajubas (Black hooded body cover) to hide myself."

"You'll have to wear your Kajubas anyhow my foolish sister, or you'll never be allowed an audience with the old fool. Ayesha, you have to remember Sameer Abdalsada is a faithful follower of the Sunni belief, and as such he demands all respected Iraqi woman to wear the Kajubas. I know of at least one time where the old fool ordered the death of a woman by stoning, because she wasn't properly dressed in her Kajubas, and she was foolish enough to allow the top of her knee to be exposed to all who saw her. As much as the old man enjoys looking at young woman, he firmly believes in our sacred religion, and anyone who violates his beliefs will suffer a long and painful time, sister."

"Huh, I can't figure out the mind of a male. On one hand the fool loves to see women naked. On the other, he'll condemn any woman he sees exposing skin he enjoys viewing in private. One day, Iraq will come out of the Stone Age and allow their women to dress the way they want. I believe if you have weapons to melt a man's mind, employ them in the war of love." Ayesha offered as she struggled into the tight fitting blouse. She was rebel enough to go without her bar.

Sadiya laughed with Ayesha and when Shafiqu finished her shower and entered the bedroom, she laughed, even though she had no idea what she was laughing about. All she knew was her two young friends were in a great mood and this made her happy. She was likewise wrapped in just a towel and she announced with a smile. "Sadiya the shower is free and you have to properly prepare if you're coming to see the Elder with us."

The three dressed but Ayesha was stalling slightly. She did not want to alarm her friends, but she was fearful meeting the Elder. She did not know how he was going to react to her discovery, she had concern maybe he might be furious, especially when she informs him how she suspected was the caused the death of Saad. She wondered if the old man might blame her for the child's death and order her stoned, or he might be so angry he could turn her over to the hated American soldiers as a special punishment for her sins committed over the past days. She wondered if the Village Elder might even get angry with her two friends for daring to want to go against the invasion forces occupying Iraq. She did not know how he felt about the hated Americans.

Her mind was racing, fearing how the Elder might react to her and what she was doing. Her fears stopped her from leaving and zapping her confidence she was doing the right thing, and want to avenge what the American soldiers did to her Father in the United States. Her want for revenge was her sole driving force, now she was afraid her overpowering want for revenge might turn her entire village against her.

Shafiqu noticed the slight hesitation in Ayesha's actions and this raised concern in her and Sadiya. Shafiqu allowed her excitement to wan and now she found herself staring at Ayesha, trying to figure out what was causing this change in her friend's actions. Drawing in her breath, Shafiqu asked. "Ayesha, what changed your enthusiasm visiting the worthless old fool?"

She shook her head to clear her mind so she could reply. "I fear we might not be doing the right thing after all. I'm the one who caused the death of the young Saad, and the Elder might not like that when I tell him about the child's death. I fear he might turn me over to the cursed American soldiers so they could melt out their justice against me."

"I don't understand you and this foolishness you're displaying before my eyes, Ayesha. Why on Allah's earth would the old fool condemn you for what you're trying to accomplish for the sake of Iraq? Paradise knows the worthless fool is doing nothing to rid Iraq of the hated American invaders. I know the old fool hates these lowly infidels who patrol the heart of Iraq as if this is Allah's given right for the American jackals to do so. Fear not my foolish sister I know the old fool will honor what you're trying to do for our country and her children's sake. Come Ayesha, I believe the time for hesitation is over, and we must place one foot before the other on the sands of our homeland, and meet with the Elder and seek his wisdom and guidance in what we're doing for the sake of Iraq." Shafiqu stared in the eyes of Ayesha as she waited for a reply.

Letting her breath out in a rush, she gave in to her fears and she told her friend in a shaking tone. "Shafiqu, I don't know what would become of me and my foolishness, if I didn't have you standing behind and guiding this worthless woman and keep me on the path or righteousness. You're right sister this is not the time to start doubting myself, or what we plan for the future of Iraq and what we plan to do against the invaders of our country. We have to go, but you have to wait until I retrieve my gift from Allah to show the old man we mean business.

"The gift from Allah has given me the strength to attack the foul Americans, and it's the only thing I can offer the Elder that'd make him want to help us with our plans against the loathsome invaders. If I walk before the old fool empty handed, he'll refuse to see us and the gift of Allah's will be wasted, I have no idea how to use it properly against the infidels occupying our country. In my heart I believe this gift would've been forever lost if Saad didn't happen across it hidden in the desert. It's like my Father always told me while he was fighting the enemy's of Iraq.

"Nothing in this world happens, unless Allah places His mighty Hand on what He wants us to do for His glory. If Saad brought this gift to me, it was by Allah's will he discover it, little sister. Yes Shafiqu, I believe you're most correct with the words of wisdom you offer to my worthless ears. It's time we leave and seek an audience with the leader of our village. Allah might take back His great gift if I don't try and use it as He deems fit, to free his Sunni children from the yoke of oppression the cowardly infidels looped so tightly over the necks of Allah's children of Iraq. Come, we must leave and visit the old fool before he leaves his home, and we'll not be able to visit with him for who knows how long, once he's gone from his dwelling. Are we ready to leave, I know I am."

THE SMALL VILLAGE OF AR-RAMIDI

Ayesha al-Qaysi rushed in her bedroom and stopped in her tracks, and she found herself staring at the gleaming metal cylinder of death. Fighting off her sudden fear of the cylinder and the death it contained, she picked it up and cradled it in her arms. Once she had the cylinder securely in her arms, she left her bedroom and walked out of her home with her two friends leading the way for her, but not before she covered the cylinder with a scarf.

The beautiful Iraqi women walked down the block heading for the Village Elder's home. It was the best kept building in the entire town. It took them five minutes to arrive, and Ayesha found her way blocked by an armed and angry looking man who growled savagely at her.

"What in the devil do you three evil women want here?"

Ayesha stepped out before the other women and replied in a trembling voice to the guard. "I'd like to have an audience with the Village Elder, sir."

"Be gone lazy woman, the Elder has no time to waste on the likes of you." The guard snarled.

"Sir, it's extremely important I see the Village Elder. I found something I…"

"I just told you the Elder has no time to waste on you, foul woman. Be gone with you before I plant my boot on your rearend. The three of you, go now sharmoota (bitch)!"

"Sir I must insist I see the Village Elder, sir. It's important that I see…"

A second man appeared at the door after hearing the guard snapping at someone outside. He placed his hand on the guard's back to silence him as he got in the conversation. "What is it that's so important that you three women wish to disturb the Elder over? He's a very busy man looking after the many problems happening in this foul town, young woman."

"Sir, we found something the Elder must see, sir." Ayesha pleaded with the other man.

"What is it you have, woman? That better not be a weapon. Show me at once before I have the guard do what he threatened to do to you, young woman."

She uncovered the cylinder, and the instant the second man saw what she carried, he reacted by crying out and stepping back. "By the sacred gray beard of the Prophet, bring that foul thing behind the building and wait for the Elder there. You, you'll escort the women behind the Elder's home and shoot the fools if they run. You'll shoot anyone who dares to come near these three women and yourself, fool."

The second man disappeared back in the building and by the time the women and guard walked behind the Elder's home, the Elder and second man was already waiting for them. The second man was Mustafa Abdalhadi, an ex-General in the Republican Guard for Saddam Hussein's once feared guard units, and he was an active officer in Saddam Hussein's Mukhabarat Intelligence Service. General Mustafa Abdalhadi was well acquainted with the weapon held in her shaking arms. The guard stopped walking and went in a stance where he could shoot any of the women if they displayed a threat against the old man waiting for them.

The Village Elder Sameer Abdalsada stood with Mustafa, and the moment he saw Ayesha, he snarled at her. "Young woman, remove that rag from your cursed shoulders. If what you carry is what I think it is. You're no longer to act like the rest of the women of this village. I believe you're a warrior for our cause, and you were chosen by the Almighty hand of Allah, woman."

Her face flushed red as she placed the cylinder on the table to her right then she struggled out of the heavy Kajubas. She knew the silk blouse she had on under the robe left very little to the imagination, and she was going to be offering the men a show of her treasures. Once she was out of the black robe and hood, she picked up the cylinder, she was trying to use it to hide herself behind. To her surprise, none of the men showed the slightest bit of interest in seeing her body, because they were staring at the metal cylinder locked in her arms.

"By the sacred sands of Mecca, where on Allah's great earth did you ever find this weapon, daughter of the desert? I heard and saw this weapon when I was an active General for President Hussein in the Republican Guard. I never allowed myself to believe this weapon would ever surface since the American soldiers had invaded and destroyed our country. Here, place the cylinder on the table so I might open and see if what it is, still rests in its place." The Elder ordered Ayesha with surprising strength in his voice.

She followed the old man's orders and the moment the cylinder was on the table, he moved in and opened it like he was well acquainted with the cylinder as he suggested. Once the protective sphere was released from its lock down clamp, Sameer very cautiously lifted the metal cylinder cover and when the bottle and stand was cleared of the cover, Sameer released his breath as he proudly announced. "By the endless grains of sand in the vast desert, it's here. Mustafa, see, you see the weapon I spoke to you about many times in the past. It is here, brought home by this woman to our cause." Abdalsada turned to the women and offered her. "Ayesha is the name given you by your Father. My daughter, do you have any idea what you have returned to me? I can't believe you found this great weapon, woman."

She allowed her arms to move away from her chest, she no longer cared about what the men might see of her body. She was more interested in the cylinder and the strange effect it was having on the old man. She looked in his eyes as she answered. "Elder Sameer Abdalsada, I have no idea what I brought to you sir."

"Well daughter, allow me to explain to you. Ayesha, you might have brought Iraq's freedom. Young woman, this is what you have discovered here. Ayesha, years ago, President Saddam Hussein issued orders for our medical technicians to develop a new weapon of mass destruction for military use. A weapon that would only attack and eliminate the impure race of the worthless Persian people, this great weapon was meant to be designed as "The Sword Of God", the ultimate weapon to be employed by our military against our enemy. It was supposed to have the same power as the Hand of Almighty Allah.

"It was said if this weapon was ever released against Iraq's hated enemy the Iranian's, it'd be the same as if Allah Himself has raised His great Hand against the nation of Iran. Then by merely closing His fist on the worthless throats of the Persians, Iran would no longer exist on the face of the earth. This is the product of that order. With this weapon in our hands, we can release it against Iran as was Saddam Hussein's wish, before he was slaughtered by the American military. The mass deaths this weapon will cause to that foul land of dog eaters will demand every other nation would have to commit their lifesaving efforts, to save some of the cursed Iranian bastards from their foul fate of death.

"This unbelievable weapon will force the god cursed infidels to pull their non-believing soldiers from our lands, and once gone from our country. The Sunni faithful with the help of Arabia, will mass together as one military force, and take our country back from the fool of a non-believer placed as our leader of Iraq by the American politicians and their military forces.

"The fool in command of Iraq is of Iranian Ancestry, and this weapon will kill him and his lowly offspring, and anyone born of impure Iranian blood. It'll purge the ah-Basrah Province and the rest of Iraq of all dog eating Shiite fools, descendents from the Persian infected race. My daughter of the desert, this weapon will not attack any member of pure Arab race. As you know, the Persians are not of the Arab race, they're mix-bred bastards. What a stroke of luck for you to have found this weapon.

"Where did you find it Ayesha, you must walk with the hand of Allah protectively on your shoulder, you brought this weapon to me without suffering the ill effects from its deadly wrath." Village Elder Sameer Abdalsada stopped speaking to give Ayesha a chance to reply.

"Village Elder Sameer Abdalsada, my quest to bring this item home was not without death wrapped around its feet. It has cost the life of a very brave young child Saad Ihsaan, sir." She replied as she shifted the weight from one foot to the other

"Saad Ihsaan, yes Saad, Saad, Saad, he was the young troublemaker who'd steal the fillings of your teeth if he had half the chance, woman. Yes, I remember a report I read that announced the child was missing from the village. I had no idea he died during your quest, Ayesha." The old man offered while displaying little interest in the missing child. Over the years of occupation of American Forces, many children male and female disappeared from villages of Iraq.

"Elder Sameer Abdalsada, you're not angry for my being the cause of death of Saad Ihsaan, sir?" She asked while fearing the elder's reply.

"Blame you for the little foul troublemaker's death. Ayesha, the death of Saad is no great loss to our village or country. I say this to you Ayesha the death of this entire village would be no great loss as long as this mighty weapon was brought back into the arms of Sunni possession. It's the salvation of our nation, and the key to our freedom from the lowly infidels who have invaded our country and will not leave. I'd trade a thousand, even a million Saad Ihsaan's worthless lives for possession of this great weapon. I ask you again where you found this weapon, and is this all of the weapon where you found it, Ayesha?" Village Elder Sameer Abdalsada snapped angrily at her as he held her in his angry glare.

"Elder Abdalsada, I wasn't the one who found the mysterious cylinder that seems to cause you pleasure. It was Saad who originally found the item, he told me of the bunker constructed in the desert to our west. Saad was the one who brought me to the bunker, and lost his life to what was hidden in the cylinder after we discovered it hiding in the bunker, Elder Sameer Adbals..."

"Ebn el metanaka! (Sonofabitch) By the lowly creatures who wander the vast desert in the middle of the night in search of souls to feast their lust upon. Don't tell me you fools dared to open the container? May Paradise protect us if you fools were stupid enough to open the container to the air? It could be the cause of death to all if it's not properly deployed, foolish woman." Sameer growled as he picked up the glass container and cautiously rolled it in his shaking hands so he could check and see if any of the liquid was still trapped in its glass prison. A smile more a sneer slowly crossed the old man's lips when he noticed the amount of liquid still trapped inside the bottle.

"No Elder Abdalsada, we were not foolish enough to open the container to the air. I have no idea what was contained inside the cylinder, or how Saad became contaminated by this weapon. All I can tell you for certain is he was out to the bunker once, before he took me to it. Now, I can only imagine how he became contaminated by this weapon on his first visit to the bunker." She was trying to be overly respectful and polite by using the old man's title and name when addressing him. She was lying through her teeth, because she found a report about the weapon and understood the power contained within the liquid housed inside the cylinder.

The Village Elder replaced the glass container on its stand, and then set the cylinder top back in place to protect the weapon from accidents. Then he turned to the woman as he offered. "Ayesha, for some reason, Allah in his infinite wisdom chose you, a mere woman to be our savor of Iraq. You'll be the cause of releasing us from the suppressive yoke the hated American soldiers have placed around our necks, daughter. It's not for me to understand the confusing reason why Allah picked you to come to our aid. Since He chose you to free Iraq, it's my responsibility to protect you with all assets available. Ayesha, since Allah gave you this gift, it'll be yours to employ when I order it released against the enemy of our country, woman."

"Elder Abdalsada, I don't think of myself as a chosen child of Allah's love. If anyone was chosen to help Iraq through these terrible times we face against the lowly infidels. It was Saad, he was the first to lay down his life for our cause…" She offered, but her offering was cut off by the Elder as he growled at the woman standing before him so proudly.

"Foolish daughter, it's as I offered. If I say you were chosen by Allah to help Iraq rid herself of the jackal invaders! That is what you'll be and you'll not argue the point further with me. What good would it do if we honor a known troublemaker who wasted his foolish young life stealing goods and food from hard working Iraqi families of this village, woman? The child's dead and he's where he should be. I warn you foolish woman, you'll follow my orders faithfully, or you'll find yourself joining that worthless child in the grave." The Elder bulked up his body and sort of towered over Ayesha as he glared at her and he waited for the woman to acknowledge what he just ordered of her and her friends.

She backed down from the Elder's anger as she hung her head in shame for causing him anger, and mumbled just above a whisper. "Yes Elder Abdalsada, it must be as you say."

"I'm pleased you understand, getting back to the matters at hand. I'm honor bound to protect your life as Allah's chosen leader, and I'll do that." The Elder turned to General Abdelhadi.

"General Mustafa Abdalhadi, I command you to get in contact with the insurgent forces waiting their chance to act against our hated enemy in the surrounding villages. We have to understand it's only a matter of time before some hated American jackals show up in our village in search of what we have in our possession, General Abdalhadi. We have to protect this great weapon and this woman of respect, General. I want you to make contact with our forces waiting to attack the lowly infidels in the villages of Karbalh, Samarra, Baqubah and especially Fallujah, General Abdalhadi.

"In Fallujah, I know there are at least three hundred ex-soldiers biting their time in hopes we'll mount an assault against these infidels to our land. The rest will send any able bodied male warrior who can pick up a rifle and defend this woman and our weapon. General Abdalhadi, you know who you have to make contact with, so the other Elders of those villages will send the help we need. General Abdalhadi, make your contacts and have the other villages send help, sir." The old man held the Iraqi General in his harsh gaze until he turned on his heels and headed off to carry out his orders.

When the General was out of sight, the elder turned to Ayesha and remarked. "Ayesha, I'll maintain control of the gift Almighty Allah placed in your path. I'll maintain control of the weapon until it's employed for our cause. Once we learn what Allah has in mind for us, you'll be his implement that'll set free Iraq of all god cursed infidels who invaded our lands.

"I know with help of our faithful brothers of the Sunni religion in Saudi Arabia, we'll have no problem defeating the cursed infidels who overran our country, and dared to hang President Saddam Hussein as if he was a criminal. I don't know what the future has in store, with Allah's light protecting you you'll be successful in any endeavor He places before your footfalls. Ayesha, I offer you the protection of this fine Iraqi soldier. He's a proven warrior and has strong connections with al-Qaeda of Iraq, and if we need added assistance, he'll be the one who'll get it for us. His name's Mugtada al-Sistani and he'll die at his post rather than allow any harm to befall your shoulders, Ayesha."

The old Eelder looked at the soldier he was speaking about and replied with a slight nod and then he went on with his words. "Ayesha, you have the makings of your own protective ring about you I see. I noticed how the women with you, protect you from any wrath. This is good to understand. At least I'll know you have women surrounding you, so you're not only ringed with male protectors. A woman needs some of her own to protect her during these troubling times our country's inflicted with. I order you to return to your home and wait there for word from me. Mugtada will post himself outside your home, and stop anyone from bothering or threatening you in any manner. He's now your protector also.

"Make no mistake about it Ayesha, Mugtada understands if anything happens to you under his protect. It'll not only cost him but his family their worthless lives for his failure to protect you at all costs. In fact Ayesha, I'll order your Mother and her sons out of the home, and you and these two young women will share the home until I have further need of you and this weapon of importance. If we get word the worthless infidels are approaching our village to search it, you and these women will be moved to another village, or a secret place until the hated infidels give up their search for you and this weapon, Ayesha.

If you're forced out of this village, you'll take command of the weapon and protect it until I order you to release the evil vapor against our enemy, the loathsome Persian fools. By the sacred breath of Allah, we'll take control of our country from the occupying forces currently our evil masters.

"Ayesha, you will obey all my orders as if they came from Allah Himself. I have other things I have to prepare for and take command of, and that means I have no further time to waste on you. Mugrada, escort these three women to their home and they'll remain in the foul place until I instruct you otherwise. You'll order the Mother and her sons and daughters out of the home. I'll send someone with you, and he'll bring the Mother and her children to her new home, Mugrada. Be gone with you now so I can get my plans in operation." The old man snapped as he suddenly flung his hand in the air, crudely dismissing them.

Mugtada saluted the old man with his Kalashnikov AK 47 assault rifle, and then he took a step to his right and motioned the three women with his weapon to leave. Proudly, Mugrada walked down the street with the women until they entered their home and he took up his position of guard duty at their front door of the small structure.

THE UNDERGROUND BUNKER IN THE IRAQI DESERT

Captain Robert Walker had his specialized troops acting like a well oiled machine. The soldiers picked to relieve the CIA Operatives took positions, and the others ordered to be the defensive security ring around the bunker, were set in place and ready to defend their positions against any possible attack. Walker was surrounded with the soldiers he trusted most.

Colonel Leadbetter was making his first entry in the underground Iraqi bunker, and he was being accompanied by Agent Stockten, and just like Stockten, the Marine Colonel refused to put on his protective clothing and separate breathing apparatus. At first, he was going to get in his gear, but when he noticed the special agent was prepared to enter the bunker without his gear, he decided to be as foolish as the agent, and go in with his uniform for protection. He refused to be showed up by the spook.

Walker noticed what the well respected Marine Colonel was doing and he smiled, because he knew why he was taking such a foolish chance that could cost him his life. He refused the offer to accompany the Colonel and agent into the underground chamber, saying he had to make certain the rest of his troop were set in place, and the Colonel brought the excuse for Walker not entering the bunker.

Walker was no fool and he understood all the concerns dealing with this biological weapon, and he was not going to take any chances with his life unless it was absolutely necessary. Sergeant Dorothy Ramirez was by his side, happy that he refused to enter the Iraqi bunker with the Colonel and CIA Agent. She realized he did it because he knew she would be extremely upset with him if he followed the Colonel inside the bunker, even if he had his protective gear on. She took his hand in hers and gave it a gently squeeze, and when he looked at her, she smiled at her soldier. He returned her smile and turned his attention back to what the rest of his soldiers were up to around the once hidden bunker.

Colonel Leadbetter allowed the agent to lead him around the bunker and explain everything they discovered and where they found it. The Colonel could not hide the fact he was bored by the agent's lengthily presentation, and when he saw and heard enough and where the weapon was resting on the table, he barked at the special agent to go outside so they could talk without the dangers that might be stalking the interior of the complex.

The Colonel allowed the agent to lead him out of the bunker, and once they were outside the complex, he waved Walker over to him so he could hear what the agent had to offer them.

Captain Walker, Lieutenant Hall and Sergeant Ramirez walked over to their commander, and they ripped off a fine salute. This angered the Colonel and he snapped at the trio. "How many god damn times do I have to tell you people never to salute me in the field? You people are pushing me over the god damn falls. I can't get any of you pack rats to salute me when we're on base where it matters, but you squirrels want to salute my ass out in the field where you might identify my ass as a commander, and mark me for death from a sniper."

Colonel Leadbetter stared at the soldiers until he felt he made his point then he informed them why he wanted them by his side. "Walker, we'll finish this conversation later when we have more time to speak about this shit. Right now, I want you birds to pay attention to what Stockten has to say. Once he finishes his report, you'll gather the personnel for your unit, and you'll deploy by means of the Humvees to the second position where the other Agents found the body of the

Iraqi kid. I want you people to check that area out, maybe the CIA Operatives missed something important. Walker, you have to remember we have Agents out there with helicopters, searching for the crap we want. That's the reason I want you people to the other site Captain, so you can relieve the Spooks and commandeer their helicopters if you have need for air movement.

"Walker, we have to assume control over this mission, and locate all remains of the bug juice we're looking for. Time's critical on this mission. Better yet, Lieutenant Hall, why the hell don't you move your ass over to the Humvees and get your people ready to ship out the moment I'm finished speaking with Walker and Ramirez, that way we can save time, dammit. Get a move on it before I kick you in the ass." Colonel Leadbetter snapped at the Mutt because he was staring at Walker like he was waiting for him to issue orders to him.

Captain Robert Walker shifted his eyes over to the Mutt and made a swift head movement. That was enough and the Mutt took off to carry out his orders from the Colonel. Walker's commander noticed the movement and this angered him and he growled at his Captain in front of the special agent. "What the fuck was that shit about? You people better realize I'm the Commander and lead dog in this rat race, and it's what I say that goes. You better have a frigging talk with your people and clue them in on that fact, so it's crystal clear in their minds, Walker. If I issue an order and these shitbirds look to you before they carry them out. It's not going to be long before you find yourself out of this damn outfit, and me taking over command of these popping jaybirds. There's another conversation we're going to settle when we have more time to hash this shit out, Walker."

Walker looked at his commander and smiled, he realized the officer was making a show for the CIA Agent. He knew the Colonel would never drive him out of the outfit under any circumstances. The Colonel was the one grooming him to take over command once he decided to retire from the Corps, and besides he was in with General White for anyone to be powerful enough to cause him problems where he might be drummed out of the Special Forces.

"You better wipe that damn grin off your stinking puss before I wipe it off for you. Arrr… you people will be the death of me yet. Okay Walker, agent Stockten has a number of important points to go over with you, and he'll give you the location where his people discovered the body of that Iraqi kid. I'm going to leave you in his hands, I'll check in with General White, and inform him we linked up with the Spooks. When Agent Stockten's done with you people, you'll report to me for further orders." The Colonel turned back to the CIA Agent and nodded slight at him then he walked over to the caravan of humvees he brought his people out to the desert in.

Agent Stockten did not waste anymore of his time with going over everything his people had discovered hidden inside the bunker, and where they found the body of the dead Iraqi kid. He also informed the Captain and Sergeant of the danger this weapon threatened the world with. Once he finished his presentation, he announced that was all he had. He took time to inform Walker if his medics came up with information about this biological weapon, and how it kills the host once they finished their autopsy of the child's body.

Walker smiled at the CIA Agent and put out his hand and he and the agent shook, he then informed him he was going to report to his commander then he and his soldiers were going to leave for the second location in the desert. Stockten watched them head for their Colonel. When they were out of ear shot, the agent got on his people. He did not want them hanging around without anything to do after they were relieved of duty by these Marines. To the agent's surprise, the colonel did not draft the Marines who accompanied them when they discovered the bunker.

As they walked together, Sergeant Ramirez remarked to her lover. "Robert, for that man being a Spook, he seems like a man concerned for our well being. After the initial confrontation between you and him when we first showed up here, I thought he was going to be a bear to work with. I hope I'm not forced to change my mind about the Spooks, Robert."

"Fuck that shit, Spooks are Spooks and they're never to be trusted by any Marine. Any time you feel yourself starting to feel sorry for them pricks, all you gotta do is remember how many Marines were drafted by Spooks and never came home on a shared mission with them bastards. Hey baby we betta get a step on it, the Colonel's already mad dogging our asses." Walker pointed out the obviously fuming officer with his chin and they increased their speed.

Colonel Leadbetter was waiting with his hands resting on his hips as he glared at the soldiers walking towards him. When Walker and Ramirez walked up to their commander, the Colonel started in on them again. "You two shit sacks were walking like you had a damn piano weighing your asses down, damn. Didn't I tell you shitbirds time was of the essence on this mission? Arrr... fuck it, Walker this soldier to my left is Colonel Mark Pullman, he's on loan to us from the Airforce, and he's your acting ATO or Air Tasking Officer. He's the dude responsible for calling in air assets we might need on this mission, Captain. Walker, I'm giving you this man in perfect working order, and I expect him to be returned in the same condition."

Colonel Pullman's eyebrows arched as he turned his head and stared at the Colonel, trying to see what he meant by his last remark. Colonel Leadbetter picked up the look and snapped. "Colonel Pullman, we've been loaned other Officers and doctors for our missions, and this man and the rest of his lunatics corrupted outstanding Officers and doctors alike, until those people acted like his gombas, and they became wastes to their chosen field, sir. I assure you Colonel you're hooking your wagon to the best fighting unit in the services. If you're attached to these people, you stand the best chance of returning from your mission alive and intact. So wipe the dumb look off your puss and be thankful for linking up with my people, sir."

"Colonel Leadbetter, before I was assigned to your soldiers, I took the time to go over a number of your soldier's personal 201 files, when I was informed I was to be attached to your outfit. I read some operations your people were on sir. Colonel, I'm proud and honored to be a part of these fine young soldiers, sir." Colonel Pullman nodded to the other Colonel in acknowledgement of his soldier's outstanding fighting abilities.

"Yeah, well you can save it for the people who give a fuck about that kind of shit, Colonel Pullman. In my outfit, there's not one soldier in this thing for personal gains, recognition or glory, sir. My soldiers do what they're ordered without question or regard. They get in there and neutralize the situation and disappear as quickly as they entered the kill zone. We're classified as the Shadow Soldiers of the Marines. Dammit look at me for the love of the Christ Child I'm beginning to sound like a damn TV commercial, Colonel Pullman. Anyway Walker, did you find out the info you need from Stockten to formulate a working scenario, when you assholes start to make your way out to where the Spooks found the body of that kid?"

"Yes Sir Colonel Leadbetter, Agent Stockten was very helpful and forthcoming with giving us a detailed rundown on where and what we're facing when we get out to the second location, sir." Walker replied as he maintained eye contact with the Colonel. He was also sizing Pullman up, trying to see if he had balls to make it in his unit.

"Yeah? I wonder what that damn popinjay has up his fricking sleeve, Captain Walker. I've never known any damn CIA Agent being very forward with advice for us grunts. Never mind him for the time being Walker, I'll keep my eye on his ass and if he tries to hang us out to dry, he'll be the first to bit the bullet. You worry about getting out to the second location. I have a gut feeling it's where we're going to find, or get the lead we need to find the missing weapon, and the one who was with the Iraqi kid that died."

"Colonel Leadbetter, Agent Stockten informed me his medics were still working on the kid. He also informed me he'd keep us apprised if they discover anything on how this bug killer does its work. As far as I know Colonel, all we were given for protection against this biological strain was a carry shot of adrenalin, a lot of good that'll do against this crap. How long do you think it'll take if the Spook medics to find a way to protect us from this weapon, if they discover how it works, kills and how to stop the damn thing from doing its act, sir?" Walker asked.

Colonel Leadbetter let his breath out in a rush before responding to Walker's question. He took a moment to formulate his thoughts and then he offered. "Look Walker, I don't want you to concern yourself with that crap. You just worry about finding this shit and get it to me safe and sound. That way you won't have to worry about anything else on this mission, Captain."

Walker realized the Colonel was dancing around his question, and he was not going to let it go that easy. He was concerned over this bug killer because he and Ramirez were speaking about having another child, and he did not want this weapon affecting an unborn child of his. This though gave him the strength to challenge his commander for a more definite answer to his last question as he nearly barked at his commander. "Not for nuthin Colonel Leadbetter, I didn't hear a positive response to my question. In case you didn't understand what I asked Colonel. I wanted to know how long it might take if the medics are able to discover an antidote to this shit, to get it in our hands for this operation." He allowed his stare to sharpen until he was almost glaring.

Without thinking about it, Leadbetter's temper got the best of him because of the way his Captain just challenged him. He growled at Walker savagely for forcing him in this conversation he did not want to get involved. "God damn you to hell and back Walker. What do you want from my ass? How can I answer a question I have no answer for? You know damn well how I hate to be backed in a corner, and you pushed me against the wall. Walker, I know how you and the rest of our soldiers feel when it comes to another bug hunt as you people call these missions. We have our duty and we will carry out this mission under the circumstances, even if it costs the lives of every soldier. Walker, don't concern yourself about any possible antidote for the…"

"Why Colonel Leadbetter? Why should Walker not concern himself over the development of any antidote to this weapon? Colonel Leadbetter, if we have to put our asses on the line for this mission I want, no correct that. I demand every possible protection to be employed if we're going to be exposed to this weapon." Sergeant Ramirez growled at her commanding officer as she placed her hands on her hips and openly glared at her commander.

The Colonel's face flushed over Sergeant Ramirez's remark and he roared. "You demand! You demand! You demand shit from me, sister!

Anytime you want to demand anything from me, you better be willing to back it up with your body, soldier. You don't demand anything, if anything, you own me sister. Well look at this line of shit coming from you? Sergeant Ramirez, the always high and mighty female warrior Sergeant who just yesterday challenged me for ordering what shots to be issued that we have to try and protect us against this bug problem. That was you back there at Pope bitching like hell for ordering you people to accept the shots we have against this shit, wasn't it Ramirez?" He was actually taunting the female Sergeant because he wanted to get Walker's mind off the effects of this weapon.

"You know damn well that was me complaining about those damn shots, Colonel."

"Well little miss can't be wrong over there, what the hell changed your mind from yesterday to today about what we introduce in your body? What do you want from my ass for the love of God? First you don't want me to order protection against bug juice, now you're begging me for shots I don't have available, Sergeant. Consistency Ramirez, if you want to be the best soldier you can be, you need consistency, missy. If you change your mind over one decision then you can change your mind at perhaps the most critical time during any operation you're on, and that change might cause the death of you and any soldiers around you. Ramirez I want…"

"Colonel Leadbetter you can suck my Von Stucker for all I care. All your bull shitting and stalling isn't answering my last question, sir." Walker growled as he tried to get the Colonel off his girlfriend's back, because he did not like the way the Colonel was dumping on her.

The fuming Colonel Leadbetter spun around so he could face Walker head on, and his eyes narrowed to mere slits as he glared angrily at Walker with all the venom he could muster in his eyes. He was fighting his instants to rip Walker's head off his shoulders over the way he just spoke to him. The only thing holding him back was because he understood where Captain Walker and Sergeant Ramirez's concerns were coming from.

Colonel Pullman was taken back by the way the Captain was speaking to his Superior Officer. He was set to react against Walker when Colonel Leadbetter caught his reaction and he waved him off and he started to speak. "You better be a whole lot more careful in the way you're addressing my ass in fucking conversation we're carrying out, Captain. You even got Colonel Pullman upset enough and he was going to jump in on this mess you created. Walker, the only reason you're still breathing because of the way you're disrespecting me, is because I have no answer for your ass at this particular moment.

"Walker, this isn't the first mission we've been sent out on where the Ace, King, Queen, Jack, and Ten was stacked up against us, and it's not going to be the last one either I assure you, sir. Walker, the only thing I can tell you for certain is, no matter what the Spook medics come up with in their examination of that dead kid's ass, it won't do us a lick of fucking good. By the time they come up with a working antidote to this shit. This mission better and will be over and we'll either have all remaining product of this shit locked up safe and sound in our control, Captain. Or each and every one of the soldiers sent on this messed up operation will be dead. That's the only two finalities you and the rest of your soldiers can bank on, Walker." Colonel Leadbetter looked at Walker, and shrugged his shoulders.

When there was no response from Walker, Colonel Leadbetter turned to Sergeant Ramirez. He was looking for some kind of reaction from either soldier he was trying to talk sense into, before they panic the other soldiers. What he did not realize was the fact many soldiers picked up the confrontation going on between the officers, and they were paying close attention to what was going on between them. Both Walker and Ramirez were bringing up the same concerned the rest of the soldiers were disturbed over.

From the corner of his eye, the wise and ever alert Colonel Leadbetter, easily picked up the many faces of the other soldiers, and he realized he had to get control over the situation before he had a mutiny on his hands with the rest of the other soldiers refusing to go out on this latest bug hunt. Drawing in a huge gulp of air, the Colonel barked at the soldiers from his specialized units. "What the fuck do you shit bags call this crap? I don't remember relieving any of you Squids from assigned duties or responsibilities on this damn operation. What are you fucking people looking at me for, dammit? You people know what you have to do, so get to it.

"Dammit to hell, are we now a bunch of nosy ass girls you people have to stop what you were doing, so you pack of shitbirds can hear me ripping Walker a new asshole? If that's what you people have come down to in my beloved Corps, I'll order each one of you soldiers and killers to strip out of your damn uniforms, and I'll have crates of pink poke-e-dot dresses air dropped for you once feared killers to fucking wear on your sissy little asses. Until I can have the lot of you shipped back to the States where I can have you Sectioned Fifteen with a shitload of bad paper out of my beloved Corps.

"If you born again killers want to act like a bunch of cackling hens with nothing better to do with your damn time, but to stare at me with your damn mouths opened like a bunch of shit civilians. I'll have you people dressed like a bunch of hens, not soldiers for Christ sake. You people called yourselves fucking killers? Arrr… the hell with it, I'd trade the whole fucking lot of you assholes in for two good looking girl scouts who'll follow orders without hesitation. You people better get back to your damn work before I order all you nosy ass girls shot on general principals. All I want to see is assholes and elbows from you fucking people. Get back to work before I take some shots at you people!"

Colonel Leadbetter's stinging words were still echoing when he turned to Ramirez and Walker, and bitched at them in a seething voice. He was trying to defuse the confrontation between them as he hissed. "Do you two shitbirds see what the fuck you caused with these troops for God's sake? Dammit Walker, you two ball sacks have to understand most of these assholes don't know any better, they look to you two for some unknown reason to my ass but they do for their leadership and decision making.

"When this pack of screaming squirrels wasting their time seeing you birds questioning my abilities to command this unit, and busting my fucking horns in any fashion before this rip rap. They think we're starting to come apart at the seams and I can't blame them for this thought. Walker, I don't mind you questioning some orders if you disagree with them, or they go against your grain. As long as you question them in private, so the other soldiers don't hear your bitch.

"I can't accept having your ass challenging me in front of the troops. Walker, I'm warning you one last time, if you question my command abilities in front of the troops again, I'll have you discharged from the service with a shitload of bad paper to go with you then you can waste your fucking life in any way you chose. Remember while I command your ass, Captain Walker. No one soldier is that important to this special unit of soldiers. Any one soldier can be replaced at the drop of a hat around here, if he screws up or challenges my ass, and that includes your ass. It's about time you realize your shit does stink, soldier. Now soldier, I believe this conversation has run its course to its conclusion, and you and the Sergeant here have duties to carry out before you deploy to your next station of responsibility of this operation, Captain Walker!"

Walker was about to jump on the Colonel because he was not done with his bitch. When Sergeant Ramirez rested her hand on his elbow to get his attention, Walker turned to her and looked in her pleading eyes and noticed the silent warning from her to let it go.

Ramirez shook her head no at him and Walker knew the battle with the Colonel was over at this point. He returned the smile of his lover as his shoulders and muscles in his back relaxed. With a nod to the Colonel, Walker gave in to his orders.

"That's what I thought Captain. You made a life saving decision sir. Now Captain Hot Shot, I suggest you take command of these soldiers who'll be accompanying your ass to the second location of this operation. I want your unit heading out there before it gets dark. As you're aware Captain, the desert is no place to be moving about when it's dark. There are enough things that can kill ya ass out there when you can see the damn things coming at ya. I hate to consider what would be lurking out there when you can't see the damn things. You have your orders Captain, so I suggest you and the troops carry them out as received, before I really get pissed with your ass and settle this conversation here and now, soldier." Colonel Leadbetter relaxed his angry stance as he tried to get control over Walker, and to show the rest of the specialized soldiers under his command there was no problem between the two officers.

The Airforce Colonel Mark Pullman offered the words that broke up the tension of the moment between the other officers when he grumbled. "Colonel Leadbetter, your Captain Walker seems to be a rather excitable chap, sir. The Captain had me going there for a moment until I picked up he was a soldier who'll carry out his orders no matter what those orders might be, sir. While you birds were arguing, for a moment I thought you two were angry at each other, sirs. But seeing how the young Captain respects your command Colonel, I know this whole mess was an act, and the Captain is going to carry out his orders as received, sir."

THE MIDDLE OF THE IRAQI DESERT, THURSDAY, OCTOBER 31st, 2008

Captain Robert Walker and the rest of the soldiers from his unit left Colonel Bruce Leadbetter and the two other units at the bunker site. Walker had a mixed total of fifty male and female soldiers in special tactics and weapons, accompanying him to their second location. Traveling with the overloaded convoy of Humvees was slow and laborious. It took a full day of traveling for Walker's group to head for the second site where the Iraqi child's body was discovered by the Spooks, and from what the Captain was able to tell from their position, the troopers were seven hours from the location.

Walker's travel was plagued by a number of breakdowns and vehicles getting stuck in the soft and deep sand, because the machines ran out of road twenty five miles back. His caravan spent a night in the desert and the sun was going down, and he was considering calling it an early end to their travel for the day. The Captain was not trying to push his people too hard, because Colonel Leadbetter figured it would take his convoy two days to reach the second location.

This was the reason why Walker was not pushing his people to the bone. In the back of his mind, he was hoping the CIA medics would come up with an antidote for this weapon, before he was forced to tangle with it. That was why he did not mind having the medical spooks involved with his original caravan. He was pleased two DEPMEDS or Deployable Medical Systems were going out to the bunker site.

Walker raised his hand out of the top of his machine and the trailing vehicles slowed down. He spotted a clearing in the middle of two dunes. It looked as if this area was once a hard packed ancient wadi, or dried up river bank when the desert was once a lush tropical region.

McNip pulled the lead humvee in the area Walker wanted to bunk down for the night, and the young Captain hoped out of the machine before it came to a stop. The first thing he did was to sent out his two pointmen, so the two soldiers could check the surrounding area and make certain the soldiers did not stumble into a enemy combatant trap, or any other threat to them.

Sergeant Walter Casper, the Ghost, and Sergeant Frank Whitcomb, the Hunter checked out the area while Walker and the rest of his troopers set up camp for the night. The two pointmen spread out to about a thousand yards from each other, yet kept an eye on each other as they searched for possible threat aimed against them or their fellow soldiers. The area was void of human activity, so the Ghost lit up a smoke as they hunted for any hidden enemy combatants in the desert. The soldiers closed in until they were walking almost side by side, they were so confident there was no threats in the area against them.

Going out about a mile from the temporary encampment, the two soldiers made a wide three hundred and sixty degree sweep of the parked vehicles. When they returned to where they entered their sweep of the area. They returned to the camp to report their findings to Walker. The Ghost spotted the security guards Walker stationed on the top of the dune and smiled, pleased he was sharp enough to secure the camp before having his people settle in for the night. After reporting their findings to the Captain, he ordered one of the pointmen hunting while the second waited to relieve the other. He was not taking chances of getting involved in an ambush with insurgents while moving his troops another twenty two miles to the south.

Walker kept an eye on his elite soldiers as they set aside the areas they would rest for the night. As usual, he was surrounded with the few soldiers he trusted the most from the unit. The Mutt, Sergeant Dorothy Ramirez, Buckethead, No Neck, McNip, Roach, Baby Tee, Ice, Wacko, Siberia and Bind Date were bedding down near Walker. The Mutt was complaining as usual at the troops, and Blood Clot was getting on his back for complaining about their operation.

"Man, I can't stand this new form of Asymmetrical fucking Warfare, people."

"Man Mutt, you're getting so bad about complaining, I swear to God above you'll probably complain about a damn blow job. What the hell's getting into you lately, dog man? You're getting tough to be around with your complaining." Blood Clot fired at the grumpy soldier.

Walker was shocked and had a dumb look on his face as he stared at the Mutt. He was not staring at him because of his complaining, and when the Mutt noticed the look he snapped at Walker. "What! What the fuck did I do wrong now man? I didn't do nuthin wrong."

"You didn't do nuthin wrong this time. You surprised the hell outta my ass, that's all you did." Walker mumbled at his best friend and fellow soldier.

"How the hell did I do that man?" The Mutt asked Walker with surprise in his tone.

"I didn't know you could pronounce Asymmetrical, yet alone know what the fucking word means. You do know what the word means, right man?" Walker asked the Mutt.

"Hey man, I was always smart, it's just you didn't know it until now, Homes. And yes, I know what the fucking word means, wiseass. It means irregular, man." The Mutt replied confidently.

"Huh, the asshole might know what the word means alright, but ask the jerk to spell it, Walker. C'mon Walker, Mutt's so dumb he's still trying to figure out where the hell his lap goes when he stands up. Hell, he only got out of the fifth grade because he no longer fit in the desk." The pretty female soldier Baby Tee snapped at Mutt with sweet viciousness lacing her tone.

"Hey bitch, if you think you're so damn smart, you spell the fucking word. Hey Baby, do you believe in love at first fright?" The Mutt fired back at Baby Tee, angrily for daring to get on his ass in front of the rest of the soldiers.

"It depends on who I'm looking at, stupid. There, you see Walker you see how defensive he gets whenever he doesn't know the answer to the question asked of him. If he knew how to spell the damn word, he'd do it just to shut me up, honey. The Mutt's only spitting out words to see where they splatter. He's trying to show off his two dollar education, Walker." Baby Tee replied as she smiled at the angry Mutt glaring at her.

"You keep getting on my stinking ass like this, and I'm gonna stick my dick right up your pretty little ass for ya." The Mutt warned the smallish woman. Baby Tee was not trying to hurt Lieutenant Hall's feelings, she was only trying to make light of their situation and make some of the other soldiers laugh a bit.

"That has to be the worst proposition I ever heard coming out of your filthy mouth, Mutt. But what the hell I'm desperate, so let's go honey." Baby Tee replied, but she could not help laughing at the look now on the Mutt's surprised looking face.

"Baby look at his eyes, they're so blood shot it hurts me to look at him, honey." Neck offered.

"Hey big man, if you look close enough at him, the Mutt's whole body's blood shot." Baby Tee replied to Neck who had a crush on the other female soldier Ice.

The Mutt put a sorry looking pout on his puss as he growled at Baby Tee. "There, you hurt my feelings, baby sister. I hope you're happy with all the slugs you keep throwing at my ass, little sister. They got to me and now I gotta make an appointment with a head Doctor."

"I have my moments, but they're coming few and far in between I fear. One other thing I have to tell you though my dear Mutt, you have to have feelings for them to be hurt by anyone. And you my dear fine feathered friend, haven't heard from your feeling and conscious in many a year, ass u hole." Baby Tee was on a roll and she was not going to let up on the Mutt as she again grinned at the dangerous soldier she was getting on, and wiggled her hips sexily at him.

"All kidding aside, I want you guys to make certain the rest of our people are on the stinking ball around here. Mutt, you gotta go round and warn them to be damn careful where they're stepping. I don't want anyone stepping in any god damn puddles…"

"Puddles, hey Walker we're in the middle of the fucking desert. Where the hell is anyone gonna find any stinking puddles out here, man?" Buckethead grumbled as he smirked at the captain, thinking he made a mistake.

Walker gave a hot look at the huge man romantically interested in Baby Tee for interrupting him, and then went on with his words. "It figures you'd be the one to butt his fucking ass in on my conversation, Homes. Like I was saying to you pukes, I don't want anyone stepping in any damn puddles, or small sand mounds, or clumps of weeds for that matter. I want everyone checking around them to see if anything looks outta place or outta the normal. Even the normal out here can kill ya ass, because anything might be a weapon, man trap or IED or Improvised Explosive Device aimed at us.

"I want everyone to look alive and keep your heads on a swivel at all times, dammit. I don't wanna be forced to toe tag and bag anyone because they were careless, or stupid about their actions out here. Or you guys let down their guard for one fucking second at the worst possible time while we're on this damn bug hunt. I surrounded myself with who I classify as the cream of the crap, so you people betta starting acting like that, and make certain the rest of our people are working at their top efficiency before someone gets hurt. All I wanna see from you people is assholes and elbows and each of you looking after the soldier next to you."

Walker gave the other soldiers the look to make them move out, and when they started to follow his orders he added. "Hey Mutt, you and Raz stay with me, the uthers can warn the rest of our people. We got uther dirty work to carry out."

"Thanks a lot man, I don't like moving around the damn desert when it's getting dark out there, man. Hey Walker, what's this uther dirty work we gotta attend to? I'll tell you this, if we got uther dirty work to do, why don't we invite that puke from the Discovery Channel with us. He's always looking for dirty jobs, and from the looks of this fucking operation. There's gonna be plenty of dirty work to go around." The Mutt smirked back at Walker.

"What the fuck are you talking about? Who's always looking for dirty jobs, asshole?"

"You know the guy I mean, that Mike Rowe dude, Walker. He's always got his hand either stuffed up some cow or horses' ass, or denutting some stinking sheep on his show." The Mutt offered as he waited for Walker to realize the man he was speaking about.

"Mutt you'd be betta off if you kept your mind glued on the problem before us. Enuf about this dude will ya huh, we got bigger fish to fry. Tomorrow morning when we head out, I want the Ghost and Hunter to get out in front of our machines. I got a gut feeling we're heading for a confrontation with some crazy ass fucking sand swimmers of this godforsaken country. Those two will take the lead for the rest of the way to the second location. When we get there, I want those two out to reconnoiter the area before we set up camp, and start hunting this shit down. Those two will stop us from stumbling into any traps."

"Crap! Where the hell's that ATO dude at for Christ sake, I gotta speak to him before we turn in. Mutt, takeoff and see if you locate the ATO, and get his ass here double quick. Raz, you set up night protection, you know who to pick for duty. I want everyone on their toes at all times." Walker grumbled at his two close friends as he watched the Mutt take off for the ATO Colonel.

Just as Walker started to relax, the Mutt returned with the ATO Colonel in tow, the Mutt tripped on soft sand and took a hard tumble. This move caused Walker to laugh as he growled at the soldier. "Hey stupid, you gotta learn to fall betta than that. Or you're gonna end up spending the rest of your life pushing yourself around in a stinking wheelchair, Homes. Get up before I order you buried where you're sitting on the sand."

"Ha fucking ha wiseass, here's the Airforce Officer you wanted to see, smartass." The Mutt replied aggressively as he got up and brushed the sand off his uniform.

Colonel Mark Pullman did not salute the young Captain because he refused to salute or accept a salute while out on a mission. Walker motioned with his stubble covered chin to an overturned five gallon pail and the Airforce Colonel sat on it, and waited to see what was on the other officer's mind. Even though the Airforce Colonel outranked Walker by two rates, he was informed by his commanding officer and Colonel Leadbetter that Walker was the man for this operation, and he was to follow the Captain's orders as if they came from an officer of higher rank than the Colonel.

Walker did not mince words as he spoke to the officer. "Colonel Pullman, when we get to the second location, I don't want you waiting for me to give the order, as soon as you're set up, you're to call in the two Spook helicopters. I wanna end their part of this operation ten minutes ago. I had enuf working with the damn Spooks on this one, Colonel. Don't get me wrong Colonel Pullman, they're about as good as we are with any mission they're on. Their warriors are top notch and A Number One in my book, and they know what the hell they're doing when they're in the field. It's something about working with the CIA that bugs the shit outta my ass.

CHAPTER FIFTEEN

"Anyway Colonel Pullman, once we have the helicopters as part of our operation, the Spooks will be absorbed by my unit and given other duties to carry out, until they're pulled from us by their damn commanders. I intend to use their helicopters for our use until I get equipped with my rotary aircraft units, Colonel. You'll be in command of the helicopters and their pilots during our operation. We can use them for emergency evacuation or wounded, or send them out ahead of our convoy, and they can check out the area before us, Colonel. Hopefully the pilots will stop us from stumbling into any ambush set up by these damn enemy combatants of this country, sir.

"Dammit Colonel Pullman, why the hell am I bothering to telling you your stinking business for, sir? You know much betta than me what and how we'll employ the damn helicopters on this operation, sir." Captain Walker gave a smile to the nodding Airforce Colonel as he asked the military officer one final question.

"Say Colonel Pullman, not for nuthin sir, do you come with a moniker sir?"

Colonel Pullman allowed himself a quick laugh as he stared at Walker, and then replied. "Yes Sir Captain Walker, I have a nickname sir. But you're going to laugh like hell when you hear how I was blessed with it, sir. My flight name is Swamp Yankee, sir."

"Swamp Yankee. Now how the hell did you get tagged with a name like that, sir? Who did you piss off when the uther soldiers were tagging your ass with that moniker, sir?" Walker smirked as he rubbed his chin and stared at the Airforce Officer until he replied.

"Well sir, I was born in Brooklyn and when I was married we moved down to Clearwater, Florida. You know how it is when they're looking to stick you with a tag, sir. Someone asked me my history and when they found that out they stuck me with Swamp Yankee, sir."

"Interesting sir, okay Colonel Pullman that's about all I have for you, sir. You can return to whatever the hell you were doing before I sent for you." Walker offered to the Airforce Officer because he noticed Ramirez was returning to his position, and he wanted to see how she made out setting up the perimeter defenses for the overnight camp he ordered set up for the soldiers.

Colonel Pullman walked away from the Captain because Walker did not ask him if he had any questions that needed to be answered. The Colonel took Walker's last words as his dismissal, and he returned to where he was setting up his sleeping quarters.

When Ramirez got back to Walker, she looked at the Airforce Colonel walking away and she asked him. "What's up with the ATO, Walker? I didn't think he'd bother you tonight."

"I needed to set his ass straight, that's all. How did you make out with security?"

"I have them set up and the troopers know what to do and when they'll be relieved, so they can get some sleep Robert. When do you plan to set off for this second site tomorrow? I'd like to know when we're shoving off so I can warn the troops under my Command, Bobby." Sergeant Ramirez asked her lover as she held him in her gaze.

"At first light, I wanna get an early start tomorrow and use the cooler morning to travel there. Hey baby it's getting late so why don't you turn in. I have a few uther things I hafta look after, and when I'm done I'm gonna get some shut eye myself. Are you gonna sleep with me tonight?" Walker asked Ramirez as he smiled at her.

"Nothing can stop me from sleeping with you." She purred at him sexily.

Walker was up before the sun and was getting on his people because he wanted to head for the second location as soon as possible, and beat some heat if they left early. "C'mon strap hangers we gotta get a move on it. We're time poor and I can bet the ranch Leadbetter's already chewing his nails waiting for our report." Walker growled at the soldiers after kissing Ramirez morning.

The Mutt, sleeping next to Walker and Ramirez, grumbled as he got up on an elbow. "Yeah sure wiseass, you slept nice and cozy with your hen so you're good to go. But the rest of us pukes hadta sleep with our dicks in our hands, man."

"Don't hand me crap. You slept with Blind Date and we heard you two going at it like dogs in heat last night. Get up and get the rest of these walking sandbags moving." Walker snapped at Mutt and gave him a smile as Blind Date prepared herself to move out with the others.

After a bunch of complaints from the slowly moving troops, Walker's unit was ready to move out and the soldiers piled into the humvees, and were off in a breath of time. It took the caravan six more hours to reach the second position of the operation, and when they arrived, the Captain was the first out of the machines as usual.

He began to check out the coordinates with his handheld GPS (Global Positioning System) and he was certain this was the right location he was sent out to locate. He ordered his humvee parked where the helicopters landed when they found the Iraqi kid. Then Walker ordered his camp setup so the soldiers could start to search the area to see if the CIA Agents might have overlooked something vital to their operation when they first checked out the area.

Even before Walker started to get his camp setup for the night and without being ordered, both the Hunter and the Ghost jumped out of their machine and began scouting out the area where the soldiers were ordered to set up their temporary headquarters. The young Captain took a quick break because he was watching his people setting up camp. He liked what he was seeing, his One Charlie or Satellite Controller, the Roach, (Sergeant David Burgwald) was setting up his operation so his team could remain in contact with Colonel Leadbetter's group at the bunker, searching that place for further information about the biological weapon they were searching for.

It was starting to get late, so Walker decided to take the rest of the day setting up camp before he started his people searching for the product, and the person or persons who removed the item from the bunker at their second location. By the time the camp was setup and his security posted, it was nine p.m. The Ghost and the Hunter reported in there were no signs of any enemy combatants or man traps or activity in the surrounding area, and the two point soldiers were relaxing at the camp. The Captain choked down food, and did his last walk around his camp, and when he felt everything was right, he walked over to Sergeant Ramirez and plopped down by her side and gave her a smile and a wink of the eye.

Ramirez returned his smile, and reported. "Robert, I have the Mutt and his girlfriend relaxing, but the Mutt's scheduled to pull duty from midnight to four, and Blind Date will relieve him. I wanted to inform you, in case you wanted to speak to Frankie."

"Arrr…, it's about time he's doing something useful." Walker bitched and noticed Neck, (Sergeant Robert Abbott) heading for him, carrying the portable radio and this caused Walker to complain. "Shit, I wonder who the hell's trying to get hold of my ass, dammit. For Christ sake baby, I didn't even have time to pull my pants outta the crack of my ass, and some one's already gonna bug the shit outta my ass. I can't wait for this mission to be completed, I hate like hell going out on a bug hunt like this, honey."

Neck was grinning from ear to ear until he noticed the look on Walker's puss, and he pulled up and cautiously offered the mike to Walker like he was afraid he was going to draw back a bloody stump for a hand.

"Who the fuck's on the damn thing, stupid?" Walker snarled as he roughly grabbed the mike.

"It's the stinking Colonel, and he's hot as hell." Neck replied with another grin.

"If he's so fucking hot, maybe he should get his ass outta the damn sun." Walker added.

"This is Searcher Base to Searcher One. Come in, this is a secured net so we don't have to be careful over what we speak on the damn thing, Captain Walker." If it was not a secured net, the Colonel would have never addressed Walker by his rank or last name on an open net that could be tapped by their enemy operating in Iraq.

"Yeah, this is Searcher One to Searcher Base, what's up Searcher Base? Over sir."

"I'll tell you what's up soldier! Where the fuck are you and what the hell is that bunch of misfits you're in command of, doing? How come you haven't checked in and reported what you're up to out there? I have General White standing on my dick with both feet, because he's starving for information about this damn operation, you little prick you. Over."

"Searcher Base, we just finished setting up camp at the second site, and I'm gonna allowed the rest of the day and night to relax my people and let them rest and have something to eat. Then we'll start to search the area for any new info, sir. Over." Captain Walker reported to his commanding officer as he made like he was masturbating to the Colonel's bitch that caused both Ramirez and No Neck to laugh as they relaxed.

"Look Walker, the General was pissing and moaning he has a special meeting set up with the Big Boss, (President) for tomorrow morning at Zero Eight Hundred Hours, and they're going to hear the first report from some hot shot prick from some snot nose University somewhere in Pittsburg I believe. So I can look forward to having the General shave down my dick because anything some damn professor is going to report couldn't be good information for us. If the General gets on my ass about this shit then you can guess who I'll be coming after when the General's finished chewing on my ass. You can't get some troops out tonight to see if the Spooks might have missed something important out there, mister?" The Marine Colonel complained at Walker over the radio.

"Searcher One to Searcher Base, by the time I send anyone out for a fast search, it's gonna be as dark as three feet down a fucking cow's throat. That's why I decided to hold my people back and send them out when they can see what the fuck they're doing and going. I can't send my people out in the pitch black even though they have night optics capability. That shit works for short distances. Over." Walker reported to his commander with a snap in his tone.

After thinking over Walker's reply, the Colonel grumbled. "You're right with that order. That was good thinking. It's everyone's putting pressure on my ass and I can't do shit about it."

"I can believe that, Searcher Base. What about you, how are you making out searching that bunker, sir? Over." Walker refused to address Leadbetter by rank or last name over the radio. He was so use to not putting out information for the enemy's use on the officers on a mission.

"We ran into a mutherfucking stone wall up here, Walker. We haven't found a new thing over the item in hours. It seems the Spooks did a masterful job searching the bunker, and we have everything there was to be found about the item in the bunker. Nevertheless Captain, we're still ripping the place apart dust grain by grain. I have a gut feeling there's something we overlooked, and until I'm a hundred percent certain we found everything there is to be found in the bunker. I'll have my people working on their search until I'm satisfied we got everything that might help us with this shit, sir. Over." Colonel Leadbetter replied.

"Shit Searcher Base, I was hoping you might discover something so we know where to start our search from here, sir. The way I feel about this shit, we're starting out ice fucking cold with no direction to go off in, sir." Walker reported to his commanding officer.

"Them are the breaks Walker. You know every time we're sent on a mission, we always start off in the damn dark. There's one good think we're working on from here. We have some DNA expert puke scheduled to reach our location tomorrow morning, he's going to take some blood and tissue from the kid. He's going to try and discover where this damn kid might have came from, and that information might narrow down our search area a might for us. Over."

"Searcher One to Searcher Base, I hope this lousy puke can find something that'd help us out, sir. Am I cleared to keep my people on base until daylight, sir? Over." Walker asked and offered to his commanding officer at the same time.

"Yeah Walker, as I stated that was a good point you made, and you're free to keep your people stationed on base until morning. I'm warning you soldier, if your people aren't out and searching by first light, I'm coming out to you and taking over command, and you'll be shoveling every grain of sand until you hit hard earth. Over." Leadbetter snapped at Walker over the radio.

Walker ignored the threat from his commanding officer as he signed off with the Colonel. "This is Searcher One to Searcher Base. Out!"

"Hey man what did old whatisface have to say?" Neck asked Walker in an excited tone.

"Arrr… he's still trying to discover something that might help us out while we're schlepping around bumfuck Egypt, looking for something I don't think we're gonna find, man."

"If you feel that way then why the hell did we come out here for, Walker?"

"Neck, you know how it goes in the fucking service, when the government calls, we haul ass. You betta turn in for the night unless you pulled duty tonight, we're heading out at first light to search this miserable area to see if them damn Spooks mighta overlooked something when they first searched the place. I'm gonna have our ATO get in contact with the Spook helicopters and order them back here in the morning, and some of us are gonna do an aerial search of the area, while the rest of us search the area by ankle fucking express and elbows and assholes. Move it out big man before I find something else for you to do if you wanna stay up for the damn night, Homes." Walker warned the huge soldier still grinning at him.

"You got it and I don't feel like staying up for the night." Neck replied as he turned on his heels and took off from the two lovers and soldiers.

"Then I suggest you make like a fucking ghost and get the hell outta my sight, Neck." Walker called out after him as he returned the large soldier's grin, and then he watched him take off and head for where he was going to bed down for the night.

"I love that big tree trunk we call a soldier, Walker. He's so much like a huge teddy bear soft and cuddly, Robert." Sergeant Ramirez offered with a warm smile as she stared at the Neck until he returned to his bedroll.

"Yeah, he's like a big fluffy teddy bear alright, until he spots one of our enemy. Then he turns into a huge grizzle ready to rip apart and kill and eat the one he locked up in his sights. I'll tell you this about that big guy. I wouldn't want that guy pissed off at me for a second he's that dangerous a trooper and human being, Raz. I think we betta follow his lead and turn in for the night. I don't wanna be dragging my sagging ass around tomorrow because I didn't follow my own orders and get enuf sleep, baby."

"Yes, we're both going to turn in for the night, but not before I make love to my soldier, Robert." Ramirez purred as she looked Walker in the eyes with a dreamy stare.

WEDNESDAY, NOVEMBER 2nd, 2008, THE IRAQI DESERT

Captain Robert Walker woke with a start on the following morning and checked his watch. It was Zero Four Forty Five and still dark and he looked to his right and allowed a smile because Sergeant Dorothy Ramirez was sleeping like an angel beside him. He reached out and gave her a little shove and grumbled. "C'mon baby, you gotta get your pretty little ass up, we hafta get the uther people moving before Leadbetter shows up and eats us alive for dragging our feet, baby."

"Gees Robert is it time for us to get up already for Pete's sake? Hell, it feels like I just fell asleep for the love of God. I hate this garbage Robert, one of these days I'm going to fall asleep and wake up on my own when I feel I've had enough sleep for the night, Bobby. I'm also going to wake up in my own bed surrounded in silk instead of sand, heat and a bunch of smelly male soldiers dressed in olive drab green that should be thrown away." Ramirez complained as she got on an elbow and stared at her soldier. She fell asleep last night naked after they made love, and Walker reached out and cupped her breast as he replied to her slight gripe.

"If you're tired it's your own fault, baby. You were the one who wanted to make love instead of turning in and getting some sleep, Raz."

"Oh, I guess you hated me making love to you last night. We'll see what happens the next time you want to enjoy yourself." Ramirez retorted with a smile and sat up and looked for her undershirt. Finding it she complained as she slipped in it. "Gees Walker, this thing smells as bad as your damn boots does."

"I doubt that baby, you betta get ready to head out while I wake the uther slugs." Walker stood and stretched his arms over his head and let out a groan that would have woken the dead.

The second he growled, some of the other soldiers woke and complained at him.

"What the hell was that for the love of God, it sounded like a gut shot bear in heat? If we're still in sand land then that has to be a damn camel in pain."

"That was our fearless leader and his way of walking us up by scaring the hell outta us."

"Hell, if that's the way he wakes up, I feel real sorry for Raz when he wakes her like that." A third soldier complained as she got up and dressed in her body armor and checked her weapon.

"Yeah, yeah, you people are turning into being a bunch of stinking crybabies. I'm damn glad I don't have to wake you people for Pete's sake. C'mon, we hafta get a hop in our skip if we wanna get out there and see if we can find anything that might help our cause." Walker growled at the waking soldiers doing all the complaining over the way he woke them up.

The Mutt was the first soldier dressed and by the time he got over to Walker, Ramirez was dressed and rested her hand on Walker's shoulder and offered. "Robert, I'll have a few female soldiers prepare something to eat. Once the soldiers ate then you can send them out to search the area, honey."

"The chicks from the unit aren't gonna get upset because they're pulling the stinking chow duty for the damn unit are they, sister? I don't want them feeling just because they're women. They're expected to do all the damn cooking for the rest of these stinking slobs we have hanging around here, baby. If you want, you can always pull the regular fuckups from the group in and have them do some of the cooking for the guys, or they could pull KP and clean up for the females cooking afta the meal for us, Raz. It's up to you how you wanna handle it. I wanna keep the stinking peace between all my troops."

"You worry about what you have to worry about and leave me to handle this other crap, Robert. Look, you have your partner in crime by your side, so you two get on with what you have to handle, and I'll get the morning meal going for the soldiers, Bobby."

Walker left Ramirez to get the meal going for the soldiers so he could check and make certain the rest of his troops were up and preparing to get in the field, and search the area for the bug juice or person who had it. The Captain was proud of the way his soldiers were setting up for their search, and he found no one to get on because they were all up and dressed and milling about waiting for their next orders from their commanding officer to come at them.

When Walker spotted the Ghost and Hunter standing together along with a female soldier, he headed right for them. Walker nodded at Caviar, (Sergeant Lana Dostoyevsky) and ignored the other Russian soldier, Siberia, (Sergeant Taras Zaugnaya) because she was always ready to give the other soldiers a hard time, she did not like being with the troops. Both women were on loan to the Multi-national Rapid Response Force from Russia. There was a third Russian female soldier, and one male that represented Russia's interest in the MNRRF units. The three female Russian soldiers were part of the Russian Spetsnaz Commando troops of the elite Alfa and Vympel anti-terror units of the Federal Security Service of Russia.

Walker started to speak to the Ghost as he sucked on a smoke. "Casper, I want you and the Hunter out before any other soldier heads out in the field. I want you two to keep your eyes opened and your heads on a swivel. With the smoke from the cooking pit, I'm certain any stinking insurgents from miles around, might head over to see what the hell the smoke is about. I don't need any of them sand swimmers sneaking up on us and getting the drop on our guys. I'm gonna keep one of the helicopters from the Spooks held back and handy, in case we have to air E-vac any wounded or injured personal out of here in a fast hurry. You two betta get over where the girls are setting up the meal and grab yourselves something to eat. Then I want you two out hunting for fucking bear. Check every bush out there for any damn man traps or any sign of what we're out here looking for. Get going you two birds."

Walker watched the two pointmen as they headed over to the mess to eat, and then he started to search for the ATO Colonel. Spotting the officer wrapping up his bedroll, he went over to him and started to speak as the Colonel continued what he was doing. "Colonel Pullman, as soon as you get a chance, I want you to call in the two Spook helicopters, sir. I want them on the ground and the Spooks outta the damn machines. I'm gonna use them for our purposes like I told you. By the way Colonel, are you having any problems with my command or my people while we're carrying out our orders? I gotta know if you're doing okay with it and them so far, sir."

Colonel Pullman stopped what he was doing and he looked up at Walker and replied. "Problems Captain, the only problem I'm having is with my dick, sir."

"Zat so Colonel, and what's the problem with your dick if you don't mind my asking, sir?"

"Captain Walker Sir, it's been awful hard since I linked up with you people, sir. I have to tell you Captain, this is the first outfit I was attached to where the women are so free with walking around with nothing, or next to nothing on their bodies, sir." Colonel Pullman pointed with his jaw and Walker looked in that direction and picked up the beautiful soldier branded Ice checking her weapon, she was doing it while sitting on the sand topless, and then the Airforce Colonel added. "Damn Captain Walker, I don't know how you people ever get anything done with all the flesh I see from your fine looking female soldiers. You have to realize where I come from Captain, the females are separated from the male soldiers at all times, and Heaven forbid if we happen to walk in on one of them while they're changing, sir. You'd think you walked into a god damn mine field or something, sir."

Walker laughed over the Colonel's complain as he remarked. "Well Colonel Pullman I hope all the problems we're gonna face on this rat fuck operation is as serious as the one you're bitching about, sir. You know Colonel; I can't believe there are still some branches of the stinking service that segregate the women warriors from their male warriors, sir. I though they woulda by now, realized if they keep treating their women soldiers like they were made of glass, and they might break if they were treated like male soldiers. They're not getting the best outta their women fighters, Colonel. It took us a while to understand this shit, but there's not one woman fighter in my entire group I wouldn't trust with my back when the crunch time comes a knocking on our asses, Colonel Pullman."

"I hear you Captain Walker, but my command still demands the women be separated from the male soldiers at all times, sir. I agree with you we're keeping our women fighters down because we won't treat them the same way the male warriors are treated. I have to add I like the scenery quite a bit from your female soldiers it relieves the boredom of being on active duty, sir."

"Not to mention it makes it easier to relieve any other problem you might be suffering from, Colonel. Like the problem you just mentioned. If you're still fighting with that there problem sir, I can always have Ice. She's the one working on her weapon over there topless, sir. I can have her come by and make your problem go away fur ya, Colonel Pullman." Walker smirked as he stared at the confused looking Airforce Colonel.

Colonel Pullman laughed nervously as he offered to the grinning Captain. "Hell sir, I'd like to take you up on that offer Captain. I haven't been with my wife for almost a year and a half, sir. I've been stuck in this God forsaken country that long, Captain. But I still have to pay attention to the rules and regulations of my service, and the regs state there's to be no fraternization with the female population, especially females below my rank under no circumstances, Captain."

"Man Colonel Pullman, you come with a whole bushel basket full of stinking problems cluttering up your damn mind, sir. Regulations, what the hell's that crap sir? If my group worked and worried as much as you do about them stinking regulations you're so worried about, sir. We'd never get anything done, and our women fighters would still be operating under many restrictions, like back in the damn Stone Ages, sir. I say the hell with those damn regulations, if you have a problem and there's a soldier who can take care of the problem for ya ass, sir. I say go at it like two dogs in fucking heat and be done with it, sir. Say Colonel Pullman, allow me ask you a question, sir?"

"Shoot Captain." Colonel Pullman fired back at the younger military officer.

"Colonel Pullman, say you're in the stinking field and you need a hand with a problem that cropped up on ya, sir. Would you have trouble asking a fellow male soldier to lend a hand to settle that problem, sir?" Walker asked the Airforce Officer with a smirk.

"C'mon Captain, if I was suffering from the same kind of problem as I have now, sir. First off I'd think there was a serious problem if I had a hard on and being around a bunch of male soldiers, sir." Colonel Pullman smirked as he stared at Walker while waiting for his reply.

"You missed the stinking point I was trying to make with your ass, Colonel Pullman. What I was saying was, if you had a problem and you needed a fellow soldier's help. You wouldn't think anything about requesting that help from a male soldier. So why not think the same way about the hens from my unit, Colonel Pullman? I'll tell you this Colonel there isn't one female warrior in my unit who'd think twice about helping you out with that there problem of yours, sir. If a guy went as long as you did without sex from a woman I mean, Colonel." Walker said as he glanced at the soldier Ice, and noticed she put her uniform blouse on, and added to his words to the officer. "Sorry Colonel Pullman, it looks like the boat just sailed without your ass, sir. All I can offer sir is slap the damn thing down and get on the horn and order those two helicopters in. I need those machines here ten minutes ago, Colonel."

Colonel Pullman looked in the direction Walker was looking and he replied as if he lost his best friend as he noticed the soldier slipped in her blouse and grumbled. "I see what you mean Captain, she got dressed, sir. Dammit, I'll get on that order immediately, Captain."

"Thanks much Colonel Pullman, and once you finish with the Spooks and order their helicopters in. I suggest you get your ass over to mess and choke down food, sir. We're heading out once I make certain there are no problems with my troops, Colonel Pullman. I don't know how the hell long we'll be in the field searching this morning sir. So you betta eat your fill before we shove off for duty, soup up (drink water) while you're at it as much as you can drink, Colonel. Although we'll have plenty of water with us out there sir, there always seems to work out we never have enough of the shit to drink when you're strolling around in the middle of the damn desert." Walker looked up to the sky, and then moaned at the other officer.

"From the looks of it Colonel Pullman, it's gonna be three shades of hot as hell today, sir. I hafta check on a few soldiers I need to look after, and then I'm gonna eat something. Then we're heading out to begin our search for this shit, Colonel. I want you by my side at all times while we're out there Colonel, in case we have to call in air assets to assist us if we come under attack from insurgents while searching the damn area, sir. I don't trust this damn country and its people as far as I can throw them, sir." With that said Walker stood and left the colonel looking for his radio so he could make contact with the commander of the helicopters.

When Walker finished speaking to his troops, he headed for the mess and ate and drank his full. Sergeant Ramirez waited for Walker to catch up with her and they ate together. The two soldiers ended up being the last troopers from the group to eat, and when they were finished, Walker growled out at the rest of his troops milling about waiting for them to finish eating, so they could set out on their mission for the day.

"It's time for us to take a walk in fucking hell. Pick your people and stick with them and head out and watch what the hell you people are doing out there. Remember to keep your eyes opened and protect the uther soldier you're with at all times. Let's get a move on it before we hear from Colonel Leadbetter, and he starts eating our damn asses out again, because we're kinda dragging our stinking feet getting started on this damn operation this morning." Captain Walker bent down and picked up his weapon and checked to make certain there was a round set in place in the chamber, and the group of specially trained soldiers headed off as one to carry out their orders from their young commanding officer.

WEDNESDAY, NOVEMBER 2nd, 2008. THE WHITE HOUSE, WASHINGTON D.C. ZERO, EIGHT HUNDRED HOURS EST

All concerned politicians scheduled to sit in on the special report soon to be delivered by Doctor Johan Rosenblum, was already waiting for the College professor to arrive at the Oval Office. President Albert Cole was relieving his boredom by speaking with some of the elite people attending the meeting.

He was busy speaking with his Vice President, Mary Hirshfield, General John White, the Chairman of the Joint Chiefs of Staff, and CIA Director, John Raincloud. The White House Aide walked the University professor in the Oval Office who seemed like he was walking to his death to the Oval Office.

The moment the President noticed the professor enter the room, he broke his conversation off with the others and crossed the room and put his hand out and shook the professor's hand, as he offered. "Doctor Rosenblum, it's good you were able to make it here so quickly, sir. I trust you had a safe and enjoyable trip to Washington from Pittsburg, Professor Rosenblum?"

"My trip was most enjoyable, Mr. President. Before you ask Mr. President, I have all the documents with me to forward my presentation to the others attending the meeting, sir."

"Good Professor Rosenblum, I have my military people chomping at the bit to hear what you have to offer, so they could direct the soldiers they have operating in the field, Professor. I trust you know everyone in the room, sir. If not I'd be pleased to introduce you to any you don't know, Professor. If you wouldn't mind, I'd like to get this meeting started so I can get the other members in gear, Doctor. From what I was lead to believe by Doctor Russbinder, on duty with my Special Forces troops in Iraq, and he's the NEST Doctor I have working with this Rapid Response force General White setup for this type of situation we're facing here Professor, this is an emergency sir. Shall we get started, Doctor Rosenblum? Is there anything you need setup to help you with your presentation, sir? Would you care for any refreshments or drinks before we start, Professor?" The concerned President of the United States asked the doctor.

"I know Doctor Russbinder very well Mr. President, I had the pleasure to work with him on a number of occasions, and I'm quite comfortable and need no refreshments, Mr. President. I feel the same as you and believe we should get started with this meeting as soon as possible, sir. I fear you have no idea how little time we have to find the missing biological weapon before it might be accidentally released in the air, and the damage this weapon could cause to the earth if it is ever released against any nation in the range of war, sir. Mr. President, I have everything I need for my presentation for everyone attending the meeting sir, and I have no need for further assistance from anyone in the room, Mr. President." Doctor Rosenblum replied as he allowed the American Leader to walk him deeper into the Oval Office, to where the doctor could sit or stand to give his presentation.

As Professor Johan Rosenblum hurriedly prepared himself to speak, the President offered to the others. "Ladies and gentlemen, please allow me the pleasure to introduce you to Doctor Johan Rosenblum from the Center for Biological Security at the University Of Pittsburg Medical Center. The Doctor was given a sample of the Agent P, One, Three, Five for examination by our General White under my direction.

The Professor is here to report his finding so I want everyone paying attention to his every word, and I want input from everyone here on how we'll handle the information the Professor is about to give us. Professor Rosenblum, you may begin your presentation, sir. Errr… Professor, if it'll make it any easier for you sir, you may give your findings to the members of this meeting while seated, we're more interested in your findings than protocol, Doctor Rosenblum."

Professor Rosenblum stopped what he was doing and looked at the President as he spoke directly to him, and then replied with a smile. "With all due respect sir, I believe I'd be more comfortable if I stand during my presentation to everyone here, Mr. President."

"Suit yourself Professor Rosenblum. I was only trying to make you as comfortable as possible, sir." The President snapped back at the elderly man with a hint of anger in his tone.

Doctor Johan Rosenblum was taken aback by the President's harsh tone nevertheless the professor dismissed it by thinking the American Leader must be under tremendous pressure over this new weapon of mass destruction. The doctor started to rush so he could begin his presentation to the others. When the doctor was ready to speak, the professor stated. "Good morning ladies and gentlemen, please allow me to say how deeply honored I am to be asked to speak to America's most elite today. As President Cole has just informed you, over a week ago I met privately with General John White, and he released to my possession a small sample of the newly discovered biological weapon known to me as P, One, Three, Five. I must admit when General White first met with me at the college, I thought this weapon was just another breed in the deadly biological family. After conducting a number of detailed and intense tests on the small sample, I was forced to bring this biological weapon into an entirely new rating zone.

"As anyone who works with chemical or biological agents understand, the highest possible threat level attached to this family of weapons of mass destruction, was and still is branded as a Bio or Chemical level four threat against humanity. Mr. President, ladies and gentlemen this new biological weapon I examined, has forced me to classify it as a biological level five threat to humanity, and that's because of the overwhelming and extremely deadly characteristics possessed by this weapon. I'd like to offer I'll aim my finding mainly to President Cole, I hope everyone will believe and understand I'll be addressing everyone attending this meeting as I speak more directly to the President."

"Professor Rosenblum, you don't have to clarify everything you say to anyone in this room but me, sir. My people understand you'll be addressing me with your findings, you'll be including them in on this conversation, sir." The President grumbled while trying to get the doctor moving along with his offering, so he could start his attack on the item.

"I'm sorry and I thank you for clearing that up for me, Mr. President. Well sir, since being given the small sample of the biological product by General White, I spent every waking hour working of the dangerous subject, sir. I'll give you a brief rundown on how this extremely deadly biological weapon works it evil ways on the human body. This biological altered protein attacks the RNA of every living cell inside the infected host's body, Mr. President.

"There are a number of different situations I must inform you about, so you can properly and fully understand just how this deadly biological weapon affects the human body when it comes under assault by the weapon, Mr. President. The start of it is what we in the field commonly refer to as the RNA Transcription; that's the differences in the composition of the RNA and DNA of the human living cell have been well noted and separated over the passing years. The RNA is not usually found as a double helix in the living cell, sir.

"But its present as a single strand in the living cell however, the single polynucleotide strand might fold in on itself to form portions which have a double helix structure inside the cell under attack by this new biological weapon. Just like the tertiary structure of the proteins that forms every living cell of the human body, sir. Here's exactly how the biological weapon works its deadly business, sir. In the biosynthesis of the RNA of the human living cell which is called transcription proceeds in much the same fashion as the replication of the DNA of the living cell, and it also follows a set path throughout the base pairing principle of life itself, Mr. President.

"Transcription branded this function as the synthesis of the RNA of the living cell that is under the direction of the DNA of the human cell itself. The RNA synthesis or as we come to accept and call it, the transcription, is the process of transcribing the DNA nucleotide sequence information into the RNA sequence information that makes up every living cell of the human body. The nucleic acid sequence uses complementary language and the transmitted information is simply transcribed or copied from one molecule to another inside the living cell. The DNA sequence being changed in the human cell is enzymatically copied by the infected RNA polymerase introduced to the cell, to produce an altered nucleotide RNA strand that's commonly called the messenger RNA of the human cell. Because it now carries the infected and altered genetic message from the DNA to the protein synthesizing machinery of the living cell, sir.

"In the case of the altered protein encoding DNA Mr. President, Transcription is the first step that leads to the expression of the altered genes by the rapid mass production of the mRNA intermediate which is a faithful and absolutely identical transcript of the infected gene's protein changing instruction, which changes the original structure of the living cell of the human body.

"With all due respect Mr. President, the stretch of DNA that's being transcribed in the altered and now infected RNA molecule, is called the transcription unit of the living cell, sir. A DNA transcription unit is then translated into the protein of the cell that contains the exact same sequences that direct and regulate the protein synthesis of the human cell. In addition to the exact coding and reproduction of the infected sequence, is translated into the new protein strand of the human cell, sir. The biological weapon we're taking under consideration of is basically a genetically altered and infected protein that exactly copies, and then completely takes over the original RNA of the infected living human cell, sir.

"Once again Mr. President, a certain section of the DNA double helix is uncoiled and only one of the DNA strands serves as the new template for the altered RNA infected polymerase enzyme that helps to guide the normal synthesis and health of the RNA stored in the living cell, Mr. President. After the infected synthesis of the DNA has been completed and copied by the infected cell of the helix strand. The RNA separates from the infected DNA in the living cell, and the DNA strand with the infected RNA strand attached to the strand recoils back to its helix system of the cell again, sir. The DNA of the human cell separates the races, and separates female from male, hair color, height and weight of the subject and so on and so forth, sir.

"Another step in the ongoing evolution of the infected RNA of the cell caused by the attack of this biological weapon is called the genome wide demarcation of the RNA polymerase II transcription unit system that is revealed by the physical fractional of the chromatin of the human cell, Mr. President. Epigenetic modifications such as is in the case of this biological weapon will rapidly and completely affect the chromatin serve as an important role in the regulating of expression and accessibility of the genomic DNA strand of the human cell under attack by this extremely fatal weapon, sir.

"I'm reporting that a genome wide approach for fractionating yeast chromatin to two separate functionally distinct parts, one containing the RNA polymerase II transcribed sequences of the living cell, and the other comprising the noncoding or neutral sequence system and genes transcribed by the RNA polymerase I and III of the human living cell, Mr. President.

"Mr. President, the non-coding regions of the human cell could be further fractionated into a number of separate promoters and segments completely lacking the necessary promoters needed to change a living cell's structure and makeup to form a human body. The separations I observed during my study of this extremely dangerous biological weapon in question were quite apparent based on the different cross linking efficiency of the chromatin in different genomic regions of the living human cells under attack by the introduction of this biological weapon, sir.

"Mr. President, the most stunning results I have observed and discovered during my very limited time and experiments I had to work with on this biological weapon strain, reveal a genome wide molecular mechanism for marking the infected promoters of the human cell. Along with the normal genomic regions of the human cell that have a so called license to be transcribed or altered by the newly infected RNA polymerase II. That was introduced in the living cell at a previously unrecognized and normally accepted level of the genomic complexity of the living cell.

"Which may still exist in all the known and usually accepted eukaryotes of the human body, Mr. President Sir. My basic approach to the examination of this man made altered and infected product has employed a broad base potential use as a tool for genetic annotation, and for the characterization of the global changes in the chromatin structure usually accompany many different genetic, environmental, and or disease state of examinations I performed on this chilling biological weapon, Mr. President.

"The genomes stored inside the eukaryotic cells or as we sometimes call these human cells, the junk or useless or non-coded genetic traits contain a wealth of information not yet encoded directly in the start of the DNA sequence and process, and the forming of the infected cells in question in the infected human body, Mr. President. Three interconnected mechanisms for the storing of this vital information in the coding of the human DNA and cell structure are normally well established in the forming of the cells of the human body, which is called the covalent modification of the genomic DNA, sir.

"This process is the most important part of this sequence called methylation, or the genetic alteration of the chromatin of the living human cell, by varying its basic protein composition of the living human cell Mr. President; and the enzymatic modification of the chromatin protein of the human cell under assault by the attack from the new biological weapon. Once it was or is introduced into the host's infected body, Mr. President. The defects I observed during my limited but detailed study of the effects of this weapon on the human cell, displayed these processes produce phenotypic effects during the differentiation and development, due to their most profound influences on the underlying gene activity of the human cell as follows:"

"Excuse me for interrupting you Doctor Rosenblum, I must ask you a question troubling me. Don't tell me the experiments you carried out on this biological weapon didn't consist of you introducing it into a living human volunteer, sir? The way you're speaking of your findings, make me fear you might have used a human host to get the results you're offering, Doctor. If you did this nightmare, that makes you and us no better than the animals who developed this item in the first place, sir." Director Blaylocke cried from his seat as he stared at the college professor.

Doctor Rosenblum rolled his eyes over the terrible question asked by the National Security Director. The doctor drew in a gulp of air and started his explanation of the question asked of him in an agitated voice. "Director Blaylocke, of course we never dared to even contemplate the thought of introducing this deadly item into the host of a living human being, sir. I resent you thinking of that horrible a scenario, sir. All experiments we have successfully carried out on the item General White offered me, was carried out in extremely controlled conditions, never allowing the item to threaten the life of anyone working on it, sir..."

"I'm going to take this time to interrupt you, Doctor." President Cole offered as he leaned forward and stared at the doctor, before going on with his words. "Doctor Rosenblum, everyone here knows full well you would never place the life of any human on the line, to work with the item I ordered delivered to you, sir. I'm going to cut you off because you're going off the page for the reason you're here. Doctor Rosenblum, I want you to forget the question asked by my National Security Director, and I order you to get back to informing me of what you discovered with this biological weapon of mass destruction, Doctor."

"Yes Sir Mr. President, I was most unpleased with the Director's question, and I wanted to assure him that at no times were any humans threatened by this extremely deadly item all the while I was working on or with the subject, sir. Now where was I ahhh... yes Mr. President, as I was saying sir. The Histones that comprise the structure of the human cell is a major medium for the epigenetic information, being each of the tails of the RNA strands can easily accommodate a multitude covalent of modifications of the original characteristics of the biologically altered infection attacking the cell system of the human body. Including the acetylation, methylation, phosphorylation, ubiquitination and ADP ribosylation that comprise the main structure of the human living cell, Mr. President.

"Some specific combinations of these newly developed modifications of this process were linked directly to the chromatin condensation states, and the general transcription activity of the human living cell, which has become infected by the introduction of this biologically altered strain. This may be used by the altered protein of the living cell to help guide the recruitment of the transcription factors, and incorporating the other most usual regulatory proteins of the living cell to particular genomic regions of the infected living cell."

The doctor was able to see the strained look clouding over the President's face, and he felt he was losing the President over his long winded presentation and decided to make it easier for him to understand. "Please try and look at it this way Mr. President, just say histone H-3 lysine-4 methylation by Set1p is associated with an active but non-infected chromatin of the cell structure, that happens to be active, and it represses certain genetic growth of the living cell in question. This reaction may be distinguished by the trimethylation of the histone lysines, sir.

"On the basis of these and other normal functional recently discovered linkages for the construction of the living cell of the human body, the information stored and coded inside the histones memory of the human cell, along with their modifications has been dubbed the histone code of the living human cell, Mr. President Sir. Further recently and excitingly discovered combinations of the chromatin immunoprecipitation and microarray techniques, has allowed the genome wide distribution histone and the acetylated and methylated isoforms to be determined present in the yeast structure of the living cells of the human body, sir. It's rather difficult to assess at this precise time the global effects of these newly discovered combinations of the histone modification patterns might have on the accessibility, or the organization of the underlying original DNA template of the living cell growth in the human body, Mr. President.

"Mr. President, I have been able to report through my countless experiments with the DNA structure of the human cell over the many years I had the pleasure of working with it. The saccharmomyces cerevisiae chromatin can be fractionated physically into functionally and distinct and identified genomic regions of the living human cell structure, sir. Including the coding, non-coding and regulatory and non-regulatory regions of the human living cell, that allows me to separate the biological infected RNA from the non-infected RNA of the living cells in question in the human body, sir. I was successful in recording the two separate and distinct procedures which yielded reciprocal results for my understanding, sir.

"One of my experiments was based solely on the differential segregation of the untranscribed regions of the living cell of a body into the aqueous phase of the human cell during the phenolchloroform extraction of the formaldehyde cross linked chromatin region of the living cell, Mr. President. The other but I'm afraid weaker enrichment for any possible potential transcribed regions I been successful in discovering, which may occur by trying to cross link the dependent genome wide nuclear protection of the infected human cell, to the non-infected sections of the living human cell, sir. So this discovery forced me to propose both these usual fractionations are not so easily determined during the attack of the…"

"Err… excuse me for interrupting you at this crucial time Professor Rosenblum. Usually I consider myself a well educated and highly intelligently person, Doctor." The President offered from his chair as he held up his hand to silence the doctor for the moment. The President was no longer able to take it because the word's the doctor was using in his presentation was extremely confusing him. Once the President had the doctor's attention, he went on with his words. "I'm afraid you have lost me, as well as probably everyone else seated in this room, right after you said good morning ladies and gentleman, sir. Professor Rosenblum, do you think you might be able to break down everything you're stating here to a lay man's terms, so we who aren't as obviously educated as you are, might be able to follow what you're offering us a little clearer and easier, Professor Rosenblum?"

Doctor Rosenblum allowed a smile as he offered to the American Leader. "I'm sorry if I lost or confused you during my presentation to the members of this meeting, Mr. President. I understand the exclusive world of the DNA and RNA makeup of the human living cell might be confusing, even to those who work with these items every day of their lives, sir. Every day I work with the reproductive living human cell sir, I'm constantly discovering a number of new wonders about them, Mr. President. Yes, I can sum up most of what I've been telling you and the other members, in easier terms for you and the others to follow and understand, sir.

"Mr. President, and members of this meeting, the DNA of every human cell has what we in the field commonly call useless or junk or non-coded genetic traits, which are edited out by the normal process of the construction of the human cell. Nevertheless they have the standard codes, or we as human beings could find ourselves being born with three eyes, two noses for a lack of a better explanation of the structure of the traits, until the genetic coding of the genetic composition of the living cell can be transferred to the non-coded trait areas of the human cell, sir. These non-coded cells are more or less blank traits of the living human cells waiting for an identity to be in-coded on them through normal construction of the human body, sir. Most if not all deformities of the human body seem to occur when something goes wrong with the genetic traits waiting to be encrypted with the genetic traits that define the countless different shapes and races and male and female, the human body will soon become.

"Mr. President, this particularly developed biologically altered E Boli Strain was genetically altered and engineered and perfectly altered to activate these so called junk or non-coded receptive genetic traits of the human body, which are unique to the Persian Race, Mr. President. The altering of this deadly strain causes the rapid proliferation of this particular and deadly E Boli Strain developed singularly to attack the Persian nationality of the world, Mr. President. But this discovered biological weapon will not contain itself against the genetically targeted Persian Race of peoples it was originally designed to attack and destroy by the developers, Mr. President.

"This new designer weapon of mass destruction is so aggressive in its native state that it wouldn't take very long before the new strain of biological agent mutates to where it'll level its effects on all Arab races of the Middle East, Mr. President. Then the weapon will mutate further until it threatens the world at large. Once it runs out of human hosts to feast upon, this weapon will then mutate exponentially until it becomes strong enough and uncontrollable enough until it attacks all living things on the earth, whether it be of human or animal in nature, Mr. President."

"A little more about this weapon Mr. President, once this biological weapon is released against the peoples of earth. It'll instigate a vast cascade of further chemical and structural changes, which will allow the altered strain to mutate further, and the strain will eventually become so powerful in its own right, to where the weapon will cause the denaturizing of every living cell in the human body. Over time this biological weapon will become so aggressive until it has the power to effect the more dominate DNA strains not married to the Persian or Arab races. In a few months' time, this altered strain will integrate and marry itself with the DNA of all human and animal cells, and once married to the DNA it'll prohibit the cell's natural DNA traits all together, so it can actually attack the entire human race, Mr. President." It was at this point the professor stopped speaking to see if the President had further questions of him.

President Albert Cole sat back in his chair and rubbed his chin as he let out his breath in a rush, and then complained. "Gees, Professor Rosenblum, I don't mind telling you that you successfully scared the living hell right out of me, sir."

"I'm afraid I haven't even begun to scare you over the terrible threat posed by this new weapon of mass destruction, Mr. President." The professor replied to the shaken American Leader.

"How is that Doctor Rosenblum? I thought I heard all the dangers of this damn weapon already, sir?" The President snapped nastily as he held the professor in his angry gaze.

"With all due respect Mr. President, if this biological weapon ever comes to the shores of the United States, within a period of mere weeks, it could devastate the entire United States, and then quite quickly turn into a global pathogen situation, sir. Taking into effect the massive amount of travel people in say New York City or California for examples, and add Europe with their so called no borders then you have to add the international trade of most countries into the mix. Adding all these considerations will help to assist the rapid and uncontrollable spread of the terrible affects of this weapon at an extremely alarming and unstoppable rate, until it's introduced and infects every nation of the world, Mr. President.

"But even because of the so complicated mixing of peoples so easily, has its drawbacks against us in any attempt to try and control an outbreak of a form of pandemic it assists us in our war against any possible pandemic threatening us, Mr. President. Though this unified globalization of the world has its own drawbacks to try and contain any biological outbreak in any region of the world, it also assists us developing a sort of international disease close surveillance, and tracking systems viva the easy access internet. Along with much better communication capabilities existing between the other nations of the world, far better than if we didn't have such access to other countries of the world's alarm and warning systems, sir. The danger of this biological weapon is that it doesn't start with being forced to incubate inside the animal hosts. The development of this potential biological plague begins right in the infected human host, and that cuts down our time of reaction and discovery of the weapon dramatically against us, Sir.

"Usually Mr. President, the beginning of most pandemics that might threaten the human population, commonly develop in the bodies of certain animal types, such as the swine and bird flues, and there it stays until the disease mutates before the disease can make the leap from animal to the human host infection. We usually refer to this type of situation as the virological blenders that allow this biological weapon to attack both animal and human host at the same time, sir. Commonly Mr. President, when an infection develops in the animal population, it gives us a certain amount of time to discover it and react against the possible pandemic outbreak, sir. This is because the animal population will display the effects of being sick well before a human host would, because of the medications available to the human host, sir.

"As I stated in this conversation Mr. President, this biological altered protein has no need to develop inside the animal population, sir. This weapon develops right inside the human host, and that takes away the so called early warning system for us, by discovering the disease before it affects the human host it was aimed at, sir.

"We also have a secondary assistance offered during any threatened pandemic outbreak, sir. With the faster genetic sequencing abilities we're able to develop of late, gives us the heads up and technological abilities to create a rapid reacting early warning system, by means of our discovering the attack by this weapon quicker than ever before. Yes Mr. President, I can see and offer with confidence within six week's time, we could be facing a global pandemic situation that'll impact every nation of the world. Taking in effect the peoples who become infected by this biological released weapon and the infected host travel to other parts of the world, and the infected hosts help spread this infection faster than air currents and other means of transmission, sir. In this case we've come to the conclusion that the contagion affectability rate will be between ninety five percent to ninety eight percent saturation of the human race. This knowledge informs us just how vulnerable our interconnected globe is to disease and weapons of this sort of evil. Mr. President getting back to our medical staffers and emergency responders employed during times of a possible pandemic outbreak, sir."

"Mr. President, you must understand and take into consideration our current medical structures and staffers are in a terrible state of affairs. This failure is due mainly to the severe and countless cut backs in medical assistance and training of new medical staffers needed at times of pandemic outbreak, sir. If this biological weapon is ever released and hits the United States shores, the hospitals will be pounded by what we commonly refer to as a surge capacity influx of infected patients, sir. That's when thousands of infected and sick civilians make their way to hospitals for emergency treatment and help, sir.

"The extra beds and medical equipment and medications we'd need to defend ourselves against this pandemic outbreak, will be overwhelming to the medical staffers at best, sir. As I mentioned, we'd be hard pressed to maintain the proper medical staff during the peak of the pandemic outbreak affecting us on any release of this weapon. What with treating Doctors also falling victim to the deadly affects of this rapidly spreading disease, and with much needed Nurses choosing to stay home to care for their own family, as they also fall sick to this biological weapon's terrible effects on release against the world. I see a living hell right here on earth if this biological weapon ever makes it to the shores of the United States, Mr. President."

"Doctor Rosenblum, I hear what you're saying and understand the ramifications you're talking about at this meeting, sir. Even though I understand these factors and am able to follow them, sir. I believe the President and others attending this meeting are still kind of confused at what you're driving at, Professor. I think it'll help him along with the rest of us if you were to inform the President of the severe effects this biological weapon poses for the world at large, sir. We need to hear the entire nightmare before we can formulate our reactions to this properly, Professor." Doctor Mark Johnson sitting in for Doctor Russbinder, suggested from his seat.

"Yes Doctor Johnson, I believe it'd be rather foolish on my part to hold anything back, sir. As you stated, the full horror of this nightmare has to be exposed, sir. Mr. President." Professor Rosenblum offered as he turned to the American Leader, and went on with his words.

"Mr. President, you have to think of the severe and wide ranging ramifications if this extremely deadly biological weapon is able to reach the shores of the United States. Think about the effects this weapon will have on the population of the United States. Every hospital bed in the States and the world for that matter will be filled to overflowing their capacity for treatment of the sick. And, the sick and dying will soon be treated right where they fell. Every Doctor will think they were hit by a Tsunami of massive proportions of sick and dying patients, sir. Every emergency responder will be rapidly overwhelmed by the heavy influx of patients they'll be forced to care for, and the Doctors and other medical staff will find themselves forced to pick and choose what patients they'll help, and who they'll allow to die a horrible and lingering death before their eyes, sir. The medical staff of this country is a serious consideration than what I beforehand mentioned, sir.

"Even though we have a great medical assistance program set up in this country, there's a severe shortage of medical beds and hospital staffers. If we're hit with a pandemic outbreak of global proportions, we have to and must take into consideration and understand these shortages in our medical field, and what will happen once this possible pandemic outbreak reaches our shores, and kills the civilians in the tens of thousands. Our medical workers will be stretched to their absolute limit in the first few hours of the disease reaching our shores. The medical personal will be further stretched to their limit, when numbers of doctors and nurses and medical aides also begin to fall victim to the effects of this terrible biological weapon posses, Mr. President. As these doctors and nurses fall victim to the effects of this weapon, it'll effectively remove the medical assistance and resources offered to the civilian ill and dying, and we'll be helpless to do anything about this situation.

"Mr. President, the normal activities of the world will be forced to come to a grinding standstill. Economies of the world will begin to stagnate and fail, and any emergency survivors of this terrible weapon will find themselves scared to death to step foot outside their homes, in fear of becoming infected by this latest horror to possible plague the world. These poor souls won't be able to elude the grim reaper for long. This Biological Level Five threat will spread rapidly and unchecked, and it'll quickly find everyone living on the face of the earth no matter where they try and hide from it, and sooner or later it'll find and destroy them, sir.

"Mr. President, I'm not saying all humanity will perish from this terrible threat to us, sir. As it has been the every case whenever a plague or pandemic outbreak threatened to erase humanity from the face of the earth, there are always some survivors left to start over again, sir.

"Survivors come from many different reasons and circumstances Mr. President, natural immunities to the plague's outbreak for one, will always allow some souls to survive any possible outbreak, and take an infected male who might impregnate a woman before he finally gives into the terrible effects of the weapon or pandemic, sir. Something happens inside the impregnated woman's womb that might afford the unborn child to be born with a sort of natural immunity or resistance against this latest manmade plague to attack the earth, sir.

"If this happens, the blood of this new born child will help us develop an active and rapid acting antidote to employ against the biological weapon, sir. As I informed everyone here, this weapon kills with such proficiency that the development of any possible antidote will be a waste of time. By the time we're able to employ the antidote, the deaths will be too massive to be of use to the final outcome of this infection, sir. Other souls will be able to survive by living underground or underwater where the germ won't be able to find and destroy them so easily, sir.

"There's another situation we must take into consideration when trying to combat a pandemic situation breaking out in the United States, Mr. President. We have to understand the severe ramifications a pandemic of this nature and threat level will cause outside our medical sector, sir. As the effects of this released biological weapon quickly takes over the world, our plant workers in the pharmacy industry will suffer drastically as their plant workers fall victim to this disease, Mr. President. The supply of medications needed to at least make the infected and dying host as comfortable as possible will end, and the infected patient will suffer terribly until finally dying, sir. Let alone taking into consideration the possibility of developing an active antidote against this deadly weapon without the proper staffers, sir.

"The terrible and all consuming effects of this fearsome weapon doesn't stop there either, Mr. President. As the plant workers become ill and the States are plunged into darkness because there's no one left healthy to work the power plants while trying to defend against the effects of this pathogen. We'll find ourselves fighting a many front war not only against this pandemic outbreak. We'll be fighting to maintain the normal activities needed to keep the United States working as an active nation, as more normal services usually enjoyed or needed to keep our country operating properly, will quickly start to falter and fail under the terrible effects offered by this deadly biological weapon.

"Mr. President, I'd have to say this weapon of mass destruction has to be the most deadly one ever to be developed by the evil mind of man, sir. The damn thing will kill too quickly for us to be able to develop a working antidote that'd have a positive effect on the infected host, before he or she dies from the effects of this biological weapon on his or her body, sir. Mr. President, I found myself asking more than once while I was working on the small sample offered by General White. Is this the one; is this the one weapon that'd force the world before their maker's feet for final judgment of the wrath of God? This one weapon could well be the feared Armageddon that destroys the entire human race, and all other life on the face of the earth, sir.

"Mr. President, I see in my mind's eye run away fear, uncontrollable riots in major cities, and all sorts of civil and national unrest until the troublemakers become infected by this biological weapon, and they die off from its effects on their bodies, sir. It'll be mayhem in all countries of the world once the civilian populations realize what was released against and is killing them at the same time, sir. At the best, the overall death rate will be massive, alarming and beyond counting and human understanding, and the bodies of the dead will be allowed to rot where they have fallen, Mr. President. I see once this biological weapon has run its course and burn itself out. Any possible survivors will take a year, two, three, or maybe a full generation or two or three generations, before survivors will start to band together in large enough numbers to begin to reproduce and start the repopulation of the human race, Mr. President.

"I can only pray to God there'll be more than one possible Adam and Eve left alive, once the biological weapon has come to burn itself out, sir. To start to bring new life back to a devastated earth, if this damn biological weapon is released against the humanity of the innocent world, sir. If this weapon's released by accident or on purpose Mr. President, it'd be the final catastrophe, the long feared doomsday weapon to attack the world and her children. Mr. President, I see maybe one in ten million people possibly surviving the devastating effects of this weapon, if it's released against the world, one in ten million people surviving if we're lucky. As I have mentioned before in this conversation, the contagion rate affectability is placed at between ninety five to ninety eight percent of all deaths on the earth." Once again, the shaken elderly professor stopped speaking to allow the President or anyone else attending the meeting, to ask any questions he knew they must be suffering from.

The President was sitting on the edge of his seat, staring at the professor's eyes, as the old man continued to inform him and the others of what horrible effects this biological weapon might have on the earth and her populations. The President shook his head slowly, as if he was trying to clear his mind so he could speak coherently about the subject. Finally the President grumbled at the professor. "Doctor Rosenblum, when I told you were scaring me to death before you went on with your presentation, you said you only began to scare me, you weren't kidding, sir. Are you certain of your findings, sir? What the hell am I asking Professor? Of course you're certain of your finding, or you wouldn't be standing before me and scaring me like you are, sir."

Professor Rosenblum nodded at the stunned looking American Leader.

Doctor Johnson stood and his action caused the President to look at him and ask. "Doctor Johnson, I hope you have questions for the Professor that might make me feel a little better over this damn information I'm hearing reported here today, sir?"

"Yes Mr. President, I have a few questions I'd like to ask the Professor. But I don't believe they'll make you feel any better once he answers my questions." The other NEST doctor replied.

The exhausted and completely confused President removed his eyes from Doctor Johnson, and he leveled them on Professor Rosenblum and Doctor Johnson took this action from the American Leader as an okay for him to start his questions of the doctor.

"Excuse me Professor Rosenblum, you stated a newly born child might come with some sort or form of possible resistance the child was able to develop while living in the womb of the mother, against this biological weapon after being impregnated by an infected host, sir. How come you believe that if we use the new born child's blood, we'd be wasting our time trying to prefect an active and rapid acting antidote to this new threatened infection against us, sir? Surely the child's blood would help us to develop an antidote to this horror, sir."

"Doctor Johnson, I offered retrieving the blood of a possible antidote donor would be a waste of our time and efforts for a number of reasons trying to defeat the horrible threatened effects of this terrible weapon of mass destruction, sir. The first one is being and it's the most prevalent reason I have to offer everyone attending this meeting, sir. Taking into consideration the rapid rate of speed at which this biological weapon kills its infected host, sir. No possible antidote developed in the world would be employed soon enough to have any favorable outcome in its use against this terrible weapon. No antidote developed will be able to save the life of one infected host, before the host body gives in to the appalling effects of this biological nightmare, sir.

"Furthermore Doctor Johnson, it'd also take many years before we have enough living donors where we could milk them, and manufacture enough of the active antidote to have any positive outcome on the effects of this so deadly weapon, sir. Speaking of the impregnated woman and her unborn child again, it'd take many years and maybe even generations before the population would start to reproduce in the numbers of protected children needed, to make enough of an active antidote against this weapon, to have a positive effect against the damn thing and start controlling it, Doctor. No, I see no hope of developing an active antidote against this weapon of mass destruction, before any released product does what it was designed to do, and that's to destroy all life on the earth.

"As I stated in this conversation to all members, Doctor Johnson this manmade biological weapon of mass destruction was developed solely to attack the Persian race of Iran and all her descendents by the madman once in control of Iraq, sir. Neither the fool nor the Iraqi technicians working on this weapon took into consideration the possible mutations this weapon might employ, to survive until it became strong enough to threaten the world population, Doctor. You must understand this is a living weapon, and as is in the events controlling all living things. This biological strain being will do anything in its power and it needs to do to survive another day of its survival, Doctor. The only way this weapon can survive is if it mutates into any form to continue its life, so it can attack all living things until it runs out of living hosts to infect and feed on. Then the weapon will merely and finally turn against itself, and destroy itself by feasting on the weaker cells of the weapon itself.

"Doctor Johnson, you have to understand every time this biological germ jumps from its original target of the Persian race, and mutates itself into the strength it needs to enable the weapon to attack another race of peoples. The biological weapon changes its original properties, sir. As I stated in this lengthily presentation to the members Doctor Johnson, this biological weapon will expand exponentially at a rate of ten times ten times ten times ten until it covers the entire face of the earth, and the living weapon attacks all living things, sir.

"No one living human being or animal known to the civilized world will be safe from the devastating effects of this biological weapon, until all life as we know and understand it, ceases to exist on the earth. Then and only then will this biological agent start to burn itself off by eating on its own remains, because it has nothing else to feast upon, Doctor Johnson. This is a living thing we're attempting to confront and destroy, and we have to remember this fact while trying to deal with this weapon, Doctor Johnson." Professor Rosenblum growled, not realizing he was beginning to lose his temper trying to make every one understand how dangerous this biological weapon truly is.

"Please Professor Rosenblum, we understand what you're reporting, sir. I don't need you placing your health at risk by allowing your temper to rule your better judgment, sir. Think of your blood pressure and get a hold of yourself, and then Doctor, continue with your presentation, sir." President Cole said as he tried to calm the excited professor so he could finish up.

Doctor Johnson was not going to end his questioning of the professor, because there was something he needed to know from the aged professor. Doctor Johnson allowed the professor the time to calm down, and then he asked him his next question. "Professor Rosenblum, I have one more question for you to reply if you don't mind, sir. Although we have a pretty good idea how this infection is passed from one infected host to another, I'd like to hear what you have to offer, sir?

And, I still believe there has to be some antidote, something we have in our arsenal."

"Yes sir, by all means Doctor Johnson and that was a good question needing to be asked and answered by Doctor Rosenblum, sir." The President added as he looked at the professor, and then gave him a weak and exhausted smile.

Drawing in another quick breath, Professor Rosenblum responded politely but quickly to the last question asked of him by the doctor and he directed his response to the American Leader. "Mr. President, that's one of the most puzzling and concerning and also confusing situations of this new and extremely deadly biological weapon's properties, sir. Although it's a living thing and needs a moist and livable environment to usually survive and grow in. This particular biological strain is more than capable of surviving on the outside skin of the infected host in a sort of dormancy type of state for long periods of time. That fact allows this weapon to not only survive in the infected host, but outside and feast itself on the layer of skin of its host until it either finally enters the body of its host by eating through its skin, or is inhaled by the host with the external infection. The living germ can also be transmitted by merely coming in physical contact with the infected host. As well as being in the nearby vicinity of an infected host and he happens to sneeze, cough, laugh or even speak to another person not infected by the ugly biological germ, sir.

"Mr. President, I did however take it on myself and I ran a number of detailed experiments on the weapon's survivability on many different surfaces and conditions such as wet, dry, hot and cold surfaces, and the damn thing was able to survive and reproduce itself in a number of hostile environments that would normally hinder, or usually destroy another type of biological germ.

"I will take this time to address the Doctor's remark about something we have in our arsenal to combat this weapon.Problems exist with regard to vaccines available to DoD (Department of Defense) for immunization purposes. Only a few biological agent vaccines have been approved by the Food and Drug Administration. Many of these vaccines remain in the Investigational New Drug status. Although

IND vaccines have long been administered to personnel working in DoD vaccine research and development programs, the FDA usually requires large scale field trials in humans to demonstrate new drug safety and effectiveness before approval. The DoD has not performed such field trials because of the ethical and legal considerations involved in deliberately pursuing other means of obtaining FDA approval for IND vaccines. IND vaccines can now be administrated only under approved protocols and with written informed consent.

"During the Gulf War, the DoD had requested and they had received a special waiver from the FDA requirement for written informed consent since this was a contingency situation. If the DoD intends to use vaccines to provide protection against biological agents to personnel assigned to high risk and threat areas of designated for rapid deployment, it needs to make the required decisions for proceeding with the immunizations involving IND vaccines, or obtaining special FDA approval for the use of them. The DoD officials informed me they intend to acquire a prime contractor to subcontract vaccine production with the pharmaceutical industry, and take actions needed to obtain FDA approval for existing IND vaccines. But this weapon kills so quickly no possible antidote or vaccines will help in time, and we were forced to come to the conclusion this weapon of mass destruction will survive in countless numbers of extremely hostile or friendly environments, and that's why it's absolutely necessary for us to stop its deployment anywhere on the earth by any means at our disposal, Mr. President."

"Exactly and that's what I intend to do as we speak, Professor Rosenblum!" The President roared as he suddenly jumped to his feet and he started to pace the Oval Office behind his massive desk as he added to his words for the members of the meeting. "That's exactly what I intend to do with this damn situation Professor, stop this damn thing dead in its fucking tracks, before it can be deployed against any race of people on the earth. General White!" The President turned to his military leader, and then he growled at him.

"This is where your Special Forces troops come in again I'm afraid, General White. Your elite soldiers must be forced to understand just how imperative it is for the troops to find every trace of this damn thing before it's used against us, sir. Where's the damn Marine Operator at? Walter, I want you in here immediately." The President roared at his young aide.

Walter, the White House Chief aide to the President, rushed into the Oval Office the moment he heard the President bellow for him. Upon seeing him, President Cole snarled at the young man. "Walter, get the damn Marine Operator in here, I need to speak to that Officer, son."

General John White smiled as he decided to take a back seat until he understood what the President wanted from his operator, and where he was going with his anger. When the officer marched into the Oval Office and snapped to attention and sharply saluted the Commander in Chief, the General stared at the young man.

"Ahhhh… Lieutenant, I want you to raise those soldiers we sent to Iraq on the radio. I need, no correct that I demand to speak directly to their Commanding Officer."

The Lieutenant cast his eyes towards the Chairman of the Joint Chiefs of Staff which caused the President to growl at his favorite aide. "What the hell are you looking at the General for, mister? I gave you a direct order and I expect you to carry it out immediately, Lieutenant! Your General has nothing to do with the damn order I just issued. I suggest you carry out my request before you find yourself attached to the soldiers we sent to Iraq."

The officer sharpened his attention stance and he saluted the President and then turned on his heels to carry out his orders from the Commander in Chief. When the officer was out of the room, President Cole turned to his General and snapped the military officer. "General White, I want you with me when I speak to your soldiers in the field, sir. Then I want you carrying out my orders to them, sir."

General White nodded at the upset President as he rose and followed him out of the Oval Office. They walked together to where the Lieutenant had his communication console setup, and by the time the President arrived. The officer offered him the mike and he announced. "Mr. President, I have a Colonel Bruce Leadbetter on the line, and he's the Commanding Officer of the Special Operations Soldiers we deployed to Iraq, sir."

"That'll be all I need from you Lieutenant, you're excused. I'll call if I need you Lieutenant." The moment he abandoned his seat and post, the President plopped down and said aggressively into the scrambled radio. "Colonel Bruce Leadbetter, this is your Commander in Chief, and I have a new batch of orders for you to carry out. Are you there Colonel Leadbetter?"

Without realizing he was doing it, Colonel Leadbetter automatically straightened up as he replied to the angry sounding American Leader. "Yes Mr. President, I'm here sir. Mr. President, I'm at your disposal and awaiting your new orders, sir."

"You're damn right you're at my disposal soldier, and that's what I wanted to speak to you about, Colonel. Colonel Leadbetter, you do understand the mission you and your outstanding troops are currently deployed on sir, and I want you to understand just how crucial this operation is to me and to the rest of the world population, sir. Colonel, you're ordered by me personally to search all Iraq if necessary, until you found every possible trace of this damn item, sir. I'm telling you personally Colonel Leadbetter, none of your highly trained soldiers will be allowed out of Iraq and back in the United States, until every iota of this damn thing is accounted for, and it all is in our god damn possession, sir.

"I hate to be forced to inform you Colonel Leadbetter Sir, but if this item is somehow released to the air by accident or on purpose, I'll be forced to sterilize the entire nation of Iraq, and if forced to, I'll burn the entire Middle East to a damn cinder, to stop this crap from escaping the Middle East region and infecting the rest of the world, sir. This item will not be allowed to escape its confinement as long as there's a breath in my body. Do I make myself clear on the steps I'll employ if this thing is released against the world, Colonel Leadbetter?"

"You made your wishes perfectly clear, and I understand the steps you'll adopt if this item is somehow released, Mr. President Sir. I and my soldiers will complete our mission successfully as ordered by any means we have to employ, sir." Colonel Leadbetter replied into the radio to his Commander in the United States.

"Very good Colonel Leadbetter, complete your mission and I'll see you and your elite troops when you return to the States, sir." The President snarled as he broke off the communication with the Marine Colonel. The President did not leave his seat as he turned to the Chairman of the Joint Chiefs of Staff, and ordered him in no uncertain terms.

"General White, you just heard the orders I issued to your Colonel Leadbetter in Iraq, sir. You'll not return to the Oval Office with me to hear anything else that transpires in the room with Doctor Rosenblum. Instead, you'll get back to the Pentagon and order enough of our nuclear submarines and other nuclear assets deployed to the Persian Gulf, Indian Ocean and the Mediterranean and Red Seas. I demand enough of our nuclear arsenal waiting in the area, and one word from me and they'll launch their entire compliment of nuclear tipped missiles and other weapons at any nation, or nations I ordered destroyed without hesitation, sir. One way or the other, I'll stop this miserable biological weapon from being released and threatening the world, General White. You're dismissed so carry out your orders, General White."

"Yes sir." General White replied as he snapped to attention and saluted the President.

THE UNDERGROUND BUNKER IN IRAQ

Colonel Bruce Leadbetter released the mike he was not the least bit surprised by the President's last orders. Because he was informed by General White he was planning to sterilize the entire Middle East if needed to stop release of the biological weapon, he and his troops were sent to Iraq to discover and take in their possession. Or the soldiers were to destroy it before it became a threat to the world. The Colonel took the time to light up a smoke, and picked up his mike and snarled in it as he released the smoke from his lungs as if he was angry at it.

"This is Searcher Base to Searcher One. Come in Searcher One. Over."

Captain Robert Walker heard his radio squawk and he slowly rolled his eyes as he grabbed for the mike and he replied to the incoming call. "Yes, this is Searcher One to Searcher Base. Go with your traffic. Over."

"Searcher One, I want to inform you I just got my ass reamed out good by Eagle One. (Code name for the President) He wasn't in a very pleasant mood, and I want to know what the hell you fucking people out there are up to. It seems everyone in the real world is starving for information on our missing item, and the progress of this fucking operation." Colonel Leadbetter roared in the mike, and then he waited for Walker's response to his gripe.

"For Christ sake Searcher Base, we're in the stinking field looking for any signs of this missing person and the damn package that's supposed to be in his or her possession, sir. What the hell more can I offer, we're doing our best. As of this time Searcher Base, we haven't uncovered any new information of the item or missing subject, and we haven't been able to detect a warm trail as of yet, sir. If the people in the real world are busting your stinking horns for information on this crap, I suggest you tell them to get their asses out here and help us search for this crap, so they wouldn't be busting your horns so much, sir. Over Searcher Base."

"You're being a fucking smartass as always, soldier. You try and get someone sitting in a nice safe office in the real world to leave it and come out and do some schlepping around of their own in the animal world with us ground pounders, Captain. You pay attention to your mission and find that crap so we can get the hell out of this lousy desert. I have enough of a tan to last me for the rest of my life, mister. All kidding aside Captain, how the hell are you doing sir, and do you need more people to help you to locate this missing shit, soldier?" Colonel Leadbetter was refraining from using Walker's last name or rank over the radio this time, even though they were operating on a secured net for communications.

"Searcher One to Searcher Base, I believe I have enuf personnel to carry out this operation successfully, sir. I ordered the Dragon Flies (helicopter) back to my camp and once they're back here, I'll employ one of them in my search pattern of the surrounding area, sir. Have the extra personnel you have held in reserve in case I might need them at a later time during this damn mission, sir. Over Searcher Base." Walker replied with a snap as he stopped walking and held the mike to his ear with his shoulder as he lit up a smoke.

"Roger your last and will do as suggested, Searcher One. Over." Colonel Leadbetter replied as he cursed himself for not being in the thick of it with his other soldiers.

"Searcher One to Searcher Base, before we break off communication. I'd like to know if the Spook medics were able to come up with any new information for our use. I sure could use some kinda help from someplace on this damn operation, sir. Over." Walker asked his commander in hopes the medics were able to come up with something that might help him and his team, as they searched the area for signs of the missing person and biological agent this person supposedly removed from the bunker.

"Searcher Base to Searcher One, I haven't heard jack shit from them damn pain in the ass people since they first disappeared in their miserable medical tent some hours ago. I'll tell you what I'm going to do though Searcher One, once we finish with this communication. I'll check in with them people and see if they were able to find out anything new on that dead Iraqi kid, or this missing crap. All I know now is, we had three different medics turn up here, and they disappeared in that stinking tent never to be seen again. For all I know, they could be in there smoking grass and sipping booze, Searcher One. Yeah, I guess it's time I get on their god damn asses, soldier. Keep me advised on the progress you might make, and if I have to check in with you before you check back with me. I'll have the artillery unit open up and fire off rounds at your ass to remind you to check in with my ass more often, soldier. Searcher Base Out."

Walker grinned over the threat from his commanding officer, because he knew there were no artillery units in miles of their locations as he checked off on the mike. "Searcher One. Out."

The Mutt worked his way over to Walker's side the moment he noticed him on the radio, and knew he was communication with the Colonel at the other site, and he wanted to see what Colonel Leadbetter has to say. "Hey Walker, what the hell did the fucking Colonel want from our damn asses this time around, man?

"Arrr… he wanted to tell me he has some stinking people climbing all over his fucking ass about this shit we're looking for, that's all man. Add that to his usual threats from the prick, and you get the jest of what he wanted to bust my horns over, man." Walker replied as he finished off his cigarette, and check on what his troops were doing. At least the ones he could see from where he and the Mutt were speaking together.

"Man that little fuck working this operation from the damn cheap seats back there has to get himself a fucking life, Walker. What the hell does the prick think we're doing out here for the love of God? Taking a stroll along the beach looking for fun and games with any A-rab chicks we might come across out here." He bitched angry the colonel was getting on their ass again.

"C'mon man, you know he's under the gun with the rest of us for this operation, Homes. I don't see Hunter and the Ghost, are they still pulling point duty? I want them two in front of us, they're the only ones I trust to keep us from falling into an ambush by a pack of insurgents working this country, Mutt." Walker grumbled as he tried to locate either of the pointmen.

"You know them two pricks are in front of us man. Where the hell didja think they'd be Walker? The last time I picked up either of them two birds, they were working off to the left of the main body of our people, Walker." The Mutt reported as he looked off in the direction he last spotted the two soldiers working in, and then he tried to locate them as well for Walker.

Walker did not try to locate the point soldiers after realizing they would always be walking point for his troops. He looked over his shoulder and picked up Colonel Pullman, and waved the Airforce soldier to his side. When the Colonel reached Walker he almost growled at the officer. "Colonel Pullman, didja get in contact with them two Spook helicopters as I order? I don't see either machine coming back to our location, Colonel. I want the machines back here ten minutes ago. Colonel, if I had those damn machines available, I'd have them over us scouting out the area in search of the prick we're looking for, and keep an eye out for possible ambushes, sir. A pilot in a helicopter can see a helluva lot further than my point soldiers can, Colonel."

"Captain Walker, I made contact with the lead pilot after you ordered me to do so, sir. I keep looking for any sign of them sir, as of yet I haven't picked them up, sir. I don't know where the hell they were searching, for all I know they could be a hundred miles from our position, Captain. Do you want me to get in contact with them again and see where the hell they are, sir?"

"I sure as hell do Colonel Pullman, I need them damn machines working for me." Walker growled at the higher ranking officer, and regretted his display of anger aimed at the officer.

Colonel Pullman did not notice the way Walker spoke to him as he headed off to find their One Charlie Operator. Finding the soldier branded Roach, the Colonel ordered him to open a communication link with the lead pilot of the CIA helicopters. In a matter of seconds, the pilot was on the radio with the Airforce Colonel. "Yes, this is Tracker One to Searcher One. Go with your traffic sir. Over."

The Colonel took the mike and replied. "This is Searcher One to Tracker One. Tracker One, where the hell are you sir? I have an extremely excited Commander waiting for you people to get your asses over to us pronto, sir? How far out are you at this time sir? Over."

"Tracker One to Searcher One, I'm sorry for delay returning to the base, sir. We had to fuel up before returning to the main base as ordered, Searcher One. As I see it sir, we're fifteen minutes from your location, sir. We're turning on final approach to your Papa, Papa as of this time, sir. Any further or change to my standing orders as received, Searcher One? Over." Commander Peterson asked as CIA Lieutenant Carl Bryant listened to the communication the pilot sent out.

"Searcher One to Tracker One, there are no changes to your standing orders as of this time, sir. You're ordered to return to main base of this operation as soon as possible. Over Tracker One."

"Tracker One, Roger last Searcher One, am returning to main base. Out." Commander Peterson replied as he broke off communications with Searcher One.

Colonel Pullman did not bother to sign off with the pilot he disconnected the communication and handed the mike to Roach, and then he went off to report to Walker. Spotting the Captain standing with the soldier he left him with, the Colonel rushed over to the

Captain and reported. "Captain Walker, I just finished speaking with the Commander of Tracker One, he reported the reason for their delay getting back here sir, was they needed to refuel their machines, sir. ETA our position is ten minutes out, sir."

"Good, going Colonel Pullman, when the helicopters get back here, sir. I want the machines to land at our main base setup, sir. I'm gonna order some soldiers back with you, sir. Colonel, you're in command of my people and I want you controlling the helicopters at the same time. I want one of the damn things out before our point at all times while we're in this desert, sir. I want the people to keep their eyes opened for our subject, also looking for groups of possible insurgents or ambushes being setup against our forces as we move out here, sir. From reports I read before leaving for this second location Colonel, they mostly state this area we're working in was a hot bed for insurgent engagements and activity, sir. I have no intention of getting caught flatfooted by these sand swimmers where they might get the upper hand on us, sir…"

"Captain Walker, here comes the helicopters now, sir." Colonel Pullman interrupted the officer and announced, and both officers watched at the two war machines flew over their position, and continued heading to the temporary camp about three miles behind the group of special operations soldiers in the field searching for the packages.

"It's about time them damn things got back here, you betta start back for our main base, sir. I'll order the uther soldiers I want to follow you back to the base for security reasons, Colonel Pullman. Err… look Colonel I don't want you taking any crap from these assholes I'm assigning to your security, sir. I'm certain they're gonna try you out for size, and if you don't step hard on their throats, you won't be able to control them for a fricking instant, if they get away with any crap on you, sir. I know none of my people are gonna enjoy taking orders from a fly jock, sir. So I'm afraid you might have your work cut out trying to control my troops with ya.

"Colonel Pullman Sir, my troops are the handful, sir. They're still the best soldiers you'll link your wagon up with in your life, Colonel. Good luck working with my people because you're gonna need it sir, and get the lead helicopter up in front my people before we stumble into something I have no intention of enjoying out here, sir. Get it done as quickly as possible, Colonel Pullman. Shove off sir." Walker offered with a snap as he stepped out of the Colonel's way, so he could follow his last orders.

"You got it Captain Walker, I'll have the helicopter up and out before your people immediately sir, and then we'll assume point duty for your foot patrol, sir. I'll make certain the pilot knows what's expected of him, Captain." The colonel replied as he took off.

BACK AT THE ONCE HIDDEN UNDERGROUND BUNKER IN IRAQ

When Colonel Bruce Leadbetter broke off his communication with Captain Walker, he decided to head to the portable medical center the CIA Agents setup to continue their examination of the body. He walked through the first layer of protection as if he owned it, and he was immediately stopped by an agent seated between the two layers of protection leading into the main body of the medical center. Upon seeing the Colonel coming at him, the agent stood and sort of growled at the officer. "Can I be of assistance for you, Colonel? You know you're not allowed in this area without having an environmental suit on, sir."

The way the agent was speaking to him heated the Colonel up, and he snarled at the younger man without hesitation. "And, who the fuck are you to be speaking to my ass like this, mister? If you fucking remember correctly buster, I'm the god damn Officer in command of this entire fucking operation, and if I want to walk in there the way I'm dressed. I'll do exactly that and enjoy myself while I'm at it, mister. Now get the hell out of my fucking way, I have to speak to one of your damn medics right now, pal."

"Colonel Leadbetter, you might be in command of this operation, sir. But once you enter this installation Colonel, you're under the command of the medics. If they order me to stop you, I'll stop you in your tracks Colonel, by any means I have to resort to accomplish my orders, SIR."

After a tense and rather hostile stare down, Colonel Leadbetter realized the agent was correct, and the medics superseded his command and he blinked as he offered in a much calmer voice. "Okay, right, yeah young man you got it, I want to speak to the medic I was speaking to before. The reason I want to see this man is because I have a number of soldiers out in the field looking for this missing person, along with the carp we're looking for in this desert. I need to know if the medic was able to find out any new information that might help them in the field. I just finished speaking to my commander and he wanted to know if your people were able to find out anything that might help him and his troops, sir. Dammit to hell and back, I don't remember the name of the damn medic I was speaking to, mister. Let me poke my stinking noggin in there and see if I can spot the man and get his fucking attention, and get him out of the main section of this damn structure so I can speak with him again."

"I can't allow that, Colonel Leadbetter. You're not dressed in protection gear, or authorized to enter the quarantined area of this installation, sir. This is what I can do for you Colonel. I can go in there and speak to Medic Lieutenant Richards, and see if he wants to break off his examination of the body, and if he wants to leave the quarantined area so he could speak with you, Colonel. I don't know if you're aware of this or not, sir. You're already breaking the regulations that govern this medical installation, Colonel Leadbetter.

"Colonel, you're not allowed to enter this far into the quarantined medical ward without being dressed in the environmental suit and separate breathing apparatus, sir. With you standing this far in this medical structure secured area, you're placing both of us in serious trouble, Colonel Leadbetter. I suggest you leave this area immediately, and I'll go in and speak to Lieutenant Richards, and if he wants to come out of quarantined area for a break and speak with you, he will sir. Please Colonel you must leave the quarantined area immediately, sir." The CIA Agent waved his protected arm out before him and drew the officer's attention to the see through heavy plastic flap doors he plowed his way through moments ago, and motioned for him to leave the area.

"I guess you're throwing my ass the hell out of this place I see, mister?" Colonel Leadbetter nearly roared at the young man as he tried the glare he always used on his troopers.

"If you choose to look at it that way Colonel, yes sir I'm throwing you the hell out of here, sir. It's for your own safety that I'm doing this, Colonel Leadbetter."

"Okay buster I guess you win this round, I'm warning you though in no uncertain terms, sir. If this Lieutenant Richards of yours isn't standing before my can by the time I finish starching my nuts. I'm coming back in here, and I'm coming in here with armed soldiers, and I'll see this fucking Lieutenant Richards one way or the other, sir. Do I make my intentions perfectly clear to your ass, Mister CIA Man?"

"I read you loud and clear on your threat Colonel Leadbetter. I wouldn't attempt that, sir." He cocked his head to the side and displayed no fear over the Colonel's threatening words.

"Hmmmm.., you got some guts there and guts are enough, buster. Get in there and inform Lieutenant Richards I want to see his ass outside this dump as soon as he can leave the fucking quarantined area, and I'll not wait for long for him to come out of there."

"I'll get on that order for you instantly I assure you, Colonel Leadbetter."

With that said the angry military officer turned on his heels and stormed out of the temporary medical unit. Once outside, Colonel Leadbetter lit up a smoke, and started pacing in front of the medical unit while waiting for the medic to come out and speak with him. Ten minutes later, the medic came out dressed in his scrubs, and he lit up a cigarette after drawing in a few quick deep breaths of fresh air. The air inside the heavy environment suits could become stale after breathing it for long periods of time while working in a possible biological contaminated area.

Colonel Leadbetter gave the medic a few moments to himself so he could collect his thoughts, and when he felt the medic was calm after finishing off his cigarette, he snapped at the man. "Well Lieutenant

Richards, have you been able to find out anything that might assist my people in the field, sir. I had a number of bitches from my Commander, and he's concerned about this damn weapon, and the protection of his fellow soldiers out there, sir."

"As well as he should be in fear of that, Colonel Leadbetter. Sir, so far we're able to determine how the child was infected by the biological weapon, sir. The point of infection centered on the child's right leg at about the pocket area, sir. We determined the child must have removed the missing vial and placed it in his pocket and one way or the other, the vial either broken, or somehow leaked in his pocket, sir. Don't get upset Colonel Leadbetter because the small amount of the biological agent this child had on his person is dead by this time of exposure, sir. It was absorbed by the cloth of his clothing and dried up and died off, and if any of the weapon had leaked out of his clothing, judging from where we found the kid's body buried, it had to be dispersed on the sand. The obvious hostile environment if the biological agent seeped into the sand, dried up the agent rapidly, and that was the only way for the germ to die off, sir.

"Colonel Leadbetter, I further believe the biological agent once stored inside the vial is dead, because even if it was able to survive in the hostile environment of the desert. The germ had no other living host to attack and survive in or on. When we found the body we figured he was five hours dead, sir. And, there was only a minute amount of the biological agent left alive in two of the child's internal organs, and they were the largest in his body. It was dead in the rest of his body, sir. So we came to the conclusion the biological germ still remaining is the main supply stored in the missing cylinder removed from the bunker, sir. If we find that container sir, I believe we'll have the entire supply of this shit, Colonel.

"I'm telling you Colonel Leadbetter the more we get into what this biological weapon can do to the human body, the more I come to fear the damn thing, sir. This weapon has to be the most dangerous item ever developed by man's evil mind, sir. The longer this germ is allowed to survive in an uncontrolled environment, the more it mutates, and more the damn thing mutates, the more dangerous it becomes. Colonel Leadbetter, this biological germ will change itself until it has the ability to attack any living thing we expose the damn weapon to, and the weapon mutates at an alarming rate, sir. If this thing's ever released against any nation, there won't be any living thing left on the earth that's not threatened by the damn thing, sir. It'll change until it can kill everything and everybody and we'll have to find some way to stop it before it kills…"

"Look Lieutenant Richards," Colonel Leadbetter interrupted the medic and growled in his harshest voice. "I don't give a flying fuck what this damn germ can do to the human body or animal for that matter. I'm only concerned if you people were able to come up with something that might help protect my people in the stinking field, that's all Lieutenant Richards."

"Err… Colonel Leadbetter, I'm deathly afraid there's not a helluva lot we could develop that'd help protect your soldiers in the field, or the human race from this weapon, sir. This weapon mutates so rapidly and grows unrestrained that an active antidote against it would be totally useless and out of the question, Colonel. If we're able to come up with an active antidote against the weapon, the damn germ kills its human host so rapidly that by the time the antidote is introduced into the infected body, it has already suffered massive internal damage to every major organ in the body, sir. Furthermore Colonel Leadbetter, we have come to the horrible conclusion that if we're successful in developing an active antidote against this weapon, and we introduce it into an un-infected human, the antidote will do absolutely nothing to protect the treated host.

"Now before you ask Colonel Leadbetter, allow me to explain a little further what I mean by my last statement, sir. As we continued to carry out further experiments on the germ, we discovered if we try to inoculate the host prior to being infected by the germ. Any possible antidote will be attacked and absorbed by the white blood cells of the human body sir, and it's destroyed before the host becomes infected with an active strain of the biological weapon, sir. Thus rendering any possible antidote completely useless, sir.

"Colonel Leadbetter, the normal function of the white blood cells of the human body is programmed to attack most invaders or infections to the body. This is the problem we're facing when it comes to this germ and its effects on the host's body, sir. Normally, the white blood cells would attack any infection, and in doing so it builds up a quick resistance against further attacks by the infection or the attacking germ, sir. But in this case Colonel Leadbetter, as the white blood cells attack a much weaker version of the germ, which is the foundation of any active antidote, this is what happens, sir.

"Once the white blood cells attack this weaker version, the weaker version of the weapon is still so powerful it has a negative effect, and the weaker germ is strong enough to kill the attacking white blood cells, sir. Thus Colonel, the supposed antidote is being destroyed by the white blood cell and the body's natural defense against any invading infection sir, but the infection is also killing the defender of the body and removing the protection the white blood cells usually offered to the infected host, sir.

"This weapon was designed so perfectly by its developer that there's no way in hell we can possibly come up with any active defense against the weapon, before the evil thing works it intent against the host and kills it, sir. This weapon scares me to my soul Colonel, it kills so rapidly and any weapon we can use to create some kind of protection for the human body. Is likewise destroyed by the weapon before the defense against it is activated to where it might make the infected host survive the attack from this damn thing, Colonel Leadbetter." The medic complained as he removed another smoke from his pack and he lit it and drew in the smoke.

"God dammit what the hell are you people being paid for, for the love of the Christ Child? I can't believe with all the fucking assets you guys have available for use for this type of god damn situation, you fucking people can't crack this damn thing in half and come up with something that might work against the damn thing for Christ sake, sir." Colonel Leadbetter snarled angrily as he held the young man in his ugly gaze and waited for a reply.

"That's not quite fair Colonel Leadbetter. Allow me to assure you Colonel Leadbetter Sir, we've been bending over backwards trying to find something that might work against this terrible strain of damn germ, sir. You have to understand our work on this biological strain is still in its infancy stage, Colonel Leadbetter. Heaven knows how long the Iraqis have been working and perfecting this terrible weapon, sir. We only been working on it for a few days now Colonel, and to try and come up with something that works against this horrible item that quickly is almost impossible to achieve, sir.

"Don't get me wrong Colonel Leadbetter, sooner or later we'll come up with something that'll work well against this damn germ. Heaven knows when the breakthrough will come Colonel and I can only hope it won't be too late to develop something that works for the human race to survive this possible biological pandemic attack against it, sir." The CIA Medic snapped back at the upset military officer as he angrily pitched his cigarette at the ground by his feet.

Drawing in a breath, Colonel Leadbetter backed off his anger aimed at the medical technician as he replied. "Yeah Lieutenant Richards, I see what you mean by your efforts on this crap, sir. Perhaps I was a little off base with my gripe at that, sir. You have to understand I have a mess of soldiers out there in harm's fucking way. I want and demand something be made available to them that might help them survive any biological contaminated environment from this god damn thing we have here, sir. And, I want it ten minutes ago at that Lieutenant Richards."

"I feel you Colonel Leadbetter and understand where you're coming from, sir. All troop Commanders want nothing more in life than to protect their treasures on the field of battle, sir. You have to understand we're doing everything in our power to try and come up with something that might protect your outstanding soldiers, sir. We're working against time here, Colonel Leadbetter. Time we don't have to work with at that sir. If this damn thing is released before we come up with something that works against it. Not only your soldiers in the field will be placed in harm's way, every living thing on the earth will likewise be placed at risk and death, Colonel."

"Christ Almighty Lieutenant Richards, ever since finding out this damn thing existed, I've been spoon fed a constant flow of extremely unpleasant information about the damn shit. In my wildest dreams

Lieutenant, I would've never though these backasswards technicians in Iraq had the damn smarts and would've never been able to develop something this dangerous." The fuming Marine Colonel grumbled as he looked around for something to hit, to help calm down his mounting anger.

"Colonel Leadbetter, I assure you we're leaving no stone unturned in our ongoing search for something, anything that might help us against this biological weapon. Colonel, we even employed a DNA expert from the States for our search, and he's trying to figure out where this child might have come from in this country, sir. What possible village or vicinity or region where he might have lived, in hopes of trying to narrow down the search area for the missing weapon, Colonel Leadbetter. We're trying everything in our power for help with this damn thing, sir." The medic offered to the still fuming Marine Colonel.

"And how is that going, Lieutenant Richards. By the way Lieutenant, how come the CIA placed a Lieutenant in command of such an important situation as this one, sir?"

"Sorry for my lower rank Colonel Leadbetter, before I was enlisted by the CIA, sir. I worked in the biological field for many years, Colonel. I guess they must have classified me as there most experienced operative they have for this biological type of situation, Colonel Leadbetter. As far as the DNA expert's concerned Colonel, he's working with countless DNA samples removed by our soldiers in both actions they took part in during the Desert Storm action, and the Iraqi Freedom action, Colonel Leadbetter."

"What the hell do you mean by that statement, mister? What fucking DNA samples is this so called expert of yours working with here, Lieutenant Richards? I was unaware we have soldiers doing this kind of shit during those two engagements. All of a sudden I feel like I'm being kept out of the stinking loop, Lieutenant." Colonel Leadbetter snorted with a snap, while searching for anything that might help his soldiers in the field, while accepting the reason for a mere Lieutenant to be in command of such an important operation as this one was to the world.

"Allow me to explain what I meant by that statement, Colonel Leadbetter. You see Colonel our soldiers in both aforementioned actions came across so many killed in action Iraqi soldiers and dead civilians. It was ordered by the higher ups for some soldiers to remove samples of the body's flesh, so we could develop a sort of store of samples, so we'll be able to match where some of these bodies came from in Iraq, sir. These removed DNA samples will allow us to trace the genetic roots of the dead through the samples, so we might locate where this dead child came from, sir. It has added to our own growing bank of DNA stores for future reference and considerations against crimes committed by a criminal, and dead soldiers so damaged the only possible identification of the dead has to be made by the remaining DNA of the corpus itself, sir.

"Colonel Leadbetter, we're removing mouth swatches from convicted felon criminals so we can continue to expand our DNA information banks in the United States, sir. This is breaking down to a world wide effort by most nations so if God forbid, we're faced with a world threatening situation. We'd be able to follow the ancestry of the massive amounts of possible dead, and find out where they might have come from at the same time Colonel, or where we might have to deliver the body for burial, sir." The medic offered the concerned Colonel.

"I got it Lieutenant Richards and I want to know, no correct that. I demand to know if this so called DNA expert, is having any luck placing a stinking village or region of this god forsaken miserable land to this kid's dead ass, sir. If this supposed DNA expert is able to narrow down our search area for where this kid might have come from. It'd help my people out enormously trying to find the rest of this missing shit, so we can get the hell out of this damn place, Lieutenant Richards." Colonel Leadbetter hissed hotly at the young medic.

"Colonel Leadbetter, we understand this, and that's why we've employed the services of this expert from the States. With the wealth of stored samples he has to draw from in this country, we feel it's only a matter of time before this expert is able to offer a close proximity as to where this dead child might have live, or at least came from at this point, Colonel Leadbetter."

"How soon do you think this expert might come up with something useful to work with, Lieutenant Richards?" Colonel Leadbetter snorted.

"Soon, very soon we believe he'll find out for us, Colonel Leadbetter. Because from the first moment he arrived at this site of the bunker, he's been working with all known samples our people were able to amass on the Iraqi population during those past two wars, sir."

"That's the first bit of good news I heard from anyone connected with this fucking operation since it started, Lieutenant Richards. You have to stay on top of this damn DNA expert, I need that information he's working on ten minutes ago, sir." The Colonel offered in a hot tone as he removed his cigarettes and offered one to the medic. Taking one the Lieutenant replied.

"Colonel Leadbetter, I assure you this DNA expert will come up with the ability to narrow down your search area, and soon at that sir. That's why we drafted him in the first place, and also why we started the DNA banks of information for just this type of situation, sir."

"How the hell long am I going to be forced to wait with my thumb stuck up my ass and spinning on the damn thing, sir. Until this DNA expert of yours comes up with this damn information for my use Lieutenant Richards?"

"Colonel Leadbetter, I'm expecting a positive response from the DNA expert at any time, sir. From what I was led to believe about his experiments Colonel, he has already established the kid had to come from this region of Iraq sir, and he's been successful narrowing it down to an area of some fifty square miles, Colonel Leadbe…"

"Jesus H. Christ and miracles Lieutenant Richards, I could have told you that much without using these damn DNA samples and tests this expert of yours is employing for this shit. Where the hell do you think this damn kid came from anyhow? We found his dead ass out there in the middle of the desert which easily informed me he couldn't have lived too far away from where we found his dead ass. There are at least fifty to sixty small villages, not counting the damn Nomad Tribes living in this part of the desert, within this fifty square mile region this expert's offering us. I don't have the time or luxury of searching every damn one of them before the nut who has this shit in his or her possession. Accidentally or on fucking purpose, decides to see what the hell he has and he or she opens the damn thing to the air, and we'll end up with one helluva god damn mess stuck on our fucking hands, Lieutenant Richards.

"For the love of God man, if this is the best this damn DNA expert has been able to come up with so far, sir. I don't think he's that fucking good an expert, and he's just blowing fricking smoke up our damn asses and wasting our fucking time, while he fumbles around with his damn DNA samples he's playing around with in that medical tent, buster."

"Please Colonel Leadbetter calm down, I understand the stress you must be operating under, sir. My DNA expert will narrow the search area down quite a bit when he finishes with his experiments on the DNA of the child. I'm certain once he finishes his tests, he'll have the search area down to ten square miles at the most, and that will eliminate many of the smaller villages you're concerned with, Colonel Leadbetter. He just needs a little extra time…"

"Time! Time! Lieutenant Richards, what the hell's wrong with you? What the fuck, do you have shit packed in your damn ears? Didn't I just tell you we're piss poor on time with this operation." Colonel Leadbetter's eyes narrowed as he pointed his finger at the media as if it was a weapon, and growled savagely at the man. "Now you look here Lieutenant Richards, if you can't light a fucking fire under this so called expert of yours. I'm going to step in and by the time I'm finished with his ass, he'll have the answers I need, even though he might not look like he does now. From what you're telling me, he's our best fucking hope of narrowing our search area down, and if you can't get him moving on this crap, I'll certainly get his ass in gear for him, sir."

"Colonel Leadbetter, I'm aware time's not on our side with this operation. You have to understand some experiments our DNA expert's conducting can't be rushed. Some experiments have to grow in a special environment, and that takes time, and once the results are in then he might come up with a positive conclusion on where this kid came from, sir."

"There you go again, using a possibility in the word might, Lieutenant Richards. I can't run this damn operation on a supposition. You have to understand I have soldiers in the field, and they're operating with their dicks or tits in their hands. I'm not enjoying having my fucking people working with such a threat of death hanging heavily over their damn heads, and they have no idea in what direction they should go from here, sir…"

"Colonel Leadbetter, your soldiers are not the only ones working with the odor of death hanging over their heads. The entire population of the world is hanging in the balance I'm afraid, Colonel. The population's banking on what we and your soldiers can accomplish on this operation, Colonel Leadbetter." Lieutenant Richards snapped back as nastily at the military officer, while interrupting him.

Colonel Leadbetter had to swallow before he replied. "Yeah, I guess you're right, Lieutenant. It's just I'm working with my back against the wall, and it seems no matter which way I twist and turn on this mission. I find my nose planted against this wall blocking my every move, Lieutenant."

"I understand what you must be going through, Colonel Leadbetter. I can only assure you we're doing our best to help you and your troops to get over this damn mess, sir. That's the best I can offer you, Colonel. We're trying our best, and we won't give up until we have positive results, Colonel Leadbetter." Lieutenant Richards replied as he let his breath out in a rush, and cast his eyes towards the portable medical structure they had set up for their experiments.

As if on cue, Major William Millstadt strolled out of the medical installation still dressed in his environment suit after it was decontaminated in the chemical shower. The Major had his plastic helmet and breathing apparatus lying over his back. He was struggling walking in the suit as he walked up to the Colonel and Lieutenant Richards and requested to speak with him.

The Lieutenant was relieved to see this man as he replied in an excited tone of voice. "Major Millstadt, this man standing by me is Colonel Bruce Leadbetter, and he's in command of this operation, sir.

In fact Major he's the reason for you being ordered out here, sir. So anything you have to offer can be discussed in front of this Officer at the same time, Major."

Major Millstadt offered his hand to the middle aged military officer. Colonel Leadbetter didn't shake it as he barked savagely. "Who the hell are you Major Millstadt, and what the hell are you doing still dressed in that damn suit? What if anything have you been able to discover that might assist me with this operation and protecting my damn troops while you're at it, sir?"

Taken back by the way the angry Colonel just spoke to him, the second agent replied with a little concern lacing his voice. "Colonel, I'm Major William Millstadt, I'm the Agency's Chief DNA expert. I'm used when the Agency has to identify a body and it's my job to find out where the dead person might have come from, sir."

"That'll make me sleep a lot better tonight, sir. Look Major, I don't give a good god damn for any of your titles. I'm more interested in what you found out that could help me and my soldiers, Major Millstadt. If you found something then I suggest you give me your damn report, so I can transfer it out to my Commander in the field and he can then act on it, sir. If not, you're wasting my fucking time, time I don't have to waste Major." Colonel Leadbetter snarled not removing his eyes from the second CIA Agent.

"I get that you're working under time constraints Colonel Leadbetter, and I'm proud to report my experiments were rather successful, sir. It took me quite a while to grow the cultures I needed and when they were complete, I was surprised to see such great results with the…"

"Come on will ya for the love of God, Major. You're stalling your damn report, and you're walking around in a mine field with snow shoes if you continue wasting my fucking time. Cut to the chase and report your findings before I reach in there and pull them out of your ass, Major."

"You better watch the way you're speaking to me Colonel, or I'll write you up sir."

"Look Major Millstadt, after this fucking mess is over, you can do whatever the hell you please with my ass for all the good it will do ya, sir. I need your damn report and I'm issuing you a direct order to get on with it, before I have you shot for disobeying a direct order from a Superior Officer, Major." He fired hotly at the other officer, waiting for his report to begin.

"Colonel Leadbetter, as I started to say sir. I was pleased with the results of my experiments on the DNA of the dead child, sir. I've been able to narrow it down quite a bit as to where this child was born in this country, Colonel. I linked this child's genetic sequence to one of three possible locations in Iraq, sir. The first and strongest location I came up with that had most DNA codes matching the dead child, was the small Iraqi village of ar-Ramadi at an eighty percent possibility marker, sir. The sequences from this location matched the child's DNA footprint the strongest, Colonel. The second location I came up with was the much larger village that's a good size city in its own right, Fallajah was the second possible strong point of where this child may have come from, sir. But this hit only carries about a sixty nine percent match ability with it, Colonel Leadbetter Sir.

"The third place the dead child might have come from, but this hit was the weakest point of the three hits, is the village or city if you will of Karbalh, sir. This hit came up with a thirty one percent positive hit. So I offer to you Colonel Leadbetter, the first village I'd order you soldiers to check out thoroughly is the village of ar-Ramadi, Colonel Leadbetter. I believe this village is the strongest possible hit I was able to come up with, sir."

"That's all I needed to know from you Major. Now I have something to aim my troops at. By your leave Major, I have an operation to get off the ground and thanks to your outstanding efforts, I have something to aim them at, Major." With a nod, the Colonel dashed away from the two CIA Agents and headed for his radio net.

Colonel Leadbetter rushed for his radio and pushed the soldier commanding the net out of his way, and he pressed the button and growled in the mike. "Searcher Base to Searcher One! Come in Searcher One, this is a direct order Searcher One. Over."

CHAPTER EIGHTEEN

Roach was carrying the portable Prick-25 radio as the group of specialized soldiers continued their search for the missing item and second missing person. The machine went off and Roach searched for Walker to let him know he had a call coming in from their command center. Spotting the Captain checking out an area of scrub brush, Roach made his way over to him.

"Hey Walker, you have a fricking call coming in from the stinking Colonel, man." Roach reported as he offered the mike to the young Captain.

"Fucking great, that's all I needed to fuck up the rest of my damn day. What the hell does that pain in the ass want from my sagging ass for Christ's sake? I just finished speaking with the prick about an hour ago, man."

"I ain't got a clue but the radio's a squawking and it has to be the damn Colonel, Walker."

"Give me the damn thing." Walker took the mike and snapped in it. "Searcher One to Searcher Base. Go with your traffic. Over."

"It's about time you replied, Searcher One. Searcher One, I have a flash for ya ass, and you're to respond to this information. Searcher One, I was just informed our dead package likely came from the village ar-Ramadi, the village is about twenty two miles north your location. You're instructed to concentrate your efforts at this village. I have a second location and that one's the city of Fallujah, and I'm dispatching my remaining helicopter to this city to scout it out. The most likely place this dead damn kid came from is the village you're ordered to check out, sir. Searcher One, it's going to take you at least two hours to get there by Humvee express. I'm ordering you to dispatch one of your helicopters before your column, and allow it to get to the village before your soldiers arrive there and check it out.

"Searcher One, you're instructed to surround the village before entering. Is there any way you can stop anyone from entering or leaving the village before you can secure the population of the dump? You have the power to arrest every damn one living in the village, and check them out. Anyone of no interest is to be released, and anyone you deem connected to our package, is to be detained by any means necessary, until you can locate our package. Make no mistake about my orders Searcher One. I don't give a rat's ass if you have to kill every living soul in that village, and then have your soldiers dismantle the place stick by stick until you locate our package.

"That possibly infected package and weapon our package is more than likely carrying, is the most important part of this entire operation, sir. I want both items laid out feet up if necessary before my damn ass by the end of this day. Do you copy your orders, Searcher One? Over." Colonel Leadbetter growled in the radio and then he waited for a reply from Captain Walker who was in command of the second search site.

"Searcher One to Searcher Base. I copy and understand orders as issued, sir. I'll carry them out to the best of my ability, Searcher Base. Over sir."

"Searcher One, you'll carry out your orders better than the best of your abilities! You and your troops will carry out your orders successfully, or you shitbirds will not return to the real world until you do, Searcher One. Get on with your orders and report the moment you reach your target area, Searcher One. Out!" Colonel Leadbetter abruptly broke off his communication with Walker, to display he was serious with his order to get the job done.

"Well fuck you too!" Walker snarled in the dead mike, and shoved it back at Roach as he looked at the soldiers surrounding him.

They pulled in when Walker started to speak in the radio with their commander, and now the soldiers wanted to know if there was a change in their orders.

"What the hell's up with the prick, man? You look really pissed off all of a sudden, man." The Mutt asked his lifelong friend with concern lacing his tone.

"We got a target area to concentrate on. I gotta make contact with the ATO dude and get him airborne. We gotta hustle our asses back to base and get in the Humvees and head for ar-Ramadi. Since you got the biggest mouth of our troops, you get the job of locating this shit village on the map so we know where the hell we're heading by the time we get back to base, wiseguy. Roach, get the SATCOM unit setup I gotta make contact with the ATO pronto."

"Right away, I'll take me a few seconds to set it up and align it with the satellite, Homes."

Walker gave the order, "Light'em if you got them. We're on a break until Roach gets the SATCON up and on line, and then we're moving out double quick."

"Walker, I got a linkup and the ATO's waiting orders." Roach called out.

Walker pitched his cigarette on the ground and walked to Roach and he handed him the mike and he offered on the secured net to the Colonel. "Searcher One to Tracker One. Over."

"I take it that's my call in, Tracker One, Searcher One. Over." Colonel Pullman responded while asking the Captain if that was the way he wanted him to respond to his call.

"Roger Tracker One. I have orders so listen up. You're instructed to head for ar-Ramadi, sir. I don't have an exact location on the target area, sir. So you're gonna hafta pull up the location and information on your own, sir. Once you have your target pegged out, you're to head for the location and hover over the village until my forces arrive on site and surround the town. I want you to keep your eyes open for ambushes setup once you're in the vicinity, sir. You do understand the moment your helicopter arrives on site, any insurgents in the area will know we're coming, and they'll likely setup something against us when we arrive on site, sir. Over."

"Tracker One to Searcher One, I understand my orders, and Commander Peterson has already located the target village and is setting in the GPS location on his control panel, sir. The Flight Commander informed me we should be arriving over the target village in ten to fifteen minutes from takeoff time at the latest, sir. Over."

"Roger that last Tracker One, don't waste anymore time speaking to me on this damn thing. We're pulling up stakes and heading for base and our Humvees, sir. You're instructed to be airborne immediately sir. Out Tracker One."

"Out Searcher One." The instant he was off the net with Walker, Colonel Pullman looked at the commander of the helicopter and he put power to his motors, and the helicopter lifted off the ground. In less than a heartbeat, the helicopter was flying at one thousand feet heading for ar-Ramadi at one hundred and fifty knots.

When the Captain was off the radio with the ATO Officer, he looked at his soldiers and then grumbled at them. "Okay people we have orders so let's get a stinking move on it. We have the helos heading out, so let's not be the ones holding up this damn freak show. Make certain we're not leaving anything we might need behind because we're heading back to base. Colonel Leadbetter was able to discover where that dead kid mighta came from, and he has ordered us to take over the stinking village and rip it a fucking part with our bare hands and find our missing packages so we can get the hell outta here."

"Out fucking standing Walker, I'm beginning to see a stinking end coming to this operation, man." The Mutt offered with a grin plastered on his stubble covered chin.

"Don't get ahead of yourself stupid. We're far from seeing a damn end to this operation." Walker warned the Mutt as he shoved him on his back to get him moving.

The special ops soldiers quickly wrapped up their equipment and supplies, and then the soldiers headed back for their temporary base. When the helicopters were in the air, Colonel Pullman maintained constant communication with Walker over their radio, reporting their progress by the mile heading for ar-Ramadi.

Just as Walker and his soldiers reached the base, another report came in from Colonel Pullman. "Tracker One to Searcher One. Come in sir. Over."

"Searcher One, send your traffic Tracker One. Over."

"Searcher One, we're about a mile and a half from target area, and I'm able to make out some buildings of the village. I'm deploying Tracker Two to the south end of the village to form up a protective ring around the village, and stop anyone from leaving until your troops arrive on site. We should be in position in two minutes. I repeat we'll be in position in two minutes. Over."

"Good deal Tracker One, I want that damn village buttoned down tight until we arrive on site and secure the dump for searching, sir. Over." Walker responded to Tracker One.

"Tracker One will do as ordered Searcher One, one question before signing off, Captain. What the hell do you want me to do if some of the villagers try and leave the town once they see our helicopters over the village, sir? Should I open fire on them and kill the lead group, or should I buzz them or just allow them to leave the damn village, sir? I suppose you understand the moment anyone in the village sees us approaching the town, the male population will automatically order their female population out of the village until your troops leave, sir. These damn Arabs have a real problem with us searching their women folk, sir. We ran into this problem in the past a number of times, sir. Over."

"Dammit to hell and back again, I didn't give that fucking problem a second though Tracker One. You just mentioned you ran into this same type of situation before, sir? How did you people handle it when you were faced with this problem, sir?" Over."

"Tracker One to Searcher One. We were forced to allow the women population of any village about to be searched, to leave the area until we had our people set on the ground, and were able to stop anyone else from leaving the intended search area, sir. Over."

"Okay Tracker One, that's what you're gonna do in this case as well then, sir. I can't allow you to open up on a stinking group of Arab civilians, especially a bunch of stinking women and children fleeing the damn area before we get on site. Tracker One, I guess all you can do at this point is your best to try and stop anyone from leaving the damn area until we finally arrive on site and secure the village. One question to you, when your people checked the village that gave you trouble. What was the stinking reason for the search in the first place? Over." Walker asked, fishing for added information from Tracker One.

"Searcher One, we were ordered to the Iraqi village to search for any possible hidden weapons, sir. When we secured the village and searched it, we found just a few weapons, but it was decided the fleeing women and children hid the weapons we wanted under their Kajubas. We were stuck because it was almost impossible to search any Iraqi woman and kids, even though we knew damn well they were smuggling the weapons we wanted out of the village on their persons. Over." Tracker One reported to Walker.

"Shit, okay Tracker One then I am sticking with my original order to you then, sir. You'll try and stop anyone from leaving the damn village until we foot soldiers arrive on site, if a flood of women and child cut out on us. We'll get stuck hunting them down one at a time if necessary, and search them somehow later on, sir. That's the best I can offer you at this point, Tracker One. Over." The Captain responded to Tracker One's report.

"Tracker One to Searcher One, I'll follow those orders as received sir. I have to break off this communication at this time because we're rapidly closing in on the village in question, and I have to pay better attention to the situation my helicopter will cause in the damn village, Searcher One. Over."

"Copy that Tracker One and secure the village the best you can, sir. We're leaving the base at this time, and we'll burn up the fuel and get to the village as soon as possible, sir. Good luck with your orders, Tracker One. Searcher One Over and Out."

"Out." Was the last word Tracker One reported before he broke off the communication.

IN THE SMALL IRAQI VILLAGE OF AR-RAMADI

The moment anyone living in the village spotted the approaching American helicopter, the man rushed to the home of the Village Elder and reported the fact of the helicopter to him.

Instantly the Elder and former General in the Republican Guard, Sameer Abased sent for Mustafa Abdalhadi, one of the Baath Party cronies who exerted control over Iraq's Intelligence Services, and likewise a former General in Saddam Hussein's once feared Republican Guard. When Mustafa arrived, the Elder informed him of the rapidly approaching helicopter, and Mustafa understood the ramifications of the machine and offered the Elder. "Sameer, I'll get to Ayesha's home and order her immediately out of the village for her own safety. It has to be the god cursed infidels coming for the weapon and woman who has it in her possession."

"Yes General Abdelhadi, do as you offered, first you'll return the metal cylinder to our daughter, and then you will order her to protect it with the last breath of her worthless body. General Abdalhadi, I cannot tell you how important to our cause it is for us to maintain this cylinder in our possession, until I get it to the right hands, and they know what to do with it from that point. You'll order the great fool we have protecting Ayesha, Mugrada. He's to protect Ayesha and before you ask, the other two foolish women with her are expendable. I'm only worried about Ayesha's life, and the protection of this cursed cylinder. Mugtada will stay with Ayesha until I find out where we're to deliver the cylinder. General Abdelhadi, how are you making out getting fighters from the surrounding villages?"

"I'm doing well having a number of al-Qaeda of Iraq fighters to infiltrate our village, and prepare to defend it from American attack. It was reported there are two hundred Arab fighters in the village, with more reporting here by the minute, Elder Sameer. I believe we'll have enough fighters to stop any Americans discovering we have the cylinder in our possession."

"This is good to hear, General Abdelhadi. Now you must get in contact with Mugtada, and have him escort Ayesha and her lowly friends out of the village to safety, before the cursed American soldiers arrive in our village, General."

"I'll leave for Ayesha's home and order her out of the village for her safety at once."

"Good, first you'll follow me and I'll give you the cylinder to return it to Ayesha. For the life of me General Abdalhadi, I have no understanding as to why Allah in His infinite wisdom, has entrusted this great gift to the hands of a lowly god cursed woman. For some reason He chose to do so, and that makes it my duty to see Allah's will carried out, until He shows us the path to take His gift in. Be gone with you General Abdelhadi, because soon the hated infidels will carry out their insult to our village and children." Sameer handed the cylinder to the General, and stared until he turned on his heels and left his presence with the cylinder in his arms.

THE CARAVAN OF AMERICAN HUMVEES HEADING FOR THE VILLAGE OF AR-RAMADI

The Mutt, (Lieutenant Frank Hall) was going over a number of reports he found inside the CIA commandeered humvee, while he was being bounced all over as his heavy duty military jeep ripped through the desert on the road the machine was making for itself. He was sitting in the back seat of the machine while Captain Robert Walker sat in the passenger seat of the machine. When he finished reading the report, he called to Walker with concern. "Hey Walker, you won't believe the fucking shit I just read, man."

"You read something without pictures of naked women in them, man? Mutt you're beginning to surprise the shit outta me, buddy. What the hell did you find back there that's got you so worked up, Mutt?" Sergeant Dorothy Ramirez snapped at him with a pretty smile.

"Ahhh… nagging your way to fucking ecstasy at my expense I see little sister. I can read, write and trace, and I can conjugate at the same stinking time, baby sister." The Mutt fired back at the pretty Sergeant Ramirez as he shot her a disgusted look.

"Cut the shit out and tell me what the hell you found in the stinking report, Mutt. I need all the damn input I can muster for this damn bug hunt operation, man. The frigging Colonel's starting to get really pissed off at us for wasting so much damn time as it is." Walker snapped at the Mutt as he grew angry at him for dumping on Ramirez.

"Walker, you're not gonna believe this shit for a stinking minute when you hear it man. Do you remember that little prick of an Iraqi Colonel who came to the States and started to pick off some of our stinking people, because we did in his hot shot General back in Iraq, man?"

"Yeah, his name was Colonel Harmoodi al-Qaysi if I remember right, or it was something like that. The lousy dude was on a stinking mission to free or kill that fricking Iraqi Colonel Abdulaziz Majd al-Adwani we took back to the States as a fucking prisoner, so we could've prove Saddam Hussein was behind the plot to assassinate our President a few years back, man. I'll never forget them two fucking names as long as I live. What's the stinking point you're trying to make here Mutt?" Walker asked the Lieutenant.

"Walker, it states on this stinking report that Colonel al-Qaysi came from the damn village we're heading for now man." The Mutt reported to Walker in a calm tone.

"Now that's troubling to my ass, I wonder if this dead ass Iraqi Colonel had anything to do with the stinking item we're out here looking for, buddy. Did the Iraqi bastard have any stinking kin living at this lousy Iraqi village we're heading for, Mutt?" Walker asked with concern as he maintained his vision in front of him.

"Yeah Walker it states here the lousy prick left behind a wife and five male and four female children in the village, before we turned him into Iraqi salsa. Well will you look at this shit, it states here a group of stinking Marines gave the bastard's personal effects to one daughter, and she got a red flag by her damn name, man. The bitch's name is Ayesha, and the red flag warns this is the only child from this family that's worth keeping an eye on. It states further this stinking chick has the same terrorist tendencies as her old man did, Walker."

"Good find there buddy, when we reach this damn Iraqi village, this chick is the first one I want placed in custody. I wanna question her slimy little A-rab ass personally, if she's a hot one from this dead ass Iraqi Colonel shit. Then she bares close examinations when we get hold of her rotten ass. Where the hell didja find this stinking information from, buddy?" Walker questioned his fellow soldier as he turned in the seat so he could look at the Mutt dead in his eyes as he waited for his reply.

"Shit Walker it was printed in one of the Spook's handbooks, man. There are a number of uther books and reports back here along with this one, buddy. I hope you don't want me to read all this shit back here, it'd take me forever to get it done and understand it."

"No, I wouldn't want you to hurt yourself doing some important reading, dog man." Walker grumbled at the Mutt for giving him a hard time over reading the CIA information.

"I'm not lying to ya stinking ass, I'm not gonna read all this shit piled up back here, Walker. It'd take me a fricking week to read through all this shit." The Mutt fired back, not giving into getting stuck reading all the papers in the rear of the machine.

"Walker, we know the Mutt's not a liar. Gees Walker, between you and the lie detector technician he doesn't stand a chance in hell of getting away with anything anymore. The reason the Mutt's not in jail is because he was released because of the overcrowding thing back in the States, honey." Blind Date, (Sergeant Regina Raphael) offered as she got on her boyfriend's back and smiled.

"I see I'm gonna start to have some trouble with your lovely little ass now, sister. Look sister, I just got Baby Tee offa my stinking ass, and now I got you taking her place." The Mutt growled at the beautiful female soldier and stared her in the eyes.

Blind Date continued to smile one of her sexiest smiles at her lover and soldier, until the Mutt smiled back at her. That move got the Mutt off Blind Dates backside, and they both relaxed.

IN THE SMALL IRAQI VILLAGE OF AR-RAMADI

The Village Elder, Sameer Abdalsada watched as his General took off with the stainless steel cylinder containing the biological weapon, to collect Ayesha and her two female friends. Then get them safely out of the village before the American soldiers arrived, and the invaders took over the village. The old man picked up a number of Arab people he did not recognize rushing around his village. The group of strangers seemed to be armed to the teeth for battle. The Elder picked up two men and watched them as they set up a heavy machine gun, and they stacked up four RPG's against the side of the building where they setup the machine gun by.

A number of more young Arab men rushed in two building, and the Elder noticed they kicked out the windows on the second floor of the structure, and they took up position in the windows. The Elder was able to see the AK 47's held in their arms and the men started to scan the sky.

More heavily armed Arab men ran down the center of the main street of the village, and they took up positions behind a number of parked vehicles in the road. It seemed everywhere the old man looked in his village, he easily picked up more Arab men running while carrying assault rifles or RPG's, (Rocket Propelled Grenades) and most of them he was seeing were strangers to his village. In no time his village was turned into a heavily armed camp, with many young Arab males looking for someone they could attack with their weapons.

The people Sameer relied so heavily on to help him solve the many problems in his village, rushed in his home. They wanted to get the old man out of the way so when the fighting started against the soon to be arriving American invaders by the Arab men flooding into their village. His friends did not have to worry about losing the old man to the fighting about to take place in the small Arab town.

Tracker One reached the north side of ar-Ramadi. The ATO Officer was shocked at what he was witnessing going on in the town. Every where he looked he picked up small groups of women and children fleeing the village, and the civilian groups were heading for the desert surrounding the village. Colonel Pullman ordered the pilot, Commander Peterson to move in closer to the town, so he could better observe what was taking place below them.

Again, the ATO Colonel was shocked at what he was seeing. All he noticed was men heavily armed running all over the town, taking up positions of defense against the soldiers about to reach the village. The Colonel had the pilot move his helicopter and he picked up more armed men running from his machine hovering over the town. Some of the wild acting males turned and aimed their weapons at his machine. For some reason they refrained from firing at the helicopter. Instead the Arabs took to waving their fists wildly in the air at the helicopter, and then quickly disappeared in the clutter of the town.

"Uh oh Commander Peterson, it looks like the entire village is setting up to defend it against our troops when they get here, sir." Colonel Pullman mumbled at the pilot as he continued to watch masses of armed Arab males running all over the place below him.

"What the hell are we going to do about it Colonel Pullman? We can't allow Walker's troops to walk in the town without knowing large numbers of enemy combatants are setting up, and they're ready to defend the village against his incoming troops, sir." The pilot offered as he watched the same thing the Colonel was seeing below them.

"I'm going to make contact with Walker and inform him of what he's walking into, sir. I can't allow his troops to walk into a beehive without warning him first, sir."

In the village, the Elder Sameer Abdalsada allowed two of his bodyguards to drag him and his wife out of the home. They dragged the old man and his bitterly complaining wife over to a concrete bunker constructed months before Saddam Hussein ordered the invasion of Kuwait, and the bunker was abandoned since that time. It was the only structure in the entire village that would stand up to a heavy attack against the building.

Before Colonel Pullman was able to raise Captain Walker over the radio, Tracker Two reported in to the lead helicopter, and the pilot of the second helicopter informed the ATO Colonel of what he was observing taking place in the village from his end of town. It was the same uncontrolled mayhem happening there. The second pilot reported spotting tens of women and children fleeing the village for the safety of the desert. He was also reported seeing many armed Arab men pouring into the village and taking up defensive position throughout the town.

"God damn! What a fucking mess we have developing against us, Commander Peterson. Shit, shit, shit, it looks like Captain Walker's troops are going to be forced to fight these bastards from building to building in the town. The way the enemy combatants are setting up against his incoming troops, sir." Colonel Pullman growled at the commander of the helicopter as he grabbed for the mike and placed the call to Walker. "Err… Tracker One to Searcher One. Come in Searcher One, this is an emergency sir. This shit's real important sir. Over."

"Searcher One send your traffic, Tracker One. Over." Walker replied, it just so happened he had his Charlie One standing by his side when the call came in.

Inside ar-Ramadi, General Mustafa Abdelhadi reached Ayesha's home amid the mayhem occurring in the town. The once powerful Iraqi General stopped by the guard he posted, Mugtada al-Sistani who took a threatening stance against the strange Arab men running around his town like crazy people. When the Iraqi General reached the security guard he growled at him. "Mugtada, come with me my brother! We have to get these three foul women out of the village until the loathsome American soldiers leave us in peace. We know the cursed infidels must be coming to find this weapon and Ayesha. The Elder gave us the chore of keeping the unclean women safe, and that's what we're going to do. Get in the building Mugrada."

General Mustafa Adbalhadi along with his security guard Mugtada al-Sistani, charged through the front door of Ayesha's home. Inside they split up and went searching for the three young Iraqi women hiding in the home because of the activity in the town. Finding the three women hiding under the overturned mattress of Ayesha's bed, the General ripped the mattress off them and growled at the women.

"Come with me you young fools, I have been entrusted with your worthless safety by the Village Elder, and we have reports a large number of hated American Crusaders are heading for our village, women. We'll take you fools to safety in the deep desert, far away from where the cursed infidels will be searching for you three, and Allah's gift, women. We have no idea how close the lowly infidels are to our village. So we have to rush to leave before the American soldiers attack us. There are two of their helicopters taking positions on each end of the village. They are not stopping anyone from leaving the village yet, so we must leave immediately.

"I believe it's only a matter of time before the evil ones who have invaded and destroyed so much of our country, will stop anyone from leaving the village for the safety of the desert. So the cursed by Allah infidels, could search everyone from the village and find what they are looking for. We have to leave this place immediately. I warn the three of you creatures of the earth not to say a word if we're challenged by anyone we might be confronted by in the village. I'll do the talking for the five of us from this point on, is that understood by you worthless women?"

Without waiting for a reply from the women, the angry Iraqi General went on with his words. "Come foul women, we have to get a move on it while there's still time for an escape route to travel on from the village. No, don't take any of your worthless belongings with you, we have to travel light. We don't have god dom time to wait while you gather what you believe is important to you and want to take from this foul structure.

"We must move quickly and extra weight will only serve to slow us down and rob you of your strength, and place your life in danger in the desert. Get dressed in your Kajubas so you can hide the Sword of God under your dress, Ayesha. I trust you with the weapon given to us by the sacred Hand of Allah, and you're not to stop for anyone who might challenge us as we flee to the desert. If necessary, Mugrada and I will engage in talk or combat against anyone who tries to stop us from leaving the village. You women must keep going no matter what happens.

"If we're stopped by any cursed fools running over our village, and Mugtada and myself are forced to fight them for your freedom and we are killed. You women must keep going until you're out in the desert. Once you find a safe place to hide, you're to use your Kajubas as a Howli, and dig yourselves in the sand. Then you're to pull the sand over your bodies and hide until someone comes for you. I order you to remain under the sand until either I come for you, or the American soldiers leave our village and you can return.

"I promise Ayesha al-Qaysi and your foul friends, if we're separated for any reason. I'll find you and if the cursed infidels destroy our village before they leave its remains. I'll find another village in Iraq who'll protect you in the same manner as your village is protecting you and Allah's great gift. That's good you must travel light, let us go before the evil ones arrive in our village, woman. Come, come women before I leave the other two of you behind to the fate of the hated American soldier's hands and abuse. No we don't have time to look for items you want to take with you. We must leave this foul place at once, even if I have to take you out of this foul home naked." Mustafa growled at the three pretty Iraqi women, as he tried his best to get them moving faster, because he understood he and they were running out of time to escape the town.

Once the three women were read to leave with Ayesha carrying the cylinder tucked safely under her robe, they left her home with Mustafa leading the way for them and with Mugrada protecting their flank. The five Iraqis went down a narrow alleyway and came out on the next block of the village. They rushed across the open street and down another alleyway, and then out on the third block. Here Mustafa cautiously looked around and picked up the two black painted American helicopters blocking the main road heading north and south of the end of the village, and their escape route.

Mustafa looked across the next street and saw he had another block to make before he came out on the east side of the village. From where he was standing, Mustafa was able to see a number of low sand dunes in this area that should hide their escape from the helicopters and the infidel searchers, unless the two machines change their position against them.

Suddenly, twelve heavily armed Arab men ran down the block where Mustafa and his wards were stopped at, and one of the Arab protectors picked up the two men and three women hiding in the shadow of the building. They stopped and aimed their weapons at the five and one of them snarled at who he thought was the leader of the group they spotted.

"You, the big one with the weapon locked in your foul hands, why the devil are you wasting your time looking at us for, stupid. Get your cursed women out of the village before the hated American infidels arrive, and they defile your lowly women before your worthless eyes, fool. We have come down this block and it's still clear, so get your women out of the village while it's still safe for you to move them out. Once the fighting starts with the lowly infidels in the village, anyone moving around the town will be killed on the spot by either the American invaders or us. Once you have your worthless women hidden in the desert, you two are ordered to return to the village and help us defeat the invading infidels. Allah knows we'll need all able body men of fighting age from this village to help us with our war against them. Return to aid us, fool." The man speaking moved the barrel of his weapon in the direction he wanted the five to move in.

Without waiting to be told twice, General Mustafa Adbalhadi nodded at the angry man, and then he took off with the four others following behind him. It took the group two minutes to reach the safety of the sand dunes and desert, and once they were in this area. They ran along the side of the dunes that barely covered them, moving until they came to a number of larger sand dunes where they could run in a standing position. This protection enabled them to move faster and in no time, the small group of five was about a mile out of the village suffering exhaustion. General Mustafa Abdelhadi would not allow the women a second to rest as he pushed them forward. He was able to hear the roar from what he understood was the motors of the American humvees, and yelled at the four with him.

"Come and keep moving, we have to get further out in the desert because the hated American soldiers are about to enter our village. You three women keep moving or I'll shoot anyone who cannot keep up with the others. Your worthless lives depend on how far we can get away from the village before the enemy soldiers arrive, and the infidels attack our homes and kill our loved ones. Keep moving or your fate will catch up to you from behind, and destroy your foul souls." Mustafa continued to roar at especially the women, driving them further away from the village as he continued to run from the town for his life.

THE CARAVAN OF HUMVEES KNOWN AS SEARCHER

"Tracker One to Searcher One. Warning, warning, warning! You're heading for a village heavily armed and well prepared for your arrival. The village is setup for countless ambushes and attacks aimed against your incoming soldiers. I see many I repeat, I see many heavily armed young Arab males setting up positions to defend the village from your presence while employing automatic weapons and the likes. Many hostiles are setup to attack as your units as they enter the village. I see many RPG's, heavy machine guns and many attackers are set up on rooftops of a number of homes and other building in the village. I also picked up a num… huh, what the hell was that god dammit…" Colonel Pullman suddenly yelled in the radio as the hovering helicopter was forced to make a number of extremely erratic maneuvers to avoid an RPG round fired at the helicopter from somewhere in the village.

Tracker One helicopter rapidly rose in the air, and then dipped down hard to the right and then the machine dove wildly straight for the ground. The pilot pulled back on the stick with all his might as he growled in the helicopter. The pilot was forcing the helicopter to vibrate violently because of the tremendous stress he was placing on his machine's flying capabilities. Then the pilot drove the machine back towards the ground as the rocket propelled grenade went flying past the cockpit of the helicopter, and the round dropped harmlessly to the sand on the other side of the machine and exploded in the dust.

"Tracker One Searcher One, report back god dammit! Tracker One, what the hell's going on out there, dammit! Where the hell are you Tracker One I need input and I need it immediately, sir? Report, what the fuck's going on out there!" Walker roared in the mike, fuming he just lost contact with his Air Tasking Officer.

"Tracker One to Searcher One. Holy shit, we just dodged an RPG round fired at the damn helicopter. This shit's going down the drain quick. Damn Searcher One, I see another Arab asshole lining up an RPG. What orders do you want me to follow, we have to start worki…"

"Tracker One, Tracker Two, get the hell outta range of those fucking RPG's. I can't afford to lose one of your helicopters Tracker One, not if we're about to head into a fucking Hornet's nest. I need eyes in the air, break off recon and get fucking air between your machines and those damn RPGs. We have the village in sight and we are deploying three quarters of a mile from the village on the north side. Reply to last order Tracker One and Two. Over."

"Tracker One, received and am carrying out your orders, Searcher One. Over." Colonel Pullman replied to Walker's order.

"Tracker Two, I just received a number of new orders and you are instructed to act accordingly with these new orders, sir. Over."

"Roger last reply, Tracker One and Two. Take up new positions outside known RPG range, and you're free to lose weapons on anyone who tries to attack your machines. Tracker One and Two, weapons free and active to employ from this point, protect yourselves and your machines at all costs. Over." Walker commanded the pilots of both Tracker Helicopters over the radio.

"Roger last." One pilot replied to their orders from Walker.

As Walker's troops piled out of the humvees and took positions of defense before the idling war machines. The ATO contacted AWSCB or the Air Wing Support Command Bahrain, and the Colonel reported on the situation facing the ground troops he was ordered to protect.

"AWSCB, Tracker One on special mission Rapid Fire. Come in. This is an emergency request for immediate heavy air support of ground troops involved in the operation, sir. Over."

"AWCSB we copy your transmission Tracker One, and understand your mission and we're ordered to support your request for immediate air support for top priority mission. What's the nature of your emergency request for air cover and backup support? Report your situation as observing…" AWSCB response was cut off right in the middle of his reply by a second air wing support stationed in Iraq.

"Tracker One this is AWCSI (Air Wing Command Support Iraq) Baghdad and we can support any mission request for Operation Rapid Fire quicker than AWSCB. We're ordered to support any unit involved in Rapid Fire Mission from the start, sir. This mission was given top priority for requested air support or cover of said troops involved in this operation. What's the nature of requested air support, Commander? Over."

"AWSCI, Tracker One ATO Colonel Mark Pullman reporting I have thirty six Special Forces troops about to enter the Iraqi village of ar-Ramadi. I tracked an unknown number of positive insurgents and enemy combatant groups setting up armed resistance in the village against our troops on the ground. The enemy combatants are heavily armed with RPG's, heavy and light machine guns, and a number of ground insurgents operating inside the village are preparing to attack said American units as they enter the town, sir. Over." Colonel Pullman was not the least bit concerned using his name and rank and report over the opened radio net while requesting added air support for the mission, because he was aware they were working on a secured system.

"Roger your last and am prepared to support your operation with four rotary support Apache aircraft fast attack platforms, sir. Sorry to inform you there's no Super Cobra's available for Marine ground support operations at this time, Colonel Pullman. I'll be supporting your enemy combatant engagement with fixed wing of six A 10

Thunderbolt II Warthog strike platforms, employed for close in ground support of said troops, sir.

"I'm further committing a wing of six F-15 Eagles for strong air to ground support, and am committing a pair of AC-130 A/H Spectre Gunship platforms for additional close in ground support for your operation and ground force protection. The reason I'm supporting your operation with twin Gunships is so one can work each side of the village at the same time. ATO, are you going to be the main and controller of air support platforms during this engagement, sir? Colonel, I'm aware of what you people are searching for, and that's an added reason for so many close ground support systems I'm sending for your support request, sir."

"That's a Roger on last, Command. I'm Air Tasking Officer for the mission and directed any air attacks against insurgents in the village will come through me. Using the close in air support platforms are a good idea for this mission, sir. We can't blow this village off the face of the earth until we're certain our package isn't located in the village. I have heavy numbers of exposed enemy combatants running all over the town like a pack of sprayed roaches, and have large number of Iraqi women and children fleeing village for safety of desert at the same time, sir.

"It seems the presence of my helicopters woke up an enemy combatant stronghold, and we're going to have our hands full with dealing and searching this place, Command." Colonel Pullman reported in an excited tone as his helicopter leveled off at a safe distance away from the small Iraqi village. A sudden action caught his eye and without knowing it, the ATO Officer just picked up the five Iraqi people with the cylinder make it out of the village safely, and he noticed the five quickly disappear behind low sand dunes.

The concerned pilot spotted the five Iraqis fleeing the village and he mumbled at the ATO Officer. "Shouldn't we try and stop them people from leaving the town, Colonel Pullman?"

"Naw its two males taking their family out of the damn village before any fighting starts. Quite frankly Commander Peterson, I'm kind of happy they left the village. At least its two less males we have to worry about when our troops invade the village and they take it over, sir. Damn, I never seen such a small village with so many people running around the damn place with weapons exposed like these nuts are doing below us, Commander. It almost seems like they're not the least bit interested over the fact we're detecting the armed Arabs preparing to engage our troops when they enter the village, sir."

"I agree Colonel Pullman, I say the hell with those sand swimmers getting out of the village and let's concentrate our efforts on the combatants setting up against our troops, sir." The helicopter commander growled at the colonel as he watched what was going on in the town.

"Tracker One, AWSCI Command, am reporting ETA first air support strike platform systems I engaged for this operation, are two minutes out your current position. The advance air support platform is the six fix wing F-15 Eagle aircraft, and they're armed for air to ground support efforts. I'm further reporting ETA heavy Spectre Gunships should arrive your position thirty to sixty seconds behind first air support platforms I dispatched your position. Third air support platforms, the Warthogs are one minute to a minute and a half behind the two Spectre platforms. Last committed air support platforms are the Apache rotary support systems, Colonel. Their ETA your position five minutes after last arriving air support strike platform systems approaching your present position. They're the slower moving support systems dispatched your position, they'll arrive your position last. Over."

"Roger last and am looking for air support platforms arrive my position, Command. Over." Colonel Pullman replied as he checked the air over his helicopter.

Walker had his special operations troops spread out in a protecting pattern, and had them slowly and cautiously approaching the village. The Captain knew what he was doing while stalling slightly, because he understood Colonel Pullman would be on top of his game, and he would have requested any nearby air support for his troops. He was also having the sixteen humvees in his unit protecting his lead advance. Five humvees had fifty caliber machine guns mounted to the roof of the machine, and another three humvees were equipped with the MK 19-3 40mm Automatic Grenade launchers mounted to the turret positioned in the humvees. These weapons were the only heavies he had available outside a few 40 mm mortars. As his troops advanced, the Captain kept looking towards the sky to see the first signs of his air support arriving overhead his position.

He let his breath out in a rush when he noticed the telltale white vapor streams streaking the cloudless sky heading for his position. Just as he picked up his air support coming at him, all hell broke out before his troops. Some Arab insurgents moved out of the village to engage his troops before they were able to reach the town. The enemy combatants were firing AK-47 assault fire at his people as Walker bellowed out. "All troops get down and return fucking fire!" Walker dropped down and fired his M-16 in the direction of the heavy incoming enemy fire.

The Mutt was pounding away with his weapon, and he rolled over until he was by Walker's side and he complained. "Man, you know someone can get killed around here?"

"Fuck you, keep firing at the dopey little bastards, air is almost on top of us man."

A round hit the sand separating the two soldiers and it caused the Mutt to grumble. "Hey man, someone around here is being awful careless with their use of fire arms. By the way, I picked up fricking contrails. I take it we're engaging about fifteen to twenty heavily armed combatants out there, Walker. This is great man, it's about fucking time they decided to stand and fight us, so we can get some stinking kill time in on them. I like it, I love it, I gotta have fucking more of it." The Mutt screamed out as he emptied his weapon in the direction of the attacking insurgents.

The three humvees with grenade launchers mounted on them opened fire on their attackers, and in seconds there was a large wall of death hitting the enemy insurgent's positions. Almost instantly, the enemy fire slackened off and as quickly as the enemy fire started, it ended and the combatants pulled back into the village for safety.

The Mutt got Walker's attention and he pointed with his chin as he ranted. "That's why the fricking assholes broke off their stinking engagement against us, Homes."

Walker looked in the direction the Mutt pointed and noticed six F-15 Eagles do a quick low flyover of his position. The retreating Eagle aircraft dipped their wings to their fellow soldiers on the ground, and then the screaming aircraft assembled at their standoff positions. The go fast aircraft waited to be called in to attack the insurgents fighting their people.

"Well that scared the shit outta the lousy bunch of flaming assholes, Walker. I wished they pressed their fucking attack against us, so we coulda wiped the whole lot of them lousy bastards out that fricking easily." The Mutt bragged as he snapped his fingers and rolled on his back and lit up a smoke and took a drag and blew the smoke out over his head as he relaxed a bit.

The next support platform to arrive on site was the Warthogs, and the commander of this wing of aircraft immediately checked in the Searcher One troops, and he informed Captain Walker of their presence in the area, by flying low over his ground troops. Then their aircraft likewise headed for their standoff positions, and commenced to hovering in the area while waiting for a call in to support the friendly ground troops if they came under attack again.

Without waiting to be called in, one of the Warthog aircraft suddenly broke formation, and the aircraft charged at the beginning of the village and it opened fire with his GAU-8/A Avenger 30mm Gattling Gun. The rounds ripped up the soft sand and Captain Walker saw three enemy defender's bodies get tossed in the air, and then spun about like rag dolls caught in a hard wind. The chilling sound from the Gattling Gun was more than enough to break off the enemy insurgent's attack against them.

Colonel Pullman made a call to Walker because he wanted to inform him of what his people might be walking into, and what he was able to setup as a defense against what the insurgents had successfully setup against his troops. "Tracker One to Searcher One. I have a flood of information to transmit to you, sir. Over Searcher One."

As soon as he received the incoming call from the ATO Officer, Roach quickly made his way over to Walker and handed him the mike. The Captain took it and barked. "Yeah this is Searcher One to Tracker One, go with your fucking traffic. Over."

"Searcher One, by now you noticed the Eagles and Warthogs positioned on their ordered standoff station to support your attacking troops, sir. I have two Spectre Gunships moving in momentarily for added close in ground support of your ground troops, sir. I have four Apache fast attack platforms coming in. Their ETA is stated six minutes out of target area. I repeat, Apache attack helicopters ETA is still…"

"What the fuck are the Apache's doing supplying our fucking air cover for? Where the hell's our god damn Super Cobra's for this action for Christ sake? We're fucking Marines and we don't need any stinking Army crap doing support over our stinking noggin." Walker bitched at the ATO Officer over the Apache helicopters assisting them.

"Evidently, the Super Cobra units are out of the attack loop, Searcher One." Colonel Pullman responded, not understanding Walker's bitch. He figured the ground troops would not mind who was supporting them, as long as some form of air coverage was overhead.

"Then I guess the Apache's will have to do. Tracker One, you did well getting these damn strike platforms overhead so quickly, man. I own you a stinking beer when we get back to the real world for your efforts. Tracker One, I'm gonna hold my people back until air support is set in place overhead, and once it is then I'll make my first entry into that Iraqi rathole, sir. Tracker One, I see the main street of the village if you wanna call it the main street that is sir. This is what I intend to do Tracker One so listen up. I'm gonna send in my Humvees first, and we're gonna follow the war machines in on foot and disperse and find some stinking cover for our asses, before we start securing the damn village. I want you to keep that fucking air positioned over our heads Tracker One. You gotta make certain them flying jock straps don't go and open up on my people by fucking mistake.

"Tracker One, you gotta inform them crazy ass fucking pilots that my troops are equipped with marking strobe lights. If they see anyone not sparking like a fricking lightening bug, they're to be classified as enemy targets and taken out that fucking quick, Tracker One. If your flying braggers hit any of my damn troops on the ground. I'm gonna hunt them crazy ass bastards down and the enemy combatants will be the least of their problems when I get my stinking hands on their damn asses. Tracker One, you're to inform me the moment the Apache's arrive on station. I wanna coordinate my attack of the village with their arrival on position. It's your job to have your fly boys protecting my troops down here, so you betta be fucking good at what you're supposed to do for us, sir. Searcher One. Out!" Walker warned the ATO Colonel in no uncertain terms, and then he broke off his communication and reported to his troops surrounding him and looking for any information they could gather about their opening attack of the village.

Tracker One had his communications setup according to protocol. The ground troops will inform him where they needed a strike package, and Tracker One would relay this information to a hovering AWACS aircraft working in tandem with a JDAR air to ground support platform, that in turn would relay the strike profile to the attacking ground support aircraft. Tracker One had the power to communicate directly with the strike attack aircraft, thus elimination the AWACS and JDAR aircraft. In this case, Colonel Pullman decided to communicate directly with the attack aircraft to better control their support of the ground troops.

A shot rang out and Walker looked to where it came from, and he immediately noticed the Ghost lowering his weapon, and he looked to the village and picked up an enemy combatant falling from the roof of a building. He looked back at the Ghost who gave him the thumbs up signal, and he held up a finger and pointed it down to the ground, signifying to the Captain one enemy combatant spotted, one enemy combatant down.

Most of the Special Forces soldiers were lying low on the sand, and holding back and using the small surrounding sand dunes to protect them from any enemy fire coming from the Iraqi village. Walker stubbed out his cigarette in the sand when another call came in from Colonel Pullman.

"Tracker One to Searcher One. Come in. Over."

"Go Tracker One, whatdaya got for me? Send your traffic. Over." For the first time Walker got a little sloppy over the radio communication with his ATO controller.

"Tracker One to Searcher One, reporting Apache helicopters are on station. Over."

"Roger your last, we're moving out, keep me advised and protected in there. Out." Walker again got sloppy over the radio as he waved his arm, and his troopers instantly started to move for the village. This time the American soldiers were moving low to the ground, and the seven humvees were leading the way for his advancing troops. A few shots rang out from the village, and they were answered by heavy return fire from the fifties mounted on top of the slow moving humvees, as they raked the entire area the shots were just fired at Walker's troops from.

Walker's troops were spread out for the assault on the village. When the first of the humvees reached the foot of the village at the beginning of the main road leading to the town, his troops pulled in and assembled behind the forward humvees. Allowing the military machines to lead the way into the village, and afford the ground troops a small degree of cover protection, as the soldiers continued their slowly advance on the village. As the specialized soldiers cautiously entered the beginning of the village, the mixed nation soldiers violently smashed their way into the first few homes they came across, and they took up defensive positions inside the buildings. This move was so the advanced soldiers could afford protective cover fire for the follow on forces taking up the middle and rear positions of the soldier's formation.

As quickly as the group of multi nation soldiers worked their way inside some of the buildings, the area was streaked with telltale trailer coming from fired RPG's and small weapons fire, as the insurgents opened up on the invading American troops entering their village. Instantly, the lead humvee exploded in a shower of sparks and roaring flames. The soldiers riding inside the machine struggled to get out of the burning humvee, and the injured soldiers were then quickly pulled into one of the commandeered homes, so the medics could start to look after their severe burns and other wounds.

Colonel Pullman observed what was happening on the ground as the American forces entered the village, and he notified the hovering Spectre Gunships. "Tracker One to Tiger Impact Flight Leader. I have heavy enemy weapon fire pinning down advancing friendly forces at the head of the village from north side of the town. I need an immediate response by your strike platform to break the stalemate friendly ground forces are engaging in. Over."

"Tiger Impact Leader to Tracker One, I observed action and am reacting to enemy fire. Over." The commander of the Gunship reported to the Colonel on board Tracker One.

"Tiger Impact Leader, be advised friendlies are in the area. Watch for strobes, all strobe identified are classified friendly forces, don't fire on friendlies. Over."

"Roger last, all strobe pickups on ground are classified friendly forces, we'll hold fire on all marked and identified friendlies on the ground with strobes as detected. Am picking up large numbers of suspected enemy targets hiding on rooftops of three buildings on the second block in of the village, am taking these identified targets as enemy insurgent targets. Am I correct with this assumption of enemy targets as stated? Over Tracker One."

"Tiger Impact all identified targets picked up in the open and especially hiding on the rooftops in the village, are classified enemy targets from this point on. No friendly forces made it to rooftops of any building in the village as of this time. Prepare to engage all targets caught in the open. Am tracking many targets you brought up to my attention. They're definitely identified hostile in nature. You're cleared to light'em up, go hot on all identified targets, Tiger Impact Leader. Crew, be advised many friendly ground forces operating extremely close in the area in question to be attacked by your platforms. Over."

"Tiger Impact Flight Leader to Tracker One. Roger that last, noted there are a number of detected friendly forces closely working in the area in question, understood warning and will act accordingly, Tracker One. I have a number of military type vehicles stalled on main road leading into the village, and one seems to be disabled and burning, Tracker One. What's the situation with the vehicles I'm picking up stalled at the mouth of the village? Are they classified friendly forces for this fire mission, or are they enemy targets of opportunity? Over Tracker One."

"Tiger Impact Leader negative, negative, negative. Don't pull don't engage military type vehicles stationed on main road leading into village. They are definitely friendly ground forces. I repeat Tiger Impact Leader, don't pull on military vehicles, all military vehicles on main road leading into village are classified as friendlies and not enemy targets. Over."

"Roger that, all military vehicles on ground are classified friendlies. Am feeding hostile positions into my targeting and aiming computer system, for attack and annihilation of all identified enemy combatants on the ground. Will open volley on enemy combatants with trainable 25 millimeter Gattling Gun, and assess results of my first attack on hostile activities from that point on, Tracker One. Over."

"Roger that, bring it down Tiger Impact Leader, you're cleared to open fire on all selected and known enemy targets spotted and identified, Tiger Impact Leader. Over." Colonel Pullman replied confidently to the commander of the Specter Aircraft Gunship.

"Roger that, bringing it home Tracker One. Weapon's hot and clearing. Over."

In less than a heartbeat, the entire roof area of the three targeted Iraqi homes the combatants were setup on was ripped apart by an unbelievable wall of lead fired by the hovering Spectre Gunship. The bodies of nine combatants were picked up in the air and tossed off the roofs as if they were rag dolls, and the defenders fell in the middle of the street and died where they fell.

"Oh my God that was a good kill, good kill god damn, that was a good kill keep on them damn bad guys, Tiger Impact Leader. I have a number of enemy combatants detected running out of said building under attack by your platform in plain sight of your weapons, Tiger Impact. Ten, eleven, twelve as identified enemy targets are confirmed as hostile in nature. Nail those guys running down the street Tiger Impact Leader." Colonel Pullman roared in the radio as he witnessed the destructive force breached out by the massive Gunship stationed above his position and following his orders.

A second heavy burst of weapon's fire from the Spectre's Gattling Guns, ripped up not only the fleeing hostile's bodies. The rounds ripped up what was left of the once blacktop classified as the main road of the village, as the bullets hunted down their enemy targets. The rounds even destroyed the building the enemy combatants were using as their hiding place.

As the Spectre aircraft carried out its fire mission, Captain Walker was on his feet in a flash, and had his troops racing deeper into the village using the attack for cover. The appointed follow on troops started to secure the area behind Walker's rapidly advancing troops, before moving forward themselves. A mass of small heavy weapons fire criss crossed before Walker and his troops, as they continued to move forward in a controlled standard leap frog type formation into the heart of the Iraqi town. The Captain watched Ice, opened fire on a pair of Arab men carrying AK-47's. Her rounds ripped into the unprotected bodies of the enemy combatants, and the pair dropped to the ground, dead before their bodies came to rest on the sand blanket of the town.

The Mutt went racing past the female soldier branded as Ice, as he quickly made his way towards an over turned civilian vehicle. Once he was set in place, he got down by the side of the car and waved Ice forward as he took up the protective stance for the moving soldier behind him. When Ice reached the Mutt's side, he took off again for a small pile of bricks stacked up and scattered about on the sidewalk. When he reached this position, he again waved Ice over to his side. Before the Mutt could move out for a new position, an RPG round suddenly smashed into the pile of bricks, and the heavy impact threw both soldiers back until they crashed into the wall of the heavily damaged building behind them.

"God damn!" Walker roared as he watched No Neck charge up to the building, and he smashed his foot against the wooden door and sent it flying from it hinges. Then with one large paw he reached down and grabbed Ice by the collar of her body armor, and he easily dragged her hurting and battered body into the safety of the building. The Mutt followed the two soldiers inside the building on his own power, grinning at Neck, who sort of had a crush on the pretty female soldier known as Ice.

The Captain was on his inter squad helmet radio barking. "Neck, how the hell is Ice and the fucking Mutt, mister! Report their condition immediately, tree stump."

Before Neck could reply to Walker's concern, Ice got on her radio and replied in a sexy voice. "Gees Walker, I never knew you cared so much for me, baby. I'm fine, I just had the wind knocked out of me, that's all honey. If I knew you cared so much for me, maybe I'll give you a little tumble between the sheets when we get back to the real world. The Mutt's with me and Neck and he has their weapons sticking out the window hunting for moving targets, Walker."

The concerned Captain was relieved his two close friends were all right as he replied to Ice's comments. "I sure hope the Mutt has his M-16 sticking outta the window, and not his uther weapon, Ice. Hey honey, how many times do I hafta tell you to keep that lovely little ass of yours closer to the ground, so no enemy shooters can put a cap in it fur ya, baby? And, as for taking a tumble between the sheets, any time any place, baby. I'm glad you and that dopey bastard with you are okay, honey. I don't want anything to happen to my two favorite turds, little girl…"

His conversation was cut off when an enemy round pinged off his protective body armor high up on his shoulder. It stung like hell, but the round did not make it through the protective armor. He shook his arm in an effort to get some pain out of it. This action did nothing for the pain he was suffering, fuming he started to look for the shooter who just tagged his ass.

Another group of insurgents suddenly took off on a dead run from the building next to the one home the Spectre Gunship basically destroyed moments before. The combatants ran out of the building and dropped behind a pile of rubble lying and piling up on the street, and they started to shoot at the invading allied soldiers. Two RPG rounds exploded in front of the building the Mutt, Neck and Ice were holdup in, and Walker felt the Arabs were trying to zero in on the three trapped soldiers, and kill them before help could get to them. The Captain was about to call Tracker One when he heard Colonel Pullman order a Warthog to drop on the hunkered down enemy attackers.

"Tracker One to Talon Flight Leader. I have four hostiles in front of the destroyed building, and they have a number of friendlies pinned down. I need the insurgents erased. Over."

"Roger your last and am starting my run, Tracker One. Talon Flight Leader out. Over."

Walker poked his head up just in time to see the 'Cross of Death' the Iraqi military branded the Warthog, as the aircraft opened up on the enemy position assigned to the pilot with his Avenger 30mm Gattling gun. The young Marine Captain watched in amazement as the rounds churned up the rubble and bodies of the enemy fighters as if they weighed nothing. In one breath, the five attackers were done and out of the fight.

Buckethead, (Sergeant Vincent Lambardo) caught up to Walker and he dropped by his side and complained. "Hey man, where the hell are our two stinking Vampires (Snipers) working at for Pete's sake? They should be out there working like hell picking off some of these scumbags. We're taking too much fucking enemy pop from them assholes fighting us for them two to be doing their damn job. You beta raise the Ghost and Hunter on the horn and get on their asses."

As Buckethead voiced his complaint, the crack of a sniper's weapon rang out above the mini war taking place inside the village, and both excited soldiers looked in the direction of the crack. Walker noticed one insurgent hiding in a window fall out, and his body crumbled to the ground in a heap of death. A second round from a sniper's weapon rang out, and another enemy combatant caught in the open, went down and Walker replied to the huge soldier staring at him.

"Hey big guy does that answer your fucking question about our two Vanpires? The next time you wanna complain about our Vampires, I suggest you complain to them and see where that'll get your ass, big man." Just as Walker bitched at Buckethead, he picked up an Arab man running directly at them, and he had a weapon in his hand trying to site Buckethead up for the kill, as the attacker continued to run at them. Without saying anything to Buckethead, Walker reached out and pulled the huge soldier down with one hand, and he sighted up the attacker with his MP-5 and ripped off five rounds at the charging man. Each bullet tore into the Arab's unprotected body, dropping him dead in his tracks. Buckethead looked over his shoulder to see what Walker was shooting at, and then mumbled when he noticed the enemy combatant go down in a heap.

"Hey man, thanks a lot buddy, you saved me a helluva lot of stinking pain here, sir."

"No I didn't tree trunk, because if that lousy bastard tagged you, I woulda finished ya dopey ass off for your being stupid enough to get tagged in the first place, asshole." Walker growled at the large soldier. Between Neck and Buckethead, one or the other was always getting tagged when the troops were out on a mission. Walker believed their size made them easy targets.

The two soldiers grinned at each other, and then they moved out together with Walker using the side of an Iraqi home to inch his way towards the main street of the village. Reaching the end of the building, he cautiously poked his head around the corner in time to catch a moving Arab man, and he immediately sighted him up and pulled on the guy. The insurgent dropped down with his weapon ending up falling a few feet away from his mangled up body. The Captain moved out and picked up another target moving and fire and killed that combatant as quickly. All the while he was moving a rain of enemy rounds bounced all around his feet and against the wall behind his head and body. The heavy incoming enemy fire reminded him of an angry swarm of bees flying around him.

Mother Flanagan, (Sergeant Richard Flanagan) who received his unit tag name because when any new soldiers were assigned to their elite unit, he always got stuck helping them until they understood how the unit operated. He caught up to Walker and reported out of breath. "Hey man, I got fricking Siberia, McNip, Six Pack and Coco-G hanging back some, they're securing any damn civilian pukes we picked up hiding or wandering around the stinking village with flex cuffs, Walker. The lousy civilian Doctor puke's with this group, and they're sorta out of most of the heavy fighting for the time being, man.

"We're not taking chances with these flaming Arab assholes of this damn village, man. We're arresting everyone we come across until we can determine if they're innocent god damn civilians. Or they're combatants who didn't have the stinking stomach to continue fighting us, when we entered this lousy dump, man. You should see how the trailing soldiers are cuffing up the dopey bastards we take in custody, Walker.

"I'm telling ya man, Siberia musta had some sorta fricking training with taking and hooking up any frigging prisoners, and she's doing her fucking job masterfully with getting these rat bastards under control for us, Walker. She's hooking up the stinking prisoners back to back and entangling their arms together, and then the right leg from one to the left leg of the uther dopey prisoner. If the stupid assholes try anything against us, they'll trip all over them fucking selves, and we'll level them for any damn infraction they might try and commit against us, Captain. I think the stinking Russian babes have a helluva stinking way of crippling prisoners they take control of, man."

The humvees started to cautiously move forward again, heading deeper into the Iraqi village, and the following humvee crashed into the burning and destroyed humvee, and the second machine easily pushed it out of the way for the trailing machines to follow. The new leading humvee did not move another five feet into the village, when it was smashed into by an RPG round that hit the passenger front door, and the grenade ripped through the front of the machine of war. The power of the exploding round inside the machine blew off the driver's door, and the soldier branded High Spade, (Sergeant William Glenallen) was blown completely out of the disabled machine. He was dead before his body hit the ground.

The RPG round blew the second soldier to the group, Small Change, (Sergeant Edward London) out through the top turret of the burning humvee, and he ended up sprawled out on top of the destroyed machine, he was still alive and moving under his own power.

Walker watched Small Change roll off the top of the destroyed humvee, and then he quickly made his way safely to the side of a building. He was slightly dragging his right arm, and he was limping badly on his left leg when he crashed up against the wall of the structure. The worried Captain watched until he was able to get his attention, and Small Change gave him the quick nod, informing him he was still in the fight.

One of the grenade launcher humvees opened fire and laid down a heavy suppressing fire in the direction where the RPG was fired from. The grenades ripped apart a home, and three insurgents ran from the crumbling structure. They were easily picked off by Walker's troops.

This response from his troops seemed to anger a large number of the enemy combatants hiding inside the village, and they committed themselves to a large frontal attack on the invading American soldiers. The Arab combatants though were cut off from the bulk of their other supporting soldiers. Over forty combatants made a wild charge at his troops. Tracker One was on the horn reporting this enemy action directly at Captain Walker.

"Tracker One to Searcher One. Come in this is important. Over."

"Go Tracker One, Searcher One, whatdaya got for me sir? Over."

"Searcher One, the combatants are committed for a fontal charge at your position. They seem to want to get in close to your troops, so I can't support you in the field with air coverage, sir. It's a wise tactic if the enemy fighters can pull it off against your troops, sir. If the attackers get in your ranks, it'll stop me from sending any air support in to help your troops. You gotta get separation from the damn attackers, or air isn't going to be able to attack them, and you'll be on your own fighting the bastards off. I can't have air support firing at the enemy if they're in your face. We'll be hitting our own troops while trying to get at the enemy attacking your people."

"I read ya Tracker One I don't have the time for a fucking conversation right now. I have a shitload of crazy ass screaming A-rab bastards stuck in my fucking face. You do the best you can and we'll pick up any fricking slack in your air cover on our own. Over." Walker replied.

"Roger that and I'll stay on any reinforcements the insurgents try to get at you with. Out."

Walker's troops picked up what the enemy attackers were attempting to do against them, and the allied soldiers quickly spread out and took up defensive positions aimed against the sudden wave of Iraqi attackers. The elite soldiers laid down a horrendous cross fire with their rounds ripping into the attackers wildly charging at them. Even though it was a well organized frontal attack employed against Walker and the rest of his troops by the hard hitting defenders. The attackers were ill prepared for the heavy well directed response from the thought to be trapped defending elite Allied soldiers. It was a terrible sight, with many insurgents dropping by fives until the attackers were finally forced to break off their engagement without doing much damage to the American troops the enemy attackers thought was caught flatfooted.

As the combatants broke off their initial attack on Walker's troops, the Arab defenders continued firing at the emplaced soldiers who continued to fire on the retreating attackers. Bullets from both sides flew wildly about, but few soldiers from either side were being hit. But when the combatants created separation from the American soldiers, the Specter gunships moved in and took over the fight. The aircraft weapon fire started to mow the enemy attackers down with deadly accuracy. Out of the twenty or so attackers left, seven Iraqi fighters were able to make it back to the safety the homes and buildings the village offered them.

CHAPTER TWENTY

Many poorly constructed Iraqi homes in this area of the village had a good number of enemy snipers planted on the rooftops, and in almost every window of the surrounding buildings. As the American soldiers cautiously continued to move deeper into the village, the advancing allied soldiers came under a hail of enemy small weapons and RPG fire. As the allied soldiers walked down the thought to be main road of the town, they returned the enemy fire the best they could. The fighting became almost impossible for the Spectre Gunships or F-15 Eagle or Warthog aircraft to support the advancing American troops further on the ground. That left any remaining air support and cover to the Apache fast attack helicopters, which came in as an angry swarm of Dragon Flies hovering some twenty feet above the rooftops of homes in question in the village.

One Apache helicopter came in so low it was targeted in by a pair of shoulder launched RPG rounds fired by insurgents hiding inside the buildings. The pilot was so good flying and understanding the ability of his war machine, he was easily able to dodge the twin launched rounds, and the pilot turned his helicopter to the side and leveled off and let loose with five, two point five missiles from his right side rocket pod. The missiles ripped the buildings the pilot felt the RPG's were fired from, apart in a wave of flames and small follow on explosions. The pilot finished off the remaining structure with a string of rounds from his 30 mm chain gun.

The Spectre Gunships were surgically working over any combatants they picked up in the open, or moving about in the village. Or the pilots of the Gunships were directed to attack certain sections of the village from the ATO working Tracker One. The Gunships were working over the buildings further from the advancing friendly forces, as they moved deeper into the village.

The Captain had no idea the soldiers he left behind to arrest anyone from the village they came across, as the allied troops secured large sections of the village behind the rapidly advancing allied troops, already had over one hundred and fifty prisoners. Most of the Arab prisoners were obviously scared to death and exhausted civilians. A number of other prisoners were classified as enemy combatants, and they were being treated as such.

"Walker, where the hell are all these scumbags coming from, for the love of God? No sooner do we get on top of some of these fucks and clear them outta their damn ratholes in this stinking dump, we're attacked by more of the bastards coming outta the stinking woodwork around here. A fricking village this damn small couldn't possibly support such a large male population as is hitting us, Homes. I'm telling ya man, we musta killed off more stinking combatants than people who actually lived in this fucking A-rab village." The Mutt, who had skillfully worked his way over to Walker's side, bitched at his commander as he took time to light a smoke, and took a drag from the cigarette.

"Give me that fucking thing before it kills ya ass, stupid." Walker growled as he took the cigarette out of the Mutt's mouth, and started to smoke it as he replied. "Of course all these pricks didn't come from this one god forsaken A-rab village. They musta knew we were coming for this dump and they called in the rest of rat bastards from the surrounding villages to help this dump fend off our attack against this fricking place, Homes. I'll tell you what Mutt, that makes me believe we're in the right place, and the crap we're looking for hasta be hanging around this dump, or the damn assholes wouldn't be fighting us like this man."

"I agree man, but now I'm worried about this fucking shit we're looking for, Homes. With the Gunships ripping this stinking place apart like they're doing, what the hell happens if some of their rounds accidentally hit and destroy that damn cylinder thing we're looking for my friend, and that releases this shit in the air against us? That's gonna really suck the big one if you were to ask me, man. I want the hell outta here ten minutes ago, friend." The Mutt griped bitterly as he looked in the air to try to locate one of the hovering massive Gunships still pounding away at the Iraqi village and the enemy insurgents attacking them.

"You know the answer to that question, Mutt. I bet every responding aircraft and helicopter surrounding us, is equipped with a chemical or biological detector on board their aircraft, and if they detect the slightest trace of this shit in the air. They're gonna bug the hell outta the area in a fast hurry it up like their assholes are farting sparks, and the stinking General's gonna hit the area with nukes, and they'll burn the shit outta the stinking air that quick. That's the only uther door they'll have left opened to their actions, a complete sterilization of the entire area, my good friend." Walker replied as he finished off the cigarette and flipped the butt at the sand.

"What the fuck Easter egg hatched that frigging brainstorm because that fucking means we're gonna buy the stinking dirt farm if they do nuke this fricking place on our damn asses, buddy."The Mutt declared angrily as he stared Walker dead in the eyes and waited for his reply to his latest complaint.

"So, you got a stinking problem with that order, man? You know damn well we're operating under the rule we're expendable for this damn operation, stupid. We have orders to find this crap and that's what we're gonna do, and if we can't find the shit then the General's gonna place the period at the end of the sentence for us. So we betta find this crap and protect it from harm, if you don't wanna be turned into a bunch of nuclear ash. This ain't the first mission where our asses were hung out to dry in the damn wind, man." Walker smirked at his friend.

"I'm so fucking happy you can take your pending death so damn lightly man. I gotta tell you something, buddy. I got plans for my future Homes and they don't include being burned to a fucking cinder in a nuclear hell fire, man! How many more times are we gonna be sent on a mission with the threat of being burned alive with nukes? I'm getting sick and tired of all this lousy bullshit and threats of death, Walker? Why can't we go out on some normal fucking missions once in a while, where we go and kill the damn enemy then we go home nice and easy to get buzzed on suds in the real world, man?" The Mutt hotly countered to his fellow soldier.

"Hey man, I assure your ass I ain't got no fucking intention of being burned to death in a nuclear fire, man. That's why we're gonna find this shit and then we're gonna get the hell outta sand land like our asses are farting fucking sparks, Homes. C'mon man, we gotta get a move on it, we're starting to collect flies and the buzzards are starting to circle over our fucking heads where we're standing, and that my friend means we've been in one place too long for my likes." Walker replied as he shoved the Mutt forward with his forearm and followed him in the village.

"You lead the way for my sagging ass then oh fearless leader of mine. I hear the sound of small weapons fire popping off from maybe the next block or so up from where we're jaw jacking. I guess the stinking Vampires are doing their act as trained for, man. We might as well give them a stinking hand with the rest of these A-rab assholes from this fricking village, man." The Mutt offered with confidence, he was referring to the Ghost and Hunter continuing to engage the enemy combatants of the village they spotted and eliminated.

"Go ahead, you wanna go first, buddy." Walker offered the Mutt.

"Hell man, I don't even wanna go second, Walker." The Mutt fired right back at his commanding officer.

Walker laughed over the Mutt's replied, but he was having a hard time listening to him, because the inter squad helmet radios of the ground troopers were being flooded with incoming calls and reports from the spread out American soldiers engaging the remaining combatants operating in the village under attack from Walker's troops. Other reports informed him over the growing amount of prisoners and dead combatants, the clean up follow on troops were picking up, and finding dead or hiding in the crumbling buildings behind his advance troops.

Buckethead, hanging around Walker's side because he felt the commanding officer possessed a sort of charmed life during any enemy engagement the troops were involved in, mumbled at the Captain. "Hey Walker, not fur nuthin but I can't believe how well fucking organized these sonofabitches are in this damn shit filled village. I might be forced to believe some of these lousy creeps were trained, and they deserve some respect from my stinking ass. Naw, fuck that bullshit, these assholes are too fricking stupid to know what the hell they're doing around here. I wonder how long they were preparing for our arrival in this dump. Judging by the amount of enemy and weapons and setups they have aimed against us, the bastards musta been preparing for quite a while for us to come after their asses."

"These assholes were preparing for us long enuf I guess, and it's our fucking job to show the bunch of fucks any further resistance is a waste of time on their part. No matter how organized these lousy cocksuckers seem to be out there, they're still no match for our asses and training, big man. So let's place a fricking period at the end of their fucking sentence, and find this shit so we can get the hell outta this place once and for all, friend. I got a bad feeling if we take too fucking long finishing off the rest of these assholes. The Colonel's gonna come up and take over the mission on our asses, so he can take the stinking credit for the success of our mission once we find this shit." Walker remarked as he grinned at the huge soldier before shoving him forward.

Colonel Bruce Leadbetter broke in and overpowered the squad radio and reported to Walker. "Searcher One, Searcher Base, I'm moving backup units to your position to fill in for the wounded and dead of your outfit. You're ordered to leave the wounded and dead behind and continue your search of the village, once you secured the town. You have an order to DIP (Die In Place) if air is unable to support your action. I need that fucking crap in our possession, and that order's top priority for this operation. Don't worry about leaving anyone behind, they'll be picked up and cared for by the follow on forces, or Grave Registrations. You're ordered to keep moving forward until you secured the entire village, mister. Over."

"Well that was short and right to the fucking point I guess, man. C'mon people, we got orders and we gotta carry them out before the stinking Colonel hurts himself back there. The Colonel's getting hot under the stinking collar, and he wants a quick end to this damn operation ten minutes ago, or we're ordered to DIP if we can't knock this bunch of untrained A-rab assholes trying to shut out our damn lights on us." Walker growled at his troops as he lifted his weapon to a better firing position, and moved forward with the rest of his troops who had gathered around him when he answered the call from the Colonel.

A number of complaints came over the squad radio calling for needed ammunition which caused Walker to bitch angrily at the Mutt standing by his side as always. "What the fuck's wrong with some of our fucking troops for the love of Christ. I thought I told everyone before we engaged the damn combatants to max out on their fucking ammo on their asses when we first started this fucking mess, dammit."

"Hey pal, no matter how many rounds we took, with the amount of resistance we're picking up by these stinking defenders. There was no way in hell any of us coulda carried enough stinking ammo to complete this fucking engagement, Homes." The Mutt snapped back at Walker.

"Yeah Homes, I guess you have a good point there, buddy. Drop back and see what you can do bout getting some ammo out to the troops eating it up like there's no end to the crap, Mutt. I can't have any troops coming under attack, and not having enuf stinking ammo to fight back, dammit." Walker grumbled at the Mutt, (Lieutenant Frank Hall) and then he waited for him to shove off to follow his last orders.

"No need for that last order Walker, I just moved up the supply humvees and they're handing out ammunition to the soldiers who need it most right now, honey. How are you doing with ammo? I saw you doing your John Wayne act out there like you were bulletproof, and I thought you issued the order of no spray and pray from the damn hip on this mission, Robert." Sergeant Ramirez grumbled as she informed her soldier she was on the lack of ammunition for the advancing soldiers in the village.

"I'm fine, but I'm taking what ammunition the Mutt has on his ass, and then I'm sending him back for more ammo for the both of us. Glad to know you're on top of your game as usually." Walker offered to his long time girlfriend and fellow female soldier.

"I'm always on top of my game when we're on an operation, Robert. You just remember to be careful up there with these nuts, Bobby. I don't like you being so close to all the action. I have plans for your body once this mess is over, and I need a living partner to carry out my threats against you, Robert dear." Sergeant Ramirez purred in the radio in her most sexy voice.

"Hey baby, if anything happens to John Wayne up here, you can always take advantage of my body, if you need a living partner to screw round with." The Mutt offered over the squad radio.

"That has to be the dog man butting his damn nose in where it doesn't belong, and the only plans I have for your filthy body and ugly mind, involve a rusty nail and red hot branding irons, Mister Wiseass." Ramirez fired back at her friend.

Any soldiers listening in on the squad radio said "Wow" in it.

The remaining humvees moved deeper in the Iraqi village and started to make time for a change, until the machines turned a corner and found a roadblock of burning tires and junk cars piled up in the center of the road, stopping their forward progress. The instant the military machines stopped moving, they immediately came under attack by another group of combatants. Small weapons fire raked the length of the lead humvee and the second humvee opened up with the fifty caliber machine gun, and drove the attackers back inside the surrounding buildings in this area. The hovering Spectre Gunships followed the retreating combatants with their tracking equipment, and they opened up on some buildings the bulk of the enemy combatants retreated to. One Gunship concentrated so much firepower on one building, it collapsed in on itself from the amount of damage the weapons did to the structure.

The lead humvee laid out a number of grenades in the roadblock, and when the rounds ripped the defense apart, the humvee then plowed through the rest of the debris and then the machines continued down the road firing weapons at any attackers they spotted from inside their machines.

Walker was some twenty feet behind the lead humvee on foot, and when two insurgents suddenly made a mad dash from one building heading for a second structure fifty feet away, he opened fire on the two attackers and they never made it to their objective. So many trailing allied soldiers opened up on the two combatants, it forced Walker to bitch in his squad radio. "C'mon you fucking guys and try to conserve some frigging ammo will ya huh. Keep the damn spray and pray down to an absolute minimum. Start picking and choosing your targets, and remember one shot one kill until we get extra ammo and more support up here, dammit."

It was taking so long for the advancing American soldiers to secure the village it was starting to get dark on the troops. Captain Walker and the rest of his troops knew they owned the night, so this did not bother the elite group in the least. When it was dark, the allied soldiers shifted to their issued night vision equipment, to assist them in their ongoing fight with the Arab defenders from the village. The night made it much easier for the air support platforms to pick out the heat signatures coming from the enemy combatants hiding in the village, and the support systems were relying less and less on Colonel Pullman's directions and help, and where to attack the spotted combatants deeper inside the village.

Walker noticed Snatch, (Sergeant George Weaver) go down to one knee and check himself, and he tapped his squad radio and snapped in it. "Snatch, you hit man?"

"Yeah man, the armor stopped the damn round from getting at me, so I'm still in the fucking fight." Snatch replied once he was certain he wasn't hit by the round that struck his armor.

There was a white streak from a launched RPG round, and it struck Tracker One's machine in the tail rotor system, and the machine started to smoke heavily while enduring major problems staying in the air. Walker watched as his eyes in the air pulled itself out of the attack area before being forced to make a hard landing in the already secured section of the town. He saw the helicopter spinning to make up for the loss of the tail rotor on the machine.

What Walker did not see was one of the Apache helicopters followed Tracker One's Blackhawk all the way to the ground as fire support and protection. When the Blackhawk landed hard, so did the Apache. The gunner of the Apache platform got out and the pilot picked up the Colonel which turned his helicopter into Tracker One for the rest of the mission. When he was airborne again, the ATO Colonel immediately checked in with Walker. "This is Tracker One to Searcher One. Come in. Over."

"Searcher One to Tracker One, where the hell are you and what condition are you in? Over. I need your fucking eyes in the air or these attackers are gonna start getting the best of us, man." Walker growled in the radio as he searched the sky for Tracker One flying over his troops.

"Tracker One is on position directing air support as ordered, Commander. Over."

"How the hell's that fucking possible Tracker One, and how the hell didja pull that stunt off, man? I saw your stinking machine get hit in the ass end, and your fucking machine go down hard minutes ago, Tracker One? How the hell are you still in the air if your machine's down and out of the fight, mister?" Walker asked in the radio of the ATO Airman.

"I'm no longer in Tracker One, my new Tracker One is an Apache helicopter. I displaced the weapons co-pilot and took his place in the Apache, sir. Over."

"Out fucking standing Tracker One, I have new orders fur your ass then buddy. I want you to swing the heavier air support out in front of us. We'll control the Apache's actions from down here. You hafta keep support attacking any damn insurgents we're pushing right outta the stinking town before us. We only have a few more blocks of this dump to secure, and then the fucking combatants aren't gonna have a rotten place to turn to or hide. We're gonna force the mutherfuckers right out of the damn village, and you betta have the Gunships and uther crap level anyone we drive outta this stinking dump. I'm counting on you to control the air support for my ground troops, Tracker One. Over."

"Roger last orders, Searcher One. I'll have heavy air support concentrate efforts on the south end of the village. Anyone you force out of the town will be history by the time I'm done with their asses. Besides Searcher One, I have a personal score to settle with these pricks. They took out my damn helicopter, and someone's going to pay big time for that move. Over." Colonel Pullman bitched at Walker over the radio net.

"You know you're right with your vengeance flight, but you and air betta be where I want you, or I'll take on a vengeance mission of my own on your ass, Tracker One. By the way Tracker One, I wanna thank you for getting back in the air so quickly. I thought I lost my damn eyes in the sky when you went down a few moments ago, Tracker One. Over."

"That's no problem Searcher One. I'm only carrying out my orders as received. Over."

Walker did not get a chance to respond to Tracker One's response, he was hit in his body armor by another round fired at him from an insurgent, he cursed because of the pain the round caused his exhausted and battered body, even though the round did not make it through his protective body armor. The Mutt saw the round hit Walker's armor and asked him. "Hey man, you hurt bad Walker?" Then Mutt gave a smirk at his friend.

"Hey stupid, didja ever see anyone hurt good you fucking idiot?" Walker growled back at Mutt as he glared at him while trying to take his mind off his pain.

"Well, there was this girl I once took to bed, and she liked it real rough, so I took a brick…"

"Spare me your sexual exploits will ya. I shoulda had my head examined asking you a serious question, asshole. God damn, I feel like a can of crushed assholes. I never expected such resistance coming from these backassward people." The Captain complained as he drew in a gulp of air, and let it out slowly as the pain started to let up on him.

"If you don't mind my saying, you look like a can of crushed assholes. By the way Walker, look at it this way. Right now because of being beaten up so bad, you become a prime candidate for medical Marijuana for ya pain." The Mutt smirked again.

"Keep pushing my ass stupid. You betta remember I have a loaded fucking weapon in my hands, and you wanna go screwing around with my ass like this, buster."

"All joking aside Walker, how the hell are ya doing? Didja experience any pain, buddy?" The Mutt asked seriously as he continued to stare at his lifelong friend and fellow soldier.

"No stupid, I experienced a fucking blow job, you asshole. Of course it hurt like fucking hell, man. I'll make it alright, but I feel real sorry for the first lousy prick from this dump I get my fucking hands on to interrogate. He's gonna wish his father never porked his damn muther by the time I'm done with his god damn ass." He raged as he rubbed the spot on his armor where the bullet struck him, it did not do a thing to help the pain.

Heavy weapon fire broke out on the next block up from where Walker and the Mutt was hold up, and they ducked down and observed the action occurring before them. It was like a scene out of the movies. Heavy tracer fire in the darkness was hitting a number of buildings in the village, and a streak from a missile fired at the firing combatants erupted in a wall of flames, when the Hellfire missile hit the target. In response to the attack on the trapped combatants from the allied soldiers, the enemy insurgents responded with a new barrage of RPG rounds streaking across the night air. Their explosions brightening the night, and momentarily rendering the night vision equipment of the American soldiers almost useless until the flames and explosions settled down.

The night vision equipment employed by the specialized soldiers was picking up the constant flashing strobe lights from the American troops, who wore them to identify themselves to the other friendly forces employed for this hard hitting operation inside the small Iraqi village. Between the flashing strobes and countless explosions and tracer fire, it created sheer mayhem for the soldiers attacking the dug in combatants, and the insurgents involved in defending their village against the American soldiers.

Slowly, Captain Walker's attacking troops started to make huge advances in the village, and soon the enemy combatants were running out of homes or rubble to hide behind, and continue their war against the advancing American soldiers. Many of the combatants decided it was much wiser for them to surrender to the quick moving soldiers, rather than trying to continue to fight to the last man. Or daring to flee the safety or what there was of safety left in the all but destroyed village. Every Arab male who picked up a weapon and aimed it at the American soldiers, knew what was waiting them if they were foolish enough to try and escape the village after that action.

The Iraqi defenders were either already attacked by the heavy air support the American forces were enjoying protecting them. Or they witnessed the onslaughts of the air attacks on their fellow insurgents being attacked by the aircraft and helicopters. Not many of the defenders wanted to face the death waiting them from the air, if they dared to expose their positions to the American support systems, or to the allied ground soldiers attacking them.

As Walker stepped out and started to lead the way for the remaining humvees, as the elite soldiers continued to advance forward in the all but destroyed Iraqi village. The enemy combatants started to come out of the homes they were hiding in for protection, with their hands held in the air unarmed. Trailing allied soldiers assigned to take command of the surrendering prisoners, rushed out before Walker and his advance units, and they took charge of the combatants giving up in large numbers. The soldiers flung the enemy fighters to the ground and roughly searching them, ripping the robes and clothing from their battered and bloody bodies. Once the enemy combatants were searched, they had their hands pulled behind their backs and secured with flex cuffs, rendering them harmless and out of the fight.

Not all the fighting came to an end in the town. There were a large number of enemy combatants who chose to continue their fight with the American forces, and the special ops soldiers kept pushing the defenders through the street until there was only one block of buildings left, until the defenders were forced completely out of the village. These were the hard line fanatical fighters, the more radical of the enemy insurgents defending the village, and they put up a valiant fight against overwhelming odds mounted against them.

Captain Robert Walker and his troops kept the pressure on the hard line Iraqi fighters who he believed were likely members of al-Qaeda in Iraq, resorting to fighting the remaining insurgents from building to building inside the village. Forcing the insurgents into the few structures left standing until their backs were against the wall, and they had to die in place or flee the safety of the buildings and be forced in the open desert. Into the waiting air support foaming at the mouth to attack any Arab fighters forced out of the village, by the advancing American forces.

Fifty insurgents suddenly made a mad dash out of the village into the desert, hoping the darkness of night would keep their move hidden from the trailing American soldiers. As the group of insurgents charged into the desert, Walker's troops pulled up and allowed air support to move in and finish off the defenders of the village for them. The Captain was not very interested in trying to save these Iraqi defenders, because he knew they would never surrender peacefully to his troops. These Arab fighters had to be part of al-Qaeda in Iraq, and there was no way in hell they were going to give up to his troops to save their own lives. He decided to allow the aircraft to take this group of fighters out of the picture, so they would not come back in the future and cause his troopers or the new Iraqi government any further problems or attacks.

Captain Walker and the rest of his troops bunched up on the edge of the village, and stood by and listened in as Tracker One communicated with the air support platforms above them. "Tracker One to Talon Flight Leader, Raven Flight Leader and Tiger Impact Leader. I have a large group of enemy combatants trying to make it to safety in the desert. As of this time, the combatants are completely exposed and trapped in the open. I'm requesting a run on the fleeing combatants immediately. Over."

"Raven Flight Leader to Tracker One. Roger that. We're setup and in position and am starting approach on enemy combatants fleeing the village. What order of attack if any do you prefer employed against the fleeing enemy forces? Do you want 20mm or missile attack on enemy fighters? It's up to you so make the call. Over." The commander of the lead F-15 wing asked Tracker One over his radio net.

"Raven Flight Leader, Tracker One, you're to clear guns, you're to clear missiles, go with everything. Employ everything you have on board your attack platform, sir. You're operating under a complete destruction order, Raven Flight Leader. Over."

"Roger last Tracker One, am engaging combatants trapped in open with everything I have on board my platform. We're operating under the complete destruction order, beginning attack profile on targets. I hope you understand this is going to create one helluva mess down there, Tracker One. Over."

"Roger that but remember Raven Flight Leader, we have many friendlies on the ground in the surrounding area. Confirm you see strobes coming from friendlies in the area, before opening fire on the trapped enemy combatants, Raven Leader. Over." Colonel Pullman wanted to know if the commander of the F-15's had Walker's troops clear of his attack area, before he let loose with the weapons on board his aircraft.

"Roger that Tracker One, receiving good report from strobes of many friendlies on the ground in the surrounding area of attack. They're marked and well out of the attack area. Preparing to begin my opening attack on exposed enemy combatants as of this time, Tracker One. Over." The commander replied to Tracker One's orders.

"Tracker One, Roger that Raven Flight Leader, don't fire on the strobes, they're friendlies. You're clear to engage combatants. Clear guns, clear missiles, clear bombs on targets identified. Over."

"Roger last Tracker One, clearing missiles, clearing bombs, clearing guns, clearing everything on board my platform, sir. Need immediate BDA (Bomb Damage Assessment) after my run's completed over the target area. Over Tracker One."

"Roger that, BDA after your attack run's completed, Commander. Begin attack on insurgents Raven Flight Leader. Over." Colonel Pullman replied to the attack pilot of the F-15.

"Beginning my approach, weapons away Tracker One. Danger Close, I repeat Tracker One, Danger Close. Over." Danger close was a warning the attack aircraft was going to employ CBU-52 B/B cluster bomb system during his attack on the enemy attackers, and he wanted all friendly forces in the area to be aware of his attack plan.

Tracker One watched as Raven Flight Leader led the way for the rest of his trailing F-15 aircraft, and then he concentrated his attention on the fleeing combatants as the weapons from the aircraft closed in on their position. When the weapons hit their target, Colonel Pullman called in his radio in an excited voice. "Good kill, good kill, keep it coming. You have a secondary group of combatants trying to make for the road leading back into the village, stay on top of these guys Raven Flight Leader. Over."

The second attacking F-15 Eagle aircraft came in for the attack, but the enemy combatants who survived the first attack, split up into smaller groups. They were making themselves harder targets for the attacking aircraft by spreading out like they were doing, and trying to make themselves as small as possible on the ground. This action forced Colonel Pullman to get back on the radio and warn the attacking F-15 aircraft. "Raven Flight Leader come around again, target's moving Two, Two from point Three, One. You have to stay on top of these guys. I want all down and out of the fight. Over."

"Roger last, targets moving Two, Two, from point Three One, will comply Tracker One. Coming around for second run at enemy targets still active on the ground, and will stay on top of said targets until all resistance has ended. Over Tracker One." The second Eagle pilot came around again and started a run on the moving Iraqi fighters.

As the second, third and then forth F-15 Eagle aircraft combined their attack on the trapped, dispersed combatants. The overpowering weapons lit up the area where the enemy insurgents fled to. This section of the desert was instantly bathed in a shower of sparks and flames from many bombs and missiles let loose on the trapped Iraqi fighters below the aircraft. Tracker One's ATO Colonel had to wait for a few moments for the flames and smoke to die down, before he was able to give Raven Flight Leader an accurate Bomb Damage Assessment of the attack area and Iraqi fighters. When the earth settled down, the Tracker One platform closed in and checked out the attack area. There was nothing left alive in the entire section of the desert, so he report to all assets taking part in the operation for the search for the biological weapon.

"Tracker One to all friendlies operating in attack area. All resistance from the enemy insurgents in the village and surrounding area has been sanctioned. All enemy threat has been likewise sanctioned, and has stopped except for a few small pockets of resistance trying to fight it out with our troops on the ground, and they're ground forces problem now. Raven Leader, Talon Leader, you're instructed to return to nest for rearming and refueling. You're further ordered to be held on ready standby alert status for future assistance if needed by said ground forces. Over."

Both wings of American warplanes checked in and replied to Tracker One's last order, before they left the attack area.

"Tracker One to Tiger Impact Leader, you're instructed to receive in-flight refueling, and remain in general area in case we have a flare up in enemy combatant resistance aimed at our ground forces. Wild Fire Flight Leader, you're instructed to land at the north end of the village at a safe distance away from the town and out of RPG range. You'll remain on the ground and on site and be ready to assist any needed air support for friendly forces operating on the ground dealing with Operation Rapid Fire. Over."

Both Commander of the Spectre Gunship air support platforms reported in and informed Tracker One they understood their orders, and they were complying with the orders they received from their commander of this operation inside the Tracker One helicopter.

Captain Walker was with the Mutt, Neck, Buckethead, Sergeant Ramirez and Blind Date, and they watched as the aircraft made quick work of the hard liner Iraqi fighters he wanted dead. When the shooting was over, the Captain grumbled at his friends as he pitched his cigarette at the ground. "Well that's that. It's a fricking shame those assholes didn't want to live and chose to go out like soldiers, such a fucking waste of a bunch of brave men and women fighters. Shit."

"Hey asshole, they're fricking enemy soldiers, and now they're good enemy soldiers, because the lot of the stinking shitheads are on their fucking way to Paradise like they wanted to be heading since they were born in this messed up frigging world, man." The Mutt growled at his friend because he was displaying some remorse over the death of the enemy combatants who would have been happy to kill, cook and eat any American soldiers if they had half a chance to get at Walker and his elite troops.

"You got a point there Mutt, but because they chose a soldier's way out doesn't mean I have to hate the sonofabitches for their actions. No matter what the assholes were or what they did in this country, they were fucking soldiers guilty of carrying out their country's political aims and military orders. That means they should have the respect any soldier enjoys for carrying out their orders faithfully." Walker snapped back at the Mutt.

"Hey man, I'm not gonna get involved in a pissing contest over a pack of stinking dead ass terrorists being slaughters by our forces. Let's say they're dead and let it go at that, Homes." The Mutt replied as he shot Walker a smile, this softened his stance and he groaned.

"I guess. C'mon, let's get back to our troops and see what they're doing about securing the village, pal." Walker remarked as he gave the field of battle a quick glance then headed off.

Suddenly, all weapon fire in the village stopped, and an eerie silence filled the area. The only traffic the soldiers heard was from the prowling Specter Gunships. Sergeant Dorothy Ramirez worked her way to Walker's side and she asked him. "What do you make of this ration of shit we're seeing, Robert? I don't like this crap one bit."

"Neither do I, it's like the quiet before the stinking storm. Raz, while there's a low in the fighting, we hafta concentrate on getting our troops betta organized, before shit hits the fan again. We're operating like a bunch of armatures with some of our people running around like a bunch of crazed lunatics." He growled as he scanned the forward area of the village.

Without informing Captain Walker of his actions, the moment Colonel Leadbetter was made aware his troops were entering the small Iraqi village, and were encountering heavy resistance from the enemy defenders. The Colonel immediately ordered up a UAV or Unmanned Aerial Vehicle, and he was watching the action going down in real time, as it occurred inside the village. He was fuming over the combatants were putting up a good fight against his highly trained and elite soldiers. He wanted a quick and final end placed to the fighting in the village, before someone made a mistake, and they accidentally destroyed the cylinder containing the biological weapon, and then all hell would break out in the country.

The Colonel was aware if any aircraft or sensors stored in the humvees working in the village picked up the slightest trace of the biological agent in the air. An automatic signal was to be transmitted by the sensors, and a flight of B-2 Stealth bombers would be dispatched with a pair of nuclear bombs storied in their bays. The aircraft would drop those weapons on the heads of his troops in the field, and then Iraq and most of Saudi Arabia, Iran and any other nation near the blast area. Would be erased from the earth in one flash of nuclear hell and destruction, in an effort to burn up the released biological weapon before it could infect human or animal life.

Walker did not mind taking a few moments after the support platforms eliminated the insurgent resistance in and around the Iraqi village of ar-Ramadi. This was because he trusted his troops and understood the rest of them would be busy securing the village and civilian population. The Captain was giving his soldiers the chance to arrest everyone they found alive in the village, and sort out the important civilians and separate them from the rest who would be of no important intelligence worth to his mission.

He wanted the leader of the village and his closest people taken into custody, and the more important factions of the insurgency operating in Iraq held together with the members of the insurgency vital to interrogate. Because he wanted to know their affiliation, and where the nucleolus of their command structure of the insurgency was situated in Iraq. This knowledge would be vital in the ongoing fight against al-Qaeda in Iraq, and any other insurgent factions operating in the ravaged and war torn country.

The main soldiers to Captain Walker's command were surrounding their officer, and they were getting extremely antsy over getting back in the fight, even though the bulk of fighting was over in the village. There was still some sporadic small weapon's fire continuing as the other soldiers of the unit continued their mop up operation, and securing the village.

The Mutt, dared to approach and break Walker's daydreaming trance as he stared at the death the support platforms carried out against the defenders of the Iraqi village by offering him. "Hey chum we still have a minor fucking war going on in the damn village, and the rest of us wanna get involved in the action before it's ended. I hate to say this, but some of the uther guys feel you're giving too much honor to the dopey bastards out there who decided to die, rather than give up. C'mon Walker, we gotta get on with this mission so we can get the hell..."

Walker took his eyes off the death created by the aircraft and then he seethed at his lifelong friend and fellow soldier. "Hey look pal, don't talk to me about things that are above your stinking pay grade. I know damn well we have to secure the fucking village, and get on with our operation. I want you to order some of the villagers out there, and have them bury the enemy dead. With respect and you'll assure their bodies will be respected by the grave diggers. Dammit, yeah, you're right Mutt, order one of our people to get on the burial detail, and I'll turn the rest and head them back to the village and we'll finish up with securing the place."

CHAPTER TWENTY ONE

Wacko, (Sergeant Salvatore Tomassi) ran up to Walker and waited to be acknowledged by the exhausted looking Captain. When Walker looked at the Sergeant he reported. "Captain, we have the village secured from further major enemy engagements. Although there are still some minor pockets of resistance continuing in the dump, it's unorganized and aimless at best. We have the Vampires out and they're making short work out of further resistance from the combatants still operating in the village, Captain. We also secured a main building, and we assembled any persons we classified as important enuf for close interrogation, Captain Walker."

"That's an outstanding report from you Wacko, and you surprise the hell outta my stinking ass by acting like a soldier for a change, buddy." Captain Walker snapped before he caught himself, he was still extremely upset over having to kill so many soldiers only guilty of defending their country. Once he got control over his emotions, he went on with his words to the stunned looking fellow soldier.

"From what I know about these backassward people, I was led to believe every stinking village or town had a sort of leader running the damn place. Either an Omar or Village Elder or someone like that, were you able to locate the head dude in command of this stinking village? By the way Wacko, I'm upset at myself for snapping at you like I just did. We still tight soldier?" Walker asked the other soldier hoping he was not pissed at him.

"We're tighter than two coats of fucking paint, Walker. Yeah Captain, we were able to locate the Village Elder. The dude was hold up in a concrete bunker obviously constructed by the nut once running this miserable country a few years back. We had to root the dude outta the place by threatening to blow the bunker up with him and his family inside the bunker. Walker, the dude's really pissed off and he's refusing to speak to anyone we had try to question the fucker. There was a few uther dudes with him we classified as ex-military, and some of us feel at least one soldier who was with the old man mighta been Republican Guard trained. We separated the thought to be soldiers from the old man, and we are waiting further orders on what we should do with the leader of this place.

"We also took in custody a few insurgents we feel mighta worked directly with the command structure of the combatants, sir. We have them secured in the building we commandeered as our makeshift command HQ while stuck in this bug infested miserable Iraqi town, Captain."

"Good, good, I betta see if I can loosen up the old man's tongue a little, Wacko. Hey Mutt, when you were reading the report you found in the CIA humvee, were you able to find out if there were any pictures of this stinking dead ass Colonel al-Qaysi's fricking brood. I'm interested in the chick the CIA creeps were showing some concerned with her that forced them to go so far as to place that red flag next to her name in their damn report." Walker remarked as he turned to the Mutt and waited for his reply.

"Yeah, there was a picture of the good looking chick with the report. In fact Walker I got the picture of the bitch with me, man." The Mutt offered as he went fishing in his pocket looking for the picture, and then he added. "She's a real good looker, and I was kinda saving the picture for my private collection…"

"Oh God, the Mutt's really starting to get disgusting, Walker. You know the only reason the Mutt took the picture of the woman was so he could jerk off to it while he was in the head doing his business. I vote we neuter the dog man when we get back to the real world, so the women back there will be safe from his debauchery and evil ways,

Walker." Baby Tee snapped while she maintained a sweet but vicious looking smile on her lips.

"Man little tits, any chance you get you jump on my stinking ass, bitch. Why the hell don't you go and get on someone else's ass for a stinking change will ya, Baby? Or at least go and grow some tits for yourself, baby." The Mutt fired back at her.

"Because it's fun getting on your ass and besides, you give me so much ammunition to use against you, any time you open your disgusting mouth and say something, dopey."

"You two birds betta get married, or at least get offa each uthers asses while we're on this damn mission. You guys fight worse than married folk do. We ain't got time for this kinda bullshit you birds. Let's get a move on it and start questioning some prisoners we have in custody. Wacko, you wanna lead the way to this building were we're holding the prisoners?" Walker grumbled as he looked at Wacko, and nodded at the wild and fun loving soldier.

The troop's who forced the remaining combatants out of the village to their slaughter, turned as one and followed the other soldier to the building containing the prisoners to be interrogated. After a few moments of hustling, the soldiers came up to the largest building in the village, and the front door was being guarded by two of Walker's troopers. The Captain nodded at the soldiers as he climbed the three steps and entered the building with the Mutt, Sergeant Ramirez, Buckethead and Neck following him. He needed the two largest soldiers he had in his unit with him because he was planning to intimidate the Iraqi prisoners with the larger men's presence. Inside the building, a few specialized soldiers were ripping the place apart, looking for any information on the biological weapon, or who might have it.

Wacko had to get Walker's attention and he directed him towards a room, and he crashed through the door like an angry linebacker attacking a quarterback on the field, making an impression by the hard entry in the room, shaking up the prisoners in the room. He was a bad sight to see, his uniform and body armor was covered with dried sweat, blood and whatever other fluids came from his body, or anyone who happened to lean against him. His chin was covered with a four day old growth of stubble that seems like he could use it as a weapon.

He had two straps of rounds for his M-16 crisscrossing his body, and an extra canteen hung from his web belt by means of a tattered shoelace. His holster was ripped and the pistol missing, the damage to the holster obviously caused by a round fired at him. The Captain's helmet was bent in two places where bullets bounced off his head protection, and his face was covered with dirt and dried blood from his mouth and the corner of his right eye. A crust of dry sand circled his mouth and eyes, and his angry expression warned everyone in the room he was not to be messed with. The young officer's eyes were ablaze and his chin stuck out, displaying he was not in a good mood, and he was looking to take someone out.

The six soldiers assigned to guard the over thirty prisoners and civilians, snapped to attention when He stormed in the room. The soldiers still kept their attention glued to the prisoners and civilians trapped in the room. Walker smirked slightly at his troops, and he aimed his questions at the one soldier he chose as the leader of the guards from his unit controlling the prisoners.

The soldier he smirked at was Sergeant Christopher Danko, just called Danko for short for lack of a better nick name for the soldier. When Walker acknowledged his presence, Danko offered a report on the situation and prisoners. "Sir, these are the prisoner and civilians we picked out for close interrogation from the village, sir. We feel these few people might have vital information we need. The rest of the civilians pukes of this town, along with possible insurgents we captured alive, are being held prisoners throughout the rest of the stinking village, until we have further orders as to do what with them, sir."

"Very good soldier." Walker was pleased Danko did not address him by name or rank in front of the prisoners and civilians. Because he believed the less the prisoners and civilians knew about their interrogator, the better off it was for him to force information they had from them. He wanted the scared looking prisoners to think he was working for the CIA, because many of the Iraqis feared the interrogation tactics the Spooks always employed. He drew in a breath and held it for a moment as he tried to calm himself down a little.

The other soldiers that followed him into the building instantly took up defensive positions surrounding Walker, and they glared at the Iraqi prisoners like they were just daring them to try something against them. This was another form of breaking down the resistance of the prisoners before their interrogation began. These soldiers were in the same rough shape Walker was, and their presence was extremely intimidating.

Captain Walker did not say a word to any prisoners as he started to pace wildly before them, and then he stopped and lit a cigarette. With his eyes narrow and seemed like they were on fire, he looked at each prisoner lined up with their backs against the wall. He was trying to pick out the Elder of the village on his own. There were ten old men who could be the Elder, so he was forced to ask Danko which prisoner was the one he was looking for.

Danko walked up to Sameer Abdalsada and rested his hand on the old man's shoulder. This action caused the Elder's bodyguard to react and he made a threatening move at Danko. The Mutt was on him in a flash and shoved his forearm under the neck of Emad al-Battat, and savagely forced the man back against the wall, choking him with his forearm at the same time. The Mutt had no idea the man he was assaulting was once a Major in the feared Republican Guard under command of Saddam Hussein, when he was in power over Iraqi.

Walker watched what the Mutt was doing to the prisoner and he did not react until he saw Emad's face starting to turn a red, and the man was desperately struggling to get air in his starving lungs. When the man started to go limp under the Mutt's attack, Walker moved up and placed his hand on his arm and pulled it away from the throat of Emad. Then he growled at the Mutt. "He's had enuf, we won't have any further trouble with this little prick. Let him go and if he's stupid enuf to cause us more problems, take the fuck outside and shoot him in the fucking head and be done with him. It's that simple man."

Every word Walker said was immediately repeated in Iraqi by Sergeant Diane Morrison. The soldier branded Ice was one of three soldiers in Walker's group who spoke fluent Arabic.

When the Mutt released his death hold on Emad's throat, Walker turned to the man and hissed in his face. "Look Mac, I don't have the fucking time or patience to waste on you. If you give me further trouble or resistance, I'm gonna shoot you and the man standing to your right for any infraction you're stupid enuf to commit in front of me." He waited until Ice translated his words to Arabic, and heard her leave in the curse words and nodded to her for that move.

"Okay pal nod your fucking noggin if you understood mine, or my soldier's warning." Walker snorted at the shaking prisoner.

Emad slowly nodded at the fuming American soldier in the positive.

"Good, now we understand each uther betta. The rest of you people listen up, I'm looking for a small shiny stainless steel metal cylinder, and the assholes who has the damn thing in their possession. If someone steps forward and tells me where this damn thing is, it's gonna go a helluva lot easier on the rest of you fucking puds. If I'm forced to go the route of questioning every one of you fucking people privately, I'll work every one of you fools over until you tell me what I wanna know, or you end up fucking dead. Either way, it doesn't matter shit to my stinking ass as long as I get the information I'm looking for from you fucking people." Again, he had to stop speaking to allow Ice to catch up to his threats in Arabic.

When Ice was done translating his words, Walker moved over until he was standing in front of the old man, and he leaned forward until his face was just inches away from the Elder's face, and he hissed at the old man. "Okay pal, since you're the fucking head cheese of this stinking dump, you gotta know what the fuck's happening in this place. I hope you like the taste of dick cause I'm gonna cut yours off and shove it down your throat, if you don't tell me what I wanna know from your ass. So I'm gonna start my interrogation with your fucking ass first, pal." He knew what he was doing, and was cursing up a storm to further insult and intimidate the Arab males of the village, in an attempt to soften them up until he started questioning them in earnest.

All he read in the eyes of the old Iraqi leader of the village was unfettered hatred for him and his uniform. The Captain decided to move whoever he was going to question first from the group to another room. He was hoping separating the prisoners from each other would make the ones left in the room, believe if the one being questioned did not answer the soldier's questions, he killed that one and would come in for another man to start questioning. At least this was what he was banking on. It was the first step in properly interrogating a prisoner taught to him when he went to classes on training how to interrogate a prisoner.

Suddenly Walker roughly grabbed the old man by the collar of his robe, and he dragged him out of the overcrowded room. The two were followed out of the room by the Mutt, Buckethead and No Neck. Once Walker had the Elder out in the hallway, he released the Elder and even helped him get his balance. The Mutt drew Walker's attention towards a door and Walker led the old man and the others in the empty room. Once in the room, he calmed down and told the Elder to take a seat and relax. This time he had to rely on Neck to translate his words to Arabic.

The Mutt offered Walker a bottle of warm water and he took it and offered it to the Iraqi Village Elder as he remarked at him. "Look sir, I didn't mean to be so damn nasty to you in the uther room. I'm in your village and I've been assigned to find this damn cylinder I asked you about in the uther room, and the person who has the damn thing with him or her. If you know who the hell has the damn thing and where the cylinder is, I'll collect it and the person and my soldiers and myself will leave your village in peace and in haste. I don't wanna be the cause of destroying anymore of this peaceful village than was already destroyed, because your people thought they were going to get the upper hand on my soldiers. I didn't want that, but your fighters didn't leave me any uther choice in the matter, but to defend ourselves against their stupid attacks and respond accordingly against it."

Once his words were translated by Neck, Walker continued his words aimed at the Elder. "I have a picture of the woman we're looking for, and if you tell me where she's hiding, and if she has the damn cylinder with her. We'll leave your village." This time Walker did not wait until his words were translated as he removed the picture of Ayesha al-Qaysi the Mutt gave him earlier, and he flashed it before the Elder's eyes.

As good as he was and how historic the old man was trying to act before the American soldier, Sameer Abdalsada was unable to hide the shocked look in his eyes at seeing the picture of Ayesha locked in the soldier's filthy hand. Now, he was fighting a battle with himself, wondering how much this savage and lowly infidel knew of Ayesha, and the cylinder with the biological agent trapped inside it.

Both Walker and the Mutt noticed the sudden change in the Village Elder's expression and stance, and Walker understood he just struck a nerve with the old man, and his anger returned with all its fury as he hissed at him again. "Okay pal, no more playing mister fucking nice guy with your stinking ass. I saw by your look that tells me you know this fucking woman I'm looking for. Where the fuck is she and this damn cylinder I need, god dammit?"

Drawing in his breath and releasing it slowly, Sameer Abdalsada replied in an angry tone. "Lowly American infidel from the sewers of the slums of Baghdad, of course I know this faithfully Arab woman, who has lived in my village since the day she was born. As is my duty and responsibility as Village Elder soldier, I was present at her birth. That was the reason for the shocked look in my eyes. What is it you want from this daughter of Allah, cursed infidel?"

Walker had to wait until Neck told him what the old man said to him, hearing his words infuriated him, and he was back on the old man. "Look pal, I told you I didn't have the fucking time or patience to go dancing around with you over this fucking situation. If you don't tell me what I want to know about the cylinder and this damn chick. I'm gonna allow the twin tree trunks standing behind me to have a little go at getting this information from your sagging ass, pal. It's up to you on how much pain you wanna suck down before you tell me everything I want and need to know from your ass, mister. Believe me my friend, by the time those two big slugs are done with your ass, you'll tell me everything I need to know from you and more, pal."

"God cursed American fool who has commanded the hated soldiers who have destroyed my village. I'd willingly and proudly give up my worthless life to protect a sacred daughter of Allah. I'd be cursed to hell for all eternity by Allah's mighty breath, if I turned His lovely daughter over to your blood coated evil hands, American savage. So you can defile His daughter's sacred temple. You do your worst to my old and broken body, and see what it'll net you for your wasted efforts, infidel. Not one single word of betrayal will ever cross my weather beat parched lips against His faithful daughter. As the trusted Elder of ar-Ramadi, it's my sworn duty to protect all faithful daughters of Allah from the hands of any lowly infidels who have invaded Iraq and slaughtered His children." When Sameer Abdalsada finished his speech, he set his eyes and jaw and stared into the burning and hate filed and most threatening eyes of Walker.

After Neck translated the elder's words for Walker, he moved to his side and rested his hand on his arm, and when he had his attention, the Mutt made a swift head movement towards Walker. This action informed Walker he wanted to speak to him in private, because none of the other soldiers in the room knew for certain if the old man understood or spoke English.

Walker moved in the hall with the Mutt and allowed him to speak.

"Walker not for nuthin man, but I saw that stupid look before from uther Arab pricks in this country. When they make that kinda stupid ass puss, nuthin we can do to them this side of judgment day, will break them down to where they'll talk to us."

"You got me Mutt, whatdaya suggest we do with the fucking old dude, dog man? I need to know where this bitch is hiding, and if she has the damn cylinder with her or not, buddy. Or we're gonna end up wasting a helluva lot of fucking time looking for the damn thing, if we have to resort to searching what's left of this lousy dump, my friend."

"Walker, we have a number of uther stinking prisoners we can work on, why not let the uther pricks think you did something to the old man, and now you're gonna work over their asses the same way, man. Some uther pricks in the uther room looked like they were on the verge of talking even before we turn our attention on the little pricks." The Mutt offered with a smirk as he stared at his commanding officer while he waited his reply.

"How the hell are we gonna know who are the fucking weak ones in the uther room, without wasting a ton of fucking time and energy with trying to break them down first, Mutt?" Walker asked as he took a quick breath and returned the Mutt's look.

"I don't know, maybe we should show each mutherfucker in the uther room the picture of the chick we want. If we get any reaction from any of them like we got from that old man. Then we take the one who reacted outta the room and work on that one first. It's the only thing I can come up with to save us some fucking time you keep saying we don't have much of, man."

"That's a damn good idea Mutt. I knew if you applied your noggin to this problem, you could come up with a good reaction. We're gonna do what you suggested." Walker replied.

"Hey man I was always smart, it's just you never paid much attention to any of my uther my suggestions." The Mutt retorted as he returned Walker grin.

"Hey stupid don't go and allow my compliment go to your stinking head. You betta remember even a stinking clock that's stopped is right at least twice a day." Walker fired back at Mutt.

"Oh man that was good I didn't see that one coming. Yeah, you're like the stinking chick I was once dating, she'd give me a compliment and take it back when I started to enjoy it. You know Walker, when we get back to the States, I think I'm gonna go into politics, so I can go to Washington and turn Gold into Lead like they do." The Mutt complained at Walker.

"C'mon Homes let's see if we can shake any of them uther rotten pricks up, and maybe place a quick end to this damn mission we're on before I die of old fucking age." The young Mari ne Captain grumbled as he took the lead with the Mutt following him, they both entered the room with the prisoners gathered in it. Then Walker looked at the faces of the few soldier's he left guarding the Iraqi prisoners and then he turned to the prisoners, as he motioned Ice over to his side and he whispered to her.

"Hey honey I want you by my side and translate my words for these popping jays as quickly as you can. We came up with a plan, we're gonna try it on some of these damn jerks here. I hafta get this damn interrogation moving along before Colonel Leadbetter gets his ass over here, and he gets on us for not moving quick enuf for his likes. I was forced to leave the two tree trunks out there guarding the old man from the village, and I want these fools to think we mighta done something bad to the little prick, because he didn't wanna tell me what I wanted to know from the old goat chaser, girl."

"You got it honey I'm going to make it look like you told me something terrible about the Elder, and then I'm going to put a surprised look on my face. Maybe that'll help make the other prisoners think you hurt the old man, Walker." Ice replied as she put a shocked look on her face.

Walker turned to the prisoners and held the picture of Ayesha up so they all could see it, and then he barked at the group as a whole. "Okay you people, this is what I want to know from anyone of you assholes. I want to know if any of you people know this woman, and where she's might be hiding in this village. Your fucking leader decided not to acknowledge he knew this woman, and he's paying dearly for refusing to answer my fucking questions. Unless you turds wanna join him, I suggest someone steps up and tells me what I wanna know before I lose my god damn patience with the lot of ya."

While Ice was translating his words, Walker and the Mutt studied the faces of the prisoners. The Captain picked up the change in one prisoner's face and he immediately drew the Mutt's attention to him, and the Mutt nodded in agreement with his pick. The instant Ice finished speaking, Walker headed for the prisoner he picked out, and he glared as he looked the Iraqi man dead in his eyes. The look was more than enough to make the Arab react, and when he moved away from Walker's face, he grabbed the man roughly by the throat and he literally dragged the stunned Iraqi man out of the room. As a few of the more threatening Arab men grumbled their displeasure over the way the wild acting American soldier was manhandling one of their own in right front of them.

The prisoner's reaction to the way Walker was treating one of their own made the American soldiers guarding the prisoners to tighten their grips on their weapons, and they assumed a more threatening stance against the Iraqi prisoners.

Walker practically dragged the second prisoner he believed was an enemy combatant out of the overcrowded room and across the hallway, and then he almost threw the prisoner in a third empty room of the Elder's home. The Elder was being held in seclusion in the room next to the one the Captain entered with the second prisoner in tow, with the Mutt and Ice this time.

When they were in the room, Walker slowly and purposely removed his razor sharp Marine K-bar knife, and he started to pick the dirt out from under his fingernails with it. He refused to look at the stunned prisoner. He was giving the Arab a few seconds to contemplate what he was going to do to his body with the knife. The Marine Captain was sitting on the edge of a desk in the room, and suddenly he threw the knife at the desk, and the blade stuck in the surface of the old desk which served as a warning to the prisoner. The suddenness of his actions made the prisoner flinch, and he picked that up and knew this man was going to break under his questioning.

Walker got off the desk and started to walk around the room until he ended up standing right in front of the prisoner. Then, ever so slowly, he started to circle the prisoner and when the Arab man was forced to turn his head in order to see Walker moving behind him. He slapped the prisoner across the face, and then ordered him to look forward until ordered to do otherwise.

This Arab was present a number of time when Iraqi prisoners were being interrogated by the military when Saddam Hussein was in command of Iraq. He knew what he would soon be facing at the hands of this American soldier, and he was not looking forward to the pain he was about to suffer because he would refuse to admit he knew the woman they were looking for. The Iraqi prisoner started to sweat as he waited for the first blows to fall on his body, and the pain the beating would soon cause him.

Walker bumped into the prisoner's shoulder on purpose as he walked back to the front of the scared Iraqi. This forced the prisoner to take a short step forward or fall to the floor, and when Walker gave him the look. The prisoner took the step back until he was standing in the same spot where he placed him when they first entered the room, and he growled savagely at the prisoner. "You betta get back where you were fucking standing asshole, if you know what's fucking good for ya damn ass."

Ice instantly translated Walker's words to Arabic for the prisoner, as he continued speaking to the man as if he believed the Iraqi understood his words, and it was impossible for Ice to keep up with his angry words.

"Listen up mutherfucker, I got some stinking questions to ask your slimy ass, and the first time I feel you're fucking lying or stalling and jerking me off. I'm gonna start cutting the flesh from your miserable body, nice and slow man. So you can enjoy the fucking pain I'll be causing your ass shortly buster." Again, Captain Walker was flooding his words on purpose with a string of angry curses, because he understood how insulted the Arab race always got whenever they heard someone cursing in front of them. All his actions were committed to breaking down the resistance of the Iraqi prisoner, to get the information he needed from him as quickly as he could gather it from the prisoner.

Walker was right in the face of the prisoner again, invading his space so completely it was overwhelming to the prisoner, as he fished around in his pocket without looking at his hand, until he found the picture he was searching for. He removed it and shoved the picture in the face of the Arab, and stared him dead in the eyes for a long moment as he snarled, sending spittle flying on the Arab's face, further insulting him and breaking down his resistance on the Iraqi.

"Okay you lousy fucking A-rab prick, when I first showed you this fricking picture of the Iraqi bitch I wanna talk to in the uther room. You reacted like you recognized her ass when you saw her damn puss. So I'm gonna ask you once more if you know her ass, and if you lie, say good fucking by to the fingers on your left hand, one at a time nice and slow. I'm gonna enjoy working on your A-rab ass, because I know you know this lousy woman I want, and until you give her up. I'm gonna continue ripping your ass apart, one piece at a time." He moved away from the prisoner and scooped up his K-bar and moved in on the prisoner as he roared.

"Answer me mutherfucker, do you know this damn woman and if you do, where the hell is this bitch hiding in this village? Don't wait for the fucking translation, you know fucking damn well what I just asked your ass, fucker. I want an answer from your ass right this god damn minute, if you wanna keep breathing like you are scumbag."

The prisoner displayed an act of defiance as he stared back in Walker's red face and wild looking eyes. But Walker was able to see his lip tremble, and realized the man was trying to make a show of it before he started to talk like a school girl, and the prisoner told him everything he wanted to know about the chick. He was good at interrogating and getting information from any prisoners he was working on one way or the other. The Captain understood he had to one up this Arab, if he wanted to get his information while it mattered to him and his operation. He backed off the prisoner a few feet and moved over to the Mutt and grumbled in a low whisper.

"Hey man, we gotta hit this Arab bastard, and we gotta hit him fucking hard and fast with the number three act, if we wanna break him down fast enuf for his info to matter to our asses. We gotta find out where the hell this hen's hiding and if she has the damn cylinder with her ass, dammit. You wanna pull it off or do you want me to be the bad guy? It makes no difference to my ass who is the good guy in this act, as long as we get this guy singing like a canary."

"I got ya ass on this one Walker. Here's what we're gonna do with the dumb asshole. You go at him and I'll make my move on the lousy prick, while trying to shove your ass outta my way and then I'll attack the fuck in front of ya. Once I get on him we'll have the fuck where we want his ass. Luck with the mutherfucker, I don't think this dude's gonna be that hard to break down, Walker." The Mutt offered confidently as he gave Walker a quick slight nod.

Captain Robert Walker stomped the four feet up to the prisoner, and he placed his forehead up against the prisoner's head, and pushed him back with his head as he growled savagely at the shaking man. "Look stupid I told your dopey ass I don't have the fucking time or the want to waste with cutting you up into nice little pieces. So I'm gonna end this damn thing real fast for ya ass, fucker. I'm gonna ask you one more fucking time, and if you don't answer me truthfully, I'm gonna start slicing you up into nice even pieces, and then I'm gonna feed the parts of your body still wiggling to the fucking dogs in the middle of the streets of this dump, scumbag. And, anything that's left over of your ass, I'm gonna have wrapped up in pig skin and buried and you know what that means to your stinking beliefs. Where the fuck is this fucking chick hiding in this god damn village, buster?"

Again the Iraqi prisoner just stared back with a dumb expression on his face at the fuming Captain, but he was unprepared for what happened next to him in the room. The second soldier suddenly made a dash at his helpless body while he drew his nine millimeter pistol out, and the second soldier pulled the slide back and the prisoner thought the wild American soldier chambered a round in the weapon. The crude actions of the second soldier forced Walker out of the way as the Mutt charged at the helpless prisoner. He grabbed the Iraqi prisoner roughly by the throat and he slammed his weapon against his forehead, and leaned his head so close to the prisoner's face that the stunned Iraqi could actually smell his vile breath, as the second soldier snarled in his face.

"You wasted enuf of our fucking time on this bullshit act of yours, buster. I'm gonna blow your stinking head offa your shoulders, and then I'm going back in the uther fucking room and pull one of your uther friends in here and get the fucking information from his stinking ass, pal. So your ass doesn't mean a fucking thing to me and my cause, stupid. So say goodbye to Allah, and then kiss your ass goodbye, because I'm gonna take you out of the equation, mutherfucker."

The Mutt shoved the barrel of his pistol harder against the prisoner's head, and he glared, leaving no doubt in the Arab's mind he was about to die by the hands of this wild acting American soldier. The prisoner ripped his eyes from the Mutt's glaring face and he looked at Walker with pleading eyes, as he begged him in English. "Please Mr. American Soldier, remove this madman from my face, and I'll tell you everything I know about the woman you're searching for. Please American Soldier, I don't want to die. American Soldier you must stop this one before he does something rash and kills me, you must help me please."

Walker smiled, the Mutt pulled the number three move in interrogation off so perfectly, and it did what he wanted. He moved over until he was standing by the Mutt and he put his hand on Lieutenant Hall's arm, and forced him to remove the pistol from the Arab's face, and said. "C'mon man, he wants to talk to us, buddy. But if the little fucker lies to my ass, do him in and do him in real fricking fast without question, man."

"You got it here you take the little prick because I wanna kill the dopey bastard." The Mutt growled as he roughly pulled the man forward and shoved him at Walker.

The Captain caught the shoved prisoner and stopped him from tumbling to the floor. The Arab would have fallen hard because Walker ordered his hands secured behind his back before they entered the room. He helped the prisoner right himself and moved the Iraqi to the desk, and allowed the confused captive to sit on it and relax and get his composure. Walker reached around him and cut the flex cuffs to gain the Arab's trust. The Arab put his head down and moved his hand to his face and wiped the sweat running in his eyes. The prisoner was struggling trying to get his breathing under control, and was breathing heavily. His body was shaking and Walker noticed the Iraqi pissed himself when the Mutt was manhandling him.

The Mutt moved over to Walker's side and whispered to him. "I bet the scumbag Code Brown (shit) himself. I can't want to check. This dude was nuthin to break, man."

"Shut the fuck up, we got him right where we want him, so let me work on the lousy bastard before he realized what we done to him and he clams up on us again." Walker snapped at the Mutt, keeping his voice low so the Arab prisoner did not hear what he said to the other soldier. Then he turned to the prisoner still trying to get his breathing under control. Walker pulled his smokes out of his pocket and tapped a cigarette out and offered it to the prisoner. He was entering the good cop stage of bad cop interrogation phase. The Captain knew once he gained the prisoner's trust, the Arab was going to sing like a canary, and the prisoner would tell him everything he wanted to know about the missing chick and biological item.

With a shaking hand, the prisoner took the offered cigarette from the calm acting American soldier and placed it in his mouth. Walker snapped his Zippo lighter out and it exploded in a flame which caused the Arab to flinch, and move his face a little away from the flickering flame. Staring at the flame, the prisoner moved his face forward until the tip of the cigarette ignited, and then Walker snapped the lighter closed to scare the Arab again by his sudden and sharp moves. Everything Walker was doing was geared to shake the confidence of the prisoner, and then assure him he was his friend at the same time.

"Thank you Mr. American Soldier, I am afraid your other soldier has upset me. Mr. American Soldier, you must keep the other soldier away from me."

"Look pal as long as you fucking tell me everything I need to know about this chick friend of yours, we'll get along just fine and the uther soldier won't bother your ass again. If you screw me over about what I wanna know from you then the uther soldier will deal with ya ass and I'll wash my hands of ya that quick." Walker was trying his best to keep the surprised look off his face over the fact this prisoner spoke and understood English so well. He was fuming none of the other soldiers from his unit picked up this fact, before he found it out for himself.

"I thank you Mr. Brave American Soldier for stopping the other soldier from killing me. What is it you need to know about this woman you came to this village to seek, Mr. American Soldier? Ask me any question you want a truthful answer to, and if Allah grants me the knowledge to answer faithfully. I'll answer your questions truthfully." The Arab asked and offered as he snuffed out the cigarette on the surface of the Elder's desk without regard for the fine furniture.

That crude action from the prisoner informed Walker this man was more than one of the regular insurgents working in Iraq. This guy's actions displayed he was obviously once a soldier for the madman of Iraq. He gave the prisoner a few seconds to collect himself, and then he asked as he showed the prisoner the picture of the woman again.

"Hey look pal, I'd like to spend the rest of the stinking day jaw jacking with ya ass, but I gotta know what you know about this woman we're looking for?"

Some words the fearsome looking American soldier was using served to confuse the prisoner for a few moments. But the Arab was able to figure out what the foreign soldier wanted to know from him, and he offered calmly to the glaring military officer. "Mr. American Soldier, I fear you are wasting your time continuing to look for this Arab woman in the village."

Captain Walker knew what he was doing dealing with the Arabs, he was purposely keeping as many colorful slang words in his conversations to add to the insult, and to confuse his prisoner as he roared at the man again. "Whatdaya fucking mean by that god damn remark? C'mon man, you're stalling my stinking ass again, and if you don't want the uther fucking soldier to ask you these fricking questions I'm asking ya. You betta be a whole helluva lot more forward with your fucking answers." He allowed his anger to get the best of him as he snapped nastily at the prisoner, and then he glared at the man as he waited his reply.

"Please Mr. American Soldier you must learn to control yourself. I am no further a threat against you or your fellow soldiers in this village. What I meant by my remark is, when I was with my fighters we were charging down a block in the village, when we came across this woman you search for. Mr. American Soldier, she was fleeing the village before your powerful soldiers arrived in the village to take it over."

"Shit, God dammit are you fucking certain it was this stinking woman you saw leaving this dump?" Walker snarled at the almost grinning prisoner as he waved the picture of Ayesha in his face one more time.

"Yes Mr. American Soldier, I'm certain it was this woman I noticed leaving the village before your fearless soldiers arrived." The prisoner offered, feeling he was now helping the Americans.

"Crap! Was she alone when she took off from the stinking village?" He asked, searching for any added information from the prisoner.

"No Mr. American Soldier, this woman was in the company of General Mustafa Abdelhadi. I recognized the once feared General because he was in command of my unit of the Republican Guard when Saddam Hussein owned the world. That fact Mr. American Soldier was the reason I didn't challenge and stop them from leaving the village. The woman was with two other Iraqi women, they were helped by a security guard in the employ of the Elder, Mr. American Soldier."

"Do you know the names of the uther women with this bitch?" Walker asked.

"Yes Mr. American Soldier, I know one woman with the one you want, her name is Shafiqu al-Quraishy. I know her because she was once dating a foolish soldier from my unit. The insolent woman was too hard for the fool to control, and he refused to use the lash on her cursed back for her insolence she displayed for the fool interested in her. The fool allowed the woman to control his life, instead of the other way around where the male is the true ruler of his hom…"

"Look pal, I'm not interested in any of your backasswards customs. Keep talking about these five fucking people you spotted leaving this dump when you and your friends were setting up to hit my troops, fucker. Do you know the name of the guard helping this General whatever the hell his damn name was, and the three women who escape with the damn General before we arrive? By the way fella, were any of these people carrying something that looked like a small shiny garbage can, a cylinder type thing of highly polished metal?" He asked the prisoner with concern as he held the Iraqi in his gaze, feeling he was getting some place with the prisoner.

"No Mr. American Soldier, I did not notice any of them carrying anything of metal when they left. The only thing I noticed was the weapon in the General and security guard's hands. I do offer this, the three women were wearing Kajubas', the heavy robes are so flowing and wide I fear they could have been smuggling anything out of the village at the time I spotted them on the run. I would not have been able to say with certainty if they had anything hidden under the Arab garment, Mr. American Soldier. I did happen to see Ayesha, and she seemed to be suddenly pregnant, and I found this to be strange to observe.

"Because Mr. American Soldier, I was told over the passing years the foolish woman refused all advances from any available males in the village. Every since her Father met his fate in the country you are from, Mr. American Soldier." The prisoner offered as he drew in his breath, and stopped speaking and stared back at the military officer from the United States.

CHAPTER TWENTY TWO

"f you don't think this chick was screwing around with anyone who mighta made her fucking pregnant? Could she have been hiding the damn cylinder under her damn robe, Fella?" He questioned as he glared at the prisoner.

"That is a good question Mr. American Soldier. Alas I fear only Allah and the god cursed woman would be able to answer that question truthfully for your satisfaction." With each response the Iraqi fighter replied to Walker, his confidence and English grew to where the once enemy prisoner was feeling this American soldier was going to ask him for his help to find this woman obviously so important to him.

"Shit, right, yeah okay buddy. Look pal do you know where these people might be heading for? You gotta know if there's a fucking safe place somewhere around here for this stinking Iraqi General to take the women to?" Walker question the prisoner, feeling this guy was enjoying sticking it to his fellow Iraqis now he was talking.

"No Mr. American Soldier, where the fools entered the vastness of the desert from the village, made no sense to me I fear. Because that course they headed out on would bring them out to the deepest part of the desert sands, far away from any other Iraqi village, or needed help from anyone living in my country. You have to remember one thing Mr. American Soldier, when the five fled the village, two of your helicopters took positions at the north and south end of the village. Your flying machines of war closed off all normal routes of escape offered to any villages in the surrounding area by the wise move."

"Shit, shit, shit. Okay friend, can you take me out to where they entered the fucking desert from the village?" The Captain asked giving in he was going to be forced to head out in the desert in search of these people.

"Yes Mr. American Soldier, it'd be simple to assist you, for a fee I fear." The prisoner put on the widest grin Walker ever saw.

The Captain's eyes narrowed as he glared over the balls this prisoner was displaying as he seethed. "Huh, I see you fear much my friend. Now you want me to fucking pay your ass for your fucking help? How about if I fricking pay you with your worthless life?"

"I'm sorry for my last remark Mr. American Soldier. Over the passing years, there has been many of my foolish people who when they offered their assistance to the American soldiers occupying my country. My fellow neighbors were paid well for their assistance by the American government. Just think of how valuable I would be for your cause if I was being by your side all the while you are in my country, Mr. American Soldier. Not only do I speak my country's language, I speak the words that'll allow you to understand me when I discover something you need to know, Mr. American Soldier. I can work as your interpreter if and when you have to speak to my people in search for the ones you're here to capture.

"Kind and brave Mr. American Soldier, I know the desert like the back of my hand, and I also know where any drinking water lays in the unending desert. I can read tracks in the sand of the desert you would not recognize as tracks, if you don't know the countless ways of the vast desert, Mr. American Soldier." The Iraqi prisoner offered proudly to Captain Walker, with the feeling he was offering the foreign soldier something he could not possibly pass up if he truly wanted to capture the ones he was so interested in finding.

"Yeah, I'm sure you can help us. But I don't have the power to hire ya fricking ass, let alone pay you. I'll tell you what power I do have over your lousy ass. If you don't take me to the part of this village where you last saw this bitch, I'll shoot your ass where you stand and then I'll find her myself. So what's it gonna be friend, you wanna play ball and take me where you saw this bitch, or do you wanna die here?" Walker growled at the prisoner, not giving an inch to him.

Letting his breath out slowly while giving up his want to work for the American soldiers, the swift Iraqi prisoner offered in a submissive voice. "Mr. American Soldier, it'll please Allah if I took you to where I saw Ayesha and her friends living the village. When do you want me to take you to the place I know of, Mr. American Soldier?"

"Right after I check on my troops in this building. Mutt, you'll stay with this prick and if he tries something stupid, waste his fucking ass." Walker growled at the Mutt as he snapped his fingers, and turned to Sergeant Morrison and barked at her. "Ice, you're with me, we gotta check on the uther troops, and there are a few uther things I gotta check out before we take off with this prick and find this Iraqi chick. Come with me." Walker offered as he led the way and rushed in the room with Neck, Buckethead and the Elder and growled at the soldiers as he walked in.

"Bucket, get in the uther room and pull a soldier out to guard this prick here. I need you two turds with me. I don't want anyone speaking to this prick until we find what we're here for. Neck, stay with this dude until the uther soldier relieves you, and then linkup back with me. We know where this chick left the village and once we pick up her trail, we'll bring her down and then we're gonna get the hell outta fucking Dodge."

The Captain and Ice waited until Buckethead came back in the room with a second soldier in tow, and as soon as they were in the room. He left with the three soldiers following. He entered the first room where the bulk of civilians and prisoners were being held in the building, but he noticed a lot more of his fellow soldiers standing in the room and barked at CoCo-G, (Sergeant Milton Pettibone) who received his tag name because McNip, who was part Japanese and part Irish. He wanted a name for the black man and since the Japanese language did not have a word for the usual derogatory name for a black man, McNip dubbed Pettibone, CoCo-G. Walker growled at him. "Hey stupid, where the hell did all these uther soldiers come from?"

"Walker, this is our backup unit Colonel Leadbetter sent to help us with securing this damn village, sir." CoCo-G offered with a grin, happy to have the extra help.

"Man, that's great fucking timing the stinking Colonel's on the ball with our follow on forces. We can leave half the backup unit behind to finish securing the fucking village, and look after the damn prisoners until we can figure out what the hell to do with the damn assholes." The Captain replied with a grin as he nodded to the soldiers who just arrived in the village.

CoCo-G leaned closer to Walker and asked him barely over a whisper. "Hey man, it seems like you have a purpose in your step, Walker. What the fuck's going down and when the hell are we gonna get the fuck outta this flea infested dump, and get our asses back to the real world, Captain? I'm tired of this fucking place already, man."

"CoCo, we just got word on where the bitch left the stinking village and headed in the desert. We got one of the A-rab bastards gonna take us to where he spotted our missing chick, and then we're gonna track them down in the sand until we catch up to her ass, and we take her and the cylinder back to Leadbetter. So he can do whatever the hell he wants to do with the damn thing, and then we're gonna place distance between us and this stinking dump, CoCo. I can't wait to get back to my place in the Keys. The first thing I'm gonna do is drop my World Cat in the stinking water. Then I'm gonna fish for a week while taking time to make love to my lady on the water." Walker explained to the other soldier.

"That's outstanding news Walker. Can I watch you guys going at it like dogs in heat? Hey buddy, are you that certain this damn chick has the crap with her ass?" Sergeant Pettibone asked as he looked Walker in the eyes and waited his reply.

"Shit, I was until you asked me that question, stupid. I guess the only way we'll know for certain is when we find the missing chick and search her ass and see for our fucking selves. Before you ask me, if she doesn't have the crap on her person, we start our search over and keep going until we finally find the shit. The Colonel warned me none of us are gonna get outta this god forsaken place until we find the crap for his ass, or he burns the Middle East to a fricking cinder with nukes. So this Iraqi chick betta have the crap with her when we find her ass."

"Hey Walker, what the hell is a World Cat? When you mentioned that, I was trying to figure out what the damn thing is." CoCo asked ignoring the fact he might be in Iraqi if and when the colonel has to resort to nuking the place.

"It's my boat I got at my place on Marathon in the Keys, its one helluva boat. She's a thirty three footer with an eleven foot six inch beam with twin hulls and she's as stable as shit in the water no matter how rough it is when I head out fishing." Walker offered with a grin.

"You said you're gonna stay on the water a week fishing, how you gonna cook, what are you gonna do for drinking water and showers? A week's an awful long time to be out on the water, man. You're gonna smell five times as bad as you do now, Road Kill." CoCo questioned Walker as he used his unit's name to address him.

"Shit I guess you never saw my boat, she has a small barbeque on board for cooking, and I have an inboard head and shower with one hundred gallons of fresh water stored on board. I have enuf fuel on her to take me almost anywhere I wanna go. Hell man, I can make Mexico without needing to refuel before I get there. She's got a fourteen foot tuna tower with twin helms, powered by twin electronic Mercury two hundred and fifty horse four stroke outboards. I can hit speeds of fifty knots on water. The Cat's stable enuf to go out even with small craft warnings issued by the Coast Guard, and most uther boats are forced to stay moored up and…"

"Not for nuthin Walker, we gotta find this A-rab chick and this stinking crap the Colonel wants, if you wanna get home and play Captain of the sea." The Mutt complained as he stepped up and grumbled at Walker having fun telling the other soldier about his boat.

"Yeah, you're right. We betta get a move on it before the Colonel comes down here and starts trying to eat our asses for supper, cause we didn't locate that shit yet. Mutt, order the new guys to secure the prisoners, and you take the uther soldiers you need from their ranks to fill in for our dead and wounded. By the way Mutt, you have numbers on our dead and wounded? I gotta know how many of our people are down." Walker asked as he waited for the bad news to hit.

"Yeah I got some numbers for ya, our dead was low, real low thank God. We lost a FNG, (Fucking New Guy) High Spade, Sergeant William Glenallen. He brought the dirt farm when his humvee took a direct hit by an RPG round. The uther soldier in the humvee was Small Change, Sergeant Edward London he was wounded, he's among the walking wounded. We lost two uther soldiers from the unit, I don't have their names yet, and I read a report stating we have fifteen wounded to the degree of walking wounded to critical." The Mutt reported after linking up with Walker once he was relieved of duty guarding the prisoner doing the talking, and the prisoner even wanted to work with them and get paid to boot. The Mutt hated getting stuck guarding prisoners, he was of the mind to let someone else pull this shit duty. He believed he was made for killing enemy, not playing nursemaid to any fool who surrendered to them.

"I knew about High Spade. I saw him get hit and blown outta the damn machine when it happened. I'm sorry about his loss, I felt he was gonna fit in well with the rest of us shits in the unit, Mutt. The report was good and we did well for this kinda engagement to lose three soldiers to this bunch of Iraqi popping jays. What about the combatants, any numbers on their body count come in yet? I'd like to know how many we sent off to Paradise."

"Shit man, I read three different reports on them assholes, and the numbers on the enemy were all over the frigging place, Walker. I decided to pick the middle report to go by, until I got positive info on the enemy dead and wounded. The report I'm going by stated over two hundred and fifty combatants were KIA (Killed In Action). I know that's not including the assholes we drove outta the village and the aircraft worked their asses over for us. Their wounded is pegged at two hundred and most wounded are classified critical. We didn't leave many asses alive, Walker. I read a report stating we have seventy four identified combatants in custody." The Mutt gave Walker a smile of victory because of what they did to the defenders of the village.

"Damn, we did a helluva lot betta than I expected on this one so far. What with the heavy amount of resistance the insurgents were giving us when we hit the fricking rat's nest here. I was concerned we mighta suffered our own deaths in the teens or twenties at worst. Well enuf jaw jacking bout this shit, we gotta get after this bitch and that crap we want. We also gotta assembled our people and get them betta organized, and pick up the talker and have his ass take us to the spot where the assholes he saw were heading for the desert when we entered this dump.

"You get the rest of our people assembled and I'll get our friend and we'll head out in the desert and get this fucking thing over with." Walker looked at his watch and was amazed at the time. It was Oh, Nine, Ten Hundred Hours, and there was plenty of light left to this day. He found himself starting to believe he was going to complete their mission, and by sometime tomorrow they would be heading for home.

The Mutt took off to carry out his orders, and Walker headed for the room with their prisoner who offered to help them, for a fee. By the time Walker got back to the prisoner and moved him out of the building. The Mutt had the rest of the unit assembled and ready to head out. The Captain addressed his troops from the top step of the porch he was standing on while he held onto the prisoner's collar with his right hand. "Okay people listen up this is important. Before we shove off on the next part of our operation, I want everyone to max out on ammunition and water. Our water hogs have the duty to make certain we have enuf drinking water for a three day walk in the damn desert and you selected soldiers will make certain our people dri…"

Some of the soldiers in the ranks grumbled over the Captain's remark about a three day hike in the desert. He ignored their complaint as he went on with his orders. "We have five people we're looking for out there, and two are known to be Iraqi regular soldiers, and the uther three are identified as women, and they entered the desert on ankle express. (foot) So we're forced to use the ankle express during our pursuit of the flaming assholes. We're still gonna have our air cover overhead, and we can use this support to supply us if we run low on water, food or ammunition. I have no idea where these scumbags are heading, or what backup support they might find by the time we finally catch up to their asses.

"So I want each one of you to be prepared for any possibility out there against us. This operation's far from over, and I don't want any of you swinging dicks or bouncing tits letting down your guards by thinking this thing's finished. We're in a land that's flooded with enemy combatants who wanna kill, cook and eat our asses. So you people betta be on the alert and keep your noggin's on a swivel for this last part of our mission. That's it."

"That's e-fucking-nuf." One soldier smirked, and his comment made the rest of the troops laugh as they lifted their rucksacks and looped them on their backs. Then they checked their weapons and when everyone was satisfied with their equipment. The soldiers made a half turn to the right and then waited for Walker and the Arab to lead the way for them.

Walker shoved the prisoner in front of him as he growled. "Okay pal if you wanna remain sucking up stinking oxygen, I suggest you betta get me over where you last saw these five puds. Remember this while you're at it buddy, if you try anything stupid or I feel you're waste my fucking time, this will be the last time you'll be walking on the sand of the desert, asshole. If you screw around with me, you're gonna find yourself buried under the fucking sand you love so fucking much. Get your ass in gear before I hop you in the damn can."

"Yes Mr. American Soldier, I'll take you to the spot where I witnessed the five you want, walk out in the desert from the village. May Allah take my worthless eyes if I fail you on my mission, Mr. American Soldier." The prisoner looked at Walker, and placed a grin on his lips while looking for some sort of approval from him over his offer.

"Yeah whatever you fucking say buddy, so stow the stinking commercial and get on with it will ya." Captain Walker again gave the Arab prisoner a shove to get him moving. As the rest of the elite specialized soldiers followed the Captain and the Iraqi prisoner, they moved like a well trained military unit with a real purpose in mind. Some of the soldiers checked the sides, front and rear of the formation, and moved like they were just daring any Iraqi troublemaker to make a move on them as they moved off.

The soldiers followed the prisoner and Walker down one block in the village. Then they crossed over a street and cut between two homes until they came across another street. They crossed that one and walked between two other buildings until they came to the edge of the village where the desert started. The prisoner walked until he found the spot he was looking for, and then he announced proudly. "Mr. American Soldier, this is the spot where I came across General Abdelhadi and his four friends. My people were coming down that road, and the five were coming out from between those two buildings. Mr. American Soldier, we stopped them and spoke to them for a moment, and then we ordered the General to take his cursed women and leave the village before the shooting started with your soldiers. I believed the General was bringing the Elder's family to the safety of the desert, Mr. American Soldier."

"Yeah yeah what fucking ever you say." Walker growled at the prisoner as he crudely shoved the man out of the way, and looked at the sand for tracks that would clue him in on where the five Iraqis entered the desert. Without being ordered, both the Ghost and Hunter broke ranks and they rushed up to Walker and studied the distorted footprints in the soft sand. The concerned Captain looked over his shoulder to see who just moved up to him and smiled at the soldiers. The Ghost spoke first to the Captain.

"Walker I'm picking up at least five separate sets of footprints, and they're heading out that way. They're pretty messed up, I make it two sets of footprints are heavy, that makes me believe those two belong to male movers, and the other three are light, which makes me believe three sets of prints belong to either women or children breathers." The Ghost pointed straight ahead to show Walker where the footprints were heading in the desert, and added. "Walker, the footprints can't be any longer than fifteen hours old. The way the desert so quickly erases evidence of people moving around, makes me believe the footprints couldn't be any older than that long."

"You're certain at least three sets of footprints belong to women movers?" Walker wanted to make certain he was going to be following the right sets of footprints out to the desert.

"Like I said man, they're either women or children footprints. Three sets are much too light to belong to male movers, Walker. Yeah, looking at the footprints closer, the strides are too large to belong to kids, so they gotta be adult chicks I figure." The Ghost corrected his report.

"That's all I need to know man. Have a soldier take charge of the A-rab fuck. I don't want him tagging along with us in the desert, because I don't trust him as far as I can throw the dopey bastard. I don't need the lousy prick calling out an alarm when we catch up to these uther assholes. Well we can't put this shit off any longer, Ghost. It's time we take our little walk in the fucking desert." Walker grumbled as he straightened up and removed a cigarette from his pack and lit it after giving one to the Ghost. A soldier from the ranks moved up and roughly grabbed hold of the prisoner by the arm, and started to walk the prisoner back to the almost destroyed village and rest of the prisoners being held there.

Once the prisoner was out of the way, Walker called to his troops gathered and resting until needed. "Okay people we have our stinking package's point of entry in the frigging desert. I want everyone to spread out but keep a good formation. Keep your eyes open and your heads on a swivel for any possible ambushes or mantraps. Remember we're in an extremely hostile fucking environment, and we're not only threatened by enemy combatants or any nut who picks up a fucking weapon against us. Also, about every stinking poisonous thing God ever placed on the earth is waiting out there to get a chunk from our asses. Keep good spacing, and protect the soldier in front of ya. Let's move out."

THE DESERT FIVE MILES FROM THE IRAQI VILLAGE OF AR-RAMADI

Iraqi General Mustafa Abdelhadi, in great physical shape for his age was in the lead of the small group. He was followed by Ayesha al-Qaysi, Sadiya Sadjadpour and Shafiqu al-Quraishy were next in line, the security guard was protecting the rear of the rag tagged group as they struggled through the desert. Ayesha was having the hardest time, because she was carrying the nearly twenty pound metal cylinder, the added weight robbing her strength. The sun was high in the sky and there was not a single cloud in the sky to be seen, and the heat and burning sun was helping to take more of Ayesha's strength as she continued to trudge along in the soft sand.

General Abdelhadi was pushing the women as hard as he dared move them along, because he knew of a group of Arab fighters who constructed a sort of underground hideout about twenty miles away from his village. As the group fled, they were able to hear the weapon fire and explosions taking place behind them, and this forced the Iraqi General to push the women harder on their beginning trek. Twice since the group left the village, the General stopped and turned and witnessed a number of large columns of bellowing black smoke as it rose in the air, and he was able to see a number of aircraft circling his town. Since it grew dark, the General never turned to look back at the town again.

After a few hours of walking which was extremely dangerous, the General allowed the small group to take their first break of their forced march. He controlled the little water they had, allowing the women to take one swallow each when it was absolutely necessary. The men refrained from drinking any water. After resting for twenty minutes, General Abdelhadi ordered everyone to their feet. The group set out again on their quest to locate the underground shelter the General knew of. Since it became light again, the general started to push everyone harder. General Abdelhadi reasoned they were about twelve miles from the village. The General did not fool himself and was reacting as if he knew the Americans picked up his trail in the sand and hunting them. The General's only thought was to get the cylinder and biological weapon to the hands of these desert fighters.

Iraqi General Mustafa Abdelhadi knew this group of Iraqi Sunni fighters was active with their ongoing war with the invading Coalition Forces that destroyed his country so completely. The General understood if he was to place a weapon with this much destructive power in the insurgent's hands. They would know where, when, and how to employ the weapon where it would do the most damage to their enemies. This was the General's driving force, to get the biological weapon to the desert fighters.

About five miles back, the General had his group commit an almost ninety degree right turn, and now they were heading in an easterly direction. The Iraqi Commander was praying if the Americans were in pursuit of him, they would assume his group was heading straight north towards the more populated region of the area. General Abdelhadi took a breath and looked behind him and was disgusted to see his tracks were still so clear and easy to follow in the soft sand. He cursed the sands for not erasing their tracks quicker, he knew if the Americans sent out one of their helicopter, the pilot would easily be able to follow their footprints right to them.

Ayesha struggled to the General and plopped down on the sand and let out an exhausted sigh. General Abdelhadi noticed the cylinder in her arms and growled at her, hating he was ordered to protect the lives of these three lowly women by the elder. "Foolish bitch of the sands who does not possess the smarts to know when she is exhausted, and doesn't have common sense to allow one of the other worthless women to carry her burden for her. Why do you alone carry the cylinder? I don't understand such foolishness you're displaying before me, cursed woman."

"General Abdelhadi, I carry the cylinder because it was entrusted to my hands by the Almighty Allah and Village Elder. I sworn an oath to Allah that I alone will bring His gift to those who'll use it where it'll carry out His will. I'll carry this cylinder until my heart bursts in my chest, to honor the trust Allah bestowed on my worthless shoulders, General Abdelhadi. The cylinder is of no true burden I assure you General." As if she was carrying out an act of defiance, Ayesha struggled to her feet, and started to walk in the direction they were originally heading in.

General Mustafa Abdelhadi continued to stare at the strong minded woman until she walked fifty yards ahead of him and the group. Letting out his breath in a disgusted sigh, the fuming General started to walk and he rushed himself until he was walking alongside Ayesha, and then he grumbled at her again. "Foolish young woman, be like a male camel and continue to carry that foul cylinder, and when your heart burst within your foul chest. I'll order one of the other foolish women to carry it like you should have done while you were still breathing. Ayesha, I admire your strength, but I curse your stupidity, woman. If you continue to refuse to allow one of the other cursed women to carry the foul cylinder for you, allow me to carry your burden for a while so you can rest until you regain some of your strength. Then you can have this gift of Allah's back in your worthless arms for all I care, woman."

Ayesha stopped walking and looked into the eyes of the feared Iraqi General. Relenting Ayesha offered the steel cylinder to the Iraqi Officer. The instant she was released of her burden, she realized how heavy the cylinder was in her aching arms. Her arms pained her and she found herself shaking them to get her circulation going in them again. Even her shoulder hurt, and she rubbed the back of her neck to get some pain out of it. The general smiled because of the discomfort Ayesha was suffering. The experienced General believed it was Allah's way to punish the woman for not using the brains He gave her to think with, by carrying the cylinder so long.

When Shafiqu noticed the General and Ayesha speaking together, and then the Iraqi Officer take command of the cylinder, she increased her pace until she caught up with her friend. Shafiqu knew what she was doing and she leaned her body against Ayesha, and allowed her sister to lean her weight against her body, and she carried some of Ayesha's weight for her. After they walked about a mile, most of Ayesha's strength returned to her sore body. She then asked. "General Abdelhadi, I'm in command of my worthless body, and I'm willing to take the burden of the cylinder from you. For some reason, I feel naked without having Allah's gift to wrap my arms around, to give me comfort."

The officer stopped walking and he looked in the sand coated red eyes of Ayesha. Without giving it a thought, he willingly returned the cylinder to her. Pleased to be able to walk in the desert without carrying the weight of the canister in his arms. With his weapon he had looped over his shoulder, and each step he took in the soft sand, the AK-47 weapon constantly slipped off his shoulder, and it dropped to his elbow then interfered with his walking and carrying Allah's gift. When he returned the cylinder, Ayesha wrapped her arms around it and pulled it close to her chest in almost the same way a baby was hugged by the mother. General Mustafa Abdelhadi shook his head because as long as he lived, he felt he would never be able to understand the extremely confusing ways of the woman world, like he knew the ways of the desert. He longed to be in control of vast Armies for the government.

THE SPECIAL FORCES ENTERING THE DESERT

Captain Robert Walker and the rest of the soldier's of his search team were about a mile away from the village already. The going was tough for the troops because in this area, the sand was soft and deep and extremely hard to walk in. Especially for the soldiers who had the burden of sixty eight pounds of military equipment, the extra ammunition, food and survival gear, not to mention the extra water and weapons on their persons. Some of the soldiers complained it was like walking in seven inches of snow, the way the sand constantly gave way under their feet and closed in on them as they tried to pull their feet out of the sand. The Captain was in the lead, and he was flanked by the usual soldiers. Buckethead, Neck, Sergeant Ramirez, Blind Date, Baby Tee, the Ghost and Hunter were nearest to him.

There were a few things that got away from Walker's attention because he was so concerned with catching up to the Iraqis and hoping they had the biological weapon with them when his soldiers caught up with the group. The first and most important thing he happened to overlook was his air cover was not on top of his group. He was basically heading in the desert blind with no protection from the air if they ran into trouble. The other thing he was not paying attention to, was the fact his two pointmen were walking by his side as they struggled through the sand.

The Mutt forced Walker to pay closer attention to what he was doing when he complained at the Ghost who stepped in front of him, and the Ghost ended up cutting the Mutt's way off. "Hey stupid, don't cut across my fucking beam like that for Christ sake. This shit's hard enuf to fucking walk in as it is, without my having to dodge your stinking ass like this, Ghost. Watch where the hell you're going man."

Walker immediately registered the Mutt's bitch and he pulled up and barked at the point soldier. "Ghost, Jesus H. Christ, what the fuck are you doing in the fucking formation? You and the damn Hunter should be five hundred yards ahead of the fucking unit, and you two shitbirds should be scouting around so we don't walk into a fricking ambush, dammit. You shitbirds betta get the hell out there where you belong and take point duty, and keep us on the right trail of these stinking pukes we're afta for Pete's sake. God dammit, if I don't keep on your asses, this unit would go to hell in a handbag in minutes."

"Yeah Walker, we're taking point so don't blow a fucking head gasket and hurt yourself." The Ghost growled, not liking the way the upset Captain was speaking to them, especially in front of the rest of the soldiers and he snapped back at his commander. "Why the hell don't you people take ten and give me and the Hunter time to get out in front of the unit?"

"That's a fucking idea Ghost, we'll take a break while you two head out and scout around the area. I'll use this time to check in with Tracker One, and see what the fuck he's up to, dammit. I gotta keep my eyes on the lot of you birds, and this operation at the same time." Walker bitched at the Ghost as he held up his hand to stop the soldiers moving, and they could take a break.

The Mutt was considering informing Walker when they left the village for their trek in the desert he failed to inform Tracker One they were heading out of the dump to search for the Iraqis. Walker was busy lighting a cigarette and the Mutt knew he had to inform him about his blunder. So the exhausted Captain could order up the helicopter, and they would have their air cover and protection over their heads again. "Hey Walker, not for nuthin man, but you never took time to inform Tracker One we were heading out in the fricking desert."

"Dammit. For Christ sake Mutt, this is what I fucking mean when I told you you hafta start taking some of this god damn crap offa my stinking ass for me, Homes. I'm only one fricking person and I can't possibly think of every god damn thing that has to be looked afta every second on my own for a damn operation this large and important, man. Where the hell's our damn Charlie One hanging at for crap sake? That sonofabitch should be walking at my side at all time in case I need him, or a call is coming in for me, dammit." Walker snarled as he threw his cigarette at the sand and kicked sand over it.

"I'm right behind you Captain. You ordered me to stay close to your ass, sir." Roach, (Sergeant David Burgwald) called out as he moved closer to Walker while lugging the satellite communication system on his back.

Walker waited for Roach to move up to his side, and he growled angrily at the soldier as he waited for him to set up communications. While Roach was setting up the satellite unit, the upset Captain snarled at the rest of his soldiers. "Okay people, we're on fucking break until I finish getting Tracker One in the stinking air, and protecting our damn asses. Smoke'em if you got'em and wanna use'em people, we're down for at least fifteen minutes."

When Roach was ready for Walker he looked at the officer. He picked up the look and pitched his half burned out cigarette at the sand as if he was angry at the world, and then he took the mike and snarled in it. "Searcher One to Tracker One. Come in for Christ sake will ya. Over."

Colonel Pullman was supervising the refueling of the Apache helicopter he turned into the new Tracker One aircraft, after his Blackhawk was knocked out of action by the RPG round, and he was kind of startled by the way the Captain just snapped at him over the radio as he replied. "Yeah Searcher One, Tracker One. Where the hell are you? I was waiting for a call from you, Searcher One. Send your traffic. Over."

"Tracker One, we're at new coordinates Three, Three, Seven, by One, Six, Niner. Spot us on your tracking board and get back to me at once, Tracker One. Over."

The Commander of the Apache platform quickly checked the GPS coordinates as he listened to Walker's report then showed the

Colonel were the special op soldiers were at in the desert. The ATO Officer went back to Walker. "Gees Searcher One, that's a mile and a half in the damn desert sir. When the hell did your people pull out of the damn village, sir? No one informed me your troops were pulling out of the village and were on the move again, sir. Over."

"That was my fault Tracker One. Never mind that crap. What are you up to?" Walker replied as he fought off his anger of his blunder over Tracker One.

"Searcher One, I'm in the midst of refueling my aircraft. It should take me another ten minutes at the most to complete, and another ten minutes to get over head your position, Searcher One. Over." Colonel Pullman reported with concern as he looked at the commander of the helicopter, and nodded in the positive over the Colonel's words to Searcher One over the radio.

"I copy Tracker One. I'm ordering you to finish your refueling, and then get your ass in the air. We're not taking another step in this shit until I have a ready air cap over my troops, Tracker One. So we're shutdown until you're in position over my formation, Tracker One. Over."

"Roger last Searcher One, we completed refueling, and the machine's spooling up for takeoff, sir. We should be over your position in ten minutes. I repeat, ten minutes, Searcher One. Over."

Walker's sudden leaving the village took Colonel Pullman by surprise, and he rushed the refueling of the Apache he was using as replacement Tracker One aircraft. He dreaded flying the attack helicopter in the desert, because it was noted if the Apache was flown too close to the surface of the sand. The powerful motors would suck up huge volumes of sand in the engine ports, and sooner or later the sand would foul up the machine's engines, and force the helicopter to the ground until the engines were overhauled and repaired for flight again.

"I copy last and will wait for you at this point, Tracker One. I'll hold up my troops until you're overhead and protecting our asses, sir. Over." Walker replied.

"Am airborne and armed for any situation you come across Searcher One, ETA your position seven minutes. Over." The Colonel reported to Walker so he knew his situation.

"Roger that Tracker One be advised we're hunkering down until your arrival our position, sir. I need you following the tracks of our target on the stinking sand. You betta get over our asses ten minutes ago, sir. Over." Captain Walker replied, feeling a little better now he was going to have air cap over his troops again. Absentmindedly, he lit another smoke as he broke off communication with the ATO Officer.

As he rested, a second thought hit Walker like a sludge hammer, and it sent a chill down his spine as he roared at any soldier near him. "Dammit, where the hell is that civilian Doctor at for Christ sake? We betta not have left the turd behind, or someone's fucking head is gonna roll."

CHAPTER TWENTY THREE

D octor Joel Russbinder standing with the three pretty Russian female soldiers stepped forward and announced from where he was as he smiled at Walker, as if he done something right. "Captain Walker, I'm right here sir. I was ordered to deploy with your soldiers by Sergeant Ramirez, sir. She assigned these three soldiers to guard and assist me while we're in the desert, Captain. The three soldiers have been protecting me very well, Captain Walker."

"Thank God at least someone took some shit offa my stinking back." He grumbled, relieved the doctor was with his troops. The doctor had the responsibility of taking command of the biological weapon once the soldiers located the package. Doctor Russbinder was the only person with the unit who knew how to handle and secure the weapon for transit. Also to deal with the weapon if it somehow gets damaged if the soldiers were forced to engage the Iraqis who had the weapon with them. The civilian doctor was needed as well to help any soldiers who might become infected with the germ inside the cylinder if it somehow escaped its container.

Walker looked at Ramirez and gave her a thumb up, for her help with the mission. Walker was proud of Ramirez for making certain the doctor was with their unit when they left the village. He liked Ramirez had the smarts to stick the civilian with the Russian soldiers for his protection. He felt the women fighters would help the doctor feel more secured and at ease with the operation, until it concluded for them. Then Walker remarked to his lover. "Hey Raz, make certain the Doc's protected during this shit. The rest of you pukes Russbinder's the most important puke on this mess, if he's the only one who survives this damn thing that's what's to be. We need him a fucking live so he can properly look after this shit once we find the crap."

"You worry about what you have to look after, Bobby. The Doctor's my responsibility." Sergeant Ramirez replied as she returned Walker's smile, knowing why he aimed it at her.

"I knew you'd do your job so you didn't hafta tell me about it, Troop." Walker replied as he took out another cigarette because he had nothing to add in his bitch. He was using the smokes to sort of kill some time off until Tracker One assumed her air cover and protection over his troops trudging through the sand. He was still cursing himself over his blunders under his breath, as he took a drag from his smoke like he was trying to kill it off with one puff.

The Mutt was bugging his girlfriend Blind Date. He was trying to talk her into flashing him, Blind Date refused to remove her body armor so she could do what he wanted.

Walker caught this action and he warned the Mutt in no uncertain terms. "Hey stupid, if Blind Date removes her fucking body armor, I'm gonna put a cap in any exposed skin I see on her purdy ass. What the fuck's wrong with your stinking noggin, asshole? Trying to get her to step out of her damn armor while we're out here is plain crazy. It was a damn good thing she refused to do it, or I woulda took my anger out on your can and not hers, screwball. If you can't wait for any fun and games until we completed this miserable operation, find a dog in heat to screw will ya, and put your lousy life on the line and not hers. We have enuf frigging problems facing us without you creating new ones for us, Mutt."

"Gees Walker, you're getting to be no fun since you made rate, man. I guess that's what happens when you make rank and it goes right to your stinking head." The Mutt snapped at his friend as he tried to get Walker off his ass.

"Look Buddy, I like fun and games as much as the next fella, but there's a time and place for it. Out in the middle of Injun badlands isn't the fucking time or place to remove one's armor for any fucking reason, stupid." Walker fired back at Mutt as he struggled not to smile at the man.

The Mutt was about to add to his gripe when Tracker One turned up over the formation, and the Colonel was right on the horn to Walker as he reported in. "Searcher One, Tracker One. I'm set in position waiting further orders. We're armed for any situation, sir. Over."

"Damn, you did real well with getting your ass out here Tracker One, I thank you for that. Okay, this is what I want you to do. Tracker One, we're tracking five separate sets of footprints in the sand. But the trail's getting hard for us to following by foot, because the sand's starting to erase the stinking trail on us, Tracker One. I want you to fly ahead our formation on a set course due north trying to keep the tracks on the sand in your field of vision as you head out. Get out in front of our unit and find these five missing packages, and once you discover them you're to hinder any further progress of our packages, until we can catch up with the flaming assholes and take them in custody, Tracker One. Over." Walker ordered Tracker One as he stared at the hovering helicopter some fifty feet above his head.

"Roger last Searcher One. I'll get out in front of your formation and follow the tracks I picked up in the sand, all the way out to your packages, sir. Once I find the missing packages, I'll buzz and stop them from continuing to move away from your trailing troops, Searcher One. I'll report to you once I find them, sir. Over Searcher One." Colonel Pullman reported as he continued speaking to the Captain, with his hand he signaled the commander of the helicopter to head off in front of the soldiers hunkered on the ground below them, on a break from their forced march.

"You have orders so follow them, Tracker One. The moment you come across our packages, make contact and give me their Papa, Papa (location) so I know where they are in sand land, and I can make my way to them Tracker One. Over." Walker added to his orders for Tracker One.

"Tracker One to Searcher One, will comply with orders, breaking off contact, and am heading out before your unit as ordered, Searcher

One. I'll find our packages Searcher One. Over." The ATO Officer replied confidently as he tapped the pilot and once he had his attention, he pointed further towards the north heading deeper in the desert.

Captain Robert Walker kept his eyes glued to the attack helicopter as the Apache went to full power, and it took off heading north at a good clip of speed. Then he called to the soldiers resting. "Okay people saddle up we have a fucking job to complete for God and country. Unass yourselves and let's get a move on it. The sooner we complete our mission and find these people and the fucking package, the quicker we'll get the hell outta this damn place. Tracker One is on the trail of our packages and we have to catch up to them pronto."

A flood of curses and complaints came from the exhausted Special Forces soldiers, as they got off the sand and struggled to their feet straightening out their backpacks. The soldiers started to walk further out in the desert as they followed Walker as he took the lead. Walker knew his two pointmen had to be well in front of his unit by this time. So he felt secure about his mission with the Apache and his pointmen before his unit searching for the Iraqis. Walker no longer felt his troops might stumble into an ambush or trap, or come across someone they were not prepared to engage. Everything about his mission was starting to take good form again.

Sergeant Dorothy Ramirez worked her way by Captain Robert Walker's side, after she made certain the female Russians were doing their job with looking after the civilian doctor who was having some serious problems being in the desert, and keeping up the pace with the younger soldiers. All the doctor was doing was bitterly complaining about anything and everything, even his equipment and Ramirez whispered to her soldier. "I can't blame our people for complaining, Robert. It's pure hell trying to walk in this soft sand carrying so much crap on our backs, Bobby. But no matter how much our people complain about it, you know every one of them struggling behind us will follow you to the gates of hell if you order them to do so, lover."

"I know that and that's why I love what we do. It's a helluva thing to know you have people behind ya willing to follow me on any mission I'm sent out on. Nowhere on the earth will you find what these soldiers share with each uther. Dammit to hell and back again, I can't wait until this op's completed, and we can get home so we can start living again in the real world. You know, when we get home we're gonna haft do some serious talking about our futures. I know you want another kid and so do I. But our lives in the service are taking time from our one kid as it is, and if we continue with our lives in the service, we'll be taking our time away from two kids if you have another baby. Crap, I don't know what the hell I wanna do. On one hand I want a normal stinking life with you and our kid, on the other I don't know if I'll be able to survive without doing our act for the government and these troops…"

"Look Robert, now is not the time to get involved in this conversation, my dear. I know what you mean and once we're home and have clear minds to think with and some real time on our hands. We can talk over our options and see where we might want to go from there. Right now, we have to place our attention on our mission and nothing else, Bobby. It's almost over as it is, remember what you want to speak to me about once we're in the world, and anything you want to do with our lives is fine with me, Robert. I'm opened to anything we can do to make our lives better for ourselves and family." Sergeant Ramirez offered to her lover and soldier.

Tracker One moved out about three miles in front of Captain Robert Walker's troops. The pilot picked them up first and then pointed out two men walking in the desert to Colonel Pullman. The Colonel ordered the commander to circle the unknown targets until they got a positive ID on the two walkers. This was another blunder on Walker's part not to inform the ATO Colonel he sent his pointmen out before his unit as his advanced trackers.

Tracker One did a flyover of the two soldiers, and when the Colonel received the signal from the walkers, he realized they had to be part of Walker's troops. The helicopter swayed from side to side, and the two targets on the sand gave the pilot the thumb up signal. The pilot reported to the Colonel he was also picking up a positive strong strobe signal coming from the two obvious American soldiers. So the helicopter moved forward, and the Colonel reported his find back to Walker.

"Tracker One to Searcher One. Reporting we have just come across your two point soldiers about three miles ahead your present position, sir. After identifying the walkers as friendlies, we're continuing on with our search for your five packages, sir. Over Searcher One."

Walker was embarrassed by the rebut from the Colonel in the Apache. He looked around and noticed no other soldiers heard the slug, or if they heard the report, they did not care about it as he replied. "Err… Tracker One Searcher One. I'm afraid I'm slipping up command over my troops and this fucking op, sir. Sorry for not informing you my point personnel out before my formation. It looks like I own you another beer after this damn mission is done. Over."

"Tracker One to Searcher One. I didn't mean for my report to be a slap in the face, sir. I was merely reporting my findings as is my duty, Searcher One. I'm continuing my search for your packages. Over." Colonel Pullman offered with a smirk, he knew what his report was going to cause the sharp and confident Marine Captain when he first sent it out to the officer.

"God dammit." Walker bitched at no one in particular from his group as he broke off his communication with Tracker One. His anger caused Sergeant Ramirez to close in on him, and she asked her soldier with concern. "What's up with you, you look pissed off Bobby? You better calm down or this mission's going to get the best of you, Robert."

The Mutt was walking to the Captain's right and he heard Ramirez's question and popped off. "What's new with Walker being pissed off? Don't you know Raz when Walker was a bitty baby his mother was forced to feed him with a sling shot, because she was scared to death to get too close to her kid, for fear of him biting her fingers off when she was feeding the jerk. Ever since I met the crazy ass dude, I never saw him when he wasn't pissed off at someone or thing."

Walker looked angrily at the Mutt as he growled. "Fuck you and the horse you rode in on, buster. If I want any more shit outta your damn ass, I'll squeeze your stinking head." Then Walker turned to Ramirez and mumbled at her. "Hell baby, I can't believe how much I keep fucking up on this miserable operation. Dammit to hell and back again, I even failed to inform Tracker One I had our two pointmen out and about, and the stinking Colonel reported he came across the Ghost and Hunter in the damn desert. His report embarrassed the shit outta my stinking ass. That's the third time I screwed up on this damn mission. I promise you, it's the last fuck up I'm gonna commit on this stinking operation."

"Go a little easier on yourself Bobby. You can't believe you'd be able to remember or control everything happening on this mission. You're only one person, so cut yourself some slack with this operation before it drives you crazy. If you want to believe you screwed up three times on the mission, looked at the rest of our people, Bobby. You'll see none of them are paying the least bit of attention to these slight screw ups, and they're still following you as they should. That's the only thing any Commanding Officer could want and demand from his troops, for them to follow him without complaint or hesitation, Robert." Ramirez offered while trying to take some stress of command off his shoulders, with her words of approval of his actions.

"Yeah, I see what you're driving at and thanks for your vote of confidence of my command abilities. I need to hear those words every now and then. You took some sting outta the puke's report. But if you think for one moment any of these pukes aren't listening to all our communications. Wait until we get back to the real world, that's when you'll see these walking sandbags are gonna dump on my stinking can for my screw ups."

"What will it matter by then Walker? At least every one of them pukes as you call them will know you got them through another unbelievable operation with an almost zero rating for success, safely. That knowledge comes with an awful lot of respect for your command abilities. Besides Bobby, would you have it any other way with these soldiers who love one another to no end? You know damn well you'll enjoy every minute of them getting on your ass for screwing up, as long as they're home and safe, Robert. You'd do the same thing to any of them if they screwed up on a mission. All you have to do is buy the beers for the night, and they'll get off your ass real quick, it's that easy Robert." Sergeant Ramirez replied to Walker's concerns with a beautiful smile, as she took his hand in hers, and gave it a slight but reassuring squeeze. Their quiet time was interrupted by another call in from Tracker One.

"Tracker One to Searcher One. This is an important communication. Over." Colonel Pullman was checking in with Walker again.

"Searcher One, Tracker One, send your traffic, whatdaya have for me? Over." Walker grumbled in his radio as he let out his breath, and waited for the report from Tracker One.

"Searcher One Tracker One, I'm about nine miles forward your position. I'm suddenly being flooded with many separate footprints. It looks like a small Army, or at least a large herd of camels are out in front your position. Every track and print I'm picking up seems to be fresh, and they couldn't have been made long ago, sir. I figure whatever the hell I'm tracking, has to be four hours or less old. I'm heading for a large sand dune about two thousand yards ahead my machine. Searcher One, I'm picking up a column of smoke from the crest of that sand dune. I'm betting the ranch the smoke has to be from a campfire, Searcher One. On the other hand, the smoke could be from something attacked by possible band of Nomads, and the items were left to burn out on their own, Searcher One. I won't know for certain until I discover what the hell's burning, sir. Over."

"Searcher One, Roger last traffic Tracker One. Do you have a MOE (Mark One Eye) on any possible insurgents hanging around this damn sand dune you're so concerned with, Tracker One? I need to know what the hell you have on your hands, sir. That way I can prepare my troops for a possible ambush, or maybe an outright attack by a bunch of enemy combatants, or whatever the hell's going on out there, Tracker One. I need updated Intel, and I need it in a fast fucking hurry it up. Can you spot anything from your position that might be a serious threat against my troops, Tracker One? Over." Walker growled in the radio.

"Searcher One, I copy your last and that's a negative on request. I can't see anything that might be a threat against your troops at this point, Searcher One. I'm about to break over the crest of the dune, and will report the moment I figure out what's waiting for your troops over this dune. I'll report once I see what it's about. Over." Pullman reported to Searcher One Leader.

"This is Searcher One, Roger that Tracker One. I'm pulling up until you report on your discovery, Tracker One. I gotta know what the fuck's before us, before I take another step forward and commit my troops with this damn operation. Over." He replied with a snap as he held up his hand and the soldiers stopped their forward progress. Many exhausted soldiers dropped on the sand and shed their heavy ruckpacks, and took a breather for themselves.

The troopers responsible for making certain the soldiers drank enough water while they were in the desert. Quickly fanned out among the Special Forces soldiers as soon as a halt was called against their progress, and they supplied the bushed soldier's with warm bottles of drinking water. Even though the specialized soldiers had plenty of water with them, each of them had the so called Gardner's shoving more bottles of water at the highly trained soldiers, to make certain the troops were drinking enough water to keep them alive and active on the mission.

Walker was waiting for the next report from Tracker One, and the wait was starting to upset him. The officer did not like being forced to wait to find out if they were heading for trouble.

The Mutt moved up to Walker's side and offered him a bottle of water.

Walker grabbed the bottle without looking at it, and slugged the water down in four quick gulps. This caused the Mutt to ask him with a smirk. "Hey man, did you even taste the stinking shit you just slugged down like a fucking horse rode hard, Homes? You know you're supposed to sip the stinking water and not slug it down like that, man. Drinking the fucking water that fast could make you croak, or could cause you to choke on the shit."

"Who the hell gives a fuck about that crap? I got more important fucking things stuck on my stinking mind than a damn bottle of water, and how I drink the shit. I don't have any further communications from Tracker One, and the stinking Colonel reported he was picking up a shitload of new tracks covering the damn sand out before us. The puke also reported he picked up some smoke over a sand dune he was heading for. Right now the stinking Colonel's checking out the situation, and I'm stuck waiting for his fricking report so I know what the hell he found, and how I'm gonna react against it, dammit. That's why I have everyone hunkering down until the Colonel reports in, Mutt." The Captain complained as he looked due north of his position. Subconsciously he was trying to see Tracker One's helicopter in the air, and it was impossible because of how far ahead Tracker One was before him and his troops.

"Hey man I know a shitload of Iraqi's, women and children left the damn village as we were preparing to attack the dump. Maybe Tracker One came across some of the damn civilians who fled the stinking village, Walker. That's the only thing I can think of being out there. This deep in the desert, not many people live here." The Mutt offered as he tried to calm Walker down.

Baby Tee was by both soldier and she took a shot at the Mutt by commenting. "Hey Walker, you have to understand the Mutt's not afraid of any fight, after all the fights he was in his entire life, he only lost one of them, and that was against illiteracy sir."

"Boy, you're right on my ass again I see, Baby Tits." The Mutt snapped back hotly at her.

"Yeah, that's what I was thinking these new tracks were about. That's the only thing they could be, Homes. The Colonel said they might be coming from a heard of camels, the asshole he is. Camels, he should have his damn head examined." Walker added as he ignored the shot Baby Tee just took at the Mutt, and laughed over how ridicules the Colonel's explanation for the tracks he discovered was.

"Hey man what the hell can I tell ya, the stinking Colonel's Airforce, and I wouldn't think anything betta could come outta the flaming asshole's mouth, Walker. I hope when the stinking dude gets to Oz, the damn Wizard has an extra brain to give out. If this dude don't find these assholes, I'm gonna go out there and find them for myself, dammit." The Mutt's comment made both soldiers with him laugh over the Colonel's remark about camels making the fresh prints he was tracking in the sand.

The Mutt's comment also made Baby Tee get on his ass again. "Did I hear right, the stinking Mutt wants to go out in the desert and find these people himself. Walker don't allow him to do that because the Mutt couldn't find a prayer in the Bible, sir."

"You think and let me tell you something baby sister. When this damn operation is completed, I'm gonna get drunker that I ever been." The Mutt fired back at Baby Tee.

This comment from the Mutt cause Baby Tee to get on him as she retorted. "Walker, the Mutt's such a drunk I once saw him trying to squeeze the juice out of scotch tape."

"Funny, knock it off you two, we gotta stay on alert while we're waiting for Tracker One to report back to us, dammit." Walker growled at the two bickering soldiers.

Tracker One broke the crest of the large sand dune, and the pilot and Colonel instantly found themselves staring at over a hundred people who had obviously gathered, and they setup up a makeshift place for them to hunker down and rest. There were a number of small tents setup, and surrounded a cooking spot in the middle of the Iraqi camp. Colonel Pullman started to count anyone he was able to pick up roaming around the camp. Most of the people he observed were women or children, with a small number of male men the age of defending themselves at the site.

Many Iraqi's Tracker One was hovering over were looking at the sleek helicopter, and the Colonel was able to tell they were most likely cursing him. A good number of smaller children who did not know any better, were waving and smiling at them. Suddenly, a number of rounds were fired at the hovering machine from small arms weapons the defenders had, and the pilot placed the Apache in a steep climb to get out of range of shooters firing weapons at them as quickly as possible.

Once the helicopter was safely out of range of Arab shooters and weapons, the commander and Colonel spoke before the ATO Officer made his report to Searcher One. The pilot was the first to speak of the two officers inside the helicopter. "Well Colonel Pullman, what do you make of that load of bullshit below us, sir?"

"Commander, I make it these Iraqi's have to be the horde of women and children we picked up leaving the village when we first showed up outside the town, sir. I knew sooner or later we were going to get some pot shots fired at us as we hovered over their encampment. Judging by the few male adults I pick up at the camp, I don't think they'll give us too much trouble when Walker's troops come in to check these Arabs out, sir. I'm disappointed they're armed and were stupid enough to pick a fight with us by firing weapons at the helicopter. I'd think they'd try and be peaceful so they don't tangle with our ground forces coming at them, sir. As poorly as they're armed, they wouldn't stand a snowball's chance in hell against our guys, sir.

"For all I know, the three women and two males Walker's troops are out here looking for, could be hunkered down at that site below us, Commander. There are over fifty women and I was counted up to seventy children running around. Of course I have no idea how many children I might have counted two and three times, because of the way they were running around at the site. I was able to get a half ass count on the adult males. I pegged their number at over seventeen males of the age and want to fight against us, sir.

"At least I was able to get a number on the totally of people down there before they started to shoot at us, Commander. I'm really upset there are some weapons at the camp, and that makes them fair game if the fools try and shoot it out with Captain Walker's attack crews. Dammit to hell, I can see it in my mind's eye this thing getting out of control, and then the slaughter will start for those poor souls down there. These damn people never know when someone's out here trying to help the damn fools for Christ sake." Colonel Pullman reported to the pilot as he glanced out of the side window of the helicopter again.

"Yes Colonel Pullman, I was kinda disappointed myself with seeing the few weapons the males at the site had with them, sir. You'd think after what happened to their village a few hours ago. You'd figure the assholes wouldn't dare aim a weapon at any American made vehicles or aircraft, or our foot soldiers they happen across. Do you want to take another close observation of the Iraqi site before checking in with the Captain, Colonel Pullman? I can do another check of the people and what they're doing down there if you'd like, sir?"

"No Commander, I'm not fond of getting shot at by them bloody nuts down there, sir. Being hanging around with these damn foot soldiers of late, that's all it seems like is happening to me sir, getting shot at by some very angry Iraqi's and enemy combatants, Commander. I think one flight over the group was more than enough to last a lifetime, and get a good report off to the Captain at the same time, sir." Colonel Pullman offered as he continued to look out of the side of the cockpit, and noticed more Iraqi's moving around inside the makeshift camp like they had a purpose in mind to some of their actions.

"God dammit Commander, I hope to the good Lord them damn fools below us aren't trying to setup to defend their encampment against our soldiers they have to know are coming at them, like these fools tried to defend their village when we first showed up to search the place for that missing crap and the female who might be in control of the weapon, sir. If the Iraqi's are foolish enough to try and attack our ground forces, Walker's troops are going to move in and slaughter them to the last, if they're that stupid to try and put up any resistance against him or his troops, Commander. I can't believe these foolish ass people don't know when they had enough of fighting, and they settle down and try to get along with each other and the rest of the world while they're at it, sir." Colonel Pullman added to his gripe, as he looked at the commander and flew his helicopter further out of range of the continuing small weapon's fire.

"Anyway you want to look at it Colonel. If the fools cause Captain Walker's troop's any problems, they're going to end up dead in a fast hurry it up, sir. After all my years in the service Colonel Pullman, I never came across a better trained unit of troops these soldiers make up we're attached to, sir. Do you think Walker's crews are going to come in and check this site out before continuing with their search for this crap? After all Colonel from what I saw of these Iraqi's, they're comprised of a horde of sacred women and children, sir." The commander of the helicopter offered the Air Tasking Officer in a concerned voice. The commander was hoping Walker's troops did not have to enter the Arab encampment for fear of what his troops might be forced to carry out against the civilians trapped between the deeper desert and no water, and the American soldiers rapidly closing in on them.

"Of course Captain Walker's crews are going to be forced to check out the people of that damn camp, Commander. After all Sir, the soldiers are looking for two male and three female people from the village they destroyed, sir. What they're looking for is something that can destroy the world, Commander. So picking up these many Iraqis in the desert who obviously came from the destroyed village, makes it imperative Walker's troops check out these civilians down there, sir."

"Dammit Colonel Pullman Sir, I can only hope these damn Iraqi's don't give Walker's troops any problems or resistance, when the troops move in to search the camp, sir. If the fools put up resistance to these troops then I'm going to feel real sorry for the civilians once the Captain's people get through with their asses."

"Let me tell you something you're overlooking in this conversation, Commander. If Captain Walker and his troops don't find the item they're searching for. You better start feeling real concerned for the world, because if the damn fool who has control over the package ever releases the shit in the air against us. Most of the damn world we know will cease to exist, and I know the Middle East is blanketed in with nuclear weapons scheduled to be launched from the United States, Russian, France, Chinese and British ships of war and submarines. If this biological item is accidentally or on purpose released to the air from its container, sir. That's why I told you, you better worry about the world and the hell with these few civilians below us, sir.

"Don't go and get me wrong about what I'm saying in this conversation, Commander. If it comes down to where Captain Walker's troops are forced to go lethal on this group of Arabs if they decide to try and stop Captain Walker's crews from checking them out. I too would feel sorry for the soon to be dead civilians, if this item isn't at this civilian site, sir. I also have to take in consideration the severe ramifications of what would happen to the Middle East and any other section of the world for that matter, if any of this damn biological weapon gets released somehow or the other against us, Commander." Colonel Pullman explained his fears he was so concerned with to the stunned pilot of the Apache fast attack helicopter.

"Well in light of everything you just informed me of Colonel Pullman. I think it's about time you check in with Captain Walker, and inform him of what we have discovered here, sir." The pilot offered as he did a minor correction in his flight path.

"You made a good point and I better get on it right off, Commander." Colonel Pullman replied with a grin as he reached for the mike and offered. "Searcher One, Tracker One reporting. Come in Searcher One, this is important. Over."

Captain Robert Walker was enjoying a second bottle of water when the call from Tracker One came in, and he grumbled at the Mutt resting by his side. "It's about frigging time this little puke decided to check in with me, dammit." The Captain grabbed the mike from Roach and he barked in it. "Searcher One, I'm waiting for the report on your findings out there, Tracker One. Send your traffic sir. Over Tracker One."

"Tracker One to Searcher One. Sir, we discovered a large camp of obvious Iraqi civilians, comprised mostly women and children, who surely escaped the village before we moved in and searched it, sir. Their numbers are put at over one hundred and thirty civilian adult and child personnel as best able to count the movers in the encampment, sir. Be advised there are male adult members of fighting age, and they're poorly armed at best, but aggressive, Searcher One. We're nine and one half miles out from the village at true north, and more than five miles ahead of your present location, Searcher One. I'm taking position over the encampment well out of range of their small weapon's fire, and I'm able to observe the civilian site from my present position clearly, sir.

"I'll intercede if any civilians try and leave the encampment before your arrival at said site, sir. I'll retain plan of action as laid out unless you advise otherwise, Searcher One. If anyone tries to leave the site before your arrival, I'll stop them if I have to lay down a row of rounds before the movers. If that doesn't stop them, I'll pick off the leader of the group and see if that move turns them back towards the encampment, sir. Over."

"Searcher One to Tracker One. I copy your last and you're correct with your suggestion on how to stop any movers from the encampment. You're ordered to hover over the civilian camp, and stop any civilian whether male, female or child from leaving that damn site until our arrival at said position, Tracker One. It's imperative no one from this civilian group of assholes is allowed to get out of the area, until we have cleared them first for leaving the site, Tracker One. You're cleared to stop anyone from leaving by any means you have to employ against any possible leavers, sir. Be advised Tracker One, if you're forced to use weapons on any of the damn civilians, keep in mind what the fuck we're searching for, Tracker One. Over." Walker warned the colonel in no uncertain terms over the secured radio net.

"Roger your last and will comply, Searcher One. No one from the camp will leave the area until your troop's arrival. Be advised, be advised, be advised Searcher One, a number of male civilians are involved in piling up heavy items, and it looks like some of the members are setting up a defensive position inside the encampment aimed at your arrival on site, Searcher One. Another advisory Searcher One, it seems some other male members are moving the women and children out of the way, and the other males are setting up a defensive station on site, sir. This is Tracker One. Over." Colonel Pullman reported to Captain Walker as he continued to observe everything taking place inside the camp, as Tracker One remained hovering over the site.

"I copy your last Tracker One, I'll prepare my troops to approach the camp set for some minor resistance and an even more minor fight, sir. Remember Tracker One, it is imperative you stop any civilians from leaving that damn site until my arrival, and we take command of the situation there, sir. If any civilians get out of that fucking area it's gonna be your ass that'll be on the line for your failure to comply with my orders, sir. Remain on site and carry out your orders as received, I'll set a fire under my troops and estimate our arrival at the camp in forty five minutes at the latest, Tracker One. Out." Walker growled in the radio and snapped it off. Drawing in a gulp of air, the Captain bellowed for the rest of his troopers to hear.

"Okay Troops listen up we hafta hot foot it over to a stinking Iraqi camp Tracker One located out before us. Tracker One states the encampment is comprised of mostly women and children. Tracker One is also reporting a small number of males of fighting age and poorly armed, are preparing for our arrival with resistance and defense. Tracker One further states the males are constructing a stronghold in the center of the fucking puke camp, and the fools are moving their women and children outta harm's way. The encampment's five miles ahead our position and we have forty five minutes to get our asses on site, and then take over the damn encampment and search for this missing woman and the shit she's believed to be carrying on her person. Tracker One will stop anyone from leaving the damn site until our arrival…"

Because of the stifling heat and dryness of his throat, Walker was forced to take a breath before he went on with his orders to his troops. Already in the back of his mind, he was kind of taking it for granted the two males and three females and the biological weapon, was being stored somewhere at this Iraqi camp. He was that certain this was the reason why the few males were preparing to defend the camp against his troop's arrival.

"Saddle up, unass your fucking selves and get ready to hot foot it over to this stinking site. I want every swinging dick and bouncing tit from my unit to remember this order as if it was given to you people by God Almighty, because if I catch anyone of you entering this damn encampment shooting at troublemakers from the fucking hip. I'll send you on your fricking way to meet your maker myself. People, all kidding aside, we're entering a civilian camp obviously made up of mostly women and children.

"The few fricking Iraqi cocksucker's who wanna make a stinking fight of it, are our only combat targets when we enter the damn camp, if we come under attack by any of them stinking people out there, period. If it's at all possible, I don't want to see one single woman or child fall from our weapon's free fire. We're not the savages here the defenders are people, civilians. Before we enter the area, I'm going to take Ice with me, and I'm gonna have her try and talk sense into these assholes to save them from our slaughter.

"I'm only gonna talk to them assholes once, and if they don't wanna listen to reason. We're going in there and we're gonna search every person we find there whether they like it or not, troops. The ones who don't like it will be left on the stinking ground for the uthers to bury when we leave the puke campsite. I don't want anyone getting creative, if you wanna impress me then just do your fucking job, and do it perfectly. Let anyone in there give us any stinking trouble, and we'll see who shits themselves first, people.

"You troops hafta remember this warning, we're gonna be forced to deal with a bunch of civilian pukes scared shitless this time, and I want any killing held down to an absolute minimal while we're shaking these civilians down. If we discover the items we're looking for first, we'll break off any further searching of the civilians at this damn site. I don't give a shit about the supposed Iraqi General reported to be helping this bitch out against us. All I'm concerned with is this god damn biological package, and if the stinking chick gives it up right away, she's okay to carry on with her worthless life in fucking peace. I don't give a flying fuck about her stinking little ass as long as we come outta there mess with the package we're sent here to locate, troops.

"Well people that's about all I have for you Squids. Once we're on site all previous orders are subject to change depending on the situation we're confronted with when we reach this supposed civilian campsite. Any fucking resistance will be replied with extreme prejudice against any fool aiming a weapon at us. Okay troops, it's time to start putting one foot before the fucking uther and head out for this damn campsite Tracker One discovered. We have forty minutes to make five miles up in this damn desert to the fucking site in question. Let's shove off before we lose any stinking civilians Tracker One's trying to keep a damn eye on for our asses." Walker growled as he flung his heavy ruckpack over his shoulders, and picked up his weapon and headed off for the north without saying another word to his people following him.

CHAPTER TWENTYF FOUR

Tracker One was suffering a serious problem over trying to keep an eye on the horde of Iraqi civilians running wildly around the encampment. With about fifteen males constructing a pretty good defensible bunker in their attempt to fight off Walker's troops when they arrived at the site and more male members moving a bunch of wild acting screaming women, and the children, laughing and making light of the dangerous situation they were in. Colonel Pullman did not know where to look first below him.

The excited Iraqi children were starting to give the adults real fits trying to control them, and make them follow their orders. Each time a male collected a number of kids and placed them in one spot in the campsite, and when that male went to gather more children, the other kids would cut out and run from where they were placed by the male. Soon, many women who had their children separated from them, started to give the males as much trouble as the kids were giving them. It was getting so hectic in the encampment that some males started whipping the scared and upset women and wild acting children with canes, while trying to get control of the mayhem erupting inside the campsite.

Every five or six minutes Tracker One was forced to move its position while hovering over the campsite, because of the way many of the excited civilians were running all over the site. A few times Colonel Pullman thought he picked up a number of civilians setting up to make a fast break from the campsite, and when he noticed this the Colonel immediately ordered the pilot to change position over the campsite. The instant the helicopter moved to the new position where the civilians were bunching up, they instantly dispersed and moved deeper towards the center of the campsite again, and got lost in the milling crowd of civilians.

The pilot of the Apache was starting to have fits trying to stay on top of the wild acting civilians below his rotary aircraft. Between trying to dodge sporadic rounds fired at his machine, and keeping the civilians crowded in the bounders of the encampment, and with a good wind starting to kick up forcing the pilot to have to almost constantly correct his machine's flight, while maintaining his flight pattern over the civilian site.

Colonel Pullman was moving his head from one side of the cockpit to the other, trying to keep an eye on the horde of moving civilians below him. But when the pilot was forced to do a hard correction to his flight, the Colonel lost everything and had to wait until the helicopter settled down again, before he could concentrate on what was taking place below the machine. All the while the Colonel was watching the moving civilians the officer was trying to keep an eye open for any signs of an RPG aimed at the machine. At the height the helicopter was flying, he was within effective range of a hundred yards for the RPG weapon. In the back of his mind, Colonel Pullman remembered what an RPG round did to his Blackhawk helicopter, when it was struck by the round fired at it while he was working over the Iraqi village they searched hours ago.

The on loan Colonel Mark Pullman from the Airforce understood he dodged a bullet because the RPG round stuck the tail end of his Blackhawk. The ATO Colonel knew if the round hit the main compartment of the helicopter, no one on board the Blackhawk would have survived the attack or the following crash, when the helicopter tumbled out of the air while exploding from the round that would have done so much more damage to his machine.

The Colonel was sweating up a storm with the fear of one of the males of the civilian campsite below him, picking up one of the weapons and firing an RPG at their low hovering war machine. With the way the commander was trying to hold his machine basically in one spot while hovering over the Iraqi horde, the helicopter was an easy shot by any RPG round fired at it. Although the ATO Colonel never breached the subject to the commander, he understood this threat was in the back of the mind of the pilot of the Apache.

Things were not going well for Walker's troops. He was trying to force his troops to almost double time their march through the sand, making up some of their lost time to reach the civilian site before all hell broke loose, and the Iraqis had enough and they bolted from the campsite. The Captain knew if the civilians ran from the camp, it was going to take him and a mess of other soldiers weeks to track everyone down and search them before allowing them to go on their way again. The pressure was mounting on Walker's back, and he was beginning to take it out on his troops by trying to force them to move faster heading for the site the Colonel discovered.

Every once in a while, one of the soldiers would stumble and fall, and this would cause at least two other soldiers to stop and help the fallen soldier back to his feet. Also, while the soldiers were almost running in the desert now, between sweating and open mouths, the troops were starting to suck down a lot of fine sand and dust, and it was beginning to affect their lungs, making it harder for the specialized soldiers to breathe and move properly. The sand was clogging up their noses, further causing breathing problems for the specialized soldiers. The sand was starting to cake up around the mouths and eyes of the soldiers, and packing in their ears. Everything about the desert was nothing but trouble for the highly trained American soldiers trying to move over the sand.

Even eating was becoming a problem for Walker's troops. Everything they ate in the desert had a fine mixture of sand mixed in with it. Even taking a dump was causing extra problems for the troops, because of sand that got into their systems. Taking a crap was becoming a painful experience, and the soldier's rearend were as sore as an open boil. The soldiers grinned and bared the discomforts they were forced to endure for the sake of their mission and country.

Captain Walker did not bother taking time to check his Global Positioning System to see how far he was from the reported civilian camp. He was traveling due north and knew sooner or later, he was going to come across Tracker One and the group of Iraqi civilians the ATO Colonel discovered making their campsite in the middle of the desert. As his people pushed themselves to move through the desert, one of his soldiers called out.

"Hey hold up a second will ya Walker, I just spotted another set of footprints out here, sir."

Walker heard some of the call and held up his hand and his soldiers stopped charging forward on the dime. All the groans and complaints started anew as the soldiers stopped rushing ahead, and they dropped to the sand and started to suck in huge gulps of air, and downing almost hot bottles of water. Other soldiers started to hand out more bottles of water, so the exhausted soldiers could drink and wash the caked on sand away from their eyes, noses and mouths. This time many of the troops did not even bother to take the time to relieve themselves of the overwhelming weight of their backpacks, because they were too exhausted as they dropped on the sand to take a break from the pushing the soldiers were doing.

Walker let out his breath in a disgusted sigh as he, the Mutt, Sergeant Ramirez, and Blind Date headed for the soldier who called out. As they walked, the Mutt grumbled at his commanding officer. "I wonder what the hell's wrong with Blood Clot, he rarely bugs us over anything? Maybe he's having some trouble with the Doctor and the Russian babes. I know Blood Clot was hanging back keeping a stinking eye on the puke. I think he's worried the pussy ass Doc might drop dead, and he wants to be there if he does, Walker."

"I wish to hell the puke would keel over then we wouldn't hafta worry about his stinking ass so much." Walker replied as the four soldiers stomped up to Blood Clot.

When Walker and the other soldiers got up to his side, Blood Clot, (Sergeant Richard Burmbach) explained to the Captain why he wanted him. "Hey Walker, I just came across another set of footprints and they're veering off that way. I think some of the stinking Iraqi's headed off in that direction." Blood Clot pointed to the footprints in the sand.

Other soldiers formed up around the five troopers and looked at the other footprints Blood Clot discovered. The three Russian soldiers along with Doctor Joel Russbinder, also gathered around the Captain to see what the problem was.

"Shittttt man, some of the stinking shitbirds musta peel off from the group of Iraqi civilians, and this second group of puds headed off east out to the middle of fricking hell. From the maps I read of this area, there's nuthin out there but a fucking Ocean of unending sand, and sure fucking death if you're not well prepared to make it in the desert. Crap, I wonder who these other shitbirds that left the uthers pain in the asses are, dammit." Walker complained as he continued to stare at the footprints showing up in the soft sand, but they were so distorted it was almost impossible for the Ghost to offer how many people left the group at this spot.

"Maybe it's the five assholes we're afta, Walker!" Blood Clot remarked.

"Yeah, and maybe it's a heard of fucking camels. I can't split up the group in case we run into trouble with the fucking civilian assholes we're heading for. Besides, why the hell would the stinking Iraqi General split offa the other group of civilians, and head out to the middle of no fucking where while dragging three bitches along with his ass? Naw, I'm gonna follow my instincts and keep heading for the group of civilian we know where they are. We'll check this lot out first, and if the assholes we're afta aren't part of this damn group then we'll drop back, and follow these stinking prints and see if they were made by the ones we want. Mutt, I want you to set this position in your GPS, and if we don't find the nuts at that uther site, we'll use your GPS to bring us back to this location, and we'll trail these prints until we find out who the hell made the damn things, and hope there from the ones we want.

"God dammit, this is what I was afraid of for Christ sake. This is all I fucking needed to find out here, a second set of god damn footprints leading to nowhere but hell. If we're not careful, these damn Iraqis will have us schlepping all around the fucking desert, searching for the assholes. Do what I said and mark this position in your god damn GPS Mutt, and then we're heading off again. We wasted enuf fucking time staring at these damn prints in the sand." The upset Captain growled as he turned and headed for the lead of the group with one of his troopers chasing Walker with a bottle of water in hand.

The Mutt pulled out his GPS unit and entered the coordinates where they located the second set of footprints on the sand and once he was done, he headed off to catch up with Walker and his fellow soldiers. Besides, the Mutt did not want to be anywhere near the civilian doctor during this military operation.

Doctor Russbinder watched what the Mutt did and when he left, the Russian soldier Caviar, (Sergeant Lana Dostoyevsky) rudely shoved the doctor forward with her arm, to get him moving along with the other soldiers struggling to their feet. None of the three beautiful Russian female soldiers were pleased with being saddled down with the civilian doctor who was having so much trouble trying to keep up with the rest of the soldiers as they trudged along in the desert.

Walker started off he felt his troops wasted enough time checking out the new footprints Blood Clot discovered. He was trying to get his anger under control. He was torn checking out the new footprints, or continuing on for the civilian camp. He breathed a sigh of relief as he decided when his people reached the camp, he was going to feed the GPS coordinates to Tracker One, and he was going to send the helicopter off to check out the other footprints, while he and his troops handled the civilians they were about to search. Walker's anger did not leave his body because he realized they we're making the time he felt the soldiers would do, and they were going to arrive late by Tracker One's position.

The Mutt rushed until he was again walking by Walker's side, and he grumbled after spitting some sand out of his mouth. "Man, this little walk out in the stinking desert betta be fucking worth it. I got sand in fucking places where I didn't even know I had fucking places."

"It's almost over because I got a gut feeling we're heading for the right place, and the damn item and people we fucking want, are effectively trapped in that damn campsite about a mile and a half ahead of us now." Walker replied as he put his hand to his eyes and looked to the sky. He was trying to locate Tracker One hovering over the civilian camp in the air. For a brief second he thought he caught a speck in the sky, but the heat from the desert distorted his vision, and he knew he did not detect Tracker One yet.

About another half mile hard walking, the Mutt picked up Tracker One and informed Walker.

Once Captain Robert Walker and his soldiers picked up Tracker One hovering over a set position, the soldiers increased their pace. In seven minutes of pushing hard in the sand, his troops were spreading out taking up defensive positions practically surrounding the large civilian camp comprised of mostly women and children. Walker grabbed a pair of field glasses and scanned the camp and cursed when he picked up the fortifications the males of the group prepared for when his troops entered the site.

The Captain dropped the glasses and then bitched at the Mutt, who as always was by his side. "God dammit to hell man, these damn Iraqi assholes created a sorta fucking bunker in the middle of the damn messed up campsite. It fucking looks like they wanna try us on for size some, the fucking idiots they are, shit! I'd sure hate like hell to be forced to engage the few older male assholes in this fucking bunch of stinking civilians, with so many damn women and children hanging around all over the damn place, and will sure as hell get in our way when we hit the fucking place, Mutt. Jesus H. Christ Mutt, you look like shit, are you okay?"

"I never know until I sober up. Hey Walker, didja happen to pick up any fucking heavy weapons on your scan of them dopey asses?" The Mutt asked his best friend.

"You're some shit man, don't ya ever take anything fricking serious in your wasted life? All I was able to pick up displayed by them pack of nuts, was a number of AK-47s, I spotted some hand guns also, Mutt.

I didn't pick up anything heavier than those few weapons though. It looks like the few stupid ass defenders are dug in fucking deep, and they seem willing to challenge us to dare step one foot in their stinking campsite against them, dog man." Walker replied as he spat out his words in anger.

The soldier branded CoCo-G, Sergeant Milton Pettibone moved up to Walker and the Mutt's side and popped off at them. "Walker, what the fuck are we waiting for, man? Let's get this fucking game on with those assholes out there. We have the dopey bastards trapped, I say we plow into them fucks and find this shit so we can get the hell outta here yesterday, man."

Walker glared at CoCo for interrupting his conversation with the Mutt, and he snapped angrily at the black soldier. "Hey stupid shouldn't you be off shoplifting some fucking watermelons or something? I just finished telling the stinking Mutt there are too many god damn women and children in the camp, for us to make an all out frontal attack on the mess of civilians idiots out there, buster." He would have went on with his bitch at CoCo-G, but the Mutt asked him a question in an attempt to get his commanding officer off the other soldier's back, and get his attention back on the situation at hand with the horde of Iraqi civilians in their camp.

"Never mind CoCo, how the hell do you wanna fucking handle this mess with these damn civilians, Walker? I'm not too fricking happy with the possibility of mowing down a bunch of fucking women and children myself. You know if the damn fools open fire on us, we're gonna be forced to return fire man. And, in the damn fog of fucking war man, we're not gonna have the stinking luxury or time of picking and choosing our targets when we hit them asses, unless the assholes identify themselves quickly to our asses, man." The Mutt warned Walker.

"That's what I was trying to say, Walker." CoCo offered while trying to take some of the heat off his shoulders, because he realized he said something stupid to his commanding officer, and he was trying to make up for the mistake with Walker.

The upset Captain ignored CoCo's words as he replied to the Mutt. "I'm of the same mind as you are man, and I have no fricking intention of opening fire on a bunch of stinking civilian assholes. I'm gonna do what I planned to do with this fucking situation in the first place. I'm gonna have Ice talk to these flaming assholes, and see if she can talk them out of firing on us…"

"What if she can't talk the pricks outta firing on us? You know we hafta search all them damn asses, and they aren't gonna take too kindly to our searching their stinking women. What are we gonna do then oh fearless leader?" Mutt questioned his commanding officer in an upset tone.

"Look Mutt, I wasn't trained to be a fucking looser, good or utherwise. We're gonna act accordingly if we're forced to go in action against these god damn fools. If the dopey bastards fire on us then we'll return fucking fire, and hope to hell the women and children are smart enuf to get the hell outta the damn way, so they don't get caught up in the fricking action. One thing I can tell ya ass for certain I'm not gonna do, and that's allow anyone to fire on my fricking troops without they paying dearly for their actions with their worthless fucking lives. And, before you ask me Mutt, if the damn women and children are stupid enough not to seek shelter if and when the shooting starts then they're all gonna end up fucking dead. But I'm warning you and I'll warn the rest of our troops, if we're forced to go postal on the civilians. We're going in there WFD, and that's Weapon's Fire Discipline if you don't remember the damn term, buddy." Walker growled as he followed the Mutt's eyes and ended looking at the Iraqi campsite.

CoCo decided it was in his best interest to leave the officers speaking to one another, and he silently left them and went back to his original position of defense.

The Mutt and Walker stared at the makeshift civilian camp, and all they noticed was a mess of scared women and children looking for someplace to hide, and a number of male adults acting like they were waiting for his troops to dare enter the site against them. The Captain picked up the field glass and scanned the camp area again as he bitched at the Mutt.

"God dammit man, the flaming assholes are making like they wanna engage us in combat, and that fricking move is gonna cost them their stupid lives, if they try that kinda crap against our troops when we go active against the damn fools." Walker growled as he dropped the glasses and then he asked the Mutt. "Hey dog man you got any frigging idea where the hell Ice is hanging around, dammit? I need her little ass up here with me so she can do her damn act with these fucking A-rab nuts, man."

"Shit Walker the last time I saw her can, she was kinda hanging around Neck like he was her lover, man. I think Ice had cold feet and she's kinda using the big dope to hide behind."

"I can understand that easy enuf. I really thought we were gonna lose her on that mission she was so badly wounded on, buddy. She hasta be concerned with getting tagged again by another round, and if that happens, any god damn civilian in that damn encampment is gonna pay big time, if she gets hurt. Mutt, how bout you doing me a favor and takeoff and locate her, and tell her to get her ass up here on the double?" Walker grumbled as he took time to light a smoke.

"I'm on it Walker." The Mutt replied as he took off.

When the Mutt left, Buckethead moved up to Walker's side and he asked his commanding officer. "Hey Walker, it looks like we're gonna be forced to do some wet work against them stupid ass people out there, man. I picked up at least fifteen male adults with weapons, and they seem like they were setting up against us out there."

"You picked that up all by your fucking self, huh man? Look tree trunk, you're not telling me anything I don't already know for myself, dammit. Before we head out for that damn site, I'm gonna have a little chitchat with all our people first. I'm gonna tell our guys I don't want any heavy shooting, because of all the damn kids and women trapped in that fucking place. I only want return fire if fired on, and that's it. But first I'm gonna have Ice talk some stinking sense into the supposed leader of this damn Iraqi hell hole, pal. I figure with Ice speaking to the leader, he might feel less threatened if a chick's trying to talk to the

451

god damn main asshole, and stop any killing before it fucking starts, buddy."

"That sounds like a stinking plan to my ass because I wasn't looking forward to mowing down a bunch of god damn kids and hens. If Ice is successful with talking sense in some of those dopey bastards, it could turn out to be the best thing that happen since Dracula discovered the Bloody fucking Mary, man. I'd rather have some stinking fun and games with some of the Iraqi chicks, than having to kill them all Walker."

"You'd be thinking about that kinda bullshit instead of what we're facing here, stupid. Let me tell you something Homes. If you try any of that shit with them damn Iraqi chicks trapped in that place, you're gonna find the end of your stinking dick missing on ya ass, buddy. So get any thoughts of fooling around with the damn Iraqi chick's outta your stinking noggin but fucking quick. We're not here for any damn fun and games, we're here looking for a biological weapon and nuthin more than that, man." Walker warned the huge soldier as he held him in his angry gaze, until Buckethead nodded in the affirmative.

Walker again looked at the Iraqi campsite with his field glasses, but his concentration was interrupted when he received a check in from the hovering Apache helicopter.

"Tracker One to Searcher One. Come in Searcher One. Over Searcher One."

Walker did not have to look for Roach or the radio, the trooper was almost glued to his hip since they first entered the desert in search of their weapon and female who had it on her person. When Tracker One called in, Roach moved up to Walker and offered him the mike.

"Yeah, this is Searcher One. Go with your traffic Tracker One. Whatdaya got? Over."

"Searcher One, I picked up at least seven, I repeat Searcher One, I spotted at least seven Iraqi civilians who worked themselves over to a sort of empty corner of their site, and they seem to be gearing up to make a break to the desert, before your troopers move in on them, sir. Over."

"Tracker One, give me a stinking report on those frigging packages preparing to make a break for it. Over."

"Searcher One, I peg the civilian packages as three women, two adult males and two children. Over." Colonel Pullman reported to the concerned Marine Captain over the radio.

"Shit Tracker One, they could be the stinking packages we're after, and they're probably taking the two kids along so we don't open fire on them so easily. Okay Tracker One this is what I want you to do. Keep a close eye on those moving packages, and if they make a break for it, stop them. You're cleared to lay down a line of suppressing fire before them to turn them back to the damn camp, sir. If the asses still refuse to turn back then you're instructed to track them, and keep the reports coming to me. I'll leave you to cover the packages, I'm gonna try and talk to the chosen leader of this bunch of stinking nuts, sir. I have one of my female soldiers gonna open a communication with the damn leader. I figure he might be more willing to speak to a woman rather than me, or a fellow male soldier because a female might be less threatening to his ass…"

"I don't know about that Searcher One. You know how these damn Arabs regard the women of their country. They might be insulted by a female trying to talk to them. You know Searcher One, their cultural insecurities and all that other crap, sir. Over."

"Yeah I hear ya on that one Tracker One, and that's a good point you raised. Where the hell is Geraldo when you need his stinking ass, dammit? Shit Tracker One, what uther fucking choice do I have in the matter? Besides that Tracker One, I don't give a flying fuck about the Arab's and their cultural insecurities. I have a bunch of fricking soldiers I'm responsible for, and I'm fighting off the damn feeling about going into a civilian camp flooded to overflowing with god damn women and children under a live fire weapons free action, sir.

"Especially if the damn package happens to be hiding in the stinking campsite with this pack of assholes. If we go in there with our fucking weapons lit up and hunting bear, there's a strong possibility of one of the rounds striking the fricking package, and that move could spell the end for all of us in this stinking country. No Tracker One, I'm gonna stick with my original fucking plan I formulated as it stands. You keep your damn eye glued on those seven moving subjects, and if they make a break for it you'll stay on top of the asses, and once we secured the campsite, we'll hunt them uther fools down. Over."

"Roger that last Searcher One. Good luck with your penetration of the campsite, sir. Be aware Searcher One, if the seven packages make a run for it, you'll have no air cover if I'm forced to track the other packages, sir. Over."

"I copy your last and understand possible lack of air cover I'll have for my entry into the civilian campsite, Tracker One. I'm prepared to make my move against the camp without air cover. You stay on those uther assholes for me, Tracker One. Over!" Walker growled in the radio, he was that upset he was going to be forced to deal with armed civilians, and he was not going to have Tracker One overhead for air support.

"Roger orders as received Searcher One. Tracker One is assigned to the seven packages and will cover them and try to turn them back, if they make a run for it, sir. Over."

"You have your orders Tracker One. Good Luck with them. Out."

"Good luck Searcher One. If you need air support, call for it and we'll break off our coverage of the moving packages and return to support your ground forces, Searcher One. Over."

"Negative on last Tracker One. You're ordered to stay on top of break outs and nothing else for this fucking operation, sir. Repeat your orders as received. Over!"

"Searcher One my orders are as stated and I'm ordered to stay on top of possible runners from the campsite, sir. I'll comply with my orders as received, Searcher One. Over." Colonel Pullman snapped in the radio, he was that angry because he was not going to be part of the air protection for the ground forces when they make their entry into the civilian camp. The ATO Officer felt like he was not living up to his part of the operation he was engaged along with Captain Walker and the rest of his crews.

"You'll follow those orders as received whether you like them or not, Tracker One! Out!" Walker replied to the Colonel.

"Roger that Searcher One. Out!" Colonel Pullman offered and then turned to the pilot and grumbled. "Well Commander you heard the orders, sir. We have to stay on top of this group, and if they make a run for it, we have to stop them. If they don't stop we have to track the pain in the ass civilians and report to the Captain on their movements and where they're heading, sir."

"I got'em in sight sir. They won't move an inch without my being right on top of them, sir." Colonel Pullman reported to the commanding officer of the ground forces.

When Walker broke off communication with Tracker One, he complained at Buckethead staring at him. "God dammit Bucket, these fricking civilian assholes are giving me more problems than any stinking military engagements I shared with the Iraqi military, man. I'd rather be forced to deal with fucking soldiers than a bunch of god damn civilian pains, buddy."

"I know what you mean, but their stupid ass actions aren't leaving us with many uther stinking possibilities opened to us on how to fricking deal with them assholes, Walker. I say the hell with it and we go in there and level the god damn lot of them that easy, and get this thing over with. That way we won't lose any of our troops in this action, Walker." Buckethead growled over the problems this operation was causing them as he lifted his weapon into a better firing position.

"Shit, I'm almost ready to agree with you on that, Buckethead. The way this mess is shaping up, I might be forced to regard these civilians as enemy combatants, and level the whole lot of them as you suggested, big guy. I gave the Mutt the WFD, and we're gonna stay with that stinking order for the time being. Crap, I wish to hell they weren't damn civilians, that way I wouldn't feel bad if I have to order their deaths, buddy. God dammit to shit and back, where the hell's the stinking Mutt and Ice at for Christ sake, they shoulda been here by now, dammit?"

The Mutt caught up to Ice and snapped at her after seeing how she was trying to use the huge body of Neck to hide behind. Lieutenant Hall was upset with her for lagging behind trying to stay out of any action. "Hey Ice, you gotta move up to Walker, he has a detail for your ass, and he wants you up by him on the double quick."

"Fuck you Mutt, I like it where I'm stationed. If Walker needs any help, you give it to him, asshole." Ice actually growled at the Mutt which angered him, and he snarled right back at the beautiful female American soldier.

"Hey Ice, my name's not a fucking dick so keep it the hell outta your stinking mouth will ya."

The Mutt's angry words heated Neck and he glared at the Mutt which made Lieutenant Hall turn on him to shut down the big soldier before things got out of hand. The Mutt knew why Neck was upset he was trying to protect Ice who he had a crush on.

"Back off big man, I'm following Walker's fucking orders to get Ice up to his position pronto. You betta back off before I release some fucking hell on your god damn ass, big man."

"You and what fucking Army, dog man?" Neck snapped back at the Mutt.

Ice did not want this, starting trouble between the two soldiers on her behalf, and she turned and looked at Neck and offered him. "Neck, Bobby, the Mutt's right, if Walker wants me by his side to carry out a special detail, that's where I have to be. You two make peace before I leave with the Mutt." Ice looked at the huge soldier branded Neck, and then at the Mutt and when neither soldier backed down, she warned the both of them again.

"I told you two jerks to make peace, and I'm not going anywhere until you two do."

The Mutt finally nodded at the larger soldier and Neck immediately returned the nod, which caused Ice to add to her words to the two young soldiers before she left to be with the Captain.

"That's better I don't want to be the cause of trouble between two friends and fellow soldiers." Ice turned her attention to the Mutt and remarked. "Come on, it'd be foolish on our part to keep Walker waiting too long." With that said, the two soldiers took off to linkup with Walker.

Just as Walker snarled his last words at Buckethead, the Mutt and Ice charged up to his position then they dropped by Walker's side with the Mutt offering to his commander as he tried to catch his breath. "Hey Walker, I had a problem locating Ice out there, man. She was hanging back there with Neck and the three fricking Russian babes and the stinking Doctor pain in the damn ass we're dragging all over the fucking place with us lately, man."

"That's not a fucking problem buddy. I'm kinda happy with Ice trying to stay out of the line of fire, man. Not after how bad wounded she was on that mission we were on…"

"Now you hold it right there Mister Super Cock Soldier. I wasn't holding back because of my being wounded in the operation back when, Captain Walker! I was called back there to help the Doctor, because he was having some problems with one of his instruments, and I helped the poor man clean the sand out of the damn machine. That was the only reason I was back there with him, and when Neck saw me he came over to see if he could lend me a hand. I'm telling you Mister Soldier Boy. If any shit goes down on this operation, I'm going to be right in the middle of it along with the rest of the soldiers from our outfit, Walker!" Ice snarled as she lifted her weapon and slapped the stock of her M-16, and then she glared so angrily at Walker's face.

"Hey baby girl calm the fuck down, I didn't mean you were hanging back because of your being wounded back when, or you might be concerned engaging any enemy forces, soldier. Look girl, I'd want you fighting by my fricking side on any damn battlefield we're deployed to no matter who the fuck we were engaging, baby. I was pleased you were back there, that's all I fucking meant by that statement, Ice." Walker offered in his defense, even though he did want Ice out of the line of fire, because he was aware she was still not completely over the effects of the serious wound she received on that other mission. She was trying to tough it out so she was not dropped from the outfit. Walker smiled at the calming down extremely beautiful female soldier. But the calm instantly left Ice, when the Mutt opened his mouth and mumbled.

"Yeah Walker, I know the fucking instrument Ice was helping the stinking Doctor with back there, man. I wish she'd help me with my instrument once in a while, man. She's so tied up with the stinking Neck so no one can have any fun with her any longer, man." The Mutt snapped because he was still pissed off over the confrontation he had with the other soldier, because of Ice being with Neck and out of harm's way as he saw it.

Ice shot a look at the Mutt that would have melted ice in the middle of a snow storm, and then she growled savagely at him. "Now you look here buster, just because your reproductive organs are on the outside of your wasted body. It doesn't mean you don't have to respect me, mister. I don't mind you joking around with me every once in a while, and I'll happily give it right back to you in spades. But when you start making statements like the last one you crapped out of the side of your filthy mouth. It shows me you don't respect me. You own me an apology and if you don't give me one right this minute. I'll stick my hand down your filthy throat and pull one out of your miserable ass myself, mister."

The Mutt glanced at Captain Walker in the hopes he had something to say about what was going down between the two soldiers, but Ice thundered angrily at him. "What the hell are you looking at your other damn partner in crime for, buster? The both of you were born under the same slimy rock if you were to ask me. He's not the one who just insulted me you are, and you better clear it up right this minute, stupid. Mutt, if you don't give me an apology, you'll regret it for the rest of your wasted life, mister."

Ice added to her threat against Lieutenant Frank Hall by lifting her weapon to a clean firing position, and then she chambered a round, and glared at the stunned looking officer while still waiting for his apology.

Again, the Mutt looked at Walker and he replied. "Don't go looking at me, asshole. You're the one who opened his stupid mouth so if I was you, I'd apologize to Ice or she's gonna put a fricking cap in your stinking ass for ya, pal."

"Don't you help the stupid fool out Walker. This problem is between me and the Mutt. Well mister, I'm waiting and you'd be awful foolish to keep me waiting too long, Mutt!" Ice added aggressively at the Mutt as she held him in her angry glare.

The Mutt finally spread his hands apart in submission to the beautiful and young but angry female soldier, as he offered her. "I'm sorry Ice, sometimes I talk to hear myself talk I guess, baby. Are we cool again Ice?" The Mutt automatically put his arm up and Ice smiled as she moved closer to the Mutt and did what the soldiers referred to as banging sticks, as she slapped his forearm with hers. Ice then went to move from the Mutt, but he was feeling so bad about his foolish remark, he stopped her by grabbing her arm, and then he hugged her to his body.

Instantly, Ice, (Sergeant Diane Morrison) melted in the powerful arms of the young Marine Lieutenant, as she allowed him to kiss her on the forehead before the Mutt released the hold on her and asked again. "Ice, we're cool, right baby?"

CHAPTER TWENTY FIVE

"We're always cool Mutt. Can we be any other way, mister? You just have to watch how you speak to me and any of the other female soldiers of the unit, stupid." Ice turned to the grinning Captain and asked her commander. "Walker, the Mutt told me you wanted me by your side, sir. What's up and what do you want me to do about it, honey? Anything you need from me, you have it Captain."

"Yeah Ice, I sent for ya purdy little ass because I need your help, sister. Look Ice, I got a helluva mess of stinking Iraqi civilians trapped inside their damn makeshift encampment. Some of the damn fools obviously decided to construct a stinking bunker type mess to try and defend themselves against us when we decide to enter the fricking encampment to search it for the weapon and this missing Arab chick, honey. I'm stuck between a stinking rock and a hard place with this situation, because I don't wanna open fire on a bunch of stupid and mostly unarmed Iraqi civilians. This is why I sent for you and I want you to…"

"I picked up that much for myself from where I was stationed, Walker. Exactly what is it you want from me, sir?" Ice asked as she interrupted her commanding officer, but her beautiful smile stopped Walker from getting upset with her.

"Yeah, right, well Ice I pulled you up here because I want you to call out to the supposed ring leader of these stinking popping jays, and see if you can get him to respond to you, and then I want you to convince the asshole we don't meant them any harm. I want you to explain to anyone who might respond to your hail that the only reason we're out here, is because we're trying to locate a stinking Iraqi chick named Ayesha al-Qaysi, and her four friends. Lie through your damn eye teeth to the bastard if you hafta, and tell the ass this chick's mother's dying, and we were sent out here to find her, and bring her back to her mother's side before she dies.

"Lie to his damn ass, and if you can come up with a betta lie than the one I just offered ya, you're free to employ it when you start speaking to these turds. Look honey, I don't mean to heap this shit down on your shoulders, but if you can't get someone to respond to you from that group. Then we're gonna be forced to go in there in force, and being there are only a bunch of stinking civilians in the site, you know what that means, honey. So you gotta try and get someone in there to respond to your hail, baby." Walker stopped speaking and sort of put a stupid look on his face as he waited for Ice to speak.

"Jesus Christ Walker, you're not putting too much crap on my damn back, sir. That's a hell of a terrible thing I have to live with you just stuck on me, Captain. If no one in there will reply to me then we're going in there hunting bear and killing anyone who looks at us the wrong way, and I have to live with the fact if I failed to get anyone to talk to me. Any women and children in there who die will be on my conscious, sir. Thanks a hell of a lot, that's a hell of a responsibility you just dumped on me." Ice complained at Walker.

"Ice I feel ya and know how this might upset ya, but you gotta get that way of thinking outta your stinking noggin but quick. You gotta look at it disway baby. If the stinking fools don't respond to you then nuthin this side of judgment day woulda saved their damn lives for them. They have to be looked at they were living with so much hatred in their stinking hearts that it caused their deaths. Ice, you're their best fucking chance of living through this nightmare and if they don't take the opening you're trying to give them then they deserve their fate. But if you think if we're forced to do them in is gonna keep you from sleeping at night. I'll dismiss you from this duty and pull Neck up here, and allow him to try and talk some sense into these flaming assholes. Nuthin will stop the Neck from sleeping at night, baby girl." Walker offered to the pretty female soldier while giving her a way out of his orders for her.

"Captain Walker, you know damn well the ones preparing to defend their position against our troops entering their camp will never listen to a male soldier trying to speak with them, who might give them life instead of death, sir. I know if I was trapped in there and some big dumb male soldier was trying to talk me out of there in peace. I'd have to think twice the soldier wanted me out of there so he could rape me, or something like that sir. No way Captain Walker, no matter the outcome to this mess at the end of it, I'm the soldier who has to speak to these civilian trapped in there, sir." Ice offered as she flashed one of her best smiled at the intense looking and highly upset Walker.

"That's why I picked your pretty ass to speak to these trapped Iraqi assholes in the first fucking place, Ice. I knew the jackasses would never listen to reason if I allowed the massive Neck to speak to them. You're gonna be up to the task, right Ice? I don't need you starting this damn thing, and then falling apart if you can't talk any stinking sense into these damn people. If you start this you gotta finish it, so don't step up to the plate if you can finish it off." Walker warned the female soldier as he stared in her eyes to make certain she wasn't talking out of her ass, while attempting to save the Iraqi civilian lives.

"C'mon Captain, if I'm the only chance these people have, you know damn well I'll be strong enough to finish what I started with the civilians. When do you want me to start to communicate with someone from the group, Walker?" Ice asked her commander while she was trying to think about what she was going to say to the obviously frightened group of Iraqi civilians.

"I got a stinking megaphone hanging around here someplace dammit, and when I find the damn thing I'll give the shitting thing to you, and you can give it a shot talking some sense into these assholes out there. Remember Ice, if they don't wanna listen to you it's not your fault, it's there's. It's like you just said sister, you're the only chance these damn civilians have to live. So if they don't take fucking advantage of what you're offering them, it's their tough luck, baby girl." Walker replied as he looked for the megaphone.

Ice moved up until she had a good view of the civilian site, and then she tried to pick out the one Iraqi male she thought to be the leader of the trapped civilians. Walker found the megaphone and moved to Ice's side and offered the speaker and words to her.

"Here you go Ice, take this damn thing so you can speak to the fools and they can hear you betta than just yelling at the asses." Walker noticed a number of soldiers out of place and he growled at the Mutt. "Hey man, who the hell is that bunch of fucking refuges over there by that damn sand dune, and what the fuck are they doing there?"

The Mutt looked to where Walker was pointing and then he replied to his commanding officer. "That's Six Pack (Sergeant Joseph Jesposito) and three uther soldiers with him sir. I sent them over there to protect our side flank if anything went down with these damn popping jays we have surrounded, Walker."

The Captain let it go as he handed Ice the speaker and she complained. "I tried to pick the guy out who I thought was giving commands to the civilians in the camp, Captain. I haven't been able to pick out any one person in charge of the civilians, sir."

"I believe I pegged the sonofabitch, Ice. Look to the center of the makeshift bunker. You see that dude with the black robe with the checkered Kaaffiych headdress on his noggin. I kept him under observation most while I was here, he seems to be the main dude for the uthers. I think you should aim your words at that prick. If he's not the dude, at least he's a start." Walker offered as he pointed out an Iraqi male ordering the other civilians around at the site.

"I got him Walker, when do you want me to start on him and the others, sir?" Ice replied as she stared at the Arab man while waiting for Walker's next orders.

"You got the damn megaphone, now is as good a time as any. You know what you're gonna say to the dopey little prick?"

"I'm going to have to play this one by ear I guess Captain, until and only if he replies to my request to speak with him, sir. Okay Captain wish me some luck. Attention in the camp, Alhamdulilah

463

(Praise be to God) this is Sergeant Diane Morrison of the United States Marine Corps, and I wish to speak to the Emir (Military leader) or Sheik (Religious leader) of the Iraqi civilians in the camp please." Ice's Arabic was absolutely perfect as she added the correct religious phrase to get the male Arab she wanted to speak to, talking before she went on with her words aimed at the Iraqi leader. She held her words as Ice and Walker watched the sudden stirring in the camp by some upset defenders, and the Iraqi male they were trying to communicate started to yell at the others.

The leader listened to the woman's words, and warned the others with him. "The god cursed lowly infidels arrived and are wasting their foul breath and time trying to speak to us. My faithful Arab brothers, we must remain strong and prepare our hearts for battle with Satan's spawn. Follow me and I'll lead you down the path to Allah's side. I pray to Allah for revenge on the worthless heads of all who invaded our land. Remember the sacred words of the Holy Qur'an and the lines from the Surah, known in the al-Anfal, or the spoils of war my brothers. 'Against them make ready your strength to the utmost of your power, including steeds of war to strike terror in the enemy of Allah and your enemy'. The time for words passed; it's actions of our faith that matters. Those who encroach on the province of Allah face His mighty wrath.'"

Walker grabbed hold of Ice's arm and once he had her attention he asked her. "What the fuck is the lousy dude babbling about?"

"He's trying to rile up the others so they defend against us, Walker." Ice replied as she refused to take her eyes off the leader of the civilian hordes.

"Is the scumbag having any success with his line of bullshit to the uther assholes out there?"

"Look and see for yourself Walker." Ice and Walker watched as the other male members and a few older female civilians made themselves ready to defend themselves.

"Shit, we'll try this crap again on his ass, Ice. You're the only chance these assholes have." Walker grumbled with disgust as he shook his head over the thought of attacking a bunch of basically unarmed Iraqi civilians trapped in the camp he and his soldiers had surrounded.

Ice started to speak by addressing the Iraqi with the title of Emir to give him more power than he deserved. "Emir, my intention is to speak with you in the name of peace. Emir, there's been enough death visited upon your people to last a lifetime. I need to speak with you, and it's your responsibility to Allah to save the civilians in your charge. Emir, Allah will not look upon you favorably if you allow the innocent to die for a foolish cause, because you refused to speak with someone offering you the olive branch of peace and life. I assure you Emir, we're not here to kill anyone in your camp. We're here to locate a certain young Ayesha al-Qaysi and bring her back to her village. She's needed there by her dying mother, sir."

Ice stopped speaking when she noticed the Iraqi she wanted to speak with, started to speak sort of calmly with another male of the group.

"What the hell do you think they're talking about now, Ice?" Walker asked the female soldier.

"Beats me, but I'll give him all the time he wants as long as he's not making any threatening motions against us, Walker." Ice replied as she refused to take her eyes off the Iraqi leader for a moment, while she waited to see if he would reply to her last call.

Mohsoun Abdella al-Assad, who was the appointed commander of the civilians trapped by the American troops, spoke to his second in command, Abdallah Salim Agazadek. "My brother, what do you think about that American sharmoota (bitch) trying to speak with me? She has to be lying about the female she looks for. I wonder what the cursed infidels have up their foul sleeve, and what is it they truly want from us? I must ask you my brother, is it wise for us to try and fight the lowly infidels, or would it be wiser for us to speak with the lowly jackals first?"

"Mohsoun, Allah's way is the way of peace and words are not deadly. Besides my brother, you must remember what happened to our village because the more radical ones from our country decided to fight the hated infidels, when the jackals first arrived outside our town. I fear the jackals have destroyed our village because of the useless fighters who came from surrounding villages, to make a worthless stand against the foul infidel invaders.

"Mohsoun, if the hated American soldiers were able to defeat the better armed and prepared fighters from our village so swiftly. Then what possible resistance could we offer against them, and hope for any success in defeating the beasts of Satan's breast. I fear the lowly American soldiers are too powerful, and they'll slaughter everyone we removed from our village with hopes of saving their lives. The male fighters of our village were better armed and organized than we, and they were slaughtered by the greater force of American Forces. Mohsoun, it was our responsibility and duty to save the women and children of our village. So what was the worth of it all if we now allow the jackal American soldiers to come out to the desert and destroy those we have originally saved from their attack?"

"You speak words of great wisdom to my worthless ears my faithful brother. Yes Abdallah I believe you're correct to offer me it was our responsibility to Allah's word, to save the women and children of our village. We have come this far, so I must not allow them to die now at the foul hands of the lowly infidels in a battle we have no chance of success. I feel the wiser course of action on our part, would be to speak to this god cursed American sharmoota, and see what she wants, and what she offers for our survival, Abdallah." Mohsoun Abdella al-Assad replied as he looked in the eyes of his fellow Arab brother and noticed the fear etched deep in them.

"Mohsoun, the foul infidels are offering words of what they call peace, as long as they're offering us words, they're not killing our women and children. I believe it'd serve you as our chosen leader and future organizer of what might be left of our village, for you to speak to the infidel witch of the desert sands. Let's see what she has on her mind, and what she's willing to offer so we can carry out our sacred duty of protecting the women and children of our village. That's of the most concern in my mind, and it should be likewise in your mind, Brother Mohsoun." Abdallah remarked as he gave his fellow Arab a reassuring but quick smile.

"Yes, yes my brother, you're wise beyond your years of existence on Allah's lands. My Allah grant you a lifetime of a thousand years, and many healthy male children to enjoy for your guiding wisdom to me, Abdallah. Yes, I decided it's correct to speak to the American witch, and see why her cursed soldiers are hounding our people so. I must make them wait until the last possible moment before I respond to her foul pleads. I fear I don't trust the hated infidels if they came to me bearing great gifts of fabulous worth, Abdallah."

"Mohsoun, I don't understand the reason with your delay to speak to this lowly female foreigner. What's the reason for this delay on your part, Mohsoun? I fear the longer it takes for you to respond to her request for words, the larger the chance the hated infidels will attack our camp and slaughter everyone we were sworn to protect. I say we speak to this worthless infidel trying to communicate with you immediately."

"Abdallah, you possess great wisdom yet you're a very foolish man. The reason for my delay wanting to speak to the witch invader, serves me by allowing me to remain in power with our dealings with this witch of the desert sands. Abdallah, if I was to speak to her now, she'll be in the position of power over our conversation, fool. If I delay and make her and her foul soldiers believe I'm not interested in speaking with them. You must think of the relief they'll suffer when I finally chose to speak with them. The hated infidels will be so pleased they'll do everything in their power to appease me." Mohsoun snapped as he glanced at where the woman's voice was coming from. He cursed because he was only able to see countless heads of the soldiers looking at him. Fear rose in his chest as he thought the entire American Army was pitted against him.

Agazadek thought for a moment, the time trying to one up the powerful American soldiers was over. He knew the American Forces were the true power in Iraq, and any resistance placed against them was a pure waste of time and lives on their part. Abdallah realized nothing any Iraq man or soldier could possibly do against the American troops, would make the slightest difference in the final fate of Iraq and her civilians. He believed everything was lost to Iraq and her people, and it was up to the occupying American soldiers what was going to become of his country in the future. Abdallah decided to remain silent until he understood what was on Mohsoun's mind, and what he was going to do to get the women and children out of the sights of the American's weapons.

"Abdallah, this is what I want. I want you to go to our defenders in the camp and have them lower their weapons. Don't make the worthless fools drop the weapons all together though. The foul fools are only to place them out of sight of the lowly infidels. I'm hoping this action will make the foolish American soldiers hesitate with their attack against us, my brother. If our defenders do this and it causes the American witch to call out to us, I'll know I am the one in control of the conversation we'll engaged in with the hated infidels. Leave my side and carry out the orders I gave you, and once this has been accomplished and I observed the reaction from the American fools. Then I'll know how to properly proceed with my conversation with the lowly animals. Go and carry out my orders Abdallah."

When conversation between the two Iraqi's ended, Ice reported. "Uh oh, they stopped speaking and one Arab is running over to the defenders of the camp. Jesus Walker, they're lowering their weapons, I think they're going to speak with us. I can't believe this Walker, if they're lowering their weapons, it looks like they're going to talk, and we won't be forced to slaughter them, sir. What's my next move Walker?" Ice asked her commander as she watched the Iraqi defenders lowering their weapons and taking up a less threatening stance.

"Get back on the damn horn and see if you can get that lousy sonofabitch in charge of these people to speak with us. If they're lowering their damn weapons then maybe we can get outta this stinking mess without killing the civilians we have trapped in their encampment. Speak to the lousy dude in charge Ice, and see what he's up to and what he's offering us. But I'm warning you, if I detect them Iraqi's trying to set up a betta defense against us, I'm not gonna wait until they're betta set up before we hit the dopey asses.

"I'm gonna issue the attack order and place a quick period at the end of this damn drama, and the hell with trying to talk to this popping jay who thinks he's the one in command of this situation. The balls in your park, so see if you can get this turd talking, and find out what the hell's he's up to, before he and the rest of them damn civilians run outta fucking time, and I take matters in my hands and act the way I was trained to do when threatened by hostile forces." Walker growled as he held the Iraqi leader in his line of sight, so he could see what he was doing.

"I'll do my best with the Iraqi Walker, but because they're lowering their weapons, doesn't mean the leader's going to speak to me, and he does what we want him to do. I think this Arab's on a power trip if you were to ask me, sir. I don't think you should fall victim to his little head game if that's what he's up to. Walker, I think you should show him a power play of your own by ordering some of our troops to move around and make it look like our people are preparing to attack this site, sir. I'm willing to bet the bank on it a move like that will force this Arab to cry like a baby, and demand to speak to us quicker than he's planning, Walker." Ice offered to her commander with concern as she also watched the activity going on in the civilian camp.

"That's a great call there and that's exactly what I'm gonna do. Mutt, get some of our troops moving around, have the fifties (Fifty caliber heavy machine guns) setup and have the shooters move them like they're scoping out the crossfire of the damn campsite, man. I want the flaming asshole out there to believe we're planning to attack their damn camp." Walker called to the Mutt, and then he watched the soldier move to carry out his commands.

Abdallah Salim Agazadek carried out Mohsoun's orders and once he had his Arab defenders lowering their weapons and getting them out of sight of the American's view, he returned to Mohsoun's side and they watched what the American soldiers were doing, and observe their reaction to the less threatening stance his defenders were adopting against the invading soldiers.

Mohsoun was the first one to pick up the new movement from the American soldiers, but it was Abdallah who cried out the warning. "Mohsoun, your foolish actions have failed to impress the cursed infidels. Look, look Mohsoun and see what the god cursed animals are up to against us. The savage invaders are preparing their defenses for an attack against our people. You see Mohsoun, your foolish thought to delay speaking to the devil infidel witch backfired, and the American soldiers are showing us they'll just as soon attack than speak terms of peace between us and them. Mohsoun, you have to…"

"Abdallah, you have to hold your foul water and strap a stout board to your cursed back to keep your backbone straight and proud, fool. I believe the foolish American Commander saw what I was up to, and he decided to display a show of force of his own against me to bend my will to his, and then he'll command our conversation and terms of peace. I see I underestimated this wise American who thinks like an Iraqi Commander. But I'll not commit the same mistake twice against this hated man from the land of Satan.

"Yes Abdallah, you may again start to breathe properly, I'll call out to the hated American Commander's lowly bitch, and ask her what her and her troops want from us. In my mind I see we're of no threat or need to these hated infidels drooling from their savage jowls to attack and slaughter a group of innocent Iraqi civilians. So they must have something else on their evil minds they need from us, my foolish brother. What they want is probably from the female they want us to believe they're looking for, to bring her back to the village for some foul reason. It looks like the only way I'll find out what the devil invaders want, is by speaking to the fools."

"I agree with your wise thoughts Mohsoun, I urge you to communicate between this female infidel before the jackals take matters into their own hands, and they attack our wards because they grown tired of waiting for you to reply, my faithful leader."

"Abdallah, don't be in a hurry to speak to the fools. The hated infidels will not dare attack, not with the fools knowing we're civilians fleeing their slaughter of our village. We'll hold the upper hand in dealing with the lowly infidels from the West, because we Arabs choose death, while the fools from across the cursed sea choose life. It's so precious to them fools, Brother Abdallah."

There was a second burst of activity inside the camp, and it immediately drew Walker and the Mutt's attention to the sudden activities. A number of Iraqi males left the bunker area and started to mill around the campsite. The two men Ice and Walker were keeping their eyes on remained standing in the middle of the defense they set up.

"What the hell do you thing those crazy ass scumbags are up to, man?" The Mutt asked.

"Beats the hell outta my ass, it looks to me like they wanna die by the damn sword." Walker complained as he watched the activity going down in the Iraqi campsite.

"You know what they say about that shit? Those who live by the sword evidently never come across a stinking dude carrying an automatic weapon, man." The Mutt retorted with a grin.

Roach made his way over to Walker and warned as he handed him the mike. "Captain, you got a call from whatisface back in safe land, he's really pissed off this time, sir. He nearly blew out my damn eardrum when I answered his call with his screaming crap, sir."

"That's all I needed, the fricking Colonel getting on my case now dammit." Walker growled as he snatched the mike from Roach and barked into it. "Searcher One to Searcher Base, send your damn traffic sir. Over."

"I'll send your fucking traffic and it'll run right over your dragging ass, mister. How the fuck many times do I have to order you to remain in contact with my fucking ass, mister? Where the hell are you and what the fuck's going on out there, dammit? I have the big man (President) and General White standing on my dick looking for answers, and you're the only bastard who could answer their damn questions, Searcher One. What the hell's going on out there for the love of the Christ Child, Squid?" Colonel Bruce Leadbetter roared in the radio, and if he shouted any louder, Walker would not need the radio to hear him because he was that upset.

"Searcher Base, we tracked our missing package to a makeshift civilian campsite made up of mostly Iraqi women and kids who obviously fled the damn village when we came to search the place, sir.

Right now Searcher Base, we have the civilian packages surrounded, and we're trying our best to get the resident prick to communicate with us, so we don't hafta mow down and slaughter a bunch of innocent asses, sir."

"Searcher One, you have your orders, and they're to retrieve the item no matter what you have to do to get your damn hands on the shit and accomplish your mission. If you have to mow them assholes down, you'll give the order and live with it. Searcher One, you're instructed to find this crap, and your orders are to DIP (Die In Place) if need be, to get the order carried out by you and the rest of your troops. I can't impress on your ass how important it is to find this crap before it's released from confinement, and we end up with a larger god damn problem on our fucking hands. You remember your orders and they're to be carried out as received, DRT (Die Right There).

"I don't give a flying fuck what you have to do to carry out your orders I issued you soldier, as long as you find and confiscate that item, and you people get it to me ten minutes ago. Once you finish up with these Iraqi pains in the ass assholes, and your troops find this crap, your troops will report to me on the double quick, soldier. In fact, give me your GP (Global Position) and I'll dispatch a fucking drone to your Papa, Papa (location) so I can see what the hell's going on out there in real fucking time for my damn self." Colonel Leadbetter continued to roar at his field commander while trying to light a fire under him at the same time.

"Searcher Base my GP is Five, Three, One by Niner, Five, Five, sir." Walker reported.

"I'll repeat that for confirmation Searcher One. Your GP is Five, Three, One by Niner, Five, Five. Is that correct as stated Searcher One?" Colonel Leadbetter repeated.

"That's a Roger as repeated, Searcher Base. We'll remain at position and move against the flaming assholes as soon as we try to make contact with the head cheese of the Iraqi group, sir. My aim is to try and speak some sense to the dude's noggin with an attempt to not be forced into engaging the unarmed group, and we have a free hand with our search of said packages, sir. I assure you Searcher Base, if our attempts to speak to the leader fails, I'll issue the order to advance and whatever we have to resort to carry out orders will be accomplished, Searcher Base. Over." Walker reported to his commander over the radio, hoping the Colonel would allow them time needed to speak first, before being forced to attack the trapped group.

Colonel Leadbetter hesitated for a brief moment as he milled over what Walker just reported to him. He was of the same mind as Walker, and he was not looking forward to having his troops attack a bunch of civilians, especially if the package was not with this group of Iraqi people. Finally, he responded to his commander in the field. "Searcher Base to Searcher One, I received your intention and agree with your planned course of action. But I have to remind you Searcher One, time is not on our side on this mission, and if all efforts to talk sense to the leader of this group fail, you'll break off all further communications and act accordingly. How do you read orders as issued and received Searcher One? Over!"

"Searcher One to Searcher Base, I read orders five by five and will carry out orders as issued and received without hesitation if attempts to speak to the leader fail. Over."

"Fine Searcher One, there's no sense wasting time speaking with me further Searcher One. Report once you searched the civilian camp, and I can only hope to God this package is with this group you have trapped, Searcher One. Good luck with your orders and I'll be waiting for that report the moment, and I mean the exact moment you people are finished searching those damn assholes, Searcher One. Over?" Colonel Leadbetter growled in his mike, hoping to inform Walker he was done wasting time on anyone connected with this item.

"I read you and will accomplish orders as received, Searcher Base. Over." Walker replied angered by the way his commander growled over the radio. It took a second for the Captain to realize the Colonel broken off the communication, and he did not hear Walker's response.

The Mutt and Ice were staring at Walker as he finished speaking to the Colonel, and the moment he handed Roach the mike, the Mutt asked his commanding officer. "Well man, what the hell did the hot shot Colonel have to offer, man?"

"He's getting his rocks off running this operation from the cheap seats where he's safe and sound back there. The Colonel informed me we're running outta time, and wants a period to this lousy sentence ten minutes ago. I don't give a flying fuck how much pressure he's putting on my ass, we're gonna take time and talk to these people before I'm forced to go Postal on the asses."

"I agree with you Walker. We hafta try and talk these scumbags into allowing us to search their damn asses. You know I hafta admit I'm feeling a little sleazy over this order which is really weird, because generally I like the feeling of sleazy, man. Walker, I've done a number of things I'm not particularly proud of, and some things I done that I'm proud of is rather disgusting buddy. But hitting a bunch of unarmed stinking civilian goes against my stinking grain on all fucking accounts, Walker." The Mutt moaned with a smirk.

"Whether you fucking agree with me or not is not particularly relevant in my stinking life, man. All you're here for is to carry out my frigging orders and nothing less..." Walker growled before being interrupted by the Mutt.

"Hey man that was colder than the uther side of the fucking pillow. You're starting to let the Colonel directing our actions from the cheap seats to get to ya ass, buddy. We've been on tougher missions than this one, so fucking hack it man."

Walker stared at the Mutt for several moments and then snapped at him. "Fuck you man!"

"Hey man, you're gonna turn my head with all this stinking flattery you're shoving at me lately, Walker. You wanna know something Walker...?"

"Naw, I think I know e-fucking-nough as it stands, you mook." Walker remarked, interrupting the Mutt's words.

"Hey Walker, you have to get off the Mutt's case. He smoked so much pot in his wasted life, the last time he was in a bar and farted, he got everyone in the place stoned. Walker, we have a situation and we have to solve it double quick, sir." Ice offered while trying to get Walker's mind back on the matter at hand of the Iraqi civilians.

"Now wait a minute sister." The Mutt started but was cut off by Ice who fired back at him.

"Don't get on my ass, and besides if I thought for one moment there was any possible truth with my being your sister. I'd disown both my parents." Ice countered at the grinning Lieutenant.

The Mutt and Walker stared at each other while milling over Ice's stinger aimed at the Mutt, and then laughed as Walker added. "The pretty lady has a good point there Mutt, we got a pack of assholes we gotta contend with, and this bickering isn't helping the damn situation out in the least, man. Ice, I think you betta get back in communication with that damn Iraqi leader you were trying to speak with and see if you can get him to talk with ya. If he starts to talk that's half the stinking battle we hafta deal with in this Romeo Foxtrot (Rat Fuck) situation, baby. Time's rapidly running out on us and if we don't get this mess moving, then the Colonel's gonna do it on his own and then the shit's really gonna hit the fucking fan."

"I'm on it baby." Ice replied as she lifted the megaphone and called in it. "Emir, I must speak with you. It's a matter of life and death, and Allah knows there has been enough death to fill everyone's cups, sir. Please Emir, you must respond before it's too late, sir."

Mohsoun Abdellah al-Assad was being flanked by Abdallah Salim Agazadek, and they were listening as the American soldier called out to him. It was Agazadek who spoke to the leader from the village. "There Mohsoun, the foreign witch is trying to speak again with you. Her words ring with the old beliefs and words, my desert brother. This lowly infidel must have knowledge of our ways. She even calls upon Allah for His help speaking to us. We must respond to her before it's like she offers, too late Mohsoun."

"When in Allah's grace will you be strong like a proud Iraqi soldier, fool? Even though I don't want to be forced to deal with this foreign bitch, I'll do as you offered and speak to this cursed daughter of Satan." Mohsoun drew in a gulp of air and then called back to the American.

"I speak to the female with the loud voice who calls to speak with me. What is it you soldiers want from us, woman? We're no more than mere faithful followers of Allah's divine words, and we offer and wish no harm from anyone in my country. There are no soldiers with us, we're innocent Iraqi civilians, and I must know why the American soldiers are threatening innocent Iraqi citizens only guilty of running from endless fighting and death visiting my country."

"He's responding Walker, this is great sir. Maybe we won't be forced to kill the civilians after all, sir." Ice whispered to her commander, pleased she had the Arab man speaking to her.

"Never mind that crap, you keep talking to the dopey bastard. Ice, tell the dude all we want to do is come in their camp and search it to make certain there are no wanted insurgents hiding in their group, and no heavy weapons either. Tell the prick if we find nothing on them or any combatants in their group, they'll be free to go on their way in peace." Walker growled at Ice.

"Emir, I assure you we only want to make certain there are no insurgents hiding in your group, and your civilians have no outlawed weapons prohibited to be carried by Iraqi civilians for their protection, sir." Ice called out to Mohsoun.

"Huh, and I though these lowly American infidels were harassing us because they were looking for this young Arab woman they called Ayesha al-Qaysi. You see how the daughter of evil lies to us, Abdallah. This is why I keep telling you we can't trust a single word that spews forth from the American witch's worthless mouth. They are incapable of speaking the truth from their foul breath, my brother."

"Be that as it may Mohsoun, the worthless fools are talking to us, and as long as they're speaking, the cursed animals are refraining from killing more of our faithful Iraqi sons and daughters." Abdallah cried as he stared into Mohsoun's unblinking and burning eyes.

"You see things in simple ways and light my desert brother. Yes, as long as the hated infidels are speaking, they're refraining from shedding more of Iraq's blood on the desert sand. Abdallah, I must concentrate on what the witch has on her evil mind, and for me to accomplish this I fear I must ignore you my brother." Mohsoun Abdella al-Assad offered as he turned his attention to where the female voice was coming from, and called to Ice in poor English.

"Foreign woman who dares to address a faithful Iraqi man like she is my equal in the matters that concern my country, what is it you want from us peaceful civilians? We offer you no threat or harm, and every man, woman, and child in my group are no insurgents. As I offered you, we are no more than faithful followers of Allah's faithful words of peace, and that's how we chose to live our lives, in peace foul woman."

"Boy these Arab's are so damn arrogant, Captain." Ice complained at her commander as she replied to the Arab's words. "Emir, all we're asking is for permission to enter your camp in the name of peace and politely search it to satisfy ourselves you are what you claim, peaceful and true followers of Allah's words of peace. We wish you no harm Emir."

For a second time Abdallah Salim Agazadek cried. "Mohsoun you must allow the hated infidels to enter our camp and search it until their hearts are content. We have nothing to hide from these lowly jackals, and we are free of crimes committed against them. Our only guilt was we fled our once peaceful village when the American animals first entered it. Mohsoun, we're charged with protecting the lives of the women and children we lead from our village. I fear if we offer the American dogs resistance, they'll use it as an excuse to slaughter us."

"If you do not be still, you'll not live long enough to see what the cursed jackals want from us, Abdallah! It is not I who makes these faithful decisions in life; it's the will of Allah, my foolish Arab Brother. I'm merely the worthless instrument in which He employs to see His will carried out faithfully on the earth. What good is our future when He shows us roads we can no longer thread upon, Abdallah? With your complaining, it's stopping me from deciding what I want and must do. I told you once and I'll repeat it one last time to you. Strap a board to your worthless back to keep your backbone straight, son of a foul jackal. Open your worthless mouth again, and I'll tie a hot bag of ash to your face." Mohsoun snarled at his second in command, and then turned to the female voice and offered.

"Lowly female, how do I know if I allow your brave soldiers to enter my camp, you'll not slaughter my people before my eyes? Why is it you want to search my people, woman? We are innocent civilians, and the only weapons we have are for protection and that is all. As you know, Iraq is a dangerous place in which to dwell. We don't only fear the Americans we fear the lowly dogs who call themselves al-Qa'eda in Iraq, or any of their foul followers. A faithful Iraqi civilian would be the fool not to leave his home with weapons for his protection, woman."

"We understand Iraq is an extremely dangerous place to live. That's the reason we're here, to bring peace and security to the innocent civilians of Iraq. Emir now is the time for trust and you must trust us. We're not here to attack good civilians of Iraq, we're here to fight the insurgents and stop the attack from anyone on any innocent civilians of your great country. Emir there'll be no harm caused to your civilians, all we want to do is search your camp to make certain no insurgents have infiltrated your group, and they're using your civilians to hide from us, sir." Ice replied and held her breath and waited for the Iraqi's reply.

Mohsoun smiled proud of the fact he was stalling the powerful American military with words. In his mind, he knew he was stalling and would allow the soldiers to enter his camp and do whatever they want to his innocent civilians, and he was completely helpless to stop them because of the power the American soldiers had in his country. Drawing in another breath, Mohsoun called out in his commanding tone.

"American female who offers me and mine life, it seems Allah has placed all the power in your arms, and I'm powerless to stop you and must bend a knee to your demands. Yes, I'll allow a few of your soldiers to enter my camp to search for what you fear is hidden within my civilians, as long as you commit this outrage in the name of peace. I warn you female soldier, I'll not disarm my defenders and if your warriors attack any unarmed man, woman, or child, we'll react against you and your foul soldiers with vengeance."

479

CHAPTER TWENTY SIX

"Emir, I'll not demand your defenders to disarm, but if your defenders are holding weapons when we enter your camp, they'll be subject to attack. I can't allow your defenders to banish weapons when my soldiers enter your camp. You have to understand the circumstances that forced my soldiers to request to search your camp in the first place, Emir. Your people can maintain their weapons as long as they're defensive weapons, offensive weapons will be confiscated if uncovered. I suggest if your defenders are in possession of Rocket Propelled Grenades, they're to leave them out in the open on the ground in plain sight, along with any other weapons classified as offensive in nature, sir.

"Emir, this is not a request it's a direct order, any weapons offensive in nature will not be allowed to be carried by any of your defenders, period. This is important and my orders have to be adhered to at all costs, Emir." Ice replied after she received the nod of approval from Walker over what she was saying to the leader of the civilian group.

"Female American soldier, I understand your caution and I assure you there are no such weapons in my camp. I'll go over this order with my defenders, and if these weapons happen to exist, they'll be laid out before your feet, and you can do whatever you want with the foul things of death for all I care. Again, there are no such weapons here, woman. We're faithful Iraqi's who had enough death visiting my country, female. I invite you to my camp and we'll share a cup of bitter tea and speak of peace returning to my land of deserts. When do you want to start your lowly search of my people and camp, woman?"

Mohsoun replied, amazed he was speaking so friendly and reassuring to the female invader.

"Emir, we wish to begin our search of your people immediately. Time is of the essence I fear."

"So be it then, you may come to my camp with twenty of your soldiers and begin your search." Mohsoun replied while allowing a trace of anger to creep into his tone.

Walker grabbed Ice by the arm and stopped her from answering the Iraqi, and he growled at the Mutt. "Hey dog man, drop back and get the Doc up here, and tell him to take the instruments he needs to detect any trace of that fucking bug bomb, man."

"Yeah Walker, I'll have him bring up the instrument Ice was playing with before, man."

Ice gave the Mutt a terrible look that did not allow him to respond, and the Mutt took off to get the doctor to be one of the people who would enter the Iraqi camp. In seconds, the Mutt was back by Walker's side and he had the doctor and a biological agent detector in his hands.

Walker glared at the civilian doctor because he was still angry they were stuck taking him on this mission as he snorted at the man. "Doc, you're one of the people who's gonna enter that dump. I'm assigning the stinking Mutt to protect your ass out there. You got that Mutt?" Walker turned to his friend and added. "Mutt, if the Doc hasta take a dump, you help him."

"You got it man, who else is coming wit us?" The Mutt asked Walker.

"As I call out your names, you people betta muster behind my ass double quick. Ghost and Hunter, Neck, Buckethead, Roach, Blind Date, Caviar, Siberia, Wacko, Mother Flanagan, CoCo, McNip, and Blood Clot, I want you people in there in case any Iraqi assholes are hurt, you're to help them. Baby Tee, you're with us, Snatch and you too Sweat Stain, that's makes twenty one including myself, the Mutt, Ice, Ramirez and the Doc over there. The rest of you are to keep an eye on us, and if we're forced to open up on them scumbags, you people betta take out any lousy pricks we don't get right off. Ghost, Hunter, you two will lead the way and the rest of us will protect your flank. Okay let's shove off and get this fucking thing over with, so we can get the hell outta Dodge and back to the real world." Walker snapped as he stood up and the two pointmen moved out in front of the others. The soldiers moved out like soldiers prepared to defend themselves against any attack.

"Mohsoun, look at how many cursed infidels are there, and see how many are coming at us. The lowly jackals seem like they're coming to slaughter us." Abdallah warned as he took a step back and seemed like he was one step from running.

Mohsoun ignored Agazadek's words as he stared at the heavily armed soldiers coming at him. Ice maintained eye contact with the Iraqi responding to her words, and walked right at him.

The Ghost and Hunter split off and they walked past Mohsoun with one soldier walking on both sides of the Iraqi leader. Ice and Walker stopped before Mohsoun and Ice offered. "Emir, this soldier to my right is my Commander, and his name is Captain Robert Walker."

Walker put out his hand and Mohsoun shook it as he offered. "So I see you know many ways of us Arabs, Commander. A hand is the first thing you offer. Captain Robert Walker, my name is Mohsoun Abdella al-Assad, and I'm the one placed in command of these civilians from our Elder. I'm entrusted with their lives and will protect them at all costs, Captain."

When the Iraqi leader identified himself to Walker, he looked at the Mutt and Lieutenant Frank Hall understood the silent order and left the two men alone. The Mutt rushed back to his One Charlie Radio Operator, and he had Roach open up a line with the CIA Agent, so he could get information they had on a Mohsoun Abdella al-Assad that Walker might be able to use against the unsuspecting Iraqi when he began to interrogate him in earnest.

Walker was pleased the Arab was speaking English that was poor at best, but at least he was able to understand the man when he spoke as he replied. "Mohsoun, we wish you no harm and we'll try and make this imposition as painless as possible for your people. How are you people making out, do you have enuf water and food? Mohsoun, you're free to return to your village, I have soldiers there who'll feed and look afta your injured. As long as you're no threat to my soldiers, we're no threat to you and your people. I'd like to start my search of your camp, that way I can leave and you can lead your people back to their village. The fighting is over and my soldiers are looking afta any of your wounded, sir."

"You are a concerned Commander for an infidel, Captain Robert Walker." Mohsoun replied with a smirk and then went on with his words. "Alas Captain Walker, we are quickly running out of clean drinking water and food, and I'd appreciate any provisions you can spare for us. I was planning to keep my people out in the desert until your soldiers leave our village, and then I was going to bring my people back home."

"I'm afraid I was forced to leave a number of my soldiers in your village until my mission is completed in Iraqi. Mohsoun; my soldiers will not harm any of your civilians if you return them to the village on their own. I think it'd be awful foolish to keep these women and children in the middle of the desert while waiting for my soldiers to depart your town. I have no idea how long my operation might take." Walker replied politely to the Iraqi man.

"What is your true mission in my village, Captain Robert Walker?" Mohsoun asked while trying to gleam information about what so many American soldiers were doing in this area of Iraq. As far as he was lead to believe, this section of Iraq was basically free from American military operations because there were few if any insurgent attacks in the area.

"I'm not at liberty to divulge the reason for my soldiers to be in this area of your country, Mohsoun. When I'm positive what I'm looking for isn't with your civilians, your people will be free to return to their village in peace. In fact Mohsoun, I must insist you return your civilians to the village. If you want, I can leave you with an armed detail, and they can escort your people to the village." Walker made the offer, but he left no doubt in Mohsoun's mind it was an order.

Mohsoun nodded, giving Walker the impression he was going to comply with his order, and return his people to the village under escort, as he watched Walker's soldiers spreading out and start to search the countless items his people carried to the desert. Mohsoun picked up one middle aged man who did not act like a soldier, and he was being assisted by a few soldiers who entered his camp. The uncomfortable looking soldier was aiming what looked more like a medical instrument than a weapon at his people he passed at his camp.

Walker picked up what caught Mohsoun's attention and smiled as he watched Doctor Joel Russbinder checking the civilians for possible containment from the item they were looking for.

The Captain decided to break Mohsoun's attention aimed at Doctor Russbinder as he removed a warm bottle of water from his overstuffed fieldpack, and he offered it to the parched looking Iraqi man as he remarked. "Here you go Mohsoun, you look like you could sure use some water to drink, man. We'll be outta your hair soon enuf and then you can lead your people back to the village in peace under my protection. I hate to say this Mohsoun, but I can tell you still don't trust my people very much, sir."

"Yes Captain Robert Walker, I fear the Iraqi peoples will never trust any infidels and non-believers. As it is written in our sacred book of the Holy Qur'an, Captain Walker, 'O Believers! Take not the Jews or Christians as friends, for they are but one another's friends only.'"

"Yeah Mohsoun, I read your sacred Holy Book, and I understand you can interpret the sacred words and fashion them into whatever you want them to believe. Your Holy Book preaching death to anyone who is not Islamic, but the words I remember the best goes like this, and I see these words offering tolerance. They were spoken by Prophet Muhammad in his final years of life and understanding. 'Allah tells humankind he has made you into nations and Tribes, so that you might come to know one another'. Mohsoun."

"Captain Robert Walker, you cannot make me believe Allah or Muhammad wanted we Arabs to live side by side in peace with the hated Jews of the world."

"Mohsoun, if you read the words written in your Holy Qur'an, the way they were meant to be read, you'll see the Christians and Jews received a favorable position in the Islamic tradition as 'the people of the Book' and the Holy Qur'an repeatedly stated the Christians and Jews are eligible for salvation." Walker was willing to trade verse for verse of the Holy Qur'an with Mohsoun, to get him to relax his angry stance against him.

"I see I might be forced to change my most unfavorable opinion of you, Captain Robert Walker. Because it does my heart good to see a lowly infidel, a non-believer and Crusader aimed against we Arabs, has taken time to read the sacred words of Allah's faithful messenger, Muhammad. But alas, through the eyes of a non-believer I see you have missed interpreted the words of the Holy Qur'an, and what those words truly mean to we Arabs. We're ordered to kill all polytheists wherever we may find them…"

"Yes, I understand those words are printed in the Holy Qur'an, and they're written somewhat in our Holy Bible, Mohsoun. Our Bible states, 'you shall annihilate them, the Hittites, the Amonrites, the Canaanites, the Perrizztes, the Hivites and the Jebusites as your Lord and God has commanded you.' But in the Holy Qur'an if you read further, you'll come across a passage that softens Allah's harsh stance against the non-believers of the world when it's stated, 'To you be your religion; to me be my religion.' Correct me if I'm wrong, but I believe Muhammad is saying the Islamic world should be more tolerant about uther religions of the world."

"Ahhh my young infidel, you give me good battle of understandings of the Holy Qur'an. But I fear now is not the time or the place to get involved in such discussing religious beliefs and understanding, Captain Robert Walker. I must ask you again what is the reason for your warriors to invade my camp? I brought my people out here to save them for your loathsome attack aimed against my village."

Walker knew what he was doing with the Iraqi after meeting him. He was trying to gain Mohsoun's trust so he could interrogate the Iraqi man without his knowing what he was up to against him. That's why he engaged Mohsoun in the phrases of the Holy Qur'an. Walker was trained for weeks in the ways of interrogation, both non-invasive, and the more harsh ways to gain needed information for a prisoner. Here he planned to use the friendly ways of persuasion, and if that failed then he was prepared to use the harsher interrogation methods on the Iraqi. His driving force was to discover if the woman and biological agent was in the camp without his having to rip the entire place apart to find them. He wanted the Iraqi in a friendlier mood in case the woman and biological item was removed from the camp by her.

All the while he was speaking with Mohsoun, in the back of his mind he was going over the interrogation methods he intended to employ against the unsuspecting man. He understood he had to use friendly persuasions because he had no intention, or time to employ the use of the harsher sleep deprivation, or slapping the man across the face, and hollowing threats of more pain inflected on his body, or forcing the Iraqi to walking around until he was thoroughly exhausted. No water boarding event, even though he was prepared to use harsher and more painful methods than he planned, if he did not get the requested information from the Iraqi. That's why he gave Mohsoun the water when he first met the man. Sometimes that was all that was needed to make someone talk. That's why he gave the Iraqi his name and rank in the service, it was geared to gain Mohsoun's trust. He was hoping the water was the turning point to get this Iraqi to talk to him truthfully.

Walker knew there was no definitive textbook on the proper ways to interrogate a dangerous prisoner, and he was taught the usual nineteen techniques commonly employed in most interrogations which ranged from real or emotional rewards for truthful replies from the prisoner. To the employing of repeating questions so many times the subject becomes bored to death, and he finally answers questions put to the prisoner candidly. He also realized he did not have the luxury of time to go this route.

He planned to use the more emotional approach with Mohsoun, and he would work on his over inflated ego by flattering his command he had over his civilians, or if he had to attack his competency and leadership over his people, or even force Mohsoun to defend the way he was trying to protect his horde of civilians under his command and protection, and give up his information that way if at all possible. He understood he could not go too far with this line of interrogation on the Arab man. He did not want to end up humiliating and degrading the subject so much and run the risk of Mohsoun completely shutting down on him and refusing to answer any further questions of the Iraqi man.

Walker had to break down the psychological barrier between the Iraqi and himself, so he started to speak about the Holy Qur'an with Mohsoun. He entered the cat and mouse game with his Arab prisoner who did not even understand he was a prisoner. Walker searched his mind for a common bond with the Iraqi to further forward his friendship, and he was even prepared to lie to the man. He knew if he could convince Mohsoun he knew everything about him, his family or anything else he could learn about the man. He would enjoy a positive advantage over the Iraqi. Any advantage would work out in his favor, and once Mohsoun felt Walker knew everything about him, there was no need for him to resist or withhold any further information from the American soldier. That was why he sent the Mutt off to learn what he could about Mohsoun from the CIA Agent, and now he was looking over his shoulder waiting for the Mutt's return.

He understood if he was forced to apply pain to the subject, he would rapidly lose control of the situation, the subject to be interrogated and himself. Nevertheless he was prepared to resort to pain and torture and other harsher techniques, if Mohsoun refused to tell him what he knew of the missing Iraqi woman and biological item. Because Walker was classifying this situation as an emergency because of the time factor he was working under.

Mohsoun broke Walker's concentration when he asked him. "Captain Robert Walker, I hope your soldiers will take care when they approach our women. I fear a most unpleasant reaction from a male if he feels your soldiers are taking liberties with our women."

"Huh? Yeah, right, okay buddy. Look Mohsoun I know how you people respect your women as it should be, and I assure you that none of my soldiers will dare insult your women needlessly. Mohsoun, you hafta understand I'm here not of my own want, I was ordered to come to your country by my government. I'd much rather be back in my country having a beer and sitting my crack in the sand on a beach, than be here hassling your people, sir." Walker was lying through his eye teeth because he was trying to convince Mohsoun he had no other choice but to be in Iraq following orders from his commanders.

Mohsoun looked hard in Walker's eyes for a moment, and then he replied. "Do you know Captain Robert Walker I happen to believe your words ring with the sound of truth to them. I feel if you had a choice in the decision, you would never have invaded my country. Now I wonder how many of your other soldiers I once hated, were forced into this unholy Crusade. Captain Walker, many men from my country fell victim to our own government's dreadful orders. There are thousands of men who would have never lifted a weapon in anger against any country, if it wasn't for the orders given by President Saddam Hussein."

Walker had all he could do not to smile at the Iraqi prisoner. He noticed the tension in Mohsoun's shoulders leave. He found himself thinking, 'God dammit I got your ass, you're gonna tell me everything I need to know, and you're not gonna know you're doing it, stupid.'

The Mutt rushed back to Walker and waited for him to acknowledge his presence. The Captain looked and the instant he noticed the Mutt standing behind him, he turned to his prisoner and offered. "Will you excuse me for a moment Mohsoun, one of my soldiers has a problem and I hafta help him with it right away, sir."

"Yes, please look after your soldier, Captain Robert Walker." Mohsoun replied as he lifted the bottle of water Walker handed him, and took a good pull of the warm water.

Walker turned and placed his hand on the Mutt's shoulder as he led him out of earshot of the Iraqi prisoner. Once the two were far enough from the Arab, Walker asked the Mutt. "Please tell me you were able to find out something on this fucking pain in the ass Iraqi bastard, man."

"I sure did, the CIA had a file on his ass and his family." The Mutt went over everything he was found out about Mohsoun, and when he finished his report, Walker grumbled at his soldier.

"Man that was good. Mutt, I want you with me but not standing by my side. Hang back a few feet and act like you're not paying attention to what I'm speaking to this popping jay about."

"You got it Walker." The Mutt replied as the two soldiers walked back to Mohsoun.

When he was by Mohsoun's side again, he asked the unknowing prisoner. "How you doing with the water, you need another bottle Mohsoun?"

"Yes please Captain Robert Walker, I did not understand how thirsty I truly was."

Walker handed the Iraqi another bottle of water and before Mohsoun opened it, he offered. "Mohsoun, you took great care of the civilians in your trust. It takes a great leader of people to be able to carry out what you have done for them." Walker was inflating Mohsoun's ego by flattering him. He noticed the prisoner's chest swell with pride and he went on with his words.

"Mohsoun, the only reason I'm forced to hassle you is because I was ordered to locate a certain Iraqi woman, and take what she has in her possession and bring it and her to my Commander. The sooner I locate this woman and missing item, the sooner we can get the hell outta your hair." As Walker spoke to Mohsoun, he removed the wrinkled picture of Ayesha al-Qaysi and flashed it at Mohsoun and then he went on with his words. "This is the woman I'm searching for, and if she gave up to us when she discovered we wanted to speak with her. It woulda not been necessary for my troops to enter your village in the first place and destroy so much of it. Mohsoun, I know how your people never give up another Iraqi, but in this case you hafta look at it she's the reason for the destruction of your village. She took something that's extremely important to my government, and we're here to have the item returned to us.

"Mohsoun, I know fifteen uther members of your family are currently being held in Iraqi prisons for various crimes they're accused of. I know your wife fled Iraq for the safety offered by Syria, until the fighting ran its course in Iraq. I further understand you have two boys missing since the commencement of the Iraqi Freedom action. Mohsoun, if you help me locate this woman and missing item she has in her possession, I promise before I leave your country in peace, I'll have my people find your two boys, and make it possible to have your wife return to your home in Iraq. Furthermore Mohsoun, I'll do everything in my power to gain the release of most if not all of your relatives being held in Iraqi jails. What do you say Mohsoun, are you willing to help me locate this woman and item?"

Mohsoun Abdella al-Assad could not hide the astonished look over the knowledge this American soldier had on him and his family. As Walker hoped, the Iraqi felt there was no sense holding anything back from this Marine. Drawing in a breath, Mohsoun let his air out slowly as he replied. "Captain Robert Walker, I am forced to admit I don't know this woman."

Instantly, Walker puffed up and acted like he was going to blow up, but Mohsoun's actions stopped him from getting angry at the prisoner when he held up his hand and offered.

"Please Captain, don't allow yourself anger until you have heard all my words. Captain Walker, may I have another look at the picture of the young Iraqi woman you want to speak with. Perhaps if I don't recognize her, but someone else from my group will know her, and if I show them the picture they'll respond truthfully to me."

"Yeah sure Mohsoun, here you go as long as you're going to help me."

"Believe me Captain Robert Walker, I have every intention of helping you locating this missing Iraqi woman and what she might have stolen from your government, because by helping you, I'm also helping myself and my honorable family." Mohsoun replied as he took the picture from the American Officer and rubbed his chin with his other hand and then grumbled. "Yes, it is like I have stated Captain Walker, I have no real knowledge of this woman from the village. But there is one person who knows everyone who lived in the village of ar-Ramadi."

Mohsoun turned away from Walker and called out. "Abdallah Salim Agazadek, I need your assistance." After calling out, Walker and Mohsoun waited until the Iraqi man came forward.

What seemed like a short lifetime as Walker waited for the man to step forward, he noticed some movement in the crowd who gathered around their leader.

A second elderly Iraqi man stepped forward and walked over to Mohsoun and bowed to the leader of the horde as he brought the tips of his fingers up and kissed them. Upon seeing his friend, Mohsoun announced for the benefit of Walker.

"Ahhh… my old desert friend, allow me to introduce you to Captain Robert Walker, Commander of these American soldiers who have entered our camp, and they are offering our people water and food. Abdallah, this man Captain Robert Walker, has a few questions to ask of you. My wise desert brother I'm instructing you to answer his questions of you faithfully and truthfully. Please Abdallah, he is of no threat to us and our people gathered here and waiting for you to help the American Captain."

Abdallah Salim Agazadek was shaken to his very soul because he could not fathom why Mohsoun was ordering him to assist the hated invaders to his country. After knowing Mohsoun for much of his life, he felt Mohsoun would die with a weapon locked in hand fighting the god cursed Crusaders. Shaking his head to get his concentration back on Mohsoun, Abdallah stood dumbly before him and Walker.

"Do not stand there like a foolish woman sharing gossip at the watering well. This American soldier is looking for a foolish young Iraqi woman who committed the crime of thief against his government. The Captain has assured me once they take this woman and thing she stole from them in custody, the soldiers will leave us in peace. Abdallah, the American soldiers are more interested in this woman then they are with the lives of our wards. Please my brother, you must look at the picture of the foul woman, and then tell the American Captain if you know of this woman, and where she might be hiding from them."

Again, Abdallah remained standing by Mohsoun without uttering a word to either man.

Mohsoun understood the dilemma Abdellah was suffering from and he respected the man for wanting to hold his tongue, and display loyalty the Iraqi people were well noted for. Knowing this forced Mohsoun to draw in a breath and order. "Abdallah, you must free your tongue and tell this American if you know of the woman on this picture. Here, you must look at this picture and you must answer truthfully if you know of this woman and where she might be hiding…"

"And, who the hell she is with, buster." The Mutt called out from behind Walker.

Walker and Mohsoun gave the Mutt a terrible look for throwing his two cents in. Then Mohsoun added. "Abdallah, pay no attention to the other soldier, you must obey my command and tell me if it'll make you feel better by admitting if you know this foul woman."

Mohsoun's order to Abdallah caused a few other males of the group to grumble over Mohsoun ordering Abdallah to help their sworn enemy of life. A stern look from Mohsoun quieted the angry mood as he waited for Abdallah to look at the picture of the woman he was offering him. Finally, Mohsoun growled at his friend. "Abdallah, take the foul picture of the cursed woman and see if you recognize her face, and if you know where this worthless creature is hiding."

Abdallah took the picture and looked at it. Fear flooded him because he immediately recognized the woman and he was aware her father went to the United States to follow his want to seek revenge on the heads of the hated American soldiers who invaded Iraq two years ago. Abdallah knew Ayesha's father lost his life in the United States for the sake of Iraq, and now he feared these American soldiers were here to finish their revenge by murdering Ayesha who was guilty of being Colonel Hamoodi al-Qaysi's favorite daughter.

Mohsoun realized Abdallah recognized the woman and remarked. "Come, I can see by your look you know this woman. You must tell me who she is and where this woman is hiding, fool."

Abdallah heard a woman's voice but he did not know the soldier Ice, was translating every word being said between the two Iraqi males to her commander, Captain Walker.

Finally, Abdallah gave in and he replied. "Mohsoun, this worthless woman is Ayesha al-Qaysi. Her family has lived in ar-Ramadi for countless generations."

"That's good you were able to place a name to the face for the American Commander. You must tell me where this worthless woman is hiding in our group, Abdallah."

Drawing in a gulp of air, Abdallah responded. "Alas Mohsoun, I know Ayesha al-Qaysi is not among the civilians we protect. I saw her and four others heading for the desert when the American soldiers first entered our village and slaughter our friends and families. Two were males, and two were women. The five fools turned to the east halfway here from the village."

"Please my brother, take the inflammatory words from your spirit, they serve to upset our brother and sisters. We must help the Americans and in return, they'll help us survive in our country." Mohsoun was intent helping Walker he completely sold out the rest of his people.

Ice informed Walker the five people they were after were not among the civilians they trapped in the camp. She also told him the man speaking with Mohsoun, informed him the five Iraqi's cut off and were heading east about five miles behind their position.

Walker realized the five people he wanted had to be the ones who made the other footprints in the sand, and he had the Mutt place the position in his GPS. That system will bring them right back to where the five fleeing Iraqi people turned off on them. The upset Captain stuck the whistle in his mouth and then he gave three loud blasts on it. Then he watched as his specialized soldiers quickly assembled and he then informed the troops.

"okay people listen up, the ones we want aren't here so we hafta hotfoot it five miles back and pickup their trail. At least we know where these assholes are heading. Saddle up, we're moving out in two, and I mean two minutes. Any soldier who has extra water or MRE's (Meals Ready to Eat) you can spare, leave them with Mohsoun. Let's get a move on it while we have daylight left to operate. Mutt, I wanna see your ass up here immediately. I need you and your GPS, buddy."

Walker did not realize it, but the Mutt was standing right behind him, and when he laid his hand on his shoulder, Walker jumped and then spun around and took a stance warning the Mutt he was going to take his head off his shoulders.

"Hey Homes take it fucking easy man, it's only me and you called me, old buddy."

"Jesus H. Christ, how the hell many fucking times do I hafta tell ya never sneak up behind me like that, dog man? I coulda blown your damn head offa your shoulders. God damn man. Mutt, you're enuf to give a fucking headache to a stinking Aspirin." Walker was ignoring Mohsoun and his civilians. His soldiers were not ignoring them as they assembled before him, one out of every two soldiers kept an eye glued on the civilians as they moved closer around Mohsoun.

"Calm down Walker, what the hell's up with you man? You wanted me, buddy." The Mutt moaned as he tried to get his commanding officer to relax.

"Hey pal, you still have the position locked in your GPS where we picked up the uther stinking footprints we came across heading for this fucking place, man?" Walker growled at him.

"Sure I do Walker, whatdaya think I woulda done with the damn thing, erase them man? You ordered me to save them and that's what I did, Homes." The Mutt grumbled at Walker.

"Don't bust my fucking horns right now. I'm not in the stinking mood for your usual bit of bullshit, buddy. Pull up the coordinates and lead the way back to the damn things. Those damn prints are where the assholes we want turned off on us. You head out while I start the others following ya. First I gotta get Tracker One and inform the ATO Colonel where we're heading. Mutt, while you have our people leaving, order them to keep an eye on these pains in the ass. While we're moving out is a perfect time for the assholes to try something against us. If they try, mow them down and carry on with your orders as received."

"Don't talk about it, be about it Walker. You worry about getting in contact with the puke, and I'll take command of our troops and when you're finished with the Colonel, catch up with our asses. Don't worry about these slugs Walker, if they try to go hot on our asses while we're leaving, they'll receive a wall of lead for their fucking trouble." The Mutt replied confidently as he started to work on his portable Global Positioning System.

"It's about time you took some of this stinking crap offa my shoulders, dog man. Where the hell's Roach hiding at, I need him?" Walker roared at his other troopers in earshot of him.

"I'm right behind ya as ordered man, but after seeing how you reacted against the Mutt when he stepped up, I'll be dipped in shit if I'm gonna walk up behind ya, man." Roach complained.

"Cut the shit out and get your ass up here. I gotta get in contact with Tracker One."

"Hey man, I had an open key with Tracker One all the while we were in this camp, sir. I was keeping in contact with Tracker One, in case we ran into any trouble with these assholes and we needed his weapon system's help, Walker."

"Great, give me the mike." Walker waited for the soldier to give him the mike. When he had it, he moved away from Mohsoun Abdella al-Assad and the rest of his civilians, so the Iraqi leader could not hear what he was saying to his ATO spotter. Walker hated being around these Iraqi civilians.

"Tracker One, Searcher One. Come in Tracker One. Over."

"This is Tracker One, go with your traffic Searcher One. Over." Colonel Pullman replied.

"Tracker One listen up. We just received word from an Iraqi puke on where the five slugs we want went. I have my people saddling up and preparing to move afta these damn assholes. I'm gonna send you a set of number on the GPS coordinates, these numbers are where the five turned off some five miles back of my present Papa, Papa (location). I need your weapon's platform overhead then in front of my troops. I want you to locate these people then lead our asses to them, Colonel. Before you head off Tracker One, how are you doing with munitions and fuel? I can't afford to have you run out when I might need your air support platform down here, sir."

"Tracker One to Searcher One, I'm fine with munitions and fuel for five hours flight time, sir. I've been in contact with Command and requested they deliver fuel to my location and have it in the area if and when I need some it'll be available, Searcher One. They're also shipping out extra munitions for my platform in case we have need, Searcher One. Over." Colonel Pullman reported to his temporary commanding officer.

"That's using your head Tracker One, glad to have you on board. Tracker One, here's the coordinates as stated, Charlie, Five, Five, One, at Bravo, One, Niner, Niner. Repeat coordinates as received Tracker One. Over." Walker ordered the Colonel over the mike.

"Roger that Searcher One, coordinates I received follows; Charlie, Five, Five, One, at Bravo, One, Niner, Niner. Are these coordinates correct as repeated, Searcher One?" Colonel Pullman replied as he watched his pilot place the coordinates in the helicopter's GPS.

"Roger you last, your GPS coordinates are correct as repeated, Tracker One. Over." Walker informed the Colonel. He wanted to make certain he was heading for the right location.

"Very well Searcher One, when do you want me to commence carrying out these orders, sir?"

"That's a good question Tracker One. Here's what I want. You're instructed to stay over my position until my troops are out of this camp. You're to remain ready air cap overhead until we placed enuf distance between my troops and these damn civilian. Once we're clear of the pains in the ass, you'll commence to carry out my uther orders. Do you copy all as stated, Tracker One? Over."

"Roger that and understand orders, Searcher One. Over."

"Roger Tracker One, follow orders as stated, good luck. Over."

Walker cast a quick look at Tracker One as the helicopter hovered over his position about a thousand feet in altitude, and smiled as he noticed the weapons hanging ominously off the pods and hard point of the rotary aircraft. He was relieved to have such a powerful weapon platform supporting his mission. When he had enough with the helicopter, he ordered the Mutt to move his troops out as he walked over to Mohsoun and offered to the Arab.

"Mohsoun, it was a pleasure to meet with you and I thank you for your help with this situation. Mohsoun, I'll remember my pledge and I'm a man of my word, and I'll do everything in my power to get your family out of jail and get your wife back to you as well." Walker offered as he struggled to keep a straight face while he spoke with the elderly leader, because he knew the moment he walked away from the Arab, he was going to forget his name.

Mohsoun had the dumb look plastered on his face because he did not relay the words of Abdallah, and he had no idea how he had just helped the young American soldier in his quest.

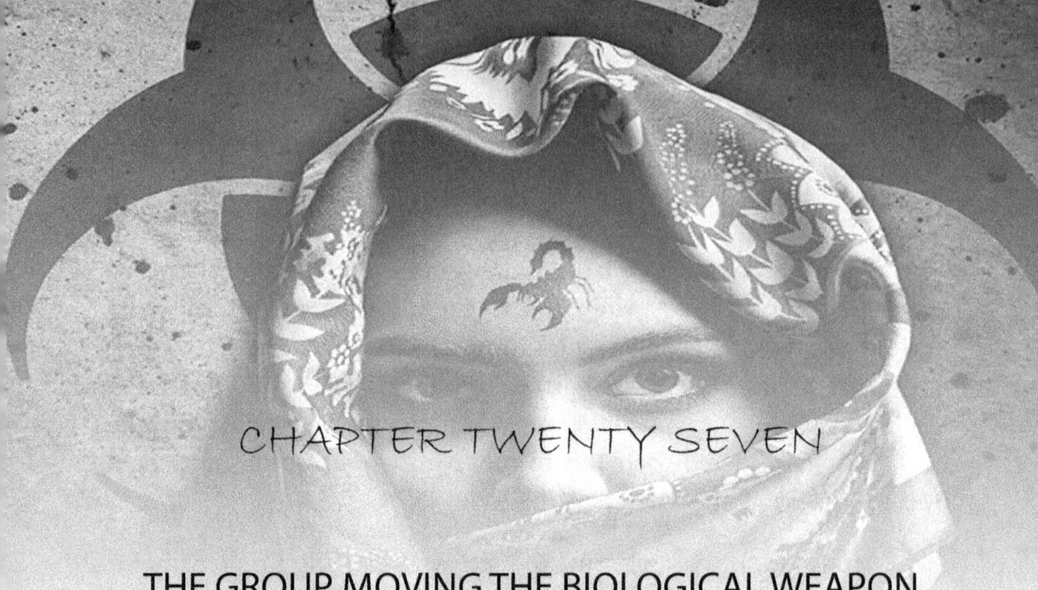

THE GROUP MOVING THE BIOLOGICAL WEAPON

Ayesha al-Qaysi struggled mightily with her efforts to stay in step with the much stronger General Mustafa Abdelhadi while carrying the heavy metal cylinder, as the Iraqi General pushed his people as fast as he could possibly move them forward. He was fearful the American soldiers likely picked up his trail, and they were rapidly closing in on them from behind. For the past half hour he never once looked behind him to see how Ayesha, or her two friends were making out following him. He knew Mugrada al-Sistani who was pulling up his rear would call out if the three women were having problems.

Ayesha stumbled and fell to the sand and ended up rolling down the side of the sand dune they were walking on the crest of for easier walking in the sand. Instantly, Shafiqu al-Quraishy yelled at the General to warn him of Ayesha's fall and sliding down the dune. "General Abdelhadi for the love of Allah, you must give us time to rest. Ayesha has fallen and I must assist my sister. General Abdelhadi, we must stop for a few moments and rest, sir."

General Abdelhadi growled at the angry Shafiqu as she rushed to Ayesha's side to help her, knowing the woman was afraid the sand might cover over the fallen Ayesha as he roared at Shafiqu. "God cursed foul woman who dares to order me like she had divine right of command over a man. Take care in your foul words you address me with woman, or I'll order your loathsome back opened with the bite of the lash. Help your worthless friend, but make certain the Sword of God is not buried by the sand. I'll give you women five minutes of rest, and then we'll start on our trek again."

General Mustafa Abdelhadi watched as Shafiqu moved to Ayesha's side and brushed the sand from her eyes and mouth. Ayesha was having trouble breathing and hurt her hand when she fell. When her senses came back, she started to look for the cylinder she lost when she tumbled down the side of the sand dune. Fear filled her as she searched for the stainless steel cylinder, she did not start to breathe normally again until she noticed Sadiya coming down the sand dune, in her hands she carried the metal cylinder.

Shafiqu helped Ayesha to her feet and when Sadiya reached the two of them at the bottom of the dune, Ayesha immediately and greedily pulled the cylinder out of her hands and hugged the object to her chest as if Sadiya had no right to touch the cylinder with her hands. Then Ayesha looked at General Abdelhadi and noticed he and Mugrada were standing on the crest of the dune looking down at her with nasty grins on their parched lips. Neither of the men offered any assistance to her or her two friends, as they waited for them to join them back on the crest of the sand dune. Ayesha cursed not only these two conceited Arab men, she also cursed all men because of the way they treated women.

Ayesha struggled up the loose sand of the dune while trying to maintain control of the cylinder, and it was only with the help of her two friends was she able to reach the top. She was suffering exhaustion and none had any water to drink for over two hours. Fighting her sheer exhaustion, she stood proudly before General Abdelhadi and she glared at the once powerful Iraqi military officer which prompted the General to snarl at her savagely. "You dare much, foolish woman born from the pits of the underworld of Satan to look upon me in such a foul and disgusting manner. If it was not for my duty to protect you, I'd order you staked down to the sand, and allow the desert scavengers of the night to have their evil way with your loathsome being, for daring to look at me like you are, woman. Allah's gift or not, I'd beat you to death with my bare hands if you look at me again in this foul manner, evil one who has made love to the scorpion." General Abdelhadi looked hard in Ayesha's eyes and waited for her reply.

Ayesha realized she might have just overstepped her bounds with the Iraqi Officer, and she bowed contritely as she offered. "General Abdelhadi, savor of my country, please excuse this worthless woman for daring to disrespect you so. I'd gladly receive the sting of the lash to atone for my disrespect I have offered you. My defense is merely that I'm extremely exhausted, and in desperate need of rest and water to help quench my unending thirst on this day. How much longer do we have to walk before we get to the help you mentioned was waiting for us?"

He was deeply impressed with Ayesha addressing him as the savor of Iraq, and that remark softened his angry stance against the woman. Then General Abdelhadi replied in a much calmer tone of voice. "Yes my foolish young daughter of the desert, our trek has caused all of us to suffer for the sake of Iraq. I've been trying to conserve the water remaining for our use, but what good will the water be if we die from lack of it, and the water is left to the scavengers of the land. Yes Ayesha, we'll rest as you have suggested and finish our water supply. I know we're but a mile or two away from the ones who'll offer us their protection from the hated American soldiers surely following us, woman. Sit down and take the weight from your feet and drink from the skin of life I offer you. We'll rest until our strength returns to us, woman."

General Abdelhadi offered Ayesha the goat bladder containing the last of their water supply. She was shocked by the slight amount of water remaining for them to survive on, and she barely wet her lips with the life giving hot liquid, before offering the almost empty bladder back to the General. Ayesha's drinking so little water again impressed the once feared Iraqi Officer, he was certain she would have drank greedily the remaining water, and left none for the other women.

General Mustafa Abdelhadi looked at the other exhausted women and offered Shafiqu the bladder of water first. He felt this woman was worth keeping alive because he was not happy with the last woman.

All she did was complain about everything happening to them on their venture in the desert. The General watched as Shafiqu did as Ayesha and barely drank enough water to wet the inside of her mouth, he then watched as Shafiqu offered the bladder to the last one from their group, Sadiya. This woman drank a good mouthful which reassured the Iraqi Officer this woman was not worth saving as he suspected as he got to know her during their trek.

When the bladder was returned to the General he shook it and noticed there was at least two mouthfuls of water left, and he offered the bladder to Mugtada who waved it off as he knew he would. Pulling in a lung full of hot air to settle himself down, General Abdelhadi refrained from drinking the last bit of their water supply. He felt like Mugtada that they should be the strongest of the five, and leave the water for the women, so they could survive until they reached the others who would protect them from the pursuing American soldiers he knew were close.

Ayesha's lips were so dry when she opened her mouth to drink water, her cracked lips started to bleed. To the General's surprise because he felt she did not have the strength to speak, she asked him. "General Abdelhadi, how much further is it to the fighters who'll protect us from the cursed infidels pursuing us, and who'll know how to properly employ Allah's great gift to where it will do the most damage to our hated enemy of Iraq, sir?"

"Ahhh... my faithful Iraqi daughter, you have greatly impressed me with the show of strength you offer to our just cause, woman. If I didn't know better, I'd swear to Allah's hand I was dealing with a well trained male soldier, rather than with a lowly woman. But alas evil woman, we're but a few miles away from the fighters whom I know are in this section of the desert. They live to assist us, woman."

"Then I don't believe we should waste any further time resting when our helpers are so near. If it's as you have informed me General Abdelhadi. The foul American Crusaders are trailing us then we must reach the safety offered by these desert fighters willing to offer us help, sir." With that said Ayesha stood on exhausted legs, and stepped out before the general sitting on the sand.

General Mustafa Abdelhadi remained seated on the sand and watched Ayesha until she walked nearly fifteen yards ahead of him. Shaking his head, he rose and barked at the others still seated on the sand behind him. "Come you wasted camel eating fools, I fear Ayesha is setting the pace we must follow. If this woman is able to continue walking, it's our duty to do likewise, and follow her to the safety offered by our other desert fighters. If you female creatures have not the strength to follow us, prepare your souls to feed the cursed desert night scavengers, I'll not offer you any further assistance from this point forward. We're on our own except for Ayesha. She's the only one decreed by Allah's breath to survive, until we reached our fellow desert brothers who'll protect us from the evil infidel pursuers."

The Iraqi Military Officer followed Ayesha, but his steps were larger and in a few strides, he caught up to and passed Ayesha without word, as he assumed the lead for the group again.

The rag tag wanders walked another mile and a half from where they rested on the sand when General Abdelhadi caught out of the corner of his eye, an Arab man suddenly duck behind a low sand dune. Instantly, the alert officer moved his weapon from his back until it rested properly in his hands to protect himself. The trailing security guard noticed the action of his General and he did likewise and moved his weapon until it was in his hands ready for use. Mugtada al-Sistane realized his General noticed something that caused him alarm before them, and Mugrada was now acting like an alert soldier ready to defend his wards and Allah's gift with his life.

After five more steps, General Abdelhadi picked up another fighter. He looked to his left and picked up another man dressed in a desert robe watching them. He turned to his right and picked up another fighter and realized they finally reached the ones he searched of. He raised his hand and bellowed to his exhausted survivors. "You'll stop walking, we reached our help."

The General turned his attention and aimed it at the desert fighter who did nothing try to conceal himself from his view. "You, my desert brother who holds a weapon like we're a threat against you, we're survivors of the loathsome attack by the evil American invaders who destroyed the village of ar-Ramadi. We have successfully escaped their slaughter and ventured to this section of the desert seeking your help. You great fool who does not react to my words, I am General Mustafa Abdelhadi of President Saddam Hussein's Republican Guard, and I demand to speak to your leader. I am waiting for some kind of response from you, are you deaf, or do you not possess the manners to respond to another faithful follower of the Sunni Religion?"

The fighter still did not react to the angry sounding General's words as he just stared at him.

Drawing in another breath, General Abdelhadi was about to yell at the fighter again, when another voice suddenly called out to him in a commanding tone. "General Abdelhadi, I see you're still nothing more than a large bag of wind and countless foul orders and words. It is I, General Ahmed al-Shugairi, and I was ordered to your endless desert to help our Sunni brothers in their ongoing fight against the cursed invaders to Iraq. I trust you'll remember your desert brother from long ago, General Abdelhadi?"

Instantly, General Abdelhadi relaxed his guard as he replied to the unseen voice. "Do you think I'm but a foul camel merchant that I would not remember my brother over these many decades? Of course I remember my Sunni desert brother who has assisted me many times over the past years. Salaam Alaihum (Peace be upon you) General Ahmed al-Shugairi."

"Bi Izn Allah (If God permits) me peace General Abdelhadi." General al-Shugairi replied as he stood some fifteen feet from where the General and his group were stopped, and the Saudi Arabian Officer exposed his presence to the Iraqi and others. Then the Saudi General started to walk proudly at General Abdelhadi as he removed the desert Howli fold from his face.

General Abdelhadi moved forward to greet the other General half way and as they met, both of them hugged each other as General al-Shugairi offered to his exhausted Sunni brother. "Allahu Akhbar General Abdelhadi, it has been a long time since we last shared a tent together, my brother. You're twice welcome in the name of Allah to my camp, and all I have to offer and protect you and your friends with, my brother. Come, let's get to my camp where we can share water and food together, General Abdelhadi."

"Allahu Akhbar General al-Shugairi. You offer me your hospitality which I warmly welcome my brother of the desert sands." General Abdelhadi replied to the other General's offer.

Stepping back a few feet for separation, al-Shugairi looked in Abdelhadi's eyes before asking. "Alas my faithful brother, what has brought you so far out in the vastness of the desert? The last word I had on you, you were enjoying yourself living in the small village you profess to be destroyed by the hated American invaders to your land, General. In Allah's grace, what happened and why have I not been informed of this tragedy to befall Iraq until I met with you? What is this I'm forced to witness, the once powerful General Mustafa Abdelhadi now leads a small Army comprised of three cursed women and one soldier who acts ill trained?"

"I fear it's true, my village was destroyed by the American Crusaders to my country…"

"You strike me with words as hard as steel my desert brother. Those who dare to encroach upon the province of Allah, face His unfettered wrath. Excuse me for interrupting your troubling words General Abdelhadi, continue to inform me of the tragedies that fell upon your shoulders."

"What have we lowered ourselves to General al-Shugairi? Are we a bunch of hackling old women who stand in the open exposed to the hot breath of the desert, while we gossip about all that has happened in my country?" General Abdelhadi grumbled as he looked over the shoulder of the Arabian Officer.

"I see the years have not softened you and you still suffer from the disposition of an angry scorpion that has feasted upon sour mother's milk, and would sting his own brother if he had half a chance, General Abdelhadi. Yes General, forgive my poor manners and I invite you and those who follow you to my unworthy tent for food and water." General al-Shugairi offered as he stepped aside and then he bowed towards the Iraqi as he flung his hand out before him in a guiding gesture for General Abdelhadi to follow him to his camp.

Without another word uttered by General Abdelhadi, he moved in the direction General al-Shugairi offered as a horde of fighters under his command, suddenly exposed their positions to the strangers who their commander gave such a friendly welcome to.

As they walked together, General Abdelhadi offered to his counterpart. "General al-Shugairi, I see you have a good number of well trained highly disciplined Saudi fighters in your command, sir. This is great news for me to witness, because I fear we'll have much need of your desert fighters. If we're to be successful with carrying out our mission entrusted to our hands by the Almighty Allah Himself, General al-Shugairi."

"Am I to believe you have a mission in your mind, General Abdelhadi? What am I asking of you my desert brother, of course you must have a mission in your mind, or you'd not be this far out in the desert with so motley a group of brothers and sister fighters. Once we reached the safety of my tent and had refreshments to enjoy, perhaps you can inform me of this chosen mission you're on in the name of Allah's will and your country's fate, General Abdelhadi."

"I expect your hospitality General al-Shugairi." The Iraqi Officer snapped proudly at the other General as he nodded slightly at the Saudi Commander.

"It is given happily as is expected from you, and anyone else who I happen across in the unending desert of our two lands, my brother. I caution you to employ much kinder and more respectful words when addressing me. Especially before my followers General Abdelhadi, if you dare to continue to try my patience, you'll live long enough to regret your foolish follies, General. There's an old saying in Arabia, General Abdelhadi, 'do not throw stones in the well you drink from', which means don't upset those you seek help from, General Abdelhadi."

General Abdelhadi stared into the burning eyes of General al-Shugairi for several long moments before he finally nodded at the Saudi Officer, while heading in the direction General al-Shugairi was directing him towards. As tired and exhausted and in need of water and food to renew his strength, the Iraqi Officer was in no mood to get involved in an extended argument with the other Sunni Officer.

General al-Shugairi remained standing where he was and waited for the four others with General Abdelhadi to pass him. Once they followed their officer, the Saudi Officer headed for his tent with twenty Saudi Arabian fighters protecting every step he placed in the sand.

General Abdelhadi and his exhausted group were fifteen minutes out of General al-Shugairi's encampment, and when they entered the protected area, General Abdelhadi was amazed at what he was witnessing. He entered a massive camp with over a hundred tents set up, and there were countless wood boxes stacked everywhere he realized contained military weapons and supplies. There was a herd of over fifty camels bedded down, along with a well for drinking water in the middle of the camp. The Iraqi General noticed there was no need for a cooking fire, because there was a sort of mess tent set up for the fighters needs.

General Abdelhadi looked at one wooden crate and noticed the American Flag painted on the side of the crate, and understood this Saudi General was equipped with military supplies sent to Arabia from the United States. The Iraqi smiled for he thought how ironic it was to be fighting against the infidels using the same weapons they sent to Arabia to protect themselves with.

General Al-Shugairi quickly caught up to General Abdelhadi and his small group before they entered his camp, and he led him to his tent which was the largest, and the Saudi Officer opened the flap for the Iraqi and his friends. General al-Shugairi walked over to a long bank of plush sitting pillows and seated himself in the middle of them, and then he motioned General Abdelhadi over to his right. The Arabian Officer never motioned the others with the Iraqi to the pillows. So Ayesha and her two friends and last soldier remained standing by the entrance to his tent. A large number of Saudi Arabian fighters entered the tent, and they sort of kept the strangers under close watch with their weapons held at the ready in the best possible firing positions against the Iraqi refugees.

With a sudden clap of his hands, five women entered the tent and offered the two Generals water and fresh dates to nibble on. The servers never offered the others with the Iraqi water or food. Once General Abdelhadi drank his fill and was comfortable, General al-Shugairi leaned closer and asked barely over a whisper. "Allahu Akhbar General Abdelhadi, would you be so kind as to explain to me why you led these worthless women to this part of the desert, my foolish brother of years past?

Remembering the customs of his land, the Iraqi offered. "I thank you for the hospitality of your tent, my brother. It's an honor for me to share your tent."

The Iraqi's response forced a reply from the Saudi Officer. "You honor the unworthy greatly, my desert brother. Enough of the niceties, I asked you why you're this far in the desert, and I am waiting your reply, General Abdelhadi."

Drawing in a deep breath, the ex-Iraqi soldier offered in a rush of words to the other officer. "General al-Shugairi, the hated and god cursed infidels have entered my village in search of the woman and the gift entrusted to her worthless hands by the Almighty Allah. With this weapon she possesses, it'll cause the deaths of countless foreign infidels to mount up like the dead leaves of the winter autumn, fall to the ground…"

"General Abdelhadi there is another old saying in my country, 'Never allow the head of the camel to enter your tent, because if you do then the rest of his body would surely follow and fill your tent until there is no room for you'. That's what happened to your country my faithful brother, you have allowed the head of the worthless American Crusaders to enter your country, and now they are as many as the Locus that once plagued Egypt countless years past. As it is stated, 'To kill one lowly infidel is not murder it is the true path to Paradise', General Abdelhadi. Bah on the old beliefs and ways of the past, who is this lowly woman you hold in such high esteem that you have led to my tent, my desert brother?"

"General al-Shugairi, she's the daughter of Colonel Hamoodi al-Qaysi…"

"I know of this Iraqi Colonel Hamoodi al-Qaysi who has surrendered his life for his belief in Allah, and for the freedom of your nation of Iraq. He was well respected in my country of Arabia. So this worthless woman is the daughter of this Colonel al-Qaysi, General Abdelhadi?"

"Yes, and that's why I'm protecting this female so faithfully, General al-Shugairi."

The Saudi General rose from his pillows and then walked across his tent to Ayesha, and then he looked deeply in her eyes and offered. "So you're the daughter of the honored Colonel Hamoodi al-Qaysi of Iraq, huh?"

"Yes General." Ayesha replied even though she had no idea who she was speaking to.

"Allow me to introduce myself to you then. I am General Ahmed al-Shugairi of the Saudi Arabian Fifth Army, special branch. I offer my daughter your Father's kingdom was in his heart and mind, and that kingdom cannot be surrendered to anyone, friend or foe. I'm honored to meet the daughter of such a brave and well respected Iraqi fighter as your Father was. Come with me my daughter of the desert sands, you should not be allowed to stand a moment longer in my presence, while laboring under the always angry Eye of Allah (Sun). You must be thirsty and in need of food to regain your strength, woman. What in Allah's name is this god cursed metal can you hold and protect as if it is a new born child you hold to your breasts?"

"It's the gift of Allah's endless mercy and love, General al-Shugairi."

"Gift of Allah, gift of Allah! It seems to me that you need some breaking with the bridle woman, because you speak in riddles to me. I believe you have to spend some nightmares upon the rack so you answer a faithful Arab man correctly when he asked you a question. You're the second person to speak of this supposed gift given you from the sacred Hands of Allah. What is this great gift Allah entrusted to the foul hands of a defiled woman?" General al-Shugairi bellowed as he glared at the lovely Ayesha.

The Saudi's sudden outburst made his guards flinch and they intensified their coverage over the strangers sharing the tent with their commander.

General Abdelhadi went to move towards the Saudi General and Ayesha, but the guards aimed their weapons at him when he moved. The guard's actions caught the attention of General al-Shugairi and he held up his hand as he turned to the Iraqi and growled at everyone in his tent. "What by Allah's great wisdom is this, I'm in command and no one will move unless I order it so. Guards, these people are visitors to my tent, and they're to be treated as such. General Abdelhadi, you'll not move a muscle unless I allow it." General al-Shugairi turned back to Ayesha and bellowed at her. "And you foolish woman, you'll join your unwise General, and you fools will explain to me about this supposed gift bestowed upon your defiled hands by Allah's unending mercy and grace, woman."

Ayesha moved like she was walking to her death, all the while she moved across the tent, the Saudi guards kept a close eye on her every movement. When she was standing by General Abdelhadi, the Saudi General snarled at her. "You'll be seated by your General and protector because when I am seated, I'll not look up to you or any other foul woman from this lice infected land of Iraq, witch!"

When Ayesha was seated on the left side of General Abdelhadi, General al-Shugairi crossed the tent and took his seat on the stack of pillows, and glared at the Iraqi Officer while he waited for him to explain about this supposed gift from Allah.

Drawing in a breath and holding it for a second, General Abdelhadi began his words. After a lengthily and rather detailed explanation of what the group had in their possession, General al-Shugairi allowed himself to relax for the first time since the Iraqi General arrived in his camp, he was aware of the biological weapon and in fact. His mission in Iraq was to locate this supposed weapon of mass destruction, and then smuggle it into Saudi Arabia. After a few moments of thought, the

Saudi leaned back on his pillows and began to bellow with laughter, as he thought how easy General Mustafa Abdelhadi and this Iraqi woman made his mission.

Ayesha and the Iraqi Officer stared at the Saudi as he continued to laugh.

Slowly, General al-Shugairi stopped laughing and then took a moment to wipe a tear from his eye. Then he looked in the Iraqi Officer's eyes and demanded of him. "General Abdelhadi, I want to witness Allah's gift to this lowly woman you protect so well!"

"Alas General al-Shugairi, the gift is extremely dangerous to remove from its protective housing. I'd be reluctant to do so until we're ready to deploy the gift against Iraq's enemy…"

"You trouble me like a lowly woman, General Abdelhadi! You'll display this gift of Allah you claim, or you'll suffer the death of a thousand cuts for refusing a direct order from me, General Abdelhadi! If this supposed gift is as you speak, I'll fill your foul mouth with pearls and other riches. On the other hand General Abdelhadi, if you dare to lie about this supposed weapon of mass destruction. I'll fill your god cursed mouth with hot ash, and you'll die slowly I assure you, General." The Saudi General roared at his counterpart as he stared harshly at him.

"General al-Shugairi, it'll be as you ordered. Ayesha, place the cylinder on the floor, and remove the security ring and cover as you witness me do when I first opened the cylinder, woman. You'll follow my orders if you wish to see the next sun rise grow, foul woman."

With trembling hands, Ayesha moved forward and knelt on the rug covering the sand, and she carefully placed the cylinder on the rug before her. Ever so slowly, she cautiously unscrewed the metal locking ring, and once she removed it from the cylinder's base, she placed it next to the cylinder on the rug. Then she rested her fingers from her left hand on the base of the cylinder, and her other hand wiggled the top half of the cylinder, until it released its grip of the base of the object. Once it was freed, she used her hands to lift the top half of the cylinder to expose the metal holder and glass vial which contained the biological agent.

When the glass vial was exposed, the guards in the tent mumbled and took a step away from the item being displayed before them. But the grumbling stopped when General al-Shugairi gave the guards a harsh look. Then the Saudi General studied the vial, he was shown what the agent was contained in. Once he was certain the item was what he was in Iraq for, he straightened and ordered Ayesha. "Foul woman, replace the cover on the cursed weapon and secure it properly, and once you have accomplished this, I'll take control of the weapon from you, woman."

"General al-Shugairi, the weapon is Ayesha's to control until it's needed against the hated infidels following us. I fear the cursed infidels are about an hour behind us, General. I protest your want to control what is Iraq's to control, and I'm angered by your statement you will…"

"Be still General Abdelhadi before I order your insulting wagging tongue to be ripped out of your disgusting mouth by the roots by hand, and fed to my dogs. In case you don't understand your position in this situation, General. You and the ones you have entered my camp with are still alive at the whim of my mercy. If you continue to try and enforce your will upon my shoulders, you'll live long enough to regret your foolishness, General. I care not one grain of worthless sand about the American infidels who followed you. My only interest in this affair is with this weapon. A thousand pardons fool of fools, but what do you think I'm doing in this god cursed desert of yours? I was sent here to locate this weapon and bring it to my King."

"General al-Shugairi, a King might rule his people and his lands, but the people's souls are theirs to rule on their own. General, you must see what we have in our hands, and the death blow we could deliver against the god cursed Crusaders who have invaded our lands. After all General al-Shugairi, if the lowly American soldiers are allowed to keep control over Iraq, how long do you think it'll be before the hateful things will aim their cursed eyes and desires at Saudi Arabia? General al-Shugairi, I implore you…"

"General Abdelhadi, Allah must have sent you to me on this glorious day, because you have just answered your own worthless question of me, fool. That's the reason I was sent to the desert of Iraq to discover if this great weapon truly existed, or if it was just another worthless threat from the madman who once ruled the worthless lands of Iraq. I never dreamed Allah in His infinite wisdom would have ever delivered this weapon to my faithful hands as you have done today. If the enemy of Allah dare place one uninvited foot in the lands of my country protected by the sands of Mecca, they'll be greeted by a wall of germs that'll destroy them in one great breath of death." General al-Shugairi announced to the ex-Iraqi Military Officer.

"You'll remove the control we have over the wonderful weapon, General al-Shugairi?" The Iraqi General asked the Saudi Officer as he stared at him hotly.

"Yes fool of an Iraqi General, I have orders if we're confronted by the American soldiers in this miserable country. We're to destroy the weapon to keep it out of their loathsome hands, or we're to employ the weapon against the lowly infidels to ensure my country cannot be connected in any way with this cursed weapon of mass destruction, General Abdelhadi."

"I warned you General al-Shugairi, the hated American Crusaders are close on my heels, and they must know of the existence of this great weapon if they're so serious with their want to capture us. It's the only reason I can see why they are after us so desperately. If the cursed jackals have destroyed my village in their search of this item, the evil ones will not stop until they have their foul hands upon this great weapon they are searching our lands for." General Abdelhadi offered in an excited voice to the other General.

"If the American soldiers are in pursuit of you, they're pursuing their own fate to their impending deaths in Iraq, General Abdelhadi. With one great cast of the fabled sword of Damascus, we'll rid Arab lands once and for all of those lower than the regurgitated filth of the Vulture until the scales of justice are balanced, you miserable sand crawler. If we're forced to use this weapon against the hunting infidels, we'll disappear like a mirage and leave their dead covering the sands of our deserts to rot in the burning sun.

"You son of a god cursed sand flea feasting on filthy camel dung, your mother has mated with a scorpion! I don't fear the hated American infidels in the least as you obviously do, General Abdelhadi. I'm not trapped in a vaginal vice as you have saddled yourself with these three women you protect. We must remain strong so we can enjoy our claim to the Prophet Muhammad's Mantle, until we're called before Him in the Hall of Judgment. As it is written, only if you hate can you join the ranks of haters, and I hate the West and all it stands for, General." General al-Shugairi snorted at his friend as he held him in a loathsome stare.

"All of what you have stated General al- Shugairi is true. If we must engage the enemy troops following me, we must begin to prepare for their foul arrival, General."

"Again you display before me why you're no longer an active General in your own country that collapsed around your worthless ears, your foolish fears make you weak of mind and back, Mustafa. Who do you think Allah favors in the web of life, the spider or the worthless fly who eats dung? With this weapon in our hands, we're the spider favored by Allah's will. During one of these moments of clarity in the dust storm of violence that swirls through inchoate movement, we hold the upper hand against the cursed invaders of Arab lands, General Abdelhadi. Remember the Hadith or Histories of the Prophet and Surah's, the chapters of the Holy Qur'an and draw strength from the written words. I assure you General, we'll be well prepared for the arrival of the loathsome infidels who follow you." General al-Shugairi boasted proudly to the Iraqi General and his friend of many years.

SEVEN MILES BEHIND GENERAL AMED AL-SHUGAIRI'S ENCAMPMENT

Captain Robert Walker's group of specialized soldiers reached the place where his targets had turned off on his troops marching towards the Arab fighter's camp in the desert. But there was a major problem with the Captain's mission, and the officer received a flash emergency message from Tracker One.

Tracker One was about a mile in front of Walker's ground troops when his air platform suffered a severe backfire report from its port engine. Instantly the helicopter lost at least half its flight power, and the pilot was having a hard time struggling to keep the machine in the air and in level flight. After fighting the controls for a few moments, the commander of the helicopter warned Colonel Pullman in an excited tone. "Colonel, you better prepare for a hard landing sir, we're going down in a controlled crash."

The Colonel pulled his seat belt harness as tight as he could possibly stand it, and then he grabbed the handhold over his head and held on for dear life. The sleek helicopter dropped in the air like a lead weight and landed hard on its wheels and spun around on the ground before coming to a complete stop as the engines spooled down. Colonel Pullman regained his senses and bellowed at the pilot. "What the hell happened to the damn machine? Were we hit by an RPG, Commander? Are we down for good on this endless mission, or is this a minor setback, sir? We have soldiers we have to protect with our platform, sir."

"Calm down Colonel Pullman, evidently we sucked up enough sand in our intake ports to stall out the engines. We're out of the game until I can remove the filters and clean them with water and air, so we can complete our mission as ordered, Colonel. I think you better warn Captain Walker we're out of the game for the time being, and he no longer has any air cover over his troops, until I can check the engines and see if I can get them back on line."

"Right Commander, I'll do as suggested. The Captain has to be informed he's operating with no air cover over his troops." The Colonel replied to the commander then he reached for the mike and snapped it on, and reported to the ground commander. "Tracker One to Searcher One, come in. This is an emergency request for secured communication Searcher One. Over."

Roach picked up the call from Tracker One and caught up to his Captain. "Walker, I got an emergency call coming in from the puke commanding Tracker One. The Airforce ninety day wonder seems upset, maybe the little prick found the damn turds we're after. I hope he has something good to report for us, sir."

"Oh great, now what's the problem with that pain in the ass. I never knew an Airforce prick could be so much god damn trouble to us ground pounders." Walker complained as he snatched the mike from Roach and then growled in it. "Yeah Tracker One this is Searcher One, send emergency flash. Over."

"Searcher One, I'm reporting that we have just suffered a major malfunction with the Tracker One aircraft sir, and your ground troops are now operating without any air cap protection securing your operation and protecting your soldiers, sir. I have no idea if we're down and out for the damn count sir, or if the Tracker One platform can be repaired and brought back in flight with the tools we have available to work on her out in the field, sir. Over." Colonel Pullman reported to the ground commander.

"November, Foxtrot, Whiskey man. (radio slang for No Fucking Way) God dammit Tracker One, what the hell's the fucking nature of your major malfunctions with the support platform? I can't afford to have your platform down, not when we're so close to closing in on our missing subject and the package she's carrying, sir." Walker growled angrily in the radio.

"Searcher One, our helicopter sucked up sand in our intake ports to stall and cripple our engines on the aircraft. The pilot's out of the machine working on the engines to try and correct the situation as quickly as possible. Over." Colonel Pullman reported to the Marine Commander.

"Shit, yeah, right, okay Tracker One this is on helluva shit storm we got on our damn hands now, man. I need your fucking support platform over our noggins to make certain we don't stumble into a possible ambush. I lost enough of my people to this Romeo Foxtrot (slang meaning Rat Fuck) operation, and I have no intention of losing any more of my troops to this damn operation, Colonel. How long do you think it'll take the pilot to clear the filters and get your strike platform back in the fricking air, if it's at all possible to be corrected by the fucking pilot in the damn field? I need to know this shit because if I can't have your support platform as a ready air cap over my ground pounders. Then I'm gonna be forced to request another air cap over my troop's noggins, Tracker One. Over."

"Hang on a moment Searcher One while I check on that request with the pilot. Over." With that said, Colonel Pullman went to the pilot and asked. "Commander, Searcher One is demanding to know if you'll be able to correct the malfunction with the aircraft, and if you're able to correct the situation on the ground with what you have at your disposal to work with. Searcher One, is also demanding to know how long we'll be out of commission."

"Colonel Pullman, I was able to get the cover off the filter I believe is clogged with sand. It's going to take me fifteen minutes to clean the filters, and then I have to try and restart the engines. Colonel, if the engines sucked up too much sand and it scored the cylinders of the motors we might be out of the picture for the duration of this mission all together, sir. That's the best I can offer until I see what's going on with the engines, and if I can repair them in the field, sir."

"Dammit, I have to report this to Walker. He's not going to enjoy this report, Commander. You keep working on the filters and report to me when you have something positive to report, Commander. Err… Tracker One to Searcher One, come in sir. This is important and will help with your decision, Searcher One. Over." Colonel Pullman offered as he went back to his radio.

"Roger Tracker One, this is Searcher One, continue your report. Over."

"Searcher One, the pilot stated he's working on the filters and should have the answer if we're operational in fifteen minutes, sir. Over." Colonel Pullman reported to Captain Walker.

"Roger your last Tracker One, requesting your position. Over."

"Tracker One reporting we're down four miles your position east of same, Searcher One."

"That's good Tracker One it should take us forty minutes to reach your position. Sit tight where you're at and I'll refrain from calling in a backup Tracker for this damn mission, until I find out your status with the aircraft. When I reach your Papa, Papa, I'll make my decision on whether or not to call in a backup support platform, and relieve you of duties or not. Over."

"Roger last Searcher One and will comply. I want to get off the net and see if I can lend a hand to the pilot, and get this repair completely in less than fifteen minutes. Over Searcher One."

"You're free to clear the net and assist the pilot on his repair of the damn machine, Tracker One. We're increasing our pace to your Papa, Papa (location) to make a determination on the situation with your support platform. We'll get to you as quickly as possible. Out Tracker One."

The moment Walker broke off the communication with the Tracker One ATO Colonel, he bellowed at his troops taking time to rest sitting on the sand in full gear. "Okay people, Tracker One's down and outta it and we hafta hustle to get to the aircraft and see if we can lend them fly jockies a hand with their repairs of the strike platform. Let's get a move on it. Saddle up!"

Walker moved his troops as fast as he could push his beat out soldiers con the soft sands of the desert. He was fuming he was forced to be heavy handed on his exhausted soldiers as they trudged along without complaint. He wanted his troops to take all the time they needed for rest, but he also understood his troops were working under time restraints for this operation. He had to find the biological agent before it was somehow released in the air, and he would find himself in an entirely different situation, and could end up facing a nuclear discharge over his trooper's heads for their trouble on this mission.

The going was hard for the soldiers, the sand in this section of the desert was fresh blown and soft, the hard walking was draining the strength out of the soldier's bodies. It was like walking in a foot of fresh fallen snow in the States. Walker was still able to find a footprint from his packages here and there every now and then in the sand, but for the most part their target's footprints were completely erased by the blowing winds and soft sands of the desert.

The Mutt worked his way up to Walker's side and complained. "Hey man, not for nuthin but with Tracker One down and outta it for the count, we lose our Intel overhead. This is getting like being back in the States. Them civilians back there are getting so bad it seems they can no longer tell the difference between the arsonist and the firefighters, the way they wanna attack our Intel people. It's getting so bad Congress and this Administration is under the assumption protecting the rights of the terrorists are more important than protecting the lives of the American people.

"I don't know when the bleeding hearts are ever gonna learn no war either against a nation or a terrorist organization, can be won without strong intelligence gathering, and the way we keep stopping our Intel people from carrying out their duty in the States or elsewhere. Their actions will stop us from winning the war against terrorism, or the fight raging in Afghanistan or Pakistan. These people hafta learn a strong offense and intelligence gathering system, is the grand equalizer in the scheme of things against these damn mass murderers who wanna call themselves terrorists, and the fucking war they're pitting against our asses, man."

Captain Walker stopped and looked at the Mutt a few steps behind him before groaning. "I agree with you. Those pricks who have a moral equivalence for the cycle of violence fail to act against terrorism, and attack the people we depend on the most to protect our backsides. I'll use what you just said, 'the assholes are no longer able to distinguish between the arsonist and the fucking firefighter'. What matters most to the damn terrorists isn't the technological complexity of the weapon they're deploying against our asses, but how many people the damn thing kills. They can either be a fricking sophisticated failure or an amateurish mass murderer. Even if their stinking attack doesn't work out perfectly for the damn terrorists, they still win that stinking round, because any attempted terrorist attack against our country will cause major problems for our civilians to endure in the way of security precautions, and being put out while trying to board one of our stinking aircraft back in the States, man."

With that said the two American soldiers began to walk towards where Tracker One was reported sitting on the surface of the sand again.

By the time Walker's troops moved forward about three miles to the reported downed support helicopter, he was able to see the war machine resting on the sand about another one to two miles ahead of his troops. The concerned Captain looked over his shoulder and was angered by what he noticed. His troops were burnt out and exhausted, and he was fearful some of the troopers might not be able to react if they came under attack by insurgents know to be lurking ahead of his people. He held up his hand and stopped his soldier's progress as he called out to them.

"Okay people, I got a good MOE (Mark One eyeball) on Tracker One, so we're gonna take a little break before continuing on towards Tracker's Papa, Papa. Soup up (drink water) and suck in air, I need you fresh and ready for anything coming at us when we finally reach Tracker's position. The scumbags we're tracking could be using the Tracker One platform as a setup against us, and they could hit us hard when we reach the downed support platform. Ghost, Hunter, I want you two pukes out and reconnoiter the surrounding area by Tracker One, and make certain we're not walking into a fucking ambush out there." Walker stopped speaking and waited for a reply from his two dangerous pointmen.

The Ghost and Hunter replied to Walker's order by giving him the thumbs up signal as they stood, and then they started to march out before the unit to assume the point position and protection for the other troopers.

Captain Robert Walker watched the two soldiers head out as another of his soldiers ran up to him, and handed the Captain a bottle of hot drinking water. He barely took notice of the soldier as he grabbed the bottle and sucked down the warm, almost hot water in a few gulps.

The Mutt was by Walker's side as usual, and he kept an eye on his commander and close friend. The Mutt wanted to make certain he was following his own orders of drinking as much water as he could stand while the troops were operating in the desert searching for the biological item, and the ones who had the item in their possession.

CHAPTER TWENTY EIGHT

When some of the specialized soldiers stood up and started to mill about, Captain Robert Walker felt the troops had rested long enough and he barked at the rest of them. "Okay you ball sacks we gotta make our way to Tracker One and see if we can help getting the strike platform back in the air, so they can assume air cap over us. Saddle up we got a date with an Arab bitch."

His soldiers did not gripe as much as the last time he forced them back on their feet, and in seconds they were heading for the downed helicopter. The Captain had his eyes locked on the machine resting on the sand while the Mutt kept his eyes out for the Ghost and Hunter.

Walker did not realize how hard he was pushing himself walking towards the downed helicopter. He was the first one from his unit to walk up to the disabled machine and see what kind of damage was caused to the platform. Colonel Pullman was standing by the pilot's side, offering him any help he could possibly give the pilot, when he turned and happened to spot Walker standing near him and he reported.

"Captain Walker, we're closing up the engine compartment now sir. We have the filters cleaned and replaced and once she's buttoned up, the pilot will try to start the engines. I think we have everything under control and from the looks of it, sir. The sand didn't harm the engines, because the filters stopped much of it from reaching the engine pistons, sir."

"Out fucking standing Colonel Pullman, I need this damn platform flying cover for my troops ten minutes ago, sir. Huh, what's your problem?" Walker growled at the Mutt who interrupted him and the Colonel's conversation.

"Man you gotta get yourself a fucking nuther life or something, my problem in life is I find my ass in this desert, getting a god damn sand enema for my fucking effort. Walker, I wanted to inform you I picked up Ghost and Hunter. They're doing their act about two Klicks ahead of our position. Any orders, I'm not getting any younger hanging around here like this you know?"

"And, you're not gonna get any fricking older if you don't get the case of ass outta your damn tone when addressing me, buster. Your orders are to sit tight while I see if this ever loving fucking machine's gonna get offa the stinking ground. Have the troops rest and suck up air and drink water during this down time, buster." Captain Walker turned to the pilot who stepped away from the engine compartment, and he was walking to the cockpit of the stalled machine. The concerned Captain watched as the pilot climbed into the helicopter, and then he heard the motors turning slowly as the pilot tried to restart the engines.

All the while the pilot tried to restart the engines, Walker held his breath until the two engines caught and coughed back into life. The pilot added more power to the engines and they backfired a few times before smoothing out and running correctly. The pilot looked at Walker and then he gave him the thumbs up signal and motioned for Colonel Pullman to get back on board the aircraft. The machine lifted off sending a small sand storm at the ground soldiers.

Roach was standing by Walker's side as they watched the helicopter slowly climb in the air, and when a call from Tracker One came in, he handed the mike to Walker. The Captain grabbed the mike as if he was angry at it and snarled in it.

"Yeah, Searcher One, send your traffic Tracker One. Over."

"Searcher One, Tracker One reporting we're mission capable. We're continuing previous orders unless you want to change them, Searcher One. Over."

"You got it Tracker One carry out your previous orders. We'll follow your machine from the ground until you located our package. Over." Walker turned to his troops and growled. "You people betta unass your fucking selves, we got Tracker One back and our mission's operational. Let's put a period to the end of this fucking operation, so we can get the hell outta sand land."

When Tracker One was five hundred feet in the air, the helicopter's front end dipped slightly and the machine instantly swept forward at full power. In seconds it flew over the Ghost and Hunter's position as it headed due east looking for the missing Iraqi's.

As the Apache rapidly closed in on the Arab's position, a watcher rushed in General Ahmed al-Shugairi's tent and he reported picking up the helicopter heading directly for their camp. General al-Shugairi jumped to his feet issuing orders for his officers in his tent. He aimed his words at his second in command, General Kaswara al-Khatib a Saudi Military Officer.

"My Commanders, a god cursed infidel helicopter is heading directly for our encampment, and I believe there are cursed foot soldiers following their flying machine to our position. The lowly infidels are coming for us, may the wombs of their mother's cry for their pending deaths. Commanders, we were ordered on a special mission that would freeze the worthless blood of a coward in his foul body. Prepare our fighters for the fight of their lives, their actions have to protect me and this lowly woman, while we escape to the safety our homeland Saudi Arabia offers. General al-Khatib, order the mortars setup to defend us while we leave for our country. You Commanders have your orders, carry them out and get your fighters prepared for Allah and for your country's cause." General al-Shugairi glared at his unit commanders until they rose and quickly headed off to follow their orders.

As the spurred to action commanders cleared the tent to take control of their warriors of General al-Shugairi, Tracker One flew over the large and active encampment. Instantly, Colonel Pullman was on the radio reporting their findings to the Marine Officer trailing behind him.

"Tracker One to Searcher One, come in sir. This is important. Over Searcher One."

"Yeah, this is Searcher One, go with your traffic Tracker One. Over."

"Searcher One, we just cleared a large sand dune due east your present position and happened across an expansive encampment of Arab what I'm classifying as positive enemy insurgents, and possible civilians with them. From what I was able to detect from our first flyover, we caught them by surprise and that caused them to go in defensive action against your arrival. The moving group of insurgents is heavily armed, and they seem to be preparing for your troop's arrival their position. I detected what I believe to be from one hundred to maybe upwards to at least one hundred and fifty heavily armed insurgents. All combatants seem to be male of fighting age and are armed and preparing to defend their position against your troops. I suggest your troops activate your strobe detections so our strike platforms will be able to detect them as friendly forces, Searcher One. Over."

"Shit, dammit Tracker One, it looks like we're gonna be forced to go fucking postal on their damn asses. Have you been able to detect our packages at this camp you just located? If not Tracker One, do you believe it's possible our packages to be mixed in with these assholes? If you say no to my question then I might bypass this group and continue with our search for these five missing fucking Arab pukes, and what they have on their damn person. Also Tracker One, I'm following your suggestion to have my troops activate their identification strobes. Over Tracker One."

"Searcher One, we were forced to clear the camp when we flew over it by three miles, before taking a standoff position against them, sir. We're waiting for further orders Searcher One. As we overflew the camp, I maintained a search of the desert for other footprints from our packages. Searcher One, the last detected footprints of our missing packages were leading right for this camp, and they were heavy and seems fresh. We found no further prints in the sand after the camp. So I'm forced to believe our packages are using this insurgent camp as their safety net, and your soldiers will be forced to enter and take command of packages and item. Over."

"I Roger your last Tracker One and I concur with your report. Tracker One based on your report, I want you to make contact with Flight Command and get some heavy air cover and strike platforms over our fucking heads for this operation we're about to engage. You know betta than I do of what we're gonna need for the success of this operation, so order it here ten minutes ago. We're continuing to move for your position, Tracker One. Over."

"Roger last Searcher One, I'll order heavy close in air defense capability for your ground in this case, sand pounders. I peg you at being four miles from my location of the camp. I intend to make a second pass over the encampment to see if I can detect heavy weapons the insurgents might have at their command, and to make certain there are no civilians with these people. I'll try and map out their positions so your troops will know where to and how to attack against the defenses these people are setting up against your troops. Over Searcher One."

"You do that Tracker One, but before you make your flyover of the camp I want you to get our heavy protection and uther support platforms heading our Papa, Papa. I want that crap here before we're forced to engage the dam n horde of insurgents. I'm gonna use the platforms to cut their numbers down drastically, before we attack them in strength. I have no intentions of engaging enemy forces this size with the exhausted troops I have at my disposal. Tracker One, don't worry about civilians mixed in with these assholes. Any civilian stupid enuf to be walking hand in hand with these insurgents are as good as they are. That's dead, if any civilian is with a terrorist or insurgent, I classify all the asses as terrorists or insurgents. Over Tracker One."

"I Roger last and will do as ordered and understand what you're saying about civilians. As far as I'm concerned, there are no civilians mixed in with these enemy fighters, Searcher One. I'll be back to you once I get a confirmation on the air assets I'm requesting, and when they're on the way to our Papa, Papa, sir. Over."

While Tracker One was setting up air cover for the ground troops, Walker had the rest of his soldiers stepping up their pace and spreading out as they approached the camp. He did not want to approach with his troops bunched up and easy targets for the insurgents to hit. After two miles of marching, Walker was able to pick up Tracker One in the air. At the same time he picked up his air cover, his squad helmet radio went off, it was the Ghost checking in with him.

"Walker, Ghost, we picked up Tracker One and headed his location and came across a large insurgent camp. The pricks are fucking armed with mortars and heavy machine guns, and the assholes are setting up a professional type defense against you people coming at them." The Ghost used Walker's name because the squad radio was a secured net system.

"We already got the warning from Tracker One. Ghost we're heading your position. I want you and the Hunter to setup and detect the leaders of this group of nuts, and set them up for first hits when I order you two to take them out. Ghost, I want you two shitbags to keep your eyes opened, you know who we're looking for. If you pick them up in that mess of shit before we hit'em, take out all but female breathers we want. Once you clear the insurgents around our package, protect her ass and item. Don't allow any uther A-rabs near her or the package until we get our hands around her chicken ass neck, and we take her and that item in custody and secure both of the damn things, man."

"I read you loud and clear Walker, and by the time you get here. We'll have the leaders of the scumbags sighted in for erasing, and if the A-rab bitch is in this camp along with these uther assholes, we'll find her fur ya, man."

Walker broke off his communication with the Ghost and he kept his eyes locked on Tracker One, as the helicopter moved all over the sky. He did not look behind himself because he knew his troops were there as always. The worried Captain moved his troops forward until they were two thousand yards away from the insurgent camp, when the first enemy rounds were fired at his troops from the insurgent's side.

The rounds fell well short of his position, and he held up his hand and his troops dropped to the ground and rapidly shed their heavy fieldpacks and extra equipment, and then they prepared to engage the combatants firing at them. Some of the specialized soldiers used their discarded fieldpacks as cover to fire at the enemy combatants firing at them.

The Mutt and Sergeant Ramirez crawled up to Walker's side and complained. "What the fuck's wrong with those dopey bastards out there man? Their stinking rounds are falling way short of our asses, the stupid fucks they are. All they're doing is marking their stinking positions so we know where to concentrate our fire when we engage the lousy scumbags, man."

"I got news fur you buster, we're not gonna engage the bastards until air support and strike platforms get here, and they soften them up first for us. Once the aircraft worked them over then and only then we'll move out and mop up the bastards nice and easy. I hope the stinking Ghost or Hunter picks up our missing package and they can separate her from the rest of the flaming assholes." As Walker was speaking with the Mutt, they heard the first report fired from either the Hunter or Ghost's sniper weapon, and Walker announced to the Mutt with a grin.

"It looks like our fucking Vampires took out a slimy ass leader of these nuts. I guess they think they're a stinking fight for our asses, man?"

Another report and the Mutt added. "It seems like our Vampires aren't done yet man."

Walker looked over his shoulder to check on his troops, and smiled because he was pleased at how well they spread out on their own, and assumed their best attack profile for when he sends his troopers against the combatants pitted against them. Then he turned his attention back to the insurgent encampment, he understood the Arab's set themselves up in their best possible position in the area to better defend their position, and attack his troops if they had the notion. The enemy forces set themselves up in a mess of ancient long ago abandon ruins, and the insurgents had plenty of hiding places available to them within the fifteen or so buildings constructed centuries ago. Some nearly buried in the sand buildings were huge, and looked like they were constructed to be sort of fortresses, and capable of sustaining heavy weapon fire before the building would collapse in on the Arab fighters.

A number of contrails streaked the cloudless sky and Sergeant Dorothy Ramirez drew Captain Walker's attention to the obvious aircraft coming in from the west, as their strike platforms were closing in on their position.

"God damn girl, it looks like Colonel Pullman's gonna be busy as hell as he was when we hit the Iraqi town, sister." Walker remarked to Ramirez.

"At least with the aircraft supporting us, we won't suffer as many causalities as we would've if we had to go at these puds with small arms we have available, Bobby." Ramirez replied.

"You got a good point. The attacking aircraft will whittle them down good enuf for our asses." Walker fired back as he shot off a smile at his girlfriend. He looked at Tracker One and noticed the helicopter was backing off the area the strike platforms were about to hit. The incoming fire from the enemy was picking up in its intensity, and some of the rounds were starting to get to his troops. None of his troops was getting picked off by the increasing sporadic weapon fire from the insurgent's camp.

Walker sucked in a huge gulp of air and then barked at his alert troops. "Okay, the assholes are starting to get our range so keep your asses low. If I see anyone's ass sticking up in the breeze, I'm gonna put a cap in it myself. The Go Fasts are overhead, and it looks like Tracker One's lining up our attack platforms to open their assault on the stupid ass insurgents. Keep low cause hell's about to visit our fucking sand swimming friends out there, people."

Roach moved up to Walker's side because Tracker One opened communications with the leading aircraft hovering over the ground soldiers, and he was able to hear what Tracker One was ordering the Commander of the F-15s to do.

Walker, along with the Mutt and Ramirez gathered around Roach as they listened in on the communications going on between Tracker One and the Raven Flight Leader.

"Tracker One to Raven Flight Leader, glad to have you people on board as air support and strike aircraft for this next phase of this unending operation, Commander. How are conditions up there? I fear we're going to need all air support systems we can muster for this one." Colonel Mark Pullman offered to the leader of Raven Flight.

"Raven Flight Leader to Tracker One, I'm pleased to be part of this operation again, sir. Conditions for attack on enemy positions are classified as severe clear. I'm reporting I have two Spectre Gunships as added attack platforms, and their ETA's ten minutes out. We're scheduled to have Talon Flight joining our attack forces for this part of the mission. I'm sorry to report we're too far out to expect any help from Wild Flight, because we're operating well outside the scope of Apache range, and we couldn't setup support systems in time to be of assistance to our cause. We tried to pick up a unit of Super Cobra's, but the Marines were already operational and couldn't break off their support. Do you have targets picked out for our attention? Also Tracker One, anything on civilians mixed in with these people, sir?"

Walker grabbed the mike from Roach and he growled at the Flight Commander. "Searcher One to Raven Flight Leader. What the hell's that bullshit you're spouting off to Tracker One? I was under the impression we were main for any fucking operations and any supporting fixed or rotary support platforms were instructed to break off ordered support to aide our asses. Did the fucking orders change and I wasn't made aware of that fact, pal? Also Raven Flight Leader, I'm telling you right off there are no stinking civilians mixed in with this group of fucking enemy combatants. Every damn target you pick up moving on the ground, are to be classified as targets for destruction. Over Raven Flight Leader!"

The surprised commander of the Raven strike package over Walker's communication replied to the ground commander. "Raven Flight Leader to Searcher One, I copy last, sir. We're operating under the same impression, and that's why we're ordered held in reserve for your mission. In case you needed extra support for your operation. Evidently Wild Fire Flight was involved in a high profile engagement, and their aircraft were ordered not to break off support of their ground troops, sir. Tracker One's request for support platforms came in to Command. It looks like you people will have to do with what we have coming as support platforms for this mission, sir. Searcher One, I understand last orders, all targets on ground are that, targets and hostile and to be engaged and sanctioned."

Walker was angered by the Commander of Raven Flight's response to his bitch, but he had to let it go as he listened to the commander's orders. His concern was his mission and nothing else.

"Raven Flight Leader to Chicks, we have ordered bomb run to accomplish for the ground pounders. Our friendlies are going to be paper close to bomb run, so we have to be better than perfect on your runs near their positions, and we have to pay close attention to Tracker One's damage assessments, and any new orders once we completed our initial bomb run of the enemy area. Pay attention to shifting friendly forces positions after we completed opening runs over intended targets. To follow on Chicks, there's no civilians pegged out on ground, so keep eyes opened for all strobes down there, they're to be marked as friendly units and not engaged under any circumstances. You Chicks will reply to last orders as received, so I know you guys are following me. Over."

The Commander of Raven Flight listened as his support aircraft pilots checked in after affirming their orders. Then the Raven Flight Leader turned his attention to Colonel Pullman on the radio link and asked. "Tracker One I need a clear vector on the first targets you want eliminated for our beginning run on the enemy camp. Over Tracker One."

Even before Tracker One could respond to Raven Flight Leader, a number of enemy combatants opened fire with mortars against Walker and his troops.

When the first mortars landed fifteen feet short of their position, Captain Walker bellowed at his troops. "God dammit, these sonofabitchs have mortar support with them. Break up and spread out more, I want twenty feet between you people. I'll get on Tracker One's ass and have him have his fly jocks concentrate their first attack of the damn mortars." With that order given, Walker switched back over to Tracker One's frequency, and then he growled at the officer commanding the strike platforms for his ground support.

"Tracker One, be advised we're taking heavy hostile mortar and small arms fire from the enemy encampment. C'mon Tracker One, you gotta break up them fucking mortars for us, or I'm not gonna commit my people against these fucking combatants. With the mortars hitting us, the scumbags will rip us new assholes if we move out against them, Tracker One."

"Tracker One to Scarcher One, I copy last and observed mortars fired at your troop's positions. Searcher One, I'm giving the mortars top priory for first runs of the combatants defenses. Let me get back to Raven Leader and have him aim attack on the mortar locations in the camp. Over."

"You betta do something out there beside sucking up fucking oxygen Tracker One, there's no reason trying to talk any sense with these lousy bastards now they opened up with mortars against us. These A-rab assholes wanna make a stinking fight of it, and that's exactly what I'm gonna give the pricks. I intend to send them on their way to Paradise. I'm not gonna allow my troops to be slaughtered by mortars, I want your aircraft to destroy them damn things." Walker replied.

"I Roger last Searcher One. Your troops are ordered to sit tight and make yourselves as small as possible targets, while I have Raven Flight vector in on the mortar sites and eliminate them on first bomb run against the insurgents, Searcher One. Over." Colonel Pullman did not wait for a reply from Walker as he made contact with the flight leader of the Raven attack aircraft.

"Raven Flight Leader, Tracker One, I have a priory high value target requests for first bomb run against the enemy combatants. You first targets are the mortars sites firing at our friendlies on the ground. Be advised Commander, your target will be paper close to our friendlies on ground, and you and your follow on Chicks will have to be extremely careful on your bomb run against the enemy installations, and not over bomb requested targets and hit any of our friendlies on ground. Keep your eyes opened for any and all strobe markers on the ground from our friendlies. Over Raven Flight Leader."

"I Roger your last and will comply, Tracker One. We've been able to sight up the mortars firing at our friendlies on the ground, Tracker One. I see friendlies paper close to ordered targets, and we'll drop perfect on enemy positions to avoid any possible over bombing and hitting our friendly troops operating on the ground. I have a strong pickup of strobes from friendlies, and we'll avoid them on bomb run. I have them setup in my HUD (Head's Up Display) and we're ready to hit the mortar sites before they're able to get at our friendlies. Over Tracker One."

"Roger that Raven Flight Leader be advised we have friendlies in the area. Crew friendlies, keep a close watch for strobe markers, all strobes registered are classified friendlies and you're instructed not to hit any locations with strobes blinking. Over."

"Roger that Tracker One, all strobes picked up by my aiming system is registered and classified as friendlies, and they're not to be engaged by our weapon attack systems, Tracker One. We're marking all strobes on our aiming computers, and that should keep our friendlies well out of harm's way on our opening attack of enemy positions. Tracker One, I'll need immediate BDA (Bomb Damage Assessment) on first run over enemy positions, so I know how to correct if needed if any enemy targets survive first bomb run over their positions, sir."

"I Roger last and will give immediate bomb damage assessment on enemy positions on first run over insurgent's site, Raven Flight Leader. Good luck and keep in mind I have a good number of friendlies close to enemy target area be alert for them moving around on you. Over."

"Roger Tracker, am requesting clearance to begin run on the mortar positions. Over Tracker One." Raven Leader asked as he checked his aiming computer for response to his commands.

"Roger that, prepare to engage, you're cleared to engage all hostile personnel on ground. You're first run will be Danger Close Raven

Leader. Over." Tracker One ordered Raven Flight Leader to employ the CBU-52 B/B cluster bomb for a full spread on the enemy target.

"Roger last Tracker One, am employing Danger Close for first run over enemy positions. Warn ground pounders of intent and order them to keep their heads in the sand for this run over enemy positions. I don't like having your ground pounders so damn close to my run, there's not much I can do about it at this point. Tracker One, remember I need BDA over targets so I can correct if need if I'm ordered to hit mortar sites a second time. I take usual command structure for air to ground operations will not be employed for this operation? Over Tracker One."

"Roger last Raven Flight Leader, you're correct to assume normal command structure for air to ground operations suspended for duration this operation. I'll be commanding your aircraft to targets. You're cleared to engage hostile installations on ground. Raven Flight Leader, ground pounders are prepared for your attack on enemy positions. All personnel picked up in the area marked M, Five, One, Niner by C, Two, Three, Niner are classified as hostile in nature, and you're cleared to engage all targets you discover operating on the ground on your first run of said positions. Be advised you're aware of what we're looking for, any female targets located in enemy positions are to be overlooked on your attacks if possible, Raven Flight Leader. Over."

"Roger last, will refrain pulling on any located female targets picked up in target zone if possible, Tracker One. Be advised my aircraft is classified as Killer Scout aircraft for this mission, and I'll post friendlies as well as selected enemy targets picked out for this attack to my follow on Chicks. Tracker One, am beginning bomb run on vectored enemy targets. Remember Tracker One, I need immediate bomb damage assessment the instant I finish bomb run over the target, so I can correct further runs for my air wing on said targets to be eliminated. Over."

The other aircraft making up Raven Flight Wing lined up on their commander's lead, and the pilot's traffic started between the attacking American aircraft. "Killer Scout to Raven Chicks, remember not to fly at even numbers for bomb run, we don't know if these bad guys have anti-aircraft shoulder launch weapons or Oil Sites (Pilot slang for Sam

Missile weapons) with them, and we might as well make it as hard as possible for the bastards to pick our asses up with their tracking radar, if they have these weapons. Raven Two, Psycho (pilot), I don't see your flight beacon on and blinking. Set beacon for double pulse and correct situation immediately, before we being run on the enemy positions. Over."

"Roger that Killer Scout, I lit up my beacon and am turning it to double pulse setting for bomb run, are you copying it now sir? Over."

"Roger Raven Two, your beacon's working. Over.

"Killer Scout to Raven Chicks, AMC (At My Command) ATT, (Advance To Target) Estimated TTT (Time To Target) fifteen seconds. Ordered thirty second spacing between aircraft for run on posted targets and positions below, all Chicks acknowledge order. We're cleared to hit targets picked out. Over." When the other pilots replied in the affirmative, Raven Flight Leader continued his orders to the pilots in his flight wing.

"Killer Scout to Chicks, speed is set at Five, Zero, Zero for run over enemy positions, time to target seven seconds. I want you people in and out of there as quickly as possible. Don't lag around attack area to avoid possible mid-air collisions. All targets acquired by aiming computer, am arming master switch for opening attack. I have good response from weapon payload. All weapons hot and am ready to pull and drop on located targets below. Weapon's away. Deployed and follow on explosion are activated. Weapons are working fine. Tracker One, I need immediate bomb damage assessment, so I can correct follow on Chicks to targets not destroyed by first run over said enemy targets and positions, sir."

"Oh man Killer Scout, good hit, that's a good hit and kill man, keep it coming. Your first target's a confirmed kill. Killer Scout keep your Chicks set on same target area and positions as you vectored in. Over Killer Scout." Colonel Pullman reported in an excited voice to the lead pilot as he observed the bomb damage to the enemy positions.

"Tracker One, confirmed secondary explosions in constraints and hit target good. Target's exploding and is on fire. We look good on this run, Tracker One. Over."

As Raven Flight Three began his run on the enemy targets, a Russian made shoulder launch missile system was fired, and the weapon streaked across his windshield. The missile struck his right wing, crippling his aircraft and sending it down.

Raven Flight Leader picked up the missile hitting his Chick and screamed orders in his radio to the crippled aircraft's pilot. "God dammit Raven Three, punch out, your aircraft's coming apart at the fucking seams, pilot. Buzz Saw punch out, punch out, punch out Commander Thomson. To all Raven Chicks, Raven Three Pilot Buzz Saw is out of his aircraft. Raven Two, Psycho don't pull on the enemy positions. I have a pilot down at Alfa, Seven, Niner, Eight. Give him time to get the hell out of the area before you continue your bomb run on the active enemy positions below."

Raven Flight Leader did a low pass as his pilot's chute deployed and slowly drifted towards the ground. Raven Leader was protecting his pilot from the enemy combatants the best he could by hovering his aircraft so closely over his pilot, and he only broke off his protection of the pilot when Raven Flight Leader picked up an American soldier's strobe, as the ground soldier made his way for his pilot. The Ghost was the first soldier on the ground to get to the endangered pilot, and he helped the pilot remove his chute harness, and then the Ghost nearly dragged the hurting pilot out of the area.

The Commander of the Raven Flight let out his breath when he realized his pilot was in friendly hands, and he reported to his follow on aircraft. "Killer Scout to all Raven Chicks, be advised Buzz Saw (Pilot) was picked up by friendly ground pounders, and he is in the foot soldier's control safe and alive. Our pilot is safe and you're cleared and ordered to continue hitting vectored in enemy targets. Remember pilots now we know enemy have shoulder launch missiles deployed, we have to attack targets from nine thousand foot level which will make our job harder to accomplish safely. Raven Four, get in there and hit that mortar installation. Over."

On the first run from Killer Scout and his Chicks, six of the seven insurgent mortar sites were destroyed, and their bombs sent many of the enemy combatants trapped in the open, scurrying for protection of the ancient buildings in the area of their massive encampment. This action by the Iraqi defenders caused Tracker One to remain in constant contact with the leader of Raven Flight as he tried to keep the Raven Flight aircraft on the combatant targets he was able to pick up in the open after their first run against the insurgents positions.

"Tracker One to Killer Scout, I have a number of enemy targets picked up in the open near the front of building with dome type structure. It seems like these combatants are trying to protect this building from attack by your aircraft. Get on these targets and take out. Over."

"Roger that Tracker One, am lining up my aircraft on the suggested enemy target now..."

When the ground support aircraft started their runs, Walker ordered a number of his troops to work their way around the enemy positions, and had them come in from the flanking position on the insurgent area he wanted his troops to take over. He wanted to cut off any possible escape routes for the insurgents, so he could keep his target from escaping his troops, and he would be forced to track her again in the desert until he could catch up to her and the missing item.

"Tracker One, Killer Scout, this is important, am picking up secondary group of breathers moving nearby targeted building I'm aiming aircraft at. Am I to take these movers as hostile in nature against friendly ground forces? If so do you want them neutralized on this run? I'm also picking up a number of friendly strobe flashes coming from same area. What the hell's going on out there Tracker One? Who the hell are these god damn people? Over."

"God dammit Killer Scout, I have no idea what the hell's going on? I have no orders from Searcher One reporting he's moving any of his ground pounders in this area of the attack zone. I haven't picked up any secondary group of breathers you reported. Give me a second to confirm this group of movers." Tracker One's helicopter moved position until he was able to pick up this new bunch of movers and instantly, the soldiers from Walker's group strobes registered with his equipment, and Colonel Pullman growled 'what the hell are these damn fools doing so close to my attack area' as he reported to the pilot. "Negative pull on second group of movers Killer Scout, they're identified as friendlies. I repeat Killer Scout, second group moving is marked friendlies. I'll get them out of the way so you can hit the building, Commander. Over."

"Tracker One to Searcher One, this is important. Over Searcher One."

"This is Searcher One go with traffic Tracker One. Whatdaya got sir? Over." Walker replied in his radio as he observed the attacking aircraft on the enemy targets.

"Searcher One, am about to target area, Three, One, Three marked on your funny papers (map), and I discovered a group of your ground troops have suddenly entered the target area. You have to get them soldiers out of the area so I can hit that requested target, Searcher One. I have a number of armed insurgents located that position, and the enemy is acting like they're trying to protect this building from attack. Over Searcher One."

"Roger that Tracker One, I'll get them outta the area. Searcher One to Neck."

"Neck, Searcher One. What's up man? I'm about to go fucking postal on these suckers over here. I have a good number of insurgents trapped in this area and am looking forward to sanctioning them, sir. Over." The soldier replied to Walker's radio traffic.

"Neck, you gotta get your people the hell outta the area immediately. The air jocks wanna hit the building directly in front of ya puss, man. Over."

"Hey man, I was wondering why those fly jockies were kinda hovering above my stinking head. I'm pulling back my people. We should clear area in five seconds, man."

Tracker One was following the troops on the ground so near his target, as they rapidly pulled out of the marked area. The moment the soldiers were clear of the area, Colonel Pullman was on his radio to Killer Scout.

"Tracker One to Killer Scout, be advised friendly forces are clear your target area. Killer Scout, you're cleared to destroy target as ordered, Commander. Over."

"Roger that Tracker One, am commencing final approach on target, Tracker One. Be advised, I need immediate bomb damage assessment on target after completed attack on the enemy structure. I need to know if you want a second run on same target. Over."

As Raven Flight Leader began his second attack run on the enemy target, the two AC-130 A/H Spectre Gunships showed up over the target area, and the moment the commander of these aircraft communicated with Tracker One. Colonel Pullman immediately assigned the massive Gunships to a target in the insurgent area.

"Tracker One to Tiger Impact Flight Leader, I have numerous tent type targets just north of main target area. You're to work over with twenty five millimeter Gattling Guns. All targets in this entire area are classified as hostile in nature Commander, and they are to be neutralized. These targets are the last of the main targets on site, after your assault, ground forces will move in and you'll be called in to assist mop up operation ground forces engage with any surviving enemy combatants with close in weapon fire support, if and when needed by the friendly forces on the ground. Clear Tiger Impact Leader? Over."

"Roger last and will comply, Tracker One. Have intended targets clearly vectored in on attack computer, and will commence my opening attack on said insurgent targets. As soon as I'm cleared to begin my attack on the combatants located below aircraft. Tiger Impact Leader over."

"Roger that Tiger Impact Leader, you're cleared to open fire on assigned targets located by your aircraft. Remember Tiger Flight Leader, there are friendly forces stationed in the surrounding areas of your attack profile, they're paper close to your intended targets, so concentrate assault as instructed to keep your attack angle tight, and don't allow your weapon fire to wander out of assigned target area. If insurgents escape assault against them, these moving combatants become friendly ground troop's problem to deal with, sir.

"You're not cleared, I repeat Tiger Impact Leader. You're not cleared and are ordered not to pursue any enemy forces out of assigned attack profile with weapon fire under any circumstances, sir. Is that clear as received Tiger Impact Leader? Also Tiger Leader, you have to keep your eyes opened for any possible female insurgents picked up operating on the ground. All female subjects are not to be hit for obvious reasons. Another warning, be advised insurgents are armed with shoulder launch ground to air missiles. Over."

"Roger last Tracker One, acknowledge fact we're only cleared to attack tent area of the combatant campsite. I'm further ordered not hit any female subjects picked up operating on ground if possible. We're unauthorized to pursue enemy targets moving out of assigned attack area under no circumstances. Is this correct as repeated Tracker One? Over."

"Roger that last Tiger Impact Leader, all correct as repeated. You're cleared to begin your assault on the enemy combatant's positions. Tracker One Over." Colonel Pullman's attention was torn between the two wings of attack American aircraft working over located enemy positions, and he was beginning to have some serious problems with trying to keep up with both attacking wings at the same time. To add to the Colonel's problems, Captain Walker was requesting to speak to his ATO (Air Tasking Officer).

"Searcher One to Tracker One. Come in Tracker One. Over."

"Jesus H. Christ, this is all I need on this fucking mission, dammit." Colonel Pullman grumbled at the pilot of the Apache as he replied to Walker's request for communications. "Searcher One, Tracker One. Go with traffic. I kind of have my hands full at the moment with trying to control assault on insurgents below us. This better be important. Searcher One."

"Tracker One, be advised all my fucking communications are to be classified as important. I want to warn you I just committed a third of my ground forces to make their way over to the uther side of the enemy encampment. They have orders to stop any combatants possibly trying to escape attack area until I had a chance to check out the survivors of attacks aimed against enemy positions first. I can't allow this bitch a chance of escaping us now we're so damn close to her stinking ass, and that fucking item she got with her. Over." Walker grumbled over the radio while ignoring the bitch from Tracker One's ATO.

"Tracker One to Searcher One, what's the reason to move your forces so close to attack area? Their move might cause attacking aircraft fits. Over Searcher One." Pullman snapped hotly in his mike, peeved Walker was moving soldiers so close to the attack area at this point.

"If I have to explain my god damn orders to you, the fucking reason for this troop movement Tracker One, is as I just stated to your ass. I need these troops set in place in case our stinking package tries to escape the area with the damn item we're trying to take in custody, Tracker One." The way Walker replied to Tracker One's bitch, left no doubt in the Airforce Colonel's mind that the Captain felt he was an asshole for requesting a clarification for troop movement he ordered carried out by his ground forces.

Colonel Bruce Leadbetter who was still stationed at the underground Iraqi bunker, was constantly monitoring all communications taking place between his troops and the attacking aircraft, and he cut into the conversation between his commander, Captain Walker and Colonel Pullman. He directed his angry words right at the officer.

"Tracker One this is Searcher Base, you're to listen to my fucking orders and carry them out as receiver. First off Tracker One, I have an unmanned drone heading your position, so I can see what the hell's happening out there in real fucking time. Here are your orders I take it you're marking a number of ancient structures the combatants are using for protection and defense…"

"That's correct Searcher Base, the structures are offering the insurgent's a certain degree of protection. There are…" Colonel

Pullman remarked but was cut off by the commander of the entire search operation.

"Tracker One, I didn't fucking ask for you to respond to my god damn orders! All I fucking remember ordering you were to follow my commands as received! Tracker One, you're ordered to have your attacking aircraft destroy all structures in the insurgent area offering these assholes any form of protection from our troops. Now before you shit in your damn pants over this order, allow me to explain my reasoning for this order. This is important so pay attention, Tracker One.

"Tracker One, I'm in command of this little brouhaha we find ourselves involved in, and this is the reason why we're going to start being a lot more heavy handed with these damn people during the rest of this operation. I don't mind telling you Tracker One, I'm getting a little sick and tired of ordering a surgical strike where we destroy just one fucking building or vehicle in a convoy of vehicles. When we know damn well a batch of known terrorists are using this convoy or buildings to move safely in or with. It's time we start fighting this fucking war against the damn terrorists correctly.

"The way we've been fighting this war against the damn terrorists is screwed up from the start. These nuts see we took the 'H' out of the phrase Heinous war. We've been fighting a PG fucking war and from this point on, we're going to fight this thing with an X rating. The way I see it, we're allowing the terrorists to feel they can enter any village in that miserable country of their choice, and then takeover the village. Or enter a convoy and all they might lose is one fucking building, or vehicle. Tracker One, those days are over because I'm going to change the fucking orders. We're going to add shock of war back in our attacks aimed against any damn terrorists we engage, by taking out the whole block of buildings where any enemy combatants are hiding inside an infected village.

"It's the only way to get the damn villagers to get on the terrorist's ass, instead of our asses during any and all engagements we enter with the enemy combatants. Tracker One, the villagers are allowing the terrorist bastards to remain safe in their village, believing if we go after these nuts, all we're going to do is destroy one building in the village. Once we start to drop an entire block in their village, the fucking civilians will start to stop the damn terrorists from entering their village, for fear their entire village might be leveled to the ground if we come for the terrorists they're protecting.

"The same fucking thing goes for any convoys transporting possible terrorists around the country, dammit. These miserable bastards are employing the civilians as a cover for their fucking movements. Tracker One, we're going to start destroying the entire convoy we sight in on. In this manner we'll seriously curtail the fucking movements of the terrorists in any other nation we decide to hit the assholes operating freely in.

"Before you cut me off and start to cry in the breast milk about civilians in the village, or who might be part of the convoy and caught in our attack against the terrorists. It's about time we start to see things in a different light, and that light is. If any civilian is stupid enough to be paling around with any terrorists in his country, in our eyes that puke has to be classified as a terrorist or sympathizer in nature, and is aligned with this pack of mass murderers. Tracker One, I issued you hard hitting orders, and you're to carry them out as received. Over."

"Roger your last and I'll carry them out as received Searcher Base. Over."

"You're damn right you'll carry out my fucking orders as received. Tracker One I'm done speaking with your ass and you're dismissed from this god damn conversation. Searcher Base to Searcher One, come in Mister. Over." Colonel Leadbetter snarled in his mike again.

"Searcher One to Searcher Base. Go with your traffic Searcher Base. Over."

"Searcher Base to Searcher One. I'm certain you monitored the orders I just issued to Tracker One's ass? Here's your new fucking orders for this operation. Searcher One, I'm as tired with chasing these assholes all over the damn globe, and only taking out some of these nuts, and allowing others to escaping their deaths because of civilian deaths involved in our hits against them. I'm employing your attitude against the asses, we're going to take out any insurgents we come across in this country, or anyplace else we happen to engage them on the face of the earth.

"Searcher One, you're ordered to eliminate any and all resistance and hostiles you come across who are caught carrying a weapon, or looking at you with cross eyes, mister. You and your troops are about to engage a good size group of classified enemy combatants inside a hostile nation to our interests, and I don't want any god damn prisoners taken by your fucking troops out in the field. The only prisoner I'd be slightly interested in having for interrogation purposes is this A-rab bitch carrying our missing package. Searcher One the only prisoners I want you to think about taking is any nuts who throw their damn weapon away and they drop down and bury their damn heads in the fricking sand before your ass.

"I know you won't give me any lip shit over your new orders Searcher One. So I'll leave this damn conversation and finish my speech this way. Searcher One, you know what you were sent out there to locate and take control of, and that's the only worry you should have clogging your damn noggin, mister. Order your troops accordingly Searcher One and find that missing item and you'll notice I eliminated you looking for our female breather. I feel I have to remind you so there's no confusion on your part over this latest order, Searcher One. You have a number of insurgents trapped in a small area in the middle of the fucking desert where no one knows what's happening, and I don't want to end up fighting the same pack of idiots somewhere else later on, you got my fucking orders right, mister?

"Searcher One, I'm giving your troops two hours and that's it, if I don't hear from you in that time, and you report all enemy combatants and resistance have been eliminated, and you have our missing item in possession. I'm going to order one of our support platforms to turn their weapons on your pack of screaming squirrels you call a fighting force, and I'll have the aircraft pepper your asses for not carrying out my orders as received, mister. Do I make myself perfectly clear on these orders I issued to your ass, Searcher One?"

"I read your orders loud and clear Searcher Base, and I'll have the missing item in possession in that time allotted to my operation. Searcher One Over."

"Searcher One, I knew I could count on your troops to follow their orders as received. All threats aside Captain Walker, good luck on this mission, because the fate of your nation and possibly the world is resting on your shoulders and the success of this latest mission." Colonel Leadbetter was pulling out all the stops over trying to impress his commander in the field, how important his mission was to everyone concerned.

"Searcher Base. Out." Was all Walker replied to his commanding officer.

Colonel Leadbetter smiled as he broke off the communication with his Captain, because he knew if anyone was capable of carrying out this mission successfully. Walker and his chosen crew of specialized soldiers were the ones who could pull it off.

Walker dropped the mike and Roach replaced it in its holder, as the Captain surveyed what the aircraft and insurgents were up to on the field of battle. Without thinking about it, he rose so he could see the battlefield better from his position. As he was standing, a mortar round suddenly exploded twenty feet by him. The exploding mortar round caused the other soldiers with Walker to duck and tried to protect themselves from the powerful explosion, but it did not make the Captain even flinch as he intensely studied what was happening before him between the aircraft and the enemy combatants being slaughtered on the ground.

Tracker One picked up the exploding mortar and was on the radio to get his aircraft on the surviving mortar setup.

"Tracker One to Killer Scout, I have a surviving mortar setup and it has to be eliminated immediately sir. After the mortar site is eliminated, the ground pounders will move out and you and your Chicks will assume standoff positions, and your aircraft will be called in one at a time to help mop up any possible surviving enemy insurgent pockets until all resistance is completely eliminated, and this operation comes to a conclusion. Over."

"Roger last and I have ordered Raven Chick Five to eliminate remaining mortar setup, Tracker One. I and my follow on Chicks have already assumed standoff position, and we will remain until Tiger Impact Flight completes their assigned mission. Tracker One how is my pilot, Buzz Saw making out sir? Was he injured in his punch out of his crippled aircraft, sir?"

"Killer Scout, I just received the first report on your pilot's condition. Your pilot had received some minor flash burns on his neck and chin from the ejection of his aircraft, and has himself a black eye and received a wrench or possible broken right shoulder from ejection. Other that those few minor injuries, your pilot's reported to be in good shape for his experience, and is in possession of ground pounders protecting him. Over."

"That's outstanding Tracker One, I'm happy to hear, inform the ground pounders with my pilot I own them a beer and steak supper when we get back to the real world, for their assistance with my wayward pilot. Killer Scout signing off. Over."

"Tracker One to Killer Scout, I think you might have that wrong, and I'm willing to bet my wings the ground pounders feel they own you a beer and steak supper for your close in air support on this operation. Over." Tracker One fired back at the commander.

Killer Scout did not have a change to reply to Tracker One's last transmission. Raven Chick Five was reporting to Tracker One he just destroyed the last mortar setup. Tiger Impact Leader was also calling in and informing Tracker One he was ready to rip the tent area apart.

Tracker One allowed the report from Chick Five to go as he replied to Tiger Impact Leader's report, he classified Tiger's report more important. "Tracker One to Tiger Impact Leader. Commander, you're cleared to begin your attack on the tent area of the insurgent encampment. Be advised Commander, you're ordered to clear all enemy personnel discovered on the ground. No enemy combatants are to be allowed to escape the area alive. These are orders and they're to be carried out as received. Over."

Colonel Pullman really hated to be forced to give that last order out to the Tiger Impact Leader pilot, because he understood he just signed the death warrant for all the enemy combatants trapped in the tent area of the large encampment, as he went on with his orders. "Tiger Impact Leader, be advised and remember we're looking for one lone female and what she has in her possession, and there's a possibility our missing package is in the tent area. If possibly located on the ground during your attack Commander, this is the only target to be allowed to breathe after you ended your action on the enemy campsite. Over."

"Tracker One, I received orders, there are to be no enemy problems left alive once I begin my attack on tent area. I understand orders as I'm to keep my eyes opened for lone female combatant believed to be in the tent area, she's the only one allowed to remain breathing after the completion of my attack. If these are orders as received, be advised Tracker One I'll be forced to attack from Angels One Zero, Zero, Zero Feet so I can pinpoint my operational targets, and allow any female targets to survive attack on said target. If these are my orders as I read them, you'll be forced to get Raven Flight Leader and support out of my way for operating at Angel's One, Zero, Zero, Zero Feet. Over."

"Tracker One to Tiger Impact Leader. Your orders are correct as repeated, be advised Killer Scout has assumed standoff position for this operation. Their aircraft are well out of the way of your attack scope on said targets, Tiger Impact Leader. Reporting for your information, Raven Flight is mustered at prescribed standoff area at Angel's One, One, Five Zero, Zero Feet. Raven Flight aircraft are positioned out of your requested operating altitude and target area, Commander.

"Tiger Impact Leader, you're cleared to employ requested Angel's One, Zero, Zero, Zero for attack altitude against site. You understand orders as stated, and no insurgents are to be left operational except for possible female target, if she happens to be located during your mission. Over Tiger Impact Leader." Colonel Pullman was being clear and precise with his orders to Tiger Impact Leader, because he was leaving no doubt in his orders to the Specter Gunship Commander of what he wanted from him, and how he was ordered to attack the target, and who he wanted dead and left alive if possible after the pair of Gunships carried out their orders.

CHAPTER TWENTY NINE

"Tiger Impact Leader to Tracker One, I understand my orders and I'll carry them out as ordered. Over." The Commander of Tiger Flight snapped at Colonel Pullman over the radio, displaying he was beginning to lose his temper over the way the Colonel was going over his orders, and making it seem like the commander did not know what he was doing.

The lead Spectre Gunship branded 'Spooky' dropped down to his assigned altitude, and when his aircraft was at the designated location in level flight, the commander gave the word. "All gunners, you're cleared to attack insurgents on the ground. Be advised gunners, we're to keep our eyes opened for any females picked up. Females are off target list and are to be avoided at all costs to our operation. All other personnel vectored in on your aiming computers are fair game, and are to be neutralized. That's the orders, carry them out accordingly. Over."

Tiger Impact Leader began his attack from the south heading north over the tent area of the enemy insurgents. The second Gunship was ordered to come in from the west heading east at a twenty second time difference at Angels One, One, Zero, Zero feet. The reason for the timing schedule and altitude difference was so the Gunships did not crash into each other being both Gunships were operating so close together with only a one hundred foot separation between the two flight attacks.

On Tiger Impact's attack, the co-pilot and soldier operating the attack on his computer aiming system were paying close attention to the mission progressing. Each soldier was following orders to keep their eyes opened for any female personnel located on the ground. Both officers were prepared to cut off the attack, if they picked up a female mixed in with the insurgents in the target area.

On the ground, Saudi Arabian General Ahmed al-Shugairi was standing with Ayesha and her two female friends, Sadiya Sadjadpour and Shafiqu al-Quraishy. The well seasoned Saudi Commander was also with the ex Iraqi General, Mustafa Abdalhadi and together, they watched how their Arab fighters were fairing against the American soldiers massed near the camp. When the planes attacked, it angered General al-Shugairi.

General al-Shugairi angrily threw his hands in the air and cursed when he saw his mortar installations attacked in quick succession and completely destroyed by the almost invisible American aircraft, he had no idea were hovering over his camp. Once the battle tried Saudi fighter realized the American soldiers were enjoying protection from aircraft, he realized all was lost with his mission, and his only chance of survival and getting the biological weapon back to his commanders and country, was to flee the area with the weapon and woman controlling it.

The Saudi turned and headed for his command tent when the first Gunship opened fire on the edge of his tent area. The Saudi turned back and stared in amazement at the twin lines of rounds rapidly working their way right through the very center of his camp. Anything caught in the two lines of death was instantly ripped apart by the countless rounds fired at his people. The Saudi stared as he watched many respected Arab fighters get ripped apart in the hail of bullets tearing through his camp. He was forced to turn his body as the rounds passed him and continued through the heart of his camp to the other end. Instantly, a second paid of rounds started to rip through his camp heading for the other end.

General al-Shugairi had no way of knowing, the instant Tiger Impact Leader broke off his attack, the aircraft rose in altitude and did a hard loop over, and then headed back for the other side of the camp, and prepared to hit it again once he received a bomb assessment damage report from Tracker One. The flight commander also had to see if Tracker One wanted his aircraft to hit the target again, or report to their standoff position, and wait to see if they would be called in to help the ground forces, if they happen across any pockets of enemy resistance still operating.

As the second Specter Gunship worked over the enemy camp, the co-pilot picked up three women standing in the open with other insurgents in the camp, and he called out to his gunners. "Erase, erase, erase, don't pull on the target! Negative pull, negative pull, you're ordered to hold fire gunners. I just picked up three female targets on the ground about dead center on the camp."

When the co-pilot excitedly called out, the commander and pilot of the second Gunship immediately pulled back on his control stick and picked up the nose of his aircraft, so his gunner's weapon systems would automatically shut down once he broke off the command order placed in the attack computers. The pilot turned to his co-pilot once he had his aircraft flying in level flight and asked his co-pilot. "Bill, how did we do breaking off the attack? Did we break off in time before the female targets were hit?"

"We pulled off in time. The three female and two male targets with them are breathing."

The commander of the second Tiger Impact aircraft reported their attack to the commander, and Tiger Leader reported same to Colonel Pullman. "Tracker One, we're forced to break off our attack. Reason was three female subjects were picked up during our second run over target. Tracker One, I need orders and BDA on target. Do you want us to hit the target again? I'm forced to report there are still a number of hostiles breathing on target. Over."

"Tracker One to Tiger Impact Leader, you're ordered to standoff position and wait further orders. I'll contact Searcher One and see what the Commander of the ground forces wants to do about this situation. Sit tight Tiger Impact Leader, I'll be back to you moment I find out what Searcher One wants to do. Over."

"Roger am reporting to standoff position to wait further orders. Over."

Colonel Pullman ignored Tiger Impact Leader's last remark as he went over to Walker. "Err… Searcher One, Tracker One, come in Commander. Over."

Walker was with troops including his One Charlie or communication's soldier, and Roach handed him the mike and he growled in the radio. "Yeah Tracker One, go with traffic. I wanna jump off and get my guys hitting the rest of these A-rab pukes out there still breathing. I'm done with hanging around this desert like a jackass. I see your fly boys are working over these assholes hard, and I wanna thank you for support of my troops on the ground man…"

"That's what I wanted to speak to you about, Searcher One." Colonel Pullman interrupted the Captain and then went on with his words. "Searcher One, the second Impact Flight detected three females in the camp and broke off his attack. I have both Impact Flights holding at standoff positions while waiting further orders. Both flights concerned carrying out orders in fear of hitting the female you want, or worse, hitting the missing item and releasing all sorts of hell, Searcher One. Over."

"Shit." Walker growled and collected his thoughts and continued with his Air Tasking Officer. "Tracker One, your pilot did right when he broke off his attack for reasons you mentioned. Shit, shit, shit, okay it seems we're gonna be forced to go in there on foot and clean out the rest of these lousy scumbags one by one, until we find this bitch and the missing crap she has with her. Tracker One, how do you wanna handle the rest of this mess? You know you're the only vertical lift aircraft (helicopter) we have, and you're the only one who can afford us close in support we might need in there. Over."

"That's not true Searcher One, Tiger Impact Flight and Raven Flight aircraft can offer close in support. The flights can assist ground forces if you come under attack from insurgents. Over."

"Tracker One, if I'm gonna allow those aircraft to work so damn close to my troops, you're gonna hafta work real close to the sonofabitches, and keep them from hitting my troops. Tracker One, I don't need those fly jocks getting over excited and hitting some of my troops. Over."

"That's not going to happen while I'm controlling the air support for your ground assault, Searcher One. I'm the control for support your troops need, and I'll make certain no aircraft's fire come close to your forces on the ground to be a threat. Err… Searcher One, we're getting off the point. How do you want to handle the rest of the operation? Do you want Tiger Impact Flight to continue working over the tent area, or do you want me to keep Impact Flight at standoff, and fly support missions if your troops come under attack by surviving insurgents, sir? Over."

"How the hell am I gonna allow Tiger Impact Flight to continue ripping into them god damn enemy insurgents without risking weapon fire hitting that damn item, Tracker One? I don't give a Frenchman's fuck about that damn female's ass. My only concern on this operation is what the hell that damn A-rab bitch is carrying with her, and the damn harm that damn thing could do if the stinking canister's destroyed by our weapon's fire, pal." Walker did not bother signing off with Tracker One as he glared at the helicopter still hovering in the nearly a mile away from his position.

"I understand the situation and pressures you're working under Searcher One, and all I can tell you is I'm doing the best I can with this damn operation, sir. Over." Colonel Pullman did not try to keep the anger out of his tone of voice as he addressed Walker.

"Yeah, I feel ya there Tracker One. I'll move my people in and get this damn woman and item. I hafta rely on you to get any heavy resistance, offa our asses when we go operational against these flaming assholes. Shit Tracker One, you have a more important assignment to carry out than just protecting our asses. Tracker One being you're the only vertical lift platform I have available for real close in air support. I'm forced to cut you out of that part of the operation. You're gonna hafta keep an eye on this bitch on the ground, and if she tries to make a break for it, or takes a position about to be hit by aircraft. You hafta call off the attack and protect that bitch before she and that damn item gets splattered all over the fucking desert by us, man."

"I copy and understand what you're concerned with and agree with you, Commander. What orders? I request you repeat so I understand and there's no confusion, Searcher One. Over."

"Roger Tracker One, I need you to keep your eye on this bitch, and keep your fire offa her ass. Tracker One if possible, I need you to pull double duty controlling aircraft fire on top of enemy when possible. The last part of my order is low priority. Your main priority is to keep that bitch safe until I get my hands around her neck, and I ring it for causing us so much trouble. Over."

"Roger all as received Searcher One. Good luck Searcher One. Over."

"Roger last Tracker One, I'm moving my troops forward to engage enemy forces. Tracker One, how will Tiger and Raven Flight Leaders respond if I request air support? Will they respond to my commands, or will they only respond to your orders? Over."

The Commander of Tiger Impact Flight responded to Walker's last question. "Searcher One, Tiger Impact Leader. Commander, all you have to do is call out the coordinates you want hit, and my flight or aircraft from Raven Flight will respond. Commander, we understand the situation your troops are facing on the ground, and I assure you Commander. We're willing and more than able to do as much as possible for you to lessen the trouble from any possible surviving enemy combatants on the ground. Over."

"I copy last Tiger Impact Leader and thanks for clearing my concerns. Okay, this is for Tracker One. Colonel Pullman, you have orders. We're moving out against all enemy resistance so stay alert, and remember, you major responsibility is to protect that Arab bitch until we can get our fucking hands on her, sir."

"Roger your last and will comply, Searcher One. Tracker One Out."

The Mutt moved a few steps closer to Walker and then he grumbled after seeing the strain his friend was operating under. "Hey man, when we get back to the real world, you oughta take Raz to Mexico for some fun and games outta the States."

"What the fuck do I gotta go to Mexico for? If I wait long enuf, all the damn bean eaters will be in the States and Raz can see all the Mexicans she wants from our front porch." Walker stared at his friend and then added. "C'mon man, we gotta place an end to this stinking fucked up mission ten minutes ago. You take command of Second Squad, Raz you got command of Third Squad, First Squad, you pack of refugees are with me. We're gonna hit the assholes from three points, and remember we're looking for one A-rab bitch and what she has. When we find her and the item, our mission ends that quick and you people go to a fall back situation, and only engage surviving enemy forces if they try and hit you. Once we're outta the picture, we'll allow the fly guys to finish any surviving insurgents off. Get a fucking move on it we got bad guys out there that we gotta get after."

Walker watched as Raz and the Mutt took command of their assigned squads, and once they were ready to move out, he waved his hand and the units moved out as one. Only sporadic small arms enemy fire was leveled at his advancing American soldiers, and Walker figured the aircraft broke the strength of the enemy combatant's resistance.

Walker's group was heading down the throat of the defenders, while Raz's squad moved to his left and fanned out to hit the enemy from the left, while the Mutt's squad moved in from Walker's right. The Captain kept glancing at the hovering helicopter and noted how low and close the machine was suddenly flying by his advancing troops. He was taking it for granted Tracker One's aircraft was marking the location of the woman he was looking for.

The Captain led his soldiers in a straight line for Tracker One's location. As he pushed his troops, the enemy's weapon fire was beginning to get a little better organized against his rapidly advancing soldiers. This forced Walker to raise his hand and all moving troops stopped forward progress and dropped down to the sand. He bellowed one word to his troops. "Engage!"

The troops returned fire at the enemy positions, crippled much of the resistance offered by the enemy combatants before Walker's troops. His troop's fire was on the mark and so accurate and picking off many defenders they located in their sights. Soon, much of the enemy fire waned off until it was back to just some sporadic and unorganized and not coming anywhere near his troop's enemy weapon fire. When Walker realized the resistance was rapidly falling off, he stood and waved his hand and his soldiers rushed forward.

Walker's group was the advance unit for the ground attack aimed against enemy positions, and his soldiers bolted over the first line of enemy defenders operating in the insurgent camp as if they were not even there. He smiled when he realized most enemy soldiers he was pushing over, was either dead or severely wounded, as his troops pushed for the heart of the camp. He took a second to locate Tracker One's aircraft and he was surprised the helicopter moved to the far end of the large enemy encampment.

A small war was raging around Walker as his troops engaged remaining enemy forces offering resistance they came across, as they entered the camp behind him as he dropped to a knee and waved his One Charlie over to his side. Then he grabbed the mike and barked angrily in it. "Searcher One to Tracker One. Respond. Over."

"Tracker One to Searcher One, send traffic. Over." Colonel Pullman responded as he looked for where Walker was on the ground below.

Bullets were pinging in the sand at his feet as Walker snarled at the ATO Colonel. "What the fuck are you up to out there, dammit? You're moving all over the damn place! Are you marking our fricking female target or what, Tracker One? Over."

"Roger that Searcher One. I was forced to change positions many times to keep up with the woman and her four friends." Colonel Pullman replied while ignoring the way the Captain spoke to him over the open net as he went on with his report. "Searcher One our target's moving to the far end of the camp and is in company of two female and two male combatants. All but the one I identified as our target are armed. Searcher One, it seems our target's going to make a break for it. The five targets are acting like they're preparing to make their way to the Saudi Arabian border, sir. Over."

"What the hell would the assholes wanna be making way for the stinking Saudi Arabian border? That doesn't make any fucking sense to me sir. Arabia's our ally and if these assholes make for that border, they're gonna be arrested and held for us." Walker howled in the radio as he stood and headed for where Tracker One was hovering. Walker dragged Roach along with him as he continued to speak on the radio.

"Beats the hell out of me Searcher One, I'm staying on top of the combatants you want as ordered." The Colonel replied as he kept an eye on the five subjects below his aircraft. The pilot was keeping his machine hovering over the top of the targets in an attempt to blind then with hard blowing sand raised by his rotors, in hopes of forcing the group to hunker down until Walker's troops can catch up and take them as prisoners and end this mission.

A couple of rounds came close to Walker and he looked to his right and picked up the Mutt, and his friend aimed and took out the shooter trying to pick off Walker then the Mutt gave the Captain a quick thumbs up signal.

Walker waved the Mutt over to his side and when he was heading for Walker, he located Sergeant Ramirez operating on his right. Getting her attention he waved her over to him as well. When Raz and the Mutt were with him, he snapped at the pair. "Okay you turds, you're with me. Tracker One's hovering over our target and it seems three women are trying to make a break for the Saudi border for some unknown reason. Raz, I want you with me so you can take charge of the lousy bitch when we catch up to them. I want a woman controlling her ass."

Walker stopped speaking and turned to the other soldiers of his attack group and bellowed. "The rest of you ball sacks are with me I guess. Your job's to keep the rest of these A-rab assholes offa my ass, so the three of us can get this bitch and item and place an end to this god damn mission, and then we can get the hell outta here pronto."

Without a word of complaint from the selected soldiers Walker wanted with him, closed on his position and once they were setup, he moved the troops forward.

The Captain was charging forward not paying attention to the surviving insurgents firing at his troops. His actions were dictated with the knowledge his troops would make quick work of any enemy foolish enough to take a shot at him. He was charging for Tracker One's platform hovering over their targets. By the time his group worked their way to the far end of the camp, there was little if any enemy fire aimed in his direction. Walker took a look over his should and noticed the mini war still raging between his troops and the surviving combatants trapped in the camp.

Walker shook his head as he continued to move forward, he picked up the five Arabs fighting the small sand storm being kicked up by Tracker One's rotors, as they fought the blowing sand under their feet trying to get out of the camp. When his group was close enough to challenge the Arabs, Tracker One pulled back so the blowing sand would not interfere with Walker's soldiers.

When the whirling sand calmed down, the five Arabs stood up and tried to climb the side of a small sand dune, but when Walker called out to them they froze in place. The Iraqi's turned to see who was barking at them so forcibly from behind. Ayesha's heart skipped a beat when she noticed the ugly look in the soldier's eyes. Instantly she realized everything was lost and she came back to reality when General Mustafa Abdelhadi growled at the soldier, as he went about leveling his weapon at the invaders at the same time he snarled at them.

"God cursed lowly infidels to the sacred words of the Holy Qur'an, and who have invaded my country. I shall be pleased to send you on your way to hell to be with your evil master, and rid the sands of my ancestors of your ugly presence…"

Without waiting orders from Walker, the Mutt leveled his weapon on General Abdelhadi's chest and fired five rounds that ripped into the angry Iraqi's body, cutting his words off in mid sentence. Walker looked at the Mutt and then asked him. "What the hell did ya do that for? I wanted to see what the lousy dude had on his fricking mind before we wasted his ass, man."

"Arrr… it was the usual old fucking bullshit always coming from these A-rabs, they keep firing off at us all the damn time. They wanna tell us we're the damn infidels and invaders to their stinking country that's all. They'll never learn not to piss off a dude carrying an automatic fucking weapon in his hands." The Mutt smirked at Walker. But their attention was caught when Sergeant Ramirez suddenly lit up her weapon and fired at someone from the group they stopped from leaving the encampment.

Walker looked in the direction Ramirez fired in and noticed an Iraqi drop to the ground. He did not realize it was Mugrada al-Sistani trying to protect General Abdelhadi from a distance from the group trying to make it to the Saudi border. He turned back to the three females and barked at them. "I hope you stinking chicks under fucking stand English, because I can't speak your damn mumble jumble. Listen up because I'm only gonna say this shit once, and if you don't understand me then you slugs betta be able to read my fucking mind, or your asses are grass and I'm the fucking lawn mower. I only want what that one bitch has in her arms, and if she gives it up without a struggle. You people will be free to go anywhere you wanna go without my bugging your asses any further. What say, you chicks gonna turn that fucking cylinder over to my ass nice and peaceful like, or you hens gonna make me take it from you, bitch?"

Without thinking about it for a second, Ayesha hugged the metal cylinder a little closer to her exhausted body, as she glared angrily at the ugly American with hatred burning in her eyes. She wanted to kill the foreign soldiers who attack the camp offering her safety.

The usually outspoken Sadiya Sadjadpour stepped in front of Ayesha and then she hissed at the American soldier savagely, mustering all the hatred she could build in her tone. "Defiled infidel invader, how dare you make demands of a faithful follower of the sacred words in the Holy Qur'an? You foul thing who has invaded my country, have no business remaining in my country a moment longer, yet you make demands of one of her children. Be gone with you and all your followers and allow us to continue a peaceful way of life in our own country your worthless soldiers have so completely destroyed." As Sadiya said her words at the American soldier, the AK-47 she had looped on her shoulder dropped down to her elbow.

Ice, (Sergeant Diane Morrison) noticed the sudden movement of the weapon and she fired a single round at the woman snarling so angrily at her commanding officer, from her hip. This caused the soldiers with Walker to open up on the remaining Iraqi's as Shafiqu al-Quraishy roared. "Do not fire at us, we shall give you what you wan…"

Seven rounds ripped into her body, killing Shafiqu instantly. General Ahmed al-Shugairi lived long enough to see Shafiqu drop down dead to the sand before his life was snuffed out. The soldiers who fired at the Arabs made certain they did not hit Ayesha, or the metal cylinder.

Ayesha stared in horror as her two friends were savagely slaughtered before her eyes. She cared nothing for the Saudi General's life. Her sharp mind registered the soldiers did not kill her like they just slaughtered the others. She understood the infidels did not want to fire at her for fear of hitting the container locked in her arms. Slowly, Ayesha started to back up the low sand dune behind her, she had the smarts to move the cylinder out before her body, to make certain the hated soldiers did not fire on her as she continued to try and escape what seemed impossible.

The moment she started to backup, Walker stepped forward and snapped at her. "Hey bitch, where the hell do you think you're fucking going? I'm warning you bitch, you take another fucking step away, I'm gonna splatter your head all over this stinking desert." With that said, he leveled his weapon to leave no doubt in Ayesha's mind what he growled at her.

She stopped dead in her tracks as she milled over the words she understood aimed at her from the American soldier. She was searching her mind as what to do next. Suddenly she sat down on the sand and moved the cylinder further out in front of her body. She was actually trying to hide behind the object as she snarled at the ugly American soldier. "Non-believer to the sacred words of the Holy Qur'an, there's an ancient Islamic creed you'll not know of, a customary we faithful believers offer to the followers who died, and once I release this gift from Allah against the lowly Crusaders. The sands of the desert will be littered with the dead of all hated infidels. The saying is this, 'there is no true God but Allah'".

"Hey Walker, the dumb bitch is trying to hide behind the fucking cylinder. Why the hell not let me take her out nice and clean so we can end this fucking drama? I'm getting bored to fucking death with listening to her usual crap." Neck grumbled as he stepped forward and trained his weapon on Ayesha's face.

"Back off big man, I don't need you doing something stupid that might cause her to overreact and do something foolish with that damn thing. I'll let you know when it's time for her to head off for Paradise." Walker warned his trooper without looking at him. He wanted to keep this female in his vision until he had the cylinder in his hands.

"Man, you're taking all the stinking fun outta this mission." Neck fired back at Walker.

"I said shut the fuck up and stand pat and that's what you're gonna do, stupid."

"Again with stupid huh?" Neck complained at Walker, but he stepped back and allowed him to finish handing the female Iraqi.

Although Ayesha understood English well, and what she did not understand she was able to figure out for herself. But she could not understand all of what the soldiers were arguing about. Now, her mind was screaming, demanding she do something about her situation and do it quick. Fighting back the fear of being slaughtered like her friends, she was trying to find a way out of her dilemma. Not seeing any other way out of this nightmare, she began to open the cylinder. All she could think to do was to release the deadly weapon to the air, before she was killed by these American soldiers. Her trembling hands continued to work on the locking spring, and she looked at Walker and hissed with all the venom she could possibly muster in her stinging words. "Once this gift is released against the foul infidels who pollute the sands of Allah, it'll be like hearing the anguished shriek emerging from the throats of millions." Ayesha continued to stare at Walker as her hands continued to work on the stainless steel cylinder, but she stopped when the soldier suddenly growled at her.

"Hey sister, you open that damn thing and you'll not only kill every stinking Iranian on the face of the stinking earth, but you'll kill every uther Arab asshole living in the damn world at the same fucking time." Walker warned Ayesha as he got her caught up in his cross hairs of his weapon, and he concentrated on her face through his sights of the weapon.

Ayesha stared back at the man aiming the weapon right at her face, and then she raged as nastily as she could speak in broken English at the foreign soldier. "You shoot me if you dare lowly infidel to the word of the Holy Qur'an. I'm not afraid of death, life is but a luxury held precious in the hearts of all cursed infidels who pollute the world of Allah with their evil presence. Once I opened the gift of Allah and release His breath to the air, His will and command will take over, and He will seek revenge upon all those who refuse his words of wisdom. Allah will leave the faithful to enjoy his world."

All the while Ayesha said her words of hatred at the American, her hands continue to work on the restraining strap keeping the cylinder together. She was having trouble freeing the spring while keeping her eyes on the soldier and the weapon aimed at her.

Ramirez moved up to Walker's side and she warned him in no uncertain terms. "Walker, you know she's about got that damn thing opened. What the hell are you waiting for? Kill her before she does what she threatened. Walker, if you don't kill her I will. I'm not going to wait until she had that damn weapon free and places my life in danger."

"Shut up for the love of the Christ Child and allow me to think for a moment will ya. You know damn well I'm not happy thinking bout killing some pretty ass A-rab chick in cold blood." Walker growled at his fellow soldier as he refused to take his eyes off Ayesha, and what she was doing to the cylinder resting on the sand. Drawing in a breath, he exploded at Ayesha.

"Hey bitch, you betta stop what the fuck you're doing to that damn thing, or I'm gonna take you out toot sweet. I'll not allow you to open that damn thing and expose it to the air while I'm alive. You betta back off and release that damn thing so I can take command of it…"

The American soldier's last words made Ayesha's blood run hot and she yelled back at him. "I warn you cursed invader, you're too late to scare or stop me from carrying out the mission Almighty Allah placed in my unworthy hands, for I released the locking spring of the cylinder. Lowly infidel from the land of Satan and sin, prepare your evil self and foul soul to witness the gift and mighty power Allah has placed in my unworthy hands to deal out His justice and will against the non-believers of the world." With that said, Ayesha removed the locking device from the cylinder and threw it defiantly before the feet of Walker growling at her, trying to talk her out of opening the weapon to the air, and yet he still aimed his weapon at her face at the same time.

"Now all I have to do is make a turn of the cylinder housing of the weapon held in the metal prison, and you'll see the revengeful breath of Almighty Allah be released against the evil of the world, hated infidel invader."

"Hey bitch, if you touch that cylinder again, I'm gonna blow your fucking head offa your shoulders as sure as I'm talking to ya, sister. I'm warning you bitch, chick or not. I'll kill your ass right the fuck where you sit, if you don't stop what the hell you're doing with that damn thing." Walker warned Ayesha as his hands shook as he continued to level his weapon at the forehead of the Arab woman.

The way Walker snarled at Ayesha, made her hands tremble with fear of the angry man threatening her for a moment. The hesitation was all he needed as he fired one round at her beautiful face. The brass clad bullet ripped into the unprotected forehead of Ayesha, and the force of the bullet hitting her skull made her body brutally pitch back and to the right side from the cylinder locked tightly in her hands.

When Ayesha's body was ripped away from the cylinder by the force of the round striking her head, the metal cylinder fell to the side and started to roll down the low sand dune Ayesha was sitting on. Sergeant Ramirez was as quick and she dropped her weapon and dove on the sand and stopped the base of the cylinder from rolling the rest of the way down the sand dune, before the container was able to fully separate.

The Mutt moved forward and picked up the locking spring and handed it to Ramirez and she figured out how it worked, and secured the two ends of the cylinder together with the spring. Once the cylinder was secured, she looked at Walker and gave him a smile of victory.

Walker smiled at her, but Roach interrupted the moment of triumph when he moved to Walker and announced. "Walker, the Colonel's on the horn demanding to talk with you, sir."

Walker took the mike and answered the call. "Yeah Searcher Base this is Searcher One. Over."

"What the fuck's going on with that damn item, mister?"

"Searcher Base, Sergeant Ramirez retrieved the item and has it secured and Doctor Russbinder is moving up to take command of said item. Searcher Base, I'm reporting our mission a success and we accomplished what we were sent to find and secure, sir. Over Searcher Base."

"Searcher One, now you have the damn cylinder secured and in your command. I'll dispatch a Slick (helicopter) heading your way. You're to maintain control of the cylinder and when the Slick lands by your ass, you, that Mutt thing who's a poor excuse for a fucking soldier and Sergeant Ramirez, are ordered to board the damn thing along with Doctor Russbinder with the item, and then get your asses back to my fucking location pronto. Your mission has been completed as ordered, and once I have that damn thing in my fucking hands, I'll get the rest of your troops the hell out of the desert heading for home. Captain, you and yours did an outstanding job as usual, well done, well done Captain. Over."

Walker looked to the sky and noticed the drone hovering over his position and then understood how the colonel knew they got control of the cylinder and biological weapon contained in it. Letting out an exhausted sigh, Walker allowed himself a few moments to relax for the first time since starting this mission, while he and his soldiers waited for the helicopter to come to their position and pick up the item that caused them so much grief and trouble over this operation.